WIZARD

IN

EXILE

Wrath of the Stormking
Volume 1

By

Michael G. Manning

Cover by Christian Bentulan
Map Artwork by Maxime Plasse
Editing by Keri Karandrakis

ISBN: 978-1-943481-47-7

For more information about the Mageborn series check out the author's
Facebook page:

https://www.facebook.com/MagebornAuthor

or visit the website:

http://www.magebornbooks.com

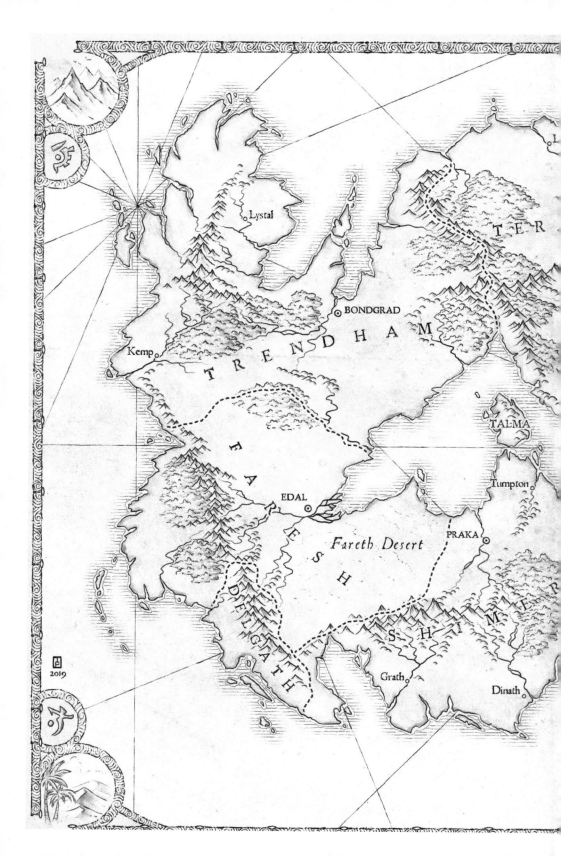

CHAPTER I

"You're a Turdian," declared Len Strayth. "I bet you eat turds for breakfast and dinner!"

The other boys laughed, then Galli Maremin added, "I bet that's why he smells so bad."

Alver was an inch taller than the ones making jokes, but he ignored them and kept walking, determined they wouldn't ruin his first day at the new school. Then someone's hand ran down his back.

"That might improve the stink," announced the third boy, Trig Blenner. He tossed a piece of fresh horse dung to the ground.

The smell confirmed what Alver already knew. A streak of fresh shit had been smeared across his back. The coat he wore was new, as was his shirt. Both had been made by his Nana in preparation for his first day at school. Alver's father had impressed on him the importance of caring for the clothes, but it hadn't been necessary. Alver loved his Nana more than anyone in the world. Turning, he glared at Trig, noting the shit stains on the other boy's fingers. "If anyone likes turds, it's you, playing with your own shit."

Trig leaned in immediately. "Say that to my—" Trig's head snapped back as Alver's right fist caught him under the chin and he fell backward, landing hard on his tailbone. Len came to his defense, attempting to push Alver off balance, but he encountered a wide left hook that sent him sprawling.

Galli was unable to react and merely stared at Alver in shock. Two of his friends were down, and only Trig seemed likely to get back up any time soon. Meanwhile, Alver's angry eyes were focused purely on him. He ran.

Alver was breathing hard, but his anger wasn't gone. When Trig started to rise, he kicked the boy in the stomach. Then he leaned over and grabbed the unconscious Len by one leg and dragged him over to the dung pile, and then through it. He stopped only when Len's head came to rest on the slick fecal remains that hadn't already coated his backside and clothes.

Looking down on the helpless boy, Alver's anger faded, and he tried to figure out what to do. He couldn't go to school now, not with horse shit on his coat. A man from across the street yelled at him from a doorway, "Hey boy! What did you do?"

Alver ran, ignoring the shouts behind him, and he kept running until he was home, though he was scared to go inside. Nana would be upset if she saw the filth on his clothes.

There was a bucket full of water by the back door. Alver knew this because it was one of his chores to refill it when Nana asked. Sneaking around the side of the house, he went to it and took off his jacket and shirt. Then he found the washtub, which she kept hanging on a nail by the back porch, and put his clothes inside.

He added some water and tried to scrub the stains out, but without soap, it seemed he was only making the problem worse.

"What are you doing, Olly?"

It was Nana's voice and he turned in horror to see her standing behind him. With the filthy clothes still in his hands, he looked up at her and tried to answer, but tears filled his eyes and his voice refused to work. Sitting down in the dirt, he hid his face in his arms.

She laughed. "Olly, you silly thing. Next time, just tell me!" Dumping the filthy water from the washtub she took the clothes from his hands and returned them to the tub. "You've never washed clothes before. What possessed you, child? Look here, watch what I'm doing."

Peeking his head up from his arms, Alver watched her add fresh water before going to get a half-used cake of soap from a box on the porch. "Rub just a little on, like this. Use too much and your clothes won't last. This is the scrub board, see?"

For the next twenty minutes, she patiently showed him how to use the washtub and scrub board to clean clothes. She finished by rinsing the clothes and putting them through a wringer to squeeze out the excess water. After hanging them up, she put her hands on her hips. "I appreciate that you want to help, but you're only eight, Olly. This is a good age, but ask me next time."

Alver nodded, not quite trusting himself to speak.

"Go refill the water bucket, then you can help me with the apples. I wanted to surprise your father when he gets home."

"Apples?"

"For cider mash," she clarified. "Don't get your hopes up. I doubt there will be any good enough for pie."

He followed his Nana around for the rest of the morning, helping her load the cider press and fill clay jars that she had already cleaned in preparation. When noon arrived, he followed her into the house and watched as she peeled and cut a few choice specimens that she'd saved. Her eyes twinkled when she glanced at him. "I wonder what I should do with these? They're too good for mashing. Grab that bowl for me."

Alver sliced the peeled apples up while his Nana made a quick pastry dough. Her question came then, when it was clear he had fully relaxed. "What happened this morning?"

"I got in a fight."

"Why?"

"Some of the boys said I stink, then Trig wiped shit on—"

"Language!"

Alver bobbed his head apologetically. "Trig grabbed a horse apple and smeared it on me."

"And then what happened?"

He shrugged. "I got mad and said something, then Len came toward me, and I punched him. Trig shoved me and I laid him out."

Nana frowned. "How many boys were there?"

"Galli was there too, but he ran when he saw what I did."

She nodded, rolling out the dough with a wooden dowel. "How do you feel about what happened?"

Alver couldn't help but notice his apple slices were far thicker than the ones his Nana usually produced when making a pie, so he tried cutting them into smaller pieces, which only resulted in small, thick pieces. He didn't know how to answer the question, so he simply said, "Angry." In reality, he felt something else, but he didn't know how to express it.

"You and Galli have been friends since we moved here," observed his grandmother.

"He said I smell," Alver told her. "He's been a jerk ever since Len showed up."

"Do you think you smell?"

"I did after Trig rubbed sh—dung on me," he answered, barely catching himself in time. When his grandmother didn't say anything, he asked, "What was I supposed to do?"

"No idea. I'm glad you were able to defend yourself, but it sounds like you went too far. You still have to go to school tomorrow. Your father won't change his mind on that."

"Is he going to be mad?"

His grandmother paused, and Alver saw a number of mysterious thoughts flicker across her features. Her visage finally settled on a faint smirk that vanished seconds later, then she replied in a serious tone, "Probably."

The afternoon passed slowly, and Alver wondered if he would be allowed a piece of pie when it was ready. His grandmother was kind, but she could be stern at times. If she felt he'd done wrong, it was entirely possible she'd made the pie just to teach him a lesson at the end. The thought made him sad, but his biggest worry was what would happen when his dad got home.

Alver's father worked as a cook at the Laughing Goat, a large public house and hostel in Lystal. He left early each morning and returned for a short break in the midafternoon for a couple of hours. Then his dad would go back and work until supper was done. He usually returned an hour after dark and ate with Alver and his grandmother.

Alver felt a sense of trepidation when his father's voice came from the front yard. "Alver, come out here please." Running outside, he could see the disappointment on his father's face.

Kelvin Wiltshire was a slim but muscular man with dark hair and piercing blue eyes. He was taller than average, but not so much that people felt inclined to mention it when describing him. He waited patiently as Alver ran to meet him, then declared, "I heard you had a busy morning."

Alver nodded, his eyes on the ground.

"Daniel Strayth came by and told me what you did to his son. Len was covered in horse shit. Said you dragged him through it while he was unconscious. Is that true?"

"There was three of them, Dad."

"That boy could have died, Alver! Do you understand that? That punch could have killed him, and if that didn't do it the fall could have. Did you think about that before you started dragging him around?"

"No."

"I haven't been teaching you to fight so you could bully the other kids!"

"They started—"

His father cut him off, "And you sure as hell finished it, didn't you?" He looked his son up and down. "Did any of them even swing at you?"

"Trig pushed me."

"Go inside." Kelvin rubbed his face with one hand.

"Am I in trouble?"

"I'll practice with you tonight and you're likely going to be sore when you go to bed," said his father.

Alver winced. He normally looked forward to lessons with his dad. Ordinarily his father was careful, but on occasion Alver came away with a welt or even a bruise. *Please don't let it be sword practice,* he prayed.

"Wiltshire!" A deep voice rang out. Looking up, Alver saw it was Darren Blenner, Trig's father.

Kelvin turned and faced the other man, touching his brow and dipping his head as a respectful greeting. "Darren."

Blenner was a farrier, and his wide shoulders and muscular forearms showed the results of his labor. Though he didn't quite stand eye to eye with Alver's dad, he had a considerably heavier frame. Curly hair normally gave the man a friendly look, but today he was obviously angry. "Your son cracked Trig's ribs."

Kelvin seemed embarrassed. "I'm sorry about that, Darren. If you want to bring him over my mother can take a look at…"

The farrier swung, his right-hand curving through a wide arc that ended at Kelvin's jaw, sending him crashing to the ground. "I never cared much for you turds moving here, but my patience ended today."

Alver was on the porch watching, but he stayed silent. He knew his father had to have seen the punch coming. It had been easy to see. *Why'd he let him do that?* Kelvin stood slowly, his lip bleeding. "Boys will fight, but…"

"But nothing, Wiltshire. He kicked Trig after he was on the ground. Tell your son to come over here!"

"I'll discipline him myself," said Kelvin.

"The hell you will!" ground out the farrier. "He needs a proper lesson."

"Go in the house, Alver," ordered Kelvin.

Darren struck again, this time driving his fist into Kelvin's stomach. He pointed at Alver. "Come here, boy."

Paralyzed, Alver watched as his father slowly straightened up, then ordered, "Don't step off that porch, Alver."

Kelvin stared hard into the farrier's eyes. "You've got a right to be angry, but you'll have to take that up with me. No one touches my family."

Darren glared at the other man, then swung again. He stopped at the last second, his fist an inch from Kelvin's nose. "You're just gonna stand there and let me beat the shit out of you?" He shook his head in disgust, then brought his other hand around in an open-faced slap that sent Kelvin staggering to one side. "Fucking turd. Cowards, all of you."

Thunder rumbled in the distance. Alver's dad regained his balance and glanced at the sky. "Looks like rain."

"Go to hell, Wiltshire." The farrier turned and walked away.

After a minute, Kelvin walked to the house and sat down in the rocking chair on the left side of the porch. Alver approached his father hesitantly. "Are you all right?"

Kelvin rubbed his jaw ruefully. "Nothing a few days won't cure."

"Why'd you let him do that?"

His father's eyes locked onto him, piercing his heart and filling him with guilt, though he didn't understand why. "You think I should have fought him?"

"You could beat him, right?"

"No fight is certain, Alver. A man can trip and die just from landing badly, but that's not the point. What happens if I beat the hell out of Darren Blenner? Does that make me right? Does that make what you did right?"

"No."

"Let's say I take his dignity and send him crawling home. Where does that leave us?" Alver shrugged, unable to answer. His father continued, "The next day every one of Darren Blenner's friends and family would be angry and things just get worse from there. Keep fighting and eventually we wind up in jail or we're forced to move."

Frustrated, Alver asked, "Why are you teaching me to fight then?"

"Good question," said his father. "Think about that for a while and forget the practice later."

"You're not going to punish me?"

"I was, but I think Mister Blenner already made my point for me. You still have to go to school tomorrow."

Alver spent the rest of the day helping his grandmother, and after supper she did let him have a piece of pie. Strangely, he didn't enjoy it. The flavor was as good as ever, but the memory of his father's one-sided fight kept intruding on his thoughts. He went to sleep that night feeling worse than ever.

CHAPTER 2

Alver had a rough time the first few weeks of school. His one-time friend, Galli, wanted nothing to do with him, and Len avoided him like the plague. Trig was scared of him as well, but he covered his fear by spreading rumors about Alver. The worst was that Alver's dad was a coward. When a few boys that Alver didn't know got the courage up to tease him about that, it took all his reserve to avoid repeating what he'd done the first day of school.

No one was foolish enough to poke the bear, though, at least not physically. They would point, laugh, and whisper, but the other boys knew well enough not to touch him. Over time, even the taunting and rumors lessened, as Alver refused to be drawn into a fight, verbal or otherwise. Each time he was tempted, he remembered his father's humiliation at the hands of Darren Blenner. Alver was determined not to be the cause of such a thing ever again.

Although Lystal was a moderately large city with thousands of children, the new school only had five teachers and fewer than a hundred students, mostly from well-to-do families that weren't quite affluent enough to afford private tutors. The ages ranged from seven to fifteen, which was the age that most aspiring young men sought work or an apprenticeship with one of the guilds. Girls were allowed, but only a fifth of the students were female. Given the numbers, the girls were all in one class with one teacher.

Alver's family wasn't considered affluent, but his father insisted that he attend the new school. Their family was also unusual in that they lived in such a well-built and relatively spacious home, especially considering that their only income was from his dad's work as a cook at a public house. Fortunately, the school only charged a modest fee for entry, as it was funded by a grant from an anonymous donor, but in practice, few students were from lower-class families.

The poor saw little to gain in schooling, and the populace of Lystal in general had mixed opinions regarding the school. Most regarded it as a waste of time. The wealthy usually hired private tutors, and everyone else could expect to learn what they needed during apprenticeships, assuming they weren't destined to work in an unskilled trade or in the fields. That ambivalence was the reason Gabet's Academy had less than a hundred students. Compounding the poor opinion with the fact that most thought only unsavory or unlucky women needed jobs, and it explained why even fewer girls were enrolled.

Lystal, like the rest of Trendham, didn't have separate classes, officially anyway. While technically there weren't any aristocrats or landed nobles, the rich still held sway. Five great merchant houses ruled Trendham indirectly. The Council of Five elected a chief executive to manage the government, and while the Prime Minister was supposedly free to act as he pleased, everyone knew who pulled his strings.

The five great houses worked in concert with the smaller merchants and the guilds to keep Trendham in order, and for the most part, it worked. They'd avoided being embroiled in outside wars for so long no one could remember the last time they truly needed an army. They'd avoided being drawn into the war between Terabinia and Darrow, just as they'd avoided being involved in the original civil war that split Greater Darrow into those two nations.

The only outside trouble that bothered Trendham came in the form of raiders from the steppes of Faresh on their southern border. Most of Trendham's professional army was posted to the south because of that, with only a token force near the border with Darrow.

Politics and larger matters were of little concern to Alver and his peers, unless something bloody happened. Wars, disasters, and similar events grabbed everyone's attention, but things had been quiet for most of his childhood. He turned ten and entered his second year at Gabet's Academy before the first news arrived that grabbed Alver's interest.

"Did you ever see a troll, Alver?" asked Douglas Rushton, a small boy who, despite his small size, was one of the few who dared to make friends with him despite his reputation.

Alver frowned. "A what?"

"A troll. You're from Terabinia, right? I heard there's trolls there."

"I don't even know what that is."

Doug's eyes lit with excitement. "They're giant monsters. They've got arms and legs like a man, but they stand ten feet tall and use trees as clubs."

Alver snorted. "Sounds like a story to keep children from sneaking out at night."

"They're real," insisted Doug. "The last time they were seen was before we were born. My dad said they ate half the people in Darrow before the Stormking wiped them out. But a courier from Bondgrad brought news yesterday that they've been spotted again, this time in Terabinia!"

"Stormking?" Alver was confused. Stormking was the name for one player in a game of tag who had to chase down the other players. "Are you talking about a game?"

"No, dunce! I'm talking about the real Stormking. Don't you know anything?" Doug had few reservations when it came to his words, a trait that had often gotten him in trouble with the other boys, until he and Alver became friends.

"I guess not," agreed Alver with a sigh.

They were outside during the long break after lunch, so Doug motioned for Alver to sit next to him in the shade of one of the large oaks that grew in the yard. After they were both seated, Doug began educating him. "The Stormking ruled Terabinia before they conquered Darrow, but after they conquered it, the Patriarch cursed the land by summoning these incredible monsters, the trolls. Wait, I think I messed up the story. He wasn't the Stormking until after that."

"What was he then?"

"Just the king? I dunno," replied Doug. "Anyway, to stop the trolls he made a deal with Marduke and sold his soul for the power to defeat the trolls."

"What kind of power?"

Doug's face took on a sly expression. "Why do you think they call him the Stormking? He controls lightning. To stop the trolls, he created a huge storm and used lightning to kill them all."

"That's ridiculous," scoffed Alver. "If the devil gave people that much power just for a soul, the whole world would be overrun with stormkings by now."

His friend thought for a moment, rubbing his chin. "You're right, but I think there was more. Oh! That's it! I almost forgot. He went to Shimera and sacrificed the people there, trading *all* their souls for his power."

"That would make more sense," agreed Alver. "But I'm pretty sure traders still come from there."

"Maybe some of them hid." Doug shrugged. "Anyway, the important part is that he's dead now, but the trolls are back."

"How'd he die?"

"No idea. But you're missing the point. The trolls are back, and this time they're in Terabinia!"

"What do they look like?" asked Alver.

"I was hoping you'd know!" declared Doug. "Everyone says they're huge, but that's all anyone can agree on."

"Well, I've never seen one."

"If they eat all the people in Terabinia, they might come here next," suggested his friend. "They say that Minister Strommen is calling on the merchant houses and guilds to send at least half their wardsmen and regular mercenaries to guard the border."

Alver frowned. "What's the difference between a wardsman and a soldier?"

"Don't you know anything?" said Doug in disbelief, but after a pause he added, "I forget you're from Terabinia. Wardsmen are soldiers, but they're magic too. Their bodies are covered in spell tattoos that make them unbeatable. If the trolls do come to Trendham, they're probably the only ones that can stop them."

"What about the wizards?"

Doug snorted. "They make the wardsmen, but I don't think wizards can fight."

"Oh."

Alver got home in the late afternoon and was greeted by an unexpected surprise. As soon as he stepped through the door, he saw his favorite person in all the world. "Aunt Ess!" He dropped his book bag and launched himself across the room into her arms.

It had been several years since she had moved to Bondgrad, and while she visited two or three times a year, it was never enough. She caught him in midair and twirled him around in a circle before setting him down on his feet. "I won't be able to do that much longer, Olly. You'll be taller than me in a few years if you keep growing like that!" she exclaimed, tossing her head to get a strand of hair out of her face. His aunt was easy to spot in a crowd thanks to her unusual red hair.

"Then I'll swing you around instead," he suggested, earning a smile from her.

His nana broke in, "We didn't expect you until the fall."

Aunt Ess grimaced. "There's been some news. I came to talk it over with W—Kelvin."

Erisa gave her a curious look. "We heard about the elves in Cerria. Are they really planning to resume normal trade?"

Ess nodded. "Yes, and they're sending a delegation to Bondgrad as well, but that's not the news I was referring to."

"She means the trolls," announced Alver proudly.

Erisa frowned. "The trolls are dead, and if they aren't, they're none of our concern. You didn't have to come all this way to give us such news."

"He'll want to know," said Alver's aunt firmly.

"What would you like for supper?" asked Erisa, changing the subject abruptly, a sure sign she was upset.

"Won't Kelvin be cooking?" asked his aunt.

Erisa's eyes were hard. "He's worked over the years cooking for ungrateful customers. I think he deserves a rest. How does a minced lamb pie sound?"

Alver could sense the tension between them, but the suggestion overrode his concern. "Good! That sounds really good."

When his father returned that evening, he seemed genuinely pleased to see Aunt Ess, but the tension in the house seemed to grow stronger, especially after they finished eating. Alver was banished to the drudgery of washing dishes, but the house wasn't large enough for that to be a problem for his young ears.

"Relax, Mom. I already heard the news. It's been all over town today," said Kelvin.

"I hope you're going to be sensible about this. You don't owe those people anything," declared Erisa.

"I'm quite happy here," agreed Kelvin. "But Lettler asked me to make a trip to Bondgrad to arrange orders for supplies for the Laughing Goat over the next year."

Aunt Ess laughed. "I knew it. I'll be coming with you, of course."

Erisa growled in frustration. "A cook is being sent to arrange business matters? Who will believe that? You might as well speak plainly—" Her voice cut off suddenly.

Alver could barely hear his father's next words, but he caught two words clearly: "sharp ears." A moment later, Kelvin's voice returned to its normal volume. "I'm sure I won't be away for more than a few weeks."

"The Stormking is dead. The queen is responsible for Terabinia now," protested Alver's grandmother.

Kelvin's voice returned with a soothing tone that was sure to irritate Erisa. "Of course he is. That's got nothing to do with me. I'm just going to Bondgrad, but since it's closer, I might hear more current news. I'll be sure to tell you about it when I get back."

"Traveling is dangerous and there's no need for it," argued Alver's grandmother. "You should stay home."

"I'll be traveling with him, Auntie," said Aunt Ess. "With me there it won't be that dangerous, I'm a wizard after all. I can protect Kelvin better than anyone." She laughed at the end as though she'd made a joke.

Alver forgot what he was supposed to be doing and left the dishes to run into the other room. "Is that true, Aunt Ess? Are you really a wizard now?" He'd been younger when she had left, and while he'd heard them mention her trying an apprenticeship, nothing else had been said of it in the intervening years.

His aunt's eyes sparkled as she saw him come in. "Did you ever doubt I would succeed, Olly?"

Suddenly skeptical, Alver crossed his arms. "Show me some magic then."

Aunt Ess made a theatrical flourish with one hand, and a blue ball of flame suddenly appeared in the air. Seconds later, it split into four balls which moved to hover at the corners of the room, overwhelming the soft candlelight and flooding the room with a vivid blue glow. "How's that?" she asked.

"Mother's tits!" swore Alver. "You really are a wizard!"

"Alver!" snapped his grandmother. His father quietly chuckled, earning him a sharp glance as well.

"Sorry, Nana," apologized Alver. Unable to control his curiosity, he asked his aunt, "Does that mean you can make wardsmen now?"

His aunt shrugged. "I suppose. If I studied the wards and spells used. Why?"

Alver had been thinking about wardsmen all afternoon. Training with his father over the years had given him a certain degree of confidence, and now that he knew there were men who made their living fighting, not just with normal weapons but with magic as well, a fire had been sparked in his heart. He knew his grandmother wouldn't like the idea, though, so he was cautious in how he replied. "Nana was nervous about Dad travelling; if you make him a wardsman it will be even safer, won't it?"

His aunt stared at him oddly for several seconds while a variety of responses flashed behind her eyes. Eventually, she settled on one. "Olly, I think you overestimate how dangerous a trip to Bondgrad is, especially if you're worried about your f—"

Kelvin stopped laughing long enough to interrupt, his tone suddenly stern. "Sam."

Aunt Ess glanced at Kelvin in frustration, then turned back to Alver. "Don't you think my magic can keep us safe enough?"

"My friend Doug says wizards are no good in a fight, that's why they have wardsmen to begin with," replied Alver seriously.

His aunt's eyes narrowed with irritation, and she started to argue, "Now listen here you little—"

Kelvin broke in again. "Your friend is right for the most part, especially if you're talking about the wizards here in Trendham."

"You shouldn't encourage this nonsense," spat Aunt Ess.

Alver's dad grinned. "But he's right. That's why the Terabinians have the Driven and it's the same reason Trendham has the wardsmen." Then he turned his attention fully to Alver. "Your aunt isn't like most wizards, though. You'll understand when you're older. She's quite capable of keeping the two of us safe."

Alver nodded, then looked at his aunt. "Don't worry, Aunt Ess, when I grow up I'll be your wardsman."

His aunt smiled, but for some reason his father didn't like the idea. "Absolutely not," declared Kelvin. "I won't have you wasting your life that way."

"Why not?" asked Alver. "You told me I have a natural talent for fighting. I know I'm not supposed to use it at school, but I could be a great wardsman!"

"Wardsmen live short lives, son—very short."

"Only if they aren't very good," insisted Alver.

Kelvin stood and ran his hands through his hair in frustration. "No, son, always, without exception. That's why the wizards here use them. If you're interested you can start the foundations for being an exceptional wizard in a few more years, but being a wardsman is out of the question."

"But Dad—"

"No buts. I'm not changing my mind on this."

Alver's frustration boiled over. "I don't want to be a stupid wizard, I want to be a wardsman!"

Kelvin glared at him. "That's just about the dumbest thing I've ever heard you say." Sighing, Alver's father glanced around, then spoke to the air. "I'm too tired for this conversation today. We can talk about this another time. There's a lot you need to learn, and I don't have the patience right now." Alver turned around and headed for his room. "Where are you going?" called his father.

"To bed. Isn't that where you were about to send me?" Alver didn't bother hiding his bitterness.

"No, but if you're taking that tone then we can both agree you need some time to cool off," said Kelvin angrily.

CHAPTER 3

The sun was low in the sky when Will and Sammy passed through the arches that decorated the western entrance to Bondgrad. It was merely decorative because a large portion of the capital of Trendham was outside the old city wall that defended the heart of Bondgrad. They were now in an expansive area that included residential sections and a few private houses, but also bordered on the western dockyards that adorned the Trent River. The road they were on cut through the middle of it and would pass by the docks before reaching the Breville Causeway, a massive stone bridge that crossed the river and joined the two halves of the city.

Causeway wasn't really the proper term, but it had retained the name from its most distant past, before the city had built it into the marvel of modern engineering and stonework that it currently was. The Breville Causeway ignored the downward slope of the riverside, supported by ever larger stone bulwarks that eventually became stone pillars supporting arches beneath the main road, which was an incredible hundred feet in width across the entire quarter-mile span. Several lanes were reserved for wagons and commercial traffic while the rest was occupied by an unceasing stream of citizens, merchants, and tradesmen.

The Breville Causeway was so substantial that it truly welded the two halves of Bondgrad into one city. At one time, entrepreneurial vendors had even gone so far as to build shops and stores along the edges to capture a portion of the money flowing across the bridge each day, but sixty years ago the mayor of Bondgrad had mustered enough support to have them torn down and cleared away since the buildings were beginning to choke the traffic.

The only building to survive was a massive inn that served as both a tavern and public house. It remained for several reasons, the primary one being that it had been constructed and designed as part of the bridge by the original architect, Lloyd Breville himself. It didn't occlude the traffic because the central support pillars and been built far wider there, to support not only the roadway, but the great stone building that nestled there, serving as a crown to decorate the triumphant architecture.

Two hundred years past, it was meant to be Breville's home, but the master builder died before his project was finished. In the decades that followed, his heirs had fallen into financial ruin and the house had been sold to cover their debts. It had changed hands between prominent families for a time, before finally becoming the embodiment of Trendham itself, a commercial establishment. It retained its historic value, it didn't block the road, and its foundation was an integral part of Breville's Causeway. It would remain so long as the bridge itself stood.

These days it was officially known as the Roc's Roost, denoted by a colorful sign displaying a giant bird nesting on a stone pinnacle. For those that could read it was spelled out as well, but despite those efforts, the locals knew it as Breville's Cock, and after they'd had a few drinks within they would gladly tell any and all that they weren't referring to a bird. The joke was as old as the building and never seemed to grow tiresome.

The building was visible long before they stepped foot on the bridge, and Will studied it as they approached. He'd seen it several times since moving to Trendham, but he'd never ventured inside. When he'd first passed through Bondgrad, he'd made a point of avoiding such visibility and in the years since, he hadn't cared enough to bother. The building rose five stories, towering over the road, but there was more to the Roc's Roost than what could be seen. More floors lay beneath, built into the enormous stone foundations.

From the street, the building was open with wide arches exposing most of the first level as an open pub. Stairs led from entrances along the sides down to a cozier bar and café that boasted long balconies and an excellent view of the river. Only the wealthier citizens and merchants frequented the lower tavern.

Beneath that were cellars for storing food and wine, but if one moved up from the river bar and street tavern, the next level was devoted to accommodations for those with too much money and too little sense, at least according to Will's way of thinking. The common room there cost five silvers if you wanted to sleep on the floor with a crowd of strangers. Five larger bedrooms held beds that would sleep four each, and a place in one of those beds was seven silver coins, an absurd price to sleep next to a stranger in Will's opinion. There were also four tiny rooms that were roughly the size of a monk's cell. If someone was obsessed with privacy, they could rent one of those for a full gold crown per night, assuming they weren't full already, which was almost always the case.

The next floor was primarily occupied by kitchens, more storage, and of course a multitude of staff, but that wasn't the end of the Roc's Roost. Three more floors remained, each smaller and more exclusive than the previous. The first two of those held what were essentially tiny apartments, each consisting of a small bedroom and a balcony where rich idiots could look down on those with less coin or more wisdom than to waste it on a room that cost five gold a night.

The extravagance didn't end there, however—the top floor held two suites with prices that weren't publicly advertised. As the saying went, if you had to ask what they cost, you couldn't afford it.

Sammy stopped, forcing Will to pull up short behind her. "What are you doing?" he asked.

His cousin looked over her shoulder at him, purposely striking a pose that was artfully coy and almost certainly calculated. Sammy winked. "This is it."

"This is what?"

"Our destination for the evening," she clarified.

Will's expression remained flat while his eyes occasionally moved here and there, observing the bustling crowd that flowed around them, jostling them as people went in and out of the main tavern. "The hell it is," he said, his expression making his feelings almost as clear as if he had spat on the road to punctuate his words.

Sammy's eyes tightened as she returned his gaze. "This is our first adventure together since…"

"Since the one that nearly killed you," Will interrupted.

Her eyes flashed a warning. "We're in public."

"They can't hear us," said Will. He didn't need to explain, since his cousin was already well aware of his particular talents. "I agreed to stop in Bondgrad because you said you wanted to leave messages with some of your friends. That doesn't mean I intend to fund a ridiculously overpriced night in the world's most expensive inn."

"Who asked you to pay?"

He continued to rant, "There are places just as fine on either side of the river that cost ten times less than anything you'd find here."

Sammy sighed. "I live in Bondgrad, Will. I know the prices in this city better than you do, not that the price should bother you."

"I'm not a duke anymore, and a common cook doesn't make much," Will protested.

She laughed as she put her hands on her hips. "*I'm* the one arranging the sales for your alchemical products. I can't imagine what you're doing with the pile of gold that must be accumulating after all these years."

"That money is for the school, plus the Goat barely broke even last year. I had to put more into it as well."

"You're full of shit. I know that school *and* your pretend employer didn't cost you even half the thousands you made last year, much less the years before."

"It's not as much as you think," argued Will. "When you factor in the cost of raw materials…"

"Most of which I also purchase on your behalf," she snapped. "I can do math, Will. It doesn't take alchemical stoichiometry to figure out your profit margins. By now you've probably got enough coin that half the women in Bondgrad would divorce their husbands for a piece of it, and the men would probably pay you just to have a look."

Will snorted, unable to remain serious in the face of Sammy's infectious humor. He took a moment to regain his grave demeanor, then responded, "That doesn't mean I intend to waste money. Besides, I've been thinking about a hospital in…"

"More philanthropy? The school makes sense at least, since Oliver benefits, but why—" Sammy paused, rubbing her face with one hand. "Never mind, I know how this argument ends. That's not the point right now. This is where we're staying, and as I said a minute ago, no one asked you to pay." She grabbed his arm to lead him inside.

He didn't budge. "You've been in this city for quite a while. Don't you have a place? I'd rather stay there than watch you waste your money here."

His cousin gave him a wry smile. "Oh, really? Why didn't I think of that? My goodness, I'm so thoughtless these days!" She dropped the sarcasm a second later, adding, "If you want to see where I live, you're going to have to follow me inside." She pulled on his wrist again.

This time, Will was too surprised to resist. "Oh," he replied, followed a moment later by, "Huh?"

Sammy removed the drab overcoat she wore as they slipped through the crowd. Beneath it she wore a practical linen dress that was exceptional only for the quality of its stitching and the expense of the rich burgundy color it was dyed. Without the coat she was now more easily marked as a woman of some means, but that wasn't the end of her transformation. Lifting one hand, she brought a slender gold chain from beneath her neckline and let the emerald pendant hanging from it show against the fabric of her bosom. A gold ring from her limnthal was slipped over one finger and then Sammy pulled off the ties holding the end of her braids.

If he hadn't known already, Will might have thought the magic that followed was part of an enchantment on the hair ties, rather than an original spell Sammy had designed for her own needs. Given her vivid red hair, she was easily remembered and always noticed, so his cousin used magic to color her hair a less remarkable shade of brown much of the time. Since she frequently wanted to switch between that and her natural color, she'd created a two-part spell to facilitate the change back and forth.

The magic swept along her braids, untwining them and expanding her curls while the hue shifted from brunette to fiery orange. Heads turned and the crowd began to part in front of them as people took note of the exotic woman in their midst.

"Temarah's tits!" swore Will, ducking his head and staring at the floor to avoid showing his face. "Are you insane?" He instinctively kept his voice from any ears but Sammy's as he smoothed his turyn to make himself unnoticeable. The technique was one he'd learned from an assassin, and while it didn't make him invisible, the effect was generally superior as he became difficult to notice.

Even Sammy struggled with it, and she knew he was there. Her eyes slid past him several times before finally coming to rest on his face as she replied, "I wish you wouldn't do that. It's hard to talk when I have to work so hard just to keep your face in focus."

Will was busy watching the room. Although Sammy's vibrant appearance was now drawing admiring looks, the attention was far less than he expected. Red hair was rare in Trendham, rare enough to draw stares, but most of the people in the room only studied her for a few moments before returning to their business. Others whispered, but all in all, the response was much more subdued than he would have guessed.

"Come on," said Sammy, heading toward the nearest of two large staircases that stood at either end of the street-level pub.

He followed, struggling to get through the crowd that now barely acknowledged his presence. There was still a small space around Sammy as people respectfully gave her extra room, but it was no longer big enough for him. The stairs were easier, since few people aside from the staff and wealthy customers were using them. Quite a few of the guests and all the staff greeted Sammy as they ascended.

"Evening, Madeleine."

"Good to see you back, Mistress."

"Maddy, the world is always brighter when you're here!"

Will let his turyn return to normal since they were out of the crowd, but he grew more confused as they ascended. Sammy leaned over to ask a question, softly whispering, "You remember I chose Madeleine for my name, don't you?"

"Yes," he answered slowly. *That's not why I'm confused,* he thought silently, but his puzzlement only grew as they passed each floor without stopping. "Where are we going?"

"You'll see," said Sammy enigmatically before stopping to address a maid who had just greeted her. "Cecilia, I'd like you to meet my cousin Daryl. We've just come in from the road and a bath would be welcome. Could you let Alyssa know?"

"Certainly Mistress," said the young woman, dipping her head respectfully. Her eyes passed over Will briefly before returning to Sammy. "The large bath or…?"

"Both," answered Sammy immediately. "This is Daryl's first visit and he's never had the chance to enjoy the large bath, so make sure Alyssa knows."

Cecilia directed her attention to Will. "Do you have any preferences for your bath?"

"Preferences?" His eyes darted toward Sammy uncertainly.

Sammy broke in smoothly, "She means fragrances." She turned to the maid. "Daryl doesn't like strong scents, so the rose soap would be best, as for the rest,"—Sammy paused, glancing mischievously at Will for a moment before continuing—"you and Alyssa can decide. Is Stefan here today?"

The maid nodded. "He's playing in the lower bar tonight."

"I'm in the mood for music. Have him switch with one of the others."

Cecilia smiled. "He'll be glad to know he's your favorite."

Sammy laughed. "Trust me, he already knows." Then she turned and resumed her climb up the stairs.

"What did that mean?" asked Will after several steps.

"Stefan is a minstrel," said his cousin. "I thought that was self-evident."

"No, what did you mean about letting her and Alyssa decide? Decide what?" Will demanded.

At the top of the stairs, they reached a landing that was open to the outside air. A decorative railing protected the area so people couldn't easily fall, and an archway opened onto a stone balcony that encircled the top floor. A trellis topped the stone railing, sheltering the area from strong sunlight above and curious stares below. A tiny garden with flowers and two benches occupied the center while double doors on either side led into the two suites on either side.

Will stared at his cousin. "This isn't…?"

She nodded. "Welcome to my home."

"What the fuck, Sam!"

"Do you like it?" Her eyes were brimming with mirth.

"You're insane." Will couldn't help but look from side to side. "This must be costing you a fortune. Which one is yours?"

She nibbled on the tip of her index finger. "'Which' isn't really a proper way to frame the question."

His eyes went wide. "Both? Why? That doesn't even make sense!"

Sammy patted him on one cheek, then led the way to the left-hand door. "This is the one I call home and it's more than large enough for my needs most of the time." Will exhaled, trying to relax, until she added, "I rent the other suite out occasionally, except when I want the extra space for entertaining."

"You're shitting me."

She looked up at him with a twinkle in her eye. "No, I'm quite serious. You know how much I like parties."

"You have a lot of explaining to do tonight," he told her, then asked, "Am I staying with you or over there?" He nodded toward the other suite.

She chuckled. "Don't be silly. There's three bedrooms in each— why would I put you all the way over there? Besides, you'll want to hear Stefan's playing. He's very skilled and he's got a voice to match."

Inside there was a wide parlor with chairs and couches for relaxing. Two more doors exited the parlor on opposite sides. Sammy pointed to one. "That's the main bath. The other door leads to the bedrooms."

"I feel sorry for the staff who have to haul water up here," muttered Will.

His cousin laughed as she opened the door. Within he could see a large circular pool already filled. Water poured in at a steady pace from horsehead sculptures on either side, and steam rose from the surface. "There's a cistern and an enchanted pump. The water is kept pleasantly warm too, although if you'd prefer it colder or hotter there's two valves over there which you can use to adjust the temperature."

Of course, he thought. "Why is it so large?" It could easily hold five or six people and even had a stone seat beneath the water that followed the circumference of the heated pool.

Her answer was simple enough, but something in Sammy's eyes hinted at mischief. "It was built as a family bath." She paused, then went on, "I was planning to use the private bath next to my room, but if you want to talk while we clean up, that's fine too."

They'd grown up together, and Will wasn't overly shy, but the thought of a private bath was attractive to him. "No, this is perfect," he told her. Squatting beside the edge, he felt the water with one hand, imagining what it would feel like to soak in the luxurious space. It had been many years since he'd experienced that sort of decadence, and despite himself, he was warming to the thought.

Sammy nodded. "The table over there is for you to put your things on. One of the girls will have them cleaned tonight…"

"I can clean them myself."

She held up a hand. "Spells are nice, but trust me, the laundry here is wonderful. Your clothes will be soft and pleasantly scented. They'll even oil your boots and whatnot." Sammy pointed to a wardrobe on one side of the chamber. "There are robes in there for you to wear. The clothes won't be ready until morning."

"Sammy, this is—well, it's hard to believe. How did you manage all this?"

She smiled, but her eyes were uncharacteristically serious. "I'll explain that over supper. For now I just want you to relax and enjoy yourself. Tonight, you're my special guest." Her arms went around him, and Will hugged her back out of habit. She said into his shoulder, "I'm not joking, Will. I respect what you've been doing, but you deserve much better than what you've allowed yourself."

He started to push away, but Sammy held on. Her next words were filled with determination. "This is my home. I won't watch you punish yourself, not here. In my house, you are safe and you will be cared for. Enjoy your bath and take as long as you wish. Afterward, we can eat and enjoy Stefan's singing."

After a moment Will relaxed and then squeezed her. "Fine."

Sammy let go and headed for the door. "Enjoy yourself. That's an order."

He waved a hand to shoo her out. "I will. Why are you being so emphatic?"

She ignored him and shut the door behind herself. Shaking his head, Will disrobed, carefully laying out his clothes before slipping into the deliciously hot water. He sank down and let his body float partway up, until he was supported purely by his neck pressing against the curved rim of the pool. He remained that way for five or ten minutes until he heard the door open again.

Sitting up to avoid presenting too much of himself to Sammy's maid, he turned his head to see who had entered. It was Cecilia. She gave him friendly smile as she placed a basket she was carrying down and then gathered up his clothing. "I'll be right back."

"No need," he told her. "I know where everything is."

"You'll be wanting more than a soak, I think," she answered, stepping out.

Will relaxed and began to drift again. "I guess I do need some soap. I didn't think about that."

A couple of minutes later, she returned, and Will heard a click at the door. Glancing over he saw that Cecilia had slid a small wooden bar through a cleverly made slot on the inside of the doorframe. "What was that?" he asked.

"The privacy latch," answered the maid. Her attire was different now. Gone was the work dress, and in its place was a simple robe held closed by little more than a silk cord.

He stared at her with some suspicion. "I don't think that's necessary. Why are you dressed like that?"

Cecilia laughed lightly and covered her mouth, though not before Will caught a brief glimpse of white teeth. For some reason, the sight intrigued him, since the woman's healthy smile paired well with her lips and figure. "I'm here to bathe you."

Will was familiar with a variety of bathing practices, and having lived in a royal palace for some time, he had an idea of what sort of things were allowed. Given what his cousin had said and the fact that Cecilia seemed ready to disrobe, he felt the need to clarify things. "Listen. I just want a bath. I'm not the sort who…" He let his words trail off.

"The sort who—what?"

"Takes advantage of the help."

Cecilia nodded. "That's a relief. I had a good feeling after meeting you, but then most of Mistress Madeleine's guests are the trustworthy sort." She gestured with her hands in a no-nonsense manner. "Stand up and sit on this bench for me." There was a small wooden stool near where she waited.

Her matter-of-fact attitude assuaged Will's worry, and he did as he was told. Years ago, he'd been embarrassed to be seen naked by the servants at the palace in Cerria, but he was older now and this was nothing unusual, other than Cecilia's attire. As he sat, he was surprised when she stepped past him, letting her robe slide to the floor. For a second that seemed to last an eternity, he watched her naked backside as she walked to the pool and immersed herself briefly.

When she stood and turned around, he averted his eyes, though not before seeing her fully naked. "What are you doing? I told you I'm not interested in—in that."

She was already behind him when she answered, "You said you don't take advantage, not that you weren't interested in my body." Will tensed as her hands came down on his shoulders. "Relax, I'm teasing you. I intend to bathe as well, so I needed to rinse first." Her fingers slid over his skin, spreading lightly scented soap across his back.

"I meant to bathe alone."

"Daryl, do you find my company odious?"

"No. That's not what I meant. Just wash my back and go. You're very lovely, but this isn't me. I prefer the company of those who aren't being paid to please."

Cecilia's hands went still, her nails digging into his skin slightly. "You think I'm a prostitute?"

"I didn't say that. I don't know what S—Madeleine put you up to, but—"

"She didn't put me up to anything," laughed Cecilia. "I volunteered for this, and it was my choice to bathe with you, assuming you don't find a little company bothersome." She resumed lathering, using pressure as her hands traced his muscles. The sensation was extremely pleasant.

From back to neck, her fingers worked miracles, then she washed his hair and used a bucket to rinse him off. Returning with the soap, she washed his arms, then his feet before moving to stand behind him again. Soapy hands crossed his chest and descended slowly down his abdomen. Will jerked, but her teeth nipped his ear. "Don't move. I just want to be thorough."

It was quite obvious to her touch that he was already in a state of extreme arousal, and despite his reservations, Will let her wash him. The next thirty seconds were intensely pleasurable, but to his surprise Cecilia released her grip a moment later and then poured a fresh bucket over him, sluicing away the soap. "All done. You can get back in and soak now if you wish, or..."

Simultaneously relieved and disappointed, Will responded, "Or?"

"I can wash myself, or if you don't mind you could do my back for me, though I'll understand if you don't want to bathe a servant. I wouldn't ask, but you've been such a gentleman."

The beast within was roaring, but his mind still held sway. "I don't mind." His voice was entirely too deep when he replied. He stood and started to shuffle around her. "If you'll look away until I'm behind you."

Cecilia laughed. "I've seen it—no need to be shy. I was just washing it a moment ago!" She stared directly at his waist, then handed him the soap. "Shoulders first, please."

He hadn't been so intimate with a woman in over eight years, and Will's heart was pounding in his ears as he sat down behind her. His moral compunctions had vanished, but the abrupt way she had stopped washing him had left him confused. Perhaps it was really just a bath, or his questions had insulted her. Or his first remark had created a proper boundary and he had allowed his lust to cloud his judgment.

He washed her shoulders, neck, and back, but she stopped him before he could try and wash her hair. "I'll do that later," she told him. "Can I ask you to do my arms?"

"Sure."

"Sit closer. I won't scream if it touches my back. I promise."

He had started to relax, in several important ways, but her words sent fire down his spine. He moved closer, washing her arms, leaving no space between them. "Feet next?"

"No, my thighs, please."

His sanity was nearly gone, but the memory of a few minutes earlier still haunted him. Will was determined to control himself. *Just wash and rinse, the same as she did,* he told himself.

"Now the center," she purred. "Just lightly soap the outside." She moaned audibly as his fingers circled her womanhood. It was obvious that this was no game.

Mustering the same will he'd once used to kill a dragon, Will removed his hands and poured a fresh bucket of water down her belly and across her more delicate regions. "All done. Ready for a nice soak?"

"Daryl, you are pure evil," she returned. Giving him a rueful look, she stood and stretched slowly in front of him, her eyes never leaving his. She walked languidly to the pool and stepped in, but rather than immerse herself, she stood on the stone bench, so that water only came up to her knees. Bending, she leaned forward, supporting her upper body by holding onto the statuary that poured water in on that side. The pose was unashamedly sexual, and when she looked back at him, her eyes were smoldering. "Come here."

He gave her a doubtful look.

"Please?"

The 'please' and a playful wiggle were more than he could stand.

CHAPTER 4

"I can't go out there," said Will. "She's going to know."

Cecilia laughed. "How will she know?"

"We've been in here for at least an hour and a half."

"Maybe you just needed a really long soak." She made a highly suggestive gesture with her two hands. "In fact, I *know* you needed that soak. How long has it been?"

Over eight years, he thought. "A while. Years," he admitted.

She nodded. "Thought so. You didn't relax until round two."

Will might have blushed at that remark once, in a life that seemed to belong to someone else. He was older now. He returned to the problem at hand. "My cousin is going to know what happened."

Cecilia shrugged. "She told you to enjoy yourself. What do you think she meant?"

"Aren't you worried she'll fire you?" he asked.

The maid laughed so suddenly she choked for a moment. It took a few seconds for her to clear her throat and then she continued laughing. Rubbing at her eyes, she looked at Will in disbelief. "More likely she'll give me a raise."

"But you said you weren't—are you saying she pays you for this?"

"You're really worried about me being a prostitute, aren't you?" she told him, but before he could respond she went on, "I'm not, though I'm not sure why it would bother you. Madeleine pays me well, *very well.* On rare occasions when she brings a special guest, I don't mind making their stay memorable. If I hadn't thought you were cute, I'd have let one of the other girls help with your bath, and before you ask, no, they aren't prostitutes either, though I'll admit they're less picky. If you were rude or smelly, the odds are they'd have just washed your back and left."

"Oh."

She gave him a curious look. "How old are you?"

Nearly thirty. "Why do you ask?" The question of his age was something that was beginning to bother him. The way things were progressing, by the time Oliver reached adulthood, the two of them would look like brothers rather than father and son.

"One minute you seem amusingly young, then the next you seem much older. You showed quite a bit of restraint earlier."

"How old do you think I am?"

Her face grew thoughtful. "Twenty-five? You look younger than me, but there's something about you."

If he looked younger, she was almost saying he looked like a teenager. "Close enough. Everyone says I look younger than I am. What gives my real age away, the beard?"

"That and the scars. Are you a soldier?"

"I was once," he answered. *The scars.* The words brought unpleasant memories. She was probably referring to the marks on his back, from when he'd been lashed half to death, or possibly the fang marks that dotted his skin. One hand went to his belly, where an assassin's blade had once passed entirely through his body from back to front. He would have died that day if it hadn't been for the timely intervention of someone important. A woman's face filled his mind's eye, dark hair framing vivid blue eyes, full lips beneath a nose that was ever so slightly crooked. Will blinked, trying to clear his thoughts. "We should go."

"Not worried about what your cousin thinks anymore?" teased Cecilia.

Will smiled to mask his feelings. "Not anymore." Cinching his robe tighter, he opened the door and stepped out. He froze a second later, as he realized the parlor was now occupied by at least ten people and Sammy wasn't among them.

Worse, they were all properly dressed, which meant that Will was the only person wearing nothing but a robe. He corrected that thought when Cecilia stepped up behind him, draped an arm across him, and rested her chin on his shoulder with an expression that left little doubt in any viewer's mind just how well acquainted they were. She seemed completely at ease being half-dressed in a crowd.

For a brief second, he considered retreating, but Cecilia whispered in his ear, "Relax. These are all good friends of Maddy's. They're simply curious to meet an actual relative of hers. She's always been so mysterious."

Will had played the part of a soft-spoken nobody for years, but he'd never forgotten the experiences of his time as one of the most powerful men in Terabinia. The maid's words bolstered him, not simply because he was Sammy's cousin, though. His identity was still hidden, but today he was free to act a different part. He strode forward, adopting a confident smile. "Hello. Nice to meet you all. I'm Daryl."

Two men held instruments, so Will assumed one of them was Stefan, but the first person to make an introduction was a flaxen-haired beauty in a simple dress. "Nice to meet you. I'm Alyssa." Her eyes went to Cecilia's, and they exchanged a knowing look. "I hope you're not too tired from—" she paused deliberately, then finished, "—traveling. We were hoping to enjoy some wine and dancing after the food."

What in the world have I fallen into? thought Will. "Charmed," he replied.

"Oh my, you sound like a gentleman!" exclaimed Alyssa. "I should have been more suspicious when Cici said you were probably too young for wine. I suspect she had an ulterior motive."

"Of course," laughed Cecilia.

Everyone looked up as the door to Sammy's room opened and she stepped out. Her eyes surveyed the area before coming to rest on Will with a smile. "You look relaxed." Then she turned to Alyssa. "The food isn't up yet?" Stefan moved over to make room on one of the couches so she could sit next to him.

"It should be ready soon. Should I go check?" asked Alyssa.

Sammy told her not to worry and then fell to chatting amiably with the two women and the musicians. Will watched her curiously, wondering at her strange home and the people his cousin had chosen to surround herself with. Sammy had obviously just emerged from her own bath since her hair was wet and she wore a similar robe. It was clear she trusted the people around her.

Moments later, wine was served, followed by a course of light dishes that consisted mainly of toasted bread with a variety of garnishes and roasted meat on skewers. Cecilia sat next to Will, and he felt his tension continue to melt away as the wine filled his body with a warm glow. The conversation revolved around music and minor gossip, but when Stefan asked about Will's life, Sammy quickly nipped it in the bud. "Daryl's here to relax. His work wouldn't interest you."

At most parties, that would have invited more questions, but Sammy's friends accepted the response and moved on. Stefan nodded, replying, "Certainly. Sorry if I was prying, Daryl."

Will's skin was starting to tingle pleasantly, though he didn't feel tipsy yet. After the food was taken away, Stefan and his friend Larup brought out a mandolin and a strange set of small drums that Will was unfamiliar with. Alyssa cajoled him into dancing, and shortly thereafter Will found himself outside in the central area watching the stars spin as they twirled beneath them.

He still wasn't a great dancer, but his old lessons came back, and with the help of the wine, he managed to get through the steps without injuring his partner. More importantly, Will enjoyed himself. Sometime later, he found himself back on the couch, though now Cecilia sat on his right while Alyssa was close against him on the left. He was definitely tipsy now, but not excessively so. Will's body felt energized.

Sammy winked when he lifted the wine bottle to examine it. "It's Lambruer, a new vintage."

He'd heard of it. Now that the elves had begun trading regularly, a number of new goods had entered the market and become popular. The elven wine, Lambruer, was an exceedingly expensive example of one of the new vintages. Supposedly elves didn't tolerate alcohol well, so their wine was kept low in alcohol, but it made up the difference with a blend of herbal intoxicants.

"You should have warned me," said Will, affecting a sour attitude that he didn't truly feel. He felt wonderful.

"Warned you that it wouldn't get you drunk? Or warned you that it would put you in a good mood?" asked his cousin. She rose from her seat, then gave Stefan a kiss on the cheek. "I need my rest, but thank you for the music."

The musician smiled, then bobbed his head and began collecting his instruments as he prepared to leave. Sammy headed for her bedroom with hardly a look back. Will called after her, "You're going to leave me here with these…" He glanced at Alyssa, then Cecilia. "What are you exactly?"

"Lionesses," answered Alyssa immediately, her tone playful while her eyes were hungry.

Will nodded, then continued, "With these lionesses? I need rest too."

Sammy laughed as she began to close her door. "You've had many years of rest. I'll trust my friends to know what you truly deserve. Good night!"

***

Will woke with a clear head and a crystalline memory of the night before. His memory was so good that he blushed just remembering it, for he was no longer under the influence of whatever was in the wine he had drunk. He silently reviewed the events, hardly able to believe everything that had happened—everything he had *done*. His memories were lurid, belonging more to the pages of a steamy romance than to the reality of his previous evening.

The evidence before him supported his memory, though, for his bed, large as it was, still contained the two most prominent participants from his night of debauchery. Alyssa was sprawled beside him, her mouth close to his ear, while Cecilia was lying sideways, his stomach serving as a pillow for her head. There were no clothes to be seen, and the bedsheets were tangled up on the floor, but the presence of two warm bodies meant he was excessively warm even though he was uncovered. *I can't believe this,* thought Will.

It was even harder to believe that it was Sammy who had been the architect of the entire thing. Or maybe not. She'd made no secret of being a libertine since she had rejected Emory Tallowen before they'd left Terabinia. What was most difficult to believe was the apparent wealth she had created for herself in Bondgrad.

Will had been carrying a tight knot of tension in his chest for so long he had hardly been aware of it, but now he felt lighter, as though a weight had been lifted from him. Simultaneously, he felt guilty for having enjoyed himself. Selene flitted through his thoughts, but he pushed her from his mind. *She made her choice; I made mine. Why shouldn't I be happy?* he told himself.

That was fun, said Laina. It was rare for him to hear a thought from his deceased sister anymore, but it still happened occasionally. A piece of her soul had fused with his when she died, leaving him with rare glimpses of her memories and desultory bits of dialogue that were clearly not his own thoughts.

Unable to find privacy, either in his bed or his own head, Will rose and went to relieve himself before taking another quick dip in the bath. He thought he'd been quiet enough to avoid waking his companions, but they were gone when he returned. The bed had been tidied, and his clothes were piled neatly on a chair by the window.

Once he was dressed, Will went to find Sammy, who he found eating breakfast in the central area. She motioned toward a seat when she saw him enter.

"Is it just us?" he asked, glancing around.

His cousin nodded, then answered in a dry tone, "Ally and Cici left while you were taking your bath of shame."

"I'm not ashamed," he growled.

"Then why is your face nearly as red as my hair?"

Will knew himself better than that, and his cheeks still felt cool, so he ignored her blatant attempt at teasing. Giving his cousin a dour look, he sat down and claimed a piece of buttered bread. His expression lightened as his teeth crunched through the crisp exterior to find a soft interior that perfectly matched the butter. "Is there a bakery nearby?"

Sammy's smile widened. "No. That came from downstairs. If there was another bakery on this bridge, we would have put them out of business already."

"You're selling baked goods as well?"

"Primarily to our customers, but we also have street-side vendors that take our extras and sell them to people who are just passing by."

"Who is we?" he asked.

His cousin looked like a cat who had just eaten the bird. "I own sixty percent."

"Of which part? The suites we're in or...?"

"Of the entire Cock."

Will sighed. "Sammy..."

"Sixty percent of Roc's Roost. Stop being a prude."

"Do you always have to be crude?"

"I only do it to remind you of who I am now, rather than the little girl you keep trying to pretend I am—plus it's funny. You should see your face."

His face looked just as it always did, but her words caused him to pause and think a moment, then he replied, "Can you blame me? You were a pest sometimes, but you were a sweet girl back then. It's not that I want to keep you frozen in time, I just wish we could go back."

"And now? Am I disappointing?" Sammy lifted one brow and her tone was light, but behind her question, Will could sense a hidden vulnerability. His answer mattered more than she wanted to admit.

Will shook his head. "No. I'll admit I don't know what to think about your lifestyle, but you're not disappointing. You're not what I expected, but you're also amazing in ways that continue to surprise me."

"My lifestyle?"

"The sex party last night, for example."

She gaped at him. "Sex party? You thought that was a sex party?" Before he could reply, she threw a sausage at him. Will caught it with a minor force spell and guided it to the plate in front of him. The food was too good to waste. She continued, "I slept alone. *You* were the one having sex."

Refusing to submit, he responded, "Alyssa and Cecilia too, it wasn't just me."

"With *you*!" Sammy laughed. "Having a threesome with two of my friends doesn't constitute a sex party."

Will's eyes narrowed. "You set that up, and you should have warned me about the wine. I thought they were your maids."

"That wine is less intoxicating than regular wine, it didn't make you do anything you didn't already want to do, and I employ a lot of people, but only my friends get invited up here."

"For the sex parties," Will clarified. His mock anger was spoiled by the smirk that threatened to take over his expression.

Now it was Sammy who was blushing. "For your information, I usually just socialize. What you're suggesting is fairly uncommon."

"But you're not denying it," he pressed. When she didn't respond, he went on. "You and Stefan seemed very friendly."

Sammy's brows knitted together, "He's a good friend, and *yes*, I've enjoyed his company very thoroughly on a few occasions. Larup too, for that matter."

Will held up his hands in surrender. "I don't really want details."

"Not to mention Cecilia and Alyssa once when I was feeling particularly adventurous…"

His eyes threatened to pop out of his head. "By the Mother!"

His cousin gave him a feral smile. "Oh, does that bother you? I know you're not that naïve."

"It's not that, it's just, that's practically incest!"

Sammy looked confused a moment, then laughed. "Oh, because you…"

"Stop! I don't want to think about it."

"Once again, I am the victor," announced Sammy gleefully.

Will changed the subject. "So, who owns the other forty percent?"

Sammy had already taken a bite, but she swallowed quickly, excited to answer the question. "That's the clever part. Twenty-five percent is held by the oligarchs, and that's deliberate because—"

"And the rest?" he interrupted.

She waved her hand. "Ten percent is owned by a mishmash of wealthy businessmen and the guilds, and the remainder is in the hands of the employees. Everyone you met last night owns a tiny part as well."

"Your workers?"

She nodded. "The ones who are smart. If they're loyal and hardworking, I let them buy a stake using their wages. That's part of the genius of my plan."

"Plan?"

"Can I explain now? You've already interrupted me once." She waited to be sure, then continued, "I try to keep the oligarchs' share at roughly twenty-five percent so I retain firm control—" She stopped. Will was holding up a hand. "What?"

"Why would their percentage change?"

"Because they occasionally buy or sell some of their stake when they need extra money."

"They don't have enough money?"

Sammy grinned. "This isn't Terabinia. Business is *everything* here. It doesn't matter how much money they have, they always need coin. Most of the wealth in Trendham is built on loans between the various merchants, the guilds, the oligarchs—the financial system is a complex web of debts. Unlike back home, where the nobility own almost everything, here it's all divided up between thousands of business interests. Anyway, it would take me forever to explain all that. The important thing to understand is this, even the oligarchs frequently need extra coin, or want a place to store it safely."

"Store it?"

"Not as coin, they store their money by owning things, like Roc's Roost, but *I* control how much they can buy, or sell."

Will frowned.

"Because I own the biggest piece of the pie. They sell a piece to me when they need coin and when they want to invest, I let them buy it back, but never at the same price. Each time I make a profit, either in coin, or my overall ownership. I operate almost like a bank, but I keep my greed modest. Roc's Roost is one of the most profitable businesses in Bondgrad, not to mention the prestige it holds, which has its own value," she explained.

"So, each owner gets a part of the profits?"

"Exactly, but the problem they had before was that *all* the profits were being handed out, leaving nothing to keep the business healthy. I corrected that first when I took over management." Sammy looked around, then cast a specialized shield that allowed sound to pass in only one direction. They could still hear things outside, but no one would be able to eavesdrop on them. "Originally I only owned a tiny percentage, but once I was managing the excess profits, I bent the rules a little."

"How so?"

"I used some of the excess coin to fund my personal purchases when trading shares with the oligarchs. I don't have to do that now, but early on it helped accelerate my rise to majority ownership."

Will's eyes widened. "You stole from the business."

"Technically, yes, but over time everything I took was repaid. No one could prove it now, unless they heard me confess it out loud." She gestured at the spell shielding them from prying ears. "Back to my clever plan—I try to make sure the oligarchs continue to own a small portion of Roc's Roost, so they'll have a vested interest in protecting it. All the major players have a stake, so none of them try to sabotage the business as they compete with one another in the myriad enterprises they are involved in."

"So you don't want to own it all," he muttered.

"Exactly! If I had wanted, I could have sole ownership by now, but that would set me up as a rival rather than a partner. Balancing things like this is much better."

"Because you make them money."

Sammy's grin was feral. "They fucking love me."

He nodded, beginning to understand. "And the employees…"

"The ones who save and work hard enough to buy in wind up gaining a solid income that will last them long past their youth. That makes them extremely loyal and motivates them to do their best for the establishment."

Will shook his head in disbelief. Sammy had become an exceptional wizard over the years, but she'd shown a distinct lack of interest in alchemy. He'd thought the problem lay with a dislike for math, but it was clear his cousin had an excellent head for numbers—when they dealt with money. "You managed all this with just the profits from our potion sales?"

"Primarily, although once I finished the apprenticeship with Deylon, I was able to make a nice living on my own, plus my acceptance into the guild opened many more doors, one of which was the opportunity to buy my first stake in Roc's Roost."

He nodded. Sammy had originally come to Bondgrad after he'd arranged a secret deal with one of the master wizards in Trendham's mage guild. Deylon had accepted Sammy as an 'apprentice' for a brief period before quickly raising her to journeyman. After she'd completed the required two years as a journeyman, Deylon had supported her petition to be raised to full master. As a result, Sammy had become the quickest wizard to ever reach the rank of master. Most new students needed more than ten years within the guild.

If all that sounded unusual, it was because it was. Will hadn't revealed his current or past identity to Deylon while brokering the deal, but he had employed both the carrot and the stick while acting as a mysterious patron to get Sammy into the guild. The stick had been the overwhelming power he had shown when first meeting with the master mage and his underlings, but fear alone wouldn't have been enough to accomplish what he wanted. The carrot had been secrets regarding the new 'Terabinian' magic. Initially he had given them the knowledge required to construct teleport beacons, the first of which was already operational in Bondgrad. A second beacon being constructed in Kemp and there was some hope that a deal could be made with Terabinia to facilitate travel to Cerria and Myrsta—assuming security concerns of the two governments could be satisfied.

So far, that deal had made Deylon an extremely wealthy master wizard, and trading the knowledge to other guild mages had quieted the complaints regarding Sammy's rapid elevation to full master. Will had also freely given the knowledge he had regarding the training of 'proper' wizards, but that information hadn't done much. The master wizards in Trendham were too old to benefit and no one wanted to create students who would quickly outshine their masters.

That revolution would have to wait until Sammy began training apprentices of her own.

"I was just hoping that over time you could improve the situation for wizards in Trendham. I never expected the deal with Deylon would result in *this*," remarked Will.

Sammy winked. "By *this*, are you referring to the rise of a sixth oligarch?"

"Is that your goal?"

"Maybe. Assuming no accidents, I'll live a long time. I'm already very prominent among the businesspeople in this city. Given a few decades I could likely manage it, although I'm not sure the political headaches are worth the trouble," she replied.

"What about apprentices?" he asked. It was a question he'd begun asking almost immediately after his cousin had been raised to master.

Sammy pushed her plate away, an unpleasant look on her face. "I'm not ready yet."

"You're scared," said Will.

Her green eyes locked onto him. "Why don't you train some apprentices if you're in such a hurry?"

"You know why! I'm supposed to be dead. Besides, I have Oliver to think of."

"You could train him in a few years."

The image of Seth Gabet's still, cold face flashed through Will's mind. He'd never forgotten the day he'd found his friend dead one morning, a result of that same training. "I'd rather he have a normal life."

"And die of old age while you're still young," she pointed out.

"Better than dying while still a child!" They stared hard at one another for almost a minute; it was an old argument. Finally, Will looked away. "It's still years before we need to think about it."

"Time flies," she returned. "The day will come sooner than you think, and if you don't start talking to Oliver soon, he won't be able to make a proper choice. You heard him the other day. He's got the idea that being a wardsman is a great life choice. That's worse than being a cook. Most of the wardsmen don't survive past thirty, even if they never get hurt. Besides, I heard you trying to convince Oliver to be a wizard."

"Only because he wants to be a wardsman. Anything is better than suicide." Will gave Sammy a hard stare. "I'm not sure I can do it, but you can."

She shook her head. "No, and I won't take any apprentices of my own until you train him."

"Why not?"

"You claim you're giving him a normal life. Fine. Once he's a man that excuse will fade. Oliver will need to know the truth, and you won't be able to hide your identity forever. I know for a fact you don't believe he should remain a mundane. At the very least he should be given the chance to become a first-order wizard. The risk is small, and it will double his lifespan. He can make his own choices if he wants to continue past that." Sammy lifted a hand and pointed at Will. "He's your son. You're the only one with any experience at this, so you'll give him the best chance. *You* train him and I'll observe and help. Then *I'll* have enough confidence to try risking other people's lives doing the same with my own apprentices." She waited then, and when Will didn't respond, she challenged, "Tell me I'm wrong."

"I don't think you're wrong. I'm just not sure I—" A sudden knock at the door interrupted him.

Sammy dismissed her privacy spell. "Come in."

Alyssa stepped in. "Dag Larmel is demanding to see you."

CHAPTER 5

"Who is that?" asked Will.

Sammy glanced in his direction. "A local gang boss, fancies himself the future king of Bondgrad's underworld." Returning her attention to Alyssa, she responded, "I gave that worm my answer last time."

"He's very determined. He's shown up twice while you were gone. That's why I hired the extra bouncer, for security," said Alyssa.

Sammy exhaled in disbelief. "Pffftt! He wouldn't dare try anything here. He knows who our partners are."

"Unless one or more of them have emboldened him," said the maid.

Will nodded, impressed by the suggestion, especially from a self-professed maid. "What's her real job here?"

Alyssa smirked. "Head maid, but someone recently suggested I might be a prostitute."

Sammy corrected her, "She's my number two and the head manager." Returning to the subject, she said, "So you think one of them is trying to shake me loose using that two-bit thug?"

Alyssa shrugged. "There aren't many women in business and even a master in the mage guild doesn't command much respect. Not to mention the rumors that you bought your rank. That's why I've been suggesting you invest in security, so they don't think they can intimidate you."

Oh boy, thought Will. Sammy began to chuckle, then she replied, "He's about to find out why no one intimidates me." She focused on Alyssa. "Send him up."

"I'll tell him his men have to stay downstairs…"

Will's cousin sneered. "No, invite them up as well. I'm going to shame him in front of his men."

Alyssa hesitated. "I don't think that's wise." She glanced at Will for support but he merely shrugged. Then she made a suggestion. "Perhaps just one of them?"

"All of them," insisted Sammy.

"He brought five enforcers with him," warned the manager. "I saw ink on one of them, though he tried to hide it with his clothes. Even if I bring Lawrence and Blaylock up, we'll be outnumbered."

"We nothing!" snapped Sammy. "Leave the boys at their posts. I'm going to meet Dag and his rowdies by myself. I'd rather not put you at risk either."

Desperate, Alyssa looked at Will again, but he pointedly looked away. "Your cousin is a veteran, right?"

Sammy sat up, snapping her fingers to recapture Alyssa's full attention. "This is my establishment, and my cousin is a gentle soul. I won't expose him to such rough men. Just send them up, and I don't give a damn if one of them is inked."

Will struggled to hide his smile as he raised his hands in surrender. "I'll wait in my room."

The maid-manager tried to resist, but Sammy was having none of it. "Go! Make double sure they all come up, especially the mercenary!"

As soon as Alyssa left, Will announced, "I lied. There's no way I'm missing this."

His cousin sighed. "Fine, but don't let them see you. Under no circumstances are you to interfere. It's important they learn this lesson properly the first time. Agreed?"

He nodded. "As if I would need to interfere. Where are you going to do this?"

Her eyes indicated the door to the little courtyard. "Out there. I don't want to risk my furniture. Find a spot and pretend you're a tree or something."

Outside, Will stood beside the door with his back to the wall and used his camouflage spell to blend in with the building. As an extra measure, he smoothed his turyn in that special way which made it difficult for people to notice him, visible or not. Sammy stood in the center of the little garden between the two benches. She still wore the simple bathrobe she had donned the night before, which made her seem even more vulnerable.

Will felt sorry for the criminals, until he saw them arrive. The man that reached the landing first had broad shoulders and a flat nose that looked as though it had been broken many times. The thug's long-sleeved tunic hid his tattoos, but Will could see the turyn swirling around him, the product of the enchantments on his body.

Behind that bruiser walked a heavy-set bald man who was slightly below average in height, but that did nothing to offset his predatory posture. Will guessed he was Dag, the leader. The man still had dark hair, but he was clearly entering his middle years. Behind him came four others, all clearly criminals and radiating an air of danger.

The point man, the wardsman mercenary, studied the area then stepped to one side. "I think she's alone."

Dag nodded, stepping forward. "Madeleine! It's so nice of you to invite us up. Are you sure it's wise to meet with us without an escort, or at least a chaperone? What of your reputation?" The gang leader's eyes continued to examine the area, suspicious of his luck.

"It's your reputation that will need repairing, Dag. I gave you an answer already. I don't work with people like you," responded Sammy firmly.

Dag licked his lips. Will thought he looked nervous, and he had the impression that Dag probably didn't look nervous very often; the man was planning something. The crime boss ignored Sammy's response. "You must have some guys up here. Are they hidden?"

Sammy laughed. "I like my privacy. Why would I need anyone? We're just having a polite discussion, aren't we?"

Dag snapped his fingers and two of his men moved out in either direction, following the balcony around the perimeter of the rooftop, verifying there were no hidden guards or worse, crossbowmen. A moment later, they returned. "It's clear."

"Check inside," ordered Dag. Despite the cool air, sweat was beginning to form on his brow.

"You really are paranoid," observed Sammy. "I haven't given your men leave to enter my rooms."

Dag didn't reply immediately, but after his minions had returned and confirmed that they were alone, he smiled. "I'm not in the habit of asking permission."

"Then you're obviously not a man of wisdom. You already know my answer. If there's anything else, you should be brief, before my patience runs thin."

The lead thug gave her a look of disbelief. "And what happens then?"

"I'll make you cry." Sammy's tone was so serious it made her words seem almost childish. Will knew better, but Dag had no idea.

The crime boss' face darkened. "You don't get it. I was planning to give you a stern warning, the kind that turns purple after a day or two, but you're so stupid you think I wouldn't dare touch you. A couple of guards, hell, even a maid, just one witness—that's all it would have taken to save your life. But you? You meet me up here by yourself? I've met some dumb bitches, but you're on a whole 'nother level."

Sammy frowned. "Murder will get you a noose, even you, Dag. You know who my partners are. I'm sure you wouldn't be that foolish."

"It ain't murder if you trip and fall off the balcony," said the crime boss.

"Have you forgotten I'm a wizard?" she asked calmly.

"I didn't come alone, sweetheart. I've dealt with your kind before." He nodded in the direction of the wardsman who stood slightly in front of him. "I brought Chet here as extra insurance, just in case. Ain't no wizard alive that can survive being within spitting distance of a wardsman." He nodded at his men, and they began walking toward her, closing in from different directions. Daggers had appeared in their hands as if by magic, and the wardsman now held a short sword etched with runes. "Don't fight and we'll make it quick."

Will watched carefully, while simultaneously fighting his instincts to intervene. He distracted himself by trying to guess how Sammy would react. The men in front of her obviously had no idea what a true wizard could do; they'd never met one before. Of course, Sammy hadn't trained much for combat, but given her strength, Will didn't think it would matter. The only risk was that she might freeze, but if that happened, he was more than willing to take up the gauntlet for her.

A wind-wall would be perfect. It would make a mess, but the fight would be over with one spell, Will thought. If it were him, he'd likely try to kill them in a more controlled manner, paralyze two or three with a source-link, then he would kill the fourth and fifth with precision spells. With luck, he would be able to limit the casualties and have the boss terrified and ready to talk at the end.

Sammy chose a different path. Intense flames erupted around her in a semi-circular wall that blocked vision and threatened mortal harm to anyone stupid enough to attempt stepping through them. The space directly in front of her was open, though, giving her a clear line of sight to Dag and Chet.

The tattooed mercenary feinted to the left, then took a step to the right, moving with a speed that reminded Will of a vampire. Using her innate talent with fire, Sammy launched several rapid-fire firebolts at her adversary, but the man's speed and reflexes were flawless. He dodged everything as he closed the gap then lunged forward, thrusting his enchanted weapon directly toward Sammy's unprotected abdomen.

Whether the blade's enchantments would enable it to pierce a force effect, Will didn't know, and he was relieved when his cousin didn't try the experiment. Instead, she put a point-defense shield directly in front of Chet's face.

The shield was practically invisible to normal sight, not that it would have mattered. The mercenary had already committed to an incredibly fast dash, and the shield appeared just an inch from his face. The end result was exactly the same as if he'd charged face first into an oak tree. His motion came to a chaotically abrupt pause, accompanied by a loud cracking noise. His limp body slumped to the ground a second later.

Dag stared at the dead mercenary in horror, while his four other men circled around the fire-wall so that they could see their prey. Will noted that each of them only held one dagger now, when only moments before they'd had one in each hand. He'd been so focused on the wardsman he hadn't noticed them throwing their secondary weapons. *Sammy couldn't have seen them throw either; the fire-wall blocked her vision too,* he realized.

Glancing at his cousin's face, he saw that her features were contorted into a furious snarl. Her quiet composure was gone, replaced by desperate rage. Sammy's hair seemed to catch fire as the wall of flames circling her vanished. A split second later, new flames appeared, wreathing the five men in front of her with bands of incandescent energy. Now that her enemies were all in view, she no longer had to bother with passive defenses.

Everyone froze in place. Dag and each of his men had searing flames less than an inch from their skin, giving them no choice but to remain still. They could feel no heat, despite the crimson intensity, but one of them made the mistake of touching one of the fiery bands, and his scream was enough to convince the others that the flames could indeed burn them.

The first words out of the crime lord's mouth were, "How? What are you?"

Sammy took a step forward. "I'm a wizard, you idiot. You've just never met a real one before." Bending briefly, she checked the wardsman's neck for a pulse, but didn't find one. "He's dead," she announced.

Dag's words came quickly. "That's murder. But we won't say anything. Just let us go."

She straightened up, and Will noticed an unnatural jerk in his cousin's movement. She was hurt. Staring down at the corpse, her eyes glowed red, and a large amount of turyn moved invisibly from her to the body, which erupted in white flames so bright that everyone had to avert their gaze. A wave of heat washed over them all, and then the body was gone, leaving only a pile of dry ash in its place. The wind was already beginning to scatter them. Sammy stared coldly at Dag. "Did you say murder? Who died? I only saw five of you arrive, and I'm sure if you ask any of my employees, they'll tell you the same." She put a finger to her lips. "Or was it four of you? I forget."

Will was impressed. Bodies were mostly water, and it took a lot of turyn to incinerate one so completely. He was quite familiar with the cost from his previous experience eliminating trolls. Sammy's natural talent was with fire, so it was probably easier for her, but still, it had to have been a chore. He could feel a tug in the air as Sammy drew turyn in to replace what she had used. *She must have used most of what she had.*

The five men in front of her were terrified, their eyes darting back and forth between the woman they had come to intimidate or kill, and the seemingly solid bands of fire that trapped them. One of them began to cry when he saw new flames appear around Sammy's right hand. "Then again, maybe none of you came to visit me today. There might be no one to argue otherwise."

Dag's henchmen were already babbling and begging, but it wasn't until he broke and began to beg that Sammy let the flames around her hand die down. "Please, Maddy, let's work something out! None of this was my idea! If I had known—"

"If you had known what?" demanded Sammy, moving several steps forward until the crime lord's face was just inches from her own. "If you had known you didn't have the power to make a credible threat? That doesn't sound like a good reason for mercy." She lifted her right hand, and a fiercely bright orange dot appeared at the tip of her thumb. Dag jerked as she pressed it against his face, just above his left eye. His body touched one of the bands of fire, and smoke rose from his scorched clothes. The smell of burned flesh filled the air.

Sammy pulled her hand away, and Will was faintly relieved to see that she hadn't burned the villain's face. Her flames had removed his eyebrow without marring the skin beneath. Dag's only injury had come from his fearful reaction when he attempted to pull away. Tears were leaking from the corners of his eyes as she moved her hand to remove his other eyebrow, but this time he had the sense to remain perfectly still.

"I told you I'd make you cry," she reminded him.

"Let me tell you why I'm here," Dag pleaded. "I can help you!"

Sammy shrugged. "I don't care. Now hold still, otherwise this will hurt a lot more than it has to." The flames around her hand expanded and moved to engulf Dag's head before passing down his neck and chest. The man sobbed briefly, but held his breath a moment later when he realized he hadn't been burned. Smoke rose and swirled around him as his clothes turned to ash. The fire flowed downward, removing every trace of clothing, even his boots. When the smoke cleared, Will could see that his body was entirely hairless as well.

Will was stunned by his cousin's precision. He had long known of her talent with fire, but the absolute control required to burn away hair without allowing any of the heat to burn skin surprised him. At the same time, seeing his sweet younger cousin displaying such a cold fury as she intimidated the gangster was more than a little disturbing.

Dag was still crying and pleading, but Sammy ignored his words. "I didn't have to burn away your hair. Watch." She demonstrated by incinerating the other four men's clothing, while leaving their body hair intact. "Do you know why I removed your hair, Dag?"

Despite himself, Will felt sorry for the criminal as his lips trembled and snot dripped down them to land on his chin. "Why?"

"Because eunuchs don't grow hair," said Sammy with a smile. "I thought I'd save you the trouble of watching it all fall out, since I'm about to remove your balls."

Oh, hell no! thought Will, horrified. He'd known Sammy for her entire life, but he couldn't tell if she was bluffing. He started to suppress her will, to snuff out the flames, but then he saw the fiery bands restraining the henchman flicker. If he tried to stop her, the thugs would be free to act. Then his eyes spotted the trail of blood Sammy had left behind her. She was definitely wounded.

Dag was openly weeping now and when he saw the flames appear around her hand again, he cried out, "It was Blathe and Pummen! Please! By the Mother, please don't take my balls! I never would have done this if they hadn't told me to!"

Sammy stopped and the flames around her hand vanished. Lloyd Blathe and Aaron Pummen were two of the five oligarchs who collectively ruled Trendham. She had suspected that one of the five might have encouraged the crime boss, but not two. "Why should I believe you? You might easily lie to focus my attention on the wrong people."

"I can prove it!"

"How?"

Dag fumbled for words. "I don't know. But I will."

"I'm quite sure they wouldn't do anything foolish like leaving actual proof of their involvement in this," said Sammy. Then she smiled. "But thank you for volunteering that information." The flames reappeared around her hand. "Now, let's finish this up."

"I can help. I'll work for you! Anything you want, I'll do it! Please!" begged the gang leader.

Sammy paused. "I don't need a petty henchman like you."

"I have people all over the city. I can get anything you want. Information, money, just name it!"

"If you openly defy either of those two, they'll have you killed," said Sammy. "It would be kinder for me to let you go." Her eyes drifted downward. "Minus those two, of course. Lessons must be learned."

"No, wait! They don't have to know. I can be your inside man," begged Dag.

"Hmm," Sammy seemed to consider the idea. "Perhaps you're not as stupid as you look, but that won't be enough."

"Anything!"

"You'll belong to me. I want ten percent of everything you take. You'll take my orders and tell me anything and everything you learn." The negotiation from there was nonexistent. Dag capitulated to every demand. When it was over she dismissed the fiery bonds and pointed to the stairs. "Go, and don't forget to send the first payment before the day is done. Your men can turn it over to Alyssa."

Dag and his men hesitated. They were still naked. Sammy smirked as she realized their problem. "Oh. Turn around," she commanded. Once they had complied, she removed her bloody robe and tossed it over Dag's head. "You can wear that. Your dogs will just have to put up with the embarrassment. Now go, and don't look back unless you want to die. You aren't worthy of the view." Without her robe Will's cousin was entirely naked as well, and now he could see the blood running down the inside of her left leg.

None of them dared turn their heads. They moved woodenly, stiff with fear, making certain she wouldn't mistake their actions until they were down the stairs and out of sight. Sammy turned toward Will, who now revealed himself. "That went better than I hoped."

Will hurried forward, guiding her to a bench. "Better would be if you weren't bleeding. Let me see the wound."

"It's fine," she replied nonchalantly, summoning a potion from her limnthal. "I have these. I get them straight from the only supplier in Trendham."

He confiscated the regeneration potion before she could unstop the vial. "That's overkill and an unnecessary risk. You know what can happen if you use those too frequently." Will was referring to the risk of tumors and consumption.

Sammy argued, "I haven't used one since the time I nearly died. Besides, even if you use healing spells, it will scar and ache for weeks. Give me the potion. I'll risk it."

"No chance," said Will. "Lean back and let me examine it."

His cousin let out a sigh of long-suffering but did as he asked. "This is embarrassing."

"You're the one who gave away your robe. I thought nothing could fluster you," remarked Will. Placing one hand at the junction of her leg and pelvis, he cast a spell to block nerve conduction and prevent pain. He followed it with a specialized cleaning spell to clean blood and any debris from the wound. As much as he liked Selene's Solution it wasn't appropriate for injuries of the flesh.

Sammy kept her head turned, staring off to one side rather than watch him work. "It's not that, it's where the stab wound is located."

Will's tension faded as he saw the depth of the wound. It wouldn't require anything complicated. He snickered at her remark; the blade had hit the inside of her left thigh as she had been taking a step forward, putting the wound close to her groin. If their roles had been reversed, Will thought he might have died from the embarrassment. Using a styptic spell, he stopped the bleeding of the multitude of tiny vessels that had been cut, then repeated the cleaning spell to make it easier to see.

He already knew it had missed the femoral artery, otherwise Sammy would have lost consciousness long ago. The rate of blood production was slow enough that once he'd closed the capillaries, he could see that only two minor veins had been cut. Using another specialized spell he rejoined the veins rather than simply sealing them off. More spells followed, one to reknit the damaged muscle, another for fat, one for the fascia, and then one to rejoin the subdermal fat and smooth it out. Some of the spells he had to construct, which he did quickly, while others were familiar enough that he could reflex cast them, but all told, it took him less than five minutes to undo the damage the knife had done.

"How bad will the scar be?" she asked as he finished with the final spell that would rejoin the dermis.

"There won't be one," he replied. "Just a bruise for the next few days."

"What?" Sammy looked down, examining herself. It was now Will's turn to look away.

"You should take a bath and get dressed," he suggested.

She whistled. "I don't even see a mark. Are you sure it's going to bruise? It doesn't hurt at all." He'd forgotten to dismiss the nerve block, so he did so then and she hissed in response. "Oh, forget I said that. It's sore as hell." She rubbed it lightly, looking thoughtful. "You didn't just seal the wound. How many different spells was that?"

Will shrugged. "Quite a few. I told you I haven't stopped studying. Did you think I'd spend my time learning more ways to kill and maim? I've had more than enough of that."

"You were serious about opening a hospital," she remarked. "Is this your attempt to assuage your guilty feelings, or is this your way of competing with *her*?"

"No," he snapped, perhaps too energetically. "I mean, I do feel guilt, but I'm not a child. I did what I had to do, and nothing I do now can bring back the dead, and this most certainly isn't some foolish competition. She's much better at healing, and probably always will be. Besides, I'm not willing to delve into necromancy to accomplish miracles."

Sammy stood up, limping slightly as she headed toward the entrance to the large bath. "Terabinia is famous for the hospitals she's founded in Cerria and Myrsta. Do you think she's delving into dark magic to accomplish some of those miracles?"

Will shook his head. "No. I honestly don't. I saw how skilled she had become before I left, which is part of what inspired me to study. She's going further than I'm willing, but I don't think she's doing anything evil."

She paused at the door. "Why not?"

"Because she doesn't have to."

"But you won't forgive her. Even though she's doing nothing but good, even though she's made the people of Terabinia happier, healthier, and safer than they've ever been before."

Will grimaced. "I've already forgiven her; that's not the point."

Sammy seemed genuinely curious. "She's done nothing but good and you've already forgiven her—remind me again why you're hiding in Trendham?"

"What she did was unforgivable…"

She cut him off, "But you've already forgiven her."

"She's not human."

"For all intents and purposes she might as well be. Even if she did something bad back then, it doesn't mean she—"

"She will," declared Will. "I don't think she'll ever need to sacrifice more children, but she will need new bodies, even if it's just from aging. That's not the point. She *would do it again*, if she had to. When I said she isn't human, I didn't mean because she's a lich, I meant she never was. She was raised by a dragon, and it twisted her soul."

"You're saying she's evil?"

"No. I'm saying she scares me. Good, evil, none of it matters to her. She'll do whatever she thinks is necessary and if that means innocents have to die, she won't blink an eye," explained Will.

"The Stormking is afraid of his wife. You weren't afraid to take on Grim Talek, or Lognion, but she scares you. Make it make sense, Will."

Standing, he glared at his cousin. "Because I still love her, Sammy. I can't kill her, even though someday I'm probably going to have to try. Sooner or later, she's going to test my principles again, and I'll have to try, and when that happens, I'll likely die—because she doesn't suffer the same weakness. When the day comes that we're enemies for real, I won't be able to do it, but she will. That's what I mean when I say she scares me."

A silence grew before Sammy finally replied, "You've forgotten something important."

"What's that?"

"Who your cousin is. When the time comes, I'll do it." With that, she entered the room and closed the door behind her, but smoke rose from where she had held the door in her hand. Black marks outlined where her fingers had touched the wood.

CHAPTER 6

They wound up spending another day in Bondgrad. Sammy's deal with the crime lord had necessitated a lot of new instructions for her employees, plus she'd wanted to make sure the man made good on his first payment. She also told Alyssa to hire guards, something she'd never felt the need to do before, aside from bouncers.

Will offered to help, but his cousin politely declined his aid and given what he'd already seen, Will wasn't surprised—it was more than clear that Sammy had developed into a highly competent businesswoman. *And a terror for anyone that thinks they can threaten her,* he added mentally.

He was left with nothing to do and no one to be responsible for, something that felt odd after having been a father for so many years. Feeling strangely liberated, Will decided to take a walk and explore some of the city. He headed east first, to see the older and more prosperous half of Trendham's capital. The eastside docks were owned by the oligarchs and some of the more successful businessmen, so they were better kept and better patrolled. The residential districts were clean and peaceful.

Lunch at an upscale public house proved disappointing. The fare was better than could be found at cheaper places, but it didn't live up to the prices charged. As always, Will was disappointed, but he'd expected that. Arrogan's training had spoiled his tastebuds, and his brief time as a rich nobleman had only reinforced his culinary prejudices.

His job at the Laughing Goat didn't give him many opportunities to show off his deeper cooking skills, but given the budget and the supplies provided to him, Will never served food he was ashamed of. Using humble ingredients, he produced quality food. Food that shamed most of the housewives in Lystal, truth be told. As a result, the Laughing Goat did a brisk and steady business throughout the year. The manager, Lettler, who most believed to be the owner of the 'Goat, had never expected to oversee such a profitable establishment.

Banishing thoughts of work, Will turned back to Breville's Causeway and crossed over to the west side. There was little to be learned from the neat, prosperous streets of the eastside. He had no overt goal, but his curiosity pushed him to examine the poorer part of the capital, the places where the wealthy swept their dirt to be hidden from view.

Throughout his walk, he hadn't bothered using magic to go unnoticed. Terabinia was in his distant past, and no one was looking for him anymore. No one paid him any heed, although he did garner appreciative looks from some of the women he passed.

A brief visit to a dockside tavern allowed him to wet his throat with an ale that had been so watered down it was hardly worth drinking. After two sips, he put it aside and resumed his walk. Outside, he noticed a group of men sizing him up, likely thinking to rob him. His attire marked him as slightly more prosperous than most in the area, and though he was tall and well built, Will didn't appear to be armed.

He had a multitude of easy answers to the problem, but Will didn't even consider the more exciting options; he had nothing to prove. With a bit of wild magic, he smoothed his turyn in a special way and just kept walking. He was still visible, but the men didn't have the focus to maintain his presence within their small minds. Glancing back and forth, they wondered where he had gone, even as they failed to pay attention to the unremarkable stranger strolling past.

After two blocks, he dropped his efforts at concealment. The afternoon sun was low in the sky, and it was probably a good time to head back to Roc's Roost. A woman's voice brought him to a halt. "You look like you could use some company."

A middle-aged woman stood under the eave of the building bordering the street. She looked tired and dirty. Her clothes had seen better days while the lip paint and rouge on her cheeks proclaimed a youth that was long gone. Will recognized her as a lady of the evening immediately, but despite his protests of the day before, he had a lot of sympathy for women in her situation. Dipping one hand to his waist, he pretended to fish around in a pouch as he summoned ten clima from his limnthal. He offered the silver coins to her. "Thanks for the offer, but I don't need company. Have this and take a rest instead of working tonight."

Her eyes lit up as she accepted the coins. The breeze blew toward Will, and though he caught the scent of her unwashed hair, he stifled the urge to wince. "Thanks," she responded. "We could still get a drink, even if all you want is to talk." The prostitute's gaze studied him a second time and then she focused on his face.

Their eyes locked, and Will couldn't help but think she looked familiar. Her mouth opened. "William?"

Recognition dawned and Will froze, unsure how to react. The haggard looking woman in front of him was Annabelle Withy, Oliver's mother. He'd mistaken her for someone much older, but she was the same age as Will, not quite thirty yet. Some of the difference was because of his lack of discernable aging, but most of it was due to the hard life she had lived since running away from Will's mother's home in Barrowden. *Correction, the hard life she lived after abandoning her child,* he observed mentally.

Dark circles under her eyes indicated a chronic lack of sleep, and the green stain on the inside of her lips showed she was a regular user of chaka. The narcotic leaves were popular among those with hard lives and little hope of anything better. Chewing them gave a double benefit of euphoria and extra energy to many who labored in Trendham.

"Annabelle," he said as the moment dragged out.

She'd been studying him as well, her eyes taking in the quality of his clothes and the healthy glow of his still young skin. "You look just the same," she said wistfully, then her expression changed to confusion. "You're the Stormking, but everyone said he died. I thought you were dead. How are you here?"

Will's eyes darted to either side, making sure no one was close enough to have overheard them. Using his talent, he muffled their voices to ensure that nothing else they said would escape the space between them. "I am dead—for all intents and purposes. It's better that way."

Annabelle noted the way he glanced around, then frowned. "You look as though you're doing very well for a dead man." She hefted the silver coins in her hand. "Don't you have anything better for an old friend?"

She hasn't even asked about Oliver, he observed silently. "I'll be glad to help you, but you have to promise you won't tell anyone you've seen me." Summoning a gold coin, he let her see the metal glinting between his fingers, since that seemed to be the only thing she was interested in. "I can—" He was about to promise more in the future, but she cut him off.

"Is that all the Stormking can afford?" She gave him a sly smile, displaying a missing tooth. "Talk is cheap these days."

His eyes widened, shocked at her gall. "You realize my anonymity is what protects Oliver, don't you?"

"Who?" She stared at him, uncaring. Seconds passed before she remembered the name. "Oh! You have him?"

Will nodded.

"Is he well?"

"As well as a child can be with no mother. He's grown tall for his—"

"Save it," she interrupted. "I don't want to know." Reaching out, she plucked the gold crown from Will's palm. "I'm no mother. I gave that up when I left, and he's better off without me." His temper was rising, slowly but steadily, and Will figured her last words were the only thing he would probably agree with her about. Before he could respond, she continued, "So, do you have anything else for the mother of your sweet boy, or should I spend these coins to get a drink while I tell everyone I just met the Stormking?"

He would have done a lot more, before she started talking. He could have bought her a house, a shop, given her a living. He might even have been convinced to simply provide her with money at regular intervals, to keep her from starving and provide for her unhealthy habits. Now instead, the furious shadow of his past life was suggesting darker solutions. It would take little more than a thought to end Annabelle's miserable existence and he could imagine several ways to make it happen without any repercussions and virtually no planning.

He could walk away and return unseen just minutes later. Hell, he could probably kill her right then. Or simply render her unconscious then carry her to a dark alley. Prostitutes died every day. Violent images passed through his mind, reminders of the things he had seen, the people he had slain. Blood and brains. A shiver of disgust ran down his spine and Will tasted bile in his throat.

Killing her was the right answer. It was the only way to make sure Oliver stayed safe. *Selene would do it, if she were in my place,* he thought, but he couldn't. He couldn't kill Oliver's mother. No matter how dark her heart was, or whether Oliver ever knew or not, Will couldn't kill the woman who'd given birth to the child he had raised. Within the limnthal he had more than a thousand gold crowns stored. He summoned five pouches, each of which contained twenty of the heavy coins, then he pushed them into her hands. "That's a hundred crowns. Is that enough to shut you up?"

Eyes wide, she quickly began tucking the pouches into the front of her dress. "Yes. Thank you! I didn't realize you were *this* rich!"

"Pray that we never meet again. If I find out you've been talking, I'll be back, and it won't be to give you more money," he said coldly.

"Ooh! So angry!" she exclaimed. "I didn't mean to upset you. Why don't you let me relieve some of your stress? We never got the chance back in the day, did we?"

Will turned and began walking, afraid the bloody vision in his head might become reality if he looked or listened to her for even a second longer. She tried to call after him, but he silenced her voice. With some difficulty, he calmed himself enough to smooth out his turyn as he walked. Moments later, she'd lost sight of him and everyone else on the street began ignoring him.

He tried to relax, but by the time he reached Roc's Roost, the sky was dark and rumbling with distant thunder. There would be rain that night, and if he couldn't get his head straight it would likely become a storm.

***

"What did you do today?" asked Sammy brightly, her demeanor giving no hint that she'd spent the day dealing with planning and the minutiae required by her business.

"Just a walk around the city," he answered. Will was planning to tell Sammy about his encounter with Oliver's mother, but not yet. He needed time to calm down first.

Thunder rolled in the distance and Sammy's eyes darted upward, then back to his face, studying him carefully. "Anything interesting happen?"

"Not really. I had lunch and walked through both the east and west side."

A downpour started, filling the air with the heavy sounds of rain. "You didn't like the city?"

"It was fine. Why?" he asked defensively.

She pointed upward. "The weather looked clear until just a bit ago."

Will gave his cousin a sour look and headed for the stairs leading up. "Rain happens all over Hercynia without my help. No need to assume I'm to blame."

Sammy followed him. "Oh, I'm not blaming you. But you *are* in Bondgrad, and we *are* having a sudden storm."

"That doesn't mean anything."

"Plus, you've got that pouty face you make when you're feeling pissy." Now he was truly irritated, but Will knew better than to respond, so he stayed silent. When they were almost to the top landing, Sammy mused, "I'm glad my talent doesn't affect the weather. Can you imagine? If it did and I was upset, I wonder what would happen, drought, or maybe wildfires?"

"You're already the human equivalent of a wildfire," said Will dryly.

"Thank you!" she responded in an overly enthusiastic tone. "You're so sweet today." Will worked hard to keep from growling, but he wasn't fooling Sammy. After a moment she added, "Want me to invite Cici and Alyssa to have supper with us?"

"Mother be damned! No, Sammy," snapped Will. He took a deep breath and explained, "I appreciate what you were trying to do yesterday, and I had fun, I won't deny that, but it was a mistake I don't intend to repeat."

She held up her hands. "Hey, that's fine. I'm not trying to push you into anything. I just like seeing you relax a little. We're family. My home is yours, so I want you to feel comfortable."

"I won't be visiting again," he replied with unnecessary harshness.

Placing her hands on her hips, Sammy gave him a hard stare. "You're as grumpy as I've ever seen. I knew this storm was yours."

He did growl this time. "Yes! It's me. I'm mad as hell! Are you happy now?"

She nodded. "Want to tell me about it?"

"Not today. Tomorrow, or maybe the day after that."

"Some people feel better when they talk."

"Not me. I just get more upset. I prefer to chew things over on my own first."

Sammy studied his features for a moment, then nodded. "Fair enough. We have something else to talk about anyway. Can the weather bear you being any more upset?"

Despite himself, Will smirked. "Whatever it is will probably help if it distracts me."

"There's fresh news about the trolls in Terabinia."

Will took a seat in the front room and gave her his full attention. "What is it?"

"The trolls are closer than we thought, and they're near Cerria rather than Myrsta."

He nodded. "That'll mean a shorter trip."

She shook her head. "I don't think we have time for an overland journey. They overran Fernham, and apparently it isn't a mob. Supposedly these trolls are acting more like an army."

Will frowned. The fact that the trolls were on the wrong side of the mountains that divided Terabinia had already been suspicious. When he had last cleared them out years ago, they had been near Myrsta. That they'd been able to hide and slowly grow their numbers for a decade was also suspicious, but an army? That defied belief, both in terms of number and organization. "Fernham is a rather large city, not to mention walled. Are you sure the news isn't exaggerated?"

Sammy opened a partial bottle and poured two glasses of wine, offering one to Will. "It's regular wine." After he accepted the glass, she answered, "I don't know. It takes at least a week for news to get here from Cerria at the very best, and it's usually more like ten days."

They sipped their respective glasses in silence for nearly five minutes before Will spoke. "You think we should teleport," he stated and after she nodded to confirm, he agreed, "You're right, but it's going to be awkward." Teleporting would require either a beacon or someone he was astrally connected to. While he had the power and the spells necessary to use either of Terabinia's beacons independently, he didn't have the keys required. He'd left before the beacons had been finished.

That meant he would have to teleport to one of the people he had been close to, either the queen, his past friends—Janice and Tiny, or a family member—his father Mark or his sister Tabitha. His musing was interrupted when Sammy asked, "How long has it been since you tried to check on them astrally?"

Will sighed. "Selene, five years ago, but she was shielded, as always."

"Same as you," she opined.

"I have my reasons."

"The main one being so she can't contact you."

"That's not the only reason," he snapped.

She raised her brows. "Oh? Do tell?"

"It's to keep my location a secret as well. If anyone knew where I was, it might endanger Oliver. Plus, the anti-possession spell seems to prevent storms when I'm sleeping."

Sammy's features softened with sympathy. In the first few years after they had come to Trendham, Will had caused a lot of tumultuous weather, particularly when he was sleeping, but he'd been using the anti-possession spell back then as well, so she knew his last excuse was a lie. She didn't bother challenging it, though. "You're still having nightmares?"

"Not as often."

"How often?" she persisted.

"Every two or three months," he lied. It had gotten better, but the true frequency was closer to once a month. In most cases the weather wasn't disturbed as he not only slept with the anti-possession spell on to seal his body astrally, but he also used a complex, multilayered ward. At home he'd engraved the runes into the floor beneath the rug in his bedroom, but he carried a portable rune guide embroidered on a long strip of fabric stored in his limnthal so he could use the same ward while traveling.

The ward itself was something he'd designed after leaving Terabinia, when his nightmares had haunted him two or three times a week and had threatened to destroy the livelihood of the farmers who made their living near his new home in Lystal. It included a double-layered force dome with a complex braid of elemental turyn sandwiched in-between to help disrupt his subconscious mind's ability to communicate his emotions to the sky above. He'd gotten the idea from the notes left behind by an unfortunate wizard from the past. She'd been the tenth writer in the ancient journal passed down to him by his mentor Arrogan, and according to Grim Talek, she had been named Erica. That was the extent of his knowledge about her, other than that her studies into piercing the veil of reality had driven her insane.

As a result, she had done extensive experimentation with wards and barriers, including one that allowed the caster to completely cut themselves off from reality by severing a small piece of the world from everything else in existence. Will had used that spell once, and he still worried it might have been a mistake, since he'd seen something moving in the void outside of the real world. Grim Talek had warned him that if seen, the things in the void would remember him, haunt him, but thus far he seemed to have escaped unscathed. He hadn't dared use that spell in his nighttime ward, but he had been inspired by some of the techniques it employed.

Most of the time it worked, and the weave of different types of turyn created enough noise to filter out whatever signal his subconscious used—most of the time. A year ago, he'd had a dream so bad it woke him in the night, and he'd been surprised to find he'd somehow seeded a storm despite all his precautions. He wished it was that easy when he was awake. When he was conscious, it required a large amount of turyn to forge a link with the vast rivers of turyn that flowed through the skies above—not that he'd needed the ability in recent years.

Sammy accepted his answer then returned to the subject at hand. "What about the others?"

"None of them are astrally sensitive, so I've been checking on them every year or two." That was the main reason he never tried to spy on Selene, because if she did leave herself open to contact, she would also spot him the moment he started watching her. "Janice and Tiny are usually shielded, but not Tabitha or my father."

"So, which will it be?"

He chewed his lip. "They both think I'm dead, Sammy."

"Selene or Janice must have told them the truth by now," countered his cousin. "And if they are still somehow in the dark, that's all the more reason to go."

"But…"

She shook her head. "You already agreed we need to go quickly. Is your awkwardness worth people dying?"

Will took a deep breath. "You're right."

Sammy smiled, "So, first thing in the morning—"

"Now," he said, cutting her off. "No reason to wait. We can spend the night there and start our hunt as soon as the sun comes up."

She blinked. "That was quick."

He gave her a nervous grin. "Once I've made up my mind, I like to get it over with. I won't be able to sleep tonight if I'm wondering what will happen tomorrow." After a second, he added, "With my family, not the trolls. They don't bother me nearly as much."

Sammy grimaced. "We're all familiar with your weird priorities when it comes to danger."

CHAPTER 7

Tabitha held Talia to her breast as she sat in the peaceful quiet of the nursery. At barely five months of age, Talia was the newest addition to the family and her fourth child since she had married James Wellings seven years ago. Talia wasn't the only one who was hungry. James and her other children, Edward, Elaina, and Christopher were already sitting down to supper at the main table.

They would have waited on her, but then she would have felt rushed, and that wasn't good either. Talia fed better when both she and her mother were relaxed. The peace was broken an instant later when a surge of turyn disturbed the air and two figures appeared in front of Tabitha and her daughter.

Surprise delayed her response for half a second, but once the adrenaline hit, she jerked and took immediate action. A force-dome appeared around them, and Talia began to cry at the sudden interruption of her feeding. Rising quickly to her feet, Tabitha started to issue a warning to the newcomers. "I don't know how you got in here, but you're sadly mistaken if you think—William?" Her eyes moved across each of them. "Sammy? Is it really you?"

Sammy already had tears in her eyes as she nodded, but she pushed Will forward first. Feeling guilty and awkward, Will stared at his sister and then at his newest niece. He'd checked on Tabitha every year or two, so he already knew about her wedding and the first three children, but Talia was a surprise. Not that Tabitha knew any of that, since they hadn't spoken.

His sister's face went from blank to an expression of torment, and her lips twisted as she fought to control her emotions. Without warning, she turned away, hiding her face and using Talia's blanket to dab her eyes. When she spoke again a moment later, her voice was thick with emotion. "Would you like to hold your niece?"

Will tried to answer but barely managed to croak something unintelligible. The force-dome vanished as he stepped forward to take Talia, who had been the first to start crying, into his arms. Tabitha smiled through her tears as she handed over her daughter, then she looked toward Sammy and her composure crumbled entirely.

The two of them cried and embraced while Will tried to sooth his angry niece. Nothing seemed to work until he brought his face close to hers and the babe discovered his beard. She stopped crying then and her mouth made an 'o' as she reached out to painfully clasp at the rough hair. Will ignored the pain and continued to coo at the tiny girl, using the wonder of her tiny existence to stave off his own tumultuous emotions.

At some point Sammy and Tabitha separated, and Will's cousin asked, "May I?"

He reluctantly handed over his niece and then Will was left empty handed, staring hopelessly into his sister's swollen red eyes. He didn't know what to say, and the only words that came to him were, "I'm sorry, Tabbycat." Tabbycat was Laina and Selene's nickname for her, a moniker he'd never really gotten comfortable using since he hadn't grown up with her. He might not have dared to call her that after so much time, but it might have been the remnant of Laina's soul that caused the term to fall so easily from his lips.

Tabitha's tears started again. "Will, you're such a jerk!" Then she was in his arms, squeezing him as though she would break his ribs. Will's shoulders began to jerk in response, and he returned the hug.

"Why didn't you contact me?" she asked, her voice muffled by his shoulder while she tried ineffectually to hit him without letting go.

"I figured you thought I was dead."

"You idiot!" She was inspired enough to let go then so she could beat on him with a little more force.

"Want me to hold him for you?" asked Sammy without looking away from her tiny cousin.

Tabitha growled. "You're no better, Samantha Cartwright. You're just as much to blame."

"I'm not the one who can astral project and teleport to—"

"You could have written a letter," snapped Tabitha. "Hell, it's been five or six years. You could have walked here and back a dozen times over in that time!"

Sammy didn't argue, but Will was struck by a fresh question. "You knew where we went?"

"No, but I'm assuming it wasn't Faresh and probably not Barsta either. Is it Trendham?"

Will closed his mouth, then answered a second later, "Probably best if we don't say."

Fury lit Tabitha's eyes. "Do you honestly think anyone could force me to tell them? Don't forget who trained me. My warning a few minutes ago was no bluff."

Will's sister was one of just a handful of third-order wizards, the most powerful mages in all of Hercynia. He didn't know whether she'd continued to progress her skills, but even if she hadn't, her will alone was probably greater than almost any other wizard in Terabinia, with the possible exception of Will's other students. "What if the queen ordered you to answer?"

Tabitha's features relaxed slightly. "She wouldn't dare. Besides, I haven't seen or spoken to her in almost as long as it's been since you left, not that the creature on Terabinia's throne is Selene anyway."

He frowned. "That's a little harsh. She's changed but it's still her."

"Is it? I don't know who or what she is. The first day I encountered her and realized it was a stranger in her place I excused myself and came home. I've refused every invitation and event since then. I take it you know something? It would have been nice if you'd stayed around long enough to inform me."

Will was confused. "But you knew I was alive. What about Janice? She should have told you what happened to Selene."

His sister laughed ruefully. "The duchess? She told me you exiled yourself and that was it. She wouldn't answer any of my questions about the false queen. Given her rise in power, I wouldn't trust her to tell me the truth now anyway."

"Duchess," Will repeated. He had obviously missed a lot more news than he realized. "Janice was granted a title? Is she still with Tiny? What about the lich, how does he figure into everything?"

A quarter of an hour passed while she gave them a brief rundown of the major news since Will had gone into exile. Tiny and Janice were still married and now held the Arenata estate that had once been Will's. Selene had been kind enough to rename it, however, avoiding confusion. Tiny and Janice were now Duke and Duchess Shaw and stood as the most powerful nobles in the Terabinian peerage. The duchess was known and feared by many since she had the queen's ear. Among the movers and shakers in Terabinia, it was well known that currying her favor was the best way to rise in station.

Tiny apparently avoided getting involved in the political sphere, but he had gained considerable fame in the army, where he was known as the 'Black Duke' by some and simply as the 'Demon' by others. As the royal marshal, he was now the principal leader of the military, and it was rumored that he never removed his burning black armor while in the field. The only time anyone saw his face was when he was at court, which he apparently avoided under most circumstances.

As for Grim Talek, Tabitha had no idea. Given his ability to change his body and appearance, he could be anyone at all or might have left Terabinia entirely. Will's sister avoided Selene and all court functions like the plague, so she had only hearsay to go by. Years past, she had even been privately ordered to appear before the queen, but she had simply ignored the royal summons. Selene, for reasons of her own, had chosen not to force the issue.

As for family, Tabitha was now estranged from her mother, primarily because of Agnes' treatment of Will and Selene after Laina's death. The baroness remained involved in social circles and was a public supporter of the queen, as was her husband. For his part, Will's father had accepted a permanent position as royal governor in Myrsta. Rumor had it that he and his wife were married in name only and Tabitha happily confirmed it. Her mother's anger over Laina's death had poisoned the marriage.

Tabitha's union with James Wellings had caused considerable family difficulties as well, since the man she had chosen was as close to being a commoner as possible while still technically being a member of the nobility. His father had been a landed knight and vassal to Baron Hargast, but after his sire's death the estate had gone to his older sister, Veronica, thanks mainly to Selene's modernization of the laws of inheritance. James' only personal distinction was his service in the army during the war with Darrow. He'd begun as a lieutenant but had distinguished himself in battle, earning a knighthood (without land) and elevation to the rank of captain.

For obvious reasons, Agnes Nerrow had opposed her daughter's marriage and Mark Nerrow hadn't been very happy about it either, but the matter had been decided for them when Tabitha informed her parents that she was already pregnant. A small, quiet, and very private wedding had quickly followed. Currently, she and James were relatively insignificant politically, which they both preferred, but eventually the barony would fall to Tabitha, and that would change drastically.

Despite the rocky start, Tabitha and her father had remained close, and although Mark Nerrow primarily resided in Myrsta now, he visited her frequently, using the teleport beacons that connected the city of Myrsta with the capital, Cerria. The baron doted on his grandchildren at every opportunity.

A knock at the door interrupted their conversation. "I thought I'd bring you a plate since you were taking so long," came a man's voice.

Tabitha's eyes softened and she looked at Will, saying softly, "See why I love him so much?" Not needing a reply, she raised her voice to answer her husband, "One moment, love, don't come in yet." She strode quickly across the room and cracked the door to glance out. "Don't be startled, but we have visitors."

Will hadn't planned on letting anyone else know of their presence, and he and Sammy exchanged worried looks as Tabitha opened the door to admit James. Will's first impression of the man was uninspiring. James had pleasant features and was of average height with dark brown hair. The man was unlikely to stand out in a crowd. He studied Will and then Sammy with suspicious eyes while Tabitha took the plate from his hands.

"Should I call someone?" James quietly asked his wife, taking care to keep from acting in a way that might alarm anyone.

Will could see concern in the man's eyes, and he sympathized. Finding two strangers in your nursery with your wife and infant child would set any parent's heart to racing. Not wanting to worry him any more, Will kept his hands open and spread slightly out to each side, trying to indicate that he wasn't a threat. Tabitha stretched up on her toes and whispered something in her husband's ear, then she stepped back and smiled.

James stared at her for a moment, then asked, "Truly?" before focusing again on Will, a look of wonder in his eyes.

The anger she had shown earlier was nowhere to be seen now, and Tabitha seemed delighted as she made the introductions. "James, this is my brother William and his cousin Samantha." She turned to Will. "William, this is my husband, James. It would be an understatement for me to say that he is an ardent admirer of yours."

James gave her an embarrassed look. "Tabby, please!" Then he crossed the room in two giant strides, moving so fast Will had to suppress his instinctive urge to erect a defensive spell. James seized Will's hands, holding them with both of his own. "I can't tell you what an honor is to finally meet you, Marshal Cartwright." After an awkward second, James reorganized his hands to give Will a more conventional though still enthusiastic handshake.

Will nodded, trying to put his newly met brother-in-law at ease. "Just Will. I don't carry any titles these days."

"Depending on how you look at it you might be called 'Your Highness' since you're technically still the Prince Consort," suggested Tabitha.

Mildly aggravated, Will glared at his sister. "Until death do we part," he corrected. "Selene died. She's not my wife."

James' brows went up. "Tabitha has been telling me for years that the queen is an imposter. Do you support her claims? If you were to come forward, it could change everything."

Will waved a hand dismissively. "Yes and no. Don't mistake my meaning. The queen is no imposter, it's Selene, just not quite as she was before. The truth is more nuanced."

James listened, studying Will's features as he spoke. He was obviously still confused, but his only remark was, "Fascinating." A second later he shook his head, then apologized as he turned to Sammy. "Milady, it's a pleasure to make your acquaintance. Forgive my reticence." Shifting his gaze between them, he asked, "Have you eaten? We've already supped, but I think cook has enough to set some more plates." Without waiting for an answer, the overly excited man took Talia from Sammy and tucked her easily into the crook of one arm, then he reclaimed the plate he had given Tabitha and headed for the door. "Come downstairs! You have to meet the other children. My sister is visiting today too! You might remember her from Wurthaven!"

Tabitha gave them a helpless smile and shrugged. "I *was* going to suggest the same, but he beat me to it."

"Your husband is very hospitable," said Sammy diplomatically. Will nodded, but inwardly he thought the man most reminiscent of a golden retriever.

Tabitha led them to the door, then paused. "James can be exhausting, and I have no idea where he gets his seemingly boundless energy." Her eyes focused on them, and her gaze firmed up as she added, "Some people mistake his enthusiasm for simple-mindedness and others assume his kindness is a false front. Let me assure you that neither is the case. He is exactly as he seems—genuine, kind, honest, and compassionate. I thank the Mother every day for bringing him to me." She went through the door without waiting for a response.

"I like him," said Will as he followed. "As long as he makes you happy, I'm happy."

As they descended the stairs, they could hear James talking loudly in the dining room. "Children! Vonnie! We have guests! You'll never guess who is here!" Will grimaced, then braced himself as they entered the room. James made a grand gesture, then held out his arms as though addressing a large crowd. "May I present to you, the Stormking, savior of Terabinia, slayer of demons and destroyer of dragons!"

Will blushed red and Sammy covered her mouth to stifle a laugh while Tabitha just gave them a weak smile as she whispered, "He's incorrigible."

On the other side of the table was lovely redheaded woman who seemed vaguely familiar. She had taken charge of infant Talia, while on either side of her sat three young children—two boys and a girl. They stared back at Will with curious looks. The mouth of the youngest, Christopher, rounded into an 'o' while the other two seemed unsure how to react. Finally, the oldest, Edward, clapped. James gave Will a look that indicated he should do something. "Go on. Show them."

Confused, Will gave him a blank stare. "Show them what?"

Tabitha was unamused. "James, you're going too far."

Sammy spoke up unexpectedly, in support of James. "It's all right. He can do it. Can't you?" She put her hand against the small of Will's back and gave him a small push forward. "Show them your true self."

He started to protest, but a memory came to him of a man in black and red leathers. Will wasn't sure who it was, or when they'd spoken, but the man's words had been important, and some of them came back to him then. *"These clothes represent the monster they saw me as, but I took that image and wore it with pride."* An idea entered Will's head.

Taking a step forward, he addressed James in an overly serious tone. "You realize it isn't often I show my true power in front of others. Are you sure they can handle it?"

James nodded. "My *get* are made of stern stuff." He gave his children a hard stare. "If any of them die of shock, I won't hold you to blame."

That earned the full attention of Edward, Elaina seemed slightly fearful, and the youngest, Christopher, was completely enthralled.

Will reached out through the turyn in the room, stilling the world around them and creating a silence that seemed portentous, as though the world itself was holding its breath in anticipation. His voice filled the emptiness, deep and resonate. "For your own safety, you must never tell what you are about to see here. Do I have your promise?" He waited until each of the children answered, though the youngest merely nodded breathlessly.

"Very well." For an instant there was nothing, but then they saw the electric blue in his eyes as sparks started there. Coruscating ribbons of blue quickly snaked outward to flow over Will's body, clothing him from neck to floor in brilliant arcs of lightning, but it didn't stop there. More power erupted from the top of his head, crowning him with a vivid headband of sparks with constantly shifting points.

Making the conscious effort to reach the sky just to produce thunder would have been an immense task, so Will opted instead to use his other talent to create an auditory illusion. Thunder boomed and everyone jumped, then he asked, "Now that you have seen the proof, say my name." His eyes bored into the children, waiting for their response.

Christopher was so excited he was drooling, but he jumped up and clapped his hands together while shouting something unintelligible.

Edward was completely awed and answered in a bare whisper, "The Stormking." Elaina tuned up and began to cry.

Will dismissed his display immediately, while James stepped over and snatched his four-year-old daughter into the air and caught her nimbly in his arms. "There, there, love, it's all right. Uncle Will didn't mean to scare you."

The woman holding Talia commented dryly to James, "You never learn," but her eyes kept darting back to Will, studying him surreptitiously.

Christopher was hooting excitedly, while Edward said softly, "Do it again." Meanwhile Elaina's crying faded away as her father spun in circles with her, dancing a makeshift jig. Tabitha smirked and found her seat at the table.

The redheaded woman had a sudden realization. "I'm Veronica. Not sure if you remember me." Before Will could respond, another thought struck her. "You must be hungry."

"Oh, that's right! I'll take care of it, Vonnie," said James. Finishing his latest spin, he peremptorily handed Elaina to Will. "Dance with her," he advised with a wink before vanishing through the door on his way to the kitchen.

Will did his best to oblige while Elaina stared at him with eyes that proclaimed she wasn't yet sure whether he should be forgiven for scaring her. Sammy laughed and tried to help by making silly faces. Tabitha ate, but she paused between bites to remark, "Veronica was your upperclassman at Wurthaven. Did you ever meet her?"

He remembered at last and felt rather dense for forgetting. The red hair should have jogged his memory. Veronica Wellings, she'd been a third-year when he started at the college. More specifically, his friend Rob had had a crush on her. At one point, she had provided crucial enchanting advice that Will used to devise exploding vials for his alchemist's fire. His mouth opened, and he pointed rudely. "Oh!"

Veronica nodded, blushing faintly. "I was the girl who didn't believe you about the vampires."

At their last meeting, he'd tried to warn her, after she had delivered a mysterious message to Will from their mutual acquaintance Rob. She'd taken Will's warning as a joke made in very poor taste. "Oh!" added Will intelligently before finally organizing his thoughts. "That wasn't my first thought. I was realizing that I need to thank you."

Veronica frowned. "For what?" Just then James returned, carrying two plates, one in either hand. Since Sammy had already taken a seat next to Tabitha so they could chat, he put one in front of her, and after assessing the situation placed the other in front of his son Edward.

"Scoot over, Eddie, so your Uncle Will can sit next to Vonnie while they catch up," ordered James. Hands now free, James reclaimed his daughter from Will. "Please have a seat, William."

Will nodded. "Thank you." After sitting, he answered Veronica's question. "You looked up the enchantment used to break glass vials for me."

"Did I? I don't remember that," she responded.

He smiled. "It came in handy on several occasions. In fact, I probably wouldn't have survived my first encounter with the master vampire if it hadn't been for the well-timed use of such a vial filled with alchemist's fire." Hungry, Will managed one bite of under-seasoned capon before James re-entered the conversation.

"Whenever we talk about you, Vonnie always mentions how embarrassed she feels when she reflects back on her last conversation with you. Can't say that I blame her. She nearly got eaten just a few hours later!" offered James helpfully, earning a dark look from his sister. Sammy looked up and caught Will's eye, giving him a quiet smirk before returning to her conversation with Tabitha.

"I'm just glad we survived," said Will, trying to be diplomatic.

James' face lit up. "Thanks to you! You wiped out most of the vampires with that ritual, before going on to slay the master vampire himself in single combat." Embarrassed, Will looked away, but James ignored the hint, going on to give his children a mostly accurate though slightly embellished account of Will's efforts to save Cerria from the vampire plague. Their eyes got larger and larger as he spoke, though it was obvious they'd heard the story at least once before. James finished by gesturing toward Will again. "And now he sits right here next to you, your uncle, a real hero fit for a storybook!"

Everyone was listening at that point. Veronica looked mildly annoyed, but it was Tabitha that spoke up. "James, you're embarrassing him."

Chagrined, her husband replied, addressing Will, "Oh!   My apologies! I get carried away."

Will guided the conversation in a different direction. "It's all right. Why don't you tell me how you and Tabbycat met?"

James smiled. "Vonnie was her first student."

Tabitha clarified, "She wouldn't take no for an answer, even though I insisted she was too old."

James nodded. "Vonnie and I both managed to reach the first-order. I wish we'd been younger. It was tough enough for me, but Vonnie was definitely too old. She was just too stubborn to give up, even though she was sick for weeks."

Sammy frowned, then asked Veronica, "How old were you?"

"Twenty-two," said the other woman modestly. "I met Tabitha not long after it was announced that the Stormking was dead." She glanced nervously at Will, then went on, "We became friends, and after listening to Tabitha's stories, I became obsessed with bettering myself. I couldn't stand the thought of being unable to use my magic the way she could." She blushed, then added, "The thought of remaining young longer was just extra motivation."

"Vonnie is twenty-nine now," offered James. "She's just a year older than you, Will, if I'm not mistaken." His sister shot him another warning glare.

Sammy gave Will another half-hidden smirk, but Will ignored her, asking a question of Tabitha instead. "How many apprentices have you trained?"

"Just the two thus far," answered his sister. "Once James found out about Vonnie, he refused to be excluded, and after that things just sort of fell into place for us." She smiled. "It was scary for me, but I think once the children are older, I might try to teach others."

"She's a wonderful teacher," beamed James proudly. "I've no idea what she sees in me."

"Me either," agreed Veronica happily.

Tabitha glanced at the children, taking note of Talia's drowsy eyes. "I think it's time to start putting certain people to bed."

A chorus of no's went up, and Edward begged his father, "One more story first, please?"

Their mother argued against it. "The grown-ups need time to talk, Edward."

Sammy put a hand on her arm. "It's fine, Tabby. I'd love to hear one too. James is very entertaining." Her eyes darted toward Will, and he could see hidden mirth in them.

"Tell us the one about the siege," said Edward. "The one where the Stormking stormed the gates."

Tabitha sighed, giving Will an apologetic glance. "You always want that one."

James was already rubbing his hands together. "I'm sure you remember, but during the war with Darrow, your uncle was the royal marshal, in charge of Terabinia's army."

"You mean the Stormking," suggested Elaina.

"Well, he wasn't known as the Stormking back then, since his powers had yet to fully manifest. Back then he was just William Cartwright, Royal Marshal—"

"And Auntie Laina was there with him," corrected the little girl. Her gaze went to Will. "She was a powerful wizard. Momma and Daddy named me after her," she informed him proudly, as if he might not be aware.

Will nodded, smiling and blinking to keep his eyes from watering at the sudden remembrance. "Yes, she was. She saved me that day."

If James noticed the huskiness in Will's voice, he gave no sign. "Let's not get ahead of ourselves! We aren't to that part yet."

"Sorry, Daddy," said Elaina. James went on, giving a remarkable account, which while not entirely accurate, was close enough for a bedtime story. In it Will charged the gate alone, somehow bypassing the soldiers exiting to attack the Terabinians from the rear. Once there, he had used a spell to block the gate, then single-handedly fought off hundreds of soldiers and evil sorcerers. At the end, just before he was about to succumb to the enemy's greater numbers, Laina appeared and cleared a path through the enemy so that James and the soldiers with him could come to Will's aid.

Will listened quietly, nodding along whenever his niece or nephews glanced to see if he agreed with the story. He'd been embarrassed enough already that he didn't even blush. When it was done, he felt honored to get hugs and kisses from the children, even though they'd never met him before. Veronica took on the task of getting them into bed so that James and Tabitha would have more time with their guests. Once she and the children were out of the room, Will asked the question he'd been wondering about since the close of the story. "You were at Klendon?"

James nodded. "I served in Second Division, under Commander Hargast. I wasn't in Barrentine's Company, leading the charge, but my company was close behind. I was just a lieutenant, but I was one of the men who went in after you held the gate. I remember thinking you had to be dead when we ran by, but I saw you start moving."

"It was just a story, but you got most of it right, though you embellished it a lot more than I would have," opined Will.

"Everyone in First and Second Division talked about it," said James. "A lot of the gossip was pure rumor, but over time and with the accounts of those who were able to see, I managed to piece together most of the details. It helped that I was promoted to captain after Klendon, so I got to attend the officer meetings from there on."

Tabitha broke in, "Plus he pestered me half to death with questions, not that I could tell him much. Neither you nor Laina were very forthcoming about the war."

"I wish I had met you then," said Will.

"You did," James informed him. "You shook my hand when I was promoted. My father was a proud man that day."

"James' father died later, at the battle for Maldon," Tabitha added.

Will shook his head. "I'm sorry. So much happened, I don't even remember that."

"Don't be!" exclaimed James, getting up and coming around the table. "You had the weight of thousands on your shoulders. I'm honored just to meet you, much less call you brother-in-law."

Once they were past the awkward talk of war, Will found himself taking a liking to Tabitha's husband. The man was just as she had said, energetic and positive, almost to the point of being off-putting, but once someone got to know him, James' sincerity started to shine through. Will doubted anyone could dislike the man after getting familiar with him, unless it was simply because James represented a higher standard for kindness and genuine humanity. Some people couldn't stand being reminded of their own small-mindedness when in the presence of someone who shone with such honest goodness.

In fact, Will himself felt slightly intimidated, for he knew quite well his own shortcomings. Where James was clearly an excellent father, Will wasn't so sure of himself. While James spoke with conviction, Will remembered all too well the many times he had acted in doubt, or made choices that hurt or destroyed the lives of others. Being put on a pedestal by someone like James was a sobering experience, and something Will knew he wasn't worthy of.

But at the same time, Will was long past letting his own insecurities color his view of others. He liked the man, and rather than feeling envy, he found himself feeling protective. Tabitha had found a true gem, and she and her husband had created a beautiful family, and it was such families that Will had sacrificed his own peace of mind for. *I did some terrible things, but if it means that they can be happy, it was worth it,* he told himself.

A change in tone snapped Will back from his reverie, and he realized he had lost track of the conversation. To avoid awkwardness, he asked a question, a conversational tactic he'd learned from Selene many years before. "Excuse me, I'm sorry to change the subject, but I really wanted to ask you what you do?"

"I'm a professor at Wurthaven now!" announced James proudly. "This is only my second year, so I'm still quite junior, but Master Courtney has put me in charge of developing the new pre-admission course. Vonnie actually started it and convinced them to hire me in as her assistant last year."

"Pre-admission course?"

James nodded. "Vonnie thought it should be called the first year, but then they would have had to change up the titles and classes for each successive year, so we're planning it as a sort of prep year before entering regular classwork."

"So, what exactly will they be doing?" asked Will.

James grinned, rubbing his hands together with enthusiasm. "Not sure how up to date you are on the changes the queen has made to the practice of magic in Terabinia, but elementals are banned now. She's letting the old families keep those that they have, but on the death of a holder, the family is required to surrender their elementals to the crown rather than pass them to a successor. It will take a generation, but eventually they'll all be gone.

"Anyway, the upshot is that none of the new students will have elementals. At the same time, the queen is well aware of the secrets of true wizardry, so if Terabinia is to maintain its magical preeminence as well as the strength of its military, it will need a proper supply of true wizards to replace the sorcerers as they die out. That's where Vonnie and I come in. We're setting up a program to train young would-be students and get them through their first compression before they begin classes or learn any magic." James' face fairly glowed as he paused to see Will's reaction.

Will, for his part, was impressed, both with Selene's action to slowly rid Terabinia of all elementals, as well as with James and Veronica's part in training a new generation of wizards. "That's very forward thinking," he agreed. "What about second- and/or third-order wizards?"

Nodding along, James replied immediately, "That's the problem! Vonnie and I are both just first order."

"That's not an obstacle to assisting others through the additional compressions, though," countered Will.

"No, but you can understand the hesitation parents will have if we're asking their children to take on risks when we've failed to achieve that goal. Things get even worse when you consider the inevitable deaths that will also result. The wealthy and powerful aren't going to take kindly to a high mortality rate," explained James. "Once the children are older, I'm hoping Tabitha will take a job at the college as well. With her upbringing and the fact that she herself is third-order, I think we'll have the clout and respectability to consider allowing the most promising and stubborn students to try for higher compressions."

"There are a few others," observed Will.

"Well, the queen—" began James.

"No," he interrupted. "Technically she's zero-order now, or fourth, depending on who you ask. Without a living source, her strength is slightly limited compared to a third-order wizard; part of her will is tied up simply maintaining her immortal existence."

"You really believe she's a lich?"

"Let's get into that later," said Will. "Janice Shaw, the duchess, she's second-order, and Emory Tallowen is third-order. I'm not sure what they're doing now, but you might ask them to help."

James pursed his lips. "I'm sure the duchess is sympathetic, but she's very busy and she's in close orbit to the queen. My wife is firmly against us having any more contact with Her Majesty. I don't know anything about Tallowen."

"He's a good man. Tell him I suggested you ask him," said Will.

Tabitha had been content to listen for a while, but she jumped in then. "That brings up an important topic. Everyone thinks you're dead. I don't think James should mention you to anyone, even Emory. I don't want crown investigators at the door with questions."

"I don't think Emory would tell anyone," offered Sammy.

Tabitha wasn't persuaded. "I believe you, Sam, but this is *my* family. I won't risk it."

James replied, "Then we'll just have to wait for my lovely wife. Once Tabby is ready to enter academic life, we'll push for second- and maybe third-order compressions for those who are willing to dare it."

The conversation moved on from there. Tabitha and her husband filled Will and Sammy in on what they knew of the troll situation north of the capital. As expected, they didn't have detailed information, but everyone knew that the army had been marshalled and sent north to deal with the disaster that had befallen Fernham.

"I guess we'll head north in the morning and see what we find," said Sammy.

Will leaned in. "Who is leading them? Did the queen go herself?"

Tabitha shook her head. "No, Her Majesty is still in Cerria. The Black Duke leads them."

She meant Tiny, and though she'd already told Will about the moniker earlier, it still bothered Will. "I wish you'd call him by his name at least," he complained.

His sister shrugged. "That's what he is. I told you, he always appears in black plate, usually with black flames. There's no avoiding the name given his appearance."

Sammy glanced at Will. "Didn't you say the demon-steel armor was trapped in the pocket dimension after Lognion's death?"

There it was. Will hadn't been able to name the source of his discomfort, but Sammy had nailed it. "You're right, although I suppose it's possible that they had enough left over to make a second golem." He didn't believe it, though. They'd been desperate, and it was hard to imagine Selene or Grim Talek leaving any resource left untapped when there was no certainty they could defeat the dragon. If that was the case then Selene had either found a way to get more demon-steel, or she'd found a way to re-enter the nest's pocket dimension and reclaim the demon-steel weapons and armor lost there.

And the elementals.

Lognion had had thousands of elementals bound to him. Will had long regretted that they were still trapped there, eternally bound with no hope of release. If Selene had gone back in, had she freed them, or were they now assets of the crown? *And if she didn't free them, what does that mean?* he thought darkly. Since his exile, he'd given her the benefit of the doubt, but he still remembered something she had once told him when they'd been discussing the heart-stone enchantment and elementals, *"Assume we kill the dragon and then somehow kill a lich. I'll be the last one on your list. Will regicide be your final crime?"*

Sammy waved a hand in front of his face. "Will? Are you in there?"

He blinked. "Sorry, I'm just tired." Glancing at Tabitha, he asked, "Do you have room for two unexpected guests tonight?"

"Don't ask silly questions," returned Tabitha. "We only have one guest room, but since we're all family, that should be…"

Will interrupted, "Actually, I need space to myself." Everyone frowned at that. Will and Sammy had both grown up in families that shared beds, and even Terabinia's wealthiest expected relatives to share, not that Tabitha and James were that wealthy.

Slightly puzzled, Tabitha made a suggestion. "If you don't feel comfortable due to gender, I suppose James could share with you, and Sammy and I could…"

Will shook his head. "I can sleep in the parlor. I just need extra room for my wards."

"You didn't need privacy at my house," remarked Sammy with a sly grin.

He gave his cousin a hard look. "That was a mistake, and I didn't really sleep much either. This is for everyone's safety."

James was looking back and forth between them, silent for once. Tabitha responded, "I'm confused. Why do you need wards?"

Sammy answered for him. "He sometimes has dreams. The wards keep him from creating storms." She put a hand on Tabitha's arm. "Will can use the guest room; I'll sleep in the parlor. That way there's no awkward questions if the children wander in and see the ward guide."

CHAPTER 8

They set out early the next morning after a quick breakfast. James offered to come with them, but quickly changed his mind after a few pointed reminders from Tabitha that he had a family to consider.

Will agreed, but he didn't want to hurt James' pride. If anyone were to join them, Tabitha would be the most useful choice, given her strength as a wizard, but he couldn't countenance the thought. Thankfully, Tabitha was of a similar mindset. After one last hug, she kissed his cheek and then put her hands on either side of his head. "I hate that you're doing this again, and I hate leaving you and Sammy to do it without me, but…" She looked to one side, where Veronica was holding a squirming Talia. Her eyes returned to Will, a wealth of words left unsaid.

Will smiled, nodding. "They are the future." He glanced at James and back to Tabitha. "The two of you are guarding something far more important. Leave this to me."

Sammy hugged them and then they turned away. James called out to Will as they left, "Don't forget you're a father too, William. It's important that you come back in one piece."

Will waved and nodded without looking back. He and Sammy camouflaged themselves and then started walking, heading for the city gates. While they wanted to move faster, it was important they not give away the fact that Will had been in the city. Once outside, it didn't matter as much, since Will was likely to give away his identity and status as a living person when he engaged the trolls. They just didn't want to draw attention to the fact that Tabitha had put them up for the night.

After they were out and traveling on elemental travel-disks, Sammy remarked, "I'm starting to feel jealous of you people and your kids."

"Does that mean you're thinking of giving up your lascivious lifestyle?"

His cousin laughed. "Not quite yet, but maybe someday, if I find someone worth putting up with for a couple of decades."

"Just a couple of decades?"

She winked at him. "You and James have me convinced I should put up with the father long enough to benefit any spawn I produce. After that? We'll see."

Will laughed. "Speaking of which, you should visit your dad while you're in Terabinia. After we wipe out the trolls, everyone will know you've been here. Might as well see him before we return. He might even want to move to Trendham."

"You told me he has new kids. Not sure if I can deal with that," she admitted. "I'm sure his new wife is nice, but I don't know if I want a stepmother, or new siblings."

Will shrugged, not wanting to press her. Having been raised as an only child, he felt it was a mistake not to take the opportunity. *Uncle Johnathan won't live long compared to us. She'll regret it someday if she doesn't make the most of these years,* he thought, but he had a more pressing concern in the immediate future.

They went northwest, and although there was a river road that was fairly direct between Cerria and Fernham, the river itself was even better. The elemental travel-disk didn't discriminate between traveling over land or water, and while the road had to veer around certain terrain features, the river was relatively straight and always flat. They were able to stay low, just five feet above the water, where the turyn cost was minimal and they were able to focus on speed.

The trip was ordinarily a week and a half by horse or two weeks by river barge, but they traveled quickly enough that it would likely be less than two days. They found the Terabinian army in considerably less time than that.

It was late in the afternoon of the first day's travel when they spotted the smoke from hundreds of campfires. Gauging from the direction, the army was camped on the northern bank of the river, so they crossed over and camouflaged themselves. Half a mile from the north bank river road, they spotted the first sentries beneath the edge of the forest canopy.

"You should wait here," said Will.

Sammy gave him an annoyed look. "I'm here to fight trolls. I don't think this is the place you want to start telling me to stay back."

He rolled his eyes. "I'm not worried about that. They may have wizards or sorcerers on sentry duty. They might not see you, but it's possible to notice the turyn disturbance caused by the camouflage spell." It was something he'd learned while dealing with illusions and other magical ambushes during the war with Darrow.

"Bullshit," she spat. "You never mentioned anything like that before. This sounds like an excuse."

"Believe me or not, it's true. And I never trained you with the intent to make you a military asset. We can experiment tonight if you want to learn. It's just a matter of spotting disruptions in natural turyn currents around you, but for right now I'd rather go alone since you can't disguise your turyn the same way I do," he explained.

Looking sour, she replied, "I can mask my turyn just fine. I can even mimic someone else's turyn."

Will nodded. "In a crowd. Here you need to avoid being spotted in a desert."

"This is a forest."

"It's an analogy, with people being like trees."

She pointed in the direction of the army. "If people are trees, there's a whole forest over there."

Staring at the sky, Will prayed to the Mother for patience. "But out here, it's a desert. I'll be circling the camp, which will make the turyn of my spell stand out unless I can smooth it out."

"So, you're a tree in a desert, but you're going to make your turyn look like a tree in this forest, which is actually a desert, so the other trees who somehow also have eyes, won't see you're there."

Exasperated, he said, "Now you're just being obtuse, and you've twisted my analogy to shit."

"It's a metaphor now, with some simile thrown in for good measure." There was mischief in her eyes.

Will narrowed his eyes. "You might be family, but you're pushing your luck with me today."

"Fine! Use your assassin's wild magic and leave me here, alone."

He did, following it with a camouflage spell. Moving just a few feet away, he saw Sammy's eyes lose track of him. "You've seen me do this quite a few times. Maybe you should practice."

Her frustrated voice carried after him as he walked away. "You think I haven't tried!"

They were close enough to the sentries that raising her voice wasn't wise, but Sammy knew he was already muting their voices to anyone at a distance. He sent his own words back to her ear as a whisper. "I'm moving away, so stay quiet or they'll hear you."

After that, Will walked directly into the forest, passing less than ten yards from the sentries they'd spotted. He pondered over the differences between himself and other wizards as he went. There weren't many third-order wizards to compare himself to, but he'd questioned Arrogan about it many times in the past. The talents that third-order wizards manifested were akin to wild magic in that they were intuitive and natural, but they accomplished things on a much grander scale.

Wild magic itself, which simply put was merely magic used without a spell construct, could do almost anything, but it was notoriously hard to control. Wizards often found they had affinities for particular usages while at the same time being forced to use normal spells for everything else. In Will's case, he'd developed an exceptional ability to alter his senses, especially his vision, allowing him to adjust it easily to see into different parts of the light spectrum with just a thought. He had also been able to quickly learn the Arkeshi technique of turyn smoothing.

The Arkeshi weren't users of magic, but through brutal and extensive training they managed to teach their students to smooth and blend their turyn in with the environment around them, making them nearly impossible to notice even though they were still perfectly visible. Will had learned the method simply by observing his sister Laina's Arkeshi companion, Darla, yet none of the wizards he had trained since had been able to imitate the technique.

On the flip side, Will had failed to learn any of the shapeshifting that his fae aunt, Tailtiu, had tried to teach him. Nor had he become very good at physical enhancements like his grandfather had used. Will could make himself stronger, faster, or increase his endurance, but his ability in that regard was still crude compared to what Arrogan had been capable of, or so he'd been told.

He was glad he had the talents he did, though, since at the moment they were ideal. Will wandered directly into the Terabinian camp, with no one the wiser. He'd thought to circle it at first, but going through the middle was quicker and afforded him the opportunity to listen to camp gossip. For anyone else, it would have been a foolish path, but Will had little to fear.

Once inside the picket lines, he dropped the camouflage spell. It only made the Arkeshi technique more difficult, and there were lots of soldiers milling about so he wasn't worried about sticking out anymore.

The camp followed standard army procedure, with a ditch and earth embankment around the perimeter. Against trolls it wouldn't be as effective as it was against a human enemy, but it was better than nothing. Will observed sorcerers standing watch at regular intervals within the perimeter, which definitely wasn't part of standard procedure, but he approved. Not of the sorcerers, but of the abundance of caution.

Selene needs to push James' wizard preparatory program harder, he thought. *Otherwise, they'll never get away from the crutch of using elementals.* Time would tell. After another four or five years, then Will would take a serious look. *You've been telling yourself that for almost a decade now,* a quiet voice in his mind reminded.

He stopped to listen near a campfire where several soldiers were resting after the day's march. "What do you think, Sims?" asked one of the men.

"Easy victory, but heavy casualties. I bet a third of us don't make it home," answered one of them, probably Sims.

"That don't make any sense at all. How is that an easy victory?" questioned one of the others.

Sims coughed. "Easy for the officers, not us. The elementals will do all the killing, but we'll get torn to shreds keeping the trolls from eatin' the sorcs."

"You're full of shit," declared the questioner.

One of the others put a hand on his shoulder. "Sims was in Darrow when the governor put down the trolls. He's seen what they can do."

The questioner paused, then asked, "Is that right, Sims? Was you there?"

Sims nodded, but another man spoke up. "It's different now. We've got more sorcs, more fire, and we've got the Black Duke now."

"The Black Duke can't be everywhere," muttered Sims. "And anyone that stands too close to him dies anyway. If things go tits up, he'll survive but that won't be much consolation for the rest of us."

"Too bad the Stormking ain't here."

"Stormking's dead, Gary. Stop dreamin'."

Sims shuddered visibly. "I saw him back then. Sure, he stopped the trolls, but he killed as many of us as he did of them."

Will moved on, making a conscious effort to block out the rest of the conversation. He agreed with Sims, and he was afraid the man might go on to give a full description of that terrible day, a day that was only *one* of the horrors of his past that haunted his dreams. Making his way toward the center of the camp, he found the command tent, but before he could approach it, he saw a face that caused him to freeze in place. Emory Tallowen.

Emory was one of his former students, a third-order wizard, and the first man whose heart Sammy had broken. Based on the insignia he wore, Will could see the nobleman was now also ranked as a commander in the Terabinian army. Despite his anxiety at seeing an old friend, Will's fears regarding the trolls receded slightly. Emory was experienced from the war with Darrow, and after ten years, Will assumed the man must've made considerable progress as a wizard. If Tiny and Emory were both here then the trolls were likely going to face a losing fight.

Staying still, Will watched as his friend walked past without giving him a second glance. Then a hulking figure stepped out of the tent, a massive form of dark metal. "Commander Tallowen." The voice was deep, too deep, set at a pitch no normal man would use.

Emory turned back. "Yes, Marshal?"

"We march at dawn. Meet me an hour prior. There will be more scouts returning through the night. Plans might change."

"Yes, sir." Emory nodded respectfully and continued on. Meanwhile, Will was stuck in place, fascinated and perplexed to see his one-time best friend again after so many years. Of course, it wasn't the Tiny he remembered, but the demon-steel golem Janice and Selene had manufactured for the battle against the dragon. But Tiny was there, in spirit if not in actual flesh. *His body is probably back in Cerria,* Will decided. He wondered if Tiny remained in the golem constantly or took breaks to sleep at night. *He has to sleep, surely.*

The metal helm remained pointed in Will's direction, and since there were no eyes to judge by, he began to wonder if Tiny had somehow spotted him, but after a minute, the golem turned away and returned to the command tent. Breathing a sigh of relief, Will continued on, moving around the tent to explore the other end of the camp. There might be vital information to be seen within the tent, but he didn't want to risk the confined space.

It took some time to reach the far perimeter, but by the time he had, there was no doubt. Selene had sent three regiments, comprising the entirety of First Division. Depending on how full the First was, there were likely more than five thousand men encamped. *She's not taking chances,* thought Will. Terabinia only kept two fully active divisions during times of peace, the First and Second. Discounting inactive Third, Fourth, and Fifth, the queen had sent half of her nation's military force to deal with the troll threat.

Considering the fact that they'd overrun and *eaten* a walled city, Will fully agreed with the decision. Combined with the large number of sorcerers and elementals, it was probable that he'd wasted his time traveling. He wouldn't be needed. He didn't regret it, though. It had taken the threat to force him to visit his sister and meet his nieces and nephews. He'd been a recluse for far too long.

Will moved past the line of sentries and continued on until he was far enough away that he could safely cast a spell without being observed. Shifting his mind partway into the astral plane took roughly ten seconds and then he reflex cast a teleport spell to take him back to where Sammy hid.

His cousin jumped slightly, unable to completely suppress her startlement. Without any astral sense, she had no hope of any proper forewarning before his arrival. Sammy suppressed her natural irritation, asking, "Learn anything useful?"

"There's a full division here."

"Is that a lot?" She saw him sigh in exasperation, then added, "Forgive me for not being a military genius. I can never keep all the names straight. I know squads are small, but the rest, brigades, regiments, pods—it all gets confusing."

"Pods?" Will gaped. "A pod is a group of dolphins." She stuck out her tongue at him, but Will ignored it. "A division is five-thou-sand-four-hundred men, if it's full. It's comprised of three regiments, each with eighteen-hundred soldiers. A regiment has three battalions of six-hundred, and those are broken down into five companies of a hundred and twenty. Within those are…"

Sammy covered her ears and closed her eyes. "Stop. You're giving me a headache!"

"I'm never putting you in charge of an army, that's for sure," said Will.

"Please don't," she agreed. "I'd much rather run a business and count my coins. Counting soldiers is just—morbid."

"Morbid?"

She nodded. "You're counting them because they're alive. The implication is that they'll be spent by either becoming dead or otherwise nonfunctional. It's depressing."

Will tilted his head, considering the analogy. "You're right, but a good leader is a bit like a successful merchant, he does his best to hoard and save every coin."

His cousin rolled her eyes. "No, Will. That's exactly how they're different. A poor merchant hoards his coins. A successful one spends them effectively, using them to make more coins in the future. That's fine for coins, but for soldiers it's small comfort if you're one of the ones being spent."

He thought about that for a moment longer, remembering his time as royal marshal. It didn't improve his mood thinking about it. "The point here, is that Selene sent an army big enough to solve the problem. Big enough that it will likely also limit their losses."

"So what do we do?"

"Tonight? Nothing. We'll move closer to the river and find a hidden spot to camp. I'll set up my ward and we can sleep in peace. From here on we can just watch and observe, but I don't think we'll be needed."

"Do I sleep inside or outside the ward?" she asked.

Will pursed his lips. Since leaving Terabinia, he had slept exclusively alone with his specialized ward and locked doors beyond that. The only exception had been his wild night at Sammy's home in Bondgrad, and he was firmly of the opinion that that had been a mistake. He studied Sammy's face. "Well…"

"The ward is to keep you from affecting the weather, right?" Will nodded. "You've never set fire to your own room, right?"

He gave her an odd look, then remembered her particular talent and chuckled. "No, and if I did accidentally cast a spell, I suppose your resistance would protect you."

"That settles it then."

CHAPTER 9

Will opened his eyes slowly, feeling the change that always came over the world in the hour before dawn. His layered ward made it difficult to perceive anything outside it, but something about the air itself always let him know that morning was near. His ward blocked most light, and with only starlight the inside was effectively pitch black. Even so, he saw something move above him.

A shiver of electric fear ran down his spine as Will's eyes went wide and he automatically began adjusting his vision, searching for any light that would let him see clearly. Half a second later he saw it, illuminated in shades of grey and white against the midnight backdrop of his ward, a strange creature with six legs and a sinuous torso covered in scales. It seemed to be standing atop his ward, staring down at him with a multitude of glittering diamond eyes set in a strange, triangular shaped head.

It was unlike anything he'd seen before, except in his most disturbed dreams, and Will's breath froze in his throat as he realized the legs ended not with claws or feet but with strange humanoid hands tipped in black talons. *This is a dream,* he told himself. *It's not real. It can't be real.* Heart pounding, he tried to think, to reason, but the fear made it almost impossible.

The monster opened its mouth, and a strange metallic clicking issued forth, sending yet more shivers through Will's overworked nerves. The creature was outside his ward, so they should be safe. Although the ward was meant to prevent him from affecting the outside world, it was still a double-layered force-wall with a potent combination of elemental energies locked within the layers. *And I shouldn't be able to see anything standing on top of it,* he realized. Yet he did. *I'm dreaming. That's the proof. I'm definitely dreaming.* His heart started to slow.

"Will?" It was Sammy's voice. "Are you all right? You're breathing funny."

Paralyzed, his eyes darted to one side, and he saw Sammy sitting up on her bedroll some ten feet away. She was looking in his direction, but her eyes were wide as she tried to see through what for her must be absolute darkness. Then his attention returned to the horror watching them from above, as the creature began slithering *through* his ward.

Mouth open, he screamed in silence, unable to compel his lungs to obey him until at last Will's power exploded outward. Lightning streamed from his chest to strike the monster dropping toward them, and the world exploded with sudden brightness.

Something touched his shoulder and Will tried to scream again. "Will? Are you all right? You're breathing funny."

Opening his eyes, Will realized he must have still been asleep. Adjusting his vision again, he saw Sammy kneeling beside him, her hand gently shaking his shoulder. He wanted to answer, but as before, his body still wouldn't respond—and then he saw the creature once more, still perched atop his ward, staring down at them with dozens of shiny alien eyes. Again he screamed, this time having only slightly more success as a weak stream of air made its way from his lungs to his throat, resulting in a strained whisper of horror. Looking over her shoulder, he saw the monster pass through his ward—again.

This time, it crossed the distance before he could do anything, and Will watched in horror as it somehow devoured and merged with Sammy. She screamed as it happened, writhing in pain, but when her eyes opened again to stare at him, the green irises were gone, replaced by inky black pools.

Something snapped then, and Will felt control of his body and his magic return. In an instant, he was sheathed in thick blue ropes of lightning and still more snaked out to blast the monster that had usurped his cousin's body.

"Will, are you all right?"

He exploded out of his bedroll and rolled away from Sammy's touch. Once more, he realized he had still been dreaming. But this time he was in full control of his body. Lightning covered him as he stared at Sammy. She'd been blind in the darkness, but the light from the arcs covering Will's form now cast her in a strange contrast of blue light and moving shadows. Will was breathing hard as he studied her for signs of the monster. Looking up, he thought he saw movement for a moment, but once his eyes focused, he saw nothing but the inside of his ward.

"Will?" Sammy's features betrayed worry and fear as she watched him. "Are you awake? Look at me." Reaching out to one side, her turyn moved and a globe of warm light appeared, illuminating the campsite in ordinary colors.

He watched her carefully for almost a minute, letting his eyes cycle through different types of vision before finally settling on what he thought of as 'normal' light. Sammy was Sammy. Her temperature was normal, her body human, and the turyn around her matched his memories. "Sam?"

"It's me," she answered. "Are you awake? I think you had a nightmare."

Will nodded, swallowing as he tried to get his heart to slow back down. His body was covered in sweat. Even so, he never took his eyes off of his cousin, fearful she might transform. After a minute, he looked around the inside of the ward again and the tightness in his chest began to relax.

"You're safe, Will. It was just a dream. You don't need the lightning," Sammy told him in a calm voice. She was careful not to move closer.

He summoned a knife from his limnthal, then used it to prick his thumb. After he'd seen the blood well from the wound, he held the knife out to Sammy hilt first. "Show me," he ordered.

Confusion was written large across her face. "Show you what?"

"Blood. They don't bleed. Let me see your blood." Thunder rumbled in the distance, punctuating his words.

He could tell she thought he was crazy. "Will, are you doing that to the weather? Is the ward not working?"

"Blood. Show me now," he ordered a second time.

"I don't want to cut myself. It hurts," she complained, but when Sammy took a step toward him, a strange shield appeared between them, buzzing in the air with a sound that made her teeth hurt. Sammy recognized it immediately; it was the sonic shield he'd created for his fight against Lognion. Not only could it divert fire, but if Will so chose, the shield could destroy flesh and bone. Her eyes widened. "Fine." Turning the knife over, she stabbed the tip lightly into the flesh of her palm. Blood welled up right away, for in her nervousness she'd cut deeper than she intended.

The sound shield vanished along with Will's cloak of lightning. His body relaxed, and he stepped forward to take her hand in his so he could heal the cut. "Sorry about that," he mumbled.

"You scared the shit out of me," Sammy informed him. "Why did I have to cut myself? Are your nightmares always like this?"

He looked away. "Only rarely. This is why I keep my door locked at home."

She examined the place he had just healed. "I hope you haven't done anything like that to Oliver or Aunt Erisa."

"Once again, this is why I sleep alone. I was worried something like this would happen."

"I'm not pretending to understand," said Sammy. "But if it was a dream, couldn't you dream I bled? How does it prove anything?"

Will didn't open his mouth, but inside his head couldn't help but respond, *because it isn't just a dream.* He had lived through similar scenarios before, he'd cut them before, and the invaders never bled.

"You're not going to answer?" she asked after waiting half a minute.

Sullen, he replied, "No. From now on we sleep separately, and you stay on the outside of my ward."

"Doesn't that mean I'll be in danger, from whatever it is you're afraid of? It obviously isn't *just* the weather you're worried about."

The expression on her face spoke of secret knowledge and Will felt a sudden panic. "Did you see something?" He moved forward and Sammy began to retreat. "Sammy, did you see something? Tell me! Anything? Anything other than me?"

The desperation on his face must have frightened her, because Sammy erected a force wall between them to halt his advance. "You need to calm down," she warned. "I didn't see anything but you."

He took a step back, then paused to take a deep breath, forcing himself to relax. "Good. Then no, you're in no danger. As long as you stay outside my ward from now on you should be safe."

"That makes absolutely no sense. How about an explanation?"

Will shook his head. "You're too close already. Talking about it might spark something. The less you know the better." *The less likely you are to be noticed by them.* He'd been having nightmares since before the war with Darrow, and they'd only increased after the things he'd been forced to do during the war. Combined with his trip to hell, the destruction of the dragon, and Selene's horrifying transformation and it was a miracle he was still sane.

Since his self-exile to Trendham his heart and soul had healed, at least in some ways. Fatherhood had given him a new purpose and time had taken the edge off of old horrors. His normal nightmares had faded and become less frequent, but a couple of years after moving he'd had the first of a new type of nightmare. He'd begun having dreams of *them,* the ones from outside, and he wasn't really sure they were just dreams.

It all came down to one mistake he'd made after defeating the dragon. Will had attempted to trap the lich, Grim Talek, within a special barrier that isolated the interior from the rest of reality. The spell had worked, even though he'd wound up allowing the lich to escape anyway, but the real mistake was the spell he had used. It had been created by a former archwizard, one of the writers in the journal he'd inherited from Arrogan, a woman named Erica.

The tenth writer had created a spell that let her see through the veil of reality into the void of nothingness that surrounded and encompassed all that existed. She'd been haunted forever after, consumed by paranoia and afraid of invisible monsters that only she could see. The barrier spell Will had used had been of her design, to keep the alien fiends that hunted the mad tenth writer from reaching her.

But the act of creating such a barrier involved creating an artificial separation in reality, it had exposed Will to the void. While he had attempted to kill the lich he had seen into the outer darkness and before he had dismissed the barrier he had caught the briefest glimpse of something moving. Somehow that brief moment had left its mark on his psyche, or as Grim Talek had described it, the void had seen him in return.

Nothing existed in the void, unless it was observed by those within reality, or as Will liked to call it, 'the Dream.' He couldn't remember who had first described it thus to him, but the idea seemed to fit. Seeing through the veil of the dream had exposed him to the darkness, and his brief look into the void had brought life to ancient horrors older than time, horrors that simultaneously hadn't existed at all—until he had seen them.

The tenth writer had rambled on about them endlessly, but it wasn't until he'd unwittingly infected himself with the same madness that Will had begun to understand. The thought that Sammy might have seen the creature from his dream terrified him, for it would mean she had also been drawn into his curse. Her statement that she hadn't seen anything was a relief to him, and he didn't intend to make matters any worse by explaining what he'd been afraid of.

When it came to the things that lay outside the Dream, ignorance was bliss, and knowledge was the end of sanity. Will didn't know what would eventually happen to him, but he didn't intend to drag anyone else into it with him.

The extended silence infuriated his cousin. "I'm going to throttle you one of these days. I'm not stupid, Will. That weird ward you use at night makes more sense to me now. You're not trying to shield the weather from your unconscious, you're trying to keep something out. I just don't understand what."

"It actually *is* to isolate myself and avoid affecting the weather," argued Will. "But it doesn't always work, and you're right, I have a second purpose beyond that."

"So, talk to me."

Will's mouth closed and he crossed his arms. His ward wasn't the spell barrier spell that had originally caused his problem. It didn't create an absolute barrier, it didn't separate the interior and exterior into two separate realities. But he *had* borrowed from the techniques that Erica had used in her spell. Will had hoped to block his unconscious mind's access to the outside world where it could disturb the weather, and he'd also hoped to isolate it from whatever place the invaders came from, to keep them from stalking his dreams.

He'd failed on both counts. *You partially succeeded on both counts,* corrected Laina's voice in his mind. *Fewer storms, fewer dream invasions. The question is how far will you go to stop it completely?*

Will knew what Laina meant. The barrier spell that Erica had invented would do the trick. It would protect him, but it would also expose him further. Was safety worth it if it cost him what was left of his sanity? Would he wind up killing himself, as the tenth writer had?

She was alone. You aren't, whispered his dead sister.

You're just an echo, Will replied. *I still only have one soul. You're just an impression left in me, like a footprint in the sand.*

Sammy waved a hand in front of his face. "Hello! William? Are you still in there?"

He gave her a weak smile. "Not really. I'm not going to talk about it either. Sorry. It has nothing to do with the present and everything to do with things that should never have been learned. If you're unlucky enough to inherit the book of the first wizard, you'll learn when you read it. Just don't make the mistake I did and try to use anything written within those pages."

His cousin closed her eyes and seemed to meditate for a moment, then opened them again and told him, "Fine. But you scared the shit out of me, so you owe me breakfast. I *was* planning to offer to cook, but you have to atone."

Will struggled to keep from laughing. While he had once taught Sammy some of the basics of cooking, he doubted she'd improved upon them. They both knew she'd been hoping he would cook. "We can't have a fire," he told her, but when he saw her expression darken, he hastened to add, "however, I've created some workarounds that will save the day."

Her brows went up. "Oh?"

He nodded. "Clean up the camp and roll up my ward cloth while I get started. You won't be disappointed."

Sammy did, but she watched him from the corner of one eye as he began removing food items from his limnthal and placing them in the air in front of himself. Butter, eggs, ham, sausage, bread, and more all hung suspended in front of him. As she finished rolling up the embroidered ward cloth, she couldn't help but ask, "What spell is that?"

He chuckled. "Something I dreamed up years ago. I call it a mist table. If you look closer, you'll see there's water vapor suspended in a flat plane just below the food."

"I don't recall seeing anything like that in any of the books we brought from Wurthaven, or in the guild library in Bondgrad."

"That's because I designed it myself," said Will, then he paused, giving her a curious look. "You haven't designed any spells, have you?"

Sammy glared back. "No. You insisted it was incredibly dangerous and never spent any time on spell design with me. Some of us didn't have the luxury of attending Wurthaven."

"I thought maybe your Trendish master would have explored the topic with you during your apprenticeship."

She rolled her eyes. "You know that was just a farce to satisfy the guild's requirements. Besides, most of the wizards in Trendham are afraid to do anything, much less dabble in spell design. Very few do anything other than repeat what others have done for decades and decades without variation."

Will ran through a half dozen other spells she hadn't seen before, slicing up the ham, melting the butter, and heating the sausage in an invisible pan. He cast each spell with nothing more than a thought and a bit of turyn. Sammy's eyes grew wider as he continued, browning the ham as though it lay in an iron skillet while simultaneously whisking the eggs together atop a thin layer of melted butter. "Every one of those is a new spell, isn't it?" she asked.

Will shrugged, keeping his eyes on the eggs to keep from burning them, though there was no flame in evidence.

"And you're reflex casting all of them. How long have you been doing this?"

"I've been working as a cook for years now, Sam."

"But no one knows you're a wizard. I thought you weren't doing anything besides a little practice to keep from getting rusty, but this…" Her words trailed off.

"And the alchemy too," he reminded her, flipping the eggs in a pan made of nothing but air. Small runes that she hadn't noticed before glowed along one edge. "I'm alone in the kitchen quite often, so I've come up with a number of handy spells to make things easier. I can use a lot of these inside other items too, so even if someone walked in, they wouldn't notice."

"That seems like extra effort."

"It keeps my job interesting. Someday I might write a book, *Culinary Magic for Wizard Chefs,*" Will explained.

"What do those runes represent?"

Will moved the air skillet closer to her so she could see it more easily. "It's an elemental air spell that solidifies air into this specific shape. At first, I had a dozen variations to account for different needs and sizes. They could range from pots to pans to soup pots, but eventually I streamlined the spell and added a small amount of complexity to enable a single spell to produce multiple shapes. The first rune here denotes which shape I want; the second indicates the size."

Sammy frowned. "And the rest of them?"

"One for heat and two for duration," he answered. "I added more to the spell construct later. Those essentially designate the amount of turyn stored within the spell at the time of casting and at what rate it will be used for both heat and maintaining the air's shape. Essentially, I can set how long the spell will last, how hot it will get, and how long it will stay hot. The visible runes are there so I can change those settings after casting if I decide I need something different."

"Wouldn't it be easier to use force spells?"

He nodded. "Except that I could only use one, and a single force spell can't create multiple noncontiguous objects."

She shook her head in wonder. "So you made all these spells just to replace pots and pans, to cut meat and vegetables, and—and what else?"

Will smiled. "Much, much more. I have spells to whip egg whites, to slowly stir a pot, to cut, chop, puree, you name it. I also have a master spell to clean fish, gut and skin wild game, defeather fowl. That took some doing, let me tell you. It wound up being almost as complex as Selene's Solution. I'm pretty sure it's at least seventh-order when it comes to difficulty."

He handed her an invisible plate that held a perfect omelet, hot sausage, and a perfectly toasted bun slathered with butter. Sammy stared at it in wonder, then looked up at him, her mouth dropping open. "But, why?"

"You'll need your own utensils. I don't have a spell to replace those," he told her.

His cousin summoned a knife and spoon from her limnthal, then sat down. The elemental plate behaved much like a normal plate, so she put it in her lap and began sawing at the sausage. Once her mouth was full, she reiterated her question, forgetting about manners. "No, really, why? This must have been an immense investment of time and energy, designing all these spells, using them until you could reflex cast them— it just seems like a huge waste of time."

Will's eyes narrowed, and he held up one hand. "If I dismiss the spell that omelet will be on the ground. Are you sure you want to disparage my work?"

Using the spoon, she cut the omelet in two and managed to stuff one half of it into her mouth while shaking her head 'no.' Will's eyes crinkled at the corners while he watched her, amused. Sitting down with his own plate of food, he began to explain. "You can already see the benefits. We are eating a freshly cooked meal under conditions that call for a cold camp. No smoke, no fire, no dirty dishes, but that's not why I did it. I did it because I like it. Even though I've been hiding all these years, I still like magic. Cooking relaxes me, and designing spells to make cooking easier was a natural extension of that. It's the first thing I've ever done with my power that I'm truly proud of."

Sammy finished wolfing down the omelet and started on the rest of the sausage. "The way you used to train, I figured that if you designed any spells they'd be battle magics."

A shadow passed over his face, but Will shrugged it off. "I've done some of that too, but killing is nothing to revel in. If I leave a legacy behind, I'd rather they remember me for these spells rather than anything violent I've done. Depending on how things go with the trolls, you might see some of those spells today as well, but I hope not. I could happily spend the rest of my life without touching any battle magic. It's gotten to the point I sometimes have trouble just killing chickens."

"But you still practice?" Her words were muffled by the bun she was chewing.

Will nodded. "I can't stop. I get too anxious if I don't. I'm constantly worried about someone coming after Oliver, or Mom—or you."

She finished her food and tossed her plate straight up. It didn't fall back down, nor did it disappear, it simply slowed and continued to drift higher. She looked askance at Will.

"It's made of air, and it's the same density as the air it came from," he explained, then dismissed the spell.

"Most people find it easier to use earth or water to make temporary objects," observed Sammy. "I don't know that I've ever seen anyone use a spell to do the same with air."

Will shrugged. "I was experimenting with something else and tried it. It wasn't very successful for what I was attempting, but I realized later that it had certain advantages for my cooking spells. The pots and pans I create don't conduct heat very well, so the heat stays where I want it when I'm cooking. It would be a drawback if I was using a stove, but when I'm heating the food with magic, it's a different story."

"What were you trying to do with it before deciding to use it for dishes?"

His expression turned dour. "The usual—finding ever more lethal ways to use magic."

Sammy almost stopped there, sensing the change in mood, but she pressed on. "I don't understand your fixation. Much as I hate it, killing seems easy. Is it really necessary to find new ways of doing it?"

He finished the last of his own food, then put away the remains and dismissed his airy cookware. "You're right. Especially when you can convert turyn to flame with little more than a thought."

"Lightning is just as lethal," she observed.

Will shook his head. "That's not the point." He gestured with his hands, while trying to find the words to explain. Sammy had been through bad times. She'd been there when Barrowden was burned, when her mother and brothers were murdered, and not long after she had taken blood herself, killing a Darrowan invader with a hidden knife. She was no stranger to cruelty and violence, but she hadn't seen the things Will had.

She'd been there when he went to Hell, and she'd nearly killed herself bringing him back, but she hadn't gone herself. She'd seen some of the effects of the war with Darrow, but she'd never fought in a battle. From her perspective, having the power to protect herself and put an end to anyone who threatened her was enough, and Will couldn't fault her in that perception.

Eventually the words came to him. "We aren't the same, and it's probably better that you don't think like me, but the things I've done have left a mark. Killing is easy, but when I look back on my mistakes, I often realize there were better ways to do what needed doing, ways that wouldn't have cost me so much, or cost so many other people their lives. I spend a lot of time mulling it over when I'm trying to sleep, and whenever a solution to one of those old problems comes to me, I have to pursue it."

Sammy frowned. "So you're making spells to solve old mistakes? You can't go back in time."

"If I'm ever in the same position, I'll do better."

"Those days won't come again."

He nodded, but his heart knew otherwise. "At the very least I've also designed a multitude of other useful spells as a result of some of my ideas."

CHAPTER 10

Will returned to his body and saw that his cousin was giving him an unhappy look. In fact, she looked so thoroughly disgruntled that it was hard for him to imagine she had ever been gruntled at any point in the past. "What's wrong with you?" he asked.

"Is this all we're going to do?" she responded. "Sit here?"

"Since Emory is leading the sorcerers and wizards, it's easier to observe him than try to sneak around all day. Plus I get to hear their scouting reports."

Sammy puffed her cheeks and blew out a dissatisfied breath of air. "It also seems suspicious to me that you have an astral connection to one of my old flings."

Will laughed. "He's a good friend, and at one point I thought he might be an in-law. Besides, I'm sure you have an astral connection to him as well, you just can't sense it."

"Ha!" exclaimed Sammy with perhaps a touch too much enthusiasm. "We were never that serious."

"Mmhmm," said Will agreeably.

"We weren't!"

"Whatever you say," he agreed, then looked up at the sun. "Ready for lunch?"

She narrowed her eyes. "Trying to appease me with food?"

He shrugged. "You don't have to eat if you don't want to." Thirty minutes later, they'd finished two bowls of lamb stew he'd packed away before leaving Lystal. All he'd had to do was warm it up. That and the butter-crust plum tarts he'd been saving put a distinct smile on his cousin's face.

"I'm surprised you didn't cook something fresh, given what you showed me this morning," remarked Sammy, rubbing her belly appreciatively.

"The time difference in the limnthal comes in handy when packing food for a trip, and sometimes I don't feel like cooking," he replied. Will stretched his legs, then returned to his original sitting position. "Now, if you'll excuse me, I have more eavesdropping to do."

"Remind me, why am I here again?" asked Sammy.

"Because you insisted on going on the adventure," Will replied, "and I didn't argue since it's nice to have someone to guard my body at times like these." He heard her sigh as he left his body and sought his target. Moments later, Emory Tallowen filled his vision, and he saw that things were no longer as peaceful as they had been just an hour prior.

Emory sat astride a powerful charger, yelling orders into the pandemonium that surrounded him. Trolls were everywhere, and men were dying faster than Will could count. Flames were everywhere as Emory and the sorcerers with the Terabinian army tried to kill the trolls in their midst, but there was no scenario Will could imagine that involved them recovering from having this many trolls among them. The only battle Will had seen even close to the disaster around Emory was the fight against the trolls in Darrow, when his father's contingent had nearly been wiped out.

This was worse.

Short of a miracle, the entire First Division would soon be little more than a memory. As he started to withdraw, Will noticed an odd hole surrounded by disturbed earth. Looking farther away, he saw similar holes in every direction. Understanding came instantly. *The trolls buried themselves and let the army pass over them before attacking,* he thought. *But how did they know where to be, and when?* Such an ambush required significant preparation and even more intelligence.

He noted the information and let it pass through him. Now was not the time for rumination. As he snapped back to his body, Will's eyes opened and he looked at Sammy. "We have to move now. They're dying."

"But just before lunch, you said…"

An elemental travel-disk formed beneath his feet, and Will pulled his cousin onto it as it began to rise into the air. "They were ambushed. The trolls are in the middle of the army."

"We didn't pack up," said Sammy weakly, trying to process the sudden change. "How bad is it?"

They picked up speed quickly, and the wind was already making it difficult to talk. "First Division will be wiped out," he answered grimly. "Emory is one of the officers."

His cousin's fingers tightened where she held his waist. "He's a third-order wizard, he'll be fine." The words were more for herself than Will.

Shouting into the wind, he hated himself as he responded, "There's no ley line near here. Could you burn that many trolls to ash with just ambient turyn? Even with your talent, it's impossible."

Sammy stayed silent, and tense minutes passed as they flew above the tops of the shorter trees and dodged between the limbs of the taller ones. Their speed was such that it wasn't long before they heard the screams of dying men and the roaring of trolls echoing around them. The trees cleared, and before them an open field appeared, a low place between the gently rolling hills that had been kept clear of the forest by locals who used it as a natural thoroughfare.

For as far as they could see in either direction, men and trolls fought, or to be more accurate, trolls reveled in the bloody chaos while the desperate Terabinians struggled to regain some semblance of organization. Nearly half of them looked to be dead already.

Will pulled back from the edge and directed the travel-disk back into the trees, but what Sammy had seen already was horrifying. Although she'd been through some tough moments with him in the past, she'd never seen blood and violence on such a scale, and he worried she might vomit or panic. Instead, her nails bit into him. "What are you doing? We can't help them from here. Go back!"

He'd already formulated a plan of action, and Will was grateful to know Sammy hadn't lost her head yet. Later would be another matter. "We can't help them," he told her. "There's only one thing left to do. Make sure the trolls don't escape."

"You just pointed out that there's no ley line near here. Emory needs us. Even if we can't win, we have to save him—save them, as many as we can."

Will glanced upward, to a sky that was frustratingly clear and calm. "There's power to be had, if I can reach it. When I do, I'll channel it for you so you can clean up the mess."

Her eyes narrowed. "Clean up?"

"You'll have to burn everything that's left."

"There are wounded men out there! I can't burn living men!"

"There won't be anyone left when I call you. Just wounded trolls." The expression on her face at his words hit him like a punch in the gut, but he continued, "I need you, Sammy. I can't finish it by myself. I'll do the worst, but I'll need you to make sure the trolls don't get back up. Do you understand?"

Her mouth was slightly agape. "You're just going to give up and kill everyone? No! Fuck you! I'll save Emory myself!"

"Walk out there now and you'll be dead before you reach him," Will told her.

"But you won't?" she demanded.

There was no gentle way to explain, so he didn't try. "You're powerful, Sammy. But you have no experience in this. I do. I've done this before."

"Killed thousands without thinking twice?"

"Yes," he answered flatly.

"I won't let you."

Will was beyond caring about threats, but her stubbornness matched his own wishes, so he modified his plan. "Look, I'll do what I can. After I go out, create a fire-wall. Use the trees and set fire to this side of the forest's edge. If I can, I'll get the survivors to retreat this way. Let them through, and I'll do my best to hold off until they're clear."

"All of them?"

"Do you want me to die?" he growled. "My chances get worse the more we prolong this. I'll get Emory out. That's the most I can promise."

She looked as though she would argue, but as Sammy studied his face, her expression softened. "Fine. Do what you can."

Will turned away, using a camouflage spell as he started for the battle. He wasn't sure what had convinced her, but as he walked, something ran down his cheek, and he wiped at it without thinking. His fingers came away damp. *That's odd,* he thought, but he didn't pause. Breaking into a jog, he ran toward the screams.

Beyond the tree line, the sun felt good as Will entered a nightmare as vivid as any that haunted his nights. Despite the years since his last exposure to war, it all felt familiar. The sounds, the blood, the sheer awfulness, all of it came back as if he had never left it at all—as though the rest of his life had been the dream and he had only ever existed in the midst of this rotten misery. There was no hope, no escape from it, this was his life, if it could be called such. Given what he was there to do, it was better that he had already given up on optimism, for it could only bring additional pain.

With his morbid resignation to horror, there came a strange peace, a feeling of fatalistic empowerment. Nothing mattered. Everyone was dead, now or in the near future, whether it was by his hand or from the violent excesses of the trolls. Will was free. His only task was to bring an end to the suffering, both that of the humans and the monsters that feasted upon them.

You have to save Emory, Laina reminded him silently from the recesses of his mind.

"Right," he answered. A small portion of First Division had somehow come together and eliminated the trolls among them, creating a small island of desperate humanity in a sea of violent despair. They were more than two-hundred yards to the right of where he now stood, but Will didn't want to go to them; he needed to draw them in his direction. Using an elemental travel-disk, he elevated himself until he could see over the tumult and spot the warriors of Terabinia. One part of their line featured a warrior of burning black metal, Tiny. Will sent his voice across the distance. "Tiny, this is Will. I can't hear you, but I can help. Head toward the tree line to the east of you. You'll see a great fire, but ignore it. Sammy will let you through."

To his satisfaction, he saw the metal giant's posture shift, and the helm swiveled in his direction. Seconds later, the Terabinian soldiers began trying to push in his direction. Other than Tiny, however, none of them could make much progress.

It was time to soften up the trolls. Will dropped his camouflage and lowered himself to the ground. The nearest trolls looked at him with surprise and toothy grins. Two stopped eating the liver of a man still screaming and turned their attention fully to him.

Will decided to start small and give himself a chance to warm up to his dark work. From his limnthal, he summoned his staff, a weapon he had crafted shortly after beginning his exile. His teacher had frowned on enchanted items, but Will had had a lot of time on his hands, and the enchantments on the staff were relatively simple. The staff was five feet in length, and one enchantment reinforced the oak and steel, for the staff was heeled by a steel cap while a steel strip ran from there to the head. The second enchantment controlled the blade, and when Will activated it, three feet of sharp steel sprang out from the top, turning the simple weapon into a sword staff. The final enchantment protected the wood and steel from vibrations and shocks.

Ordinarily, the first reinforcing enchantment would be sufficient for a battle tool, but this final one was necessary to protect the staff from Will's particular talent. Other than that, it was merely an extraordinarily sturdy weapon. What made it more deadly than an ordinary sword staff was the magic of the wizard who wielded it.

Will stepped to one side, avoiding the swiping claws of one troll while using a hasty point-defense shield to throw the other off-balance by preventing its leg from coming down on the ground properly. As it stumbled and fell, he swept the blade of his staff around in a wide arc, and a strange hum filled the air. The metal's shine vanished, replaced by a dull grey as Will's talent caused the weapon to vibrate at a speed too fast to be seen.

It was a frequency perfect for butchery. Will used it daily when quartering fowl or slicing up pork at the Laughing Goat. He'd had years to fine-tune his technique, turning cutlery into something that went far beyond simply *sharp*. Used with kitchen knives, it required a lot of control, for the vibration also made the implements tough to handle, numbing the hands of the user. Will's enchanted staff was designed to deal with that, though.

The blade cut through the troll's waist as if the monster was made of butter instead of tough flesh and even tougher bone. The cut was so swift and painless that the troll seemed surprised when his upper body fell away from his lower half. Will whipped the staff around, and after using another point-defense shield to block the other troll's claws, he sliced away first one arm and then a leg. He took a moment then to thrust the blade through the groin of each troll. It wouldn't kill them, but that was where their brains were located, and it would take them longer to recover from that than decapitation or dismemberment.

A sense of satisfaction began to rise within him, but this was far from being enough. Will moved on, engaging several more trolls and garnering attention from still more as he cut them down. He had disabled ten or twelve before they realized a true threat was among them. Four pressed in on him from every side, too many for him to deal with in simple fashion. A loud buzz arose as the air blurred around Will, forming a weird shield.

The claws, arms, legs, and even torsos of the trolls around him disintegrated wherever they touched that shield, becoming liquid gore that exploded around the human in their midst. It was the same shield Will had once used to slay a dragon, but he had improved it slightly. The sonic shield was a product of his talent, but he had developed a conventional spell of elemental air that he used along with it now, sluicing away the gore and keeping it from landing on him. When the wounded trolls fell back, he was still untouched by the bodily fluids that soaked the ground around him.

Will smiled. After years of hiding, it felt good to test the magics he had been honing. It was pleasing to see that his improvements worked properly, but it still wasn't enough. He needed to create a bigger disturbance, to draw all of them toward him.

Walking forward, he swatted a thrown boulder from the air with a larger force spell similar to his point-defense spell. Clearing the space around him with a few swings of his staff, he unleashed his anger and cloaked himself in lightning before sending long strokes out to rip through dozens of nearby trolls. Until now he had been conserving his energy, but he could hear the Terabinians making progress toward him. The more he occupied the trolls, the easier they would find it to advance. His turyn only had to last until then.

The lightning was so bright it left afterimages in the eyes of his enemies, the ones who weren't sent shivering to the ground. Deadly as it was, it couldn't kill the trolls, but it could disable them for several minutes at a time. Will alternated between strokes of lightning and thundering waves of pure sound that deafened and stunned his enemies. The trolls nearest to him were down now, out to a distance of thirty or forty yards, their bodies twitching and shaking as they lay senseless around him. Those further out drew back, searching for stones or other large objects to throw.

Will laughed at them, then mocked them in trollish, "What will you do now, weaklings?"

They answered him with heavy stones and thrown clubs. Will stopped those in rapid fashion using his point-defense shield, but when a large shadow blocked out the sun, he was forced to use a stronger defense. He opted for a force-dome rather than a sonic shield when he realized what was falling toward him.

One of the trolls had thrown a dead horse. Will admired the monster's creativity, but then his attention was captured by a verbal response from one of them. "Your power won't last, *tregbor*. We heal, but you *lasgit*!" It was trollish, but with a strange accent and a few words that seemed foreign.

The fact that they spoke so clearly confirmed that the trolls weren't some barbaric holdovers of the last purge, but rather some tribe that had been brought from elsewhere, though Will couldn't imagine who would be capable of doing such a thing. Their accent might be a clue, but Will was only familiar with one troll clan, so he couldn't ascertain much from it.

In the grand scheme of things, Will's stand in the midst of the troll horde was a small thing on a battlefield that spanned more than a mile, but the light and noise produced by his magic had served to distract a significant portion of the trolls within the closest hundred yards or so. Will wanted to do better. The sky teased him, for he knew the power high above was what he needed, but he didn't have the turyn necessary to bridge the gap, not consciously at least. As always, he wondered why his subconscious could often accomplish what his waking mind could not.

The sound of a Terabinian horn reminded him that the power he needed wasn't far off. Once the remnants of First Division reached him, he would have the key required to touch that distant power. For now, he would have to be more creative to attract more of the enemy's attention. A risky idea came to him, but Will was beyond worrying. With each passing moment, the cautious man who had hid for so many years faded away as the furious battle awakened his old alter ego.

As he leapt up, a force-travel-disk appeared beneath his feet and lifted him twenty feet into the air, allowing him to look down on the trolls and see farther into the distance. It also made him an ideal target, and the fact that he'd chosen to use a force spell meant he couldn't use his point-defense shield or other force spells. It wasn't a mistake on Will's part, though; despite conventional battle wisdom, he'd chosen his platform deliberately.

Within seconds, rocks, clubs, and dead bodies began to be hurled in his direction—anything within reach that the trolls could lift and throw.

The advantage of a force-disk was that it was perfectly stable and with the exception of some rare magics or extreme force, indestructible. It gave Will a solid point for his offensive defense, which turned out to be a variation of his old favorite spell, the wind-wall. He began with a sonic shield to protect himself in the short term while his new, improved wind-wall gathered momentum. Unlike the first version he'd learned years ago, this one took time to get started. It lacked the quick response of the original, but it made up for it in efficiency and duration. For a much more reasonable expenditure of turyn, the same effect could be created and maintained.

Thirty long seconds creeped by as the air moved steadily faster around him, and Will's sonic shield struggled to deal with some of the projectiles thrown at him. Bodies weren't too bad, and smaller weapons, spears, or wooden clubs it handled with only slight adjustments, but when some of the trolls began hurling rocks bigger than a man's head, he began to have problems. Stone—and even worse, metal—were the most difficult things for his sonic shield to deal with.

Small boulders shattered against his shield, but the sharp fragments made it through, cutting exposed skin and bruising him in other places. He was already juggling three magical workings simultaneously—the rapidly strengthening wind spell, his sonic shield, and the force-travel-disk, but Will added an iron-skin spell to protect himself better. The complexity of it all would have overwhelmed him once upon a time, but Will was a long way from being an apprentice.

"Kill the tregbor!" yelled one of the trolls, and the missiles began flying at Will with increasing frequency and volume. It was almost too much for him, but before it overwhelmed his sonic shield, the wind-wall began making up the difference in his defense. Lighter objects began missing him, driven off course by the strong wind, which grew more powerful by the second.

Will sneered at the monsters raging beneath him. His layered defenses wouldn't allow much in the way of sound to pass, so he used his talent to project his voice to the trolls. "Coming here was your mistake. Humans are not prey, and Grak Murra will see that only your ashes leave this place!"

Grak Murra was the title that Clegg, the troll chieftain had given him, 'grak' being the word for troll in their language and 'murra' being the new word that Clegg had created to denote mother. Trolls were hermaphrodites and had neither mothers nor fathers, but the ancient troll had coined the word in honor of Will's sacrifice.

The wind had become a tempest, and now even the heaviest stones were missing him while everything else was being caught and whipped around in circles. The trolls stopped throwing things as their missiles began striking them, but it was too late. The wind began to catch everything and even lifted some of the smaller trolls into the air. Those that didn't want to be thrown about had to flatten themselves against the ground.

Will dismissed the iron-skin spell and dropped his sonic shield to save turyn while he focused on the chaos created by his wind spell. The effect extended more than a hundred yards around him and made the terrain all but impassable. It couldn't kill the trolls, but they couldn't travel through it; even crawling put them at risk of being lifted off the ground.

He had finally gotten the result he wanted. Everyone on the battlefield knew he was there, especially the trolls. Across the field, he could see the survivors of First Division heading toward him, helped by the thinned-out and disrupted trolls between them, but as they got closer, Will knew he would have to dismiss his windstorm to allow them to reach him.

He kept it up for several minutes, then released the spell. It would take ten or fifteen seconds to taper off, but that was all he needed. Lowering himself back to the earth, Will dismissed the force-travel-disk and set off to meet the Terabinians. Sword staff in hand, he reinstated his iron-body transformation just to be safe and began using the point-defense shield for serious threats. He was nearly out of turyn, and he needed to be frugal with his remaining resources.

It took a minute for the trolls to realize he was afoot and seemingly vulnerable. Most of them were still scattered and confused. Will walked through those that dared to confront him, cutting them into pieces as he passed, his only expression one of utter disdain. He drew on the ambient turyn as much as he could, but it was insufficient to replenish him. The trolls themselves, while living, had very little turyn, so draining them wasn't an option either.

Without a ley line or something similar, Will would eventually be unable to sustain even the magics he was currently using, but he wasn't worried. Relief was close at hand. He glanced at the sky once again as he walked. *Soon.*

The beleaguered soldiers came into view, and he realized they'd stopped advancing. Even Tiny's metal form wasn't enough to make a path for them anymore. The sorcerers who were managing shields along the sides and rear of the formation were exhausted, and the warriors fighting along the active front side had nothing left to give. Their offensive advance had stalled, and now they were barely keeping the front from collapsing inward. Despite their best efforts, Will could see men being snatched from the line. The trolls often lost one of their long arms making such a grab, but they had arms to spare, while every human soldier taken diminished the remaining Terabinian force.

Sweat was heavy on Will's brow, not from the magic he had used as much as from the exertion of physical combat. His magical prowess had grown over the years, but his physical endurance was limited. Regular practice with Oliver had kept him fit, but his stamina wasn't what it had been when he'd been in the army. He diverted some of his dwindling turyn to reinforce his strength and dexterity, then leapt forward with renewed vigor. *I only need to make it a little farther.*

The trolls behind him had finally reorganized, massing to overwhelm him, while those in front of him were preoccupied with the Terabinians, so Will broke into a sprint. He could cut his way through those that were unprepared, but if the horde behind fell on him in concert, he wouldn't have the energy to repel them.

His vibrating blade cut away the legs of those standing in front of him while he ran through, leaving the trolls falling like cut timber in his wake. Half a minute later, he found himself panting in front of the human shield-wall, while a host of spearheads pointed toward him. The soldiers were too shocked by his appearance to react. Glancing behind himself, Will saw space behind him had filled in. He was about to be pinned, quite literally, between trolls and spears.

He put his back to the spears and faced the oncoming trolls. Will's turyn had dropped to a level far below even that of a normal person, to a point that would render most unable to move or possibly even remain conscious, but Arrogan had trained him for that—years ago—before he'd even been able to cast a single spell. Eyes on the enemy, Will sidestepped a giant club crashing straight down, then hopped up and to the left to avoid the angled return swing as the troll whipped it back up and toward him.

His lip curled into a sneer of contempt, and although the blade at the end of his staff had fallen silent from lack of energy, he drove the point forward like a spear into the troll's groin. Without magic, it was harder to penetrate the thick hide, but the blade went far enough to reach the brain. The troll shivered and fell sideways, unconscious.

Claws came at him from the left, and a fence-post club swung low toward his legs from two trolls spaced widely on either side of him. Reacting with a speed borne of endless training, Will ducked the claws and created a point-defense shield to stop the club—or tried to. He successfully ducked the claws, putting his head directly in line with the swing of the club, but his shield failed to materialize. There was nothing left. His turyn was gone.

In that second, he knew he'd gone too far, dared too much, and his overconfidence was about to cost him everything. Death came slowly, and Will could almost count the cuts and scratches that marred the wood as it swung directly toward his face, but he couldn't move fast enough to avoid it.

CHAPTER 11

Something dark flew across the periphery of his vision, and the wood shattered into flinders. One portion remained in the hands of the troll, while another large section flew off to Will's right amidst a storm of sharp splinters. Black flames trailed behind a massive ebon blade that continued on to shear the troll in half diagonally, from left hip to right shoulder.

"Shields on me!" thundered a deep, metallic voice. "Reform and hold it!" Men from the shield-wall raced forward several steps, and the line shifted forward. Shields and spears were raised, but before the trolls could assault the new formation, force-walls went up in front of it.

Straightening up, Will glared at the towering metal behemoth that had saved him, then put his hand on its leg. The black flames that covered the golem flickered and faded around that leg, and the metal went from black to dull grey as he drew in a substantial amount of the demonic turyn that powered it.

With his energy returning, Will studied the Black Duke. "You stink like a demon," he remarked after several seconds. "But at least your looks have improved."

A lieutenant who was approaching gaped at him. "You will address the marshal as Your Grace or milord! Show some respect—or—" The officer slowly slumped to the ground. Will had attached a source-link and rapidly drained the man of every bit of turyn the man possessed.

"Stop," bellowed the golem. "You've killed my officer!"

Will glanced up at the massive metal form. "He's just unconscious. I needed the energy."

Another officer, this one a full commander, closed in and Will recognized him. It was Emory Tallowen. He was relieved to see his old student still alive. No matter who else had to die, Sammy might forgive him if he could save Emory. The commander was equally upset. "Anyone who can't move is dead, Will! Are you planning to carry him?"

He wished he could smile, but reality was far too bleak for that. "Good to see you again, Emory. To answer your question, no. I'm planning to kill him, along with every other living person on this cursed field."

Emory blinked, then responded with a single word, "No."

A shadow fell over them, accompanied by the golem's low voice. "Why?"

Will looked up at his one-time friend and felt his chest tighten, but his eyes remained dead. "I came to help if possible, but when I discovered this disaster, it was too late. Most of your army is gone, and what's left will soon be food. There's little in the way of resources here for me to draw on, other than the sky, but I need considerable turyn to form the link. The men remaining to you have enough for my purpose. It's a poor option, but I can guarantee the trolls will be eliminated. The alternative is waiting until they exhaust your casters and eat these men anyway."

Emory's face reddened. "The man who trained me for war would never counsel sacrificing soldiers—"

"You were a squad leader then," snapped Will, cutting him off. "Now you're a commander. Grow up. The priorities are different." He glanced back at Tiny's metal form. "We're working with just the power we have here and now, in our bodies and the bodies of these men. I don't have a miracle to offer, just the possibility of making it so the deaths of these soldiers won't have been in vain."

"You need turyn to call the storm," intoned the royal marshal, the cold metal of his golem's helm giving no sign of his feelings. "Can lightning kill trolls?"

Despite their grievances, Will was glad to see that Tiny's mind was still as quick as ever. "No." He shook his head. "Sammy is here. The wall of fire in the trees to the east of us is her doing. Once I've tapped into the power up there, I can channel it for her."

After a second of silence, the marshal responded, "You can channel the power to her from here?"

Emory's mouth gaped. "You're not considering…" Tiny held up one massive hand, stopping him in mid-sentence.

Will answered quickly, "She can teleport to me, once I've pacified the trolls."

"Or you could teleport these men to safety instead," suggested Emory stubbornly.

Before Will could argue, the marshal pronounced, "Do both. If she can teleport to you, then you can teleport to her. Take the men to safety, then enact your plan."

Emory and Will both frowned, thinking Tiny misunderstood the problem. Emory replied, "He just said there's not enough turyn to do both."

Will nodded. "I'd have to make dozens of trips and drain these men of everything to cast the spell over and over. If these monsters take victory today, there will be twice as many next time. There'll be no sto—"

"Use me," said Tiny, patting the dark metal of his breastplate. "The trolls can pound on me as long as they wish. From what I've been told in the past, that can provide a significant amount of power."

Emory blinked and Will went still. After the span of a few seconds, Will asked, "How many soldiers are left?"

"Less than two-hundred is my estimate," said the marshal. "Take the regulars and the exhausted sorcerers first, and the stronger ones can maintain the shrinking perimeter."

Emory looked at Will, then added, "I'll go with the last group. Get everyone else out, then I'll let you save me," said the commander.

Feeling both weary and strangely hopeful, Will nodded. "I can take seven at a time." The marshal nodded, his metal helm expressionless, but when he started to turn away to issue orders, Will spoke again. "Leave the orders to Emory. He knows your casters better. You need to get out there and start building up turyn now if you want to have enough to allow me to finish this."

Any other nobleman in Terabinia might have bridled at Will's usurpation of authority, especially one given the rank of royal marshal, but though the two of them had parted on bad terms, Tiny didn't take umbrage. He headed for the line and made his way through. Will watched him go, a mixture of unidentifiable feelings passing through him. By the time he looked back at Emory, the first seven had been lined up for him to take.

Will stretched out his arms and addressed them, "Get as close as you can and keep a hand on me. Once we get to safety, I'll take whatever energy you have for the return."

Teleportation wasn't a cheap spell to cast. On an ordinary day, Will could use it three or maybe four times in quick succession before needing to replenish his turyn. Teleporting twenty-five times would require everything the men around him had to give and possibly more. Will hoped he could make up the difference with what he could also absorb from the environment between jumps.

All of that ignored the skill and rare combination of talent that allowed Will to slip halfway into the astral and find his target, or the fact that he had spent years learning to reflex cast the complex spell with barely a thought. The men he saved considered themselves lucky, but none of them truly understood the magnitude of their good fortune. It was unlikely anyone else on Hercynia could have done what the former prince consort of Terabinia was now doing.

Time after time Will teleported, each time draining the men he took to near unconsciousness before leaving them with Sammy. Even with his skill and practice, it took him half a minute to slip out of his body and reorient himself each time, but Will worked with the single-minded stubbornness that had proved to be his greatest strength since his first day as Arrogan's apprentice.

The ring of soldiers trapped within a sea of trolls grew smaller and smaller over the course of half an hour. The monsters definitely noticed, but they were helpless to prevent the escape, for as the group got smaller, it took fewer and fewer sorcerers to maintain the force-walls that protected the remainder.

When Will was close to the last trip, Sammy asked, "How am I going to see where to teleport to, and how will I know when you're ready?"

"Use a force-disk to gain some height and watch, but mind your eyes or you might be blinded by the glare. When you think the world has ended, that'll be the time. Just teleport to the epicenter," he explained, then added, "I'll be back with Emory next."

For his last trip, Will only had to bring Emory and four other sorcerers. They'd all been on their feet when he left, but on his return, only Emory and one other still stood. The trolls gathered around them were battering at the force-wall mercilessly, and a few seconds later, the last sorcerer collapsed, leaving only Emory, who quickly switched to a ring-wall force spell. He'd known better than to use a full dome, since a complete blockade would prevent Will's teleport from working. Some thirty feet away, Tiny's massive form fought a solitary battle, although in the face of so many trolls, he'd lost his grip on his weapons and now struggled merely to remain on his feet while the monsters batted him back and forth between them. The metal of his artificial body was pitch black and burning with toxic flames. The trolls didn't realize it, but if they beat on the demon-steel long enough, it would eventually overload in a devastating explosion. That wouldn't be ideal, however, since it would merely spread troll bits far and wide over a distance of miles. In a few days or weeks, the trolls would return in numbers beyond counting.

Will dragged the nearly helpless men close together, and Emory moved to stand beside him. The tired commander crouched down and made sure each man's hand was holding onto one of Will's legs, and then he nodded and released his spell. Will teleported them away.

Sammy's eyes locked onto Emory when they appeared, and Will could see that she was filled with more emotion than she cared to admit. For his part, Emory only glanced briefly in her direction as he began channeling his strength into Will. Will took it all and scavenged what was left in the near-unconscious sorcerers at his feet.

A minute later he, was ready, but he caught Sammy's attention before he left. "Do you have enough left to teleport?" The massive fire-wall she had created at the forest's edge had doubtless cost her a considerable amount of turyn.

She nodded. "I'm good, as long as I can see where to teleport." Her voice was steady, but Will could see the telltale signs of stress and anxiety in her stance. He gave her what he hoped was a reassuring look, then slipped out of his body for the final teleport.

With Emory and Sammy now together, Tiny was the only target he could lock onto. For a moment he worried, realizing the big man's true body was probably back in the capital, but a second later, he found the metal golem. It was the location of Tiny's soul that mattered, for in the astral realm souls were all that mattered. He took a moment to study the scene before casting the spell.

Tiny had given up trying to fight and seemed to be focusing on staying upright. The fact that even that was a struggle for his dense form was a testament to the strength and ferocity of the trolls, who were frenetically beating upon him with claws and clubs. The royal marshal understood his goal, however, for even with his weapons he couldn't effect any lasting damage on these foes. Even the black flames radiated by his demon-steel body weren't enough to destroy a troll.

Nothing less than complete incineration would do.

Will timed the spell and appeared just as two trolls on one side had finished landing colossal blows against Tiny's helm. They were no longer forced to fight with finesse, as there were so many of them that the golem couldn't retaliate, so they were now making wide, powerful swings as if they meant to drive Tiny into the earth like a metal piling.

The instant he arrived, Will erected a force-dome, then put both hands on Tiny's metal legs. In his true body, Tiny stood a full head taller than Will, who wasn't short, but in the golem, he was close to twelve feet tall. The continuous beating on his metal body hadn't left so much as a scratch, for demon-steel grew stronger and more impervious the more force one applied to it. It wouldn't dent or deform in the slightest. Instead, it would convert the kinetic energy into demonic turyn that reinforced its shape. Beyond a certain saturation point, it would begin to radiate the turyn as black flames that were toxic to most living creatures, with the exception of demons and the undead.

The enchantment on Tiny's golem powered its motion by using some of that demonic turyn, but the warrior had done his best to stay still so that he wouldn't waste any of the energy generated by the trolls' assault on him.

Will's spell had very little turyn in it, and it collapsed under the first two blows from the trolls. It was Tiny's enormous metal arms that shielded him from the attacks that followed.

Will focused on drawing power as rapidly as possible, but the feeling of being protected by someone else created a rare feeling of nostalgia for him. The last time he could recall was the night they had rescued Tailtiu from the vampires, when Tiny had shielded Will and Janice from the blood drinkers with his own flesh and bone.

It had been a friendship he'd thought would stand the test of time, but it had still gone terribly wrong. *Just like Selene,* he thought grimly.

Stop thinking about the past, he chided himself. *Focus on the present.* The toxic turyn that flowed around and into him was steadily being converted into his own type of energy, but the volume he was absorbing required conscious attention to manage safely. Will needed a lot of turyn, more than the human form could handle, but that was all right, since it didn't need to be inside him. A proper wizard took ownership of not just the turyn within them, but the turyn around them, and the greater their will, the farther the control extended.

The talents that third-order wizards developed went beyond even that, allowing them an intuitive control of turyn far beyond their normal reach, a command of power that was outside the range of will, a command that was akin to persuasion, as the wizard's turyn communicated his desires to the environmental turyn he had no direct connection with.

The battlefield that Will and Tiny stood on was far removed from ley lines or other sources of concentrated turyn, but far above them, currents flowed, powering the weather—wind and rain, snow and ice. Even clement weather possessed enormous potential hidden behind its tranquility. Will merely needed enough turyn to build a bridge, and as he steadily drained Tiny's golem, he formed the recycled energy into an invisible column above their heads. Metaphorically, Will's magic stretched, as if he was standing on tiptoe and straining for the heavens with his fingertips.

Sometimes his mind did it without effort, when he was sleeping, or during a few memorable fits of rage. Somehow, the unconscious mind could create the link with nothing more than the wisps of ambient turyn present anywhere, but for a deliberate connection, Will needed a dense collection of energy. He'd done so in the past by draining enemies and allies, and today he used Tiny.

The river in the sky seemed too far away, but Will refused to despair. It wasn't in him. He hadn't scaled the heights of wizardry by being pithless or faint-hearted. He continued drawing turyn and kept stretching, ever farther, until he felt the faintest touch, as though an electric shock had run through his hand.

The transformation happened in an instant. One moment Will was at his absolute limit, and the next he was inundated with limitless potency. The bridge he had built went from a faint wispy column to a dense pillar of turyn communicating between earth and sky, with Will at its center.

Where a moment before had stood a mortal, a god now resided, and as Will's eyes opened on the world around him, he grinned, as though reality itself was little more than a joke. His body was cloaked in pure electricity, and the blue of his eyes was no longer visible as they glowed with white intensity. A shadow loomed over him, and he brushed it aside with one hand, sending the frail metal form crashing away to one side.

The trolls rushed in, but only for a second. Touching a god wasn't permitted. Lightning flowed from his hands and branched out in all directions, impaling the brutish monsters and locking them into a shivering embrace of pain and misery. Within fifty yards of him, nothing was untouched, though beyond that the rest of the trolls continued their savagery unabated.

He released them seconds later, feeling a mild sense of satisfaction as he watched their now-flaccid bodies collapse to the ground. They weren't dead; he could tell that at a glance. His sense of turyn had been elevated to exquisite heights and he could see the difference between the dead and the still-living that lay scattered across the bloody battlefield.

Without exception, the trolls lived, but surprisingly some of the humans lying in the dirt were also alive. Most were badly injured, but a few were unharmed, hiding their faces and hoping they might escape the hungry mouths of the trolls that feasted on their comrades. A faint sense of compassion passed through him, but it didn't last long.

They are all dead. Some of them just don't realize it yet. His purpose was to end the suffering, and death would be a mercy, an end to the terror. It was time to show them his compassion.

The world vanished. For those at the forest's edge with Sammy, it vanished in a wave of light that blinded them; for Will, it simply changed to darkness as he reflexively shielded himself from the flash and the shockwave that followed. He held himself apart, in a bubble without light, wrapped in pure silence. But he felt it still, in his bones—in his very soul. Beyond his warm womb, the world shook in riotous ecstasy as cascades of lightning washed away the mediocrity of ordinary existence.

It felt good.

He was supposed to stop then, but Will wondered if he should. More would be better, and while lightning couldn't ordinarily incinerate a body completely, that was likely just a matter of how *much* lightning the flesh was exposed to. A minute might not be enough, but ten minutes? An hour? Did he have a limit?

And for that matter, why did he limit himself to the boundaries of the battlefield? What if there were more trolls farther out, hidden in the trees? The power he wielded went on to infinity—would it not be wise to use it more fully, to purify the entire region? It might kill a considerable number of humans, but wasn't safety worth the risk? The soldiers would die, but Sammy and Emory should be relatively safe. Their magical resistance should protect them, even if their shields failed. If it didn't, it was an indictment of their power, a sign of unworthiness.

A shiver of pleasure ran through him as he began to expand the range of destruction.

Is that the best you can do? asked Laina, speaking from the depths of his soul. *You have no more self-control than that? I thought my brother a true power, not an animal, a slave to his own gift.*

You're dead, he replied, but there was no indication whether she heard him. It didn't matter what Laina thought anyway, but the silence annoyed him, and the annoyance awoke something different within him, his stubbornness.

"Damn it!" he swore, and the lightning stopped. Vision and sound returned to show him a smoking field on which nothing moved, other than the electrical arcs that flowed up and down his form. The power was still there, still his, but he had to restrain himself.

Death was everywhere. Of the wounded soldiers and those pretending, none remained alive. Most of the trolls were still alive, if unconscious, but surprisingly, a small percentage had been so thoroughly inundated with lightning that they had perished. Will turned his attention in the direction of Sammy and the escapees, and from the turyn in that direction he could tell they were still alive. He hadn't overreached. Scanning the rest of the field, he could detect another small group to the northwest, and he frowned.

From the energy he could detect, they were likely human. Most importantly they weren't trolls. Had Tiny stationed some reserves there? His curiosity was interrupted by Sammy's arrival some fifty feet away. She turned in a slow circle, getting her bearings, until at last she laid eyes on him. "Close enough," she announced, walking in his direction. Her steps slowed as she got closer, and her eyes widened. "Will? By the Mother, what have you tapped into?"

He realized the cloak of lightning must be making her wary, so with an effort, he suppressed it. "It's safe to come closer."

His cousin shook her head. "It's not that, it's the turyn. You look as if you're bathing in a ley line. How? That much power should kill you."

It hadn't occurred to him, but Sammy hadn't seen him like this— few had, and most of those hadn't survived the experience. Couple that with the fact that Sammy's last experience with turyn at such a scale had nearly killed her. She'd been channeling a ley line for a ritual with Emory, a ritual that opened a gate to the depths of hell so Will could escape. Emory had lost consciousness at the end, and the power had rebounded, nearly destroying her. She'd lost the ability to use magic, or even speak, for several months.

"It's a matter of perspective," he told her. "I'm not trying to contain the power, or even channel it directly through myself. The turyn is channeling *me*. Most of it remains safely outside my body, but it bears my will. Taking it in would destroy my body, so instead, I have to become more than just my body."

She looked scared. "That doesn't make sense."

"A different way of saying it would be that I'm not controlling the power in the sky, I have become the sky itself. It's a part of me, not the reverse."

"I can't do that," she stated flatly. "That's not something a human should be able to do. I'll die."

"You don't have to. I'll feed the power to you, as much as you can handle, and I won't lose consciousness and leave you holding the bag. You just have to do what you do best—burn them." She still looked uncertain, so he added, "Trust me. I won't let it hurt you." He reached out to her with one hand.

After a second, she took it, and then her eyes widened in shock. "Oh. That's nice."

He smiled. "Of course it is. I can adapt it, shape the frequency to match yours, or even adjust it to something that will make you feel as though you've slipped into a warm bath." For a moment, he had to resist the temptation to show her more. That wasn't supposed to be his purpose. There was work to be done. "But that's not the point. *You* need to shape it. It's your talent we need right now." Carefully, he pushed more toward her, waiting until he sensed her acceptance before increasing the flow.

Sammy acclimated quickly as the turyn flooded into her. At first, she passively accepted it, but as her confidence grew, she began to pull. The energy around them resisted her for a moment, but Will relaxed his efforts and allowed her to take control. The point of exchange was strange, as it felt as though he was plunging into her, his power rushing forth in a raging cataract which she greedily consumed. Somewhere in the center was a point where their identities met, transforming from one into the other.

"Gods, yes!" Sammy shouted, her body erupting into flames.

The next two minutes were a flurry of flames as Sammy filled the nearby vicinity with sweeping waves of fire, but she eventually paused. "I can't reach far enough. The battlefield is too big. This will take forever if we have to travel back and forth."

He'd been waiting for that. Will's first experiences with his talents had been on battlefields, under circumstances that required him to use them at extreme distances. Sammy's gift with fire had appeared relatively early, but she'd never had cause to experiment with it. Laina's voice returned unexpectedly in his mind. *How often does someone need to burn down a city, or a forest? In ordinary times, no one should ever need to use a power like that.*

True, Will responded, then turned his attention to Sammy. "You can't go farther than that with direct control. Draw more turyn from me. Flood the entire area with it first. Once it reaches the density you need, let it know what you want."

"Is that what you do? How do I do that?" she demanded. "I can't talk to it. It isn't a person."

In fact, it wasn't exactly the same as what Will had just done. For his lightning storm the power had mainly been where it needed to be, far above. But he had done similar things in the past, such as when he had converted the spells of the Darrowan sorcerers into a massive shockwave that had devastated their own troops, or when he'd sent his voice across miles through city and countryside. He didn't have a good way to explain it, though. "Just flood the area with turyn. I can't describe how to ignite it. That's why it's a talent; it can't be taught. You have to feel it."

"Maybe this isn't a talent. How do you know I can do this? It doesn't feel like I can," she lamented.

Will was still drunk with power, and he knew his thinking was being affected, but he also knew he wasn't wrong. At the moment, he had little patience for doubt, and he had to fight himself to keep from cutting her off from the source. Instead, he reached up and caught her chin in one hand, lifting it and meeting her eyes directly. Arcs of electricity and ripples of flame ran back and forth between his fingers and her jaw. "Do it. Stop thinking and make it happen. I know what lies inside you. Let it out. Make them burn!" He stopped himself before adding, *or I'll kill you.*

Something was wrong with that last thought, but it felt right.

But the rough delivery had somehow reached his cousin. The fury in his gaze cut deeply, and though it instilled fear for an instant, that primal emotion quickly turned to anger in her. Sammy glared back at him, and the power coursing through her responded, filling her with strength and desire. She was burning, and she wanted everything else to burn with her.

Things escalated from there, and Sammy began drawing as much as possible, not simply through herself, but around her. Will suppressed the urge to fight her for control and continued maintaining the bridge while allowing her to take everything it offered. Turyn streamed down, spreading out around them like a billowing cloud, rolling out in every direction. It was invisible to the normal eye, but to the initiated, the turyn was so dense as to be blinding.

It took several minutes to cover the entire battlefield, and some of the trolls were beginning to move before she was finished, but they wouldn't be recovering quickly enough. Will watched it all with pure curiosity, and he wondered if Sammy would go too far and burn the surviving soldiers as well, but he said nothing. It wasn't his concern. He was impressed to see that his cousin's control wasn't lacking, however. As the edges of the turyn began rolling toward the Terabinians it suddenly stopped, as though it had come up against a wall.

There was no wall, of course, the power was responding to her wishes, creating its own boundary. Will was pleased to see that she hadn't disappointed him.

And then hell came to earth, and everything turned to flame.

The heat was so intense that everything turned to ash, and even though the flames didn't begin until at least fifty feet away, it should have killed them both, but even the heat obeyed her wishes and the air around them remained cool. It grew thin, though, as the burning zone had flash-heated its air and sent it rising toward the sky. The cool air in the center was being drawn away, and the entire area experienced a sudden pressure drop.

Will's ears popped, and he had trouble drawing breath. Sammy's talent had protected them from the heat, but he doubted there was an allowance for the lack of air. That sort of indirect consequence probably needed deliberate preparation. *Should have used a water-breathing spell,* he thought, *but too late now.* He wondered how long it would be before they lost consciousness.

Sammy was clothed in living flame, but seemed to be nude underneath it, for the fire provided infrequent glimpses of the skin. Given the control she'd exhibited in the past, Will suspected it was a conscious choice, but he didn't think further on it. *A goddess can do as she chooses.*

It had only been half a minute, but it was plain to see that the job was done. Sammy was breathing hard, struggling to get enough air, although she didn't seem to realize it. She continued to draw ever more power.

"That's enough," he told her. "We need to go."

Her lips curled. "No. I'm not done."

"It's over." He began resisting her pull, cutting off her access.

The reaction was immediate and primal. Sammy's features contorted with fury, and her hand snapped out to grab his throat as she snarled, "I'm not done!"

But while she had been lost in the throes of power, Will had been slowly regaining his usual human sensibilities. With a thought, his skin became as tough as iron, giving her nails nothing to dig into, and while his rationality had returned, his will was as strong as ever. Quickly, but carefully, he restricted the flow of turyn.

Mere seconds after her assault, his cousin's eyes widened as she realized what she had attempted to do. Shock and remorse were starkly visible on her features, while Will's face remained cold, expressionless. His former fury had passed, but his warmth had yet to return. Sammy pulled her hand away from his neck, but Will had already turned his eyes to the heavens again. Clouds began to roll in.

He caught her shoulder with his right hand and teleported them beyond the closest edge of the devastation she had created, the farthest place he could see. The battlefield was no longer on fire; Sammy's flames had turned everything to ash, but the terrible heat remained, and the place he took them was still too close. Will teleported them a second time, taking them still farther away, where the air was better and the hair on his arms didn't immediately start to curl from the heat. A cool breeze was blowing steadily inward, toward the zone of incineration. The low pressure left after her flash fire was bringing in a rush of air from around the battlefield.

He still retained the link to the sky, and once he was satisfied that they could breathe properly, he continued his efforts to turn what had been a clear day into a downpour. It was more difficult than he expected. While the lightning had been easy, the conditions were nothing close to what they needed to be for rain.

Fortunately, he didn't have to supply the turyn—that was his already, in near limitless quantities—but it did require an extensive and prolonged exercise of will—the true power of any wizard. His activities thus far had put a greater strain on it than ever before, but he didn't relent. A deep fatigue that had nothing to do with physical exertion was eating at his concentration and resolve, but he kept working.

The thin, wispy clouds that had initially appeared began to thicken, and before long the sun disappeared from view. Everything fell into shadow, but still the rain didn't come. It took another fifteen minutes as Will shifted the weather patterns for hundreds of miles around to bring in the moisture needed, along with the cold air to trigger its release. In the past, the conditions had simply been much more favorable, or he hadn't needed rain, but after the firestorm Sammy created, he felt it was necessary. While the battlefield was no longer burning, the heat had ignited brush fires all along the periphery—not to mention the incipient forest fire her initial wall of fire had created.

Sammy watched him silently the entire time, until near the end she made a suggestion. "You don't have to go that far. It would be easier for me. I can simply snuff the new flames."

His eyes flicked to her, then back to the sky. "No need to risk it. You've done enough for today."

"You're exhausted. You might injure yourself."

"Don't distract me." Minutes later, the rain finally began. Fat, heavy drops started falling, heralding the downpour that would soon begin. A crisp, cool breeze swept in, and the rain picked up until the noise grew loud enough to cover almost every other sound. With some reluctance, Will released his link to the heavens and felt a heaviness settle in around his shoulders. He had left himself plenty of turyn, but his will had been stretched to its limit. He took a long, slow breath, then focused on Sammy. "It's time to go home."

She seemed surprised. "We aren't going to say goodbye?"

"Nothing has changed. We didn't say goodbye last time."

"We said goodbye when we parted with Emory. I just saw him again for the first time in forever," she clarified.

"He's a military officer, and he's currently busy with what's left of his command. I suspect he and the royal marshal both will have some explaining to do after this debacle. First Division was effectively wiped out. It's best if we leave them to it. We have no place here."

Concern appeared in her expression. "You think he's in trouble?"

Will shrugged. "He was well connected, and if he's played his cards right over the years he still is, but losing an entire division is a disaster. That was fully half of Terabinia's active soldiers. Much of the blame should fall on the marshal's shoulders, but given his closeness to the queen, someone else might need to take the blame."

"But it wasn't their fault," argued Sammy.

He frowned. "Wasn't it? Was someone else in charge? Tiny was in direct command, and Emory appeared to be his second. They fell for a clever ambush, but that's no excuse. Ambushes are always clever. It's their responsibility not to lead their men into one."

"They said the trolls were buried underground. You think you would have noticed that?" she demanded.

"Probably," said Will immediately. "But that's not the point. I've made mistakes before. I once led the army into an explosive trap that killed quite a few soldiers and nearly killed Laina. I didn't expect it, but it was still my fault. I was in charge. A leader gives credit to those who serve under him, and he takes blame when anything goes wrong."

"That isn't fair."

"War is never fair, and military rules reflect that," Will answered. "Are you coming? Or have you decided to stay?"

Irritated, she glared at him. "I have a business to run. If you leave me behind, the trip back will take too long."

He held out his hand. "I meant stay for good, but it sounds like you plan on coming back."

"A lot of people depend on me. I'm not fickle, Will, if that's what you think of me." She took his hand.

His eyes lost focus, and after a lengthy pause, the world changed.

CHAPTER 12

Erisa was scrubbing sheets in a tub when they arrived. Will placed them just far enough away that he could call her name without startling her. "Mom. We're back."

She still jumped slightly, but she smiled when she turned her head to look at them. "Sooner than I expected. Things went well?" Rising from the stool she had been crouched upon, she made a not-so-subtle inspection of the two of them.

Looking for injuries, thought Will. He studied the washtub for a moment, then complained, "I told you; you don't have to do that anymore."

"Magic can't do everything, and I didn't know how long you'd be gone. The laundry couldn't wait." Her hands straightened his collar, while she surreptitiously searched for cuts or wounds.

"I'm fine," he told her, brushing her off with a sour look.

Erisa was already inspecting Sammy. "I'm sure you are, but I like to be certain." She hadn't commented yet on her niece's complete lack of attire. Her first reaction was to sniff. "What is that smell? Did you burn your clothing?"

Among other things, Will thought. The stink of burned flesh always brought back terrible memories.

Sammy blushed, though she didn't shrink away. Her confidence, especially among family, was legendary. She did summon a robe from her limnthal, but before she could don it, Erisa caught her hand. "Stop. No reason to make that smell as well. You need to bathe first." She cast a dark look at her son. "You too. That smell is awful." Before he could cast a spell, she held up a hand, adding, "Use soap. The tub is already out, but let Sammy go first."

Will and his cousin looked at one another, their eyes meeting to communicate a message that hadn't changed since childhood. There was no use resisting. They smirked, and Will went into the house to wait his turn while his mother fussed over Sammy. Even though he knew he would be forced into a bath before long, he went ahead and cast Selene's Solution on himself to get rid of the stench.

A few hours later, Alver returned from school, and his eyes lit up when he saw who had come home. "Dad!" A firm hug followed, but when he looked up, he could tell something was wrong. A shadow seemed to linger over his father's face. "How was the trip?"

Will's response was light, but the smile on his lips never quite reached his eyes. "It went well."

Unsure how to brighten the mood, Alver asked the question he was most interested in. "Did you see any soldiers? They say there's a lot of wardsmen in Bondgrad."

His father's expression tightened. "I saw quite a few, but only one wardsman."

"Could you see his tattoos? I bet he looked cool!"

"He was a thug, working for criminals. There was nothing cool about him."

Alver flinched. "Oh."

Before he could say anything else, the kitchen door opened, and Sammy stepped in. "Olly!"

"Auntie Ess!" More hugs ensued.

"I'm glad to see you too," Sammy said after a moment, ruffling Alver's hair. "Did your dad already tell you about the inn we stayed at in Bondgrad?"

Will frowned, wondering what she might say about her establishment. Given the debauchery, he couldn't think of anything appropriate for a child to hear. He needn't have worried, however. She spun a sparkling tale of dancing, food, and jovial minstrels playing music that filled every corner with mirth and merriment. As she went on, Will realized everything she said was true—his cousin simply didn't mention the drinking—or the fact that most of her servers were not-quite-retired prostitutes.

Listening to her, he couldn't help but wonder if his own opinion was too harshly colored by his prejudices. Growing up in a small village, his sensibilities were informed by an entirely different set of circumstances, and given what Sammy was saying, he might not be seeing things clearly. His thoughts drifted to Cecilia, and he blushed.

"Is that true, Dad?" asked Alver.

Sammy laughed. "It must be, since his cheeks have gone pink."

Will replayed the last few sentences and realized that Sammy had been telling tales about how popular he'd been with the maids at Roc's Roost. "Cecilia was just doing her job. I'm sure she's nice to all the customers," he replied, his words coming out a bit too quickly.

"Cecilia? Is that her name?" Alver looked to his aunt, who was now grinning broadly at Will's mistake.

"Hmm," Sammy said thoughtfully. "I didn't mention any names, but apparently your dad was paying close attention that day."

Erisa appeared as if by magic. "Is that true, William? Have you taken a fancy to someone?" She made no attempt to hide her hopefulness.

"Of course not," Will snapped harshly. An awkward silence followed. But Erisa quickly moved to smooth things over. "I won't tease you, since you seem to be tired from the road." She turned to her niece, then pulled out something she'd been hiding behind her back. "Sammy, you've been living in Bondgrad—have you seen one of these yet?" In her hand was a small bronze item. It was round, similar in size to an apple, with a clear crystal mounted on top and a metal switch on one side. Runes were engraved all around the exterior, though none of them were familiar to Will.

He still recognized the device, though. He'd studied them before the war with Darrow. The object was enchanted, and contained within the vessel he could sense a concentrated source of turyn stored there. It was smaller than the ones he'd seen before, but it was clearly an enchanted spell bomb. His mother smiled, then moved her thumb to the switch. "Watch this!"

"Mom, no!" Will screamed, but it was too late. Her thumb slid the switch over, and the crystal on top began glowing. Within a second, it would explode. With one hand, he grabbed the collar of his son's shirt and jerked the boy back, shielding him with his body while simultaneously erecting a force-dome over the two of them and Sammy as well, who stood a few feet farther back.

Nothing happened.

"Dad? Can you let go? You're hurting me."

"It's an elven lamp," said Sammy, keeping her tone calm. "They're new. Relax. You're scaring Olly."

Confusion reigned as Will studied the strange looks on everyone's faces. With a start, he let go of his son, who he'd been holding tightly against his chest. Alver stepped away, then bumped into the force-dome. "What's this?" asked the boy, running his hand along the invisible surface.

"It's a magical shield," said Sammy. "Your father startled me, and I created it without thinking." She gave Will a hard look.

"Wow," said Alver, impressed.

Will hastily dismissed the spell, while giving his mother and Sammy an embarrassed look. "Sorry for shouting. It just—that thing looked like a type of bomb."

"I didn't mean to scare you," said Erisa, her face apologetic. "I bought it from a trader last week. I thought you'd be surprised."

Heart still pounding, Will's body was damp with the beginnings of a cold sweat. Shame and anger flared within him, and he didn't know how to deal with the weird mixture of intense emotions. A quiet moment at home had turned into a moment of horror, and he'd scared everyone, especially his son. Worse, he'd nearly done something worse. In the heat of the moment, he had almost removed his mother's hand before putting up the shield. It had been a split-second decision, and all that had saved her had been the instant calculation that it might take too long. Using a shield had seemed the wisest move, even if it meant his mother died instead.

Bile rose in his throat, and he fought down a wave of nausea. He took a step toward the door. "It's been a rough week," he said lamely. "I think I'll go check in with Lettler at the Laughing Goat."

"But you just got home," said Alver with obvious disappointment.

"Damn it, stop whining!" snapped Will. He stopped then, seeing the look on his son's face. "I'm sorry, Olly. I didn't mean that. I'm just stressed." Backing out of the room, he crossed the threshold and was outside in just a few long strides. *I need a drink,* he told himself.

He wasn't particularly given to drinking, even under stress, but he had two pints that evening, and he stayed at the Laughing Goat until late that night. Lettler asked him a few questions, but it was quickly apparent that he wasn't in the mood for talking, or working, and the man soon left him alone. Will tried the food while he was there, and though the flavor was underwhelming, he didn't complain about the substitute cook. He didn't have it in him.

The next day when Alver returned from school, his father was waiting for him. "I need to apologize," said Will without preamble.

Alver looked nervous, but he shook his head. "It's all right, Dad. Nana explained."

Will took a seat on the porch steps and motioned for the boy to join him. "What did she say?"

"Just that you were hurt in the war. That sometimes the memories come back." After a second, Alver added, "I didn't mean to make you angry."

Will felt his chest tighten. He started to tell the boy he hadn't made him angry, but that wasn't quite true. He turned the words over in his head, then answered, "That wasn't your fault, son. I was angry, but it wasn't fair. I lashed out at the first person that spoke, and I'm sorry. You're the last person I ever want to hurt."

"Was it the magic lamp?"

It wasn't *just* the lamp. That had sparked his fear, but the bigger problem had been his recent experiences in Terabinia. Seeing old acquaintances, fighting trolls, and... *killing again*, he thought sourly. It was a combination of fear and shame, and the shame came partly from the knowledge that he enjoyed some of it. His personality shift when channeling the storm, the freedom from care, concern, or morality.

But the lamp had definitely set off his worst instincts. "The lamp looked like a type of bomb I once studied. I never saw one explode, but I did see a different sort of bomb go off in an ambush during the war. A lot of people died, and I suppose that's partly why I overreacted."

"Because it scared you?"

"Yeah. The fear took me to a dark place. Afterward, I wanted to escape. That's why I went out. Do you understand?"

Alver nodded. "Is that why you're afraid of fighting?"

Will blinked. "Huh?"

"Remember when Trig's dad hit you, but you didn't hit him back? I didn't really understand then, but I think maybe it's because of the same thing." Alver's face twisted as he tried to explain what he was thinking.

After a moment, Will answered, "The main reason was because violence isn't the way to solve problems with neighbors, friends, or family. It would be best if we never used it between people at all, but I don't know if anyone can prevent war entirely. If I had beaten up Trig's dad, it would have created bad blood between us, and then I'd constantly be worried about what would happen next. We all live pretty close together here." He paused, then added, "But there's also some truth to what you said. Because of the war, I'm a little bit afraid of myself. I've seen what men do in battle, and I've done some of it myself. I'm always scared I might do it again, and civilized people can't live like that."

When Alver was little, he had asked questions about his father's past, but he'd never gotten any real answers. In time, he'd gradually come to believe it was a lot less interesting than he'd imagined, but now his curiosity had returned in full force. "Did you kill people?"

His father's eyes had been firmly on him for most of their conversation, but they looked past him now. Will's lips tightened, and his answer came after a significant delay. "I've kept a lot from you, son. Do you know why?"

Alver had heard the excuse often enough that it immediately came to his lips. "You always said it was to protect me."

Will nodded. "That's true, but it isn't the only reason. One reason is that I don't want my past to influence your future. Boys tend to idolize their fathers, and I didn't want you to idolize any of the things I've done. I wanted you to respect me for something more important, for being a good father. I can't teach you right and wrong by giving you examples from my past, so I've tried to do so by being a good father in the present."

Alver's frustration grew. It sounded like a variation of the same old excuse, with the exception that it indicated that his father probably *had* done something really interesting. Will saw the look on his face and shook his head. "I know what you're thinking, but I'm not done. The third reason I've kept my past a secret is that I'm ashamed of some of it. Not only was I afraid you might idolize me for the wrong things, I was also afraid that you might instead be ashamed of me." The look of surprise on Alver's face made Will hurry up and add, "I'm not a criminal, if that's what you're thinking. I wasn't a deserter either. No one has judged me but myself, but that's bad enough."

His son stared at him for a minute, unsure what to say. Finally, he said, "You still didn't answer the question, though."

"I didn't," Will agreed. "I will tell you everything when you're older. For now, it's more important to me that if anyone asks you anything, you can honestly say you don't know. You're a smart boy, though. You can make a good guess. Just imagine how most people would answer that question."

"They'd say no," Alver stated slowly.

Will nodded again. "That's always the best answer. I try not to lie to you, though I haven't always been completely honest." He wrapped an arm around Alver and pulled him close. "My greatest hope is that you never have to kill anyone, that you'll be able to live with a clear conscience. The sun is brighter, the air cleaner—when you don't have that kind of stain on your soul."

Chapter 13

Months trailed into a year, and despite the trauma of his brief return to Terabinia, living as Kelvin Wiltshire served as a balm for his nerves. Kelvin's problems were ordinary, and frequently illusory as well. His boss, Lettler, was actually his employee, and while making sure the Laughing Goat continued to profit was still something to worry about, Will had deeper pockets than anyone in the town of Lystal realized.

Sammy hadn't returned to visit since their ordeal with the trolls, and while Will worried that they had some issues to discuss, he never made the effort to track her down. He did make quiet inquiries among some of the customers who traveled from Bondgrad, but only a few of them were successful enough to have spent any time at Roc's Roost. From what little he could garner, Sammy's business ventures were still going well. They'd certainly been strong enough that she hadn't bothered him about producing another batch of potions for sale.

Not that I'm worried about money, he told himself. He still had enough saved that he could fund the school and continue his plans for the hospital. It would be years before he had to worry about coin, and if he did, he had other avenues he could pursue. While none of the powerful in Trendham knew his identity, he had made contact with the movers and shakers in prior years. Sammy's sham apprenticeship and entry into the mage guild was the result of one of those secret deals.

The five oligarchs knew him, though they had never seen his face. He'd never given them the means to contact him; the relationship was entirely one-sided. Mainly because he knew they wanted too much. If they'd been able to send him letters or other communications, the requests would have been endless. Instead, his primary message to them had been that he lived among them (somewhere) and that his intentions were peaceful. The only favor he had ever negotiated for had been on Sammy's behalf, but if the need ever arose, he felt certain he had plenty of leverage to ask for considerable assistance.

He returned his attention to the onions in front of him. His lapse in attention had resulted in a lack of uniformity in the cuts. *Focus on the present,* he told himself. *The whole point of it all is to live normally, not waste time musing about how you could extort the powers that be.*

"Kelvin."

Will looked up. Lettler had stepped into the kitchen. He was the only man who could enter without triggering Will's hidden wards. The only one who knew he often cooked with magic rather than pots and pans. In spite of his sour demeanor and ugly face, Lettler was one of the few people in Trendham that Will trusted with any of his secrets.

Even so, the man still knew only a portion of them. He knew that Will was a refugee, a wizard, and filthy rich. He probably knew he was dangerous too, even though Will had never threatened the man, or treated him badly. Quite the opposite. Lettler had been forced to act the part of the angry employer, simply to satisfy Will's need to maintain anonymity.

The kitchen was a safe place, though. Just as Will used magic there, he also allowed Lettler to speak frankly within the safety of the kitchen wards. "What do you need?" he asked.

"Someone's here to see you. Says she knows a few things about Roc's Roost."

Will frowned. "Why is she asking for me? You're supposed to be the one who's been asking about it."

Lettler shrugged, then scratched at his pockmarked cheek. "I tried. She said it was obvious I wasn't the one that's asking."

"And she's demanding to see me?" Will's paranoia, which had largely faded over the quiet months, now reared its ugly head. A dozen improbable theories ran through his mind, along with dark thoughts of what he might have to do if someone had uncovered his secret.

The manager held up both hands in a placating gesture. "Nothing like that. She just said she could see I wasn't really interested. Said if there was someone who wanted to know more, they should come talk to her directly."

Will had already removed his apron and begun washing the stink of onions from his hands.

"You gonna talk to her?"

He shook his head. "You go out to the bar. I'll come out, look at the customers, then come back. Then you come back and tell me which one is her."

Lettler sighed, then nodded.

Fifteen minutes later, Will sat on a stool mulling over what he had learned. The woman had been sitting at a regular table, seemingly without a care in the world. She'd been dressed in clothes some would call masculine— trousers, a linen shirt, and a heavy coat, though all had been cut with the female form in mind. Such wasn't too uncommon in Trendham, as there were some women traders and merchants. The nation had a much looser tradition when it came to gender roles than Terabinia did.

More importantly, there had been no hint of magic. Few practitioners could hide their art from him. While many mages were inobservant, Will was not one of them. Even before he had learned to cast his first spell, he had been discerning enough to spot hidden soldiers just by the disturbance they created in the turyn around them. Sorcerers, wizards, warlocks, all of them tended to create even larger disturbances. He had yet to encounter any clever enough to disguise their unique signature from him, aside from Grim Talek and his now-deceased grandmother, Aislinn.

Selene probably could, he realized. She was talented and had a teacher with millennia of experience. Tabitha, Sammy, or Emory could probably learn too, but he doubted they'd ever had cause to practice that sort of subterfuge. In any case, the end result was that Will was fairly sure that barring someone exceptional, his visitor was a mundane.

Smoothing out his turyn, Will became unnoticeable, then walked out into the main room and took a moment to study the woman more closely. Her clothing was well made, but only enough to indicate she was likely successful in her business endeavors. She had no rings on, and her nails were short but well kept. Likewise, her hair was also short, exposing a slender neck. Her only obvious ornamentation was a gold ring hanging from one ear. Her face was attractive in the sense that it was symmetrical, and her skin was unblemished, but her features weren't exceptional or exotic in any way.

Dark hair, dark eyes, simple attire—she looks just like what she probably is, a trader, he noted mentally. The ordinariness of her appearance made him even more paranoid, but eventually his curiosity won out. Circling the room, he relaxed his turyn, then approached her from behind. It was easy enough, since unlike in the romances, the mysterious visitor had neglected to sit in a corner with her back to a wall.

He didn't make enough noise as he walked, so he lightly touched one shoulder before moving around the table to face her openly. She didn't jump, but her expression was one of mild surprise. "You aren't what I expected," she pronounced.

Something about her tone pleased him. "You sound disappointed. May I sit?"

"Suit yourself," she answered, waving a hand casually at the chair opposite her.

He pulled the wooden seat out and eased into it. "What did you expect?"

For whatever reason, his words sparked some interest, and she studied him carefully before answering, "Not someone smelling like onions." Her eyes narrowed, and she pointed one finger at his collar. "You've got stains on your shirt. Did you butcher something?"

"Earlier." Will lifted one brow, then smirked. "I'm still curious about Roc's Roost, unless you don't like talking to scullery boys."

The stranger began laughing, then stared at him again. "You're no scullery boy. You might be a cook, but as young as you look, you're definitely not a boy. I'm not sure what to make of you, to be honest."

"I'm the one looking for news—why are we talking about me?" asked Will.

She shrugged. "Because I was hoping to make a bit of coin, rather than be treated to a tasty bit of tenderloin from the kitchen." She waggled her brows lasciviously to make the point.

Once upon a time he might have blushed at such a remark, but now Will fought to hide a grin at the inappropriate compliment. "So—do you have any news about Roc's Roost?"

The trader's face turned somber. "Not really, and if I did, I probably wouldn't tell you."

"Remind me again, why are we talking?"

She sighed. "I heard someone was asking around about Maddie, so I came to take a look myself. I figured I'd make a few coins spinning harmless tales, but since you're clearly not rich there's not much point in making up lies." The trader pulled out a small eating dagger and began trimming one of her nails.

"Yet you know the owner's name," Will pointed out.

She pointed the knife loosely at him. "As do you apparently. Mind telling me what this is about?"

A good cover story would have been nice, but Will's mind had gone blank. "No?" After a second of feeling silly, he decided to go on the offense. "Why do you care? Is she a friend of yours?"

"Not really," she answered, then grimaced. "Now you're trying to sneak answers out of me, aren't you?"

Will kept his mouth shut and the two of them stared intently at one another for several tense minutes. Then he asked, "What's your name?"

"Cora Dewitt," she said promptly. "And y—"

He cut her off, "Is that your real name?"

"No. Does it matter?"

"It shows you're hiding something."

Cora grinned, and the combination of bright teeth and the sparkle in her eyes made Will's heart jump a little. "It shows I didn't like my original name. When I decided to take up this life, I figured I could choose a name I liked. What's it to you?"

"What was your original name then?" he asked.

"Wilhelmina," she returned. "But if you call me that, or Wilma, you can give up on expecting me to answer. Now for a bit of turnabout, what's your name?"

"Kelvin Wiltshire."

Cora laced her fingers together and rested her chin on them. "And is that your real name?"

He'd been having fun up until that point. Somehow Cora's native charm had disarmed his usual caution, and now Will realized he'd gone too far. The conversation had left him open, and the trader was far too discerning to be fooled by his usual answers. His primary defense over the years had been avoiding people like her. He'd learned to lie at court, but in many respects, he was still a novice. Selene had shown him that repeatedly. Now he was in over his head.

He'd let his guard down, and now his family was in danger. Something dark must have shown on his face because Cora suddenly changed course and lifted her hands in a gesture of surrender. "Whoa, sorry! No need to give me such serious eyes. Forget I asked."

Will tried to relax by taking a deep breath, without looking as though he was taking a deep breath. The end result left him feeling even more awkward. He stood up, pushing back his chair. "I should get back to the kitchen. Thanks for your honesty—about Roc's Roost."

"Wait." Cora rose quickly and caught his arm, then quickly released it. "Will you answer one question for me?" When he didn't respond, she asked anyway, "You don't have any ill will against Maddie, do you?"

The sincerity of her question caught him, and he answered despite himself, "No, of course not. The opposite really."

They locked eyes, and Cora nodded. "I believe you." He turned away, but she called after him. "Hey, kitchen boy!" Somewhat surprised, he looked back, and she grinned at him. "What time do you finish working?"

"In a couple of hours. Why?"

"I hardly know anyone in this town. Maybe we could share a drink?"

"I go home to my family after I leave."

Cora winced. "Sorry, I didn't realize. You seem young for a wife and children."

He should have left it at that, but something stopped him, and instead he clarified, "By family I mean my mother and my son. I don't have a wife." He retreated to the kitchen before she could say anything else.

The next hour and a half was devoted to cooking, but his thoughts kept returning to his conversation with the strange trader. Each time he caught himself thinking about it, he had to try harder to push the thoughts aside. *She's too old for me anyway,* he mentally chided himself. *No, she looks to be the same age, the problem is I look like an eighteen-year-old.*

A few minutes later, his mind drifted again. *She was pretty. Not in a childish way, but in the sense that she looked fit—intelligent too.* With a frustrated sigh, he put down the stack of plates he was holding. He'd intended to wash them by hand. It was a chore he didn't relish, and he often just used magic, but he'd thought the task might help him discipline his mind. Clearly it wasn't working. With a thought, he cast Selene's Solution, imbuing it with enough turyn to clean not only the dishes but the rest of the kitchen as well. He wasn't in the mood.

After letting Lettler know he was leaving early, Will left. He considered going out the front, but he stopped himself. He knew that secretly he was hoping Cora might be waiting to catch him as he left. *What a stupid thought,* he growled mentally. *I have a family, and on top of that, far too many secrets to consider intimacy.*

What about after Oliver is grown? asked Laina's voice from the back of his mind. *You've thought about revealing yourself then. If you didn't have secrets, would that change things?*

Will stopped with his hand on the kitchen door that led out into the alley behind the 'Goat. There was no one around, so he indulged his impulse to answer her out loud. It was something that sometimes helped him feel as if Laina were still alive. "Of course not." Muttering to himself, he opened the door and stepped over the threshold. "Even without secrets, power and notoriety create an even bigger problem. I'd never be able to trust anyone's motives."

As the words left his lips, he realized he wasn't alone—across the small alley a figure stood in the shadows. With hardly a thought, Will erected a force-wall between himself and the stranger. A few seconds later, his eyes and brain caught up with his reflexes, and he recognized the figure.

"You got off earlier than you said," observed Cora, and although she couldn't see the force spell, she sensed his alarm. "I didn't mean to scare you."

Will dismissed the force spell, and feeling even more foolish than before, he said, "You startled me. Do you make a habit of waiting on people in dark alleys?"

A smirk caused her lips to curl. "If I met more interesting people, maybe I would. Do you always debate the corrosive effects of power and notoriety on your ability to trust?"

He went still for a moment, before ultimately deciding he wasn't ready to commit murder yet. *I haven't fallen that far,* he told himself. Glancing over, he saw she was watching him, but he couldn't think of a good answer. Attempting to be clever would probably only give more away, leaving his only options as silence—or murder. *Silence works.* He started walking, giving the trader no response.

She cleared her throat, and despite himself, Will looked back, surprised at her persistence. "What?"

"You never answered my question." She had one hand on her hip and a look of challenge in her eyes.

Will had known a number of powerful women over the course of his years, and some of them had been quite assertive, but as a general rule, most were relatively demure. In Terabinia he would only expect such behavior from an aristocrat, and although Trendham was more progressive, it was still uncommon for most women. "You aren't timid, are you? I don't trust *you*—that's why I was mulling over the nature of trust."

Once again, he started to turn his back on her, but she spoke again. "That was just banter. I meant my question about the drink, from earlier." When he looked back, lifting one brow, she added, "That's one way people build trust, or so I hear."

"I told you I have a family."

"But no wife. Surely, they wouldn't object to you socializing a little? Or you could invite me to your home."

"I don't keep wine at home."

"I have a couple of bottles. If you're uncomfortable with me visiting your family, you could come see my wagon. It's like a house on wheels." She winked at him to punctuate her remark.

Will fought the urge to laugh. "Aren't you the least bit cautious? Most would think twice before inviting a strange man home." He walked back toward her, stopping just a foot away. Cora wasn't short, but he still loomed a head taller. It was a silent reminder of the size disparity between them.

She grinned up at him. "Timid traders don't make a profit. I think I'm a good enough judge of character that I feel confident showing you my home—unless you're afraid I might force myself upon you. Is that what you're worried about?"

He stood there for a moment, intrigued by her confidence and her brash wit. It stimulated him in ways he hadn't experienced in many, many years. As close as he now stood, he could smell her, and despite the fact that she'd been traveling, he wasn't repulsed. There was definitely the smell of the road, dust and sweat, but it was layered over the scent of leather, cedar, and cinnamon? *And maybe a hint of cloves,* he decided.

Back in Terabinia, wealthy women often used floral fragrances, or sometimes mint or other herbs, to hide unpleasant smells. In Trendham it was a wider trend, since the population tended to be more affluent as a whole, but cinnamon wasn't commonly used for the purpose. Understanding dawned on him a second later. "You trade spices."

"I do." Rather than lean away, Cora held her ground, then sniffed. "And you chop onions." She laughed as he stepped back. "I smelled them earlier, but I don't now. Whatever you wash with works extremely well. Share the secret and I could make you a fortune."

Selene's Solution, he thought, but he wasn't about to confess to being a wizard. Instead, he gave her his answer to the original question. "I'll meet you here in half an hour, then we can have that drink. Good enough?"

She nodded.

As Will walked away, he added, "Don't try to follow me home, or the drink is off."

"Wouldn't dream of it," she replied.

CHAPTER 14

As soon as he was out of view, Will vanished, using a camouflage spell and smoothing his turyn. Then he silenced himself and climbed the nearest building. He moved across the roof until he could see Cora and watched her for at least ten minutes. She showed no signs of trying to follow. When he was certain she wasn't going to tail him, he teleported home, making up for the time he had wasted.

He gave his mother the excuse that he had agreed to have a drink with Lettler, but she probably didn't believe him, as her response was far too agreeable. "That's fine. Stay out as late as you like." Erisa's smile was insufferable. "Maybe you would like to change into a clean shirt?"

"My shirt is clean, Mom. It's just Lettler."

"That's fine, dear. I'm sure you know best."

Will was still shaking his head as he walked back into town. He found Cora standing close to where he'd left her, although she had finally moved out of the alley and was waiting at the corner nearest the front entrance to the 'Goat.

There was a twinkle in her eye when she spotted his approach, and as he drew close, she whispered in a conspiratorial voice, "Were you followed?" Paranoia reared its ugly head, and a split second passed before Will realized she was teasing him. He gave her a sour look, but it only seemed to encourage her. "Because if you were, it wasn't me. I was waiting right here," she finished.

"I knew this was a mistake."

Cora caught hold of his elbow before he could turn away. "Don't run away. It's dark! At the very least you need to walk me home. You need to take responsibility."

She's trying to lure you away. It's a trap. They'll be waiting for you, whispered the angry, suspicious part of his mind. Will had to suppress the urge to flinch away when Cora touched his arm. He knew the voice in his head wasn't rational, so he focused on her words. "Responsibility for what?"

"For me being out so late," she returned, smiling faintly.

"You were the one who took it upon yourself to wait two hours in a dark alley. Don't put that on me."

Cora laughed. "Don't overestimate your appeal. I waited inside for most of that time. I only went out back when I thought the time was close."

"Most would wait out front, where there's light," he remarked.

She turned her head up and gave him a square look, then declared, "You've got a squirrely look in your eyes. I figured you'd run. I was right too. If I'd waited in front, you'd have slipped past me."

Will rolled his eyes. "Most would take the hint."

"Pfftt! A good trader never takes no for an answer. You'll need to work harder if you want to dissuade me, otherwise I'll hound you until I get bored."

"How long before you get bored?" he asked, affecting a hopeful tone.

She laughed again, then looked him up and down. "I have no idea, half an hour maybe? I'm honestly as surprised about this as you are. You really aren't my type."

Will disentangled his arm from hers. "I said a drink. I don't mind conversation, but that's as far as this goes." He felt disappointed in himself even as he said the words. *Would it be so wrong?* he asked himself.

Cora seemed to ignore his rejection and pointed to the left. "That way. I'm camped just outside of town." They turned to follow the road and then she waggled a finger at him. "See, that's what I mean. Not my type at all. Don't worry. You'll be safe with me."

He couldn't help but chuckle, though he also felt a bit curious. "What's your type then, since I'm so obviously not it?"

"Short answer?" she asked. When he nodded, she replied, "Bad boys."

"That's not much of an answer. I'm sure a sizeable fraction of your gender would say something similar."

It was Cora's turn to give him a somber look. "Long answer then. I have terrible taste in men. 'Bad boys' is an understatement. Somehow, I always find the worst ones. Antisocial, violent, criminal—you name it. There's always warning signs, but for some reason I think I can save them, that there's a good person underneath it all."

He sighed. "I'm guessing things didn't work out."

She looked at him sideways, then grinned and gave him a gentle pat on the back. "If they had, I probably wouldn't be trying to pick up kitchen help to amuse myself, would I?"

Behind the smile, Will sensed a dark tragedy hidden just out of sight. It pulled at him, drew him in. He felt a certain kinship with the trader, though he was sure their pasts were very different. They had already passed beyond the edge of town, and in the gloom, Will saw a large wagon. Four horses were staked out nearby and the rear end featured an ornate wooden door lit by an oil lamp hung on a brass hook. A heavy-set man sat on the steps, whittling something with a small knife.

The man glanced up at their approach, and he studied Will with obvious suspicion, though he said nothing, choosing to wait until Cora had come within easy speaking distance. She addressed the man first, "Jak, this is Kelvin. He works at the public house in Lystal, the Laughing Goat. I don't think you have much to worry about."

Jak sighed. Now that they were closer, Will could see the man was considerably older with thick grey hair and an impressive mustache. If he had to guess, he'd have put Jak's age at fifty, though he still seemed fit. Jak didn't answer, and after taking a good look at Will's face, he knocked on the door. "Mary, she's back. Let's go."

The door opened a minute later, and a plump, middle-aged woman stepped out. Jak caught her hand as she descended the short steps, though she obviously had no problem with her balance. Like Jak, Mary gave Will a careful going over, then nodded to herself before asking Cora, "Should we find a place to sleep in town?"

Cora shook her head. "No. Kelvin won't be spending the night." She gave Will a look of mock sadness.

Will tried to appear friendly. "I'm just here for pleasant conversation, no need to worry." Jak and Mary both gave him an odd look, then walked away, following the road back into Lystal. He turned to Cora. "I didn't offend them, did I?"

Her expression was one of puzzlement, but she answered, "I doubt it. Can you make a fire?" That was an odd question, since almost everyone learned the basics at an early age. She clarified by adding, "A campfire—over there maybe. I have a little stove inside, but it's a nice night, and I have a guest. It would be nice to sit outside." She didn't wait for an answer, pointing to the right side of the wagon. "There's some wood and kindling bundled under that side. I'll get the wine." She turned away and went inside the wagon.

Being given a task made him feel more at ease for some reason. Will found the wood, which was already cut into short lengths and quartered. The kindling was much smaller, but there was plenty to get the fire going. He gathered what he needed and cleared the leaves and litter away from a small area so he could organize the wood into a simple, tent-like structure. Glancing around, he saw Cora still hadn't emerged, so he used a quick spell to light the kindling rather than bother with flint and steel. The fire was just beginning to show merry little flames when Cora opened the door again.

She had a bottle under her right arm and two long-stemmed glasses in her hand. Her left hand was dragging a wooden frame of some sort. She deftly managed the door and the steps even though she was obviously overburdened. Will offered to help, and she pushed the bottle and glasses into his hands. Then she unfolded the wooden frames, and Will realized they were camp chairs, very similar to the ones used by officers back when he'd been in the military. Once they unfolded, one piece of fabric served as a seat, while the other formed the back.

Unlike the plain ones he'd had, these were made with expensive cloth embroidered with floral designs that matched the rose carvings that flowed along the wood legs. Given the materials and craftsmanship, Will knew the chairs were expensive. He stared at the long-stemmed glasses in his hands, which were likewise unusual in their quality. He'd expected wooden cups.

Cora had made a minor transformation as well. She still wore trousers, but she'd traded her plain shirt for a long-sleeved blue blouse. The heavy coat was gone as well, replaced by a cozy shawl knitted from what looked to be a high-quality wool yarn. She sat in one of the chairs and crossed her legs, whereupon he noticed she'd traded her boots in for fur slippers. Cora gestured magnanimously toward the other chair. "Make yourself comfortable."

He did, then opened the bottle and filled a glass for her. She drank most of it and handed it back immediately. "More please."

Chuckling, Will refilled it and then filled his own. "This is not what I expected," he admitted after he'd taken his first sip.

"The wagon, or the slippers?" Cora straightened her legs so he could see her footwear better. The fur was rabbit, facing inward to keep her toes warm. The outside was suede, with two small ears sewn on to each. She wiggled one at him.

They were cute, and so was their owner. Cora's shawl and blouse made her look like a wealthy housewife, cozied up near the fire for a cup of tea—or in this case, a glass of wine. Will had thought Cora attractive, in a simple, straightforward way, but seeing her in this relaxed state pulled at him in ways he'd never expected. She was exotically domestic, if such a thing could be said to exist. "Both," he answered, taking another drink.

She seemed mildly disappointed. "Both?"

He nodded. "I haven't seen a wagon quite like yours be—"

"Lots of people have seen my wagon," she interrupted. "A lucky few have seen the inside, but *no one* has ever seen my magic slippers. Aside from Jak and Mary, obviously. For some reason, I thought you'd be more discerning."

There was absolutely nothing magical about the slippers, aside from the love and care that had gone into making them. Will could see that at a glance, but he played along, asking, "Magic slippers? What powers do they hold?"

"Supernatural comfiness," she answered proudly. "No matter what I find on the road, or what unpleasantness I may encounter in my dealings, once I slip these on, all my cares drift away. You should try them." Without the slightest bit of self-consciousness, she pulled off the right slipper and handed it to him, then put her bare foot on his leg to keep it away from the dirt on the ground.

The gesture was both casual and familiar, as though she'd known him for far longer than an hour or two, but somehow it didn't feel strange. It just made him even more aware of how much he lacked. She had a pretty foot too, not that it mattered. Will examined the slipper with one hand, feeling it would be rude not to show some interest. He held it up, then looked at his boot. "I don't think it will fit me." Then he slipped it back onto her foot.

He made no move to remove her leg from his lap.

Cora pulled it back, shifted her chair to angle it toward him, then put both feet up on his lap. "Pity. You could have enjoyed the amazing power of my comfy slippers. I could have just kept my feet up here until you were done with them." She met his eyes and held them while taking another sip from her glass.

"You're lucky they don't fit," said Will. "Otherwise, I might not have wanted to give them back."

She held her glass out for him. "More." Will filled it and handed it back, then finished his own glass and refilled it as well. "You wouldn't have worn them even if they fit," she announced.

"Oh?" Will arched one brow.

Cora nodded, lifting her glass into the air in a mock toast toward him. "The comfy power of my slippers would destroy you."

That got him to chuckling. "How so?"

She withdrew her legs, then stood and scooted her chair over so that it was right beside his, without an inch to spare between them. Sitting back down, she leaned until her face was close to his. "There's no comfort in you," she pronounced. "If you were exposed to such a thing, you would melt away."

She was close enough that he could smell the wine on her lips, and Will fought his instincts, until at last she leaned back into her chair, restoring some of the distance between them. He sighed regretfully. "You're probably right. Which begs the question, why would you invite someone like me here?"

Cora straightened up, thinking, then she replied, "Loneliness? I'm not sure. You probably think I'm mysterious and enigmatic, but the truth is I don't understand myself any better than you do. Despite how I seem, I'm not a girl anymore. I haven't dallied much in the years since my husband left me."

"You're married?" That surprised him.

"Was," corrected Cora.

"What happened?"

She shrugged. "I loved him too much? I told you I like the dangerous ones, and he was certainly that. My man was a killer. You could see it in his eyes. He was a trader too—that's how we met—but he was also ruthless when he thought he might be cheated."

"Did he hurt you?"

Cora shook her head. "No. He never hurt me. He loved me as much as I loved him, I think. Until I cheated him of what he wanted most. He couldn't abide that."

Will frowned. "You cheated on him?"

"No, I cheated him out of what he wanted most, a family. He got into a fight, and I wouldn't stay out of it. I got hurt and lost our child as a result."

"You were pregnant?"

She nodded. "A daughter. He left me shortly after that."

The unfairness of it made Will slightly angry, but there was no use getting worked up over other people's old grievances. "Sounds like you're better off without him."

Cora was staring into her wine glass, her head down so he couldn't see her face. "No, he was right. I chose him over our child."

"You didn't know what would happen."

"No. I did. They'd have killed him, and I couldn't let it happen, but I also knew I was pregnant. I saved his life, but I did it knowing I would lose my baby."

"There's no way you could have known that," he argued. "And it's not fair for him to blame you either."

"I knew," she declared. "And I did it anyway. That's no way for a mother to be. He knew it and I knew it."

"I disagree," said Will, but when she didn't respond, he left the matter to silence. It was obviously an old wound, and he was a stranger with no right to meddle. They finished the bottle, and Cora went to fetch another. They started on it, and after a while he asked, "Did you ever think of starting over?"

"I'm barren."

Years of listening to his mother, plus his time studying at Wurthaven, made it impossible for him to keep his mouth shut. "Are you certain? A lot of people think that, but unless..."

"I travel a lot, Kelvin. There's a place in Terabinia with some of the best doctors in the world. They confirmed it." She took a large drink.

"Wurthaven," muttered Will. "I'm sorry to hear that."

"It's probably for the best anyway. I already told you: I made a choice no mother should make. I don't deserve children. Temarah knew what she was doing." Cora looked back over at him. "Wurthaven— you're familiar with Terabinia. I thought I heard an accent in your voice. Now it makes sense."

The wine had dulled his usual wariness. He'd never hidden his country of origin from his neighbors anyway, so he wasn't too worried. "Whatever you're thinking, I can assure you it's far from the truth," he told her.

For some reason, his statement shifted her mood, and Cora began laughing. "What in the world are you worried I might think? Let's see." She made a show of rubbing her chin and being deep in thought. "So, you're a Terabinian, living in Lystal, on the far side of Trendham, with your mother and son." She narrowed her eyes. "You must be a spy!"

"No..."

"No shit!" she sputtered. "Why would anyone send a twenty-year-old to Lystal to act as a spy? And what's your cover? Oh, that's right! You're a kitchen drudge. It makes perfect sense! Only here, at the Laughing Goat, could you learn all the best-guarded state secrets of the oligarchs."

"Well, now that you put it that way."

"It sounds stupid," she agreed. "And I'm a little disappointed that you think I'm dumb enough to believe something like that."

"I didn't say anything. You created the entire story without any input from me," he protested. Mentally, though, he filed the story away. Even though the tale was implausible, it might be enough of a reason to explain his secrecy and paranoia. So long as she believed he was dumb enough to believe in such a possibility, then maybe it would make sense for him to worry about alarming his neighbors.

She was watching him, though. "That's it." Leaning over, she poked his forehead with one finger. "I can see you thinking, and you're thinking *way* too hard."

"It's just that even though you're joking, I do worry that others might—"

"No, you don't," she cut him off. "And don't lie. I don't mind if you want to pretend to be mysterious, but don't play me for a fool. I can see there's a lot more to you than you want to share. Not the least of which is that you're a lot cleverer than you want me to think. But you're only a halfway decent liar, so don't bother. In my profession, I have to be good at spotting lies or I'd be broke."

Her perceptiveness annoyed him, not to mention she was leaning in again. He could feel the warmth of her breath on his cheeks. It had been a decade since he'd had a conversation half as interesting. It had been almost as long since he'd *felt* interesting to someone else. His descent into obscurity had been deliberate, but in that moment, he was sick of it. The wine was warm in his belly, and he wanted nothing more than to reach out and pull Cora's head just an inch closer, to kiss her—to live.

Do it! shouted Laina from the gallery of his mind. *Do you know how boring it is being you? Do it!*

As often happened, hearing Laina's voice brought out his stubbornness. Reining in his physical impulses, Will gave in to a bit of vanity instead, and issued a challenge. "So tell me, oh peerless trader, what do you see?"

That lit a fire in her eyes. Cora finished her glass and held it out for him to pour another. The way her hand swayed was a visible indicator that she was well past tipsy now. She downed the glass in one long draught, then set it carefully aside. "Make sure I don't break that," she told him. "They were expensive." After he nodded, she rose from her chair and circled him slowly before stopping in front of him. A slight stumble made him fear she was about to fall, but instead she simply sat down on his lap. Much like a cat, she made it seem as though that had been her intention all along. "Are you sure you want to know what I see?"

"If nothing else, it should be good for a laugh."

The firelight made her eyes seem huge as she stared at him with the intensity of the inebriated. "You have a good heart, but you hate yourself. No, wait. Not hate. You're afraid, yes, that's it. You're afraid of yourself." She reached out and turned his head to the left, then back to the right. "You're also quite handsome, except for these marks on your cheek. Bear attack, right?"

"It wasn't a bear."

"Don't interrupt." She shushed him by putting a finger to his lips. "I'm prognosticating." She put a hand on either side of his head, taking a firm grip in his hair. "You're afraid of greatness. So afraid that you decided to come here and hide, where the people who know what you're capable of will never find you. That's why you're working at that bar, and why you're pretending to be younger than you are." Cora's face swayed, then she leaned in and kissed him. Her tongue probed lightly between his lips, then withdrew.

Will felt as though his body was on fire, and the taste of cinnamon lingered in his mouth. Then Cora leaned in again, but this time she simply laid her head on his shoulder. "I'm just gonna rest my head here for a second," she told him. "I'm a little dizzy."

You're a little drunk, he observed, *and so am I, but not as much.* She was a couple glasses ahead of him, and he outweighed her as well, so it was no wonder. Cora's position on his lap was cutting off the blood flow to one leg, and he had unconsciously shifted his shoulders to support her head better, which was already beginning to make his back hurt, but he kept still. There was something precious about the moment. It felt sacred somehow.

Eventually he had to move, though. Lifting his left hand, he used it to cradle the back of her head as he shifted his weight forward to stand up. He eased his right arm beneath her hips and carefully stood, then he walked to the back of her wagon and stared at the door that stood in his way. He only had two hands, and both were occupied.

Cora was asleep, so he took a chance and used a few spells. The first was a spell of unlocking, but the door was already unlocked. The second was an air spell that could be used to manipulate small objects. It was enough to open the door for him. Then he climbed the stairs and looked around, adjusting his eyes to the near pitch darkness of the interior.

The inside was cramped, but clean and well cared for, giving the space a cozy feel. Most of the walls were covered with built-in wooden shelves that were crowded with small boxes, all neatly labeled. The smell of spices permeated everything. To the right was a broad wooden plank that had hinges along one side. It looked to be either a table or a fold out space for a bed—or both. Will wasn't sure. Farther in, below the upper shelves, was a curtained alcove, just large enough for a small mattress. Will carried her over, and once he was closer, he was sure that it was Cora's bed. He had to kneel to get low enough, which made things awkward, but he managed to get her onto the mattress without banging her head into anything. He was relieved to finally stretch his back again. Cora wasn't overweight, but she had a healthy amount of muscle on her frame.

Imagining what she must look like under her clothes wasn't productive, so he pushed those thoughts aside and started to ease back toward the door. A hand caught his sleeve. "Don't go."

"You're half asleep. Get some rest."

"I was just resting my eyes. I'm awake now. Stay."

"You're drunk."

"So are you. Besides, that's why I asked you to drink with me. So I could have my way with you." He could see a wicked smile on her face despite the darkness.

"I'm going home."

She kept a firm grip on his arm. "I'm not done prognosticating."

"Prognosticating would be telling me the future. That was my past and present you were talking about."

"Really?"

"Yes."

"Know-it-all. So much for pretending to be dumb. You've outed yourself."

"Damn. You caught me," said Will dryly. He pried his arm free as gently as he could, then started to back out.

"Wait."

"What?"

"I thought you liked me."

Will didn't have to think about the answer. "I do." Before he could stop himself, he knelt back down and leaned into the alcove. Cora could barely see him in the darkness, but her breathing sped up as she felt his closeness. He placed his lips against hers, returning the passion she had ignited in him a short time ago.

He lingered for a few dangerous minutes, until Cora's hands began questing, and he realized his own were acting on similar impulses. With an effort of will, he drew back, his fingers still tingling from the memory of soft skin. "Good night, Cora."

"What the hell was that?" she demanded.

"You weren't sure I liked you. I was just answering the question." He had his hand on the door handle.

Cora was trying to climb out of the bed. "Then come back here and let's finish the discourse of our—ow! Damn it!" She had misjudged her position in the dark and smacked the back of her head into the board that framed the upper part of the alcove. She stood, then swayed sideways before sitting down abruptly.

"You're way too drunk," said Will. "Get some rest. Tomorrow we'll have more time. Maybe I can show you my home too, if you're interested." He marveled at his own audacity as the words left his lips. *Am I crazy? I can't introduce her to Mom or Oliver. What am I thinking?*

"I won't be here, damn you!" she sputtered.

"You won't?"

"My house has wheels, doesn't it? What did you expect?"

"I didn't think you'd be leaving the same day I met you."

"I've been here three days already," she responded, exasperation coloring her tone.

"Oh." Once again, Will felt incredibly foolish. He was also crestfallen. *Did I really just invite her to my home? I'm an idiot.* His emotions had run the gamut in just a few short minutes. "Well, maybe the next time you come through Lystal…"

"I'm heading to Faresh next, and then to Delgath. I won't be back in Trendham for quite a while, much less this backwater town."

"That's months of travel sure, but eventually…"

"Then I'll go to Barsta. Do you know how much some spices sell for in Bern? I'd be a fool to cut my route in half just to come back here. I'd be throwing away a small fortune."

Will collected himself, regaining his internal balance, then gave her a sad smile. "Well, it was nice meeting you, Cora. I truly enjoyed your company. Thanks for the wine. If you do ever happen to travel through Lystal again, I'd love to meet up." With a clear conscience, he stepped out into the crisp night air and shut the door.

"No, wait!" she called. He could hear her through the door, and he increased his hearing as he walked. He winced as he heard the thump when she fell trying to get back to her feet. "Damn!" she swore. "I'm never coming back to this stupid town." The last thing he heard was her growl of frustration.

He knew how she felt.

CHAPTER 15

Will was up early, and he left the house just before dawn. Cora's wagon was gone. He spent the rest of the day with a feeling of disappointment, even though he'd expected as much. It wasn't until that evening that his mood lightened, mainly because when he got home, he found that his cousin had returned for a surprise visit.

Erisa was all smiles, and Sammy's hug was firm. It seemed to Will she squeezed him even tighter than usual. "Talk later?" she whispered in his ear.

"Sure."

Supper was good, although Will let Erisa do the cooking, much to Sammy's disappointment. His cousin did enjoy the food, but she was prejudiced in favor of Will's cooking. Although Sammy did her best to hide her feelings, everyone knew, and when his mother gave him a knowing look across the table, Will couldn't help but chuckle.

The conversation didn't venture beyond the usual pleasantries, and after discussing Oliver's progress in school, Sammy's continued business success, and the lack of change in Will's day-to-day routine at the Laughing Goat, Sammy asked an unexpected question. "Have you seen Evie lately?"

She was referring to his cat, or rather the reincarnated demigod who preferred to live as a cat. Will hadn't seen her since Oliver was four. Her last words to him had been, "I'm bored," and she'd disappeared the next day. Will shook his head. "No, not since she left."

"Who is Evie?" asked Oliver.

"You don't remember her?" asked Sammy. When he shook his head no, his aunt explained, "Evie is the cat we had when you were little." She wasn't about to explain the cat's true nature; that was a topic for Will to broach someday.

Oliver's face twisted in thought. "I think maybe I remember her. What happened to her?"

"She wandered off," said Will. "Cats do that sometimes."

"If it was when I was little, she might be dead by now," offered the boy.

"I doubt it," said Will. "She's from a very long-lived breed."

"You could look for her," suggested Sammy, giving Will a meaningful look.

"She'll come back when she's ready—or not," said Will. He knew what she was suggesting; since he had an astral connection to the Cath Bawlg, he could find her with a simple search of the astral. "There's no need to meddle."

Sammy's features showed frustration. "Aren't you curious?"

"I'm a cook at a public house on the far end of Trendham. Curiosity isn't a beneficial trait. The only thing I want is to live and let live," he told her.

His cousin switched to a different subject. "What about Tailtiu? Has she visited at all?"

A spark of anger emerged in Will's heart, and he quickly glanced at his son to see if the boy was paying attention. Oliver didn't appear to be listening. Will answered with a flat tone, "No."

Without looking up, Oliver asked, "How old is Aunt Tally?"

"I'm not sure," said Will. "She was already very old when she moved back to Terabinia."

Oliver looked up, his eyes showing sadness. "You think she might be dead? Is that why you don't want to talk about her?"

Yes, thought Will, though not for the reasons Oliver might assume. His fae aunt had rejected the very nature of her existence. She had originally been a part of the fae realm, immortal and amoral, as all the fae were, but after Will had freed her spirit, she had been cut off. Over time, her young soul had given her emotions, a conscience, and a considerable amount of pain. Mortality, particularly in the people she cared for, did not suit Tailtiu's worldview. Her first experience with suffering had been the death of her puppy, but learning she would need to drain the life from people to sustain her now-limited immortality had not sat well with her.

Will had given her options. He'd created two enchanted items. One that would allow her to receive turyn from him or other donors, and another that would allow her to tap directly into ley lines. No one needed to die. At first, she had accepted that, but as the years passed, Tailtiu had grown more depressed, and eventually the former-fae decided that she wanted to die.

Will had accepted her choice, but he hadn't told the others. Tailtiu had aged steadily once she quit accepting turyn, and while Erisa and Sammy had thought it was merely an illusion, Will knew differently. He had been faintly relieved when Tailtiu told him she was leaving. Privately, he had mourned her, but he hadn't wanted to have that conversation with Oliver yet. A 'trip' to Terabinia was a perfect excuse. Years had slipped by, and he had continued to put the discussion off, but Sammy had forced his hand. "As much as I hate to admit it, you're right, son. It's also possible that we might not get word if that's what happened. I don't think your aunt had much in the way of family left back home."

Sammy frowned, probably puzzled as to why he would let Oliver think Tailtiu might be dead. He'd have to explain the truth to her when they had their private talk later. His mom was giving him a concerned look as well, so Will added her to the list as well. Some days he just couldn't win.

Eventually, Oliver went to bed, and after explaining the situation with Tailtiu to his mom, he took a walk. Sammy caught up with him within minutes of him leaving the house. "I can't believe you never told us about Tailtiu." She sounded angry.

"She wanted it kept secret," he replied.

"*She* wanted it kept secret, or *you* didn't want to have to deal with someone else questioning your judgment?"

Will stopped walking and gave his cousin his undivided attention. "Both. She knew you wouldn't agree, and she didn't want to upset everyone. I knew that if I told you that, you would feel compelled to harass me about it every chance you got."

"Harass you? Is that what you call it when someone cares about the people around them, harassment?"

She nailed you with that one, said Laina in his mind.

Shut up, Will told his dead sister.

Laina had more to add. *Let the record show that I told you the same thing when you agreed to Tailtiu's request, but you didn't listen to me.*

"Are you even listening?" asked Sammy.

He tapped his temple. "Sorry. Laina was agreeing with you." Sammy's irritated expression shifted slightly as concern for him appeared in her eyes. "What?" he demanded.

"Are you sure it's really Laina?"

Will had been open with his cousin about his occasional conversations with Laina since her death over a decade ago. She'd never shown any doubt about his statements before. "What are you implying?"

"What if it's just your imagination?"

He felt defensive, but he knew better than to give in to that emotion. Taking a deep breath, Will responded, "I wondered the same thing, back in the beginning, but over time, the things she said fit too well, and sometimes she knows things I don't think I ever knew. Specifics about her family, or Selene, but I've never really made an effort to verify it."

"But you realize how it sounds to other people, right?" asked Sammy.

The compassion in her gaze made him angry. "Yes, that's why I only mention it to people I *trust*." Will swallowed and tried to recenter his thoughts. "I know it might not be real, but in the end, I decided it didn't matter. I think a fragment of her soul merged with mine, but it could very well just be my imagination. Either way, it doesn't matter, it's still me talking to myself. It just so happens that one of my internal voices sounds like my sister. Is there a problem with that?"

"No, it's just that after what happened last year..." Sammy's voice trailed off.

"What?"

She sighed. "I didn't come to fight with you about Tailtiu, although"—she held up one finger—"I *am* still upset about that. I came to talk about what happened with the trolls, and with us."

"Us?"

Sammy nodded. "First, I wanted to apologize, for what I did."

He chuckled. "You really wanted to kill me there at the end, didn't you? I was a little mad about that at the time, but I got over it after a day or two."

Her eyes widened. "Why are you laughing? It wasn't funny. I seriously attempted to kill you. I *would* have killed you if you hadn't made your skin as hard as steel."

"But you stopped immediately after that," he told her. "That's what matters, right?"

"No!" she growled in exasperation. "I stopped because of—because of the way you—hell, I'm not sure what you did. You weren't human. *I* wasn't human. At the time, it didn't feel like right and wrong existed—just my power, and then you took it away. I wanted to kill you for that, but you wouldn't let me."

"Of course—"

"Shut up. Let me finish. You wouldn't let me. For a little while, I was the most powerful being in the world, but then you just *crushed* me. I was mad, yes, that's when I tried to rip out your throat, but when you looked at me... my pride vanished. No, that's not quite it either. *You* became my pride. I felt like a servant, but I was glad it was you." She shivered. "Once it was over, I tried pushing it all out of my head, but the more I tried, the more disgusted I felt with myself. It's taken me over a year just to come back and talk about it."

He didn't know what to say. Will held out his hands, palms up. "I'm sorry I didn't let you kill me?"

"This isn't a joke. I went from a goddess to an animal."

"And?"

"I liked both." She looked away. "That's what disgusts me. It disturbed me, because until then I thought I understood myself."

"Power can do that," he told her. "It makes you feel different, but you're still you afterward. You just have to make sure you don't lose control. To be honest, that's one reason I'm grateful to have Laina's voice in my head. She's kept me from doing things I would regret on more than one occasion."

"It wasn't the power."

"Huh?"

"It wasn't the power," she repeated. "I tried it myself. There's a ley line that runs through Bondgrad. I tapped into it away from the city. I felt nothing like I did that day."

"Tapped into it to do what?"

"I wanted to find out if it was me, or the power. I thought I could figure it out. But I was lying to myself. I wanted to feel that rush again. I still want it. When the ley line near Bondgrad didn't work, I went back to Terabinia. Remember the place where I nearly died?"

He did. She was referring to a place in the mountains between Barrowden and Branscombe where they had found a crossing point between two ley lines. They'd used the power there to open a gate to Hell, and Sammy had almost died during the later attempt to bring Will back. "Why did you go there?"

"I wanted that feeling, but I couldn't recreate it. I drew power straight from the intersection for over an hour. I got rid of every scrap of snow and ice within half a mile of that place, and then I melted the rock itself." She looked up at him, shame written on her face. "But I never felt it again. It was just me, behaving like a maniac in the mountains. Do you understand?"

"Understand what?"

"Like I said, it wasn't the power. It was *him*. It was the Stormking."

Will frowned. "Now who's the crazy one? That's just a name some people made up for me."

"It's just a name, sure," she agreed, "but it's a name for something inside you."

"I'm just me, Sammy. Maybe it is just me, but if so, it just means there's something wrong with me and my power makes me a little crazy."

"Are you still having those dreams?"

"What's that got to do with anything?"

Sammy was insistent. "Are you?"

"I've had a couple. Nothing as bad as the one you saw," he admitted. "Why?"

"Have you ever wondered if they're connected?"

Absolutely not! Deep down, he knew that was impossible. The outsiders had nothing to do with his power. More importantly, they had nothing to do with his personality shifts. His moments of maniacal bloodthirst had started happening long before he ever made the mistake of looking into the void. Most of that had started during the war. *Agreed,* said Laina.

You weren't in my head back then.

I've seen enough since then. Plus, I see your dreams sometimes, she replied.

What? That startled him, but she refused to answer. Glancing up, he saw Sammy watching him again. "They're not connected," he told her. "And Laina agrees with me. What good does it do to speculate on it?"

"Maybe you don't need to put up the wards at night," she suggested. "Maybe you're just fighting with yourself. It might be that if you could accept that other part of you, maybe you could unify your mind. It seems like you're splintered. Laina's your conscience, or your guilt, and the thing in your dreams is your fear. If you could bring them all together, then…"

"Then what? You think I'll turn into the Stormking?"

"No. Yes. I don't know. Maybe you'll just be regular old Will. The Stormking might just be another fragment. If you can—"

"I'm regular old Will right now, Sammy. There's nothing else." *And I'll be damned before I ever unify any part of myself with that thing from the void.* Looking at her face, he could see that she wanted something. "You want me to become the Stormking. Is that it?"

"No. I want you to feel better." Her eyes darted briefly to one side.

She was lying. Will shook his head. "Try again, this time with more sincerity."

"I'm sorry," she responded. "I waited all this time so I could be sure. I didn't trust myself before." Her eyes locked onto his. "But I really do want you to feel better, to get past the dreams."

"Why didn't you trust yourself?"

Her shoulders bowed with shame. "Because I was worried that if I saw you, I'd only try to convince you to channel that power again, to share it with me." She held up her hands then. "But that's not what I'm trying to do now. I just want you to figure out what's going on with your dreams. So you can feel better."

Will understood. She was deceiving herself, but it made perfect sense. Aside from the nightmares, he sometimes had other dreams as well. Dreams in which he grabbed the reins of power and didn't let go. It was foolishness, and likely would kill him if he tried to hold onto the power indefinitely, but he understood the draw. It was like a drug, and he had to fight against the impulse to use it again. For whatever reason, Sammy had experienced it as well, and now she was struggling to regain her self-control. She *had* to convince herself that she had gotten past it, that she only wanted the best for him. The self-deception was a form of protection for her personal identity.

"Thank you," he said, accepting the truth she wished for, rather than the greed she was trying to deny. He pulled her into a quick hug. "I think you're wrong about me being fragmented, but hopefully it won't matter. I shouldn't ever need to use that sort of power again, and if I do, I won't share it with you." Sammy tensed as he said that, but after a second, she relaxed.

Then she pushed him away. "Now you need to explain why you didn't tell me Tailtiu left with the intention of dying."

"It was her choice."

She growled. "The hell it was! We're family. You should have told me. I could have spoken with her."

Will braced himself for the onslaught. He'd made the choice knowing he would eventually face such a lecture. He listened for a considerable amount of time before she finally finished. The fact that he didn't argue made her even angrier, but there was nothing he could do about that either. In the end, all he could do was promise to attempt to contact Tailtiu, to see if she had passed on or not.

The prospect of the lonely emptiness he would find was something he dreaded. So much so that he refused to check right then. Sammy finally accepted that, but in the course of their discussion, Will completely forgot that he'd intended to ask about Cora. The trader had said they were merely business acquaintances, but he'd wondered just how well they knew each other. When he finally remembered a few days later, Sammy had already gone back to Bondgrad.

CHAPTER 16

It was two weeks later when Will finally decided to try and contact Tailtiu, or at least confirm that she was no longer among the living. Seeking her in the astral, as he would do with others, was too daunting. Through the astral, the bond between people was intimate and often emotional; seeking someone that had already died would be a visceral exposure to emptiness and loss. The last time he had done such a thing was when he had confirmed Laina's death.

And yet I'm still here, with you, she told him.

Maybe, he responded, *assuming you aren't just a sign of my mental instability.* He turned his thoughts back to Tailtiu, and his lips began to move as he quietly said her name three times in succession. Although she was no longer one of the fae, many aspects of her old existence still held true, and the ability to contact her through naming was one of them.

It would also be less painful when it failed. Will expected to feel nothing but a dull lack of response. He was wrong. A sense of irritation returned to him, and he began to wonder, *did I imagine that?* Repeating the names once again, he received only one impression, a sense of denial. It was essentially a sign that she didn't intend to meet him.

Unable to restrain his curiosity, Will slipped into the astral and sent his perception out in search of her. What he found confused him, and it took him a while to understand what he was seeing. Eventually his mind resolved the strangeness, and he realized she was underwater. A large, fish-like creature was in the center of his view, presumably Tailtiu, although it looked nothing like any form he'd ever seen her take before.

The lighting was dim, but he sensed other similar creatures around her, and as he looked around, he could see that the water went on to the limit of his perception. The sun sparkled above, filtering down to where she swam, but of the bottom he sensed nothing. Multitudes of other creatures also swam there, though most were much smaller than Tailtiu and her companions.

Will studied her form carefully, remembering the pictures from a marine naturalist guide he had once studied. *Is she a dolphin, or some sort of small whale?* He wasn't sure.

Go away, she thought at him. Being astrally sensitive herself, the ability to communicate came with the direct contact he had initiated. *I'm busy.*

We miss you, Will told her.

I'll visit—someday. Not now.

Will let his sense of self fall back into his body and lay on his bed for a few minutes, thinking about what he'd seen. He had no idea why she was in that form, but he felt a great sense of relief that she was alive, and apparently living with some sort of purpose. A faint smile crept across his face without his knowledge.

Bolstered by what he had found, he returned to the astral and checked on Evie as well. She, at least, was still in the form of a cat, but the resemblance to what he had expected ended there. Her fur was a deep black that shimmered in the red glow of a pool of liquid magma which was close to where she was napping. Glancing around, Will saw what appeared to be a massive cavern lit only by a lake of molten rock.

When he returned his gaze to Evie, he saw her eyes open to stare back at him. They glowed a deep orange, matching the lava around her. *Where are you?* he asked.

She looked around, then responded, *It doesn't have a name.*

What are you close to?

Evie turned her gaze upward, toward the cavern ceiling. *Up there is the place you call Delgath.*

Delgath was the name of a small mountainous country. The coast there was a jungle, and the majority of it was unsuitable for farming, but the dwarves supposedly had several large cities under the mountains. Will had never met a dwarf, but he'd heard they sometimes traded with Trendham. *You're with the dwarves?* he asked.

No, but I saw some as I traveled. They are far above this place, she explained.

How deep are you?

She returned the mental equivalent of a shrug. *I do not know. Are you well? Are you safe?*

Yes. We are all fine.

That seemed to satisfy her, and the cat curled back up, closing her eyes and returning to her nap. Will could tell he was being dismissed. *Goodbye.*

Returning to his body, Will felt a weight lift from his shoulders. It hadn't been long since his cousin's visit, but he decided to make a quick trip to give Sammy the good news. Teleporting, he could be there and back in no time at all. *It's amazing how much easier it is to visit people when I'm not burdened by guilt,* he noted.

***

"Who would win in a fight," began Doug, "a wardsman or an iron knight?" He and Alver were walking after school. Doug was headed for home while his friend was headed to the Laughing Goat.

Alver sighed. Doug was always coming up with hypothetical situations that had no real answer. The other boy seemed to love nothing more than talking, even if there wasn't any point to it. "Why do you care? We've never even seen an iron knight anyway."

Iron knights were the new special units that were now part of Terabinia's army. Their neighbor had eschewed wardsmen in favor of sorcerers for as long as anyone could remember, but during what was now called the 'Troll War,' the iron knights had been sent to the field for the first time. They were supposedly soldiers wearing some sort of enchanted plate armor that made them incredibly strong and fast, but no one really knew for sure.

"If they thought they were good enough for trolls, then they must be tough," mused Doug.

Despite himself, Alver was drawn into the subject. "Not good enough apparently, since the Stormking had to save them. They lost almost their entire army."

"But the iron knights survived," Doug pointed out.

"Doesn't matter if they couldn't kill trolls."

"Trolls heal, so it wasn't really fair. That's why I wonder what would happen if a wardsman fought an iron knight one on one. Personally, I think the iron knight would win since the armor would keep him from being hurt."

Alver scoffed at that. "Wardsmen can wear armor too, you know, and some of them carry magical weapons."

"But an iron knight is completely protected. If a troll couldn't kill one, what chance would a wardsman have?"

Irritated, Alver held up a finger. "First off, a wardsman *is* magic. He's got his tattoos all over him, all the time. Take an iron knight out of the armor and he's just a regular person—"

Before he could finish his argument, Doug cut him off. "What if a wardsman wore an iron knight's armor? Can you imagine? Would he be twice as strong? Or twice as fast?"

"Neither," said a deep voice.

Lystal was a fair-sized town, but not so big that people didn't talk to one another on the street. Having a conversation while walking meant being prepared to entertain interjections from outsiders. Alver looked over at the stranger to ask what he meant, then nearly jumped out of his shoes when he saw a giant emerging from a provisioner's shop on their right. He stumbled into Doug, and it took the two boys several seconds to sort themselves out.

The giant laughed at their reaction. "I didn't mean to give you a fright. I just thought you should know, the magic in the suits the iron knights wear won't work with a wardsman's tattoos." His accent made it obvious he was Terabinian.

Alver stared up at the giant—no, it was definitely a man, just a very big one. The stranger had dark brown hair, cut shorter than most men liked, and while he did have a beard, it was also trimmed close. He stood far taller than anyone Alver had ever seen, and although his father Kelvin was relatively tall, this man would likely be a head and a half taller. His clothes were plain brown linen, but the tunic covered something else. Given the pungent smell of iron, Alver thought there might be mail underneath it. He glanced at the man's belt, looking for weapons, but saw only a long knife.

The stranger seemed to take note. "Looking for a sword?"

Doug was still mute, but Alver just nodded, then asked, "You're wearing mail under that shirt, aren't you?"

The big man lifted one brow, then patted his chest, which emitted a metallic sound as the rings moved against each other beneath the tunic. "Just a byrnie. Traveling can be dangerous. You've a sharp eye, lad."

"Nose," corrected Alver. "Mail always stinks."

Doug gaped at his friend in alarm, shocked that he would insult the huge man, but the stranger merely laughed. "You sound like my wife, but even she insists I wear it when I leave home."

Alver ignored the joke, instead asking, "How do you know about the armor the iron knights wear?"

"I'm sure you've figured out I'm from Terabinia. It's near impossible for a man my size to avoid being conscripted into the army at some point. I've met some of these 'iron knights' you like to talk about."

Doug was hooked. "Really? How big are they? Is the armor really magic? How does it work? Do you think if—"

The stranger laughed. "Sorry, lad, I've got places to be, but I'm also starving. Where's the best place to get food in Lystal?"

Something about the man made Alver suspicious, though whether it was the fact that he was Terabinian or that he was obviously a warrior, he couldn't be sure. He seemed too clean and well-kept for a regular soldier, much less a civilian. Without fully understanding his own motivation,

Alver pointed west. "If you go to the next corner and follow the road that way, it will lead you to a public house on the edge of town called the Red Hare. It's the best food in Lystal, other than my Nana's, of course."

Doug gaped at him in disbelief, and the Terabinian noticed. "You seem to disagree."

Alver's friend needed no encouragement and immediately blurted out, "The Hare is too expensive, and everyone knows the best food is at the Laughing Goat." Doug looked at Alver. "Your dad works there. He's the reason the food is so good."

Alver was giving Doug dagger looks, but the other boy was oblivious. Glancing up, he saw the newcomer studying him and felt the need to explain. "It's too busy. Plus, you're a foreigner, I figured you can afford to pay more."

The Terabinian laughed. "I think I'd rather have your dad's cooking if it's so good you're trying to keep foreigners away from it. Which way is the Laughing Goat?"

Alver clamped his mouth shut, flattening his lips. He was unsure what to say, but he had a bad feeling. He looked over at Doug and mouthed one word, 'run.' Then he turned back to the stranger and said, "I have to get home. Nana's waiting for me." Without waiting, he nudged Doug, then started to move.

"I think I need a guide," said the stranger, his large hand descending toward Alver's shoulder.

Everything happened in an instant. Alver leaned left, avoiding the hand while turning his body in the direction he planned to run. At the same time, he pushed Doug. "Run!" He knew there was no way someone so big could catch either of them. He had one foot starting forward when the ground came up suddenly and smacked him in the face. The Terabinian had kicked Alver's weight-bearing foot out from under him.

Doug had finally seen the light and was running, but the stranger seemed content with Alver. With one hand on the back of the boy's shirt, he lifted the youngster to his feet. "Let me help you back up." Deftly, he caught Alver's fist as the boy swung for his groin. "None of that now. That's not very nice."

Alver followed up with a kick to the knee, or tried to, but his aim was ruined when the big warrior lifted him completely off his feet. His shirt cut into his throat, choking him. Nevertheless, he continued to struggle, and when the man set him back down, he nearly got hold of the hilt of the man's knife. He gave up a second later when his arm was abruptly twisted behind his back. "Let me go!" he yelled.

"Certainly. Right after you take me to the Laughing Goat." The pressure the stranger was putting on Alver's arm was unrelenting. "Is it that way?"

"No."

"So that's it." The stranger began marching him in the direction the two boys had been going initially. A shopkeeper looked at him with a worried look, but the giant simply gave the man a jovial grin. "Not to fear. I'm just taking the lad to see his father. It seems he needs a lesson in manners."

"No, I don't!" growled Alver. "This is kidnapping!"

The Terabinian simply laughed, while deftly guiding Alver along with pressure against his captured arm. "Your father can be the judge of that."

Their trip to the Laughing Goat was humiliating, for Alver continued to loudly complain, and they drew onlookers all along their route. Some of the townsfolk appeared alarmed at first, but after hearing the stranger's friendly banter, most decided it was nothing to be overly concerned about. If there were any who felt otherwise, the foreigner's massive size must have convinced them it wasn't worth the trouble of intervening.

After a couple of blocks, the foreigner even stopped to ask a passerby for directions to the 'Goat, since Alver refused to offer any help. The man happened to be Darren Blenner, Trig's father, and he gave Alver a strange look. "The boy won't tell you? His dad works there."

The giant shook his head. "For some reason, he doesn't want me to talk to his father."

Darren nodded. "The boy's a troublemaker. I've had words with his dad in the past." He licked one thumb and then dusted his knuckles on his coat to indicate the discussion involved more than simply words. "Give him a lump and maybe he'll learn to discipline his brat better. Apparently, he needs another lesson."

Alver turned red at the words, and with his dignity already gone he lost his temper. "Another year or two and I'll return ten-fold what you gave my dad, Darren Blenner! I haven't forgotten you!"

Blenner's face twisted angrily, and he lifted one hand. "I'll give you a lesson in speaking to your betters right now, boy!"

The older man's right arm came up and he swung, but the giant caught him, massive fingers enfolding Blenner's hand as though the Terabinian was holding the fist of a small child. The big man caught Blenner's eyes with his while maintaining a firm grip. "Let's not be hasty, friend. That's his father's job, not yours. Understand?" Blenner tried to pull back, but couldn't, then his face blanched as the stranger's grip tightened painfully. The Terabinian then added, "We're all friends here, right?"

"Yeah. Of course," agreed Blenner quickly, casting his eyes to the ground. "I wasn't thinking."

Alver had gone silent watching the exchange, and if the giant's pressure on his elbow had slacked, he didn't notice. Blenner gave quick directions to the stranger and hurried on his way as soon as he was released. They took a right at the next crossing, and the Laughing Goat came into sight. That was when Alver finally spoke again. "Do you threaten everyone who doesn't cooperate with you?"

"I haven't threatened you," offered the stranger. "Trust me. You'd know if I did. This is what I call 'friendly restraint.' As for that man back there, well, there's a few like him in every town I've ever been in. Did he and your father get into a tussle?"

"I don't want to talk about it."

The big man pursed his lips. "No shame in it, lad. That's no way to solve differences, and it certainly doesn't prove anything."

"Easy to say when you're the size of a cow shed," muttered Alver.

The stranger released him, a thoughtful look on his face. "True enough, not that I can change what I was given." He took a slow breath. "Well, that's the place, so you're free as I promised."

For some reason, Alver no longer felt like running. "You're not going to take me to talk to my father?"

"Not much point. I'm actually here to talk to the owner, Lettler. I was a little curious after hearing your dad was a good cook, but from what I just heard, I doubt he's anyone I'd be interested in meeting."

Something about the large man's words made Alver feel defensive. He knew his father was more than capable of beating Trig's blowhard of a father, but at the same time, he didn't want to argue the point lest he bring trouble to his family. While the stranger seemed decent in his own way, Alver was still suspicious, and he knew his father had moved them to Trendham to hide from something serious.

His curiosity was now fully engaged, however. "Want me to tell Mister Lettler you want to talk to him?"

The Terabinian regarded him thoughtfully, then replied, "You've changed your opinion of me rather quickly. Sure. I'll go find a seat if you wouldn't mind letting him know I'd like a word."

It was hardly a challenging task. This early in the afternoon, there weren't many customers, and Lettler was tending the bar and serving tables himself. The staff who handled the evening crowd wouldn't arrive for another hour yet. Once Alver saw his new acquaintance head for a corner, he went to the bar and spoke to the manager in a quiet voice. "The big man that just came in is looking for you. Says he wants to talk about something."

Lettler frowned. "About what?"

Alver shrugged. "I don't know, but he was insistent about it. He twisted my arm to get me to show him where the 'Goat was."

"And you were talking to a stranger because…? Nevermind, I'll go see what he wants."

Alver hurried to add, "He's Terabinian, said he used to be in the army."

The older man paused, his face becoming stern. He turned his eyes to the Terabinian and studied him, then spoke quietly from the side of his mouth. "Walk out like you're going home. Then circle around to the kitchen door. Tell your dad what you told me. Try to be casual." Without waiting for a reply, Lettler put on a milder expression and wandered over to greet the newcomer.

Filled with excitement, Alver struggled to keep his pace slow as he went back outside, and as soon as he was beyond the doors, he broke into a run. He was fully invested in the drama, and he nearly stunned himself when he slammed full body into the kitchen door, forgetting his father often kept it barred when he wasn't expecting deliveries. Bouncing off, he was rubbing his bruised shoulder when Kelvin opened it a minute later.

"What the hell was that about?" demanded his father.

Alver struggled not to shout, but he couldn't manage a whisper either, so instead he whisper- shouted the news to his dad. "There's an enormous Terabinian here to see Lettler! He's huge! He told me to tell you, and on the way here he showed Trig's dad who's who! He wanted to hit me, but the stranger caught his fist in one hand and I thought he might squeeze until the bones popped! I don't think he's bad, but he might be here to arrest Lettler, I don't know, and if—"

Kelvin held up his hand. "Hold on. Slow down. You aren't making sense. Who told you to tell me? Lettler or the stranger? How does Blenner enter into this? Start from the beginning." Alver started over, though he was still stumbling over his words in his haste. With some effort, he managed to convey a semi-intelligible summary of recent events. Near the end, his father asked only one question. "What did he look like? Describe this so-called giant to me."

"He's enormous, at least a head taller than you, maybe two! He didn't have a sword, but he was wearing mail under his tunic. I thought he'd be slow, but he was quick enough to knock my feet out from under me before I could run. He doesn't seem mean, but I bet he could take on four or five soldiers by himself! I think he might be bigger than a troll!" Alver's words continued to tumble out faster than he could organize them.

"Hair color? Eyes? You already told me he's big," said Kelvin calmly.
"Dark brown, I think."

"You think?"

"I'm not sure about the eyes, but he's *huge*! That should be enough. There can't be many people that size in the whole world."

His father gave him an odd look. "You'd be surprised. Besides, if you haven't noticed, the way you're growing, you're going to be pretty sizeable yourself someday."

Alver nodded, impatient and not seeing the point of the aside. "What are we going to do?"

Kelvin gave him a hard look. "*We*? Nothing. You've had enough excitement for one day. Go home."

"But Dad! What if he tries to arrest Mister Lettler?"

"Precisely why you shouldn't be here," said his father. "I'll keep an eye on things from the kitchen. I won't let anything happen."

"From the kitchen? Mister Lettler might need help! The stranger might think twice about doing anything if there was someone else in there."

Kelvin shook his head. "That's not how hiding works, son. I sincerely doubt that giant of yours is here for Mister Lettler. I know I haven't told you much of anything, but Lettler is doing his job, which in this case is making sure I'm *not* seen. I need you to go home and do the same. Tell your Nana what you told me."

He looked into his father's eyes and saw his determination. There'd be no arguing. He made his own decision then and simply nodded. "Yes, sir." Turning around, he ran as if he were heading home, but as soon as he had turned the corner, he stopped and quietly stalked back toward the front doors of the Laughing Goat.

He instinctively began to crouch, but then realized that since the front doors faced the street, he'd only be making himself conspicuous to those nearby. Alver made a conscious effort to relax, then walked up the front steps and sat down by the door. *I've done this dozens of times. I'm just waiting for Dad's break. Nothing unusual here,* he told himself.

Unfortunately, although it was a quiet time of day for the 'Goat, it wasn't quiet enough for him to make out the conversation inside. Alver fretted for a moment, when suddenly the door opened and one of the regulars, Frank Daller, stepped out. The man glanced down at Alver and nodded as he stepped off the front porch and headed home. Without thinking, Alver caught the door with one hand before it closed, then, still in a crouch, he duck-stepped into the main room.

He already knew where the big man was sitting, and that he wouldn't be visible on that side due to a low railing, but one of the other customers who sat more directly in front of the door did notice him. Luckily this one knew him as well. He looked a question at Alver, who merely held one finger to his lips and gave a weak smile. *Please don't say anything, Mister Graber,* he begged silently.

Graber winked then turned his attention back to his food while Alver let out a sigh of relief. Carefully, he scooted along until he reached the end of the half-wall, then sat down with his back to it. He was still twenty feet away, but his ears were sharp enough to listen in from that distance and trying to get closer would only expose him.

"I already told you. I don't know anything about the hospital funds," said Lettler, sounding annoyed.

"They listed you as the donor and as a managing partner," returned the big Terabinian's calm voice. "Such a charitable act—I'd think you would be proud of the fact."

"It wasn't me."

"And the Academy?"

"I don't know about that either," insisted Lettler.

The stranger let out a deep breath, somehow making it ominous. "I think you do."

Lettler tried to sound angry, but his voice came out sounding nervous. "Why do you care? It's none of your business."

The table creaked as the big man leaned forward, putting his full weight on his elbows. "Because I'm curious how the simple owner of a public house can afford to give such enormous sums to charity. Did you have a rich uncle die and leave you his fortune?"

"I think it's time for you to leave," warned the manager.

"I'm not going anywhere until you introduce me to the man who's really paying the bills. You're welcome to try and move me if you like."

"I'm not fool enough to try that, but the town watch won't take kindly to your antics. I'm a respected citizen here. Want me to call them? All I have to do is step outside and—"

"And what?" growled the Terabinian. "Go ahead. I'm sure your employer will be excited to have them in here causing a ruckus. Have you thought about what I might say when they start asking me questions? There's a much simpler solution—just tell me who the donor is."

Lettler sounded desperate as he replied, "I keep telling you, I don't know anything about this."

"Gabet's Academy," intoned the stranger. "Dedicated to Seth Gabet. Have you ever met the man? I have. I actually knew him. He was friends with someone I was very close with, and probably with someone you know."

The tension in the air was thick, and it wasn't hard for the remaining customers to read the room. The last two wolfed down the remainder of their food and left, giving Alver warning looks on their way out the door. No one wanted to be in the vicinity if a fight broke out with the enormous Terabinian. Lettler backed away and moved toward the bar. "One second, maybe I have something back here I can show you."

Alver frowned, then heard the sound of a crank. The manager had grabbed the crossbow he kept under the counter. *Is he going to shoot him?*

There was a crash as a chair flew back, and the Terabinian lifted his table to use as a shield. "A crossbow? I've offered you no harm. Put it down and I'll leave."

"It's gone too far for that," hissed Lettler, his voice tight with fear.

Alver felt paralyzed, but before the situation could escalate any further, he heard his father's voice ring out. "Easy, Lettler, that's enough. I'll talk to him."

"Did you hear what he said?" asked the manager.

"Yeah. Looks like the customers are gone. Go home early. We'll call it quits for today," said Kelvin calmly.

"I don't think you should stay here alone," cautioned the manager.

"It'll be fine. He won't hurt me. Go home." It took a little more reassuring, but finally the manager agreed. Alver worried he'd be discovered, but Lettler headed for the kitchen. Kelvin called after him, "Thanks for trying to protect me."

Lettler grunted and was gone. Meanwhile, Alver was mulling over what his father had just said. *Why was he giving orders to Mister Lettler?*

The stranger had waited in silence the moment Kelvin had appeared, but now he spoke. "It's been a few years."

"You scared off my customers," said Kelvin. He sounded genuinely aggravated, but there was no trace of fear in his tone.

"That wasn't my intention, Will. You have no idea how hard it was to find—"

"My name is Kelvin now. Don't use that name again. And yes, I damn well know how hard it was. I made it hard to find me on purpose—I didn't want to be found."

Alver's brain was buzzing with questions, but all he could do was remain silent and try to hear as much as possible. He did know his father's name used to be Will, but it had been so long since anyone had called him that that he'd nearly forgotten it. *Did he know him before I was born?*

The big man seemed regretful. "Sorry about the chair. I'll pay for it."

"I don't need your money. It'll be fine. Just leave. The sooner you're gone the better."

"Wi—Kelvin, I came to apologize—and to thank you."

Kelvin responded without hesitation. "Don't need it, don't care. Door's that way."

"Damn it, Will, I'm serious! I want to make amends. I wanted to tell you last time, but I didn't get the chance."

"The man you're trying to apologize to is dead. Save your dignity, John. Go home and leave me in peace. That's all I want now."

So his name is John, noted Alver. *Dad really does know him.*

The big man took a slow breath. "You have no idea how hard it was for me to get here, much less find you."

Kelvin reacted angrily. "How many know about your trip? As important as you are now, there must be hundreds." He growled inarticulately. "I've built a life here. Oliver is in that school you were harassing Lettler about. All I wanted is to give him a decent life. Now what will happen? Where will we move that's safe?" Thunder rumbled in the distance.

Alver winced at the sound. Throughout his childhood, his father had occasionally had nightmares, and they always happened on nights when there was a storm. Kelvin had never admitted to being afraid of thunder and lightning, but Alver had figured out the connection. He didn't really understand why, but his guess was that some of the worst things that had happened to his father must have happened during storms.

The Terabinian's next reaction surprised Alver. Peeking around the edge of the wall Alver could see the big man's expression showed worry, or perhaps even fear. "No one knows, Will, I promise you that. Not even Jan. You need to stay calm."

"I am calm, damn it!" snapped Kelvin. More thunder punctuated his reply.

"No, you're not. It's thundering, so I know you're upset."

The big man spoke softly, as though trying to calm a dangerous animal. Alver watched and wondered. *So he knows my dad is afraid of storms. Maybe he knows why. But why is he afraid? Is he afraid of my dad? He's easily two and a half times Dad's size.*

"You expect me to believe you didn't tell your wife?" Kelvin's voice grew louder, but before he could continue, the front door opened, and at the same instant, all sound from their side of the room stopped. Alver was so startled he almost fell over, but then he saw Lettler in the door frame.

The manager looked at him then looked toward Kelvin. "Sorry, I'm just locking the door, then I'll be out of the way." He opened the door wide, staring at Alver and waiting.

Alver crawled out as quickly as possible, then the manager locked the door behind them. "What were you thinking, boy?" he demanded.

Alver fumbled for an answer. "I wanted to make sure he didn't hurt my dad."

Lettler ruminated on that for a moment. "It's good you want to protect him, but you don't need to worry. Now, you better get home. It sounds like we're about to have a storm."

Without thinking, Alver asked, "Do you know why my dad is afraid of thunderstorms?"

"No, and that's the first I've heard of it. A lot of people are scared of storms, though. I didn't know your dad was one of them," said Lettler.

Alver nodded. "That man in there seemed to know about it too."

"That's not for us to worry about. Go home, Alver. I don't want to have to explain to your dad that I caught you eavesdropping."

"Yes, sir."

CHAPTER 17

As soon as he heard the door open, Will stopped the sound of their voices from passing more than a few feet from them. He mentally chided himself for not damping down the sound of their voices sooner as he usually did during sensitive situations, but Tiny's appearance had startled him.

"Yes. She doesn't know," repeated Tiny. "At least not yet. Once I get home and we start talking—I'm sure she'll find out. I don't keep secrets from her. But I arranged this without her help, so I doubt she knows anything about it. As far as anyone knows, I'm visiting relatives near Branscombe."

"This is a damn sight farther than Branscombe," returned Will. "You don't think people will wonder at your extended absence?"

"You seriously overestimate how important I am."

"You're the Royal Marshal!" exclaimed Will.

"Terabinia is at peace!"

"You're the Black Duke. People pay attention to your comings and goings," Will reminded him.

"They pay attention to that enormous suit of armor. I almost never go out in public like this." Tiny gestured toward himself.

"I'm sure the people at court are quite familiar with you. You're the size of an elephant. A man would have to be blind not to remember you!"

"I don't go to court! I only make appearances in that stupid armor, and then it's usually just to intimidate people. I can't stand the pomp and circumstance, and I can't stand most of the nobility either!"

"I feel so sorry for you, *Your Grace!*" sneered Will.

Tiny snapped. "Don't call me that! I'm sick of it."

"Then you shouldn't have accepted the fucking title! No one forced it on you."

"Someone had to take responsibility since you up and abandoned everyone and everything!" Tiny rebuked him. He was shouting now.

Will's ears were beginning to flush red. "You made it pretty damn clear I wasn't welcome the last time we talked, or maybe you've forgotten?"

"I came here to apologize for that, you damned turd farmer! If you'd just shut up and let me!"

"You're too stupid to even swear properly—why in the fuck would I let you mangle my ears with whatever half-baked, half-assed, linguistically lame, excrement-laced excuse of an apology you think is worth traveling across half of Hercynia to deliver?"

Tiny blinked, and silence reigned for a moment as he mentally processed the sentence. Then he replied, "Because it actually matters to you, even if you won't admit it. Maybe you should get your brain checked. I think the magic has started to rot everything between your ears."

"Fine. Let me hear it," said Will.

His old friend stared at him in surprise, then responded awkwardly, "I don't want to now! You've pissed me off."

"Idiot. More likely you forgot what you intended to say. You marched your happy ass halfway across creation to deliver some sorry remarks and now you can't even remember what the hell you meant to say?" Will's nostrils flared and he sneered as he delivered the next line. "Next time, maybe get your wife to write it down for you."

"At least I still have a wife. Maybe if you hadn't abandoned yours, you wouldn't be such an asshole."

Sparks traced brilliant lines along Will's arms. "You really don't value your life much, do you? My wife is dead. That thing you serve isn't her."

"If that was true, you wouldn't have to shield yourself constantly."

"What does that mean?" asked Will.

"You have an astral link with her, same as with me and Jan. If she wasn't really Selene, it wouldn't work. Astral links are between souls. The reason you have to hide is because it *really is her*."

Will's mouth fell open, closed, then opened again.

Tiny seized the initiative. "You know I'm right."

Will rolled his eyes. "I know you smell like a bull and an iron foundry made love, then died together and have been rusting and rotting in an open field for a month and a half." Tiny's expression didn't waver, so a second later he admitted, "Fine! You're right on that point, but it doesn't matter. She died. End of marriage."

"As I recall, you've technically died once or twice."

"It never stuck. She's *still* dead. Besides, I can't forgive what she did." Tiny had no reply for that, so Will continued, "You're a father yourself, so I know you understand."

Tiny nodded. "I agree, and once I found out what had happened, I realized why you left, but..." He let his words trail off.

"But what?" demanded Will.

"I'm sure you've followed some of the news over the years. You've heard about the things she's done—the schools, the medicine. The people are healthier and happier than I've ever seen. Physicians make twice yearly trips through even the most remote villages. The sick, especially children, are treated by them without reservation. Anyone who needs special care outside of those visits is allowed to come to the capital at any time of year. It's like nothing our nation has ever seen before."

"Does that excuse what she did? If it was your son's life she spent for her immortality, would the end justify a child's murder?" argued Will.

"Of course not! I'm not saying that, and when I first heard, I almost left—"

"But you didn't," interrupted Will.

"I had a wife and child—two now. Jan and I discussed things and chose what we thought was best for them."

"Which was obviously wealth, power, and rubbing elbows with the elite. I have a family too, and I left because I found the answer was exactly the opposite of all that." He'd actually adopted Oliver after leaving, but he didn't see the point in mentioning that technicality.

"Damn it, Will. Life isn't black and white. *You're* the one who taught me that. Remember when I nearly screwed things up with Jan? You were the one who made me realize how childish I was being. The world is complicated. It's never as simple as pure right and wrong."

Thunder rolled, and the building shook as lightning struck somewhere nearby. Will's temper had been fading, but it flared anew as Tiny's words sunk in. "You think I don't know that? *That's* why she's still the queen! I *should* have ended her. It was my duty, my responsibility! If I had lived strictly according to my principles, she wouldn't have lived another day. I had the power and the right, but I couldn't do it. Despite everything, I loved her too much, and that undid me. If I truly believed the world was black and white, I'd have killed her. I couldn't, but that doesn't mean I could stay and pretend everything was all right either. So here I am."

"The power and the right?" muttered Tiny. "What right? Who are you to be the judge?"

Will looked directly into his old friend's eyes. "I'm the First Wizard. It's my duty to protect Hercynia from powers that would threaten humanity, and I swore to my predecessor that I'd eliminate the lich and all knowledge of the heart-stone enchantment. Selene and I actually talked about this before she turned herself into an abomination. I'd planned to give her a pass since she and I would both eventually die in our own time, taking the secret with us.

"Instead, she made herself into a lich, and now I have *two* to kill. If I can ever get over the weakness in my own heart." Will stopped then, letting his eyes fall to the ground. The energy had drained out of him, and quietly he added, "I bet you feel pretty stupid about coming here now."

Tiny remained silent for almost a minute, watching him the entire time, then spoke. "No. I came to tell you I'm sorry, and I am. After you came and told me you killed the dragon, I reacted badly. I didn't believe you, and after all the stress and fear of the month leading up to that, I lashed out at you when I shouldn't have. I was angry with you for not being there. I was furious that you'd left us with Grim Talek. That you treated us like children with nothing to offer, who only needed to be protected. I was damn proud of my part in stopping Lognion, and when you told me it was actually you who'd finished the job—I lost my mind.

"Jan and Selene both educated me on the facts, and once I'd had time to cool off and see reason, I realized I'd been a complete ass. What really made me say those things was the fact that I spent a month feeling lost and afraid, first thinking you were dead, then finding out you were actually very much alive, you'd simply abandoned me. That doesn't excuse how I behaved, but that's where it came from. With all that said, once again, I'm sorry. I should have listened when you came to give me the news.

"That's why I came here, to apologize and to ask you to come back. I don't know if we can ever be friends again, but I didn't want to live the rest of my life with the regret of not having told you that." Tiny sat down in the nearest chair, staring at the wall.

Will ran a hand through his hair, unsure what to do. "I already knew all that, even without you saying it."

"Still, I had to say it."

"I already forgave you anyway. I didn't leave because of you. I left because of Selene," Will added.

"I know."

"The truth is, I've wanted to apologize for the very same things you mentioned, leaving you behind, keeping you in the dark, all of it."

"I'm listening."

"I can't," said Will. "I am sorry, but I'd do it all again, and the truth is, I don't *deserve* forgiveness. That's why I didn't stick around after the last troll disaster. I figured you'd be the bigger man, but I didn't want to be forgiven."

Tiny rose to his feet, facing Will. "I forgave you not long after you left, so whether you like it or not, that's that."

Will nodded, glancing up briefly at Tiny's face, then back at the floor. It occurred to him then that they looked like two children forced to apologize after a playground fight, but he couldn't think of what else he could do.

Tiny spoke again. "And I'm always the bigger man."

"Too right," said Will. "You're like three of me, all mashed together." His breath rushed out of him as the big man's arms circled him and began crushing his ribs. Tiny released him a few seconds later, and Will returned the gesture with a hug of his own, since his arms had been pinned against his sides the first time. Afterward he stepped back, feeling somewhat awkward. "There. We're even now."

Searching for a way forward, Tiny said the first thing that came to mind. "Your son has grown well. How old is he? Fifteen?"

"Twelve," said Will wryly. "He's overlarge for his age. Something I'm sure you're familiar with."

Tiny nodded. "Everyone assumes it's a blessing, but it brings its own challenges. He seemed quick on his feet, though."

"I train with him several times a week."

"Preparing him to be a wizard?"

"Nothing like that. It's still too early. Besides which, he's currently obsessed with becoming a wardsman," replied Will.

Tiny frowned. "A mercenary? I wouldn't wish that on him. He'd be better off in the queen's service." He lifted his hands up as a gesture of peace when Will glared at him. "Hear me out. Despite how you feel, she's a good ruler and it's an honorable life. With some help he could be one of the new Iron Knights."

"I'd sooner—"

Tiny cut him off, "At least he'd live a normal life. The enchanted armor gives most of the same benefits the wardsmen have without burning up the life of the user the way those tattoos do."

Will took a deep breath, then responded, "I'm sure those positions are only offered to the sons of important lords. Even if you could make it happen, it would cause a scandal."

"When he's ready, send him to me as a foster," said Tiny simply.

"What?"

"A foster. The nobles all send their children to learn from one another during their teens. He could be my nephew. No one would dare question it if I spoke for him."

A bolt of fear passed through Will's heart at the thought of sending his son away, but he suppressed the feeling immediately. He needed to think about Oliver's best interests first, rather than his own selfish wish to keep the boy close. Still, he wasn't convinced it was the best idea. "The queen would dare to ask—and she's sharp enough to know your family tree better than you do."

"So?" Tiny shrugged.

Will gaped at him. "So? She'll figure it out."

"And you think she'll take it out on the boy? I won't defend what she did, but she's not malicious. As far as I can tell she still loves you, not that she'll talk about it. My best guess is that once she figured things out, she would pretend not to know—that or she'd take the opportunity to do whatever she could to help give the lad a leg up."

Will frowned. "Why?"

"Because he's your son."

Will rolled his eyes. "I grew up in Barrowden because my father worried his wife would have me killed when she found out about me. I'm not sure you're thinking this through."

"Do you really think that poorly of her?" asked Tiny, shaking his head. "She knows you adopted him. She has no reason for rancor, and moreover, she would likely see him as an opportunity to improve your feelings toward her."

"And when that fails, a means to get revenge," returned Will. "Besides, I think you've forgotten what I have to do."

"What?"

"Kill her," said Will, his voice flat.

"You aren't really serious," stated his old friend. "After all these years? I don't believe you."

"These years are a drop in the bucket for us. Eventually I'll find the resolve, otherwise..."

"Otherwise what?"

"Otherwise, I'll choke at the end, and she'll probably kill me instead," said Will. "Unlike me, she has no compunction doing whatever she thinks is necessary to ensure her survival."

Tiny closed his eyes as though searching for patience. When he opened them again, he replied, "First, I think you're seriously underestimating her feelings for you. Second, you should remember that I'm sworn to her service."

"You were sworn to me once. That oath was never revoked."

"You left Terabinia and surrendered your titles. Legally you're dead. Even if you weren't, the queen released me from that vow before granting me my title."

"That's only valid if you accept her as the rightful monarch—" began Will.

"I do," Tiny snapped. "If I didn't, I couldn't in good conscience have sworn fealty to her."

Will's eyes narrowed. "That's a convenient bit of logic."

Tiny's voice was even as he replied, "Unlike some, I take my oaths seriously."

"It was too much to hope you might at least be on my side."

"I never changed sides, Will!" said Tiny, his voice rising in intensity. "I came here to try and make amends, but let's be clear—we were all on the same side. *You* were the one who created this rift."

Will could have escalated things further, but he'd already gotten control of his temper and he didn't see any good in letting his anger get the better of him again. Instead, he raised his hands. "Fine. We have a fundamental disagreement here, but we can still be friends."

"That's all I wanted to begin with," said Tiny.

"Congratulations on your second child," said Will belatedly, hoping to change the subject.

"Thank you."

"Boy or girl?"

"Boy. I think Jan was a little disappointed since we already had one son, but she's devoted herself to spoiling little Emmet anyway."

"Emmet, that's a good name," remarked Will. "What did you name your first?"

"William."

"Yes?"

"No, that's his name. William."

"You didn't!"

The big man nodded. "We chose the name early, before he was born, and before all the"—he waved his arms at the space between them—"before our trouble. I tried to change our choice when he was born, but Jan wouldn't listen."

Will's mouth twisted. "It might have been better if she had agreed with you."

Tiny grinned. "She had some interesting arguments for why we should keep it as William. In her words, 'If you're mad at the first one, maybe try to raise a better William.'"

Will chuckled. "Good luck."

"The second argument was even better. She joked that if I had to punish him, I could work through my anger at you."

Will's eyes went wide. "You—no, that's not fair."

"Don't worry," said Tiny. "If anything, the joke made me think. Whenever he needed scolding, I always thought it over twice, just to be sure. In fact, I think it's because of his name that I felt compelled to talk to you again. I have so many feelings attached to one name; I couldn't bear to leave things as they were."

Once again, Will was reminded of how deep the river was that ran beneath Tiny's rough exterior. He wished he could forget everything and go back to the way things had once been, but a small voice in the back of his mind reminded him, *The good old days you're reminiscing over actually involved you living in constant fear for a good bit of the time.*

Despite that, he missed Tiny and so many others. Will was full of conflicting emotions, but he was clear on one thing: the best part of his current life was the fact that the only expectations anyone held for him, were those he set for himself. *And Oliver,* he reminded himself.

Before he could stop himself, Will asked, "Maybe you'd like to have supper with my family?"

The big man's eyes lit up. "I'd love to. I have at least a week before—"

Holding up one finger, Will interrupted him. "One night. I won't risk more. The neighbors will have questions, not to mention Oliver, so I have a few rules I'll ask you to abide by." Tiny nodded, so Will continued, "One, Olly doesn't know who I am, or who I was, other than my old name. He doesn't even know I'm a wizard."

Tiny's face showed disbelief. "How?"

"I only practice magic when I'm alone, or in my workshop, which he's never seen. Here in Lystal I am just an ordinary cook. I don't own the Laughing Goat, I didn't fund the new school, and I certainly didn't donate the funds for the hospital. Understood?"

"Surely you plan to explain things to the lad?" asked Tiny.

"In a few more years," said Will. "He's still very much a child and children sometimes talk when they shouldn't. I'm going to explain the rest when he's of age to make the choice of magic."

"So he's never been exposed to any magic whatsoever?"

Will shook his head. "He knows Sammy is a wizard."

"Why was that all right but not you?"

He rolled his eyes. "She's relatively unknown. I wasn't. When we came here, I didn't know how many people would be looking for me. I couldn't really disguise the fact that we were from Terabinia, but if I'd made my abilities known, a lot of people would have had questions. Questions I didn't want to answer."

"You're a self-exile, Will, not a fugitive. Selene never sent anyone after you, and everyone else thought you were dead. You didn't have to live like this."

Will shrugged. "I did what I thought best, and despite what you might think, I actually like this life. I like my work, and there's no one pressuring me to use my power to kill someone else's army or use my abilities to intimidate political enemies. Here I can just be me. I cook, I take care of my little family, and secretly I help people as I can—but no one's forcing me to do anything." He turned toward the door. "Come on. Mom will be happy to see you, and Oliver is probably dying to know whether you were planning to arrest me or kill me."

CHAPTER 18

Erisa Cartwright was both delighted and worried when she saw the long shadow cast by John Shaw appear on her doorstep—for multiple reasons. She shared Will's worries about the possible intrusion of the past, but the most pressing concern for her was how she was going to feed the enormous man. The supper she had been planning would be far from sufficient, though it was early enough that she hadn't started cooking yet.

Will read her concern and understood without her saying a word. Not necessarily because he was that observant, but simply because he was a cook first and foremost. It would have been what he was worried about in her place. "Don't worry, Mom. We closed the 'Goat early so I brought the stew home so it wouldn't go to waste."

"What did you carry it in?" she asked. The stew pot at the Laughing Goat was large enough for a petite woman to fit inside.

Tiny grinned and stepped back onto the porch. When he returned, the stew pot was between his thick arms.

Erisa blanched. "By the Mother! That thing must be as heavy as a millstone. William, why would you make him carry such a thing?"

"An unexpected guest should do something to lighten the imposition," said Tiny. Then he frowned. "You meant Kelvin, right?" He glanced at Will for confirmation.

"Oliver isn't home yet," said Erisa immediately. "Besides, the boy still knows his father's old name, even if we don't use it much anymore."

Unconcerned about the weight of the pot he was holding, Tiny was struck by a sudden thought. "If he knows your old name, then surely he knows who you are?"

Will scoffed at the thought. "He hardly knows anything about the Stormking, much less his actual name, and if he did hear it, he wouldn't believe it. Cartwright isn't exactly an uncommon name."

"He knows you've forbidden him to use it in front of anyone in Lystal," observed the big man.

"I'm his dad," said Will. "I'm the least interesting thing in this town for him. I'll be explaining some of it in just a few years anyway."

Then he looked at his mother. "I sent him home first. He should have been here before us."

The sound of steps on the wooden porch announced Oliver's arrival. His eyes went wide when he stepped through the doorway and saw the giant Terabinian standing in the main room. "Holy Mother!" he yelped, nearly falling over his own feet as he immediately tried to back out.

Erisa laughed at her grandson's near fall, but Will's expression was more stern. "I sent you home to warn your grandmother. Where have you been?"

Oliver kept his eyes on the floor. "I was worried about you. I waited in case something happened, but then I missed it when you left."

"And if it had been an emergency, your grandmother would have been entirely unprepared," lectured Will. "I didn't just send you home to get you out of the way."

"I'm sorry, Dad."

"When are you going to start thinking beyond your nose? This could have been serious."

Erisa tried to intervene. "There's no harm done."

Will held up one hand. "No. Let me finish." He refocused his attention on his wayward son. "You might think my orders irrelevant, or that they're just meant to punish you in some way, but the truth is our family has to be cautious. We can't have two leaders, and for now, I'm the one who sets the rules. That means when I tell you to do something, I expect you to do it—for all our sakes, not just mine. Do you understand?"

"Yes, sir." Oliver's face was red as he stared at his feet.

"Look at me when you answer," said Will.

"Yes, sir."

"That's better. Your punishment will be no supper." Will noticed the look on Tiny's face and realized the punishment might be too much considering their unique guest. Missing the mealtime conversation would be a bigger penalty than the lack of food. Mentally adjusting, Will added, "No supper tomorrow, since we have a guest tonight."

Oliver's face brightened and he nodded quickly.

Will questioned his judgment a while later when they'd largely finished eating and the conversation began in earnest. A few rounds of question-and-answer led Oliver into topics that held great interest for him.

"So you were in the army with my dad?" he asked, following up on something Tiny had said about himself.

The big warrior nodded. "Those were some of my best days, if you exclude the actual fighting and dying." He frowned. "Maybe I shouldn't phrase it like that, but in my memory the bad things are kept separate from my memories of your father and my other friends."

Oliver glanced at his dad. "I bet you were glad to have such a big friend. No one else would dare pick on you, and in battle he could—"

"Hold on, Oliver," interrupted Tiny. "Let me correct you on one thing." Will gave him a warning look, but Tiny shook his head then continued, "When I met your dad, we were both in jail. Arrested on suspicion of avoiding conscription, which was essentially just a way to conscript us anyway, but I digress. *I* was the one being picked on, and your dad stood up for me."

Oliver was visibly shocked. "But wait, what? How?"

"I didn't think I could fight back, something you should understand given your size," said Tiny. "If you fight, you're a bully because you're bigger than everyone else. If you don't fight, you're a pushover. You can't win. Know what I mean?" Oliver nodded. "Your dad wasn't really in a position to defend me, but he did anyway, and I discovered my first real reason to fight—to protect a friend."

Remembering his friend Douglas, Oliver nodded again in agreement. "That makes sense."

Will chimed in, "You're still right, son. Having Tiny on my side was always a comfort, and he saved my life any number of times. I wouldn't be here otherwise."

"Don't let him fool you," argued Tiny. "I protected your dad a lot early on, but over time he was really the one protecting me." He gave Will a sour look. "Sometimes so much that it made me a little angry."

"Dad's good at fighting," said Oliver slowly, "but you're so much bigger..."

Tiny laughed. "You have no idea. Once people saw him in action, only the foolish would dare—"

Tiny's voice vanished abruptly, and Will began speaking over him, "Because I outranked you by that point."

Oliver frowned. "You just said you started out together as conscripts."

"Actually, I joined as a private contract," corrected Will. "Thanks to some help from my father, your grandfather. I'll have to tell you about him someday. Anyway, as a result I had more opportunities to advance."

Finally able to speak, Tiny added a correction. "You would have been promoted anyway." He focused his eyes on Oliver. "Your dad was a brilliant officer—among other things."

"You were an officer? Like a captain? Really?" Oliver was learning more with every passing minute.

"Yes," said Will simply. "And that's all I'll say about it for now. I'll tell you more when the time comes for you to make certain choices."

"What choices?" asked Oliver. "I'm big and I can fight. You taught me how. I know you don't like the wardsmen for some reason, but it's obvious I should be a fighter—of some sort."

Will's cheeks colored. "Things are nowhere near that simple. There's a lot more to this world than fighting."

"When you're my size, you can either hold a sword or pull a plow," said Oliver. He didn't want to argue with his father, but he had to speak the truth, even if it meant his punishment would be worse. "Would you rather I was a beast of burden or the one who protects it?"

"Tone, Oliver!" snapped Erisa, but her stern response was spoiled when Tiny began laughing.

Will and his mother both gave the big man harsh looks, but he didn't stop. Finally, he opened his mouth to explain. "I'm sorry. I shouldn't laugh, but the boy has a way with words, and speaking as someone who grew up big, I understand the feeling." Before they could respond, his eyes focused on the youth sitting across from him. "However, let me assure you young man, that your thinking is far too simplistic. I know it seems cut and dried, but you still have a lot to learn. First, I find your sentiment toward farmers a little insulting. My parents were farmers, and let me assure you none of us would be doing anything if there weren't farmers making sure none of us starve to death." Oliver started to apologize, but Tiny held up his hand. "Let me finish.

"I felt like you once, and while I'm not saying you should become a farmer, you'll find there are a lot more open doors waiting for you than you realize, but that's for your father to explain someday." He stopped and looked at the others. "Where was I going with this?"

Will sighed. "You said 'first,' so I assume you had a second point as well."

Tiny seemed to jump slightly, then focused on Oliver again. "Oh, right! Second, look at your dad. He's a little taller than average, but he wasn't a warrior, not like me, yet I'd never want to challenge him. He's the most dangerous m—" His voice died suddenly, and Tiny's eyes went to Will. After a second, he raised his hand in a gesture of surrender, then opened his mouth once more. "I just meant to say that we all have different things to contribute, and violence is honestly the least of them."

Oliver frowned. Something about the entire exchange seemed off. "You were talking about Dad. What were you going to say?"

Tiny's expression seemed desperate, but he managed a response. "I meant that maybe he's just a cook, but he raised you, didn't he? Just like farming, or cooking, or any other profession, raising the next generation is much more important than fighting. Do you understand?"

Oliver nodded slowly, his expression still uncertain, but Will spoke up. "Let's move on to other things."

Tiny agreed quickly, then asked, "I notice you don't have any of the new lights. I thought everyone was using them by now."

"Dad won't let Nana have them. He thinks they'll blow up our house," said Oliver immediately. "They remind him of magic bombs."

Will gave his son a look of exasperation. Meanwhile, Erisa added, "He has some perfectly reasonable concerns."

Tiny seemed confused, and Will couldn't blame him. Over the past year, the new elven lights had become the biggest trend in Trendham. From the look on his friend's face, Will guessed they were equally popular in Terabinia. Many households had stopped using oil lamps, candles, and rushlights entirely. The new magical lights came in a variety of styles, and some of them were extremely cheap, barely more than the cost of the metal that went into making the housing. They produced bright, clear light with no soot, smoke, or smell, and the more expensive lamps had different settings to control the light level or even the color.

It had led to a revolution in household lighting for rich and poor alike. People still had to purchase the fuel, a form of concentrated turyn known as bluet, but which most just called 'blue.' The fuel was an ongoing source of income for the elves, who hadn't shared the secret of its creation, but they charged very little for the substance. A family could afford to light their home for less than the cost of rushlights, which had previously been the cheapest form of lighting. It was far cheaper than oil for lamps, and vastly cheaper than candles, which only the rich could really afford.

As a result, the elven traders now traded almost exclusively in bluet. Their ships made regular trips into every Trendham port to meet the incessant demand for the magical fuel. The elves hadn't tried to keep the workings of the lamps secret, so now many human craftsmen made and sold lamps. Other small devices were beginning to work their way into the market as well, all fueled by the seemingly ubiquitous fuel, bluet. Clocks, self-heating kettles, small heaters, every day some new device would begin to be sold, and they all used bluet.

Will didn't trust it. "It's not safe," he muttered. "Sooner or later, there will be an accident."

"How?" challenged Oliver. "You keep saying that, but nothing has happened. Everybody I know uses it at home, but they're all still alive."

"No one knows how they make it, but anytime you have energy concentrated like that, there's some risk," began Will.

"Lamp oil is a concentrated source of energy," countered Tiny.

Will nodded. "And I understand the dangers of oil. I know what to do to make it burn and to put it out. I can understand the risk. This bluet the elves are selling, no one knows how it's made. Enchanters know how to tap it to power magical devices, but we don't really understand it. What if there's a way to cause a runaway reaction? Could it explode? What circumstances could result in such a thing? Without knowing that, I don't know how to use it safely. Unless they share their secrets, or until we figure it out on our own, I won't have it in the house."

"Good luck finding out," said Oliver, his tone sarcastic.

Will's eyes lit on him. "What does that mean?"

"You're a cook, Dad. You have about as much chance of figuring that out as my friend Doug." The table fell silent, and Oliver looked up from his plate. "Did I say something wrong?"

Before anyone could reply, Will intervened, addressing Tiny directly. "I taught him to respect authority, and to consider the experience of the one speaking. Given that, he's right. I wouldn't know better than the town butcher. I can't fault his conclusion. He just doesn't have all the information he needs. In fact, neither do I."

Erisa spoke up. "Oliver, you need to be more respectful when you talk to your father, right or wrong."

The boy nodded. "Yes, Nana. Sorry, Dad." He glanced over at Tiny. "Do you use the new lamps at your house?"

Tiny nodded. "We do. They're very popular all over Terabinia." Then he asked, "What time do you get up? I was thinking about getting some exercise in the morning. Do you have time to practice with me before school?"

That caught Oliver's interest. "There's no school tomorrow. Can you teach me? I've never learned from a real warrior!"

The big man's eyes seemed to glow with malicious intent, and his laugh filled the room. Oliver wasn't sure what he found so funny.

CHAPTER 19

"Maybe I should delay opening the 'Goat," said Will, letting his nervousness show.

Tiny grinned. "Don't worry about it. We're just going to have some fun. I'll take good care of the boy."

"Yeah, Dad. We'll be fine," agreed Oliver.

Will looked at the two of them, then gave Tiny a hard stare. Tiny replied to his unspoken warning, "I won't forget my promise, and I won't hurt him. You know me better than that."

Once Will had finally left, he focused his attention fully on Oliver. "So, why don't you tell me what sort of things your dad has taught you already?"

Oliver listed them quickly. "Staff, spear, some wrestling and unarmed strikes, as well as sparring with sword and shield. We only use wooden weapons, though."

"And what do you think you most need to learn?"

"Sword and shield."

"Why?"

"Well, everyone needs to learn to box and wrestle, staff is good for travelers, and spear is important in the army, but only professional soldiers really need to learn the sword," said the boy.

Tiny nodded. "True enough. That's what you want to be, a soldier?"

"A wardsman."

"Your dad doesn't like that idea, does he?"

"No, sir." After a brief pause, he added, "But it's my life."

"I'm not judging your dream," said the big man. "Wardsmen don't live long and you're beholden to your sponsor, whether you agree with their morality or not. That's why I'd say becoming an Iron Knight would be better."

"They have the same problem, don't they?"

"What's that?"

Oliver took a deep breath. "They have to swear to a lord, and that lord swears to the queen. So they still have to abide by the morality of their superiors."

The big man went still, then replied, "I suppose that's true. I guess the trick is finding someone you can trust to follow."

"Well, Dad left Terabinia for a reason. So I'll probably trust that and look in Trendham."

Tiny sighed. "I guess I can't argue with that logic, but remember this: if you ever want a different opportunity, come find me in Cerria. I could probably get you into the Iron Knights too, if that's what you want."

Oliver tilted his head to one side. "Just how high-ranked are you?"

"High enough. You'll know when your dad is ready to talk." He walked over and began sorting through the practice swords that Will kept in a wooden storage chest under the back porch.

"If you're afraid to say, then it must be pretty high," suggested Oliver. Tiny shrugged. "You said Dad outranked you, so you must have gone up quite a bit after he left."

Tiny finished selecting two and tossed one to him. "Nice try. Now, show me your stance."

"Which one?"

Tiny smiled. "Good answer. What do you have?"

"Just a sword." Oliver moved to offer the big man a side profile, sword forward.

"What would change if you had a shield?" The young man turned, holding a pretend shield in the other hand and putting his shield side forward. The sword was now held back in reserve, ready for a retaliatory strike or sudden thrust. Tiny nodded, mildly impressed, then asked more questions. "What if you had a spear instead? What if you were in a line?"

"First or second line?" asked Oliver.

After fifteen minutes of question-and-answer, Tiny had to admit that Will had done a good job with Oliver's military education. The boy knew the basics of modern warfare, including formations and basic unit tactics. "You were obviously paying attention to what you were told," said Tiny. "What would you say is the biggest thing you lack?"

"Size?"

The big man laughed. "Hardly, and not for long. You're almost as big as some soldiers already. What else?"

"Experience. Dad says knowing is one thing, but you can't trust your knowledge until you've actually drilled in a line with men on either side of you."

"He's right. I was going to show you some of that, but it appears he's already taught you as much as you could hope to know without actually joining the army. Plus, if you really want to be a wardsman, you won't be fighting in formation that often anyway. Ready for some sparring?" Oliver nodded quickly. "Just swords then," said Tiny.

Their swords met with a wooden 'clack' and the first few passes were slow and basic, but things didn't remain slow for long. The big Terabinian steadily increased the speed and power of his blows, and while Oliver was exhilarated at first, fear gradually crept in as he realized that a missed block would likely result in a serious bruise— or worse. The Terabinian was good, and faster than he'd expected. Oliver's hand and arm began to ache from the shock of blocking his sword. Then it happened.

It was too fast for him to follow. He missed a block, and pain blossomed in his wrist. Before his weapon had even fallen from his hand, he was struck twice more, once in the stomach and again in the thigh. He found himself on the ground, blinking away tears as he tried to breathe.

"Not bad," pronounced Tiny. "Want to know what you did wrong?"
Oliver nodded an affirmative.
"You shouldn't have disrespected your father at the dinner table."
"Sir?"
The big man gave him a smile that was simultaneously friendly and frightful. "Do you think I'd dare to beat you like that in front of him?" When Oliver just stared back, he answered for him. "No. I wouldn't. And if anyone ever hits you that hard in training then you should suspect their motive. A good teacher doesn't deliberately injure their students. Let me see your wrist. Is it broken? If it is, I've got something for it." Together they moved Oliver's hand through its range of motion, then checked his stomach and thigh. "Damn, you're tough," said Tiny after a minute. "I really expected I'd have to use this." He held up a small vial before tucking it away. "I think we can continue, if you're up for it."

Oliver was already on his feet, stretching out his sore thigh. "What was in the vial?"

"Regeneration potion," said the big warrior. "Damned expensive, but better than risking what your dad would do to me if he came home and found you with a broken arm and bruises all over."

"Oh."

"I won't go that hard on you again. That was just a painful example to underscore what I want you to learn before we get started. Are you listening?" After Oliver nodded, he continued, "Your dad is an old friend of mine, but I'd never want to be on his bad side in a real fight. To be completely honest, he scares the shit out of me. I can see you look up to him, but it's clear to me that because of his silence, you don't have the respect for him you probably should have. Does that make sense?"

Oliver looked apologetic. "Not really?"

"I'll rephrase it then. Are you scared of me?"

"Yes, sir."

"Almost everyone is," agreed Tiny. "I'm not afraid of many people, but your dad would be one of them. So whatever you think about your old man, you should factor that into the equation. You ken me?"

"Ken?"

"Do you understand?"

"Yes, sir."

"And another thing. Yeah, your dad is a cook, but he's a lot more, and he likely knows more about just about everything than anyone you've ever met. In fact, I'm already considering whether it's safe to have elven lamps at home now, and my wife is one of the most powerful wizards in Terabinia."

Oliver frowned. "How high-ranked are you again?"

Tiny realized he'd made a mistake and coughed. "Let's get back to sparring."

From there, the practice went more like Oliver was used to with his father. Tiny pressed him, forcing him to work hard, but he didn't deliberately try to overwhelm him again. Occasionally, they would take breaks and the big warrior would point out things he could do better and places where he seemed to lack awareness.

"You've got real potential," said the Terabinian at last. "Learning early was definitely good for you, but you have natural talent as well. You do have some interesting blind spots, but I think that's probably because you've only trained with one person, and your dad, for all his gifts, has a rather unique fighting style. I don't think it translates well for you."

"Unique how?"

"I'm not at liberty to say, but if you train with a variety of different people, you'll eventually get a feel for what I mean. It will make more sense when he eventually opens up to you about his past."

"I'm so sick of hearing that," Oliver grumbled.

The big man nodded. "I'm just as sick of it. Not the secret part, obviously, but the self-exile part. I miss my friend."

Oliver's ears perked up. "Self-exile? He didn't have to leave?"

Tiny groaned. "And now I'm in trouble. Forget I said that." Oliver pestered him for a while, but the Terabinian refused to say more.

That evening, after Will returned from the Laughing Goat, he took Tiny away for a walk and a private chat. Oliver tried to follow them, not caring about the consequences, but he had to stay too far back. He lost sight of them around a corner, and when he caught up, they were nowhere to be seen.

***

Will laid a hand on Tiny's shoulder and teleported the two of them without warning. Tiny found himself in a dark space, but seconds later, lights appeared around the room, providing bright and steady illumination. Looking around, the big man surmised they were in some sort of antechamber with an archway ahead that led into a workshop of some sort. "I thought you didn't like elven lamps," observed Tiny, staring at the lights.

"Look again," said Will. "The lamps are the same, but they don't use bluet. They're enchanter's lamps. The principle is similar, but they don't have a fuel source. I have to provide the power each time I want them to work. There's a simple metal disk that holds a small store of turyn, but it will run down within an hour or two, unless I provide a fresh input."

"Oh," remarked Tiny. "Can I ask where we are?"

"You can ask," said Will, a smirk on his face. "But all I'll tell you is that no one knows, except me." In truth, they were underground, less than a mile from his home in Lystal. He'd excavated the first room immediately after the move to Trendham and had continued expanding ever since. At first, his complex of workshops had had an exterior entrance, kept well hidden, but even that was long gone. Now the only way to reach his hidden sanctum was via teleport. He had developed a variation on the large-scale beacon that the Wayfarer's Society had designed for cities and long-distance teleport. It allowed him to teleport to his workshop without first entering the astral plane and without visible line of sight, but its range was very limited. It only worked when he was within eleven or twelve miles of the beacon.

As far as he could imagine, there was no way anyone could ever find it without him deliberately showing them the beacon key or finding him through an astral connection. To preclude the latter, he'd warded the entire complex with a ward similar to the one he used when he slept at night.

The small beacon itself was disguised as one of the lamps in the antechamber. A magical device so simple (on the surface) that no self-respecting enchanter would bother giving it a second glance. Not that anyone uninvited would ever gain access in the first place. Will's paranoia had taken him far beyond the precautions most would call reasonable.

The first room beyond the antechamber housed a long row of benches and glassware. The equipment there was dedicated to the final stages of alchemical processing and refining. A hallway on the left led to a small warehouse containing supplies while a similar hall on the right led to a collection of vats for processing and fermenting a variety of products. It branched off to a separate set of rooms dedicated to metalwork and enchanting projects.

"So this is all some sort of secret lair?" observed Tiny. "How could you hide something this size? How did you find the time? From everything you've said, you spend most of your time pretending to be a cook."

Will gave him a hard look. "I take offense to that last part. I am *not* pretending to be a cook."

Tiny gave him a quick bow and a lopsided grin. "Please forgive the insult. That was thoughtless of me."

Will smirked. "Apology accepted. Come on, let me show you the rest of the place."

"Are you sure you should?" asked Tiny. "You've obviously gone to great lengths to keep this secret."

"Do you know where we are? Does anyone else? Do you know how I get here? There's secrets involved with that as well." He gave Tiny a flat stare. "Consider this my apology. I've never shown anyone else, even Sammy." Of course, that was partly because his cousin was also a wizard. He shared some of his research with her, and if she ever saw the beacon, and disassembled it, she might figure out the key. Tiny had a less than zero chance of ever finding the place on his own. Will said none of that, of course, since it would only be insulting.

"I guess I should be honored then," said Tiny dryly.

"I know it's small recompense for everything I held back in the old days, or even for the secrets I'm still keeping. But it's something, right?"

The big man rolled his eyes. "It's something."

"Let me give you the tour." Will led Tiny through the majority of the rooms, giving brief explanations of each. Near the end, he led his friend toward a bench in the first workshop, where he did most of his alchemical work.

Tiny stopped him. "You didn't show me where that leads. It looks important." The door in question was a massive set of double doors."

"It's not finished," said Will. "Currently it just leads to an empty room, but eventually I plan to create a separate complex of rooms centered around a main council chamber."

"Council chamber?"

He nodded. "I told you. I'm the First Wizard. I know it sounds like something I made up, but it's an ancient office, even if I'm currently the only one on the council. Eventually I intend to bring in the others."

"The others?"

"The other wizards—first, second, and third-order—all of them, from all over the world. There aren't many yet, but that will change with time. I'm not including non-wizards, or those who haven't completed a compression, but all the real wizards will be a part of the council, to some degree or another."

Tiny gaped at him. "You're serious?"

"Dead serious."

"What about Selene?"

"What about her?"

"Will she be a part of this as well?"

Will shook his head. "The council won't be beholden to any government or other sovereign powers. Its sole purpose will be to regulate the practice of magic and to protect humanity from the other powers that might threaten it. Did you know we still have a treaty with the fae? Without it they would be free to run amok in Hercynia."

"She's a wizard too," pointed out Tiny.

Will's eyes turned hard. "Technically she is a wizard, of sorts. But she isn't human. Previously I'd planned to appoint her as my successor, but that's off the table now."

"Off the table of your organization of one," said Tiny sarcastically.

Will shrugged. "Say what you will, but it's far older than anything else. Do you know who the first First Wizard was?" When Tiny simply stared, Will answered for him, "Grim Talek, and he had the decency to step down when he became a lich."

"Seems like you like him better than your wife."

He felt a flash of anger, but he suppressed it. "He's still a monster, but he had a purpose and he fulfilled it. His original crime is as bad as hers, but he *did* persist for millennia just so he could help rid us of the dragon's tyranny. Stepping down and leaving the council to the living was a mark of integrity, especially considering he'd decided to compromise every other principle he had for the sake of revenge. He's still on my list for removal, though."

"Why wait?" asked Tiny, his tone harsh.

"I'm a father," said Will. "I've made mistakes, but the big one that I've observed in many of the monsters I've fought is a single-minded obsession with some goal. They put everything else aside to achieve some end. As a human, and as a wizard, my first responsibility is to humanity, and family is a big part of that. I won't sacrifice Oliver's childhood for my vendetta. I'll raise him right and make my preparations in secret, for his sake as well as for the people's."

"The people of Trendham?"

"The people of Hercynia. I'm not a ruler of any nation, nor should I be. My duty is to this world, not some particular faction. Wizardry will be practiced in service to mankind, not for the pursuit of political power. That's my new purpose, and it will be the purpose of the council I rebuild—after I've raised my son."

Tiny waved a hand at Will. "Fine. I believe in your sincerity, even if I'm a little skeptical. Tell me about what you're actually doing here."

Will nodded. "Well as I said earlier, this area is mainly for late-stage alchemical processes—"

"You're making regeneration potions here?" He pulled a vial from a belt pouch at his side and waggled it between his fingers.

Will eyed the pouch. Unless he was mistaken, it was the original leather case he'd had made for his friend years ago. They had been standard issue for magical support officers, Iron Knights, and high-ranking officials ever since, though the current ones were professionally made and stamped with Terabinia's seal. The vial tucked between Tiny's overlarge fingers was much newer, however, for he recognized the glasswork. It was from a batch of potions he'd made after coming to Trendham. Glancing up, Will saw a hint of mirth in Tiny's eyes.

"I tried my damnedest to trace this back to you—without luck."

"Since I'm likely the only one producing them, I knew it was a risk," said Will. "I took a lot of precautions."

Tiny laughed. "Every batch seemed to come from a different place, and the original supplier in each case was always someone different, with no idea who it was they'd bought them from. The lengths you went to preserve your anonymity borders on obsession. If it hadn't been for the hospital you founded and the request for doctors from Wurthaven, I'd never have found the school here in Lystal."

Will shrugged. "I don't think I'd call it an obsession, since you just made it clear at least one person was looking for me."

"You still have contact with the trolls," said Tiny. "You realize that also puts you under suspicion for what happened in Terabinia."

He frowned. "You don't seriously think that, do you?"

"I don't think you'd do it on purpose. Maybe you made a mistake somehow? You showed up to haul our asses out of the fire just in the nick of time as well."

Will shook his head. "You've seen how careful I am, and I had to clean up the first troll mess. Those trolls were from a different tribe. Even their language was different."

"There were people with them," said Tiny. "Did you know that? Not captives, not food, but collaborators of some sort."

"I saw a few when I helped you," agreed Will.

"It was really hard to figure anything out about them, since they were completely incinerated. Some think that was too convenient."

"Are you trying to pick a fight with me?" asked Will. "You know damn well why Sammy and I incinerated everyone and everything on that field."

His old friend held up both hands. "I know that. I'm just letting you know what sort of dark rumors circulate in backrooms. We *did* identify the origin of some of those people, before you showed up to eliminate them."

"And?"

"They were Trendish."

"That makes absolutely no sense," replied Will. He rubbed his chin for a minute, then added, "Actually, it wouldn't make any sense no matter where they were from. No one has a motive for starting a troll apocalypse. It's insanity. It would be complete disaster for everyone."

Tiny nodded. "Assuming everyone is smart enough to know that, or that they aren't insane. But you're right, politically there's no sense in creating a doomsday scenario. That's why Selene ordered the origin of the perpetrators kept secret. Even so, we've stepped up our surveillance of the oligarchs as well as the border between Terabinia and Trendham."

"I can't fault you for that," said Will. When Tiny didn't stop staring at him, he asked, "What?"

"Do you know anything?"

"No. Why? You've seen how I live. I'm not even remotely political."

"You must have some contacts with the government here."

Will sighed. "I've met with the various oligarchs only two or three times each. None of them can contact me, nor have they seen my face. I show up, make a few demands, and disappear. That's the extent of my relationship with the powerful in Trendham. Any more than that and they would have to know more about me, and I'm not about to get drawn into their political intrigues."

Tiny seemed to deflate. "Damn. I was really hoping you might know something, or at least be able to give us a lead to follow."

"Sorry," said Will. "Not that it helps, but if I *did* have any knowledge, the perpetrator would be dead already." After a moment, he went on, "Let me show you what I'm doing here. We've gotten sidetracked. Recognize this?" He held up a sample that had been lying on the benchtop.

"Bluet."

Will nodded. "I've spent some of my spare time trying to figure it out, though without much success."

"If it helps, I'm sure there's an entire department at Wurthaven trying to figure out the same thing," remarked Tiny. "The secret to making it would be worth a fortune."

"I'm not surprised," said Will. "It contains more turyn than a turyn elixir, yet it's formed into a solid matrix, and it doesn't seem to be combustible or explosive. At a glance, it seems like the perfect storage medium for concentrated energy."

"But you still don't trust it."

Will grinned. "Not in the slightest. Since I can't seem to figure out how it's made, I've been trying to figure out how to unmake it."

"Unmake it? Just stick it in one of those lamps."

Will shook his head. "No, not like that. I'm trying to figure out if it's unstable in some way. Everything breaks down. Most things will oxidize or burn. Even gold can be dissolved by the appropriate acid, but so far, I haven't found anything that will react with bluet. Well, except for one thing." He pointed to a metal box at one end of the table. "Let me show you the latest sample I put in there, but close your eyes before I open the box."

"Why?"

"There's a forbidden type of ward inside the box. It's mostly safe, as long as you don't look at it or observe it in any way."

"That doesn't make any sense, and why is it forbidden?"

"It cuts reality into separate pieces, which would be fine by itself, but the boundaries create an interface with the void, the empty place outside our existence. Looking at it risks your sanity, and it can bring unnatural creatures into our world."

Tiny felt a cold shiver run up his spine. "That sounds like something you shouldn't be messing with."

Will nodded agreeably. "You're right. I originally used it to try and eliminate Grim Talek. I'm still suffering from some side effects. But, that's precisely why I'm very careful not to observe the ward boundaries now, even in small experiments. Turn around and close your eyes." As soon as his friend had turned his back, Will closed his own eyes and opened the box. Operating on feel alone, he found the button that deactivated the ward, then removed something small from the box and closed it again. "You can open your eyes now, it's safe."

Tiny turned around, gingerly cracking one eye open. "You're sure?" Then he focused on the glass bowl in Will's hand. It contained a greyish black powder of some sort. "What's that?"

"As far as I can tell, it's essentially very similar to soot."

"Like soot from a fire?"

"Mostly carbon, but it also has a tiny fraction of oil or fat, which you wouldn't see with real soot, but essentially it's all organic matter."

"You mean it was alive?"

Will shook his head. "No, I mean it in the chemical sense, although it *could* have been produced by the decomposition of something alive. Given the catalyst for its decomposition, it could be tempting to think it might have been alive in some fashion."

"Will, I know nothing of magic, or alchemy. Can you explain it without referring to cats or cysts?"

He couldn't help but chuckle. "The word was catalyst, but it just means something that triggers or enables a reaction. In this case, it was a negative catalyst, the lack of access to the astral plane caused the bluet to break down."

"Uh huh…"

Will continued, "There are two planes that are fully contiguous with our own, the ethereal, and the astral. The ethereal is entirely physical, while the astral is non-physical and non-local. It's a plane with only one dimension, that of the mind. For some reason, bluet loses stability when isolated from the astral plane."

Tiny nodded sagely. "Of course! And naturally that means...?" He waved his hand in a rolling motion, hoping Will would finish the sentence for him.

"I've no clue," admitted Will.

Tiny deflated, exhaling loudly. "You built the tension up just to tell me you don't know?"

Will smiled. "Don't underestimate yourself. It's possible that with a good explanation you might have an idea that hasn't occurred to me. Also, you can share this information with Janice. She might also have some insight."

"I doubt I'll be able to explain it adequately," said Tiny.

Reaching out with one hand, Will tapped a small notebook. "I've written up an exhaustive report. Take it back with you. If I'm not mistaken, your wife will be very interested to read it."

Tiny scratched his beard. "I think you underestimate how busy she is. She's essentially running Terabinia half the time."

"She'll want to read this," said Will confidently.

"Despite what you seem to assume, the queen and quite a few others at Wurthaven have done a lot of testing. This probably isn't news to them."

"They don't know about this."

"You seem very sure of that. How do you know?"

Will made no attempt to hide his smugness. "Because if they had known this, they wouldn't have allowed bluet to be freely traded in Terabinia."

"You haven't shown that it's dangerous. In fact, you already admitted it seems to be safer than you expected. You just don't understand how it works."

"I said I have no clue, but that doesn't mean I don't have some suspicions. If it requires access to the astral plane, then bluet might be conscious in some way. Or it might be an advanced tool for eavesdropping. I know it isn't produced alchemically, and it isn't a product of enchanting, but if it needs the astral then there's a high chance that it's able to transmit information in some fashion."

The Terabinian marshal's eyes widened. "You think the elves are spying with it?"

Will shrugged. "I didn't say that. I honestly don't know. It wouldn't make sense to try and eavesdrop on every trader, farmer, and craftsman in Terabinia and Trendham, *if* that's what it's being used for. As far as I know, the astral requirement could be a byproduct of how it's manufactured. Maybe the elves have special magical cows that shit bluet and remain linked to it in some way. It might be something completely innocuous. But I'm not allowing it in my home until I know the truth. It probably isn't something most people should worry about, but I'm sure a powerful monarch would want to know."

Tiny nodded. "Did you tell the oligarchs?"

Will lifted one hand, ticking off fingers one by one. "Lentam, Marlow, Coires, Blathe, and Pummen—none of them seemed interested in my warning. They don't trust me, and I can't say I blame them. No one likes finding a stranger in their bedroom at night."

The big man rolled his eyes. "You broke into their homes? No wonder. All this time and you haven't created any trust with them at all. I know you're antisocial, but I thought you understood diplomacy better than that."

Will didn't really care, and he let it show in his expression. "I'm not here to rule or exert power, political or otherwise. I chose my method of contact precisely so they couldn't make requests or demands of me—*and* to let them know I can reach them whenever and wherever they are. I never wanted to make friends. I wanted to be left alone. For that purpose, a little fear is better than diplomacy."

Tiny studied his face, then observed, "You've really changed. The Will I met in a jail cell years ago in Branscombe wouldn't recognize you at all."

"Back then I didn't understand much about this world."

"Back then you had hope," countered Tiny. "We all get a little jaded with age, but it's important to have hope, otherwise what's the point?"

Will's expression darkened. "I don't need hope, I have the present, that's enough. Rather than wishing and dreaming, I make the world what I want it to be. My family is sheltered and fed, my son is safe, and I have contingencies to protect them in every worst-case scenario I can imagine. I might be more cynical these days, but my goals are still largely the same. I work to protect humanity from horrors they don't even know exist."

"Preparing for the worst is important, but we also need hope. Hope prepares us to make the most of the good we didn't expect—"

"My hope died on a ritual altar while I was trying to kill a dragon," said Will, cutting him off. "You can lecture me about it when the day comes that your wife turns into an immortal monster who steals other people's bodies so she can pretend she's still human."

Tiny's cheeks flushed, but he held his tongue. Picking up the journal Will had shown him, he tucked it under his arm. "Is there anything else you want me to take back?"

"Actually, you can answer a question," said Will. "That demon-steel golem you were using against the trolls—where did it come from? I didn't think there was enough of the metal left after the first one was lost in Lognion's nest."

"Selene got it back," said Tiny.

"The nest's dimension was locked."

Tiny shrugged. "She told Jan it was keyed to her blood."

Except her blood was no longer the same, thought Will. *Obviously, she made good use of her corpse.* He frowned, thinking about the thousands of elementals that had been trapped there with the dragon's body. *I bet she didn't free them either.*

Tiny glared at him. "I don't like the look on your face."

Will looked up. "I was just thinking about all the elementals that were there."

"I'm sworn to protect the queen," growled Tiny. "Remember that." When Will's expression didn't change, he spoke again. "Half the time the person wearing the queen's face is my wife. If you don't care about anything else, at least remember that—please."

Surprised, Will forgot about his anger. "What?"

"She still likes to wander off and disguise herself as other people," explained Tiny. "Just like when you met her, except now she can just change how she looks. She's gotten good enough to transform Jan's face as well, so no one knows when she's gone."

"How does she rule like that?" asked Will.

"They use those enchanted tablets that Grim Talek taught you, though they hardly need them. She trusts my wife to make most decisions on her own."

Will stared blankly at him. "That's—I never expected that. How long does—that must get weird."

The big man nodded. "Tell me about it. I feel strange kissing a different face, but I've gotten used to it."

"Oh." Will frowned again. "I didn't need to hear that." He took a moment to clear his mind of the image. "Where does she go?"

"I've no idea usually, but there are new rumors regarding the Mother. Jan and I were talking about it a while back. It seems pretty likely that it's because of Selene's excursions," said Tiny.

"What rumors?"

"Miracles and the like. A stranger arrives and someone's child spontaneously recovers from an injury or deadly illness. Some of it is simply random acts of charity, but the healing seems too unlikely to be anyone else."

"You think she's deliberately impersonating Temarah?"

Tiny shrugged. "Doubtful, but she likes to be anonymous, and miracles lend themselves to being attributed to the Mother. Who else would be doing it?"

"Grim Talek is certainly capable," noted Will, "but it sounds like Selene."

"I'd hesitate to give the lich credit for anything good," said Tiny sourly. "We haven't seen him since you left, so he could be anywhere—or anyone."

CHAPTER 20

Despite Will's initial insistence that Tiny would only be welcome for one night, by unspoken agreement his old friend stayed for a second night before leaving the next morning. When he left, their goodbye was bittersweet.

Will had worried that Tiny's appearance would presage the arrival of more unwelcome intrusions, or a total loss of privacy, but nothing of the sort happened. His life returned to normal, and the months went by without interruption. A few years passed and Oliver was nearing his fifteenth birthday when a new sickness came to Trendham.

In truth it was an old disease, but one that hadn't been seen in more than two centuries, Redweep Fever. The illness got its name from the fact it caused the whites of the eyes to turn red in many victims, accompanied by pink or brown secretions as blood leaked into the tear ducts. That and the fact that many cried from the pain of the illness. The disease disfigured some and caused permanent blindness in the worst cases, if the patient didn't die outright.

The outbreak hit Darrow and Terabinia in the winter, before spreading to Trendham in the spring. In the span of just a few short weeks, one out of three people fell sick and virtually everything ground to a halt. Generally, if one person got sick, everyone in the home got sick. The only safety to be found was in isolation, so households without anyone sick avoided contact with those that were.

The illness took roughly two weeks to clear, and though most could survive, the fact that everyone in a home would catch it meant that in many cases there were no caregivers. Many of the ill died from simple lack of care while healthy neighbors hid in their homes.

Erisa had already earned a reputation in Lystal. Though she no longer practiced as a midwife, she'd sold herbs and given enough advice that their neighbors naturally looked to her for assistance with minor ailments. Because of that, she was one of the first exposed, before news of the outbreak in Terabinia had reached their ears.

Oliver began showing signs two days later, and Will's fever started a day after that. Within a day, all three were incapacitated, and it was all

Will could do just to rise long enough to relieve his bladder and make sure everyone had water close at hand.

By the third day, Will began hallucinating and at that point he was no longer sure if he'd had anything to drink or not. When he was conscious, all he could think about was the throbbing pain in his joints as he shivered beneath his blankets.

He awoke at some point to see a black-bearded man leaning over him. "You look piss poor," said a gruff voice. "You're not supposed to sleep on the floor."

Will hurt too much to care, but as his head rolled to one side, he realized he was indeed lying on the cold wood floor of the main room. An overturned pitcher sat a few feet away. *Must have dropped it trying to get water,* he mused silently. Intense pain followed, and when it faded, he realized the stranger had moved him back to his bedroom. As miserable as he was, he managed to accept a drink of water as the stranger supported his head, but he drifted off again before long. His dreams were foggy and disorganized, but at one point he heard a woman weeping. *I must be dying,* he thought, and he felt bad for making the woman cry, though he wasn't sure who it was.

A cool sensation on his brow made him open his eyes sometime later, and Will saw the stranger sitting on the edge of his bed with a cloth and a bowl of water. The stranger looked to be a woman now, and Will couldn't help but mutter, "You shaved."

Her voice found his ears, and she sounded amused. "Shaved?"

"You had a beard. The thickest blackest beard I've ever seen, like a heavy wool blanket," he murmured.

"You really know how to make a girl feel attractive," she answered, smiling faintly.

"It was a beautiful beard," said Will honestly. "It would take me years to grow one like that, and I'm not sure it would be half as thick." With his hands, he felt the covers and asked, "Did you make this blanket out of it?" His caretaker laughed, and he suddenly recognized her face. "Cora?"

"I'm surprised you recognized me without my beard," she replied.

He frowned. "Oliver? Is Olly all right?"

"Your son is recovering. He's doing better than you, though he'll probably be in bed for a few more days. Erisa is getting better too. She must have gotten sick first, I'm guessing."

Will blinked, and moisture ran from the corner of his eyes as a feeling of gratitude swept over him. He'd been so sick he had forgotten them. Guilt followed seconds later. They might have died if it hadn't been for the kindness of a stranger. "I'm sorry," he mumbled, blinking again. "If you weren't here—I might have lost them."

Cora's expression was unreadable, though that was in part because his vision was so blurry. Eventually she replied, "You might have lost *you*. Don't blame yourself. You're only human. They'll be just as glad you survived."

"My responsibility," said Will softly. His voice felt strange and gravelly. When his eyes traveled to the bedside table, Cora noticed, and before he could ask, she lifted a cup of water to his lips. After a few swallows, she put it back, then leaned over and brushed cool lips against his feverish forehead.

Then she leaned back and scrunched up her nose in look of disapproval. "Stop trying to take everything onto yourself." She rose and stepped across the room to refill the cup from a pitcher on the table by his bedroom door.

The expression and the words reminded him of another woman from another time, and his eyes began to well again. Will rolled his head to either side, using the pillow to dry his cheeks and hoping she hadn't noticed. Cora was walking back toward him when a fresh realization struck him. "You shouldn't be here. You'll get sick."

She smiled, shaking her head. "I had it more than a month ago, while I was in Edal. It hit Faresh before it even got to Terabinia. Trendham is just the latest, although I don't think it's burned through Barsta or Shimera yet as far as I know."

"While you were in a foreign city? That must have been hard."

Cora laughed. "You forget, the road is my home. The fever was bad but luckily, I had Durin there to help me through the worst of it."

"Durin?"

"My friend, the one with the beard that so impressed you. He joined me when I went through Delgath last year," she explained.

"Oh." Will felt oddly disappointed. *I should have expected it, though. She's young and bright. No reason she shouldn't find someone.* "What brought you here? How did you find my home?"

She sat down on the edge of the bed as she answered, "The man at the Laughing Goat told me, though he had to shout directions through the door. Apparently, he locked and barred the door as soon as people started getting sick, which isn't a bad strategy for avoiding it I suppose."

"Why were you looking for me?"

Cora gave him a sour look. "You left me a little frustrated last time. I had this silly idea that if I visited and didn't drink anything, I might be able to get you to scratch this itch I have."

Will's mind was still moving slowly. "Itch?" He understood a second later when she winked at him. "Oh!" Then he added, "I thought you were angry. You said I wouldn't see you again."

She laughed. "I was drunk, and that was years ago. Although now I'm half wondering if you got sick just to keep me at bay." Her eyes narrowed, and her mouth formed a sly, predatory grin.

He did his best to come up with a clever response. "I've learned a lot of tricks to protect myself, otherwise the widows in this town would drain me dry."

Cora flashed a smile. "Widows? I think you've mixed up your age, scullery boy. You're still young enough to catch the eyes of young maidens, never mind the next generation."

Will started to laugh, began to cough, and wound up hacking up something dark. Cora lifted a bucket for him before he needed it. She'd obviously faced similar problems already, and he wondered what she might have had to deal with over the previous day or two. He would have been embarrassed, but he didn't have the strength for it.

Pain shot through his chest as he coughed, growing more severe by the moment as each cough triggered another. Will had survived numerous painful events in the past, but the lengthy, debilitating weakness that came from his prolonged fever made it difficult to accept the pain with any degree of dignity. Slowly, he curled into a ball, squeezing his arms tightly around his chest as he tried to stop the painful spasms.

It took him a moment, as the coughing finally let up, for him to realize that it wasn't just his own arms holding him. Cora had slid closer, wrapping her own arms around his and squeezing firmly but gently. It was a gesture with little value, as far as his pain went, but it brought him comfort far beyond that. As he grew still, she brought a cool cloth up to wipe his face, and Will's vision grew blurry once more. "I wish you didn't have to see me like this," he mumbled.

"Like what?"

"Weak, sick—I must smell bad too."

"Stop trying to imagine what I'm thinking. You smell fine. You had a bath yesterday."

"I did?"

She nodded. "You complained the whole time, but I guess you don't remember. Your fever was bad."

He sniffed himself and didn't notice any odors, but he couldn't be sure his nose was working. A glance under the covers showed him he was undressed, though. "Thank you. I'm sorry you had—"

"Shhh," she told him, "that's enough of that. You're the strongest man I know, but you're only human. I won't listen to any apologies."

Will met her eyes, which were strong and steady. "You hardly know me."

Cora blinked, glanced away, then returned her gaze to him. "I'm a good judge of people. You might have a good eye for vegetables, kitchen boy, but I know how to spot a strong heart."

"Last time you told me you always pick bad men," he returned.

"Just because I can spot a good one doesn't mean I make good choices," she replied, chuckling. "Besides, the more I learn about you, and your secrets, the more I think that you might be dangerous, even if you aren't necessarily bad." Will was getting tired, but his heart jumped at that statement. *What did she find?* Before he could protest, she continued, "Who keeps so many weapons in their home? A lot of people keep a few in the attic, or locked up in the basement, but your son had three swords and a spear in his room while your mother had a long knife and a smallsword."

"Even my neighbors keep—"

She rolled her eyes. "Don't start making up stories. I know better. I'm sure some of your neighbors have an axe or a hayfork kept close at hand. Some might have a spear or even a sword tucked away, but I don't know of any who have practice dummies and padded gambesons. Are you training soldiers in your back yard?"

"Just Oliver."

Her eyes softened. "You really love him, don't you?"

The tone was kind, but he didn't like the phrasing. "Of course I do. He's my son."

Cora didn't mince words. "He doesn't really look like you, though."

"Family isn't about looks. I raised him; I loved him. He's my son and I'll—" Will's words cut off as he began to cough and hack once more.

Her arms went around him again as he struggled to get his lungs back under control. "I'm sorry. I shouldn't upset you. I just let my curiosity run away with me sometimes. Anyone can see you love your son. You're a hundred times better father than I ever had."

Will nodded, still trying to stop coughing. Eventually his chest calmed, and he rolled onto his side. Tired and dizzy, he drifted into a doze. Sometime later, he woke and felt an arm around his stomach. Turning his head, he saw that Cora had curled up behind him. Unsure what to make of that, he put his head back down and closed his eyes, but a short while later he felt her arm tighten and her body began softly shaking.

At first, he thought he might be imagining it, but at last he was sure. Cora was quietly crying, though she was doing her best not to wake him. She said something, but it was too soft for him to hear, so he adjusted the sensitivity of his ears. When she spoke again, he caught her words. "Please don't die."

"I won't," he answered. Her body stiffened and she started to pull away, but Will caught her arm. "Don't go. Please." She reversed course, and her arm tightened around him until it was almost painful, but he didn't complain. His body was still a symphony of misery, but his heart was more at peace than at any time in recent memory. Will's breathing relaxed, and soon he was asleep again.

When consciousness found him again, he was lying on his other side and Cora was gone. He had to pee, and as he remembered his nakedness, he wondered if she had left to spare him some embarrassment. Carefully, Will eased himself into a sitting position and displaced the cat that had gone unnoticed beneath the blankets. Yellow-green eyes blinked slowly at him, and Will stared back in confusion. "Evie?" Then he realized she had been laying precisely where Cora had fallen asleep, and his eyes grew wide. "Cora?"

The door opened, and a broad-shouldered man entered with a wood platter that carried a collection of eggs, sausage, and a small bowl from which steam was rising. "You're awake," said the stranger, speaking through a black curtain that Will now saw was a well-combed beard of impressive length. "I didn't notice you had a cat." The man's face was coarse, and his nose was large. His irises were so dark that they blended in with his pupils, giving the impression of two pieces of black coal staring at Will's waist. "You must really like that cat."

Evie chose that moment to break into loud purring and stood up to rub her head and shoulder against his stomach. Will grabbed the blanket and recovered himself, making a thick barrier between his hips and the cat. "She's not an ordinary cat," he sputtered.

The man's face showed little emotion. "Sure, sure. I bet she likes sausage, though, doesn't she?" Will had no idea how to respond to that, but a second later the stranger lifted something from the breakfast tray. "Want some, kitty?" Will was already turning red when he realized his mistake, and at the same time he noticed the stranger was uncommonly short.

Evie stared at the sausage with some interest, but made no move to leave Will's side. Then Cora's head appeared in the doorway as she looked over the bearded man's shoulder with ease. "Don't tease him, Durin."

The man, who Will now understood was a dwarf, shrugged and set the tray down on the table by the door, then backed out. Cora didn't enter, but she did smile as she closed the door. "The chamber pot's empty. Let me know when you're done."

He stared at the door for a full minute before pushing the covers back and trying to stand up, whereupon he promptly sat back down again. His balance was shot, and that was before the dizziness made itself known. Will sat at the edge of the bed, waiting for the room to stop moving.

When things had finally calmed down, he reached under the bed and pulled out the clay pot, which he was glad to see was clean. *How many days have I been in this bed?* he wondered. Will was no stranger to caring for sick people. He didn't remember much, but he guessed that he must have been sick for at least three or four days. His eyes went to the interior of the chamber pot once more. It was completely clean and dry.

Turning, he looked at the sheets and other bedding. They were also relatively clean. It was almost certain that someone had helped him to relieve himself. That someone had also emptied and washed the chamber pot, changed his bedding, removed his clothing, and bathed him. Given his size relative to Cora, he imagined she must have had help. Although she was strong for her size, it would have been difficult moving him by herself.

Of course, there were tricks to moving patients, and Will had seen his mother manage large men before, but even so, Cora had surely needed some help. Will tried to put the thought out of his mind. When he took care of others, he tried to keep from embarrassing them, but as the patient, he found it difficult to feel the same nonchalance. The past few days had to have been the least romantic introduction to his personal life he could imagine.

Bracing himself, he got up, and this time he stayed on his feet, though he still swayed a bit while relieving himself. Evie stared at him the entire time. "Do you have to watch?" he asked. Her only answer was to continue staring. Will tried to pretend she was an ordinary cat.

Once he was back in the bed, Will slid his perspective slightly out of his body so he could communicate with Evie directly. The only other option would have been for her to physically transform so that she could speak, and the demigod obviously didn't feel the need.

How long have you been here? he asked.

A week. I came when I realized you were dying, answered the Cath Bawlg.

Will frowned. *Did you take care of me?*

No. Your mate was here, so I simply observed.

She's not my mate, Will corrected.

The cat's expression didn't change, but Will felt the mental equivalent of a shrug. *If you say so.*

He narrowed his eyes. *What does that mean?*

Humans are fools. She has bonded to you. I can smell it.

That's not how people work, Will insisted. *I've only met her once before. And besides, you can't smell relationships between people.*

I can. Otherwise, I would have killed her rather than allow her near you while you were vulnerable.

Will blanched at the thought. *I appreciate the sentiment, but I'd rather you not kill people simply because they might be a threat.*

I can smell the difference, responded Evie with a certain amount of arrogance.

The door opened again, and Oliver came in. "Dad? How are you?" Will's son looked unsteady, and the whites of his eyes were brown in spots where they had bled during the course of his illness. Even so, he was obviously farther down the road to recovery than Will was.

Will opened his arms, and Oliver sat down to give his father a long hug.

CHAPTER 21

Erisa joined them not long after, and it was apparent that she was almost as far along in her recovery from the Redweep Fever as Oliver was. Will had been the last to catch it, and it looked as though he would be the last to get over it as well. He was stuck in bed while Oliver and Erisa started resuming a more normal routine.

He couldn't complain, though. The odds were good that all three of them would have died without Cora and Durin's timely assistance. Although Evie probably would have found a way to help them if Cora hadn't been there.

Durin had been doing the cooking, and now that Will's fever was dropping and his memory seemed to be working, he came to understand he was probably better off not remembering. The dwarf's meals left a lot to be desired, and seasoning seemed to be a foreign language for Cora's short but stout companion. Thankfully, Erisa began helping that evening, and the quality of the meals improved dramatically.

It seemed that Cora knew next to nothing about cooking herself, and if she'd been reliant on Durin for her meals, Will felt sorry for her. He wanted to ask, but he didn't want to insult either of his saviors and seem ungrateful. His strength seemed to be returning, and Will hoped he would have the stamina to cook the next day. If he couldn't *say* anything, perhaps his cooking could speak for itself, either as a reward for Cora, or as an example for Durin in the future.

Will was alert enough that he woke immediately when Cora snuck into his bed that night, and this time, he made a point of scooting over to make a place for her. She said nothing, but she seemed to acknowledge his wakefulness by putting her back to him and being the small spoon. Will could hear a soft sigh from her as his arm went around her midsection and she eased back toward him.

His fatigue temporarily vanished, and Will felt a familiar stirring begin. Cora's warmth, the scent of her hair, and the softness of her body awakened urges he'd been ignoring since their last meeting. His arm tightened around her waist, pulling her more tightly against him, but Cora turned slightly and pulled away. "You're not well enough yet."

"I think I am," Will replied earnestly, though he was beginning to feel short of breath already.

"Roll over," she told him. "You'll have to be the little spoon." He groaned in frustration but rolled and put his back toward her. Despite his reluctance, his energy was already quickly waning, but his heart jumped when she whispered into his ear, "You wouldn't survive what I would do to you, but when you're actually recovered, I'll take you up on that offer."

"Only if you're sober," joked Will.

She slapped his rear and growled. "You are the most frustrating man. Sleep and get better. We'll *both* be happier then."

It took him a while to fall asleep, but when he did, he was welcomed by a warm oblivion without dreams. When he opened his eyes, he felt more rested than he'd been in a long time, though his body was still weak when he sat up. It felt as though the night had passed in an instant, and he was now alone in the bed. The smell of bacon was coming from the other side of the door, however, urging him to investigate.

Weak as a kitten, he nevertheless managed to pull on some trousers and a loose-fitting linen shirt. That alone felt like a victory, and he smiled as he opened the bedroom door. Oliver was sitting in the main room, with a basket of peas between his legs. Shelling peas was a common chore that Erisa often gave him. Oliver grinned when he saw his father. "You're up!"

Will nodded and answered, "I am." He was already breathing heavily, as though he'd run a lap around the house.

Erisa looked in from the kitchen. "There's breakfast if you feel up to sitting at the table."

"I do," said Will, his eyes roaming as he shuffled over. He had yet to see any sign of Cora or Durin.

His mother answered his unspoken question as she returned to put a plate in front of him. "They left just after dawn."

Will's heart fell into his stomach, lessening his appetite. "Oh," he said simply, trying to hide his disappointment.

Erisa watched him closely, then sighed. "You don't need to pretend for my sake. I can already see you miss her."

He shrugged. "I hardly know her. I only met her once before and—"

"And she slept in your bed every night while she was here, as best I can tell," said his mother, cutting him off.

"If she did, I was too sick to know it," groused Will.

Erisa nodded. "I see. Maybe I was wrong to assume. So you two aren't close?"

"I met her briefly a few years ago. She came to the 'Goat when I was looking for information about Sammy, back when we weren't really talking."

"That's it?"

Will did his best to sound sincere. "Yes."

"Why did she come by our house then?"

He shrugged. "She's a good person. She probably just decided to check on us while she was passing through, what with the sickness going around."

"That makes sense," agreed Erisa. She rose from her seat, and Will heard a rustling as she started to walk away. There was a folded piece of paper in one of her hands that he hadn't noticed before. "No need in showing you this then, I suppose."

Will sat up in his chair. "What's that?"

"Nothing. Just some scribbling from a stranger. I'll just throw it on the fire."

"She left a note?" Will's voice pitched noticeably higher, giving away his interest.

His mother's deadpan expression was flawless. "She did, but I'm sure it wouldn't interest you."

Will looked past his mother as she turned to walk away. Through the doorway he could see Oliver still shelling peas, but the boy's eyes were looking out the front windows. With a thought, Will reflex cast a minor telekinetic spell, snatching the letter from Erisa's grasp and bringing it fluttering through the air to his hand. She gave him a look of surprise, opening her mouth as though she would protest, but Will put a finger to his lips then pointed toward Oliver.

"I knew you were lying," declared Erisa.

With absolutely no shame, Will ignored her remark and began reading with obvious interest. When Erisa walked over and tried to look over his shoulder, he held the letter closer, using his body to block her view.

> *Will,*
>
> *I should have told you I was leaving last night, but I'm terrible with farewells. I hadn't intended on staying in Lystal for so long and I'm behind on my schedule. I hope you aren't too disappointed. Please be well and stay healthy. Maybe the next time we meet we can finally settle accounts with one another. Although Lystal isn't part of the most profitable route for me, I've decided to make it a regular stop. Can you guess why?*
>
> *Before you get too excited, though, being a regular stop just means I'll pass through once every year or two.*

That's a long time, so I have no expectations, but if you're still interested in having a glass of wine whenever I come through, I'll make sure I don't overdo it next time.

I enjoyed meeting your family and I hope next time I can visit with them under more normal circumstances. I don't know what else to say so I'll end this here.

~Cora

"She was pretty enough, but it's probably for the best that she doesn't want to settle down with you," said Erisa with a deadpan expression. She'd managed to find an angle from which she could read his letter.

Will gave her a sour look as he folded up the letter. "So you've given up on convincing me to produce a few more grandchildren?"

Erisa laughed. "No chance of that, but her cooking leaves a lot to be desired."

"Did she cook?"

"No, as far as I can tell Durin did all the cooking."

Ordinarily he would be the first to criticize poor food, but instead Will immediately felt defensive for Cora, which he suspected was his mother's true goal; she wanted to goad him into admitting his feelings. "His food was bad, of that there's no doubt. I wonder what dwarves eat normally, since it seemed like he had no taste for salt, spice or flavor."

"She must be even worse if she was willing to let him cook for her as well."

In spite of himself, Will found his teeth beginning to grind. "Or maybe she was too kind to criticize him."

His mother's expression turned smug. "You really do fancy her, don't you?"

"I didn't say that."

"Hah! My sweet son, for all your talents, there are two things you've never been very good at. One is lying, and the other is being diplomatic about other people's cooking."

Will narrowed his eyes, then looked away. "I'm not that bad."

"Bad would be an understatement. You're positively rude. It's a miracle you put up with my food, and I raised you!"

"You're a good cook," he protested, but internally he couldn't help but think about the fact that his mother had improved quite a bit since they'd been living in Trendham. He'd had plenty of opportunities over the years to make suggestions, and his mother wasn't too stubborn to learn a few new tricks.

His mother watched him for several seconds, then grinned. "I bet I'd be offended if I could hear what you were just thinking."

"I'm not going to respond to that."

Erisa laughed again. "You have gotten better at holding your tongue, when necessary, though. Anyway, that aside, I found out what I wanted to know."

"Which is?"

"You really like the girl."

"I already told you, I hardly know her."

"You say that, but my eyes aren't that easy to fool. I haven't seen you look at a woman like that since…" Erisa let her sentence trail off, regretting her choice of words. She took a breath and pushed on. "Anyway, she was giving you the eye too, so I'm left with one big question."

Will ignored the bait.

"I'm left with one big question," repeated his mother.

He sighed and gave in. "Goodness, Mom, what question?"

Leaning closer, she poked him in the chest. "Why did you let her leave?"

Will gaped at his mother. "I didn't even know she was leaving. She snuck off without telling me." He shook the letter with one hand. "Weren't you reading over my shoulder?"

She waved her hand dismissively. "Did you make your feelings clear? Did you let her know there's a place here for her?"

"She has her own life, Mom. She's a trader."

"And she thinks you're a kitchen helper. She probably thinks you can't afford another mouth to feed."

"Cora is very perceptive. I'm sure she made note of our home. She knows we aren't struggling," said Will.

"You *assume*," replied Erisa.

"I'm sure that's not the issue."

"Maybe, but if she knew just how much you could afford, I don't think she'd be so anxious to travel all over Hercynia chasing coin."

"Can we afford a horse?" asked Oliver. He'd wandered in without either of them noticing.

Will gave his mother a dark stare as he answered, "No, Olly, we can't afford a horse. What would you do with one?"

"Oh." Oliver deflated. "I didn't really want one anyway. *But,* if we did have a horse, Cora would definitely know you could afford her. Right?"

Will rubbed his face. "Women aren't commodities, Oliver."

"Commodi—what?" asked his son.

"Commodities," repeated Will. "Things you buy and sell. Like horses, or beans."

"I wasn't the one in here talking about how she left because we couldn't afford her, or whatever," said Oliver.

Erisa broke in, "Your father's right, Olly. Women aren't for sale; *however,* they do look for a man who can provide for a family. Money is a good indicator of that."

"What are you teaching him?" asked Will.

His mother was unapologetic. "The truth. He needs to know these things if he's going to find a wife. The Mother knows he's probably my only chance at seeing more children around here since you're completely hopeless."

Oliver's face took on a funny expression, and he turned around as if to leave. "Since I'm not needed here, I'll just…"

Erisa caught the back of his belt. "Nana has a few coins saved up, Olly." When he looked back, she winked at him. "When you're older, you find a good wife and give me some great grandchildren and your Nana will buy you that horse."

The boy stopped trying to pull away. "I think I could probably get married sooner if I had a horse now."

Will's mother laughed at him. "Are you trying to pull one over on your Nana?"

Olly gave Will a sly grin, then answered, "Never. I love you, Nana."

Will rolled his eyes.

CHAPTER 22

The 'Red Plague,' as it came to be known afterward, passed into history, but not without leaving scars in the memory of the survivors. Over the course of a year, no nation in Hercynia escaped untouched, and millions died in the wake of the Redweep Fever. Fortunately, the disease was somewhat self-limiting. It spread quickly, burning through populations so fast that before long there weren't enough new hosts to catch it. Those who'd had it once didn't catch it again, and with proper care most who caught it survived.

It was the initial wave that proved most fatal, when there were no experienced survivors to care for the sick. Those who fell ill during the first wave suffered a high mortality rate, and often more than a third died. As a result, the population of Trendham declined by more than five percent that year. Terabinia did slightly better, thanks to the reforms made by Queen Selene, but the death toll was still high.

Even worse, a small portion of the survivors suffered permanent blindness. Thousands were left unable to work, at the mercy of family and neighbors for their survival. Thousands more, with no family remaining, starved to death.

Here again, Terabinia led the way. While magical healing could restore sight in those who had just recovered, it was unable to help survivors recover vision unless they were treated within a week of clearing the illness. Terabinia's wizard physicians treated as many as possible immediately, and Selene herself pioneered a method of restoring vision for those who were treated too late. Necromancy proved capable of regenerating damaged eyes in many cases, and when even that failed, the worst could receive transplants, eyes harvested from the recently deceased.

While some professed unease with the collection of eyes from the newly dead, the results were clear to 'see.' Almost everyone knew someone who had lost their sight, and the queen's physicians treated everyone without charge. It took the better part of a year, but Selene's popularity soared even higher, and the common folk began to refer to her as Selene the Good.

Meanwhile, Will's efforts in Lystal, particularly through the hospital he had founded, saw more modest benefits. He'd only been able to recruit one wizard physician trained at Wurthaven, a young man named Doctor Carl Lorentz. Lorentz was from the first year of students to benefit from Veronica Wellings' compression training, and thanks to that he was the only other true wizard in Trendham aside from Will and Sammy. That meant he was only first-order, but Will considered that a huge improvement over the so-called wizards he'd seen in Trendham's mage guild, or 'novices' as he called them.

Slightly more than a year after Cora's life-saving visit, Will sat in Dr. Lorentz's office, waiting for the physician's return so he could check on the hospital's current problems and progress. When the door opened, the young man walked in and around his desk without noticing that he had a visitor. That wasn't because Will was concealing himself, but simply because the doctor seemed to be deep in thought. Will tried not to smile as he saw the man jump when he saw he wasn't alone.

He also noted that Lorentz didn't react defensively, either with a force spell or even a hand on a weapon. *The luxury of living a normal life,* thought Will, reminding himself that reacting to every surprise with a shield or a potentially lethal spell was anything but normal. His life had been relatively peaceful for more than a decade, aside from the troll incident, and yet he still couldn't shed the paranoid habits of his formative years. Surviving a mad king, vampires, the fae, an ancient lich, demon lords—all of it had left Will with a warped view of life. He envied the normalcy that Dr. Lorentz had obviously been blessed with.

"How did you get in here?" asked the physician without any real fear or worry in his demeanor. "I'm certain I locked that door." The man flipped open a book on top of his desk and leafed through several pages, checking his schedule. "I don't have you in my appointment book..." He paused. "Why are you hooded? I can't see your face properly."

"I'm your employer," said Will. With a thought and a spell, he closed the door and locked it. "I'm here to see if there's more we can do."

Lorentz's eyes widened slightly at the casual use of magic. "Mister Lettler? We haven't met in person before, but you don't seem old enough. Let me see you properly."

"I prefer to keep my anonymity for now."

Though Dr. Lorentz was still relatively young, he wasn't easily intimidated. "Precisely why you should have sent Miss Taylor to relay your message like you usually do. This cloak and dagger behavior is childish."

Will sighed. "Mister Lettler works for me. He's my public face, so to speak."

"Well, I've never seen his face either, so it's not very public if you ask me."

"Listen, it doesn't matter. The simple fact is that I own this hospital and I'm here to see what you n—"

"Oh really?" interrupted the doctor, putting hands on his hips. "I've seen the hospital charter and it's Lettler's name listed there, not 'mysterious unknown stranger' or some other ridiculous moniker."

"That's beside the point," insisted Will. He was beginning to feel exasperated.

Lorentz squinted at him. "I think it's precisely the point. Anyone could wander in here claiming to be the king of Trendham, but that doesn't mean I would believe them."

Will threw his head back, nearly forgetting to keep his hood in place. "Oh, for fuck's sake! How'd I get in here then? That obviously took a bit of magic."

"I probably left the door unlocked," said the doctor. "Besides, magic is no proof of anything. I'll have you know I'm a wizard myself, properly trained and graduated from Wurthaven, so don't even think about threatening me. And while we're on the topic, spells for opening locks are restricted, which doesn't do much for your case if you're claiming to be a legitimate owner of anything."

Standing up, Will held up one hand. "I feel like we've gotten off to a bad start here. Let me explain and—"

"A better start would be giving your name instead of trying to act mysterious, and an even better one would be to step out and make an appointment with the front clerk. Sometime next week perhaps? They're going to want a name too, by the way."

Will's jaw fell open. "Next week? You're standing right in front of me."

Lorentz stepped over and held the door open. "You can either walk out or I'll send for the constable to escort you."

Will stared blankly at the man, considering his options. He was strongly tempted to use a source-link to paralyze the man, something he imagined Arrogan would have done already, but it had been extremely difficult to recruit Dr. Lorentz. Wizards trained at Wurthaven were almost impossible to hire given the fact that the majority of the students at the school were Terabinian nobility who had little interest in leaving the country. Wizard-physicians were even fewer in number, and Will had been insistent with Lettler that they could only hire one from the more recent graduating classes.

Lorentz had been the only one to show any interest in the offer. A commoner by birth, the physician wasn't wealthy, and Will had offered a very attractive salary, but that didn't mean the young doctor didn't have other options. In fact, Will knew that at least one of the oligarchs, Aaron Pummen, had tried to hire Lorentz away from the hospital.

Lorentz had shown significant integrity in refusing the offer, and now that Will was in front of him, he couldn't help but respect the man's stubbornness. If he took a heavy hand, Will might offend the good doctor, and it was easy to imagine Lorentz deciding to tender his resignation, which would be a disaster for the new hospital. Over the past year, Lorentz had worked tirelessly for the people of Lystal and the surrounding region.

He had no choice but to be diplomatic. Making a quick decision, he pushed back his hood, allowing his face to show plainly. "My name is Kelvin, and I'm the one who insisted that the hospital not use any of the new elven lamps."

Dr. Lorentz's expression changed slightly. "That's half a name. Kelvin…?"

"It's really important that my name not be made public, not just for me, but for the hospital as well."

"As a doctor, I'm required to maintain confidentiality on behalf of my patients. I'm sure I can extend the same courtesy to you."

"Wiltshire. Kelvin Wiltshire," he answered at last. "I wanted to discuss the problems you're having with patients who received treatment too late to save their eyesight."

The doctor nodded. "Fine, fine. Just make an appointment and I'll be happy to talk to you about it."

Will blinked. "What?"

"It's been nice meeting you, Mister Wiltshire, but I have a long list of people wishing to discuss that very same thing with me. I'm sure you'll understand if I prioritize the ones who are actual patients of mine, rather than strangers who break into my office unannounced."

A detailed vision flashed in Will's mind, complete with a disturbing amount of blood and gore, but as always, he pushed it aside. *Polite, I have to be polite,* he repeated to himself. *But I also have to think of something to convince him before I wind up being escorted out.* Without thinking, he resorted to name dropping. "I expected a better welcome from Dr. Morris' student."

It was the doctor's turn to reconsider. "You know Dr. Morris?"

"I learned quite a bit from him when I was at Wurthaven, although I wasn't a medical student."

The physician's eyes widened. "Why didn't you tell me you were a fellow Wurthaven alumnus?" He closed the door and gestured toward a chair. "Have a seat so we can get acquainted. When did you graduate?"

Will grimaced faintly. "I actually never graduated. The war with Darrow cut my time there short."

Lorentz nodded with interest. "So you were there before me. Were you one of the student sorcerers they recruited for the war? You'll have to pardon me, but I don't recognize your last name. I had a common upbringing, so I wasn't brought up learning the noble lineages like most of my classmates."

He repressed his reflexive disgust at being labeled a sorcerer. "Um, no. I've always been opposed to the use of elementals. In fact, that's why I insisted on recruiting from the newer classes, I wanted a true wizard." Will paused, then added, "like myself."

Lorentz frowned. "But if you were there back when war broke out, it would have been before Professor Wellings started the new preparatory compression training. I think there might be a misunderstanding here."

Mentally, Will heard Laina's voice remark, *He clearly thinks you're full of shit, but he didn't call you out directly. This man knows the true meaning of diplomacy.*

Will ignored her. "No. I'm very familiar with compression training. Veronica was a year ahead of me, but it wouldn't be wrong to say I helped introduce her to the one who taught her."

The doctor looked skeptical. "You'll have to pardon me if I don't take you at your word. May I see your pin?"

"Pin?"

Dr. Lorentz tapped his lapel. There was a silver pin there made to resemble the profile of a raven's head with a small green emerald for an eye. Will had noticed the pin earlier, but he'd assumed it was merely an ornament. Focusing on it now, he sensed a faint turyn aura indicating a subtle enchantment. Will didn't see any point in hiding his ignorance. "What's that?"

The doctor straightened up slightly, obviously proud of the adornment. "This, my friend, is what you would have if you were indeed a *real* wizard as you so proudly claimed a moment ago. Each new student who completes the new preparatory training receives one to signify the accomplishment."

Unfazed, Will followed with another question. "What does the enchantment on it do?"

Lorentz showed a look of mild surprise. "You can see that?"

"I've always been rather sensitive," Will explained. "May I examine it?"

The doctor seemed faintly offended by the suggestion. "I think not. The simple fact that you don't have one disproves your claim. The enchantment merely controls the color of the raven's eye. Green signifies that I am a wizard of the first order."

"So that isn't an emerald?"

"No. The pin's value isn't in its simple materials, silver and quartz, but in its ability to verify the relative level of compression the holder has attained." Reaching up with one hand, the doctor deftly unhooked the pin and placed it on the desk in front of him. The moment his hand was no longer in contact, the raven's eye lost its color, turning clear.

Will stared at it for several seconds, thinking. "The enchantment on it must be exceedingly clever. As far as I know, it's impossible to directly sense what degree of compression that a person has applied to their source. Is it somehow calculating a ratio between your personal turyn and the turyn you produce moment by moment?" Will shook his head in response to his question. "No, that wouldn't work. It couldn't differentiate them. Is it somehow reading the amount you absorb from the environment and calculating back from that?"

Lorentz lifted one brow in surprise. "I wouldn't know. I didn't spend much time studying artificing."

"What color does it display when worn by a second- or third-order wizard?"

The doctor looked even more suspicious. "Answering will only help you obfuscate things. You should already know if you were trained as I was."

Will sighed. "Very well. I can tell you this. Your teacher must have told you about second- and third-order compressions. So I'm guessing it will display yet another color if you put it on me." He held out his hand, palm down. "I promise I won't steal it. Just put it on my skin for a moment. You'll see the truth then."

"You're claiming to be of a higher order?"

"I'm not claiming anything. Try it and you'll see."

The doctor seemed to waver for a moment. "How do I know you won't try to snatch it away?"

"If I'm lying, I'd be foolish to try your patience, if I'm not, I could just as easily take it by force."

"Is that a threat?" Lorentz's brows lowered angrily.

He had to give the man credit. Despite the strange situation, he had a spine. "No. I'm trying to be as polite as possible. I need you here and you're too valuable as a physician for me to replace. The last thing I want is to offend you."

The doctor exhaled loudly then abruptly placed the pin on the back of Will's hand. "I feel like a fool doing this, since it's obviously not— what?" He stared at the raven's-head pin. The clear quartz of its eye had turned blood red. "That can't be." He picked it up and the quartz turned green again. He put it on Will's hand and removed it several more times, watching it change from red to green and back again. Eventually he stopped and his eyes met Will's.

"So red means third-order," summarized Will. "I'm guessing second is what, blue?"

Lorentz nodded absently, then objected, "This can't be right. The enchantment must be defective."

"It shows the correct color for you," observed Will.

"But there aren't any third-order wizards," insisted the physician.

Will's voice was firm, and his gaze never left other man as he replied, "I know for a fact there are four. Myself and the three I trained, one of whom taught Veronica Wellings." He'd actually raised four to third-order, but since Selene had become a lich, she technically no longer counted.

Dr. Lorentz stared back. "Who are you, really?"

Will smiled. "Ask around town and you'll find out I'm the cook over at the Laughing Goat. Come by and I'll treat you to as good a meal as you've ever had." He waited a moment, but the doctor failed to laugh. "That's the truth, by the way, but only part of it. My real name is something of a problem, so I don't use it anymore. Since you've forced me to reveal a lot more than I intended, I'll tell you this: I'm the First Wizard."

"The what now?"

"It's a title." Will gave a short history of the wizard's council and the fact that while it had nearly gone extinct, he'd received his training and the title directly from the last holder of the position. At the end he finished with, "I'm bringing it back, and since you're first-order you'll be included." He paused, then added, "I like the pins, by the way. I'll have to get one from Vonnie."

The doctor didn't mince words. "You realize you sound mad, don't you?"

Will briefly considered demonstrating his superior strength, but he didn't want to push his luck. The doctor was obviously a proud man, and he might not react well to having the difference between them forcibly proven. "For my purposes, it's all right if you think I'm crazy," admitted Will. "All I really need is for you to work with me for the betterment of the hospital."

Leaning back in his chair, Dr. Lorentz scratched his head. "Well, I have to admit you've piqued my interest. I'm not saying I fully believe you yet, but I'm willing to hear you out."

"That's all I could ask for. As I started to say earlier, you've done admirable work under difficult circumstances here, but there are still a significant number of people who have suffered some degree of vision loss."

"Not in Lystal," corrected the doctor. "A few, perhaps, but we managed to help everyone here who sought early treatment."

Will nodded. "Agreed. I was referring to Trendham as a whole."

The young doctor rubbed his chin. "It's unfortunate. We've had many travel here for whom I could do nothing. I've suggested traveling to Cerria to some of them, but such a journey isn't practical for most."

"Have you considered returning to Wurthaven, for a refresher? You could learn the new techniques they are using to restore eyesight."

The doctor gave him a sharp look. "I'd love to, but again, there's no one else here. Even my staff are only half trained, and none of them can use magic. A trip back to Cerria would be wonderful, but the journey itself would be several weeks. I couldn't abandon my place here for so long."

"I can see to it that travel time isn't an issue. If you're willing, I'll make arrangements at Wurthaven for you and set up a schedule. Then—"

"Giving me several months' leave doesn't solve the time problem. There are people who need me in the here and now. I'd be derelict in my duty if I left," argued the doctor.

Will repressed a smirk. "That's not what I meant. I'm sure you're familiar with teleportation."

"But there's no beacon in Trendham, and even if there was, I doubt the oligarchs and the queen would agree to the linkage between nations. Not to mention I never studied the spell and I highly doubt anyone here has such knowledge," argued the doctor before pausing. He gave Will a hard stare. "You're about to tell me you have a way, aren't you?"

He nodded. "Would I be the First Wizard if I didn't?"

"I really wish you'd quit calling yourself that."

Will ignored the remark. "Are you free in the evenings? How about during the day?"

"For this it would be worth rearranging my work schedule, but if it has to be during the day, it would be best if I was only absent for two or three hours at a time," answered Dr. Lorentz. "Can you really do this?"

"I'll come back in a day or two, after I've made arrangements. Trust me." Then Will's eyes lost focus as he slipped partway into the astral. It only took him half a minute now, and as soon as he'd located his mother, he teleported home, leaving the good doctor to stare at the empty chair he'd been sitting in. Will figured that would be proof enough.

CHAPTER 23

Tabitha was watching her children play in the garden when Will arrived. He'd actually checked several times over the course of an hour before teleporting, waiting for an ideal moment in which he'd be less likely to startle his sister or his nieces and nephews. He succeeded in that, but still received a dour look when she spotted him.

"Years, Will, it's been years, again!"

He held up his hands in surrender, even as he argued, "Not years. It's been less than two." He'd dropped in for a very brief visit that lasted all of ten minutes a few years after his initial visit before the troll incident.

"You gave me a hug and glanced at everyone before immediately saying goodbye and leaving again. That doesn't count. And it was still well over a year ago. You told me you'd stop in at least once a month!"

Will smiled and hoped his natural charm would defuse her irritation, but angry tears were starting to form in her eyes. "I'm sorry, Tabbycat, I really am." Moving toward her he opened his arms for a hug.

She gave him a look that said he was far from forgiven, but embraced him anyway. Afterward, she grabbed his arm. "I'm not letting go unless you let me give you something."

"Actually, I thought I might spend the night, if you're willing to put me up for the night." He'd already warned his mother and Oliver that he'd be gone for a few days, and Lettler had someone else covering the kitchen.

Tabitha's reaction was one of suspicion. "Why? What's happening?"

"Well, I do need to arrange a few things, but—"

Her brows lowered. "I knew it." She looked around him to check on the kids. "Do I even dare tell them you're here? You're probably planning to leave and show up just in time to sleep."

"It can wait until tomorrow. The rest of today and tonight is all yours, if you're not too busy. And if you are, I can occupy myself with the children and visit again to spend time with you. Since the fever, I've been thinking I needed to rebalance my life, and I know that was a while ago but I didn't know what to—what's wrong?" Tabitha's eyes were overflowing, sending fat teardrops down her cheeks.

"Uncle Will?" The voice of his oldest nephew, Edward, came from behind him. The ten-year-old sounded uncertain, which was understandable since the boy had only seen him a couple of times. Tabitha immediately turned around, wiping her cheeks with her sleeves.

Will gave the boy a wide smile. "It's me!"

Edward grinned back, then started yelling to his brothers and sisters. His enthusiasm was infectious, and soon they were swarming over their uncle. Talia, the youngest at four, didn't remember him at all, but Christopher and Elaina did, and they were soon peppering him with questions while simultaneously trying to inform him of every exciting new thing that had happened to them recently. The result was a happy confusion.

Tabitha joined in once she had regained her composure. Edward and Christopher began trying to teach him the rules of a game they'd created which revolved around a large leather ball, but neither was very good at explaining it. Eight-year-old Elaina wound up being the best at clarifying the confusion, even though it had been Edward who had dreamed up their new sport.

Talia was too young to participate, so Tabitha did her best to keep the four-year-old occupied while Elaina and the boys played with their uncle.

They whiled away the afternoon with an excess of laughter and a dearth of serious conversation. The sun was dropping low in the sky before Will finally called a halt. "We need to stop if I'm going to have time to make dinner." His announcement was met with a chorus of disappointment and complaints.

Even Tabitha disagreed with his choice. "I love your cooking, Will, but we have someone, let's not waste our time."

"We won't," he replied immediately. "The kids can help me. You can watch if you want, or you can enjoy a little quiet time."

His sister's mouth formed a round 'o', then she responded, "Are you sure? The children are going to slow you down."

"I'm a wizard chef," said Will. "Trust me. It will be fun. Tell your cook to take the evening off."

A short while later, James returned home, and it was all Tabitha could do to keep her husband away from the kitchen. His enthusiastic hero worship of Will hadn't waned in the slightest over the past few years, but he relented to Tabitha's stern guidance.

Being raised as minor nobility, Will's nieces and nephews had had little to no exposure to the kitchen, aside from attempts to steal food or wheedle snacks from their cook outside of mealtimes. Being asked to knead dough or stir a pot was a novelty to them, and Edward found the prospect of peeling carrots positively exciting, since it meant he got to use a knife.

Will watched the ten-year-old carefully. As he expected, the boy was clumsy with the paring knife, and Tabitha likely would have frowned on him being allowed to use the sharp instrument, but Will was confident he could prevent a serious accident. *And small ones?* he mused silently. *Small cuts are a lesson, and I can easily mend those before Tabitha sees them.*

To his surprise, Edward got through the chore without incident, and though he did slice partway into one of his fingernails, no blood was drawn.

As his sister had predicted, the children did slow things down considerably, but Will's spells allowed him to take a lot of shortcuts to make up for lost time, whether it came to cleaning up messes, washing the excess multitudes of plates and utensils that were dirtied, or finishing some of the prep work when time was running short. If anything, the complexity of managing so many small hands gave him a fresh perspective on what he usually did alone.

Dinner was a success, and although some parts of the dishes were a bit crude, with rough and unevenly chopped vegetables, the children were exceedingly proud of their work. They ate without complaints, and when bedtime inevitably arrived, they groaned at the injustice of it all.

Will watched them go with a warm feeling in his chest. James had been chatting enthusiastically throughout dinner, but now that 'adult' time had arrived, he fell strangely silent, glancing at his wife expectantly. Will asked them, "What is it?"

Tabitha smiled faintly. "My husband is dying of excitement, but he's trying to let me talk first." Leaning over, she gave James a quick kiss on the cheek. Afterward, she turned back to Will. "Earlier I warned you not to leave until I gave you something. Let me go fetch it."

The two men watched her leave and then James stared at Will with his mouth firmly closed. He looked as though he might explode.

"What is it?" asked Will, purely to torment his brother-in-law.

James frowned, then said, "No. I'm not going to spoil it." He couldn't help but fidget in his seat, however.

"How are your classes going? Are you and Veronica still doing the preparatory courses for new students?" asked Will.

"Yes!" said James, his voice emerging almost as a shout. "In fact, it's a shame Vonnie isn't here today. She will be disappointed to have missed you. But, yes, the classes are going well."

"I met one of your students, Carl Lorentz. He's a physician in Lystal now."

James frowned. "I don't remember the name."

"He graduated about four years ago I think."

"Ahh. Then he went through when it was just Vonnie. He would have already been a senior student when I started as an assistant professor."

Will nodded. "He showed me an enchanted pin that he got when he finished his compression training. I was really impressed by the design. Do you think I could look at the notes on it? I was thinking about making one for myself—what are you doing?"

The other man had plugged his ears with his fingers and was humming loudly to himself. He paused to shout, "I'm sorry, I can't hear you." He glanced over his shoulder, watching for his wife's return.

Tabitha appeared only seconds later, coming down the stairs with two small lacquered boxes in her hands. She stopped and looked at her husband, who was still humming and rocking back and forth slightly, then she asked Will, "Have you been teasing him?"

Will shrugged. "Not as far as I know."

"James, stop." She walked over and pulled one of his hands, removing the finger from his ear. "James. You're being ridiculous."

Her husband's eyebrows shot up. "I didn't say a word, dear!"

"I never said you couldn't. It's not that big a deal."

James shook his head. "I know I monopolize the conversation too much and you've been waiting for a chance to give this to him for quite a while, so I'm going to sit quiet for a bit."

Tabitha stared at him, one hand on her hip for several seconds before looking back at her brother. "See what I have to deal with?" She turned back to her husband. "I knew you talked a lot when I married you. I'd tell you if you annoyed me with it."

James kept his lips tightly sealed, though he tried to talk anyway, resulting in a comical series of sounds, as though he'd been gagged. Will couldn't help but laugh at the man's antics. He accepted one box from Tabitha when she leaned over and stretched out her hand. "Can I open it?"

She nodded, still giving James a mock glare.

Inside were two items, a raven pin with a clear quartz eye, and a silver tablet that Will recognized as a device for long-distance communication. A small stylus rested beside it and there was a series of symbols along the bottom. It appeared to be a variation of the tablet he'd first learned of from the lich, Grim Talek. Lifting the pin, Will winked at James. "So this is the pin you were telling me about!"

The other man gaped at him, then exclaimed, "I never!" He pointed to Will and then to his wife. "Tell her, Will. I didn't say a thing! Honey, you have to believe me!"

Tabitha gave James a sad but sympathetic look. "I told you it's all right. It wasn't a secret."

Will grinned. "See, James? It's fine. Now what were you saying? The eye changes color depending on who wears it? So it should be red when I put it on, correct?" He lifted the pin with one hand. "And so it does. Very lovely!"

James' eyes threatened to bulge out of his head. "You demon! I never!" Desperate, he looked back at his wife. "He's lying! One of the students told him about them!"

Tabitha put a hand on her husband's shoulder. "James, enough. You're getting worked up over nothing." Before the man could protest further, she glanced at Will. "And *you*, you need to stop teasing my poor husband. You already know how excitable he is."

Will laughed, then gave James an amused apology. "Sorry, I couldn't help myself."

"See! I was telling the truth," said James, hopping up from his chair. He looked back and forth for a moment, then sighed. "Does anyone want some wine? I need a glass." Without waiting for anyone to respond, he went in search of a bottle and glasses.

Tabitha shook her head as he left. "I don't know where he finds the energy. I worry he's going to give himself a fit if he doesn't calm down someday." Then she asked, "So you knew about the pins?"

"Only since yesterday. I finally introduced myself to the doctor I hired for the hospital last year, and during the course of our conversation, he showed me his pin."

Tabitha nodded. "I meant to tell you about them when you first came, but you and James were talking so much that I forgot about it until after you'd left. Then the last time you came, you were in and out so quickly I didn't get a chance, but the communication tablet is what I really wanted you to have."

"I should have made a pair and given you one," said Will. "I thought about it. I just never got around to it." He ran his finger along the bottom edge. "I'm assuming these symbols designate the recipient?"

"Yes." Leaning in, his sister tapped each one in turn. "The first one is me, this one is for James, and these are for Vonnie, Sammy, your mother, and our father." She stopped then, but there were two more symbols remaining.

Will gave her a curious look. "And the last two?"

She handed him the second box. There were four more silver tablets inside. "Two of those are the ones for Sammy and Erisa, and the other two are matched with those last two symbols. I thought you might want to give them to Janice and Tiny, but I didn't want to presume."

He froze, but then forced himself to relax. "I'll have to think about that. He handed her the two extra tablets. Will you keep them for me?"

She nodded. "Just let me know and I'll have them delivered."

"I appreciate that. This was very thoughtful of you, Tabbycat."

She grabbed his hair and pulled his head down, not bothering to be gentle, then gave him a quick peck on the cheek. "One of us should be, since you can't be bothered."

"I'll do better in the future," he promised.

She tapped one of the tablets. "You won't have any choice. I'll be messaging you regularly, so pay attention."

As if in response, Will's tablet shifted, showing a row of black script on its silver surface. Lifting it up, he read the words. *Has it been long enough?* The symbol at the bottom indicated the message was from James.

Will banished the box and the other materials to his limnthal, reserving only the stylus and his tablet, then he wrote a return message. *Long enough for what?*

For a touching sibling reunion. I don't want to interrupt.

"Is that James?" asked Tabitha.

Will smiled but wouldn't let her see what her husband had written. He wrote back: *We haven't talked much—she won't stop crying long enough.* Once he'd finished, he turned the tablet around so his sister could read.

James appeared in the door a second later, an expression of panic on his face. He was just in time to see Will chuckling. Will winked at him and Tabitha gave her husband a sympathetic look. "That was all him," she said, pointing at Will. Then she added, "Although I would think you'd learn by now. It's obvious he likes to tease you."

James relaxed, then gave Will a wry look. "I suspected he might be joking."

"Yet you ran anyway," Will pointed out.

James' face turned serious, and he focused his gaze on Tabitha. "Always." The mood shifted then, but only for a moment as James held up the wine bottle. "Ready for a drink? I brought glasses as well." He placed them down and began pouring without waiting.

Tabitha spoke next. "Will likes the tablets, but I think he's even more enamored with the pins you made."

Her husband's face lit up, and Will understood better why the man had been so excited about the gifts even before Tabitha had brought them out. "You made them?"

"James designed the enchantment for them," said Tabitha proudly. "He made the communication tablets too, although the enchantment for those was based on the one you recovered years ago from Grim Talek."

Will's brows lifted in surprise. He accepted a glass from James, then remarked, "I thought your sister started giving out the pins a few years before you began working with her at Wurthaven."

The other man was already blushing. "She did, and the idea was hers, but she had me do the design work."

"From what I can tell, it must have been a clever bit of work," Will said, his tone full of admiration.

James nodded rapidly. "That's why I was dying to tell you about it earlier. It seems simple on the surface, of course, being that it's just a color change, but figuring out how to get the enchantment to detect the degree of compression in a given person's source was the difficult part."

"I had no idea you were so skilled," said Will.

Tabitha broke in, "Artifice and enchanting were his primary focus when he was at Wurthaven."

"Just to be clear, a jeweler handles the artistic part. I was only involved in creating the enchanting script inside it."

Tabitha rolled her eyes, and Will nodded to her in agreement. "*Only*, you say. That's the trickiest part. Where are the runes, by the way? There's nothing visible on the outside," asked Will.

"It's made in two parts which are then welded together. There would be a seam along the edges, but the jeweler files and buffs it down so you can't even see that once it's finished. You asked about seeing the notes earlier. I have a copy of the full rune script in my journal. Shall I bring it out so you can see?"

Will smiled. "Of course."

His brother-in-law leapt from his chair and took the stairs two at a time. He returned from his study in less than a minute with a leatherbound journal under one arm. A moment later, he had it open and happily began explaining the various parts of the enchanting script. "The pin itself doesn't hold or retain turyn, so the enchantment is virtually impossible to notice, and when someone is wearing it, it's relying on the ambient turyn differential between the wearer and the environment to empower its functions.

"This section performs a fixed calculation based on that differential to gauge how much turyn someone is actually holding, which is important since it can vary when a magic user is actually doing something. It isn't perfect, but it gives a close enough approximation of the relative ratio between the wearer's current turyn and their baseline, then from there it merely has to compare that to how much turyn they're generating from their native source," explained James.

That part alone was enough to impress the hell out of Will, but he still had questions. "I'm amazed at that part, but the last bit doesn't seem possible. You can't directly sense someone else's source. Even if I use a source-link on someone, I can't detect whether that same source has been compressed or not, even though I can control it. If a person can't do it, how can an enchantment manage such a feat?"

James turned the page. "Here's the second part," he said with a smile, displaying a lengthy and extremely complex rune sequence that filled the entire page. "The answer lies in two things, clear and unbiased turyn measurement and math. This compares the turyn frequency of the person wearing the pin from one moment to the next, then—"

"How does that help?" asked Will. "Even a first-order wizard can control and modify their inner turyn frequency in order to optimize it for various spells."

"Yes!" James nodded excitedly. "But that's not the problem—that's actually the solution, because what they *can't* control is the frequency of the turyn coming in from their living source. That part is constant. They can change the turyn produced, but only *after* it emerges from their source. By passively monitoring the turyn frequency of a person, the enchantment can discern the difference between the wearer's overall turyn and the turyn being continuously produced by their source."

"But it doesn't know what that frequency is, so how can it know which is which?"

"It doesn't need to," said James smugly. "In fact, the calculation is entirely independent of what the actual frequencies involved are. It simply finds the average, then compares it to the input that doesn't match that average. Of course, that alone would give a skewed result, which is why I needed that first calculation to figure out a person's usual baseline since the current total could vary by quite a lot. But once we've calculated the baseline amount, we use that to calculate the compression ratio of the input that's solely from their source."

Will shook his head. "That's—I don't know what to say. I think I understand the idea, but how you actually implemented the math escapes me. I'll have to study this a bit before I fully understand. Can I copy this?"

"Certainly. I can write it out for you if you want to come by and get it in a few days," offered James. The actual rune script occupied two full pages, plus there were several descriptive pages that explained the individual elements. Ordinarily, it would be the work of at least an hour to copy it all out, so it was kind of his brother-in-law to offer to do the copying.

"No need," said Will. He summoned his current work journal and laid it out on the table beside James' and then used the scribe spell he'd learned from Grim Talek. The text began filling itself in on the first blank page of his journal. He still had to read carefully and pay attention, but with the spell, he could write out a copy just as quickly as he could read it, and there was no risk of bad penmanship from excessive haste.

James watched over his shoulder. "You had that spell memorized? Did you work in the library while you were at Wurthaven?"

Will paused, glancing up. "I'll explain afterward. Would you mind reading as I write it out, just in case I make a mistake? The spell doesn't make mistakes, but if I misread, it will transcribe my error."

With the two of them working together, the copy was finished in less than fifteen minutes. At the end, Will stored his journal again and thanked James for his help. Then he answered the other man's previous question. "I try to memorize every spell I think I might potentially use, then I practice them for an hour each day. Eventually, I start reflex casting them and then I don't have to worry about it anymore. I add new spells to my practice list as the old ones become second nature to me."

James blinked. "That's very disciplined of you. I've always heard that old practitioners develop a large repertoire of reflexive spells, but I hadn't heard of anyone using a routine like that."

Will nodded. "My early years were hectic, and I had to develop as fast as possible, otherwise I probably wouldn't have survived. In the beginning, it was mainly spells related to combat or survival, but it became a habit, so even after I'd succeeded with all those, I just kept it up with more ordinary spells."

"How many spells have you memorized?" asked James.

Will shrugged. "Memorized or spells I can reflex cast?"

"Both."

"I have no idea. Hundreds? Maybe over a thousand that I can reflex cast, so the number I have memorized would be that number plus a dozen more that I'm currently practicing each day," he answered.

His brother-in-law stared blankly at him for several seconds. Finally, he asked, "That's stunning. Not to doubt you, but how can you be sure you haven't lost the ability to reflex cast some of them? I hear that over time, if you don't use one, that can happen, and you might not even know unless you needed it suddenly."

"That's why I keep a list." Will summoned a different journal from his limnthal and opened it. "As I succeed with each new spell, I add it to this list. Even though I don't practice these regularly, every month I go back through and recheck, just to be sure. So far, I haven't lost any, but I'm sure it will probably happen eventually."

James let out a low whistle, then looked at his wife. "Maybe we should try something similar?"

Tabitha blanched. "Do you think we have enough time in the day?"

"We could limit ourselves to half an hour, or even fifteen minutes," suggested her husband.

"Don't stress out about it," said Will. "Sometimes I wish I could stop. I don't think my regimen is normal."

Tabitha moved over. "Why are you doing it then?"

Will's eyes met hers, then moved to James and back again. "Fear," he admitted honestly. "Whenever I try to stop, I get anxious. If I skip a day or two, my nightmares get worse."

"You're still having nightmares?" she asked.

He closed his eyes briefly, then nodded. "Not as often, but I'm not sure I'll ever shake them completely. The war, the vampires, the dragon, all of it left scars inside." He tapped his temple. "Spell practice is just one way I cope with the fear."

James put one hand on his shoulder and started pulling. Will resisted for a moment, then let the other man draw him in for a hug. A second later, his sister joined them. More seconds passed, and neither let go. A tight knot formed in Will's chest, then seemed to fade. When they finally released him, he saw tears in James' eyes.

Will glanced back and forth between them, then asked, "What?"

"We're going to take care of you," said James, his voice thick. "After everything you've done, you deserve that." Tabitha nodded along, not trusting herself to speak.

He tried to reassure them, "I think I'm doing all right."

Tabitha cleared her throat, then said, "I meant to say this earlier. I want you to bring Erisa and Oliver next time you visit, the sooner the better." Will opened his mouth, then closed it again, unsure what to say. His sister continued, "I've never met my only nephew."

His eyes felt swollen and his voice cracked slightly when he answered, "But they're not related to—"

Tabitha's expression turned angry as she cut him off, "He's *your son*. That makes him my nephew. Don't be selfish. And your mother is part of you as well—that makes us family. Bring them, and Sammy too if she's not busy. You're the only person in the world who can freely teleport, so you should at least make use of it."

Will began rubbing his face with one sleeve, but his sister didn't relent. "I know you feel like an outsider, and some of that is because of my mother, not to mention how our father treated you in the beginning, but I'm sick of you letting that get in the way. Aside from the children and Dad, you're nearly the only family I have left."

"But—"

"And while we're at it, stop feeling guilty about Laina. I know that's really why you've avoided me all these years, but it isn't fair. Forgive yourself! And if you can't do that, at least stop punishing me with your guilt. I want my brother in my life. Do you understand?"

Will nodded and more tears followed—but they were the good kind.

CHAPTER 24

The next day, Will walked the streets of Cerria. He didn't bother with a camouflage spell or even trying to disguise his face, opting instead to employ what had become his favorite method, simply blending his turyn in with the ambient turyn around himself. While most people couldn't perceive turyn directly, the technique served to make it difficult for anyone to pay attention to him, whether they could see turyn or not. It was a bit like being invisible while still being in plain sight. He'd learned the technique from a retired Arkeshi assassin who had served his late sister, Laina.

He'd originally planned on going to see Dr. Morris, the head of the Healing and Psyche Department at Wurthaven, but after explaining the situation to James, he'd decided to leave the task to his brother-in-law. Since James was faculty there, it would be far easier for him to make arrangements for Dr. Lorentz's additional training, and it wouldn't require Will to expose himself.

With his day free, Will had played with Tabitha's children for a while, then said his goodbyes. His walk through Cerria was purely an indulgence in nostalgia. Many areas were relatively new, having been rebuilt after Linus Ethelgren's ritual had laid waste to a significant fraction of the city almost fifteen years ago. He still saw a lot of familiar sights and places, and when he began to get thirsty, he stopped at an upscale tavern named the Lazy Pony.

Sitting down at the bar, Will let his turyn return to normal so he could get service. The bartender looked vaguely familiar, and Will tried to remember the man's name. *Mark? Matt? No, that's not right.* The first time he'd come to the Lazy Pony had been to sell potions, back when he was desperate to raise money and pay off his blood debt for killing Dennis Spry.

"What can I get you?" asked the barkeep.

Max. That's it. "A pint of the brown ale," answered Will. Despite remembering the man's name, he didn't use it, since the last thing he wanted was to jog any old memories.

Max left and returned a minute later with a tall wooden mug filled to the brim. Setting it down, he held up a couple of fingers. "Two."

Will fished two copper coins out of his purse and set them down on the bar. He felt more relaxed now, since the fact that he was expected to pay up front was a sure sign that Max didn't recognize him. Regulars paid at the end, but newcomers had to pay by the drink. "Thanks," he replied, taking an appreciative sip. Then he leaned back and let his eyes explore the room.

In the middle of the day, the tavern's business was light and only three tables had customers at them. All of them were too far away for a normal person to listen in, but Will's ears weren't normal. He increased their sensitivity and enjoyed his ale.

Even with superior hearing, he could only make out the conversation at one of the tables and it revolved around one of the men's troubles with his wife. Will turned his attention to the next table. It was far enough away that the background noise from outside interfered with his ability to understand what they were saying, but that was only a small obstacle for a wizard whose talent could manipulate sound. Since he couldn't clearly make out the words, he adjusted the turyn around them, bringing the sound closer, until it sounded as though he was sitting right beside the three strangers sitting at the table in the corner of the room.

Their conversation was more interesting. "He said they lost another ship," said a young man who looked to be in his late twenties.

"An' your cousin is an expert, is he?" asked the middle-aged man across from the one who had spoken first.

"Jack's cousin works on the docks," said the third man. He appeared to be in his twenties as well, though he'd already lost most of his hair. "I think he'd know, Bill."

Bill nodded amiably. "I'm not sayin' he's wrong, just that he isn't a sailor himself."

Jack responded, "You think he has to be on the boats to know? He sees 'em coming and going every day. The men talk, same as we do. If ships are being taken, he'd know about it."

"Then why hasn't the queen done anything?" asked Bill. "I'd think there'd be some reaction from her if they were taking our ships."

"What's she s'posed to do?" asked the bald man.

"Send the fleet to Karda," snapped Bill. "Burn their docks and send a message to the Trendish so they'll know what's what. Seems simple enough to me."

The bald one rolled his eyes. "You say plenty of dumb shit, Bill, but that takes the cake. That's war if she does that."

"They're destroying our ships. *That's* war, if you ask me!" Bill shot back in return.

Jack leaned in. "We don't know for sure it's them. We don't even know if the ships was sunk. Hell, they coulda all sailed off for a vacation in Barsta for all we know."

"Now who's being stupid? One captain might do something like that, but not three in the span of a few months," said Bill testily.

"The point is there's no proof. Nobody's seen anything. It's more likely to be pirates. The merchant princes aren't fool enough to provoke us," countered Jack.

"What if it's not pirates or the Trendish?" asked the bald one.

Bill coughed, then replied disparagingly, "Storms? You're reaching if you think all three were lost to the weather."

The bald one switched to a hushed tone. "No. What if it was something else? Something not human? There're things that live in the deep that no man has lived to tell about."

"Then how're you sittin' here talking about them? Idiot. And anyway, if there was some sort of sea monster out there, we'd almost certainly have a few survivors turn up, or at the very least some bodies would wash up. A serpent or kraken or whatever you're imagining wouldn't wipe them out without leaving some sort of wreckage," said Bill.

"What about the elves?" suggested Jack.

Bill wasn't having that either. "They're peaceful traders. No one's ever even seen an elven warship, if such a thing exists. Not to mention there's not that many of them. What would they have to gain from poisoning trade relations like that?"

Will listened to them trade rumors and speculate for a while longer, but it was obvious the men didn't have any solid information, other than the fact that three ships had gone missing over the past couple of months. It bothered him that one of their first instincts was to blame Trendham, but there wasn't much he could do about idle gossip.

He listened in to some of the other patrons' conversations, but he didn't discover anything else that interested him, other than the fact that Selene was indeed extremely popular. Lognion had been a relatively effective ruler, and well respected, but the people seemed to truly adore the queen. Another two ales and an hour of listening and Will heard not a single complaint about her rule. The closest thing to a complaint was when one old man mentioned he was glad the queen's husband had died. In that old timer's opinion, Will had been violent and power hungry, the natural result of a commoner trying to mix with royalty. Neither of the old man's companions mentioned that since the Stormking had reappeared to kill the trolls then Will must still be alive.

Probably a lot of conflicting rumors going around, Will decided. The most important thing to him was that he wasn't a topic of regular discussion. *Mostly forgotten, which is what I wanted,* he told himself.

He left the tavern and walked the streets for another hour, enjoying the sights and studying the people around him. The city had obviously prospered in the years since Lognion's death, which made him feel better about his decision. He'd initially doubted whether killing the king would be a good thing, because while the man had been personally evil and cruel, he'd actually done rather well for the people in general. Will had once feared that his personal grudge against Lognion might result in a worse outcome for the nation as a whole.

Selene's rule put that fear to rest. Not only were the people healthier and happier, the nation was growing richer by the year. Will had left because he couldn't countenance what his wife had become, but now he thought it might also have been the best thing for the nation as well. Near the end, before he'd finished the dragon, it had been apparent he was having trouble adjusting to Selene's ascension to the throne. *I was violent and paranoid, not a good combination in a ruler,* he thought. *Even now, more than fifteen years later, I'm plagued by violent impulses in my daily life and nightmares when I sleep.*

Terabinia was better off without him.

Things were better this way. All he needed to do was finish raising Oliver and then he could focus on his next project, rebuilding the Council of Wizards. From his personal experience it seemed best that the council should be apolitical and not beholden to any particular nation or country. Hopefully somewhere along the way, he would find a clue as to where Grim Talek had gone. The lich could be literally anywhere, or anyone, and his ability to mimic the turyn of whomever he replaced made it impossible for even Will to tell the difference.

He could have replaced my own mother and lived next to me and Oliver all these years and I'd never know it, he thought with a shudder. It was a disturbing thought, but even as paranoid as he was, Will didn't believe it. The lich could copy his mother's turyn, but over time Will would notice the difference in her personality. But the lich could easily be almost anyone else; that was the disturbing truth. Unless he revealed himself, there was no way to tell the lich from a living person. *Or Selene for that matter,* Will told himself, remembering what Tiny had said about her secret trips while Janice remained behind to impersonate her.

He realized he was holding the pin that Tabitha and James had given him, turning it over in his fingers while he walked. Looking down, Will admired the red color of the quartz crystal when suddenly a thought struck him. *Janice is second-order.* If she were wearing the pin, the stone would turn blue. His eyes widened. "James, you're a damned genius!"

Lost in his thoughts, he walked back to his sister's house. He'd have dinner with them again and hear what James had to say about his conversation with Dr. Morris. Hopefully it would be good news for Dr. Lorentz. Either way, Will had a few more questions for James about the particulars of the enchantment he'd designed for the raven pins.

***

Dr. Morris had agreed to a series of evening sessions to educate Dr. Lorentz in the latest necromantic techniques to regenerate damaged eyes. The techniques for actual grafts and transplants to restore sight in the worst cases wouldn't be taught, though. Apparently, those techniques required lengthy study and practice, and only a few specialists had mastered them. Though Dr. Morris was the head of the department, he was not one of those who had learned to do it. Only Selene and two of the younger faculty were capable of it, and having one of them teach Lorentz would guarantee that Selene would hear about the returning student from Trendham.

Tiny had already found him through his hiring of Dr. Lorentz; if Selene heard about the unusual accommodations, she would surely figure things out and trace it back to Will.

Did it really matter? According to Tiny, Selene was most likely to try and help him, and Will couldn't help but agree. There was even a part of him that secretly wanted her to know. Even after a decade and a half, he missed her. Will found himself grinding his teeth. "You made the right decision," he told himself, "and you know what you have to do—eventually."

The schedule for the doctor's training required Will to bring him to Cerria four nights a week, and since the sessions were only an hour long, he waited at his sister's while Dr. Lorentz was out. The first week passed quickly, and as the weekend approached, Will considered what Tabitha had suggested—bringing Erisa and Oliver for an afternoon.

To do that, he'd first have to explain a few things—in particular, the fact that he was a wizard. Will had been telling himself for a while that he was waiting for Oliver to turn sixteen, and his son's birthday was only six months away. His thoughts circled around the problem as always, but in the end, he admitted to himself that he was stalling. It needed to be done, and waiting would only deny Oliver valuable time getting to know his cousins.

After returning the physician to the hospital that evening, Will surprised Sammy and gave her the enchanted tablet. She loved it, naturally, and she was even more excited to discover that Will was finally making an effort to reconnect with his sister. She readily agreed to clearing her schedule for a day to have a family reunion.

Will left before she could ask him what he would tell Oliver. He worried that if he broached the topic with her, she'd insist on being present for the conversation, and he could only imagine what she might add to it when his son started asking questions. It was better he did it alone. That way he could limit the damage.

CHAPTER 25

It was Saturday morning when he broached the subject, just a day before the planned family visit. Saturdays were the one day when he and Oliver spent an extra hour practicing, since Oliver didn't have school and Will didn't work on the weekends. It was their best time to connect, the time they had their best conversations.

They'd just finished and were sitting on the back porch together when Will finally said the words. "I need to tell you something."

Relaxed and unaware, Oliver was using a towel to wipe away the sweat dripping down his neck. "What's that?" he asked.

"You're close to sixteen now, and I want you to meet some family you didn't know about, but that means I'll also need to tell you the truth about a few things."

Oliver's relaxed mood shifted immediately to intense focus. His eyes locked onto Will's features. "I'm listening."

Will realized he was holding his breath and let it out. "I'm a wizard."

Oliver nodded. "All right, and?"

Will stared at his son. "I thought you'd be more surprised. Did you already know?"

Oliver shook his head. "No, but Auntie Ess is a wizard too, so it's not that big a shock. Not sure why you'd bother keeping it a secret, so I'm guessing there must be something else, right?"

Not expecting such a bland reaction, Will took a moment to consider his words. "The fact that I can use magic doesn't mean anything to you?"

The teen shrugged. "You can't really use it though, can you? Doug told me wizards have to limit what they do since it ages them."

"How old do I look to you?" asked Will.

Oliver shrugged again. "Thirty?"

Thirty!? He was halfway between thirty and forty, but Will was confident he looked no more than twenty. He'd been worried Oliver might soon start asking questions about why they looked the same age. He fought to restrain a laugh. *Not much chance of that, I guess. He thinks I look old.* "Most people think I'm younger than that."

"Maybe."

"I'm actually thirty-four," he admitted. "But I'll have you know most people think I'm much younger."

"That's great," agreed Oliver unenthusiastically. "Is this the big secret? You're a wizard and you're using magic to make yourself look younger?"

"No! I'm not using magic to make myself look younger. I mean, yes, I do look younger, but not because I'm trying to. I don't *look* younger, I *am* younger."

"So you're not thirty-four?"

For a moment Will wanted to pull out his own hair. "No, I *am* thirty-four, but physically I'm younger. I age slower than normal people."

Oliver's face twisted into an expression of confusion and doubt. "I don't think that's how it works, Dad."

He glared at his son. "Which one of us is the wizard?"

Oliver responded hesitantly by pointing his finger. "You?"

"Exactly—me," agreed Will emphatically. "Would you be willing to admit I might know a bit more about it than you do?"

"Yes, sir?" His tone left some margin for doubt.

Will pressed on. "Your confusion stems from the fact that the wizards here in Trendham aren't really wizards."

"But last year I saw one do—"

Will cut him off, "They're apprentices, or that's what they should be called."

"Doug told me his uncle in Bondgrad is a master in the mage guild," stated Oliver in a matter-of-fact tone. "Would you call him an apprentice?"

"Yes."

"To his face?" Oliver seemed incredulous.

"Depending on the situation, maybe. I didn't move us to Trendham to pick fights with the mage guild, remember?"

Oliver nodded, looking to one side and then the other. The subject was beginning to bore him. "Did you move here *because* you're a wizard?"

"Well, no, not really," Will admitted, "but I thought it was fairly important for you to know."

His son nodded agreeably. "Can you tell me why? Or is that still going to be a secret?"

"I'm in a self-imposed exile," said Will.

"So, you sent yourself away? That doesn't make much sense."

"Let me finish. I was a high-ranking officer and although I was born common, I was given the title of duke."

"What's a duke?"

Will blinked. Even as a boy, he'd had a rough idea of the titles of nobility, though he might not have been able to rank them. "It's the highest rank of nobility in Terabinia."

"Oh." His son's face lit up at last. "So you were really important then."

Finally, he's starting to get it, he thought. "Yes. Especially during the war with Darrow, but afterward I had some problems with the king. He saw me as a threat."

"Wow, really? Is that when you exiled yourself?"

"I probably should have, but I didn't. A lot happened. You remember our original last name, don't you?"

"Cartwright," said Oliver immediately. "You said I shouldn't tell anyone."

"That's right. And my first name is William."

Oliver nodded. "I know, although it feels weird thinking of you being called that. Kelvin seems more real to me."

"My name is William Cartwright, and I'm a wizard—from Terabinia," said Will, restating everything in one sentence. "Do you understand?"

"Yes," said his son. "But I still don't know why you left. Did you kill someone?"

He nodded. "I'm not proud of it, but I killed a lot of people. That's part of the reason I didn't want to tell you. It isn't why I left and gave everything up, though."

"Did you kill people in the army?"

"Yes."

"Well, that's all right then—right? You were following orders."

Will shook his head. "It's never really right. It leaves a scar on your soul. And while yes, I was following orders in the beginning, later on I was giving the orders. I'm also responsible for the lives taken by the men who were under my command."

"But it was still during the war," clarified Oliver.

"Not all of it," corrected Will. "Sometimes it was in self-defense, or to protect others, but if I'm being honest, I also killed some people to satisfy my need for vengeance."

"Is that why you're so good with a sword?"

"Yes, but I used magic a lot of the time."

"Wow, really?"

Will nodded.

Oliver scratched at his chin. "I didn't think magic was used for fighting very much."

"It isn't, in Trendham," said Will.

"Wait, are you a sorcerer? Doug said most of the wizards in Terabinia are sorcerers. Is that what makes you different?"

Will closed his eyes for a moment. *Mother, grant me patience.* "No. I am most assuredly *not* a sorcerer. I'll explain the particulars to you when you start training, but the short answer is that sorcerers use elementals, and elementals are created by enslaving the souls of dead men. It's a disgusting practice. I'm a true wizard, one of the few remaining in Hercynia, though hopefully there will be a lot more in the future."

Oliver picked out one particular phrase from his father's words. "When I start training? What do you mean?"

"To be a wizard," said Will simply.

"I don't want to be a wizard. I want to be a warrior."

"Why? Do you have any idea how dangerous it is?"

"Yes, but even your friend said I was a natural."

Tiny, thought Will, grimacing internally. "That doesn't mean you should be a warrior. There are so many other things you can do with your life. The world is at peace. People can build, grow, create art, make music—why would you choose such a dangerous profession?"

Oliver rolled his eyes, then picked up his practice sword and moved a few steps away. A second later, the wooden blade became a blur as he whipped it through an exercise routine meant for limbering up before practice. It was highly stylized, not something to be used in an actual fight, but Will's son executed the moves with a perfect blend of speed and efficiency. A few seconds later, the sword stopped with a snap, pointing directly at an imaginary enemy. He turned back to his father and replied, "Why did you teach me this?"

"So you could protect yourself," said Will immediately, "but—"

"But I'm *good* at it," interrupted his son. "Better than you, and I'm just getting started. And more important to me, it feels right. I know you think fighting is always wrong, but it's what I'm meant to do, and if that's the case, I might as well try to do it to protect people."

Will knew he had failed then. His years of keeping secrets had backfired, and his son had learned the wrong lesson, since the only thing Will had been willing to teach Oliver had been the sword. It was only natural that the boy thought weapons and weapon training was the most important thing in the world. Slowly, he stood up, stretching muscles that had started to cool already. "Better than me, eh?"

"With a sword," Oliver clarified somewhat hastily.

Will's voice emerged in a flat, even tone. "It seemed to me we were pretty evenly matched this morning."

Chapter 25

"It's practice," said his son. "I'm not trying to prove anything, but I've been faster than you for a while."

He picked up a practice sword. "Let's compare."

"Compare?"

He nodded. "You say you've been holding back. Let's see how good you are. Let's compare your skill, and if you really are as good as you say, then we can compare it to some of the things I've been holding back." Stepping forward, he set his feet and motioned for Oliver to attack. The teen obliged, but cautiously, and after several passes, Will grew impatient. "If you want to convince me, you're going to have to do better."

"I don't want to hurt you," said Oliver, concern in his eyes.

"You can't," said Will, "but if you do, I can fix it, just like Tiny offered to fix you that day." Oliver's eyes widened, but Will continued, "Did you think I wasn't watching?" He pressed forward, attacking more quickly than ever before. "Show me, son. You think you can hurt me, show me. If you can't, you'll be the one in pain."

Oliver's focus narrowed. He knew his father was trying to unnerve him. Students always had a disadvantage against their teachers, and even more so, sons against their fathers. A fight was as much a battle of personality as it was a matter of speed and strength. He quickened his pace, blocking and attacking without hesitation. *If he wants a bruise, he'll get one,* thought Oliver.

Suddenly, Will found himself on his back foot and struggling to keep up. Oliver was moving faster than he would have thought possible. The teen's speed and the force of his blows exceeded what one would expect from someone of his size. Will had fought such opponents before, though usually such quickness was only found in supernatural foes. *He's controlling his turyn and enhancing his body.* It was something any magic practitioner could do, but in most cases, it was done crudely.

Will was already reinforcing his own body, but he could only do so much. His skills in that regard had always been limited. Arrogan had been much better at it, which had enabled the ancient wizard to always stay ahead of him during their staff practice. The feeling Will got now was similar to that.

He was forced to back up, step by step, for he couldn't match his son's speed.

It wasn't reckless speed, either. The boy was still in complete control of himself, watching Will's actions and responding perfectly to attack or defend. In a moment, he would seize an opening and land the blow Will had asked for.

Will didn't wait for it to happen, though. Abruptly, he stopped retreating and pressed an attack, leaving himself open.

Oliver didn't shy away. He knocked his father's thrust out of line and whipped his sword back with blinding speed. He didn't want to do it, for at that speed, the wooden blade would likely leave a terrible bruise, but he couldn't pull the blow if he wanted the strike to land. His wooden blade swept back to strike his father's ribs with crushing force.

Or it should have. The practice sword stopped a foot short of his father's midsection.

Will grinned at his son. "Would you look at that? It seems like you missed your chance."

Oliver defended himself from his father's attempt to capitalize on the moment, but only barely. Stepping back, he asked, "What was that?"

"Magic. It's a shame you don't have any," said Will with a smug look.

"Don't you have to do something to cast a spell?"

Will shook his head and continued pressing his attack. "You're confusing me with the pretend wizards you've heard about before. Most magic can be done in an instant if the wizard is good enough."

Oliver's foot landed on something unexpected, and he stumbled. Again, Will's blade nearly caught him, and he barely managed to keep from receiving a hard strike to his right side. Backing up more, Oliver studied the ground but saw no sign of whatever he had tripped on.

"It's hard to fight when you're tripping over your own feet," said his father with a tone of mock sympathy.

"More magic?"

His father answered with a smile.

Oliver could see the direction things were going, and it didn't look good for him. His father's abilities were completely unknown, and he was probably going to lose, but he didn't give up. Given the new situation, he had only one option if he wanted to win. Surprise.

When Will engaged again, Oliver fought hard but gave ground. When he stumbled again, he let himself fall, but he did so with purpose, catching himself with one hand and grabbing a handful of dirt. His father didn't give him time to recover, but Oliver didn't need it. With the help of that hand, he reversed direction and then sprang upward, into his father's attack. His sword was held close to his body with the other hand, preventing the attack from hitting him properly, and as he turned, he hurled the dirt into Will's face.

At the same time, he tried to hook his father's ankle with one leg and whipped his sword back in line for another attack, one Will couldn't see while he had dirt in his eyes. Magic or no magic, his father couldn't stop everything. Either he would fall, or he'd be hit, and most probably, both.

Things happened so fast that Oliver had trouble understanding what happened. The dirt failed to reach his father's face, and Will stepped over the leg attack. His father's sword was still out of line for a block, but for some reason it didn't matter. A strange buzz filled Oliver's ears, and he watched with disbelief as Will cut through his wooden sword with an empty hand. Meanwhile, the sword that had been out of line for the block came around to strike heavily against the astonished teen's shoulder. Pain flashed, and Oliver sat down, staring up at his father. Oliver blinked, but not because of the pain. He simply couldn't believe he'd lost. One word escaped his lips. "How?"

"Magic," said his father once again. "You're fast, I'll give you that, but I've fought things faster and stronger. Monsters that eat people and don't die when you cut them."

"It's not fair," muttered Oliver.

"No, it's not," agreed Will. "Neither was that fistful of dirt. Good idea, by the way. Unfortunately, it's not enough against someone like me. It will never be enough." He held out his hand to help his son to his feet.

Oliver accepted the hand, and Will spoke again. "I don't need a sword to defend myself. Do you know why I learned to use one?" When Oliver didn't say anything, he continued, "Because there are times when even magic isn't enough. For you, the opposite is true. A sword will never be enough to beat someone like me. You need more. You need magic. Why not learn? You've got a teacher right in front of you."

Stubborn as ever, Oliver responded, "Wardsmen have magic." He regretted it a second later when an evil glint appeared in his father's eye. Something happened, though he wasn't sure what at first. Then he realized he wasn't breathing—*couldn't* breathe. His lungs stubbornly refused to obey him.

"You've seen nothing yet, son. Do you think a wardsman can fight if he can't breathe? What if he can't move?"

Oliver's body seized up as his father spoke, and he began to fall. Will caught him and eased him to the ground, but that did little to ease the panic that threatened to overwhelm Oliver's mind. He still couldn't breathe, and the only thing left under his control was the movement of his eyes. Desperate, he stared at his father.

An eternity passed while Will stared down at him, and Oliver's heart gradually began beating harder and faster. Then he released the source-link spell. Oliver immediately began gasping for air. "I've kept you in the dark for too long," said Will. "For that I apologize. Are you all right?"

Oliver nodded breathlessly, then tried to stand. His head struck an invisible barrier, causing him to fall back on his rear end. Reaching out, he felt the air above and around himself. He was surrounded by some sort of perfectly transparent wall. "What's this?"

"A force-dome," said Will. "Frequently used for defense, it also makes an effective prison. You can try to break it if you like, but you'd be wasting your time."

"Let me out."

"I will. Once I think you have a healthy respect for magic."

"I do. I understand now."

Will shook his head sadly. "No. I'm afraid you don't, but you will." The ground beneath Oliver shifted, opening into a hole just large enough to fit his body. The teen scrambled to get out, but the dome overhead had vanished, replaced by flat pane that forced him down. The earth filled back in, burying him up to his neck. Reaching down, Will patted him on the head. "There's a lot more to magic than you've seen, and I'm only showing you the things that almost any magic user could do to you. In a real fight, most of them wouldn't have the skill or motivation to try something so gentle. They'd simply kill you—like this." He glanced at the practice post that stuck up from the middle of the yard. The top half exploded into splinters.

"Dad, please. Let me out." Oliver's voice was calm, but fear had taken hold of his heart.

Will saw the change, and a wave of disgust swept over him, but it wasn't aimed at his son; the emotion was reserved purely for himself. *I'm a monster.* He knew he'd gone too far. Using the grave-digging spell, he quickly freed Oliver and apologized. "I think I overdid it, Olly. Sorry."

Oliver was brushing dirt off and trying to get his heart back under control. He looked away for a moment, blinking to clear his eyes. "I'm fine."

Will sat down next to him. "Before I came to Trendham, I went through—a lot. More than I'm ready to tell. Part of the reason is that I wasn't always a good man. When it comes to fighting and killing, no one is—they can't be. It doesn't matter whether you're pushing a blade into someone or using a spell, acts of violence require a certain amount of conviction—and that choice hurts."

"I know, Dad. I'm not a kid anymore."

"You're right," agreed his father. "I'm just telling you that because I regret some of my choices. You're going to have to make your own mistakes."

"I'll think about it," said Oliver. "But I still don't think I want to be a wizard."

"Keep thinking. We can talk it over in a couple of weeks."

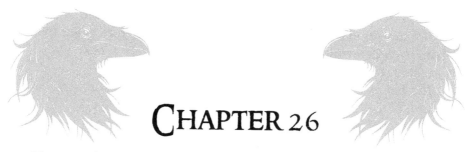

Chapter 26

The next day, just before noon, Will took Erisa and Oliver to pick up Sammy at her home in Bondgrad. It was the first time for either of them seeing Roc's Roost, and it was Oliver's first time being teleported, much less visiting the capital.

The communication tablets Tabitha had given Will made it simple to coordinate things. Consequently, Sammy was waiting in the rooftop garden just outside her rooms when they teleported to her. She smiled and stepped forward to give Erisa a hug first, as it was obvious that Oliver needed a moment to adjust.

Will put a hand on his son's shoulder. "This is Bondgrad. We're on the roof of a large public house named Roc's Roost, so don't jump over the railings."

Oliver had a tight grip on his father's tunic, as though he was afraid a gust of wind might blow him away. His head swiveled back and forth, studying his surroundings with obvious wonder. Staring upward, he marveled, "The clouds look like the ones at home."

"They're different clouds," said Will, "but it's still the same sun above us, and happily, the weather is the same. I'm hoping it will be nice in Cerria, too."

"Shouldn't it be?" asked Oliver.

Will chuckled. "It might, but there's no guarantee. It might be sunny here and raining there, or the reverse."

"Really?"

Nodding, Will added, "Yes, it doesn't rain everywhere all at once. Air currents move rain and storms around constantly. It's a big world."

"I never really thought about it before," said his son. "I just assumed it was the same everywhere."

"If it was the same everywhere there wouldn't be deserts in Faresh and jungles in Delgath. Not only does the weather vary from place to place, some places get a lot more rain than others," explained Will.

Sammy was growing impatient. Hands on her hips, she made her mind known. "How long do I have to wait for my hug, Olly?"

Oliver smiled. "Auntie Ess!" He obliged her request, and as the two of them stood together Will realized his son was now taller than his cousin. *He's growing so fast,* thought Will.

"Is this really where you live?" asked Oliver.

"It's beautiful," remarked Erisa. "Are we really standing on the top floor?"

Sammy beamed at them. "Yes and yes. I suppose I need to give you two a tour of the place. Just remember, if we talk to anyone, I'm known as Madeleine here."

"So you're in disguise too," observed Oliver. "Did you self-exile like Dad?"

Sammy glanced at Will before answering. He nodded, although it really wasn't necessary. He'd used the tablet to let her know about his revelations to Oliver the day before, so she already knew what subjects were safe. "I did," she admitted, "but in my case, it was just to protect you and your dad. No one was hunting me for my own sake. So, your dad finally fessed up about his magic? Were you surprised?"

"A little," admitted Oliver, then his eyes went past her. "Is that your room?"

"Rooms," said Sammy. "That leads to the front room. The door over there leads to the large bath. The one behind you leads to a similar suite, but I don't use that one. I rent it out sometimes."

"And you own both of them?"

She grinned and her eyes lit with undisguised glee. "I own it all, Olly. From here all the way down to the piece of bridge it sits on."

"We're on a bridge?" Amazed, Oliver rushed over to the railing to look down on the river and the busy thoroughfare beneath them. "Wow!" After a second, he added, "You never told me you were rich." Despite being the size of some men, at moments like this, the teen's enthusiasm and energy made it plain just how young he was.

Erisa joined the two, and Will trailed behind as Sammy gave them a tour of Roc's Roost from top to bottom. She gave them a brief history of the establishment and a sanitized version of how she had gone from manager, to partner, to major owner of the iconic business.

Will noticed Alyssa as they were passing through the crowd on the main floor. Irrationally, he worried that she might say something, but she merely smiled and nodded at him. Half an hour later, they were going back up to the roof, and Will realized his worries had been for naught. Sammy glanced back at him with mischief in her eye. "You should visit again, Will. You don't have any excuses now."

"Can I come?" piped up Oliver immediately.

"Absolutely!" said Sammy. "You don't even have to bring your father. Just have him give me some warning and you can spend the weekend with me anytime you like." Will frowned slightly, and Sammy saw his expression, so she added, "I'm his aunt, so whatever you're thinking, put it out of your mind."

"I didn't say anything," returned Will.

"I can come, can't I?" Oliver asked, looking to his father.

"As long as your aunt isn't busy and we don't have anything going on," said Will.

His son rolled his eyes. "We never have anything happening."

"Your father is just being cautious," explained Sammy. "You're so handsome he's worried the ladies here might start fighting over you."

Will glared at his cousin, but Oliver just rolled his eyes. Erisa spoke next, breaking the tension. "Perhaps we go. I'm sure Lady Wellings is anxious to see us."

Now Will frowned at Erisa. "Mom, please don't call her that. Tabitha will be hurt if you use titles."

"Aunt Tabitha is a lady?" asked Oliver. "What does that mean exactly?"

Will tried to explain, "It's a general honorific that can be used for most noble women, but you should only use it for those of the lower ranks. There are other terms used when in the presence of greater nobility, unless you outrank them yourself, then sometimes it's all right to use *lady* in a more informal manner."

Oliver stared at him blankly.

Sammy laughed. "Actually, it's even more complicated than that, but you don't need to worry about it today unless they have a guest. Everyone there is family."

The teen quickly asked, "If we're family, does that mean we're also ladies and uh…"

"Lords," Will supplied, "and no, it doesn't."

"But you were a duck, right?"

Sammy giggled at that, and Will smiled despite himself before correcting Oliver. "Duke. I was a duke, and no, I gave up that title, so I'm just a nothing now."

Erisa objected, "You were never a nothing."

"Oh, he was something all right," remarked Sammy.

Will sighed. "Gather around. Let's go before I change my mind."

***

Since the weather was nice, Tabitha had chosen to wait for them in the garden. She smiled as soon as she saw them appear, and within minutes, her children had gathered around for a confusing round of introductions. Once all the names had been given, Christopher looked up at Oliver and asked, "How old are you?"

"Fifteen."

The seven-year-old seemed doubtful. "You sure?"

"Christopher, manners," warned Tabitha.

"Momma, he's huge. Just look at him. He's bigger than Uncle Will!"

Edward chimed in, "Uncle Will is taller, but Oliver is wider."

For some reason, that surprised both Will and Oliver, and the two of them began eyeing one another. Oliver's growth had been gradual, and although Will had noticed the youth's growing musculature, he still thought of him as a gangly boy. It came as a shock when he realized that Oliver's shoulders were just as broad, if not slightly broader, than his own. *How much more will he grow before he reaches eighteen?* Will wondered.

James interrupted then, arriving with a tray full of pastries and other delights. "Would any of you like something sweet? No? I guess I'll just take these back then."

A chorus of no's rang out as his children swarmed over to him. Oliver hesitated, then joined them. "Save some for the others," Will warned.

Tabitha overrode him. "Don't listen to your father, Oliver. James always tells cook to make too much. There's even more still in the kitchen, so don't hold back."

When it was just the two of them, Will warned his sister, "You have no idea how much he can eat."

She shrugged. "Then we'll make more, and if he eats us out of house and home, I'm sure you've got enough stored in your limnthal to feed a small army. You always do."

Sammy interrupted them, "The house looks lovely from here. Can I have a tour?"

Tabitha grinned. "Of course, but I'll need a hug first."

Close as ever, the two were soon chatting, and Erisa went with them when they headed toward the house, leaving Will and James with the kids, and more importantly, the pastries. The two fathers stood together in a comfortable silence. When everyone had had their fill of sweets, Edward began teaching Oliver their latest game.

After revealing his biggest secret and learning that Oliver had secrets of his own, Will saw his son with different eyes. As big as some men, Oliver's speed and dexterity were far beyond those of his younger cousins. Will would have chalked it up to his son's greater age, but after their no-holds-barred fight the day before, he paid closer attention. The signs were there, right in front of him. Oliver's hands moved with speed and precision, and any time he seemed slow, it was because he was uncertain what to do, rather than any other cause.

It was normal for older children to hold themselves back when playing with smaller kids, but Will could see that Oliver had to do more than most. At times, his son was deliberately pretending to be clumsy. *How long has he been doing this?* Will wondered. He increased the turyn sensitivity of his eyes to the point that the ambient energy around him was almost blinding—but not quite.

Will didn't like increasing his sensitivity to such levels because it would give him a headache within minutes, but it was a useful ability for specific situations. Ordinarily, he would do it if he was tracking trace amounts of turyn someone had left behind, but on this occasion, he was using it to do something that most thought impossible without specialized equipment. Will studied the turyn as it moved within Oliver's body, traveling back and forth between the center of his body and his extremities.

It was difficult since simply being able to see turyn didn't enable a person to see through flesh. Will had turned up his visual acuity to the point that he could see the faint glow that emanated from Oliver's skin. By observing the changes in that glow, and the shifts in frequency, Will could get a crude view of what Oliver was doing with his internal turyn.

Comparing that to what he saw in the other children, or even James, was instructive. Where the turyn within everyone else was diffuse and moved slowly, Oliver's shifted and flowed with speed and efficiency. Will's head began to ache, so he returned his vision to normal. *He's got a natural aptitude,* he decided. *As an athlete, he would probably become a champion in most sports. As a warrior, he'll be a master swordsman, or any other weapon he puts his mind to learning.*

Arrogan had once told him never to underestimate the physical abilities of those who trained for years at sports or physical combat. Even those with no magical sense would develop the ability to reinforce themselves, to become stronger or faster. While a mage could consciously do the same, granting themselves an advantage over the average person, only those with a real affinity for it could approach the physical abilities of someone who had mastered an art, like swordsmanship.

His grandfather had had that affinity, and Will wished he were still alive to advise him now. He would know better what pitfalls and boons that Oliver's physical affinity might bring.

"You seem lost in thought," observed James.

Will blinked. "Sorry. I've been a terrible guest."

James gave him an irritated look. "Guest? You're family. You're supposed to be able to relax here."

"I'm still figuring out all the rules," he replied.

"It's very simple," said James. "Pay heed to my words. If you ever need to figure out the difference between a guest and family, this is the easiest rule to discern the difference. Are you ready?"

Will nodded.

"If you were to drop your trousers and take a shit on my lawn, what do you suppose would happen?"

Will choked briefly. "I'd die of embarrassment. Why would I do something like that?"

"Stay with me," urged James. "What would I do in that situation?"

"Ummm." Will was at a loss for ideas.

"Well, I'd probably be concerned, if it was because you'd lost control of your bowels, or angry, if you did it with deliberation, but either way we'd have a conversation. In the end, you would still be family, either way. Now, if someone else, a stranger, or even a guest, did that, what do you think would happen?"

"This is Terabinia, so it would depend on their rank in the peerage. Your response to a duke would be very different from your response to a landless knight, for example."

James held up a finger. "Shhh. Forget about the aristocracy for a moment. Let's pretend we didn't have those concerns for this."

"I'm not sure then," said Will.

James laughed, "Well, for starters, I'd be very unlikely to invite any guest who did that back again, and if it was a stranger, I might well have them arrested and put in jail."

"What was the point of this mental exercise?" asked Will.

"That's an easy way to know if someone is family or not, regardless of blood. Imagine them shitting on your lawn. If you'd have them arrested, they aren't family," said James with a grin.

Will gave him a dubious look. "Did you come up with this on your own?"

James lifted his eyes and stared dramatically at the horizon. "It's a bit of revered wisdom from my late father, may the Mother hold him forever in her arms. He was full of sage advice."

"I see," said Will diplomatically.

"Do you feel better?"

In truth, Will was now uncomfortably aware of his bowels, and he was thinking it might be time to find a privy, but he kept that to himself. "About what?" he asked instead.

"My home is your home," said James. "You don't have any obligation to entertain me with conversation. That was the point."

"Of course. It's obvious to me now," agreed Will with a faintly sarcastic undertone. Then he remembered something and slapped his thigh. "I've a question I've been meaning to ask you!"

"Oh?"

Will tapped the raven pin on his collar. He'd worn it to show his appreciation for the gift. "A math question. What will the enchantment do if it's forced to divide by zero?"

"You mean if it has to divide zero by another number? That can't happen. The inputs will always give a denominator of at least one. Actually, the numerator will also always be greater than zero, otherwise the enchantment wouldn't be active to calculate anything. Where are you going with this?"

Will was shaking his head. "No, I meant divide *by* zero."

"That's undefined, so there wouldn't be an output," said James. Then he added, "Let's be clear, though. Any person the pin comes into contact with will have turyn, so the numerator can't be zero, and they'll also have a source, so the denominator won't be zero either."

"Humor me," said Will. "Let's say I put the pin on a dead person."

"Then nothing. They've no turyn, so the pin wouldn't be active."

"And let's say that I somehow faked their turyn, so that the pin's enchantment would read them," explained Will.

"How would you do that?" asked James. "People aren't bladders. You can't just fill them up like you would a bucket with water."

"Bear with me. Assume I'm clever and I found a way. What would the enchantment do?"

James rubbed his chin. "I'd have to go through the script to be sure, but at a guess, it should do nothing."

"So the quartz stays clear?" prompted Will. "No color?"

"Yes," said James. "I'll still have to check, but I'm ninety-nine percent sure that's what would happen. Where are you going with this?"

"I'll tell you if you help me modify the enchantment. I have a special use in mind. You'll have to keep it a secret, though."

"A secret, eh?" James' eyes lit with enthusiasm, then he asked, "Can I tell Tabitha?"

"Just her. No one else."

His brother-in-law nodded. "Deal. So, what do you want it to do?"

Will smiled. "Currently, it has four output states. Clear when it's not being worn, or if a normal person wears it. Green if someone who is first-order wears it, then blue, or red, et cetera. Right?"

James nodded. "Within the script, the calculation returns a one for normal, a two for first order, a four for second-order, and an eight if it's a third-order wizard."

"So I want to add a fourth possibility, in the event that the enchantment's calculation returns an undefined number."

"Division by zero," muttered James. "I can easily add a color for an undefined result, but it won't ever happen, so I'm not sure I see the point. Unless..." His eyes drifted into the distance. "Oh! You mean—!"

Will put a finger to his lips, then nodded. "The less said, the better."

James glanced behind himself, then around the yard. "You think they could be listening? Here?"

Will shrugged. "I assume someone is watching at all times."

"Really?"

"Every day, every minute, every second," said Will.

"But that would be highly impractical," argued James. "No one has the time, or the interest to be honest. Consider who I—"

"Consider who *I* am," interrupted Will.

"He's the Stormking!" shouted Elaina. She had been eliminated from the latest game and had wandered up unnoticed.

James seemed startled, but Will nodded at his niece, giving her a warm smile. "Exactly." Glancing over, he saw Oliver had paused to pay attention. Will hadn't been entirely sure if his son had put all the pieces together, and their conversation had gone off on a tangent the day before, but Elaina's proclamation removed any uncertainty. Oliver met his father's gaze, then returned to the game. If the news bothered him, he gave no sign of it.

"It's still impractical," reiterated James.

"True," Will agreed. "And it's likely that most of the time no one is watching or listening, but I live with the assumption that someone always is. I guard my words. I guard my actions."

His brother-in-law scratched his head. "That sounds exhausting."

"It was worse when I was the prince consort," said Will. "Just being a regular person has been positively relaxing for the most part, but I still assume someone is always watching."

"No one can live like that."

"Selene did—does," said Will. "I picked up the habit from her, but you get used to it, somewhat."

"How?"

He shrugged. "It's like picking your nose. You just pay attention to where, when, and how before you do it." Looking down, he made a silly face at Elaina, who had inspired him with a finger up one of her nostrils. She pulled something out and proudly showed it to him.

"Elaina! What have I told you about that?" exclaimed her father.

CHAPTER 27

The next day, Oliver had school, so Will didn't see his son until after he had finished at the 'Goat and taken Dr. Lorentz for his evening session in Wurthaven. They didn't talk much until after they had eaten and Oliver had finished washing the dishes.

"Hey Dad?" Oliver was drying his hands with a towel as he walked out of the kitchen.

"Yes?"

"Can magic do dishes?"

Will's face twisted into a sly grin. "There are spells for it."

"How long does it take?"

"It depends on the spell. The one I use is quick and efficient, but it took me a long time to master it."

"How long?"

Will made a show of thinking about it, then answered, "Two years?"

Oliver's jaw dropped. "Years?"

He nodded. "It's the most complex and difficult cleaning spell ever created, but it's able to clean almost anything in a wide range of situations, including people."

"Did you feel like the two years was worth it because of your work at the Laughing Goat?"

The expression on Oliver's face was one of complete sincerity, and although Will was tempted to laugh, it was a good reminder that the version of himself that Oliver knew was far different from the version he saw in his own head. *To him, I'm a humble cook who happens to be a wizard.* He shook his head. "No, I actually had two reasons. At first, I just wanted a way to clean my clothes or bathe without the usual rigamarole. I was pretty busy back then and I didn't know many spells. When I looked into the subject, I discovered there were dozens, perhaps hundreds of different cleaning spells, each one designed for a different use case. Some were for dishes, others for laundry, for bathing, or simply to clean mud from boots. Although they were all much simpler and easier to learn, I didn't want to have to memorize a spell for every possible situation. So, being stubborn, I decided to learn the really hard spell that would do it all instead."

"Still, two years? How much cleaning did you need to do?"

Grinning, Will replied, "You're fifteen. Imagine how much you'll have to clean over the coming decades. I think it was worth it. Not to brag, but the last time I checked, I was the only person who fully mastered it, to the point of being able to instinctively cast it. Even the spell's designer, who did have it memorized, had to spend a minute to construct the spell each time she wanted to use it. That may have changed by now, though."

"Instinctively cast?"

"Reflex cast is the more common term," said Will. "It means I just have to think about it and I can produce the spell's effect. When you learn a spell, you have to memorize a sequence of runes and put them together in a three-dimensional construct before expressing the turyn to activate it. When a wizard uses a spell long enough, and often enough, they often develop the ability to reflex cast it."

"So you use it a lot."

"What are you more likely to do every day, wash dishes, or destroy a practice dummy in the back yard?"

"You did that really fast too."

"The force-lance is a much simpler spell, but yes, I can reflex cast it as well."

Oliver chewed on his lip for a moment. "What was the second reason?"

Will had to think for a moment. "Oh! It was the girl. The one who designed the cleaning spell. I was somewhat enamored, and I wanted to impress her."

His son hesitated, then asked, "Was she my mom?"

That struck home. Will hadn't told Oliver much about his mother, other than that she'd been from his home village and that she'd died during the war with Darrow. After a second, Will answered, "No. This was after she died."

"What was she like?"

He was tempted to substitute his memories of Selene, but Will had had a crush on Annabelle Withy for several years during his childhood. It was easy enough to share those memories with his son, and no fabrication was required—except for the ending. In his story, Annabelle was never captured. Instead, she and Will made a risky choice and Oliver was the result. They never married, as the destruction of Barrowden got in the way, and she died to a stray arrow from a Darrowan soldier a year after Oliver was born.

"Did you love her?"

The earnestness in his son's face tore at his heart. "I'm not sure," said Will. "If things had gone differently, I think I might have, but we never had a chance. After Barrowden burned, I joined the army. I didn't even know you existed until I went back home."

Oliver nodded. "Was she pretty?"

"Find a mirror and you'll have your answer. You resemble her, not me." When his son gave him a grumpy look, he added, "Yes, she was very pretty." The conversation trailed off, and Will hoped it would find a different course, so after a few seconds he asked, "Did you hear what your cousin Elaina called me yesterday?"

Oliver laughed. "Yeah. The others said it too. It was pretty funny."

He'd been dreading the response, but that wasn't what he'd expected. "Funny?"

"Yeah. I didn't really think about your name before, but after they said it, I figured out why. It's kind of awesome. I wish I could tell Doug at school; he'd lose his mind!"

Oliver was grinning from ear to ear, but Will was nonplussed. "Awesome? Why would you think that?"

"The Stormking killed a king, slaughtered a ton of soldiers, killed trolls, and fought armies!" said Oliver with enthusiasm. "Everyone was scared of him. Doug would shit his pants if he thought you were really him."

Will stared at his son with a blank expression. *Does he think it's just a joke? I did tell him that Cartwright is a common name in Terabinia, but still...*

"If you could snap your fingers and wash all the dishes, why do I have to do them?"

Oliver's words brought Will back from his thoughts. "Because you wouldn't learn anything if I did everything for you. If you want to do dishes with a snap of your fingers, become a wizard."

"I've been thinking about that, Dad. As cool as being a wizard seems, I still want to become a wardsman."

Will fought to keep his countenance calm, then played his final card. "Why not do both?"

"Huh?"

"Wardsmen use magic, in their own limited way, and it shortens their lives. That's a major reason why people say they die young, aside from the dangerous job. The people playing at wizardry in Trendham have the same problem, but it doesn't have to be that way."

Oliver was frowning. "What do you mean?"

"You've seen my weapons and armor. Just being a wizard doesn't mean I can't fight. If I became a wardsman, I could use my tattoos all day long without fear of premature aging. You could too, if you had a foundation in true wizardry—*and* you could learn to do the dishes without getting your hands wet."

His son was watching him suspiciously. "This feels like a trick."

Will sighed. "To be honest, I'm hoping you'll change your mind about being a wardsman after you see what magic can do, but if not, at least you won't be killing yourself. Either way, I promise you I won't interfere—so long as you complete the compression training."

"How many years does that take?" asked Oliver in a tone of long-suffering. "They won't give tattoos to old men."

"Mastering magic is the ambition of a lifetime, a very long lifetime, for a wizard," said Will, "but assuming you have no interest in that, you could complete the first compression within six months. You could be done shortly after turning sixteen, but I'd advise you to try for the second compression if things go—"

"Is that required?"

"Well, no. You could safely use magic, or tattoos after just the first compression. It will also double your lifespan. If you try for the second compression, that would double it again, and the third yet again."

"Would it make me a better warrior?"

"Probably not, but—"

"I'll do the first compression then."

"And after that?"

Oliver's gaze was steady. "I'll think about it, Dad, but you said it was my choice, right? You won't stop me if I do the first compression, right?"

Will nodded. "Very well."

Oliver's eyes brightened. "When can we start?"

CHAPTER 28

It had been nearly two decades since Will underwent compression training, and although his memories of it were unpleasant, Oliver's experience seemed to be plagued by pitfalls and problems. Will started with the candle spell, so that Oliver could start to learn what his source was doing as he went about his daily life, but the boy claimed he could barely see the flame.

"It's so dim," had been Olly's complaint.

It looked perfectly normal to Will, but since the flame was composed purely of turyn, he supposed it made sense that Oliver would have trouble. When Arrogan had first used the candle spell on him, he'd already developed a mild ability to sense turyn, and Will's later students had all already been partly trained, so actually seeing turyn wasn't a problem.

Realizing he had put cart before the horse, Will set out to locate some Diviner's Sage, the same psychedelic herb that had fully awakened his own sight. In Wurthaven, they used a variety of techniques, or sometimes relied on certain mushrooms, since Diviner's Sage was more difficult to find, but he had already noticed some in the area years ago.

The reason the plant was so rare was that it only grew near congruence points with the fae realm. Something about the fae energies that leaked across from the other world seemed to be vital for the plant's healthy growth. Since he'd already located the few congruence points near Lystal, it was a trivial task for Will to locate the plant. He even took Oliver along to teach him to identify it.

The problems started after Olly took his first dose. His reaction to the experience was best described as 'less than pleasant.' Afterward, his normally unshakeable son had been anxious and fearful. "That was horrifying."

"You only have to do it once. Can you see the candle flame clearly now?"

Oliver had nodded, then complained about seeing so many other extra lights and colors. "It's all making me feel nauseous."

"You'll adjust with time," Will had told him in a soothing tone.

Except he hadn't adjusted. Two days later, Oliver made a shocking revelation at breakfast as he shoveled in food. "You were right. I feel better, but I can hardly see the candle flame now."

Will nearly choked on his toast. "What?"

"My stomach feels better, though."

"But you can't see turyn?" Will shifted the currents around them, sending bright ribbons of energy directly in front of his son's eyes.

"Is that the weird lights or the candle flame?"

"Both. Although the candle spell does produce a little bit of normal light."

"Then yes, it's gone," said Oliver, visibly relieved.

"Hmm." Will did some reading after that and discovered that it wasn't uncommon for some students to require a second initiation before their turyn sight remained stable. Oliver wasn't pleased when he heard the solution.

"I'm not taking that again," declared the teen. But after some persuading on Will's part, he reluctantly agreed.

This time was worse. "Everything is melting!" Oliver's reaction went from fear to panic, and even after Will calmed him down, the teen remained in tears. Once the psychedelic effects wore off, Oliver's emotions recovered, but the nausea returned. He threw up everything he ate, and Will had to resort to Gidding's Apothecary to find a recipe for something to stop Oliver's vomiting.

Five days later, Oliver's turyn sight faded away once more. Will suspected it had gone away sooner, but the boy had been trying to hide the fact, fearing the inevitable consequences.

Olly had just gotten home from school and gone to his room. His color had gotten better the day before, although he still claimed to be nauseous. Will checked on him as soon as he returned. "How do you feel?"

"Still queasy," answered his son, but something about his tone rang false.

Will made a gesture with his hands. "Can you see this?"

Oliver nodded. "Yes, sir."

His eyes narrowed. "I didn't do anything."

"Oh. It must have been a random current I saw. I thought it was you," said Oliver, obviously lying.

"Your sight is gone again, isn't it?"

"No, Dad. I can see everything. I promise."

"What am I doing now?" Without gesturing, Will sent ripples through the ambient turyn.

Olly gave a sickly smile. "Nothing. You're trying to trick me again."

Will sighed. "We'll have to try again."

"No! No, Dad. Please, I can't take it. It'll make me sick!" pleaded his son.

Shaking his head sadly, Will replied, "It isn't poisonous. No one has ever died from Diviner's Sage. You just need to relax. It's your anxiety that's causing your problem."

"Dad, no. No. It's not just that. It's the colors afterward. This turyn stuff, it makes everything look funny. Like everything is always moving. I can't handle it. I'll start vomiting again if you make me see that stuff."

"That's temporary," said Will. "You'll adapt. Your brain just needs time to adjust to the extra sensory input."

"No, I won't!" said Oliver, desperate.

"You will, trust me," Will told him soothingly. "It's like sea sickness. Your body will get over it in a day or two." In fact, he knew nothing of the sort. While Will had suffered plenty while getting through his compression training with Arrogan, he'd had no problem at all with seeing turyn. His experience with the plant had come completely by accident, and after a pleasant but disorienting hour lying on the forest floor, his vision had been changed forever. It *had* taken him a while to get used to the new sights, but it had never made him feel ill. "Now, stand up. I already have the dose ready for you."

With an air of resignation, Oliver stood up, but a second later, he bolted for the open window. An invisible barrier blocked his way when he tried to get a leg over the sill. Oliver shifted tactics instantly. "Nana! Help! He's trying to kill me! Nana!" Oliver screamed with the full power of young lungs and the desperate energy of a boy fighting for his life. "Nana! Dad, please, no! Help! Mother save me, it's pois—!"

Will used a source-link to paralyze his son. Stepping forward, he caught the man-sized boy before he fell, then carefully leaned him over, easing him back onto the bed. He pulled out a small vial, unstopped it, and poured the contents into Olly's unresisting mouth. "Lucky for you, I thought this might happen, and I made an extract from the leaves so it would go down easier."

Oliver's eyes rolled wildly back and forth, the only sign of protest he could make, but through the source-link, Will could feel his emotions: denial, fear, and disgust. Will frowned. "You're being dramatic. How do you like the taste? I used peppermint since I know you like the flavor." More ridiculous eye movements were the only answer he received, so Will ignored them and carried on the conversation alone. "No, you don't have to worry about swallowing. It was just a few drops and you'll absorb it directly." He patted his son's head comfortingly. "This isn't my first time pois—err, dosing someone involuntarily, so you have nothing to fear." In the background, Will heard the kitchen door swing open, followed by hasty footsteps.

Will smiled, but for some reason that only increased Oliver's fear, so he shifted tactics and used a sleep spell to send his son into a deep slumber. He released the paralysis, but maintained the source-link so he could monitor the boy's condition. The bedroom door opened a second later. "What's going on here?" demanded Erisa.

"His sight faded again. So I had to readminister the medicine," Will answered calmly.

His mother's eyes narrowed. "That's why I heard my grandson screaming like he was about to be butchered?"

"He was a little reluctant, but I'm sure he understands this is necessary."

"William Cartwright! You can't force drugs onto people! Have I taught you nothing?"

"It's not a drug, it's medicine," he insisted.

His mother's hands were on her hips. "Medicine? Medicine for what?"

"Medicine to cure stupidity, hopefully," he muttered to himself, then he answered, "Medicine to give him better vision."

"It causes hallucinations," his mother shot back. "The child is terrified."

"No he isn't, he's asleep."

Erisa glared at him, her mouth wide in disbelief. "He was yelling his head off a minute ago!"

Will glanced away. "He was getting overwrought, so I had to be persuasive."

"You aren't giving him anything. Wake him up this instant," demanded Erisa.

He shrugged. "I already did. Better to let him sleep through the weird part since he reacts so badly."

She glared at him. "How? It's only been half a minute since I heard him yell."

"Concentrated extract." Will pointed at his mouth.

Erisa rolled her eyes. "A suppository is better for unconscious patients. He might choke."

Will shook his head. "That's why it was concentrated. Only needed a few drops. I didn't want to go the other route, for obvious reasons."

His mother's eyes were still angry. "You should be uncomfortable if you're going to violate someone's free will. I don't understand how you could think this was a good idea."

"It's necessary."

"Drug my grandson again and you'll find out what happens when *I* think something is necessary—for you! Do you understand me?"

Will looked down. "Yes, Mom."

"Honestly, where did you get the idea such a thing was acceptable? How many times have I told you, I never give a patient something without their full knowledge and consent. Something like this is wrong, always and absolutely—wrong."

His eyes drifted to one side. "Someone should have told Arrogan that," he muttered.

"What did you say?"

Will's eyes focused on her. "I said maybe you should have thought about that before you sent me off to live with a crotchety old man in the woods. You have no idea the things Arrogan put me through."

Erisa didn't back down. "I highly doubt he forced drugs down your throat."

In point of fact, Arrogan hadn't, but he'd forced Will through worse things—Will's own first compression came to mind. It had been a near-death experience, and despite *actually* having died once before then, and twice after, Will still thought it had been worse. That still lay in Oliver's future, and if his mother was giving him trouble over a little thing like involuntarily drugging the boy, she would definitely not be on board with Oliver's complaints during the first compression.

"We need to have a talk," he told her solemnly. Reaching out, he took her hand and started for the door.

Erisa pulled him up short. "Is he all right? It might not be safe to leave him alone after what you gave him."

"I know you think I'm heartless, but I'm currently linked to Olly. I can feel his body like my own. I'll know if anything happens. Let's talk at the table so we can sit down."

His mother's face showed a flash of regret at his choice of words. "I never said you were heartless." She followed him out of the room, then added, "Thoughtless, perhaps, and in this case, needlessly cruel, but never heartless."

Will pulled a chair out and held it for his mother. It was something she'd often had him do as a child, and although it was somewhat rare for him now, especially with Oliver around, he liked to do it when he had the chance. Today it served to remind her of his respect. After she was seated, he pulled a chair out for himself and sat beside her, angling his chair so their knees were almost touching. He took her hand in his as he started speaking. "Mom—"

She pulled away. "Doing all this isn't going to change my opinion."

He sighed. "Just give me a few minutes to explain myself. You can make up your own mind after, but I need you to know all the facts first."

She watched him silently, then nodded. "Fair enough."

"First, you're right. He's reacting badly to the Diviner's Sage, I agree. Some people do, but fortunately most of them don't need to use it more than once or twice. I'm hoping the third time is the charm, but I don't know for sure. Second, he needs to be able to sense turyn if he's going to be a wizard, otherwise he won't be able to manipulate turyn properly. Casting spells would be nearly impossible without the ability to see what he's doing."

His mother started to reply, but Will held up one hand. "I know, I know. He doesn't really want to be a wizard. Let me continue. We've already talked many times about the benefits. Even if he only does the first compression, it will double his lifespan."

"That doesn't justify torturing him," argued Erisa. "Not everyone wants or needs to live that long, and if he keeps telling you he—"

"Mom," interrupted Will. He waited until she stopped, then went on, "I'm not disagreeing with you on that, but I haven't finished." Frowning, his mother waved for him to go on. "He wants to be a wardsman, and even though I think it's a stupid choice, I can't seem to talk him out of it. There's a terrible cost to that decision, though. If he doesn't complete at least the first compression before becoming one, not only will he not live twice as long, he will probably live a much shorter life."

"I know it's a dangerous profession, but—"

"No, Mom, it's more than that. Just like wizards, wardsmen are using magic. A wardsman's tattoos require turyn, magic, just like a spell does. Even if they aren't consciously aware of it, they're burning their own lives to empower themselves. Depending on how much they use it, they could live half as long, or even worse—whether or not they ever lose a battle."

Erisa straightened up slightly. "Oh."

Will nodded. "This part is an unexpected trial, I agree. But once we get past it, the first compression will be worse, but it's necessary, otherwise I won't let him leave this house when the time comes. I'd lock him up rather than let him kill himself."

"You can't control your children, William. Trust me. I learned that the hard way with you."

"You're probably right, but I'm his father. I can't in good conscience let him hurt himself. Not if I can stop it."

"Well, I'm his grandmother, and that—"

The stern determination in his eyes stopped her. "I'm his father. You're my mother, and the last thing I'd ever want is to make you angry with me. I know you love him, we both do, but I'm his dad. This is my choice. I'll take the consequences if you decide to punish me for this, but I'm still going to make the decision that I think is right."

They stared into each other's eyes for several tense seconds before finally Erisa looked away. "It's his choice too, not just yours—or mine." Will said nothing, so eventually she asked, "You say the first compression is worse. What does that mean exactly?"

"When the time comes, I'll put a spell cage around his source. It will essentially lock the turyn he's producing into a confined space within him, preventing it from being vented normally. Over a period of hours, it will build up, producing a lot of uncomfortable sensations. For most people, it starts with itching and then burning. Some describe it as feeling the feeling you get when you hold your breath too long."

"What's the purpose of that?" she asked.

"It will force him to clamp down on his source and reduce the turyn it produces. He'll have to halve the amount coming out to feel normal again. It isn't something people learn to do consciously, not at first anyway. The spell cage essentially induces an experience that can't be escaped any other way. People generally don't figure out how to compress their source, even though they know that's what they have to do, so eventually the pain becomes unbearable and they panic. That's what happened to me."

His mother was biting her lip. "I don't like the sound of this. Arrogan did this to you?"

Will nodded, mentally adding, *and worse.* "When it gets to the point that he panics, I'll link to him, like I am right now, and paralyze him so he doesn't hurt himself." *Or us.* Will had made a semi-serious attempt to kill his grandfather with an axe after the terrifying night of his first compression. The memory was funny to him now, but at the time he'd really wanted revenge on the old man.

"And then?"

"Then I spend as long as it takes watching and waiting, until his body, mind, and spirit figure out what to do." He wanted to add an 'or' but he knew better.

"How long will it take?" she asked. "Is it safe?"

"It took me most of a night. I've helped a number of students through it before, though. Sammy got through it in less than four hours."

"And it's safe?" she repeated.

"Very safe," he answered, giving a half-lie. "The second and third compressions don't feel nearly as bad, but they're much more dangerous. A small percentage of those who attempt the second compression die."

"And you did all three, that's what you told me. Arrogan made you do all three. How dangerous is the third one?"

He couldn't gloss over the truth there. "Historically, around half of those attempting it die, but so far, I've had better luck. By paying close attention to recovery time, I think it's possible to tell which students should be allowed to attempt it."

His mother's face had gone pale. "I would have punched that old man in the nose if I'd known. That's how that friend of yours died, isn't it? Seth Gabet, the one you named the school after." Understanding dawned on her features. "*That's* why you named it for him, because you feel responsible."

Will kept his gaze on hers even though he was struggling with his emotions, then nodded.

Erisa exhaled slowly. "And yet you did the same thing to Sammy— to the only family we had left after the attack on Barrowden."

He could almost hear the words she left unspoken, *"You did this to my brother's daughter, the girl I raised and loved like my own."* The condemnation in her eyes burned. Will didn't dare to mention that he'd also done the same to his half-sisters, wife, and friends. He simply nodded once more.

The color returned to her cheeks, and a spark of anger appeared in his mother's eyes. "William Cartwright, I know you had reasons for all of it. I'm no fool. You never told me half the things that happened to you, and I'm grateful for that, because I know some of it would have left me weeping into my pillow at night. No mother wants to see her child suffer the way you did. I'm sure you probably have reasons for taking a risk like that with my little girl—" Erisa's voice cracked, and she paused until her throat would let her continue. A tear tracked down her cheek when she finished, "—but if she had died and I knew the why and how of it, I would *never* have forgiven you. Do you realize that?"

Will blinked, then nodded.

She sniffed, then wiped her cheek with one sleeve. "You're damned lucky it turned out the way it did." Leaning forward, she seized him painfully by the ear and pulled him in for a tight hug. "I love you more than anything in this world, but that would have been too much." Letting go, she pushed him back. "Now, tell me truthfully, because I know you were trying not to scare me. How dangerous is this first compression for Oliver?"

"It really is very safe, especially at his age."

"What does that mean? Why does age matter?"

"For adults it's pretty risky; some of them die suddenly. Seth was a little too old, but he still managed the first and second compression. It was the third that was too much. At Oliver's age, the first compression is very safe."

"But it's possible something could go wrong," she stated firmly. "Don't sugarcoat it."

"It's rare, but not impossible. I'll be linked to him the entire time, so I can feel every heartbeat. If anything goes wrong, I'll remove the spell cage immediately." Arrogan had done the same for him, even though it meant he'd suffered along with him. Will hadn't known that at the time. He'd learned later that it wasn't customary, since death sometimes came suddenly, and even releasing the spell cage at the first sign of serious trouble often did nothing to save the student. The old man had pretended to be tough, but he'd secretly loved his grandson. Arrogan had tortured himself with the source-link simply on the off chance it would make the compression safer. Will would do no less for Oliver.

Erisa's lips pressed into a firm line, but she nodded. "I don't like any of this, but I understand. If you think this is the best thing for him, then I trust your judgment. But you *will* explain all of this to him first."

"I already have, but I'll go over it again to be sure."

"Make sure you do." Erisa's expression was a mixture of frustration and determination. "Close your eyes."

"Huh?"

"You heard me."

Will closed his eyes. He heard his mother move, but he remained still, and an instant later he felt the sting of her palm against his cheek. It wasn't the hardest slap she could have given, but she hadn't held too much back either. Will opened his eyes again. His mother wiped her cheeks once more, then turned and headed for Oliver's room.

"That was for my niece," she said as she walked. "I'm going to go take a nap with my grandson. Hopefully I'll feel better afterward."

CHAPTER 29

Oliver woke later, and shortly after that, he threw up. His turyn sight was back, but as always, it made him extremely nauseous. He also complained to Erisa about the bad dreams he'd had during his forced slumber.

For his father, he only offered burning glares.

His magical sight only lasted two days, and Oliver was sick the entire time. When his nausea passed on the third day, Will tested him to see if he could see turyn, and despite Olly's desperate lies, Will wasn't fooled.

He didn't attempt to give Olly any more Diviner's Sage, however. A break was called for, and Will needed to do some research. Wurthaven didn't have any books on compression training, but they did have plenty of experience with awakening turyn sight in their students. Dr. Lorentz still had another week of training sessions scheduled, so Will was teleporting to Cerria and back every evening anyway. Sneaking into the Wurthaven library unseen would be child's play for him.

When he arrived at Tabitha's at the appointed time, he quickly explained that he'd be walking to the campus with the good doctor for a change, and naturally Tabitha inquired as to why. After a brief explanation of Oliver's problem, Will's sister offered some unexpected advice. "You can probably find some information in the library, but wouldn't it be quicker to ask Vonnie or James?"

Will gave his sister a blank stare for a moment as he processed her words. "Oh!" he exclaimed a second later. "You're right! Why didn't I think of that?"

Tabitha smirked at him. "The problem with being all powerful and the repository of wisdom no one else possesses is that you forget that other people sometimes know things you don't."

Dr. Lorentz was still standing nearby, waiting for Will since he'd said he would walk with him. The conversation hadn't been private, so he interjected, "Lady Wellings, you've made that joke before, but I'm not sure I understand it."

The doctor still only knew Will as Kelvin Wiltshire and was unaware that Tabitha was his sister, so he didn't have the necessary information to piece together Will's true identity. Tabitha gave the man an innocent look. "Which part confuses you, the bit about Kelvin assuming the rest of us are ignorant?"

Lorentz shook his head. "It's the 'all-powerful' part that concerns me. You've made similar statements several times over the past few weeks, and while I'm sure you're not serious, you say it as if you are."

Tabitha's face remained deliberately expressionless as she replied, "That's because I am serious, Dr. Lorentz."

Will gave her a warning glare, then turned to the doctor. "Please pardon her, Dr. Lorentz. She's been teasing me about that ever since she learned about my ability to teleport without a beacon." He took the man by the elbow. "Since I've a solution to my problem, it looks as though you'll be walking alone. I'll be waiting here to take you back when you're done." He escorted the doctor to the front gate, then returned to admonish his sister. "Please don't do that."

Despite having four children, there were times when Tabitha's own childish nature resurfaced, particularly when they were alone. Today was a perfect example as she pouted at her brother. "I'm sick of it."

"Of what?"

"Your anonymity. You're the most powerful person in Hercynia— by leagues! You don't need to hide, and it's silly for the rest of us to have to play along. There's no one left that *could* threaten you, much less anyone stupid enough to try."

"Why does it bother you?" asked Will.

She threw up her hands. "Because I want to brag about you! You're *my* brother. I want to tell people how amazing you are."

"That's a very shallow reason."

Tabitha stuck out her bottom lip. "No, it isn't. Not in Terabinia. You were a duke for a while. You should understand how society works here. Everyone brags about their relations and connections—how closely they're related to this or that important person. That's how the aristocracy works. To hell with the fact that I *used* to be friends with the queen, or the fact that I'll someday be a baroness—my brother is the *Stormking!*" Her eyes lit with an almost comical glee as she made her declaration, and Tabitha let out a deliberately wicked laugh.

Will sighed to cover up the smile that threatened to undermine his argument. "You're incorrigible. You don't attend court anyway, so it shouldn't matter."

"I still have friends," she shot back.

"There's never anyone here but you and the kids," observed Will.

"Ooh, you're going to pay for that one, mister!" snapped Tabitha. "Maybe you should think about why that is."

Will shrugged. "I'm drawing a blank here."

"I still have friends. James and I still entertain when it's our turn, and we *can* afford a nanny when we're invited out. I do have a social life, you nitwit! The reason you haven't seen anyone else is because I have to play at being a hermit for *your* sake."

In a flash, he caught her meaning. When he brought Dr. Lorentz every evening, Tabitha was his teleport anchor, so she had to stay home to enable his project. His assumption that she didn't have a social life was not only wrong—it was mildly insulting, especially since it was his fault. "Oh, damn, Tabbycat, I'm sorry! It didn't even occur to me that you were making sacrifices for my sake."

She frowned. "Stop it. I wasn't trying to make you feel guilty. I like seeing you every day, and the weekend family visits have been a dream come true. Just stop assuming you know everything about me."

"Still, I didn't think—"

"I think you're doing the right thing, helping Dr. Lorentz learn the latest techniques. It's only another week anyway. My point was that I'd love to be able to introduce you to people without making up lies, or brag about you when you aren't here. I'm proud to be your sister. Does that make sense to you?"

"A little," he admitted. "It's different for me, though. Being the 'Stormking' isn't something I enjoy, much less want people to know about."

"Why?"

"It's all power and domination. The few times I've used those abilities, it's like a transformation. I become someone else, and I don't like the person I become."

Tabitha held out her arm and he linked his in hers as they walked back to the house. As they walked, she remarked, "Maybe you should change that."

"What do you mean?"

"Forget about what other people think of the Stormking. Forget what *you* think of the Stormking. You get to decide who the Stormking is, what he means to you and how he acts. Stop thinking of it as becoming someone else. Make your alter ego become *you*. I'm not sure if I'm explaining this well."

Will mulled over her words. The Stormking was just an idea, after all, just as much as his conception of what the title 'First Wizard' meant. His power did bring a different set of feelings, but he was still the one in charge of his actions. In the past, his abilities had caught him by surprise, and he'd evaluated them later based on his early mistakes, but there was no reason to settle for those first impressions.

If there was one thing Arrogan had taught him, it was to make his own decisions rather than let the currents choose his course.

He'd spent a considerable amount of time thinking about what being the 'First Wizard' should mean, what he should represent, and he hadn't limited himself to defining it by past precedents. He intended to recreate the council and forge it into a force to properly represent humanity. In Will's mind, it came down to his very conception of the meaning of the word 'wizard.' His early lessons had been about the philosophical differences between sorcery, warlockry, and true wizardry. At the heart of it all was knowledge, wisdom, and responsibility.

A wizard learns and prepares, he repeated silently to himself. *Magic is his tool and knowledge is his goal. Therefore, the First Wizard's purpose is to ensure that wizardry is practiced in service to the greater good, and the council becomes an instrument of that.*

That was what he'd decided, the simple core of his musings over the past decade. While living in anonymity and eating and breathing humility, Will had slowly forged his idea of that title into a new identity. When he helped destroy the second troll threat, he'd used his talents with reluctance and thought of the Stormking as a kind of moral failure on his part, a moment of weakness in which his alter ego had suppressed the higher purposes of his true self.

But Tabitha's statement had reformulated the problem. *She's right,* he thought. *I choose who I am. The First Wizard is my ideal self. So what would he do with the problem?*

He would make the Stormking his tool, nothing more and nothing less.

As they reached the garden door to the house, Will stopped, then hugged Tabitha. "Thank you. I needed to hear that."

She gave him a wry look. "You've probably taken my advice and twisted it into something weird, haven't you?"

"Maybe," he answered. "But I agree with you. I'd like to be able to brag about my sister too. But I do have important reasons to stay hidden. Chief among them being safety. It doesn't matter if I'm able to kill a dragon. People will try to use my family to control me."

"I know," said Tabitha wistfully. "I just felt like complaining."

The door flew open, and James started shouting before registering their presence directly in front of him. "Tabitha! Vonnie is he—!" He stopped short, closing and opening his mouth in surprise. "Oh. William, you're here. How wonderful! Will you be eating with us? My sister will be here and I'm sure she'd love the chance to talk further." James glanced furtively over his shoulder and then returned his gaze to Will.

"The children are staying with their grandmother for the week, so it's just us adults today." He waggled his brows suggestively.

Will wasn't entirely sure the term 'adults' could be said to include his brother-in-law, nor did he really catch what James was suggesting might happen with his wildly gesticulating eyebrows. Instead, he ignored it all and jumped into what he really wanted to know. "Do you know anything about turyn blindness?"

James' face lit up with enthusiasm. "Of course! Since we have over fifty students each year, it has come up several—ow!" He gave his wife an irritated look. "Why are you poking me?"

"You just said Vonnie was visiting. Perhaps we should wait and ask her input on the matter?" suggested Tabitha.

James waved his hand. "No need for that, dear. What we know is fairly simple—oh!" His eyes lit with understanding. His tone changed. "You're right, though. Veronica is the expert." He turned to Will. "You should ask her after supper. Tabitha and I need to talk about a few things anyway. So, the two of you should have plenty of time to chat, maybe over a glass of wine?"

His brother-in-law's overacting brought out Will's inner devil. "Talk about what things?"

James stared blankly at him. "Pardon?"

"You said you and Tabitha had to talk about a few things. I'm just curious."

"Oh. Err—the laundry?" James looked to Tabitha for support, but she remained silent.

Will raised one brow. "You don't have a laundress? What about magic at least?" He took Tabitha's hand and rubbed the skin of her palm. "Is that why your hands are rough? I can't believe he treats you this way."

His sister smirked, then finally stopped him. "That's enough. Don't tease my husband too much, he might break."

"Oh! Ha, ha!" James' laugh came out stilted. "You had me again, William."

Will winked at him. "I take it Veronica hasn't arrived yet?"

"She had a student appointment, but she should be here in half an hour," said James.

"How about our other project then?" he asked.

"Let me show you. Please excuse us, dear, unless you're interested in seeing it?"

Will's sister waved him on. "I've listened to you talk about it enough. I'm not that interested in the technical details. You two go ahead."

James took the stairs two at a time as he led Will up the stairs to his study. Although Will led an active life, seeing his brother-in-law's excess energy often made him feel tired. *How does he live with all that energy inside him?*

The study itself was actually an amalgamation of what had been a proper office mixed with things that should have remained in a workshop, rather than cluttering up every spare corner. A variety of jeweler's tools and whitesmithing implements littered every potentially empty spot on the desk, the side tables, the floor, and even the seats.

"I thought a jeweler made the pins themselves," Will observed.

James nodded. "Oh, he does! Lawrence Gridstone is his name, by the way, but I designed the mold for the template he uses. Lawrence isn't an enchanter, not that it matters. I wouldn't have left it to anyone else. The enchantment is so lengthy, the chance of an error is too great for me to feel comfortable leaving it to someone else."

There was a set of burners and a crucible near the window, and a rug nearby had obvious burns in it. "Has Tabitha seen that?"

"Better luck next time," said James with a grin. "She gave me hell for it already, so you'll need to find something else if you want to make me worry." James took out a key and unlocked a small box, then lifted something small from it. He offered it for Will to inspect. "Take a look at this."

Will recognized the black metal immediately. "Demon-steel? That's a little dangerous to have in the house, isn't it?"

"The children aren't allowed in here, and I keep it locked in this box just to be extra sure. There's a transducer enchantment worked into the sides that converts any turyn that leaks from it, converting negative to positive so it won't harm anyone."

He couldn't argue with the precautions. Despite the reckless, or perhaps even harebrained impression that James sometimes gave off, the man was thorough when it came to enchanting. As Will turned the metal over in his fingers, he noted that it while it was flat on one side it had the same profile as the center cross-section of the raven pins. Something incredibly tiny was scrawled across the black metal surface, covering it almost entirely. His eyes couldn't make it out, so Will held it out with one hand and adjusted his vision. When that didn't work, he switched tactics and brought it close to one eye, changing the focal length of his eye to magnify the surface. He was barely able to see that the metal bore raised ridges in the shape of incredibly small runes. "This is the enchanting script for the pins?"

"You can read that?" asked James.

"Not really," said Will. "I'd get a headache if I tried to copy it out like this. How did you make this?"

"It's an embossing die for the pins," said James, answering a question he hadn't asked.

Will nodded. "I gathered that, but why? I figured you would cast one half of the pin with the script."

"Casting won't keep the fine details," explained his brother-in-law.

"And engraving?"

"Would work, but it would take ages for a craftsman to do. Imagine using a magnifier and tiny tools for the job. We need to make at least forty or fifty pins every semester for new students. Lawrence would flee the city if I asked him to do that. With this, we can stamp the script into one half of the pin before welding it together—it's much faster. Ask me why I had to use demon-steel."

That had been Will's next question anyway, but he obliged. "Why demon-steel?"

"Good question," said James proudly. He paced around the room with his hands behind his back like a professor beginning a lecture. "For projects that aren't as small, case-hardened steel works, but with runes that tiny, I found that even hard steel won't do. You might get eight or nine decent pins made, but even a soft metal like silver causes too much wear on the tiny ridges in the steel. Demon-steel doesn't deform, so one die will last indefinitely."

"How did you get the demon-steel?"

James made a sour face. "I had to beg Master Salsbury. He's the head of the Artifice Department. They still have a small amount left over from what you acquired."

"I remember him," said Will, handing the embossing die back. "Did you have to beg again after my request?"

"Not for anything," said James. "Besides, you wanted secrecy. They might have asked what changes I intended to make, and that could lead to some awkward explanations. I went back to steel for yours, so I hope you don't need to make more than five or six."

"I thought you said you could get eight or nine from a steel die."

"I'm making one for myself and another for Tabitha," said James. His tone made it clear he wouldn't negotiate on that point.

Will was actually fine with that, though he hadn't intended to directly involve anyone else. "I hope you haven't made it yet. The pin would be an inconvenient form factor."

James smiled broadly. "You were thinking it too! I've already started on the embossing die, but I went with a circular shape so we could use it with several different types of accessories like—"

"—a ring?" finished Will.

"You're too clever, William. Take pity and let me feel like I've contributed something!"

As if designing the original enchantment, figuring out the math, and then modifications for Will's request wasn't enough. "I'd say my part in this was pretty small," said Will. "If this wasn't a secret project, I'd be yelling your praises from the rooftops for everyone to hear."

"Tabitha will be after you for teasing me again," warned his brother-in-law.

He was actually serious, but he let it go. "I'm assuming you sorted out the other problem, since you've started working on the die."

James nodded. "It will read from the fingertip, and switch from the wearer to the person being touched when it senses a turyn shift. That was a tricky bit to add, let me tell you."

Tricky was a big understatement. Will wondered if James really appreciated the magnitude of his talent. "I hope you realize that what you've accomplished already would be a marvel for artificers of any age. Even the ones who made the relics couldn't have done some of this."

James blushed. "Now you're just buttering me up."

"I'm honest. You know I actually used a relic. I was even possessed by its creator, Linus Ethelgren. You've broken through one of the major barriers that the artificers of old faced—the space limitation. No one has ever made enchanting scripts this small before."

Normally the size of an enchanted object was a major limitation on how complex an enchantment could be. When Will had first studied at Wurthaven, the main difference between modern enchantments and the relics left by ancient enchanters had been the lack of a transducing enchantment. Transducers were used to convert turyn from one frequency to another, and were absolutely necessary for magic users who couldn't consciously modulate their own turyn.

Relics didn't include lengthy transducer scripts, enabling the artificers of old to include more of the good stuff—functional elements that produced the final effects. Before Will had come along, the researchers at the school had been stumped as to why the enchanters of old hadn't needed them. No one had been able to use the old relics, at least not until the school began using compression training with the students.

Now all the newer wizards could modulate their turyn. It was easier for second- or third-order wizards, but even first-order wizards could manage it with sufficient concentration.

With James' miniaturization of rune scripts, it should theoretically be possible to craft items with enchantments five or perhaps even ten times longer than what could be done in the past. Will struggled to imagine what could be done with that much room. "I'm still curious as to how you made the enchantment so small—without even considering how you then made it into an embossing die."

James beamed at him. "Actually, that's partly how I convinced Salsbury to let me have the demon-steel. He wanted to know my process. He even talked me into publishing." Then he held up his hands. "The process, not this specific enchantment, mind you."

"How do you do it?"

"Optical lenses."

"Huh?"

"Just like you use a magnifying glass to see something small, you can use the same effect, but in reverse. Well, that's not precisely true, but it's a good metaphor. Just as you can use a magnifying lens to burn things by focusing light, you can also use lenses to shrink an image."

Will goggled at him. "How in the world did you think of that?"

"I let the children play with one of my old magnifying glasses. Christopher was using it to burn ants, and when I saw him, it just hit me. So, I went inside and tried painting runes on glass and then letting the sun shine through to cast an image on the ground. By working with the right lens and adjusting the distance, you can make something written in large letters quite small."

"You're a genius, James," remarked Will. "But how do you create the embossing die from an image? You wouldn't be able to carve it by hand."

"That part was easy, and I really can't take credit for it. When I was a student at Wurthaven, I spent a few semesters as a library aid. One of the spells I remembered seeing the scribes use was one that could take an optical image and create an ink copy on paper. It could even copy pictures and line drawings. That's how they make new books now. Otherwise, it would take forever if they had to recopy everything by hand. It's why I asked if you studied library magic that day when I saw you transcribing my enchantment. The spell you used is extremely old, and since you have to actually read what you're copying, it's rather slow and inefficient for copying books. I don't think the scribes use spells like it anymore, since they use spells that do whole-page copying." He stopped and held up his hands. "Not that it isn't very useful for personal transcription. It just isn't as efficient for copying entire books."

Will nodded. "Don't worry about offending me. So how did you make the die? An ink copy is far from being metal runes on demon-steel."

"That part hardly bears mentioning," said James dismissively. "I just adapted the optical copying spell. The hard part was already done for me. I just had to change the functionality so that it would melt and mold the surface of the metal."

"Demon-steel is not *just* metal, James. It absorbs most forces that try to affect it, and then it's even harder to work," said Will.

His brother-in-law laughed. "Dugas helped with that."

"From the Engineering Department?" asked Will.

James nodded. "He was involved in the magesmithing when they made the demon-steel golem, not to mention all the other weapons they used against the dragon. I think he was the one that helped with your breastplate too, by the way."

"He did," said Will impatiently.

"Anyway, he shared the trick with me. They used a transducer with your breastplate, to draw off the demonic turyn while they worked it, so it would stay malleable. Of course, with the bigger stuff they did later they had the queen and Janice to help, since they were able to do the same thing directly, eliminating the need for a transducer. I didn't have anyone to assist me, though, so I built my own transducer into the enchantment that controls my luxpress. It draws off the excess and keeps the metal workable."

"Luxpress?"

"That's what I call my device. Anyway, to make a long story short, now when I want a tiny embossing die, whether it's made from steel or even demon-steel, I simply draw out the enchanting script on a large pane of glass. That's the slowest part, since I have to paint it on the glass with a small brush. Another reason why your old transcription spell caught my eye. I'm thinking of using it to speed up that part. I'll just need to modify it a little, then I can read my blueprint and it will paint it on the glass for me.

"Once I have the glass ready, I just put it in the luxpress, and it will transform a metal blank into a perfect embossing die. After that, Lawrence—that's the jeweler I work with—"

Will waved him on. "I remember his name."

"Oh, well. Anyway, Lawrence can use the die and just tap the rune script onto whatever he's working with, gold or silver usually." Finished with his lecture at last, James smiled faintly.

"I'm honored to be part of your family," said Will. "How is it that you're not working in Wurthaven's Artifice Department instead of teaching compression classes?"

His brother-in-law shrugged. "I always found artifice to be boring when I was a student. I enjoy it much more as a hobby."

CHAPTER 30

They ate at a smaller table than the one they usually used, since it was just the four of them. The seats were arranged so that Will wound up sitting next to James' sister, with Tabitha and her husband across from them. He had no doubt that the table change as well as the seating arrangement were set up deliberately.

Veronica wasn't wearing an outfit that one would expect from a school professor, either. Her dress was low cut, giving her a decolletage that would have been scandalous for a lecturer, though it was perfectly acceptable for a ball or dinner party. Will suspected that Tabitha had convinced her to change while he'd been upstairs with James.

In spite of himself, Will let his eye be drawn into the valleys. When he looked up, Veronica met his gaze, and he felt his cheeks flush with embarrassment. She smiled and turned her focus back to her food, though her face also gained a bit of color.

Across the table, Will saw his sister wink at him when no one else was looking. She knew exactly what had just happened. He gave her a stern glare, but said nothing.

The food was a bit of an extravagance compared to the usual; roast pheasant, a vegetable terrine, and braised carrots made up the majority of the meal, but it ended with a tray filled with a mixed assortment of fruit tarts. A white wine was served with the meal, but afterward, James poured everyone a fresh glass from a different bottle he fetched from the sideboard.

"What's the occasion?" asked Will.

"The kids are away," said James with a grin. "It would be a little too much to dine like this every evening, and they wouldn't appreciate it."

Tabitha nodded. "We usually plan to make the most of it when they visit their grandmother. It's a treat for us, and with you and Vonnie, here it's doubly special."

"How do you find the wine?" asked James.

Will hadn't tasted the new glass, so he raised it to his lips. A pleasant floral scent filled his nose as he took a long sip. He gave them a questioning glance. "Is this elven wine?"

Tabitha nodded happily. "Have you had Lambruer before?"

"I adore it," Veronica said appreciatively.

James clearly did as well. "It's too expensive to have every day, but tonight is a perfect occasion."

Will remembered the vintage quite well. The last time he'd had it had been when Sammy had used it to loosen him up when he had visited Roc's Roost. "I do like the taste, but I'm not so sure it's wise. I don't want to embarrass myself."

"Don't be silly," said Tabitha. "All it does is lift your spirits. There's nothing better for a party. Far better than ordinary wine if you ask me."

"I'm afraid it might give me a little too much *energy*," he replied.

Veronica laughed louder than she should have, drawing everyone's eyes. Rather than be embarrassed, she lifted her glass and took a long, deep drink. She watched Will as she did, as though daring him to say something. With the glass half gone, she addressed the room, "I for one, don't mind a little energy now and then. Sometimes it's fun to let your hair down."

James got up and leaned over Will, draping his arm over one shoulder. "At least have one glass."

"One," agreed Will, "but no more." He made good on the promise by taking another sip.

"What are you worried about?" asked James.

Will glanced at Veronica, then back to his brother-in-law. "I'm sure you know."

James laughed. "I have nothing to fear." He finished his glass and poured another. "I have my dear wife to watch over me if things get out of hand." He waggled his brows.

Will frowned. "You mean my *sister?*"

James froze. "I—I, wait, that's not what I meant."

Tabitha leaned over and lightly bopped Will's head. "Stop it." Then she smiled at her husband. "And that's exactly what you meant, dearest. Don't let him spoil the mood." She looked back at Will. "If you're lucky, you might get another niece or nephew one of these days."

A knock at the door saved the day. Will tipped his glass up and finished it. "That must be Dr. Lorentz." Veronica frowned as he hurried to the door. "Thank you for dinner. I don't want Lorentz to feel he missed out, so I'll take him home straight away."

A chorus of disappointed groans answered him. "Just come back right after," pleaded Tabitha. "You don't have to stay long, but this is too soon."

Will dashed out the door and shut it behind himself. Dr. Lorentz seemed somewhat surprised. "You seem a bit rushed," said the other man. "Is something wrong?"

The wine had infused him with a warm glow, but Will still felt relatively sober. "I'm fine, but I am in a bit of a hurry." He wasted no time teleporting the doctor back to Lystal, arriving in the kitchen where his mother was making tea. They had already established a routine, so after a brief goodbye, Dr. Lorentz excused himself.

Erisa gave Will an appraising look. "Did something good happen?"

"Just a glass of wine."

"Are you home for the evening then?"

That was when he realized he still hadn't talked to Veronica about turyn blindness. *I need to go back,* he told himself. "Tabitha and James wanted me to stay a while, but—"

"Then you should," said Erisa. "Don't let us hold you back. The Mother knows you need to socialize more."

The Lambruer had settled in already, making him feel light and optimistic. *One more glass wouldn't hurt.* "I won't be long," he told her.

"Take as long as you want, but don't try to teleport if you drink too much. I don't know how it works, but it seems like a bad idea to me," she cautioned him.

Will rolled his eyes. "I'm not going to get drunk, Mom."

"Sure, sure, whatever. You should go. They're probably waiting on you." She pushed his back, as though walking would take him somewhere.

Ever the dutiful son, Will did as he was bade, and a minute later he was back in the Wellings' parlor. Music was playing from another room, and everyone looked at him in surprise. "I thought you had abandoned us for sure," said Tabitha.

Will glanced at Veronica. He still had questions to ask, but he didn't want to be rude. Her eyes warmed when she saw him looking in her direction. *I just gave her the wrong impression, didn't I?* he realized. Pushing the thought aside, he said, "I can stay for a while. Who's playing the music?"

"It's an elven music box," explained Veronica, her expression bright. "I bought it last week and I wanted to show it to Tabitha. Do you like it?"

"Does it use bluet?" he asked.

Everyone nodded, and James handed him a fresh glass, already filled. Will took a long drink before thinking about it. *I shouldn't spoil the mood talking about my conspiracy theories and bluet,* he told himself. "The music is lovely."

"We should dance," said Veronica. She illustrated the remark with a quick twirl, passing in front of Will as she did.

Parts of her brushed up against him as she did. *Pure accident,* he decided. "I'm not a very good dancer."

Tabitha made a disagreeable noise. "Absolute rubbish. I've seen you dance. You do just fine."

"Those were court dances, and it's been years and years," he protested. "You have no idea how I abused the feet and toes of my teachers," he warned Veronica.

"Please…," Veronica enjoined him. "If you won't, that leaves me without a partner."

"We could take turns," suggested Tabitha.

"No offense, but I grew up learning to dance with my brother. I was hoping for a fresh dance partner." Veronica gave Will a sad look.

He sighed, then finished his glass. "Fine. What dance are you thinking of?"

"Nelly's Scrumble!" said Tabitha a bit too quickly, and Veronica's immediate giggle and furtive glance toward him at the suggestion made Will question his decision.

"Never heard of it," he admitted.

"It's simple," declared James, putting down his glass. "Allow us to demonstrate." Boldly stepping across the room, he put a hand on his wife's shoulder and spun her around to face him. Tabitha closed the distance, and soon they were stepping and swaying with hardly an inch between them. Will felt his ears turn red just watching them.

Veronica stepped in front of him. "Don't overthink it or you'll lose your motivation." Taking his hand, she lifted it to her shoulder, then stepped into him. "Put your other hand on my hip." Her face was entirely too close when he looked down.

He *had* danced before, however, quite a lot while he was learning, and he knew better than to let proximity make him clumsy. He placed his hand at her waist, near the small of her back, then asked, "Now what?"

"This is a folk dance," breathed Vonnie. "Your hand should be lower."

Will froze, his heart speeding up. *Is she teasing me?*

Veronica's gaze was unflinching. "If you're going to learn it, you should learn it properly. It's not a court dance." She shimmied slightly, her eyes bold.

He adjusted his hand.

"Don't be shy," she said encouragingly, so he dropped it further. "There, now we just need some rhythm. It's a spring festival dance, so there's a certain feeling to it." She rested her head against his neck and took a few steps, leading him.

Somehow, he avoided stepping on her feet. Back when he'd been a student, it had taken weeks for Janice and Dianne Young, the resident assistant at his dorm, to teach him properly before he attended the Winter Ball. Both of them suffered trampled toes and arches before he was passable.

After so many years, he was rusty, and this dance was new to him, but he'd retained enough grace to avoid stomping on Veronica's feet, despite the numerous distractions she was giving him. In particular, the dance required them to stay perilously close; whenever his partner stepped back with her right leg, he had to step forward with his left. Their legs came into frequent contact, and whenever they needed to change direction, their torsos were pressed together.

The fact that he could also feel her breath against his neck made it all the more titillating. When the song finally came to an end, he was almost panting, though the exertion hadn't been enough to wind him. His heart had run a race all on its own. They stood still for a moment.

"Not bad for the first time," said Veronica. The arm she had around his back tightened briefly, bringing their hips together just before she released him. She felt something then, he was sure of it, and her eyes held a challenge when she added, "I can tell you enjoyed it."

He would have blushed if his cheeks hadn't already been flushed from the dancing. "I need more practice."

"Let me reset the music box," said Veronica with a smile.

"One more time!" yelled Tabitha.

They all managed another half a glass before the music started again, and then it was back into the fray. Feeling comfortable now, Will was more assertive, and Vonnie responded in kind. Neither made any real effort to avoid making the dance what it was meant to be, sensual and erotic.

Afterward, they took a break, and from the glances Veronica was giving him, he had little doubt what her opinion was when it came to whether he should spend the night at the Wellings home. Despite the wine and his body's hearty approval of the idea, Will felt a sense of reluctance, though. Selene's face flashed in his mind, followed only moments later by that of Cora. He shook his head to clear it. Veronica was sitting next to him, her hand draped casually across his leg.

He glanced at his sister and her husband, and although both of them had kept a watch on developments between him and Veronica, they were currently focused mainly on each other.

Vonnie's hand moved, sending a thrill through him, and returning his attention to the woman beside him. "You probably shouldn't try any complicated spells. I think the wine has gone to your head," she told him.

His eyes darted to her hand, her bosom, and then her lips, before coming to rest on Veronica's eyes. Will knew where this was leading. *This is wrong,* he told himself. "I'm still considering," he replied.

Laina's voice spoke in his mind, *It's definitely wrong, but it seems like fun.*

Will grimaced. His dead sister's voice caused a shift in his mood. *I am not doing anything with you watching me,* he replied.

I'm not watching, I'm living vicariously. Take pity on a dead girl. This could be as much fun as that night you spent at Roc's Roost, she answered.

"Is everything all right?" Veronica's hand drifted again as she spoke, and this time it stopped even farther up his thigh. The movement was entirely unconscious and without any intent. "You seem distracted."

Unconscious my ass, declared Laina. *She's about to grab us by the root!* Will's leg shifted, moving in Veronica's direction as though it had a mind of its own.

Did you do that? asked Will.

Take a nap, I'll handle this, replied Laina.

I will not! Why are you talking so much suddenly? You go months without a word, now this.

Your life is so boring! It makes me want to die again. Moments like this, though—she snickered evilly in his mind. *Watch this.*

Will's right arm lifted, then went over Veronica's shoulder. His hand came to rest just above the valley of delights, and his fingers brushed lightly against the skin there. Veronica scooted closer, a subaudible purr reverberating in her throat. It was too low to hear, but he felt it.

He stood abruptly, disengaging and glancing around the room as though he had seen or heard something. Internally, he fought with Laina. *This is my body, and you're crossing a line,* he warned.

Don't be a prude! I was just helping you!

By some miracle, a knock came at the door. "There's someone here," said Will immediately.

James looked up. "You must have incredible ears. You heard them before they knocked."

"I'll answer it," he told them, ignoring the fact that he was the one in hiding. He was out of the room and down the hall before anyone else could respond. He opened the door without any of his usual caution.

A hooded and veiled figure stood there, making it hard to identify who it was. Light from the house glinted from the whites of the unknown stranger's eyes as they took in Will's features. A woman's voice emerged from the hood, "Master, you could be seen! You shouldn't answer doors here."

Despite the wine, Will realized who it was a second later. He looked over his shoulder to make sure no one had followed him to the door, then he hissed, "Why are *you* knocking on doors? You're never supposed to be seen—ever."

"I needed to deliver a warning. They would not have recognized me."

"Tabitha knows you," he argued.

"Only if she sees my face," replied the veiled woman.

Nervously, Will checked over his shoulder again, then commanded, "Go around back. I'll meet you in the garden." He shut and locked the door before returning to Veronica and the others.

"Who was it?" asked Tabitha.

For once, he had a decent lie already prepared. "A courier bringing a letter for me."

"For you? Here?" she asked. The others seemed equally bemused. They all knew his presence was supposed to be a secret.

"I know, I know," he said, waving his hand dismissively. "Since I've been coming to Cerria lately, I took the opportunity to make some inquiries with one of my agents. I apologize for having them deliver the report here."

"Agents? You have agents?" Veronica seemed intrigued.

Veronica's brother was equally enthused, though in a less flirtatious manner. "How many secret schemes are you working on?" asked James.

"It's nothing sinister," said Will. "It relates to our enchanting project, so you already know about most of it. This was just something extra. Don't ask me about it, though. I'd rather say nothing than lie to you." He glanced at Tabitha. "Still have those two enchanted tablets I left with you?" When she nodded, he asked, "Can I have one? I'd like to give it to someone so I can avoid putting your household at risk like this again."

A few minutes later, he had the tablet in hand, and he started to say his goodbyes. That elicited a round of protests, but in the middle of it, James asked an important question. "Which symbol is your agent going to use?"

"Oh," said Will. He hadn't considered that. He picked one of the two unclaimed symbols and pointed to it. "This one. So don't bother sending any messages to it." Then he paused as another thought struck him. "Actually, if you *do* get a message from that one, trust it just as if it came from me."

"Just who is this person?" asked Tabitha, obviously frustrated.

"Why would they message us?" added James.

"They won't," said Will. "I'm just saying that in case something unforeseen happens. Trust the message if they send one. You know how careful I am. I'm just being extra cautious. I really need to go."

"It's late," complained Veronica. "You really should wait."

"I'm sorry." Will opened his arms and gave Tabitha a quick hug.

She pecked him on the cheek. "I really hope you aren't getting into trouble again," she said worriedly.

Will held her out at arm's length and smiled reassuringly. "It's been thirteen years. I'm starting to believe I might really get a 'happily ever after,' or at the very least, a 'peacefully ever after.'"

James shook his hand then pulled him into a rough hug. Veronica followed, and Will embraced her before realizing what he was doing. He intended to keep it platonic, but there was something more to it. "Be careful," she told him, and when he looked down to answer her, he found her lips suddenly meeting his.

He pulled away quickly, and James gave a low whistle. He gave his brother-in-law an irritated look, then told Veronica, "I need to talk to you about a few things."

"I know," she answered suggestively.

He shook his head. "No, that's not what I mean. Although, yes, we do need to talk about that too." When he saw the expectant look on her face, he realized he was still leading her down the wrong path. Looking over at his sister and James, he told them, "Can we have a moment?"

They both had knowing expressions as they left Will and Veronica to themselves. Veronica sensed something was off, though. "What is it?" she asked with a frown.

"You're incredibly intelligent, attractive, and beautiful, but I can't continue in the way you might expect."

He saw the hurt register in her eyes. Then she swore. "I can't believe this—why not? We've only had a dance or two."

"There's someone else."

"Tabitha said there wasn't." After a second, she nodded, "Other than the queen obviously, which now that I say it, it sounds really strange."

"Not her," said Will, then corrected himself, "Well, yes, also her, but there's another someone else, I think. Maybe."

Veronica's face twisted in annoyance. "You've been on your own for what, thirteen years? I don't think Her Majesty should count anymore, and if she does, how is there someone else?"

"I know it sounds strange, but I've been talking to a lady trader I met a few years ago, and I think it might mean something."

"*Might* mean something? Have you made any promises to her?"

"Well, no, but—"

"Did you bed her?"

"We kissed a couple of times, though it was several years apart. Look, I know I'm not explaining this well."

Veronica lifted one brow, then replied, "It sounds to me like you're still free."

"Technically, yes. That's not the point."

"She doesn't plan to settle down or marry you?"

His expression said she should know better. "That's never happening again. Yet another reason we should nip things in the bud. I can't offer you anything."

"I never said I wanted anything," she replied flatly. "I'm a mid-thirties teacher. I live in a small apartment on campus with my one cat and I like it that way. If I intended to settle down, I'd have done it by now." She leaned in and whispered in his ear, "I just wanted to have a little fun, *Your Highness.*"

Her breath sent tingles down his spine, but Will shook his head. "I'm sorry. I can't."

Veronica pursed her lips. After a second, she asked, "What was the other thing you wanted to talk to me about?"

"Turyn blindness, but I really need to go. Will you be here tomorrow?"

"I wasn't planning on it, but I might be persuaded."

Ever an idiot, Will asked, "What do you want?" He regretted it immediately as she gave him a once over with her eyes. "I wouldn't feel right about it."

"A kiss?"

Against his body's wishes he answered, "No, but nice try."

She answered with a wry smile. "Tomorrow then, and I'll expect another dance."

CHAPTER 31

Will left through the front door but didn't immediately teleport. Instead, he made himself hard to notice, then pretended to leave via the street before circling around and entering the back garden. Rather than use the Arkeshi technique by itself, he also used a camouflage spell. Once upon a time, he would have used a spell to silence his steps, but his talent was far more effective. With hardly any effort, he could eliminate any sound he might make, without affecting ambient noise around him.

Moving slowly, he crossed the garden, adjusting his vision as he went. None of it was strictly necessary; he was meeting a friend, not a foe, but it was an excellent opportunity to practice and test his stealth skills against a true master.

It took a minute to spot her, and that took an act of will on his part. If he hadn't known she was hidden nearby, he would likely have missed her, since she was using the same technique he was to make herself difficult to notice. She had been the one he learned it from, after all.

But Will had magic, and with his silence and the ability to see heart-light, it was to be expected that he would find her first. Circling around a topiary, he stepped up beside her and then said, "It's been a long time."

The woman didn't jump. "You have improved," she complimented him. "Even my teachers would fail against you now, unless it is my age. My ears are not as sharp as they once were."

"You're hardly old," said Will.

"I am in my forties. Nothing is the same—except you. Time does not seem to touch you," she remarked.

"Show me your face."

The hood went back and the veil down, revealing Darla's face. It was still hidden by shadows, but to Will she might as well have been standing in full sun. There were lines in the corners of her eyes, and her cheeks sagged slightly. For some reason it shocked him to see her as a middle-aged woman. She had once been Laina's bodyguard, and lover, so he hadn't considered the fact that she was older than him. *And that was thirteen years ago,* he reminded himself. "It is good to see you," Will told her.

"I will not say the same," returned Darla. "Your presence endangers them."

"Have I been seen?"

The retired assassin pursed her lips, then admitted, "I did not know you were here."

"I've been careful, but I've been visiting for weeks," said Will. "What brought you here tonight?"

"I live nearby. I watch when I have time. Tonight, I had time."

Will frowned. "That wasn't my last command." The last time he'd seen her, thirteen years ago, he'd ordered Darla to protect Selene. He hadn't really expected her to remain on guard for so long, but the Arkeshi woman was strange in many ways.

"The dead need no protecting. Did you expect me to watch over your wife forever?"

"No. But that doesn't explain your presence here."

Darla's eyes darted toward the house. "She is *her* sister. I keep an eye out for her in memory of my beloved."

The thought of a middle-aged woman spending years, even decades, sitting out in the cold and watching a stranger's house made him sad. "I hope you haven't been doing this since I left."

Darla gave him a smile. It was a rare expression for her, and she wasn't good at it. "I am getting old, but even if I were young, I have never been stupid. When you died, they were safe, or at least as safe as anyone else. When you returned from the grave to slaughter the trolls, I began to worry for them."

He understood her meaning, and although it had the tone of a rebuke, he was glad that at least one person agreed with his paranoia. When he had first left, Selene had reported him dead in an accident, and his loved ones had been safe. Appearing as the Stormking had made the world realize he was still alive, and anyone who might want a lever to control him would look first to those he cared about.

Selene had loved the Nerrow family as though they were her own, so that had never concerned him, but the world was full of people who might want to coerce him in one way or another. The fact that Tabitha was his sister had never been widely known, but at the end, the news had leaked into the circles of high society. Even as a rumor, it might prove deadly for the Wellings family.

"The troll incident was years ago. Surely you haven't—"

"I watched closely for months but saw nothing. Now I come only once or twice a week, and I do not spend the entire night. Seeing what I saw tonight changes that, however, and your presence clinches the decision."

"What was your warning?"

"I arrived late, and when I first circled the house I noticed something else was here before me, and was already watching. It was looking through the front windows."

His eyes narrowed. "It?"

Darla nodded. "It had the shape and form of a man, but it moved as one of the Drak'shar."

Drak'shar was the original term for Grim Talek's experimental children, created from his experiments with dragon blood. Most knew them by the common name, vampire, and Will was all but certain they were extinct. The lich had brought an army of the creatures with him to the last battle with the dragon, including his wizard lieutenants, Mahak and Theravan. Aside from the lich himself, none had escaped. If anyone else had made such a statement, Will wouldn't have questioned their judgment, but Darla had fought the Drak'shar on several occasions, and had saved his life from them at least once.

Will fell silent, and the two of them stared silently at one another for several seconds. There were other creatures that possessed strength and speed similar to the Drak'shar. It was possible she had seen one of them. "Where did it go?" he asked finally.

"It fled when I revealed myself and approached the front door. I intended then to simply warn them that something had been at the windows. I assumed your sister would have some way to contact you. I never expected to see your face in the doorway."

"You didn't consider following it?"

"It had already seen me at that point"—Darla patted one of her thighs—"and my legs are merely human. Even when I was younger, I would have had no hope in such a chase. Besides, I have no interest in dying. There would be no warning for your family then."

"Forgive me, Darla. I did not mean to question your judgment. You were wise to do as you did." The former assassin had fought successfully against the Drak'shar in the past, but not without cost. Her body and bones had been shattered and broken on more than one occasion—even when the battle had been victorious. Chasing a vampire into the night was never a wise course for a mortal to take, no matter their age, and Darla was well aware of her own limits. Even doing what she had done was incredibly risky. *And she was alone, with no hope of support,* thought Will. He withdrew the enchanted tablet and held it out to her. "Have you seen one of these before?"

She hadn't, so he took some time to explain the functions and show her how to use the communications tablet. He also made sure she knew all the recipients and what their respective symbols were. Darla did have some reservations, however. "This is too valuable to waste on me," she said, pushing it back toward him.

"It's obvious I need your eyes, but they do me no good if you can't tell me what you've seen."

She shook her head. "I called you 'master' from habit, but I cannot serve you as I did before. I have other obligations now. My coming here was merely a courtesy to her."

Will's expression softened. "You have a family?"

"Not children, but yes. I found a new life. Too many depend on me to fight as I once did, and my body is no longer as capable."

He knew better than to ask for details. If she thought Tabitha and her children were at risk from his resurrection, she would surely not want to involve him with any knowledge of her own loved ones. Will refused to take the tablet, closing her hand over it once more. "I respect your decision, but keep it anyway and do as you will. If you see something I should know, let me know, whether it is here or in your daily life. Also, if you need me, I will do whatever I can for you or those you care for."

Darla stared at him for a moment. "I mean no insult, but asking for your aid would only bring death and danger to those you help. I will keep the tablet, though, if only to send a warning if necessary, but do not expect me to keep a vigil over them. My time is limited."

"I would ask nothing more of you," said Will. "But don't forget, if you need me, I will come if I am able."

The ex-assassin's eyes made it clear she would never call for him, but then her expression softened, and she reached out with a tentative hand to touch his chest, just over his heart. "Is she with you still?"

Are you? he asked, silently addressing his sister's ghost. Laina had been entirely silent during their exchange, and she said nothing now. "She still talks to me sometimes," he answered, "but I'm not sure if it's really her or my own madness that answers."

Darla's eyes glistened in the moonlight as she looked up at him. She patted his chest once more, giving him a solid 'thump' with her palm. "Never doubt yourself. My eyes saw her in you once. You are not mad. If she speaks to you again, tell her that I am well. Farewell, Stormking." She turned and made her way out of the garden.

His gaze followed her only because Will refused to let his attention waver, but eventually distance and the shadows took her from his view. Darla's remark regarding her eyes held weight because he knew she was astrally sensitive, like himself. Despite having no magic, the Arkeshi had once spotted him when he'd been disembodied and seeking help from his then-living sister, Laina.

That thought brought with it another idea. Will prepared himself as he usually did to teleport, slipping partway into the astral, but instead of seeking Erisa or Tabitha, he tried to find Darla. He'd never thought to do it in the past, but it made sense to him that they might have a link. Whether he'd been close enough to her was debatable, but Laina would definitely have had one.

Darla appeared in his vision, walking casually down the street half a block away. She glanced up, blinking as she stared in his direction. A moment later, she waved and continued on her way. Will returned to his body.

"I guess that settles that question."

He wanted to go home, or at the very least go back in the house. He could still hear music coming from within, but he knew better. Instead, he used the tablet to send a message to both Tabitha and James:

> *Something was spotted watching your home. Be sure to keep detection wards up at the doors and windows. It is gone for now, but I will figure out a better solution in the days to come.*

It was a quarter of an hour before he received a response, but after that, he noticed the music stopped and lights began moving around within the house. He regretted spoiling their peace of mind, but he couldn't see that there was any other reasonable choice. Will followed that by sending Erisa a message that he'd be spending the night.

He didn't mention that he wasn't planning to go inside. He intended to wait in the dark, in case the window peeper decided to return.

The rest of his night was cold and lonely, and when dawn came he had nothing to show for it. Will went home and then to work, but only long enough to tell Lettler he would need to call in his replacement for the rest of the week. Then he went to bed.

Years of healthy living had accustomed him to a normal sleep cycle, so despite his fatigue, Will only managed five hours of daytime sleeping before his body forced him to rise again. It left him feeling vaguely irritated, but unlike Darla, he was still young, with the body of a twenty-two-year-old, despite being in his mid-thirties. He did a little math in his head. His first seventeen years counted normally, but every year since then counted as only one-eighth of a year, physically anyway. *I won't count as a thirty-something until I'm around a hundred and twenty.* It was a sobering thought. He wouldn't be forty physically until he'd reached a full two centuries of age.

Chapter 31

Sitting on the side of his bed, Will saw Evie staring at him from across the room. She had continued to hang around since he had recovered from Redweep Fever, though she rarely felt the need to talk. "How do you feel about children?" he asked her out loud. He didn't expect a response. If he'd been serious about the question, he would have slipped partway into the astral so he could hear her thoughts.

To his surprise, she began shifting, her body growing and expanding into a humanoid form. That meant she intended to speak verbally, a rare treat indeed. Will looked away, not out of any respect for privacy, but rather because Evie's semi-human form was disturbing to look at. The last time he'd seen it, her facial features had been a bizarre blend of cat and human, and not a flattering mixture either. It would have given an artist nightmares.

"That had not occurred to me. I do not know if I can bear a litter, but I would not mind having more of my kind," she responded.

"That is *not* what I had in mind," said Will. Glancing over, his eyes froze for a moment. Evie had apparently found time at some point to practice her transformation over the past decade. She looked fully human, but she had chosen a dark complexion, making her look like a Fareshite, except for her long, silvery-grey hair. He would have complimented her, but she was utterly naked. He didn't bother looking away, but did manage to focus his gaze solidly on her golden-green eyes. "You're naked."

"Naturally, since I thought—" she paused. "I misunderstood. Did you mean we should try in my cat form?"

"No!" Will snapped, finally losing his composure. "I was referring to my sister's children."

"Ahh." Clothes appeared, and Evie was quickly covered in an illusory dress that matched the color of her hair. Again, it was an improvement over the last time she had transformed. Back then, she had *grown* her clothes as part of the transformation, which had led to bizarre results. The illusion was much better. "Why would I like your sister's children?"

"I think there was a vampire near their house last night. I thought maybe…" he let his words trail off.

Evie sighed, doing a passable job at seeming human. "You want me to sleep there, don't you?"

"Would you?"

"I'd rather not. I prefer home, or here."

"This is your home," he told her. "Or wherever I live, just so you know."

"I know. I meant my old home," she explained. "But it is empty. Do you think there used to be others there like me?"

Will realized she meant the Cath Bawlg's original plane. He'd been there once, while traveling with the Goddamn Cat. "You went to the dimension you came from?"

"Yes. I am linked to it, much as I am to you and certain places here. While I was away, I did a lot of exploring. The place of my origin was one of the first places I went."

"What did you think?" he asked quietly.

Evie frowned, succeeding at yet another human expression. "Desolate, empty, and barren. I have no memory of it, but I do not think it was always like that. The stink of demons was everywhere, including their anchors."

By anchors, she meant the portals and devices that Hell used to siphon off energy from planes that they had conquered, feeding their own dimension. "Stink?" asked Will. "Did you not see any actual demons?" They usually had guards at the anchor locations.

"No. I found no one, so I destroyed their machines and severed the links. It will be much harder for them if they intend to return." There was audible satisfaction in her voice, but it didn't last. "Even though they are gone, my home remains dead. I do not know how to restore it. When you mentioned children..."

Now that he understood her train of thought, it made him sad for her, and the only answers he had wouldn't help. "Evie, as far as I know, you're unique. I wish I had asked your predecessor more, or that I remembered better. From what he told me, there were no others like him—like you. I think the beings who lived there regarded him as a guardian, maybe. I'm not really sure, but if he could have produced children, I think he would have already done so, and that means you probably can't either."

"I see." Her voice was empty.

Unsure what else to say, Will responded with, "Your human form is much better now."

"The dwarves thought I was truly human. They could not tell the difference," she said smugly.

Will doubted he could either, aside from her personality and her somewhat exotic choice of coloring. "Did you spend much time with the dwarves?" After meeting Cora's companion, Durin, Will realized he knew almost nothing about them, other than their propensity for a subterranean lifestyle and their famous craftsmanship, particularly with metals. *Metal!* A sudden realization caused him to interrupt her answer with a new question. "You said you destroyed the anchors in your home plane, correct?" After she nodded, he asked, "What did you do with the wreckage?"

"I left it where I found it."

"How many anchors were there?"

She shrugged. "Many, a hundred perhaps? It took several days to destroy them all."

"May I have some of it?"

"You can have it all. It stinks of demons."

He dipped his head in gratitude. "Thank you, Evie. It might take some time to organize the recovery, and I'll need your help getting there. I'll probably want Sammy to help as well."

"I need no thanks. It will still be mine, and removing it from my home is a good thing."

"Still be yours?"

"Yes. I have told you this before. After my rebirth, all I had were my links to the things that were mine: my home world, the place I lived in the fae realm, the place I died, *you*, and Sammy."

He understood then. The Cath Bawlg's ideas regarding ownership had been somewhat broader than most, and apparently Evie had retained those views through her reincarnation. "I prefer to think you belong to me," Will teased.

The demigod was unfazed. "Yes. Is that not what I said?"

Her view of ownership and belonging was such that the joke was meaningless to her. Will sighed, then changed subjects. "I wonder what happened to the demons. I destroyed the twelve ruling demon-lords, but I know there were others waiting to take their place, not to mention the rest of their society. Do you think it was the dragonlings?" After destroying Lognion, Will had enlisted his grandmother's help to open a gate to take the hatchlings straight from the nest and deposit them in Hell. The fae queen had been forced to choose between violating a promise to him, or one of her former pacts to do so. The choice would have killed her either way, but she had chosen to fulfill her grandson's request.

"You said they destroy everything after hatching, including each other. That may be just as true in Hell as it is anywhere else." Evie sounded hopeful.

From what Will knew, the young dragons would grow over a period of years, gaining size and strength while devouring every living thing in their vicinity. As they grew, they would begin to compete for territory and the victors would cannibalize the losers until only one remained.

Then the last dragon would travel between worlds to find a new place to call home, eventually creating a new nest and beginning the process all over again.

His main uncertainty concerned the timeframe. Dragons were effectively immortal, and he wasn't sure whether it would be years, decades, or centuries before the final dragon in Hell decided it was time to move on. He also didn't know where it would choose to go. He hoped it would be somewhere else. Fighting one dragon had been enough for him.

But I know how to do it now, he thought grimly. If fate brought another draconic menace to his doorstep, he wouldn't shirk his duty. If anything, he knew better what would work and what wouldn't. *I wouldn't ask for such a thing, but I wouldn't need to bother with the ungodly preparations we used last time.*

Lost in thought, Evie's next words broke him from his reverie. "I will sleep elsewhere for a while, but do not expect me to play with them." Before Will could respond, she was gone.

"Thank you," he said softly to the empty air.

CHAPTER 32

Will survived the dance with Veronica the next night. It helped that he had time to brace himself. Veronica had also had time to cool off, so despite her ardor of the prior evening, she chose a more moderate dance to teach him.

Somehow, they managed to keep things from being awkward, which was for the best, considering they were in-laws no matter what. When Will finally broached the topic of Oliver's problem, Veronica went and fetched a small book. "Here. I had a copy made for you."

The titlepage within made it clear that the book was an academic journal from Wurthaven, so she had likely gone do some personal expense to have the copy made, but when he saw the author's name, he reconsidered that thought. "Veronica Wellings, I think I've heard of her," said Will with a smile.

Her lips quirked up near one corner of her mouth. "After several years of dealing with incoming students, I thought it might be good to compile what I could about compression training for future generations. The second chapter covers uncommon problems like turyn blindness."

"Thank you for this," Will said sincerely. "I hope it wasn't expensive."

She shrugged. "I already had a couple of extras. Maybe it will help if you or Samantha ever start training more wizards wherever it is you live now." Then her lips formed a line. "There's not a lot there about turyn blindness. You should read it, but I can give you a quick summary now."

He nodded. "Which is?"

"Maybe one in a hundred has the same problem, and it appears to be neurological rather than physiological. As you've discovered already, his eyes are capable of detecting turyn, but for whatever reason, Oliver's brain rejects the new information. The resulting dissonance is what makes him feel ill. In fact, the nausea is almost identical to what some people experience when sailing. Except unlike sea sickness, none of those with turyn blindness ever adjusted to it. If you keep dosing him with psychedelics, you'll only make him miserable."

Will frowned. "Perhaps they didn't try long enough."

Veronica sighed in frustration. "I know he's your son, so I'm not going to take offense at that, but *I* was the one in charge of many of the cases that this book draws from. I can assure you we were very determined. Several students persisted through more than a dozen attempts, and one suffered through at least twenty before I convinced his parents to relent. If that's not enough for you, there's a section in the back with citations for older texts on the topic. This has been a documented problem for some individuals for as far back as Wurthaven keeps records."

He closed his eyes for a moment, then dipped his brow. "I meant no disrespect to your work. I just—I hoped for a solution. If Oliver can't complete at least the first compression and still insists on becoming a wardsman, I hate to think how short his life will be."

"You can still try the compression," said Veronica.

Will blinked. "What?"

She gave him a faint smile. "I said you can still try the compression. Turyn blindness isn't really a barrier in that regard, he just won't be able to manipulate turyn to any appreciable degree."

"But the candle spell—he can't see the flame clearly."

Veronica laughed. "The old source-linked candle spell? I've heard about it, but I only came across references to it while doing research for this book. No one's used that in generations." She whistled. "I sometimes forget you learned from Arrogan. It makes sense. Back then, they believed it would give the prospective student an advantage in figuring out how to manage the first compression, but over time it was discovered it just didn't make a significant difference."

He stared at her, expressionless. "Son of a bitch! That old man put me through hell with that stupid candle." He growled, then exhaled and took a deep breath. "So you're saying I can just put the spell cage on Oliver and forget the rest?"

She nodded. "So long as you understand he'll never be able to express magic or cast spells."

Tabitha stepped into the parlor and interrupted them. "Will, there's a message from your mystery friend."

He pulled out his enchanted tablet. Sure enough, he'd already received a message as well. He hoped it wasn't too old as he read it:

He's outside, attempting to look in the front windows.

Will already knew the drapes had been pulled shut. Tabitha had done that the night before. Striding rapidly across the room, he went to the central window, which was six feet in width, the biggest in the front parlor. Seizing the drapes with both hands, he flung them wide.

It was already dark outside, and the illumination from within the room was enough to turn the windows into mirrors, but Will's eyes adjusted quickly so that he could see in different wavelengths. A shadowy figure darted away at a speed too quick to be merely human.

He couldn't match that speed, but thankfully, he didn't have to. Tracking the figure's progress, Will teleported, arriving directly in front of the stranger as he reached the street. As he expected, the vampire, assuming that's what it was, reacted near instantly. He was prepared for that, though. If the creature was feeling aggressive, it would try to knock him down—or worse. If it was only hoping to escape, it would probably leap over him. He had spells for either eventuality.

A simple force-wall went up to prevent both; he simply had to make sure it was tall enough to stop the jump as well. Force spells could be exceedingly cheap in terms of turyn if they were small or kept within close range, but the turyn cost scaled exponentially with distance. Planting the base directly in front of him, he was able to make the top of it twenty feet high, more than enough to intercept the vampire's impromptu leap.

Which is what it did, before face-planting against the invisible barrier and flailing awkwardly as it fell. It had struck with enough force to break bones, not that such injuries bothered vampires much. He gave it no opportunity to recover. Dismissing the force-wall before it finished falling, Will switched to a force-cage just as the creature was about to hit the ground. Timing it thus prevented the monster from leaping away in a random direction. The force-cage was essentially a cube with a solid top and bottom, and sides made of intermittent bands of force. The openings were less than four inches in width, but Will stepped back to make sure the Drak'shar couldn't snag him with a clawed hand.

The main reason he'd used a cage rather than a dome or solid cube was of course because the openings allowed him to use other spells on the prisoner within. What happened next would depend on the monster's answers.

His eyes widened in recognition. "Rob?"

Will's old schoolmate didn't struggle. Seeing the force-cage, Rob's shoulders sagged and his posture changed to one of resignation. "It was a good run, I guess," he said.

"I thought you were dead."

The vampire shrugged. "Likewise—at least until you annihilated those trolls. For what it's worth, I was glad when I heard that news. It never seemed fair to me."

"What didn't?" asked Will.

"Any of it, but in this case, I mean the way they discarded you after you killed the dragon."

"I wasn't discarded," said Will immediately. Then he glanced around. The street was empty at night, but sooner or later someone would come along. "Will you run if I take down the cage? I'd like to talk."

Rob seemed shocked. "You aren't going to kill me?"

"That depends on you. Do you want me to kill you?"

"Not particularly. Has anyone ever said yes to that question?"

Will made a mental list. *Grim Talek, my grandmother.* "You'd be surprised," he answered, then asked, "Are you planning to kill anyone?"

"To be honest, you're the only one that comes to mind, but that's just my jealousy talking. I'll get over it," said his old friend. Will dismissed the force-cage, and Rob stared at him incredulously. "That's it? I say I'm not hostile and you just free me? Aren't you worried I'll do something?"

"You've never lied to me," said Will with a shrug. "Even when you were newborn and still mad with bloodlust. I'm assuming you're past that, by the way. Right?"

"Yeah, but still. You know how fast I am. What if I'm lying?"

Will's eyes were steady as he answered, "You aren't." He was tempted to say more, but it would sound like bravado. The truth was that he could afford the luxury of mercy. Unless Will was unconscious, Rob's chance of hurting him in a fight was nearly zero, even if he surprised him. Telling Rob that he trusted his word was more likely to get him honest answers to his questions.

When he was younger, Will might have made the same decision simply out of instinct, but now the choice was deliberate, a product of the cynicism he'd developed while married to Selene. As a political figure, everything had been a calculation, and even more than a decade later, the habit was impossible to escape. He didn't like that part of himself, but he couldn't change it now.

Rob relaxed. "I really thought you'd kill me without asking questions. I'm starting to question some of my choices now."

Will was writing a message to Tabitha on his tablet. *Safe. Caught the peeper. No danger. Taking him away to talk.* Then he put it away and smiled. "I've changed. Once, I might have done that, but I got to know Theravan and Mahak before the last battle with Lognion. Meeting them changed my perspective somewhat." He gestured toward the open road. "Let's walk so we don't seem strange. We can talk as we go."

"Not worried about anyone hearing us?"

"Our words won't carry beyond our own ears. My talent will take care of that."

They were already strolling. "I thought your talent was lightning, or weather."

"I have more than one," said Will, not bothering to explain—another calculated decision. He did trust Rob, for the most part, but giving away information about his abilities without a specific reason was another thing he no longer did. His talent with sound wasn't exactly secret, but there was no need to tell anyone who didn't know already.

Rob chuckled. "So unfair. Most would be happy with just one."

"That's not what you meant when you mentioned jealousy, though, was it?"

His old friend growled, an ominous sound considering his nature. "I saw you dancing with Vonnie the other night."

Will's mouth fell open. "That's why? She's my sister-in-law now."

"Not the way you were dancing," countered Rob. "Again, not fair. First you had Janice, then Selene, and now Vonnie? How many others have there been over the years?"

"I never *had* Janice, nor is there anything between me and Veronica," said Will in exasperation.

"You and Janice weren't—? Really?"

He rolled his eyes. "No. She was just a friend. Besides, you know she married Tiny."

"I always figured that was after you broke it off. Well, anyway, whatever you claim, I could tell Veronica wanted you, and you certainly didn't look like a man who was trying to get away."

"I'd had too much wine. I politely declined later. There's someone else I'm interested in."

"Oh. So, she's not good enough for you? What a pompous ass you are!"

Will glared at his old friend. "You're awfully comfortable insulting someone you thought was out to exterminate you just a few minutes ago."

Rob smiled, showing disturbingly sharp canines. "What was it you said just a bit ago? Oh yes!" He put one hand on his chest reciting dramatically, "You've never lied to me." Then he began breathing heavily. "Oh, my heart! Now I understand why the ladies swoon over you."

Despite himself, Will chuckled. Rob's personality remained intact, even after everything else about him had changed. "By the way, my presence here is a secret, so I'd appreciate it if you don't tell anyone you saw me."

"Or—?" Rob let the word trail off.

"Or it will be inconvenient for me?"

"That's it? No threat?"

Will arched one brow as he replied, "Do I need to threaten a friend?"

"Do you honestly think of me as a friend still? That's hard to believe."

"I wouldn't have had an answer to that question an hour ago, but now that I've seen you, I think I'd like to be friends again, if you're willing."

"I knew you were mentally deficient."

Will stopped walking, giving Rob his full attention. "Actually, there's something I've wished I could tell you for a long time." His old friend waited, so he went on, "I'm sorry, Rob. I don't have the words to—"

"Don't blame yourself. It was my decision to try and help. If anything, trying to take the blame is selfish on your part."

"Not that part. I mean, I did feel bad for a long time about what happened to you. I mean after that. I've always felt bad for not trying to help you."

"By the Mother, what do you think you could have done?" demanded Rob.

"I could have tried to get you away from the lich. I still remember that day, when he was torturing you—in front of me."

Rob's expression darkened, and he started walking again, forcing Will to catch up. Neither of them spoke for a couple of minutes. "There wasn't anything you could do," said Rob at last.

"I didn't even try."

"You couldn't have stopped him. I know that, logically. And I know you had other people that needed you more—living people. You couldn't afford to throw your life away fighting for someone already dead."

"Undead or not, it was cruelty, and you were a friend. I regret not trying."

Rob sighed. "We both have regrets. That's just how it goes. Besides, for all the hell he put me through, the lich did do me a favor."

Puzzled, Will asked, "How so?"

"I can use magic again."

"I remember you telling me that last time we met."

Rob smiled. "I'm getting better, and the more I progress, the less the hunger bothers me."

Will frowned. "I thought that just happened with time. I think that's what Theravan told me."

"Age helps," Rob agreed. "That goes for ordinary vampires, the ones that can't use magic. Not that there are any others. As far as I know, it's just me. Anyway, as a magic user, it's different. The better I get at drawing turyn from the environment, the less the thirst bothers me."

"I've been waiting to ask," said Will. "How are you getting by?"

"You mean am I killing people."

"To put it bluntly, yes."

"When you mentioned regrets a minute ago—that's mine. A lot of innocent people died before I got control of myself."

Will hesitated. The next answer would be the most important one. "And now?"

His friend stood straighter. "I've lived like a human being since the last time we met."

"Like a human? Are you eating normal food or—?"

The vampire waved his hand. "No, not like that. I still need blood, but when it's necessary I buy it from the slaughterhouse." Rob shivered. "I don't mind telling you—it's disgusting, even for me, but at least I can sleep with a clear conscience. Thankfully, I don't have to do that more than once or twice a month now."

Will stared at him. "A month?"

His friend nodded. "It's the ability to draw turyn that makes the difference. Listen, a lich binds his soul to a phylactery to stay alive, and to become one you already have to be a super wizard like yourself. So drawing turyn is no problem for them, but a vampire's soul is anchored in the flesh." Rob tapped his chest over his heart. "In the blood, as Mahak used to say. Although our bodies are dead, we can't replace them. They regenerate from almost anything, but that comes with a cost—the need for blood. Some of that need is for the physical fluid, but a good portion of it is the need to replace our vital energies, ergo turyn."

"So the better you get at drawing turyn from the environment, the less thirst you have," said Will, summarizing.

"It's practically gone now," said Rob proudly. "I hardly even notice it anymore."

"What if you get hurt?"

"Healing makes me thirsty, but as long as I don't get hurt"—he spread his hands wide—"once or twice a month is plenty. Cold pig's blood turns my stomach though."

"That's wonderful." Without thinking, Will chucked his old friend on the shoulder.

Rob paused, staring at his shoulder for a moment. "You really aren't afraid, are you?"

"Should I be?"

"No, but—I, it's just not something I expected." His eyes caught Will's. "Tell me truthfully, if I'd said I was feeding on civilians—what would you have done?"

"Helped you," said Will honestly.

"You're full of shit."

"No, that's the truth. Before I met Mahak and Theravan, I thought the best thing I could do for you would be to put you to rest. But after hearing their stories, I realized they were heroes, of a sort. They had integrity and they lived as men, despite having accepted a curse that made them hated and despised by everyone they were trying to help. Obviously, Alexander and most of the others were different, but from them I saw what was possible."

"If I was still murdering people, it wouldn't be safe to try and help me," said Rob.

"For most people," agreed Will, "but I'm not most people. If it was necessary, I could contain you. With time, we could find a way."

"You're crazy. I'm still not sure I deserve to live even now." Rob closed his eyes. "I have so much guilt, you can't imagine."

"I'm pretty sure I can," countered Will.

His friend laughed. "I wasn't thinking." Rob stretched his shoulders then. "This feels good. You have no idea. For so long—over ten years—I was waiting for the day you'd find me. It's like a weight has been taken off my shoulders. This isn't what I expected."

"What did you expect?"

"Something a bit more fiery and painful. Aren't you worried I'll start another outbreak?"

It was a reasonable concern. When the master vampire Alexander had deliberately infected people, it had led to widespread chaos and the destruction of a sizeable fraction of the capital. "Mahak and Theravan—not to mention all their subordinates—they managed to get by for centuries without causing an apocalypse," said Will. "If something happens, it'll be my job to fix it, so remember that. Besides, after reading that book, the one you came to remind me about—do you remember?"

Rob nodded.

"After reading that, my head is full of dozens of terrible secrets, all of which could end the world. I can deal with one more."

"I appreciate that," said his friend. "Since we're being frank, can I ask you a possibly sensitive question?"

"Sure. I'll probably even answer it, assuming it doesn't relate to one of my seemingly endless secrets."

"Why did you let them force you out? No one understands that."

Will's eyes narrowed and he started to argue, but then he stopped and held up one finger. "Define 'no one.'"

Rob waved his arms around, indicating the city as a whole. "No one. Everyone. When you reappeared, people started talking. Most assume the queen banished you, but they can't figure out why you let her push you out. As powerful as the Stormking is, it doesn't make sense."

"Is that all people talk about?"

His friend laughed. "A few years ago, yes. Not now. Nowadays everyone is talking about Trendish pirates. Don't try to change the topic."

"I wasn't forced out," said Will. "I left on my own. I couldn't stomach some of the choices Selene had made. My pretend death was a convenient fiction. I didn't mind since I didn't want anyone trying to find me."

"What choices? I'm sure you realize she's incredibly popular."

Will didn't know if Rob knew about Selene's transformation. If he still had any contact with Grim Talek, he might, but if not, Will couldn't bring himself to share the secret. *Am I trying to protect her, or simply embarrassed?* He wasn't sure. "I don't want to say, but she crossed a line. I've made plenty of hard choices, hurt a lot of people, but I've never deliberately hurt an innocent just to get what I want."

Rob seemed surprised. "That's a hard pill to swallow. You had everything."

"Being a prince isn't all it's made out to be. I'm much happier now."

The vampire nodded. "Yeah. You really look like it."

"What does that mean?" he demanded.

"You're dressed like a day laborer and most of your expressions are grim. Grim Talek isn't as grim as you are."

"I like my clothes," said Will, making an effort to appear cheery. "They're comfortable."

Rob winced. "They're drab, and stop doing whatever that is you're doing with your face. It's hurting my eyes." He sighed. "Are you sure you left because you couldn't forgive her? Or were you just scared of success?"

"What the hell is that supposed to mean?"

"You're willing to give me a second chance, despite what I've done, but not her. Makes me think you had another reason. Going from being a country bumpkin to royalty—I wouldn't blame you if you lost your nerve because of that. It had to be overwhelming, and that's not even considering the fact that you'd just saved the world *and* pissed off most of the nobles."

Will found himself grinding his teeth. "That is *not* what happened."

"Then answer this: Why am I redeemable, but she isn't? I'm a fucking vampire, Will."

Leaning forward, he poked Rob in the chest. "First, I haven't told you what she did. So don't try to compare crimes. Second, you weren't in control of yourself. New vampires are little more than hunger and madness, and I was told that by the ones who would know."

"It's not that simple," argued Rob. "Yes, I was lost in the beginning. I got some control later, but even after a year I wasn't right in the head. I still wonder if I am, or if I'm just fooling myself."

"What's your point?" interrupted Will.

"I didn't just wake up one day and think, 'Oh, I'm me now. Gosh, I should stop murdering people and be nice!' It wasn't like that at all."

"She was never insane, Rob. She made all her choices with sober deliberation."

"Shut up and let me finish. That's not the point I'm making. What I'm saying is that *I'm* not as innocent as you're trying to make me sound. Sanity came to me gradually. In the beginning, I was an animal, then later I was a violent madman—I regained my sensibility and my morality gradually. I don't blame myself for what I did in the beginning. It's the middle I'm ashamed of. There was a period where I knew it was wrong, but I did it anyway. It's impossible to put a time and date on it and say, 'Here, this is where I became responsible for my crimes.' I can't even guess when that would be. But I'm still haunted by the ones I murdered when I sort of knew it was wrong. No matter how you slice it, at some point I was responsible for my actions, and those deaths make me a true murderer."

"That doesn't excuse what she did."

"No. I'm proving my ultimate guilt to you. Do you still want to give me a second chance?"

"I've already said so."

"Then at least acknowledge you're operating with a different standard for her than you are for me. Not that I'm complaining! I'm very relieved to not have to keep looking over my shoulder thinking you might appear and set me on fire."

Will glowered at him. "I'm starting to reconsider. Maybe you're right. If so, there's one easy way to correct my mistake."

Rob's expression shifted to one of worry. "You're joking, right?"

"That depends on how much you annoy me."

"Time to change the subject, I guess. Did you finish off the lich?"

"Almost, but I let him go at the end. Shouldn't you know this already?" asked Will. "Don't you take orders from him?"

Rob shook his head. "He set me free before the final confrontation. Said I had progressed enough in my training that I wouldn't be a threat, unless I wanted to be. I haven't seen or heard from him since."

"He just let you go?"

"I felt like he was hinting that if there was a vampire outbreak he might find me, but he didn't actually make an overt threat. I think he wasn't expecting to come back. He really thought you'd finish him off."

Will's reply was dour. "He changed his mind at the end."

"Don't we all. I can't tell you how many mornings I've stood in front of an open window, waiting for the sun, only to lose my nerve and close the drapes just before it's too late." They were dark words, but Rob's voice sounded light as he delivered them.

"I let him go to save someone else," Will growled. "I probably shouldn't have."

"What the hell did she *do*?" demanded Rob.

"I didn't say it was her," Will said with a glare.

His undead friend rolled his eyes. "Out of respect for my tenuous immortal existence, I'm going to pretend I believe you." Rob glanced around. They'd taken a right every three blocks and walked in a large square. Now they were back to within half a block of Tabitha's residence. "I guess you're going back inside now." He seemed reluctant to part ways.

"Where will you go?" asked Will.

Rob shrugged. "I've amassed an extensive list of homes with open attic windows or unlocked cellars."

"You don't have a place of your own?"

"I'll have you know I'm the most successful homeless person in Cerria."

Will frowned. "You're a vampire, and a wizard. Can't you earn money somehow?"

"Despite my progress, I'm still a very weak wizard. I still avoid the daytime because I'm not always sure I can maintain the turyn cost of the protection spell that keeps the sun from burning me to a crisp. It's hard to get a job when you're afraid of the sun."

"Night watchman? Tending bar?"

"They still expect you to show up before dusk. I'm too afraid to risk it."

"You said you buy blood. How do you pay?"

Rob shrugged. "I'm not proud of it, but I steal when I have to. I try to pick rich targets, but they're also the best protected. Sooner or later I'll probably screw up, but I've been lucky so far. I've made it over fifteen years, after all."

Standing in the road, Will thought for a moment. "Want a job?"

His friend's brows went up. "I'm an excellent evil henchman. Do you need references? Because if you do, they're all dead."

Will laughed. "I'll make an exception for you."

"Does this come with room and board?" Rob sounded hopeful.

"No, but I can afford to take care of you." Will summoned two pouches from his limnthal. They clinked when he handed them over. "There's ten gold crowns in each. Rent a place and get some clothes."

"You don't want me to come with you—to wherever?"

It was obvious that Rob was lonely, but Will would only go so far. Bringing a vampire home to his mother and son was a bridge too far. Not to mention he wouldn't reveal his home. Even Tabitha didn't know those details. "I think I need you here, in Cerria. You can keep your ear to the ground for me. There's a lot I don't know, since I don't get the local gossip. You can also keep an eye out around Tabitha's house for me."

"Can I—?"

"Don't go in. Don't even let them see you if possible. I have other protections in place as well. If you approach them, even with good intentions, I can't guarantee your safety."

Rob's shoulders slumped slightly. "Fair enough. How will we stay in contact? Regular meetings or—?"

Will smiled. "You're in luck. I happen to have a spare communications tablet."

"Like the ones Grim Talek used?"

"Almost exactly the same. Wait here. I'll go fetch it for you."

CHAPTER 33

"Are you sure this is wise?" asked Tabitha for the third time after he returned from giving Rob the final tablet.

"Very sure," Will lied.

"You realize I have four children upstairs in bed right now, don't you? He's a vampire!"

James stepped in. "Dearest, I'm sure William's judgment is good. Besides, with you here, they're safe either way."

Tabitha glared at him, then snapped, "Don't patronize me, James. I can't be everywhere all the time." She sighed. "I'll never be able to relax."

"I've already told him to stay away from the house," said Will. "I also have some wards designed specifically for the undead. You can put them around the yard, the house, the windows and doors, even the children's rooms. It won't react to living people at all."

"If it's some deadly—"

"You can choose, but I agree, a warning is all you need, so you're never caught unaware."

"He's a nice person," said Vonnie, "or at least he was when I knew him."

"He still is," agreed Will.

James' sister nodded. "I still can't believe he's been living like that, all these years. It's so sad."

Will pointed at Veronica. "Exactly! Not the sad part—I mean—yes, it's sad." He turned back to Tabitha. "He's been around all these years, and we didn't even know. The only difference now is that I'll be giving him work."

That seemed to sway his sister—a little. "Stop being so logical. Besides, what work do you have to give him?"

"I'll have him listen to rumors and whatnot. It doesn't really matter. I just couldn't stand the idea of him living like that. Not to mention it's safer and easier for him to stay out of trouble if he's got a place to call his own."

James grinned. "If he's your evil henchman, what am I? Your sidekick?"

"Sidekick? This is your saga, James. You're obviously the dashing hero of this tale."

"I like the sound of that," said his brother-in-law.

"Better you than me," said Will under his breath.

"I heard that!" exclaimed James. "It's too late to take it back. This is my epic now."

"That's what I prefer," said Will. "I was the hero last time and it was awful. I've lost count of how many times I was blown up, and those are separate from the times I actually died. The torture and assassination attempts were no fun either. You're welcome to it."

"William! That's enough," growled Tabitha.

"It was just a joke," he told her.

Tabitha took her husband's hand in her own, holding it protectively. "It wasn't funny. I'm nervous enough about this as it is. I don't want to think about anything happening to either one of you." Her eyes were on James as she spoke.

James' demeanor softened. "We were just playing, Tabbycat. The world is at peace now. Nothing is going to happen, and even if something did, I've already served in the army."

Will agreed, hoping to soothe Tabitha's nerves, but a second later he felt a strange dissonance, as though a crack had been torn in reality itself. No one else seemed to notice as they continued talking. Will tried to interrupt them. "Did anyone else feel that?"

Everyone ignored him, and Will felt the world shiver. Everything he could see moved slightly, as though he was looking at it through heatwaves in the distance. *This all happened earlier today—why am I seeing it again?*

Veronica turned to look at him, a secret smile playing at the edges of her mouth.

That's different, he thought. *That didn't happen the first time. Am I dreaming?*

"Are you looking at my breasts, William?" Veronica brought her hand up to run it over the fabric of her dress. "You can see them anytime you like."

Definitely a dream.

"First, let's get rid of the distractions, then we can do whatever you desire." A long blade appeared in her hand, but no one else seemed to notice it. Before Will could yell a warning, she turned and plunged it through her brother's heart, then withdrew it and slashed the already bloody blade across Tabitha's throat.

He stared at her in shock, a soundless scream caught in his throat. The blood from Tabitha's throat splashed across Veronica's dress, and the crimson fabric seemed to blend with his sister's vital fluids. It melted, leaving her naked and bloody flesh exposed before his eyes. Will desperately wanted to look away, but his head wouldn't move.

"You said there's someone else, but you lied. It's her, isn't it? It's always been her. Do I need to remove her before you'll see reason?"

No. That's not true, he tried to answer, but his voice wouldn't work.

Veronica stepped closer, and to his horror, Will saw that the sword in her hand wasn't a sword at all. The blade grew directly from her wrist. She wasn't human. "You like the blood, don't you, Will? I can see it in your face. You still lust for it."

She paused, studying him. "No? It's not the blood? Is it the pain? Ahh! It's the violence that makes you hard. Now I see." Her eyes drifted down to his waist.

"Let me inside and you can have exactly what you want." She licked her lips with a tongue that resembled a tentacle now, long, lithe, and covered in suckers. "You'll enjoy it." Another step closer, and now he could feel the heat coming from her body.

"Or would you rather be inside me? It works either way. We just need to join. Your soul is already crowded—what's one more?" Her hand ran up the length of his thigh, sending a thrill through his body, and visions began playing in his mind. *No, not visions, memories,* he realized. Once more, he saw himself killing Lognion's soldiers, the day he had lost his temper and chosen vengeance.

Once again, he killed servants and soldiers, men and women who had already surrendered. His pulse quickened with the feel of a skull cracking beneath his boot. *This is what I am. This is what I want.*

"Exactly," Veronica whispered into his ear. "I know what you want." He felt her hands unlacing his trousers.

She's lying, came Laina's voice. *That's not what either of us wanted.* Selene's face appeared in his mind's eye.

She'd been Laina's first unrequited love, and for Will, Selene had been his everything. Remembering his feelings for her cleared away the vision of violence. A new face appeared, Cora smiling at him. *"I'll return soon,"* she had told him.

Will's eyes opened, and he saw Veronica shed her face like a snake shedding its skin. Something terrible lay beneath it, something he didn't dare to look at. "So stubborn," she told him. "I'll have you eventually. There's no need to fight. I can give you everything."

"At what price?" he said hoarsely, having finally found his voice.

"No price at all," said the thing he refused to look upon. "You are a pillar of creation now. It all belongs to you already. You just need my guidance."

"Guidance comes at a cost too," he intoned.

"No. For the dragon's heir, it is free."

"Accept no debts!" Arrogan had drilled that line into him once, long ago. Will's head came up, and his eyes glowed with the radiance of distilled lightning. The light created holes in the human-shaped piece of void that stood in front of him. Thunder boomed from the skies above. "I will take nothing from you," he said firmly. "But I will give you this…"

The world shattered, and lightning purified everything.

***

"William! Wake up!" Someone was pounding on the door. Or was that thunder? After a second, Will realized it was both. His mother's voice came again, "Wake up!"

Rising from the bed, he crossed the room. His heart was still pounding and although he'd just woken, he didn't feel groggy at all. His most recent nightmare was still as clear to him as it had been while he was asleep.

"Open the door. Let me in," said Erisa, her voice full of fear.

Will could feel the storm in the skies above. It was connected to him as surely as the blood in his veins. Though there was only the usual ambient turyn available, it seemed to be enough to conduct his will and connect him to the rivers of power that flowed in the sky. Through that connection, he could feel the heavens trembling with pent-up power. His fear had stirred up the currents. It waited for his command to unleash itself against his enemies.

"Please, Will. I'm frightened," begged his mother through the door.

"I'm still asleep," he muttered. "Go to hell, bitch!"

She begged for several more minutes, but he ignored her, and eventually his mother's tone shifted. "This can't last forever. Eventually we will be one."

"I've already refused you," he yelled at the door. "Why do you keep tormenting me?"

Her voice replied in velvet tones. "You created me, William and you're the one who calls me. Ask yourself the question. Why do you summon me?"

"I want nothing to do with you!" he screamed.

"You summon me to give you what is rightfully yours. The power to destroy them."

"Who?"

"All of them. Those who spurn you, those who obey you, those who fail you, and those who worship you. Only when you consign them all to the void will you know peace."

"I don't want that."

"You're a broken pillar. You created the cracks and here I am."

Will ignored the voice and went back to his bed. He wanted to call the lightning, to destroy the thing waiting outside his room, but now that he knew he was dreaming, he was afraid. *I might be doing this in the waking world.* The last thing he could bear would be to wake and find he'd destroyed his own home, or worse, his family. Instead, he closed his eyes and tried to meditate. *I can't sleep forever.*

An eternity passed, while he listened to the stranger wheedle and beg from the other side of his door. Eventually, he grew bored with meditating and his mind began to wander. He thought of Cora. Her smile had warmed his heart, and he still didn't understand why she'd come and found him while he was ill.

The voice faded as he thought about her, and before he knew it, he was drifting.

***

His face was illuminated by the morning sun shining in through his bedroom window. Wincing at the brightness, Will sat up. Suspicious, he thought about his dreams. They were still vivid and terrifying, but some of the detail was already beginning to fade. *Maybe I'm really awake this time.*

Collecting himself, he thought about the day before and his conversation with Tabitha. All of that had been real, including the jokes with James and his sister's bad reaction to them. The dream had diverged from reality at some point shortly after that. But when? It was hard to be sure. *Veronica had a sword, or no, it was a sharp horn or bone, I think.*

The vagueness reassured him. It was perhaps the only way he had discovered to tell the real world from the world of dreams, but it didn't always work. *Most would think that clarity is the defining element, but it isn't. It's always clear, dream or not. It's the memory that goes fuzzy if it's a dream.* The real problem was that while he was dreaming, he often didn't remember the tricks he had learned until he'd already lost control of his emotions.

Will washed his face and dressed, then went to the door. His hand hesitated on the handle, and his heart sped up a little. "It's safe," he told himself. Firming his lips, he pulled the door open. A body was slumped against it, and his mother fell partway into his bedroom. *No!* His heart jumped, and he started to fall to his knees and catch her, but Erisa's head jerked and she caught herself.

Rubbing at her neck, his mother looked at him with bleary eyes. "You're awake. Finally."

"Mom, what happened?"

"There was a storm," she answered, as if that said it all. "A bad one."

Oliver came in from through the front door, a basket of fresh eggs under one arm. At a guess, he was probably doing his nana's morning tasks so she could sleep longer. There was relief on his face when he saw his father. "You kept screaming last night. Nana was trying to get you to wake up."

Will helped his mother to her feet, feeling guilty as he saw her struggle to straighten up. Her body was obviously sore from sleeping propped up against the door. She rubbed at her neck. "I must have fallen asleep." There were dark circles under her eyes.

"I'm sorry, Mom. Maybe you should go to bed. It's my fault you didn't sleep worth a damn."

"I'll be fine," she said, waving him away. "Oliver is late for school, and you need to go to work. Leave me be."

Will knew better to argue with her, so a few minutes later, he found himself walking with his son. They both had to get up early, but generally he left first, so it was rare for them to walk together. "Did I keep you up too?" he asked.

Oliver groaned. "I was up for most of the night, but it wasn't your fault."

"Screaming doesn't bother you?"

His son gave him a sour look. "It didn't help, but I bet most people in Lystal lost sleep. The thunder and lightning were the worst. When it first woke me up, I knew we'd start hearing you soon enough."

"Why's that?"

"You always have nightmares when there's a storm," said Oliver in a matter-of-fact tone.

Once again, it was clear Olly misunderstood. Will started to correct him, "It isn't the storm that—"

Oliver interrupted him with a chuckle. "That's why I know my cousins are wrong."

Will stopped, confused. "Huh? About what?"

"About you being the Stormking," said Oliver. "If they knew how scared you were of storms, they wouldn't say that."

Now was his chance to set the record straight. Oliver's mistake was clear to see, and they were on the topic already, but the words froze on his lips. *He already knows I'm a wizard. He's got the basics. Does he really need to know that too?*

"We studied about him a little last week," said Oliver.

"You did?"

"Were you there when he destroyed the capital?"

A chill washed over him. "Do you mean when the vampires overran Cerria?"

"Yeah!" exclaimed Oliver. "From what I heard, it's a miracle you survived if you were there. The vampires killed thousands, and the Stormking destroyed almost a quarter of the city before Lana stopped him."

"Laina," Will corrected automatically. "Her name was Laina. And I think the Stormking was trying to stop the vampires."

"By destroying the entire city!" said his son. "Isn't that insane? But what I don't understand, is how did Lania—"

"Laina."

Oliver nodded. "How did Laina stop him? Wasn't he more powerful than anyone else?"

"Well, it wasn't really him. He was possessed by an ancient wizard named Ethelgren, and Laina had some help, so…"

"Nobody believes that, though," said Oliver dismissively. "Mister Daniels told us that too, but he said it was a rumor. Most think he made that up to cover for his madness."

"Madness?"

Oliver nodded. "He had to be crazy, right? Why else would he try to kill everyone and then help Lonna perform the ritual to kill *just* the vampires?"

"Laina," corrected Will with a sigh.

"Laina," agreed Oliver. "I don't know why that name gives me so much trouble." He paused. "Did you see any vampires when everything happened?"

"A lot of them."

"Really?" His son's eyes went wide.

Will stopped in the road and lifted his tunic. Despite the many horrific wounds he had endured, he only had scars for some of them. The regeneration potions he used tended to heal everything perfectly unless there was a significant delay between the injury and taking the potion. There was no sign of either of the two times he'd been stabbed through-and-through with a sword. The only visible scars were from the lashes Lognion had given him when he'd been protecting his sister, and a few white dots here and there. The dots were puncture marks that remained from when he'd been swarmed by vampires. "See these white spots?"

Oliver nodded.

"Notice there's two? Here, here, here, and here." He pointed out several obvious ones on his stomach. "Those are from vampire fangs."

"What!" Oliver's jaw dropped. "But, doesn't that mean you were infected?"

Will produced a blood-cleanse potion from his limnthal. "If you take one of these within a few hours, it stops the transformation. It's used to stop infections on the battlefield, but it works for vampire bites too. If you insist on becoming a warrior, I'll make sure you have some on you at all times. More men die from infected wounds than in battle."

"So you really were bitten? Really?" When his father nodded, Oliver swore, "Mother's tits! Wait until I tell Doug! He's going to shit himself."

Will glared at his son. "Language."

"Sorry, Dad." A second later, Oliver asked, "So, how did it happen, and how did you escape?"

"Your Aunt Tailtiu was taken by one of the vampires, and I went to rescue her. I found her in a warehouse, but I got caught and then—"

Oliver's eyes were bugging out. "You went alone?"

Will nodded. "Thankfully, my friends followed after me, but I was running full out. We found Tailtiu in the warehouse, just barely alive, but before we could get out, they swarmed us."

"Who was with you?"

"Rob, Tiny, and Janice. Rob was a school friend, but he didn't make it. Janice was badly wounded and I got overwhelmed. If it hadn't been for Tiny covering me with his body, I wouldn't have been able to put a spell together to save us."

"Tiny, he was the one who came to see you? The giant?" Will nodded. Then Oliver asked, "If they were swarming you, what spell did you use?"

"A light spell that replicates daylight. It sends out glowing orbs. It wiped out the majority of the vampires so we could get away—most of us anyway."

"Doug is going to die when he hears this," said Oliver.

Will put a hand on his son's shoulder. "About that."

Oliver grimaced. "Aww, Dad! Really?"

He nodded again. "It's bad enough everyone knows we come from Terabinia. If you give people a specific time and place, it's a lot more likely someone will find a way to figure out my identity."

Oliver sighed. "Fine."

"I'm sorry, Olly."

"I said it was fine," replied Oliver in a sour tone.

They had come to the Laughing Goat, so it was time to part ways. Oliver started off, but Will called to his back, "Don't forget about tonight." It was the end of the week, and with no school the next day, Will had decided to begin Oliver's compression training.

Oliver gave him a look of distaste, then waved as he walked away.

CHAPTER 34

"There, it's done," said Will as the spell cage slipped into place around his son's source.

"That's it?" asked Oliver.

Will nodded, then gave what he hoped was a reassuring smile to his mother, who stood watching them warily.

"I don't feel any stronger," remarked Oliver.

He shook his head. "It won't make you feel stronger. What gave you that idea?"

"You said it pens up my turyn, right? So, it builds up inside me. If there's more turyn, I should feel more energetic, shouldn't I?"

"No. Turyn is what drives magic—it's the power behind everything, but just having more of it inside you doesn't make you feel stronger, faster, or more energetic. In fact, if you don't know how to utilize it, it can kill you. It's a bit like fire. Put to good use, you can heat your house with it, but if there's too much and it gets out of control, it will burn it down. In this example, the house is your body."

Oliver scrunched up his nose. "But you said before that the reason I'm able to move faster when fighting is because of my turyn."

"It's because of *how* you use your turyn. You have the same amount inside you as most people. What's different is that your body has learned to naturally channel it to enhance whatever you're doing, so the end result is more strength, more speed, etc."

"But I'm not even aware of it."

Will sighed. "That part seems strange to me too, but according to what my teacher taught me, many athletes do the same thing to some degree or another. It's part of what makes them so good at what they do. Some people just have a knack for it, but yours is rather extreme. It's close to what I've seen when someone uses a Dragon's Heart potion."

His son's eyes brightened. "Imagine what I could do if I took that potion too."

"Let's not," said Will. "There are limits. Just because you're close to them on your own doesn't mean the limits aren't there. I've seen men rip their muscles and bones apart using that potion. Even if they don't screw up, they still need regeneration potions and a full day's rest after using one." His son's face showed disappointment, so Will shifted subjects. "Back to turyn and your energy level. Too much won't make you feel faster on its own, but too little will make you feel tired and lethargic. During the compression training, you'll experience both. Right now, it's beginning to build up inside you, so eventually you'll start to feel uncomfortable. Eventually, you'll feel like you're on fire, and you'll be convinced you're going to die. I will have to paralyze you then, to keep you from harming yourself, or someone else."

Oliver shrugged. "I bet I surprise you. I can handle more pain than you think."

His father smirked. "I've seen how much nausea you can handle."

"That's different."

"Sure," said Will. "In any case, after an agonizing period your body will figure out that it needs to restrict the amount of turyn it produces from your source. Once it does, you'll go through the opposite effect. With only half as much turyn, you're going to feel very tired until your body learns to adapt in the second way, by absorbing turyn from your environment."

"That's what you do?"

Will nodded. "My source has been compressed three times, so I survive on one-eighth the turyn a normal person does. The other seven-eighths comes from my environment. At first, you'll be miserable, but over time, you won't even notice it."

"And how is this going to make me a better wardsman, since I can't use magic? I know, you already told me it will keep me from dying young, but will it help me fight at all?"

As far as Will knew, it wouldn't help in any significant way, other than offsetting the inevitable physical decline that overusing his source would normally produce. But there were probably some small benefits. "There are a few things that come to mind. One, the training will make you more resistant to magic, much like a normal first-order wizard. Two, you'll be able to recover faster and fight longer, because you aren't totally reliant on your source to supply you with turyn. Third, when you are tapped out, you'll be better able to function."

"Tapped out, what does that mean?"

"Suppose you use your tattoos too much and you drain yourself of energy. As I said, you'll recover twice as fast as the other wardsmen, but also, you will be able to fight even if you have almost no turyn at all. That's a benefit of what you learn while waiting for your body to start absorbing turyn. You'll be so starved for energy that you'll have to learn how to function without much."

Oliver frowned. "Can you do that?"

"Want me to show you?"

"You know I can't see turyn."

"You couldn't see it, or the lack of it, inside me anyway. I'll demonstrate. First I'll draw off most of yours, so you can see what it feels like. That will delay your turyn overload by an hour or two, so I hope you aren't impatient. Want to try it?"

Confident as always, Oliver nodded. "Sure."

Creating a source-link, Will rapidly drained Oliver's turyn, stopping just before the teen went unconscious. Oliver had already sunk to the ground and now lay there staring up at him. "How do you feel?" asked Will.

His son couldn't even speak, but he managed to open his mouth slightly. Will laughed. "I remember the feeling. Shall we trade places? Oh, that's right. You can't talk. Here." He fed half the turyn back to Oliver, taking care to match it to the boy's normal frequency so he wouldn't get sick.

"I'm still weak," complained his son.

"I left you that way so you could get a feel for it. Now I'm going to vent my turyn until I'm almost completely empty." Reaching upward, Will began expressing raw turyn from his right hand. He didn't bother giving it any form or effect, he simply forced it out as rapidly and completely as possible. To Oliver's eyes, nothing happened. "I know you can't see this, but hopefully you trust me. I'm draining myself dry." A minute later, he put his hand down and gazed at his son with a languid, dead stare.

"Did you finish?"

Will nodded. "It's not something I enjoy. But I can move."

"How?"

"Like I said, turyn doesn't give you strength or energy directly. Living beings, flesh and muscle, those things do use turyn, but they aren't entirely dependent on it. Your muscles will operate without it, or with almost none at least. Most of the time, turyn just helps communicate your will—your intent or desire—to your body. With practice, you can do that while being almost empty. The trick is focus and attention. When you are mostly empty, you have to remain fully focused on what you're doing, otherwise you'll be incredibly clumsy. Just walking takes a lot more focus than people realize."

"What if I can't do that?" said Oliver doubtfully.

"You will," said Will.

"How do you know?"

"Because the alternative is that you'd be dead. Surviving the first compression means you'll have to restrict your source, and adapting to live after that means you'll also have to learn to absorb turyn. Veronica was clear that your chances are still the same as anyone else's, even though you can't sense turyn. You're the best age for this."

"But I *could* die."

His heart clenched, but Will nodded. "Yes. A good friend of mine died that way, but not from the first compression. I don't believe that is going to happen to you. Are you still committed to this?"

Oliver nodded, but Will could see fear hidden in his eyes.

He hugged his son. "You're probably going to hate me when it gets to the worst part, but I want you to know, I'll be linked to you the entire time. I'll feel it all with you, including the pain."

"Does that mean you can stop it if it goes wrong?" asked Oliver hopefully.

"That's what I told your grandmother, but the truth isn't so simple. The body is stubborn. You *have* to get to a point of crisis for your body to be forced to adapt. If it fails, the first sign will come too late. I would remove the spell cage at that point, obviously, but according to the records, most die anyway. I saw something similar when helping students with the third compression."

"What's the link for then?"

"Because I can't bear to see you go through this without knowing what you're going through. My teacher, my grandfather, he did the same for me, but he didn't tell me all this. I think he thought it would make it easier if I didn't know. I was so furious I almost put an axe through his head afterward."

"Really? You hated him that much?"

He laughed. "For a few minutes, yeah. It took quite a while for me to realize how much I loved the old man, or how much he loved me, since he had such a strange way of showing it."

Oliver had never heard his father talk about Arrogan before. Curious, he asked, "How did he show it?"

"Mostly by insulting me, or swearing at me. He had a colorful vocabulary."

Oliver smiled. "It's the same with us."

"Hardly," said his father. "I do cuss too much, and you've picked up some of it, but I try my best not to berate you like that."

"Sometimes you fail then," said Oliver.

"You're too stupid to know the difference, idiot," snapped Will.

Olly's face registered hurt. "That's what I mean."

"And that's what Arrogan would have said to me. It was an example, dumbass. Don't prove my point for me."

"See! You just called me a—" Oliver started to argue, then realized the paradox and clamped a hand over his own mouth.

His father grinned, and they both began to laugh.

By the time evening fell, Oliver's humor had vanished. He'd chopped more firewood than they would need for the entire winter during the afternoon and then moved on to sword drills. After beating several practice swords to flinders, he'd given up on that and started running laps. Currently, he was circling the house at an impressive pace.

Erisa put a hand on Will's shoulder. "That can't be good. He's hurting himself."

"He's exhausting himself. I'll stop him before he really hurts himself." Mentally, he wondered how she would deal with the next stages. Soon her grandson would begin to beg and bargain. When that failed, he would grow truly desperate. How would she handle it if the boy began swearing at them? How would Will deal with her reaction, while trying to remain calm for Oliver's sake?

"Are you sure this is a good idea?" she asked for the tenth time.

It probably wasn't the ethical choice, but rather than answer, Will silently cast a sleep spell on his mother, putting enough power into it to keep her unconscious until morning, hopefully. He caught her as she slumped, then lifted her and carried her to bed and gently tucked her in. As he stepped out of her room and shut the door, Oliver burst in through the front door.

"Where's Nana?" His demeanor was frenetic with barely suppressed nervous energy.

"Taking a nap."

"Oh, really? I was wondering if she might want some ice." Oliver's words were coming so fast they nearly stumbled over one another.

"Ice?"

"I'm so hot. I thought I could go buy some ice in town. Actually, we should build our own icehouse. All it takes is a barn and some hay, right? I think that's right. They just cover it with hay. Of course, we'd have to cut our own blocks from the river during the winter, and that would be some work. What if we dug our own pond? We could use that. Then we wouldn't have to haul it very far, since we could build our icehouse right next to it. Where's the shovel? I can dig the pond now."

"I think it's time for you to sit down, son. You're red in the face. If you keep running around, you'll overheat."

"That's true. So if I'm still, I'll cool off? Can magic make ice? If it can I bet you're laughing, since you wouldn't need to haul blocks from the river. But you'll still need the water. So the pond is a good idea."

Most people in Lystal used one of several communal wells to get water, but Will had dug one right beside the kitchen and then built an extension of the house over it, saving them a lot of time and trips. "We have a well, Olly. We don't need a pond," he told his son.

"I should still go buy some ice, though." Oliver was bouncing up and down on his heels, unable to stand still. He took one step, but Will created a source-link and paralyzed his legs. When he caught his son and began dragging him toward the bedroom, it struck him just how much muscle the boy had put on. *He's heavier than me, I think.*

"Dad, Dad. You need to let me go. I just want to get ice."

"I know, Olly. This is just where we are now."

"But Dad, Dad, please. I just want some ice. I'll come right back."

Will got him to the edge of the bed, then cheated and used a force spell to lift Oliver's bottom half up so he could get him in without any awkwardness. Oliver continued to plead with him as he did. "Dad, I feel like I have ants all over me."

"That's normal, son."

"This isn't normal. I'm telling you. You said it would burn. I'm not burning! There're ants all over me. Dad!"

"I can feel it, Olly. I'm connected. It isn't ants, it's your body warning you that you have too much turyn. The burning will start soon."

Oliver's face scrunched up. "It itches. Please, Dad! I've changed my mind. I don't want this."

"We talked about that," said Will sadly. "I told you that you would say that. Your chance to back out was earlier. Now we have to wait."

"No, no, no, no. Please, I've really changed my mind. This isn't good. Don't you love me? Dad, Dad!" Using his arms, Oliver began fighting, trying to drag himself from the bed to the floor.

"I'm going to paralyze the rest of you now. I'm sorry. It'll be better when this is over."

"No! Dad, Dad you ca—!" his voice cut off as Will stopped the rest of his voluntary muscle control.

Reaching out with one hand, Will closed his son's mouth and tried to smooth his contorted features. He had to manually relax Oliver's facial muscles to do so, but at last his son looked to be at peace—except for the wildly rolling eyes.

Eyes were the one thing a source-link wouldn't allow control over. They were linked directly to the brain, so only magic that directly affected the mind could do something like that. Will worked hard to keep his own face calm, but it was difficult. He was acutely aware of the panic that had enveloped every part of Oliver's awareness.

He watched his son for a bit, but Oliver continued to stare desperately at him, screaming silently with his eyes. *And I'm sure I look like a villain staring calmly back at him.* This was why Arrogan had left him alone during his own trial. "I can feel everything, son, and I'm sorry. I'm going to leave the room. It might help you to focus. Just remember, it's sort of like clenching a fist, but it's not physical. That's what I was told, and at the time, it didn't seem to help. When you get it, you'll understand."

He stood and left the room, feeling Oliver's terror and pounding heart with every step he took. *It's going to be a long night.*

Sitting in the main room, he watched the fire and tried to drink a cup of tea, but his stomach was tied in a knot. The sensations coming from Oliver reminded him of when he had done the same for Selene. *This is why I don't want to train any more apprentices,* he thought. *How does Veronica endure this? She has so many—oh, that's right. She and James don't link to their students.* Should he do the same? He wanted to. The feelings of terror and impending doom were constant and overwhelming, but it was his son. He couldn't.

Then the burning started. The pain slowly grew, from mild to intense, until he could feel tears running down Olly's paralyzed cheeks. Pulling his knees up to his chin, Will wrapped his arms around them. Something wet was on his sleeve. Tears. It hadn't been Oliver crying, or perhaps it was both of them.

Squeezing his eyes shut, Will tried not to think as he relived his own compression trial through Oliver.

The night lasted an eternity.

CHAPTER 35

"William? What's wrong? How is Oliver? I can't wake him up." Erisa's voice was full of fear as she shook him awake. "You look awful."

He gave his mother a weak smile. "He did it. He's asleep now, but he'll wake up soon."

His mother didn't seem relieved. "Have you been crying? If it worked, why do you look like that?"

"It's painful, and I went through it with him. He won't have felt that, though, just his own experience."

"Why can't I wake him up?" she demanded. "And why don't I remember anything?"

"I put you to sleep. I didn't want—" The slap that cut him off brought him fully awake. Unrepentant, he finished, "I didn't have the strength to deal with your suffering and his at the same time."

"It wasn't your choice to make," she snapped.

"It was. He chose for himself, but I knew I wasn't going to have the fortitude to keep you calm while trying to keep myself calm at the same time. If you want to ground me, fine, but I'll cook my own dinner at the 'Goat if you tell me I have to go to bed without supper."

Erisa's mouth opened in surprise. "Ground you, what?" Finally, her expression softened. "Fine. I'll let you off this time. You were probably right." She hugged him, then pushed away. "Want breakfast? Will Olly be hungry?"

Will nodded. "Wait until he wakes up, though. He's tired, and he won't get much sleep this week. The worst is over, but there's a lot of misery yet ahead."

"Why won't he sleep much?"

"Keeping his source constricted is something he'll only be able to do while awake, at first. Whenever he sleeps, it will relax, and he'll start producing too much turyn again. The pain will wake him up after less than an hour. It will keep waking him up until he gets to the point that it's second nature and his control doesn't slip even when he's unconscious."

Erisa grimaced. "That sounds like some forms of torture I've heard of."

He nodded. "It's rough. But he's proven he can do it. We just need time now." Will winced as he felt panic shoot through Oliver's chest. His son had awakened. "He's up." Heading to Oliver's room, Will removed the paralysis, and the teen shot upright.

Oliver's face twisted into a snarl when he saw his father. "It's not over! I survived it, somehow, but it's come back. Just like the nausea before all this!"

Will nodded, and as he did, he felt a violent impulse pass through Oliver. *How do I keep from seeming smug?* he wondered. "You have to keep your source compressed. It's like a muscle. When you sleep, it relaxes again until you learn to keep it tight all the time, asleep or awake."

"Why didn't you tell me that before?" shouted Oliver.

"Calm down and focus," said Will sternly. "That's your only choice at this point. Anger and panic won't help you." A nearly inaudible growl came from his son, but the boy didn't say anything. "Your grandmother is making breakfast. When you're ready, come out and eat." He left the room.

Will felt the murderous intent rise as he turned his back, but Oliver managed to restrain himself. He smiled, but made sure Oliver didn't see it, then shut the door behind him. "Is he hungry?" called Erisa from the kitchen.

"He is," answered Will. "But don't expect a thank you this morning. He's very out of sorts."

"There's sausages and bread on the table. I'll have your eggs in few minutes. Grab the jam for me, will you?" Will did, and a few minutes later he was sitting down, eating.

Oliver still hadn't come out by the time he finished, so Will checked his enchanted tablet. There was already a message from Rob:

> *Saw ten elves today! There are dozens in the city. No idea why. As far as I know they've never come inland from trading at the port cities.*
> *~Rob*

Will replied:

> *Find out what people are saying. Keep me informed.*
> *~Will*

"Is everything all right?" asked Erisa, having observed him writing with the stylus.

He chuckled. "Just keeping Rob busy. He saw some elves and thought I needed to know."

"Are they something you worry about?"

Will shook his head. "No. They're probably just a trade delegation, but if it keeps Rob feeling useful, then I'm happy to read his messages."

"Maybe you should ask your sister about it," suggested his mother.

He didn't see the point, but nodded along. "Since I'm not taking Dr. Lorentz for lessons anymore, I'll just send a message to James. He likes to feel useful too."

Oliver stepped out then and quickly came over to the table. Sullenly, he ate his food and then returned to his room. A second later, he put his head back through the door. "Thank you, Nana." His words sounded sincere, but when his gaze fell on his father, Oliver's eyes hardened.

"You're welcome, sweetheart," said Erisa. "I hope you feel better soon."

"Love you, Nana." Oliver's eyes bored holes into Will until he withdrew and closed the door.

"He seems like he'll be all right," remarked Erisa.

Will chuckled. "If he's got the composure to remember his manners for you, then I think you're right."

"Being a grandmother has its perks, just like fatherhood does."

"Fatherhood has perks? I'm not seeing them," said Will wryly.

"A few. There will be a lot more when you're a *grand*father. Think of this as an investment. If you're lucky, you'll have lots of grandchildren to dote on."

Will chuckled. "I think you've got the better end of things."

Erisa gave him a severe look. "I'm being shortchanged. So far, you've only given me one grandchild. If you don't sort yourself out, I'll be too old to hold the next ones, assuming I'm alive to see them."

Will sighed. There was no way to win. "I told Lettler I wouldn't be working for the next two weeks, but there's not much I can do today. Since Oliver's feeling kindly toward you, I'll take the opportunity to spend extra time on some of my projects."

Anxiety appeared in Erisa's features. "What do I need to do?"

"Nothing. He just needs rest. He'll spend days trying to sleep, and the rest of the time he won't have the energy to do much of anything. I'll start him on exercises next week," explained Will.

"Is there anything I need to watch for? Is there any danger?"

Will shook his head. "No. But if you do need me, just write a message on the tablet I gave you. I'll teleport back right away." Leaning forward, he kissed his mother's forehead, then stepped back, and after less than ten seconds, he had achieved the proper state to teleport to his custom beacon.

***

The week passed productively for Will, and miserably for Oliver.

With James' help, Will had finished a set of four modified raven pins, one for Will, James, Tabitha, and Sammy. The pins were mainly a test article. In the future, all the raven pins given to new students would have the improved enchantment. The only difference between them and the original version was that the new ones would turn black if worn by someone without a source. Rob proved an invaluable test candidate to make sure the pins worked properly.

Will also did his best to fool the new enchantment. Since he was easily the best at modifying his own turyn frequency, Will could fool most wards and had previously slipped through many magical security measures protecting sensitive books in Wurthaven's library. If anyone could trick the new enchantment, it would be him, and if he could do it, then his target could as well.

Happily, he failed every time. Although Will could alter the turyn within and without himself to match any frequency, he couldn't change the small amount that was continually emerging from his source. Even though he altered that turyn almost from the instant it emerged, it wasn't fast enough to spoil the calculations done by James' enchanted pins.

Their second project involved rings with a similar enchantment, although there were key differences. The most obvious was that the rings performed their measurements on anyone touched by the wearer, rather than on the wearer. Although a small change, James had to come up with an extra mathematical function to eliminate the wearer's influence so that the ring's results purely reflected the person being touched. While the ring also had a plain quartz stone set in it, the colors didn't function in the same way, and the signal that told the wearer the result of the enchantment's calculation was hidden.

They'd had quite a few discussions on the reason and method for doing that. "I understand why you want the signal to be a secret, but why put a stone on it at all then? That's just an added complication," James had complained.

"I'm a bad liar," said Will. "So I usually don't try, and if I do, I mostly do it by omission."

His brother-in-law's brow wrinkled in confusion. "That is not what I asked."

Will smiled. "Or I fall back on wizardly tradition and make my answer cryptic. I wasn't very good at it in the beginning, but I've gotten better. Don't you think?"

"By the Mother, you are so frustrating!" replied James.

"I'll take that as a yes. Can you fit my request into the space we have? I know it's already tight."

"Barely. But as I said, it would be simpler and easier to just omit the stone and the colors."

"You can make the rest of them that way if you want. I only need mine to function this way."

James growled. "That's *two* different setups then! That's not easier."

"Make them without the stones then. Just help me create the more complicated enchantment and I'll make my bespoke version myself," said Will.

"I'm not making the embossing die, that's the part I'm complaining about, just so you know," said James.

Will nodded. "I know. That's what I meant. Just work out the enchantment specifics and I'll make the embossing die and all the rest. I won't even need to bother Lawrence with it."

"I'll have to teach you the spell so you can use the luxpress." James started rummaging through his desk. "I have it in here somewhere."

"This spell?" Will held up his palm, forming the spell construct for James to see.

James gaped. "You memorized it? That's a seventh-order spell. I haven't even memorized it, and I designed it!"

Will shrugged. "It's a hobby."

His brother-in-law stabbed at him with his index finger. "You, Will Cartwright, are a very odd man. I hope you realize that. How did you memorize it? As far as I know, I never copied it out for you."

"You showed it to me the first day, when you were telling me about the luxpress. I'm still impressed by that, just so you know," said Will.

James seemed to be on the verge of an apoplectic fit. "You saw me cast it and remembered it from just that?"

Will pursed his lips. "It wasn't *that* simple. I tried it right after I got home, so I wouldn't forget. Then I added it to my practice routine. I'm sure if I had slept on it without writing it down, I would have forgotten some of the key details."

His brother-in-law seemed as though he would start spitting as he replied, "It's a *seventh-order spell,* William!"

"I told you, it's my hobby. You know how many spells I've already memorized, not to mention learned to reflex cast. Some of them are ninth- and tenth-order. I've devoted an hour a day for nearly the last seventeen years to memorizing and practicing spell constructs. A person starts to develop a knack for it after a while. If it's any consolation, if it had been any more complicated, I would have needed you to write it out for me first. Seventh-order is just about the most complex I would try learning from just seeing it."

"You're a monster."

Will smiled. "Thank you. Some of my best friends are monsters. Now, back to the topic at hand. Aside from the custom enchantment, what I really need your help with is building another luxpress. The materials looked simple enough, but you never showed me the enchantment that went into it."

James frowned. "If you need one, you can just use mine."

Will clucked his tongue admonishingly, waving one finger from side to side. "I have all sorts of ideas for the future, and some of them are somewhat distasteful. If I use yours, that would make you an accomplice. Plus I'd have to explain myself."

"If I give you my design, knowing you might have some nefarious plans, then aren't I still an accomplice?"

"No, because you think I'm just joking."

"I do?" James looked very confused.

Will laughed. "You thought I was serious?"

"So, you don't want the design for my luxpress?"

His face turned serious. "No, I definitely want it. I was joking about all the accomplice stuff."

Despite his sometimes-befuddled demeanor, James was no slouch when it came to his intellect. Slowly, he said, "I—don't—believe—you."

"You're a founding member of the Council of Wizardry, aren't you?"

"But I'm only first-order."

"Council members can be of any compression level. Only the head of the council has to be third-order," Will extemporized.

"Really?"

He nodded, then lied, "It's in the charter."

"There's a charter?"

Will rubbed his chin thoughtfully. "I need to make a copy for you and Tabitha. I keep forgetting."

James nodded. "Yes, I'd like to read it myself."

"Anyway, as I said, you're a founding member, correct?"

His brother-in-law straightened a bit. "Well, yes. I suppose I am."

"And I'm the First Wizard, head of the council, right?" James nodded, and Will immediately responded, "Easy then. I order you to share the design of the luxpress with me."

James stared at him with eyes that had narrowed into slits, then sighed. Reaching into another desk drawer, he pulled out a small, new looking journal. "I already made a copy for you. I'd planned to share it anyway, until you made me nervous with your criminal implications."

Will accepted the journal graciously, with a bow and a flourish of his hand. "Thank you, kind sir."

"Do you tease everyone like this?" asked his brother-in-law. "I never know what to think."

He answered sincerely, "Just you."

"Why?"

Will shrugged, then smiled. "I'm not sure. You just bring out the devil in me." He stared at the ceiling for a moment, then added, "Actually, maybe I do have a reason. I never had a brother growing up. Maybe you feel like a younger brother to me. I just can't help wanting to torment you."

James froze, then his eyes began to turn liquid. A second later he opened his arms.

"Aww, damn," muttered Will, but he didn't retreat.

CHAPTER 36

Oliver finished his first week and began the second week of his compression training without ever noticing the new gold ring his father started wearing. He had bigger problems. Although he could now sleep three or four hours at a stretch before waking up feeling as if he was on fire, he still had no energy. He spent his days in a perpetual malaise. His lethargy was so great, it was an effort just to get up to go to the bathroom.

Having been active and physically hardy for the entirety of his life, being so sluggish came as a shock to him. When his father appeared in the door, he shared exactly how he felt. "Go away."

"Today you start exercises."

"Not happening," said Oliver. "I can hardly eat, much less move around." He turned his head on the pillow so that it faced the wall.

His father leaned over the bed and across Oliver, until his upside-down face appeared in front of the teen. "You won't be simply moving. I'm expecting a jog."

"You're insane."

"Don't make me resort to dark magic," joked Will in a voice that was both humorous and threatening simultaneously.

Oliver sat up and tried to pull on his trousers but struggled to complete the task. Managing the fabric while trying to line up his toes so he could get a foot down the correct leg of the trousers was a nigh-insurmountable chore. He would have growled, but that took energy he didn't have.

"Focus," said his father in the most irritating tone possible. "You don't have any turyn to spare, so keep your mind purely on the task at hand."

"Does it look like I'm trying to learn a musical instrument while I'm doing this?" asked Oliver in a voice that lacked sarcasm. Sarcasm took more than he had to give.

"Break it down into steps. Mind what your hands are doing, how the cloth droops, and where your foot is. You're training your mind as much as your body right now."

Oliver wanted to rip the pants in two. "I really hate you right now, Dad. I hope you realize."

Will gave him a ridiculous grin. "I hadn't noticed. You'll need to get your stamina back if you want me to give a damn."

The trousers tangled up again. "Making me angry isn't helping me focus," he whined.

"Your enemies won't give two shits about whether they're making you angry or not. In fact, they might do it just to make you act stupid."

"You're not my enemy. You're supposed to be my father."

"I agree, but I doubt you really feel that way right now, do you?" Will leaned in until his face was mere inches from Oliver's.

Oliver's anger surged, and without thinking he moved. Lightning fast, his right hand came up, forming a fist. It struck with all the force he could muster, and there was an audible crack when it reached his father's jaw. Pain shot up his arm, but Will's head didn't move.

His father blinked. "Oops. I didn't mean to do that. Your hand is broken, isn't it? Damn."

Oliver cradled his hand, hissing at the pain.

"What did I tell you about punching people in the head, Oliver?" said his father in a disappointed tone. "Never use your fist. You'll probably put them out of the fight, but you'll likely break your hand as well."

"You bastard. That wasn't your head."

Will nodded. "True. You caught me off-guard, and I didn't have time to react properly. My instinctive response is a point-defense shield. In essence, you may as well have punched a brick wall. I'm sure you feel rather stupid, so I'll try not to rub it in. Next time, use a palm strike."

Oliver's eyes were red when he looked up. "It still wouldn't have worked, though."

"But at least you wouldn't have broken your hand. Maybe. As hard as you struck, maybe you would have." His father studied him for a moment. "Let me see your hand."

Wincing at every movement, Oliver reluctantly held it out. When Will began lightly pressing on it, he ground his teeth together, but refused to cry out. The involuntary whimpers that escaped sounded worse than crying, though. Remembering what had happened when he'd practiced with Tiny, he asked, "Do you have a healing potion?"

His father gave an evil laugh. "Do you know how much a regeneration potion costs?"

"No."

"A thousand gold crowns."

Oliver's eyes bulged. "What?"

"That's what they used to cost, anyway. By the time we came to Trendham, they were down to less than five-hundred. These days you can get one for around a hundred crowns. Do you have a hundred crowns?"

Oliver groaned.

His father laughed again, then produced a vial from thin air. "I happen to have one, however, I'm afraid you can't use it." The vial vanished. As Oliver started groaning again, Will explained, "I'm not entirely sure what would happen if you tried to use a regeneration potion in your current state. Normally it uses a lot of your physical reserves, as well as turyn, which would put you to sleep. Given how low in turyn you are, you would pass out immediately and you'd probably lose control of your source. The added turyn drain would keep you from waking up for an extended period, and I'm not sure if that would set you back in your training or not. So we won't risk it."

"Dad!"

"Don't 'dad' me. You broke your own hand, and you probably would have broken my jaw if you'd connected." He stared down at his son for several seconds, then made an offer. "Tell you what, if you promise to get up and jog for me, I'll fix your hand."

Frustrated, Oliver replied, "That's what I was trying to do before—!"

"Before you lost your temper and tried to lay me out, you mean," corrected his father. "Is that a yes, or a no?"

"Yes, sir."

"Good boy. Let me have your hand again."

"What about the potion?"

Will shook his head. "I told you already. If you take that, you won't be running, you'll be sleeping, and it might mess up your compression training. I'm going to fix this the old-fashioned way."

"Will it hurt?"

"That depends on how nice you are."

Oliver gave it a moment's thought, then slyly said, "If it hurts, I might not stay still. Don't you need me to be still?"

"Nice try," said his father. Abruptly, Oliver felt his body go rigid. "As you can see, I *could* work on it and keep you still no matter how bad the pain is." Sitting down on the bed, Will deftly guided the hand to his lap and lightly probed the long bones in the main part of the back of his hand. Oliver would have hissed, but his body refused to respond.

Will's features softened. "Luckily for you, I'm not a sadist. In fact, I'm extremely fond of you." Oliver felt his arm go numb from the elbow down. At the same time, his paralysis vanished. "This is a simple nerve block, so you won't feel anything until after I'm done."

"Thanks, Dad."

"You're welcome." Will remained focused for a few minutes while Oliver watched, unsure what was happening. "You broke two bones. I used a diagnostic spell to visualize the bones, but you probably couldn't see it, could you? No? It was this one and this one. Do you remember the names?"

Oliver's brow furrowed in concentration. "The metacorpuscles?"

"Metacarpals," corrected his dad. "I know you don't plan on working with the wounded, but a warrior should still learn the basics of anatomy. It's important both for assessing your wounds and for learning how to hurt your enemies." After a brief pause, he added, "I'm going to fuse the broken ends. That won't prevent the swelling and pain, but it will restore functionality. It's going to be sore for several days. Did you know that the wardsmen have a tattoo that greatly reduces their sensation of pain?"

That caught Oliver's interest. "They do?"

Will nodded. "They do. Now tell me why using such an ability is dangerous. What are the drawbacks?"

After thinking a bit, Oliver answered, "Because you might not know when you're wounded?"

"Flex your hand for me," ordered his father. "That's correct, but there's more. It can be dangerous after a battle too, when you're recovering. After I finish, I'm going to remove the nerve block. When I do, it's going to throb and ache like the devil. If I love you, why would I want you to feel that?"

Oliver hesitated. "To teach me a lesson?"

His father laughed again. "That's just an extra benefit, but there's a more important reason. Pain is a guide. Your body uses it to talk to you. That's how you know when you've trained too hard or pushed too far. With an injury, it lets you know when you're in danger of reinjuring yourself. When you start running, the pain will help you sense the movements that disturb your wound the most. It might keep you from moving as fast as you could otherwise, but you'll do less damage to yourself. Of course, your body isn't fully aware of the fact that the bones are no longer broken, but the lesson is the same."

Standing up, Will loomed over him. "Now. Can you focus enough to put your trousers on? Or do you need me to do it for you?"

Oliver sighed. "I can do it."

"Good, because if you regress too far, I'd be changing your diapers again. Let me tell you, that wasn't fun."

"Dad, please."

Will chuckled. "I'll wait outside."

Erisa was waiting for him when he stepped out of Oliver's bedroom. "I was the one who changed his diapers. You were off conquering Darrow, as I recall."

He frowned. "Don't spoil the joke."

***

As the week progressed, Oliver learned to function without having a lot of turyn. Once he got past the hurdle of feeling tired, he performed surprisingly well—physically, at least. As far as drawing in ambient turyn, Will couldn't detect much of a change. He wasn't worried, though. The first week was like that for many. Selene had also had a slow recovery from each one of her compressions.

By the end of the third week, Oliver seemed almost normal, physically. He could sleep through the night without losing control of his source. If someone didn't know what he was going through, they might think he was depressed, for his mood was flat and he had little motivation, but aside from that, Oliver was functional. He still wasn't absorbing turyn, however.

Will was just beginning to seriously worry when it finally started, near the end of the fourth week. Despite the long delay, once it began, Oliver's body rapidly adapted and within a week he was replenishing his turyn levels at a pace that gave him a normal level of energy to work with. Unsurprisingly, Oliver was exceedingly happy about it.

They were sparring one day when Oliver remarked, "You said it wouldn't make me stronger."

"I did," said Will.

"I think it has," returned Oliver.

"Believing in yourself has a lot of benefits. It might simply be increased confidence." Will put down his sparring sword and stepped to one side. "Run through your sword drills while I watch. Do it as quickly and efficiently as you can." Will increased his turyn sensitivity as high as possible and focused on his son.

Oliver moved through the forms with the same speed and agility he'd shown before compression training, but Will could see that the turyn flowing through his limbs seemed to be more tightly controlled. "Hmm." He returned his vision to normal before the inevitable headache could set in. "I think you might be right. It could be that learning to use your body while in a state of extreme turyn deprivation helped you learn to be more efficient in how you use the energy available to you. Can you go faster?"

Without a word, Oliver sped up. "I can, but at this point it starts to hurt a little."

His father whistled in appreciation. "Wow, that's enough. Remember what I said about pain."

"I think I can go faster than that," said Oliver.

"Your body is warning you," said Will. "I'm not sure how you're doing that, but you're going way past the normal limits. You'll definitely hurt yourself if you keep that up."

Oliver frowned. "What good is it if I can't use it?"

Will laughed. "You're already using it. Physically, you're at a level that no one can realistically hope to achieve—unless they're gifted the same way you are. But since you *can* push past the safe limits, you're going to have to regulate yourself. Normal people's bodies protect them by keeping them well below their physical limits." He rubbed his chin. "You said you're stronger. Show me."

Oliver nodded. "Watch this." Picking up a sturdy wooden sword, he advanced on the post that served them as a pell for practice. He went still for a moment, then exploded into motion. The pell rocked to one side despite its sturdy foundation, and the practice sword exploded, sending flinders in every direction. "Ow!" Oliver shook his right hand vigorously. "I felt that all the way to my shoulder."

Will stepped over and examined the arm with a bone diagnostic spell. "Nothing's broken, but you're liable to sprain it doing that. It wouldn't have hurt quite as much if you'd been using a real weapon. The wood transmitted the shock right back to your wrist."

"Want me to try it with a real sword?" Oliver seemed intrigued by the idea.

"Sure." Will summoned one of his falchions from the limnthal.

The falchion was a slicing weapon with a razor-sharp edge, but it wasn't really meant for hard targets. Its ideal use was against unarmored men. As sharp as it was, against any sort of armor, the edge would dull rapidly. Oliver knew the limitations as well. "A falchion? I'd rather have something heavier. Using this is like trying to chop wood with a shaving razor."

Will shrugged. "I could put a deep cut into it with a longsword or a greatsword, but without magic I don't think I could do more than score the wood with a falchion. I'm curious what you can do with it."

Oliver got set, focused, then swung.

It happened so quickly Will's eyes didn't fully register the movement. "Ow! Shit! That hurt." Oliver began shaking his wrist again. The pell hadn't moved. "I expected some resistance," complained Oliver. "I think I hurt myself when I had to stop the swing abruptly at the end."

Will frowned, but his eyes widened as the top half of the six-inch-wide post toppled over. "Holy shit."

His son grinned. "I bet you couldn't do that, could you?"

Will shook his head. Using the silver-sword spell, he might, or if he used his vibrational weapon trick, but he didn't want to spoil the moment for his son. *Besides, he's right. I definitely couldn't do that with a normal swing.* "I think you're going to have to learn what you can do and how to do it without hurting yourself. That's going to take practice."

"I'll get lots of that when I start training as a wardsman. They have to learn to fight like this."

Will grimaced. "You're not sixteen yet. Finish this year at school, then we'll see. For now, you can practice at home."

Oliver's expression turned sullen. "You said I could make the choice if I completed the first compression."

"I didn't mean you could run off and join a mercenary company at fifteen! Wait until you're sixteen at least, seventeen preferably…"

"I turn sixteen in two months," said Oliver. The age of majority was eighteen, but in most respects, it was purely a formality. In Trendham, children were allowed to start working at the age of twelve, but usually that was in the family business, and most people considered it unseemly to put their children to any sort of serious labor until at least fourteen. Sixteen was the age that most expected to be hired, apprenticed, or sent into some other specialized training.

If he refused to let Oliver join a mercenary company at sixteen, it would be considered unusual, except in the sense that few people wanted their children to take up such a dangerous occupation. On the other hand, becoming a wardsman would increase the social standing of most ordinary citizens, so few parents would oppose the choice. Legally, Will could forbid his son from joining, at least until he turned eighteen.

But doing so would create a wealth of bad feelings between them. "Let's talk about this after your sixteenth birthday. For now, you can practice at home."

CHAPTER 37

"Is that it?" asked James, his eye going to the simple gold band on Will's finger. It held a single stone, quartz, though it looked like a ruby due to its current deep red color.

Will nodded.

"That was fairly quick. It's only been two weeks since I gave you the design for the luxpress."

Will started laughing. "I finished this a week ago. I've done a lot more since."

"More rings? Who for?"

He shook his head. "No. This is the only one. Remember those books I asked Veronica for?"

"Which ones? Since you started coming around, I've begun to wonder if you're building an annex library wherever it is you live. I'm forever having copies made."

"The books on tattoo magic."

His brother-in-law's eyes lit up. "That was months ago. I'd forgotten about them. Are you working on something for my nephew?"

Will repressed a smile. James was forever referring to Oliver as his 'nephew.' It was true, obviously, but his brother-in-law seemed to take an inordinate amount of pride in the fact since he didn't have any others, and wouldn't unless Veronica decided to have a family. "Yes, for *your* nephew, never mind the fact that he's *my* son."

"Don't be jealous, Will. It isn't becoming. It's only natural that he prefers me, since I'm the cool uncle."

"Maybe I should have let you do his compression training. I doubt your status would have survived then," said Will.

"So what are you working on?"

"I did a review of the art first, and compared the books from Wurthaven with more recent samples that Sammy obtained. I was worried the material Veronica had given me was out of date, but from what I can see, the state of the art hasn't changed much over the past two centuries. There's a lot of room for improvement."

James grinned. "And your own flesh and blood is soon going to be relying on it."

Will grimaced. "I wish it wasn't the case, but I doubt I can keep him away from it much longer."

"So what have you learned?"

"That defensive magic was an afterthought when they designed the tattoos most of the wardsmen use. A lot of the tattoos are devoted to increasing reflexes, strength, and speed—all things Oliver already excels at."

James scratched his chin. "Is there a real estate problem, similar to the space issues with enchanting? If so—"

"Yes and no," answered Will. "The wardsmen don't have a problem because they still have quite a bit of unused skin, but Oliver might because I don't want him to stand out, but I *do* want him to have more functionality. He can't cast spells, so the only magic he'll ever have access to is whatever we build into his tattoos."

"So you're trying to hide new designs amid the traditional ones?"

Will nodded. "The luxpress is a godsend for some of that, but I can't rely on it for anything requiring a high power capacity. The runes are too small. Here, look at this." Will summoned his work journal and flipped it open to a page containing a detailed sketch. "See this? Those lines run along the arms and legs, up and down the torso and back, over the skull, et cetera. They serve as all-purpose channels, while these symbols that are placed along the lines denote locations, or destinations. It's like a shorthand for the body."

James pointed at the torso drawn on the page. "Then I'm guessing they're using the space available on the chest and back for the control functions?"

"Exactly," agreed Will. "Since the tattoos on the limbs are generalized, I can use them without any significant changes, but this mess they have on the chest is just a waste of space. Even with it gone, I wouldn't have enough room for what I think *should* be on there, but thankfully, your miniaturization methods will allow the low power functions to be made small. I still have another problem, however."

"Which is?"

"Ideally I'd like to add something new, but there aren't runes for it."

James frowned. "When you say 'there aren't runes' what do you mean exactly?"

"It's magic that's never been codified. I'm not sure it *can* be done. I've been thinking of sneaking into Wurthaven again and revealing myself to Professor Courtney."

"If it's not been codified, how do you know how to do it?"

"Because it's related to one of my talents."

"Oh. So you just need to create your own runes then."

Will sighed. "I took Advanced Spell Theory, but that wasn't covered. I've been reading as much as I can, but so far there's nothing on the—"

James interrupted, "It's covered in graduate level classes for artificers. It's pretty rare for people in new spell design to need new runes. They should have discussed the theory in the classes you took, though."

A scowl formed on Will's face. "Well I'll be damned if I remember that part, but I did have a lot of things happening at the time."

"It's pretty simple, really," began his brother-in-law. "You want to avoid using a symbol already used for anything else, but that's not even a hard and fast rule. Technically, you could change all the runes around, so long as you keep the new meanings straight in your head while using them."

"Huh?"

"The meanings are a formality," explained James. "We all agree on what each rune does so we can cooperate and understand everyone else's work. In theory, you could make up new meanings for all the runes. What matters is what *you* think each one does at the moment you first initialize the enchantment. I haven't studied tattoo magic, but I'm sure it's exactly the same in that regard."

"But Oliver won't know what they mean, either…"

"He wouldn't anyway," countered James. "As I said, the rune's function is set by the beliefs of the person who scribes and initializes it. After that, anyone who activates it will get that result, whatever their own ideas are about the rune."

"So I can just make up something completely new for what I want to do?"

James nodded. "Yes, but if it's something only you can do, then you'll have to be the one to ink the tattoo and initialize it. Even if you explain the meaning to someone else, if the magic user scribing it can't do it, then they won't be able to imbue the rune with that functionality. Does that make sense?"

"I knew some of this, but I didn't realize I could just make stuff up," said Will. His mind was already working on the new ideas.

"Just remember, the big problem is that no one else will be able to understand it properly if you deviate from accepted practices, and if it's something only you can do, then no one else will be able to replicate it."

Will shrugged. "Maybe I'm selfish, but at this point all I care about is making sure my boy doesn't die a senseless death."

"You know who you really need to talk to?"

He found the use of rhetorical questions slightly annoying, but Will respected his brother-in-law enough to be tolerant. "Who?"

"The royal marshal."

"Tiny? Why? He doesn't know the first thing about magic."

"He's in charge of the Iron Knights."

Will sighed. "And—?"

"The enchantments built into those suits of armor are made for men in battle. You might not want to use all of them, and some might not work in tattoo form, but I bet there's a lot of potential crossover. Of course, those enchantments are also top secret, but I bet the man in charge of Terabinia's military has access to the research material," said James.

***

The next day, Will snuck into the house that had once been owned by the Duke of Arenata. It helped that it had been his own home for a while, but now it belonged to the Black Duke, John Shaw. It was late afternoon when Will got there, and Tiny wasn't back yet, so he made himself comfortable in the main parlor. He was on his third cup of tea when he heard Tiny enter and begin speaking with some of the servants. He called out as the big man passed the arched entry that joined the parlor to the front hall. "Tiny!"

The man in charge of Terabinia's military stared at him for a moment, then his jaw fell open. "Will? How? No one said anything…"

Will held up a finger to his lips. "It's a secret visit. No one knows I'm here. Come in and shut the door. Now that I've stopped hiding my presence the servants will notice me if they walk by."

The parlor entry had large double doors, but they were usually kept open. Tiny had to move a few things to free them so he could close off the room. Then he turned back to his friend. "You have a lot of gall. Nary a word since I visited. You could have sent a note, or something."

"You know my reasons. That's all still true." Thinking about the communications tablet he'd given to Rob, he felt guilty, but there was no reason to bring that up. "Where's Janice?"

Tiny sat down in a large, cushioned chair. "She's at her other job this week. Who knows when I'll see my wife again."

"Other job?"

Unwilling to say it, Tiny held his hands up over his head, miming a crown. Will understood immediately. Janice was standing in for Selene, pretending to be queen. "You know no one can hear our words, right? I'm very good at preventing eavesdropping."

"You're paranoid about your home. I'm paranoid about my wife's secrets. The less said, the better."

Will nodded. "Point taken."

"I've missed you. Want some wine?" Tiny got up and went to the sideboard where a number of bottles were stored.

"I've got tea, thanks."

"Did you brew that in here?"

Will grinned. "I could, but it was more fun to use your kitchen. No one noticed me."

"I wish I could do that," said Tiny. "Try being my size. Not only am I famous, but everyone can't help but see me whenever I go somewhere." After pouring himself a glass, he sat down, then gave Will a serious look. "Since you never visit, I'm assuming you want something."

Will winced. "It's pretty obvious, isn't it?"

Tiny lifted his brows, then nodded.

"I need a favor, and I wouldn't ask except it isn't for me, it's for Oliver."

His large friend smiled. "You want to get him into the Iron Knights?"

"No. He wants to be a wardsman, and I can't keep him from it much longer."

He spent a few minutes explaining the situation at home, and afterward, Tiny gave him a look of sympathy. "I see your problem. Those tattoos aren't nearly as protective as a good suit of armor. What I don't see is how I can help you. Getting him into the right unit here in Terabinia is one thing, but I don't have any sway over the oligarchs in Trendham."

"You have access to the enchanting designs for the armor the Iron Knights wear, don't you?"

Tiny stared at him. "Surely you jest."

"I'm not going to share them with—"

"You're asking me to commit treason."

He held up his hands. "Not treason, petty espionage."

"There's nothing petty about it!" snapped Tiny.

"You know me. I only want to look through them and see if I can get ideas to keep Oliver safe. I'm not planning to share any of it with anyone else."

Tiny rolled his eyes. "It will be written on his skin. How can you hide that?"

Will gave him an abbreviated version of the discussion he'd had with James. "It will look identical on the outside, and some of it will be hidden inside him."

"Inside?"

Will nodded. "You're not the only person I'm borrowing secrets from. The doctor I hired for my hospital had a few ideas as well."

"You're going to use your son as an experimental test subject?"

He glared. "Some of it will be new, but I'm trying to make him safe. You have children. Surely you understand?"

"I do, but this…"

"I can pay."

"This isn't about money, Will."

"Not money, regeneration potions. I know Terabinia is the ultimate customer for a lot of what I make, even if you're using intermediate buyers. You gave that away last time you visited. I have six-hundred potions I can donate, free of charge. That's a lot of lives saved."

"You realize the prices have dropped considerably, don't you? They're not nearly as valuable as they once were."

Just a month ago, Sammy had sold a batch for him and had gotten a hundred crowns a piece, which was a fortune to most people. "They're not what they were when I was in school, but—"

"We get them for twenty-five crowns each now," said Tiny. "That's still expensive, but they're hardly a rare commodity anymore."

"Twenty-five?" Will's jaw dropped. "How? I'm the only one producing those po—"

"Not anymore. They're coming out of Barsta now, and other than the price, there's no shortage."

Will was flabbergasted, but he didn't give up. "You said it wasn't about money."

Tiny shook his head. "It isn't. I'm just giving you some much-needed context."

"How about Dragon's Heart potions? I bet this new supplier doesn't have a way to get vampire blood," said Will, allowing his rancor to spill over into his tone. "In fact, I bet the only ones left are the ones I gave you back before I left."

"We don't need them. That's part of the reason the Iron Knights were created."

"Bullshit. I'm sure there's plenty of situations where they could be a big benefit. There are lots of times and places where armor is too inconvenient. I'll give you—"

"Stop!" barked Tiny. "I'm not selling secrets to you. This is for Oliver."

Will paused, surprised. "So you'll let me see the designs?"

The big warrior nodded. "Come by tomorrow. You can see them, but you can't take them with you, so be prepared to take notes."

"I'll bring my donation as well. The regeneration potions I mentioned, plus a hundred of the Dragon's Heart potions. That's all I have currently."

Tiny held up his hands. "You don't need to do that. I'm being sincere. This is for him."

"And I'm sincerely making a donation," answered Will. "If that's not good enough, you could do me another favor in return."

Tiny sighed. "What now?"

"How hard would it be for you to take that giant golem of yours out for a jaunt?"

"Impossible. As soon as I leave the carriage house with it, people will take notice. It's hardly inconspicuous."

Will gave him a curious look. "You keep it here?"

"It's well protected, if you're worried about thieves. Besides, no one else can use it. It's built for me alone."

"What if it never leaves the carriage house? I can teleport it."

Tiny finished his glass, then poured a second. "That would work, but you still haven't explained yourself. I'm not using it to act as your personal enforcer or something silly like that."

"This is pure adventure." Will leaned forward. "How do you feel about spiders?"

CHAPTER 38

After teleporting, Will stepped back from the massive black golem, then waved at Sammy and Rob, who were waiting for them. For the first time in a while, Will had put on armor. He wore a new arming gambeson under a mail hauberk, and his demon-steel breastplate protected his torso. A small, enchanted metal shield was strapped to his left arm, and he was even wearing a steel cap and mail coif. The coif was the part he liked the least. To be functional, it couldn't just be draped over his head; he had to wear a tight-fitting, padded head piece that covered his entire head and neck. The mail coif went over that and was then laced tightly around his chin and neck to avoid any slack between the armor and his neck. The steel cap went on top of all that and buckled under his chin. The end result was that his head itched, he was beginning to sweat, and there wasn't much he could do about it. "Here we are," he announced.

The metal golem's voice was deep and resonant as Tiny replied, "Where is here?"

"We're in Darrow. The mountains you see are part of the central range. We're less than a hundred miles from Myrsta," explained Will. "But we still have a little farther to go, right, Sammy?"

She nodded. "Is this all we have? That thing scares the shit out of me."

"Don't trust me?" asked Rob. "I meant it when I said I'd keep you safe."

The golem shifted, leaning forward to get a better look at Rob. "You look familiar. Who are you?"

"My friend Rob, from school," explained Will. "You met him back when—"

Tiny drew an enormous demon-steel sword with a speed that was shocking considering his current bulk. "The same Rob who was taken and turned into a vampire?"

Will moved to stand in front of Rob. "Yes, and he's civilized, so put the sword away."

"How sure are you?" asked Tiny.

"You worked with the lich's vampires back when you faced the dragon, plus you're in no danger given the fact that your body is still back in Cerria," reasoned Will.

"I'm more worried about you and Sammy," said the golem. Tiny never took his attention from the vampire.

Will sighed. "He's trustworthy, just like Theravan and Mahak. I'm sure you met them. This isn't going to work if you spend all your time watching your allies. The thing we're here for is much more dangerous than a Drak'shar."

Rob dusted off the lapels of his jacket. His wardrobe had improved dramatically after Will's largesse. "I think you're underestimating me. I don't have much magic, but I'm very fast. Even if I can't match that metal monster, I'm sure I can handle anything made of living flesh."

Turning around, Will wanted to roll his eyes. Rob could barely maintain his sun-protection spell. "I've fought vampires and trolls both. And I know how they'd fare against this thing. It could tear you into pieces faster than you could regenerate." He'd seen trolls and vampires fight each other, but he was making some assumptions regarding the creature they hunted.

Rob whistled. "If it's that bad, why do you want me here again?"

"You're backup," said Will. "If it gets past Tiny, you may need to buy us a few seconds, or in the worst case, you might need to drag our bodies out before it can finish us off. You can't reasonably expect to fight it directly."

"Remind me again why you want to do this?" asked Rob nervously.

Will smiled. "Curiosity. I fought one once before and it almost killed me, but it had some fascinating magical abilities. Unfortunately, I didn't have a chance to bring back its corpse for study."

"So I just have to kill it?" asked Tiny.

"Absolutely not," said Will. "They're pretty rare, so I want it alive. It took Evie a week to find this one's lair."

"A demigod would probably be a good choice for this," suggested Rob.

"If I wanted her to rip it to pieces, sure, but I want to capture it." He rapped the knee of Tiny's golem with his knuckles. "It can't hurt the golem, so Tiny is ideal for restraining it. Anything made of flesh that tried to hold onto this creature without killing it would wind up torn to ribbons."

"Let's go over the plan," said Tiny.

"I'll go into the cave, and hopefully it will try to eat me," said Will. "When I yell, you run in with the golem and *don't* squash it. Try to get a firm grip on it, and I'll cut the legs off until it's reasonably helpless. Once that's done, I'll render it unconscious and take it to my secret lair where I can perform unthinkable experiments on it."

"You're not as funny as you think you are," remarked Tiny.

Sammy was frowning. "So, you don't want me to do anything?"

"You're here for area denial," said Will. "If it gets loose and comes at you, throw a force-wall in front of it. Or if you see me in trouble, the same. Don't get close. If things go really bad, for example, if I die, then you can try to roast it, but it won't be easy."

She arched one brow. "You remember who you're talking to, don't you?"

"It can move back and forth between our world and the ethereal plane, so to really burn it, you'd have to either stop it from shifting or be able to cast spells on both planes at the same time. That's even more important to remember if it comes after you. An elemental barrier won't stop it. It will shift and go right through anything in its way, so force spells are the only thing that can restrain it, and those won't work for long."

"Why not?" she asked.

Will held up one hand and created a blob of grey turyn. "This. It eats through force spells. It behaves a bit like acid, but it doesn't damage flesh, just force effects. The phase spider I fought covered its entire body in it. In some ways, it behaves like a liquid force effect. It protects the creature from blows while remaining flexible, something no normal force spell can do. At the same time, it can melt its way through force-walls, which are the only type of spell that can restrain something that moves between the ethereal and normal dimensions so freely."

Sammy was beginning to look uncomfortable. "You said you fought one before? How did you defend yourself?"

"Reflex casting. I had to use point-defense shields in a rapid-fire manner—and it *still* almost tore my guts out," answered Will.

"Is that how you learned to create that force-eating turyn?" asked Rob.

Will shook his head. "Actually, I first saw it used by the vampire Alexander. He had a spell he used, but I never got a chance to learn it, so I've just been copying the turyn I saw. That's a big part of why I want to catch this thing. So I can study what it does and how it does it. There's a host of different offensive and defensive spells I could potentially design if I understood it better."

Tiny made a suggestion. "It would be better for me to go in if it's as dangerous as you say."

"It's an ambush predator," said Will. "As tough as it is, I don't think there's a chance in hell it would think you're a meal. That's why I'll be the bait."

"What if it tries to escape into the ethereal after I grab it?" asked Tiny.

Will replied with a quick demonstration, vanishing momentarily. "I can shift too. I'll bring you with me, and you can grab it again over there." He looked at Sammy. "If that happens, fill the cave with flames and don't let them die down until it's all over."

She frowned. "But if you cross back, you'll be burned."

He nodded. "I can *see* both sides, and I'm pretty sure the spider can too, otherwise it wouldn't know when to phase over and attack its prey. Assuming I'm right, it won't shift back because it will see the fire, limiting its movement to just the ethereal plane."

"Sounds like a solid plan," agreed Tiny.

"So, I just stand around and look pretty?" asked Rob.

"Very funny," said Will. "I'll repeat. If everything goes tits up, you either try to slow it down, or grab Sammy and run."

"Just me?" asked his cousin.

Will shrugged. "Well, I'd like to be saved too, but I'm pretty sure that if I fuck up, I'll be dead before anyone can react. You should be far enough back to have options."

"These aren't the actions a responsible father should take," said Tiny. "This is too dangerous."

"Damn it, Tiny!" snapped Will. "This is our first outing in over a decade, and you're already moralizing at me." He stared at the golem for a few seconds, then added, "This is *for* Oliver, if you must know."

Tiny responded with logic. "And you think it's worth risking your life? Is the benefit great enough to offset the loss if you get yourself killed?"

"Yes, it's worth it," growled Will. "I have enough trouble sleeping through the night. If I think Olly's running around with nothing more than those shitty tattoos to protect him, I'll be a nervous wreck."

Sammy piped up, "If it's for Oliver, I'm for it." She patted Will's shoulder. "Besides, he beat one after being ambushed. This time we're ready. We can do this."

The golem's head faced her. "Begging your pardon, Sammy, but you aren't well known for your level-headedness."

"So you're backing out?" asked Will. "You know I'll just come up with a different plan, don't you? I'd prefer to have you—"

"I didn't say that," said Tiny with obvious frustration. "I was just hoping to talk some sense into you."

Will pointed. "See that boulder over there? I'm going to move it out of the way so you'll have a clear view. The cave behind it isn't very deep. I'll go in and make a light. When you see an eight-legged nightmare jump on me, come running."

"It's going to take ten seconds or longer for me to get there," said Tiny.

Will nodded. "I can last longer than that. I still know how to kill it. I just don't want to." He started walking. "Here goes."

Behind him, he heard the others continue talking. "Why am I so nervous?" asked Rob.

The other two didn't respond to that. Instead, Sammy addressed the golem. "I liked you better when you were flesh and blood. You were less rude then."

"I'm still flesh and blood," returned Tiny.

"Have you looked in a mirror lately?" said Sammy.

"My body is back in Cerria," said Tiny with an audible sigh. "As you well know."

"Prove it," she told him.

The golem's body creaked as he turned to look at her. "How?"

Sammy was waiting for that line, and she answered instantly, "Do something human. Oh! I have an idea! Try doing something nice for a change, like apologizing for calling me crazy."

"I never called you crazy," protested the golem. "I said you weren't known for being levelheaded."

"Same thing!" she said quickly. "And how would you know? It's been ages! I'm a respectable businesswoman now, did you realize that? You may be a fancy duke now, but I bet if we got our gold out and started measuring dicks, you'd come up short compared to what I keep in my treasure room."

"Levelheaded people use banks, or don't they have those in Trendham?" said Tiny evenly.

Rob jumped in. "So, you live in Trendham now, Sammy? Whereabouts?"

"Great, you've given away a secret," snapped Sammy. "Who's the idiot now, metal man?"

"The one who won't stop talking and keeps distracting me," said Tiny grumpily. "Are you trying to get Will eaten?"

"He hasn't even moved the boulder yet," she responded. "Oh, wait. He has. When did that happen?"

"While you were running your mouth," said Rob dryly.

Will heard it all, but didn't let it distract him. He'd just finished using a force-push spell to clear the area in front of the cave. With that done, he used an iron-body transformation and used another simple spell to place a glowing orb toward the back of the cave before he entered. *Now all that's left is to walk in,* he thought. *Have I forgotten anything?*

Something was nagging at him in the back of his head, but he couldn't remember what it was. Despite his confidence when speaking to the others, standing in front of the spider's lair made him hesitate. *You've got this,* he told himself, and began walking forward with purpose.

As he entered, the cave seemed dark compared to the bright sun outside. It wasn't much of a cave, being a rocky niche some twenty feet in width. The opening was almost as wide as the interior. *Why don't I see it?* Will expected that the spider would be waiting inside, a ghostly figure waiting to cross over into the material world, but there was nothing in view.

Then he realized. He hadn't adjusted his vision to see the strange light that passed between the two planes. Panic gripped him for a moment, and he took a step back, rapidly cycling his sight through various wavelengths, searching for the right one.

The phase spider emerged directly behind him, moving in absolute silence. There was no gap to close as it plunged its fangs straight toward his neck. The only thing that saved him was the bright sunlight. The spider's appearance had created a shadow, and the shifting light alerted Will at the last second. He raised a force-dome around himself as he turned to face the arachnid.

He'd been sure his memory of the creature would prepare him, but the sight of its eight eyes, black and beady in the light from outside, still sent a shiver of terror down his spine. The fangs, mandibles, and smooth grey skin covered in coarse hair didn't help either. Encountering the force-barrier, the monster began secreting that same strange grey turyn—half a second later, its fangs and head began pushing through the hole that was forming in Will's force-dome.

Time to get to work. Will summoned his weapon, a one-handed bulova axe. It wasn't a common weapon in the northern countries like Terabinia or Trendham and was used mainly by the fighters in Faresh. The handle was lightweight, cylindrical, and less than three feet in length with most of the weight provided by a long steel chopping head that was three-quarters of a foot long. The edge was almost straight, curving faintly inward at the middle and then back at the ends, giving it a shape reminiscent of a mustache.

He'd picked an axe because his primary job today would be chopping, and while Will thought the design of the bulova axe was suboptimal against armored men, he'd chosen it for the fact that its shape made it perfect for chopping limbs, and the curve made it less likely to slide away when encountering something hard, like an exoskeleton. Overall, it was lightweight and relatively nimble for one-handed use, but with the weight balanced at the head, it would cut much more easily than a sword.

Of course, these days with his talent, he could probably succeed using any sort of edged weapon, but Will liked to be prepared, and that meant using the best tool for the job. There were too many other ways things could go wrong for him to give up any possible advantage.

Dropping the already-failing force-dome, Will slammed his metal shield into the spider's head. It was already moving forward, and despite his aggressive shield bash, he was forced backward by the monster's momentum. Razor-sharp leg tips swung inward from both the left and right simultaneously, forcing him to block one with a point-defense shield and the other with the steel shield. Seeing a flash of turyn from the shield told him that it had been scored deeply enough to damage the runes that reinforced the metal, and he lamented the fact that it wasn't made of demon-steel. With the enchantment gone, it wouldn't survive too many blows from those legs.

More attacks came, and the phase spider alternated between slashing sweeps and stabbing thrusts, using all four of its forward legs. Quick as it was, Will had fought faster opponents. Even Oliver was faster, but the spider's speed combined with the fact that it had four weapons *and* fangs meant that Will was kept on the defensive. He had offensive and even defensive spells that he didn't dare use for fear of damaging his prize, so his options were limited.

His back touched stone, and Will's backward retreat came to an abrupt end. He was already in mid-block with two other legs, and the one he had meant to dodge struck his breastplate and skipped off, sliding down to rip partway through the mail that hung over his thighs.

It was a moment exactly like that which had nearly gotten him killed the first time he had fought a phase spider, but today Will had a much wider range of options. He vanished, teleporting to appear immediately behind his opponent. Confused, the arachnid froze for an instant before realizing where he'd gone, giving him the opportunity for his first attack. The axe buzzed, vibrating in response to his talent as Will swept it down on one of the hind legs—

—and bounced off, defeated by the grey turyn armor that covered the beast.

Shit, I forgot to remove the defensive turyn first. In his first battle against a phase spider, he'd discovered that wind spells could temporarily blow the grey turyn away, or at least expose areas of the spider's body. The timing was tricky, however, as the spider would quickly replenish its defensive turyn the moment the wind was gone. The magical substance acted exactly like a force-barrier, with the main difference being its liquid flexibility and its vulnerability to wind.

The spider spun and attacked with a flurry of razor-sharp legs, and Will began retreating once more, step by step. As the seconds dragged on, he became more confident in his defense. He could keep up the battle for some time this way. His main limitation would be the turyn cost of teleporting when he was inevitably backed up against a wall again. Though he could reflex cast the spell, it took a lot of his energy. After five or six times, it would no longer be practical.

Where the fuck is Tiny? he thought. *I don't want to have to kill it!* He knew time felt different in combat, but surely, he'd been fighting for more than ten or fifteen seconds. It seemed like it had been an hour already.

The spider vanished, shifting into the ethereal as a new, larger shadow blocked out the sun. The golem had arrived. "Took you long enough," Will barked, breathing heavily. He was already taking the opportunity to finish adjusting his vision properly, and a ghostly version of the spider came into view. It was backing into the farthest corner of its cave—on the ethereal plane. Temporarily dismissing his axe, Will reached out and put a hand on Tiny's metal bulk, then used an ethereal transit spell to move them to the parallel plane.

The spider hissed when they appeared.

"I thought you'd be happy to see us, you big, hairy bastard," growled Will, relishing the moment. It was a complete reversal of his first terrifying encounter with a giant arachnid, and it felt good seeing the monster's fear. Ghostly flames appeared within his altered vision, filling the cave and some of the area outside. Sammy was already doing her part back in the regular world. "You've nowhere to hide now, Leggy."

"Leggy?" questioned Tiny.

Will resummoned his axe and pointed it at the spider. "The name should be obvious."

"It is, it's just dumb," said Tiny, his voice deep and metallic.

Will glanced at his old friend, narrowing his eyes. "Nicknames are usually sort of dumb. Take yours, 'Tiny.' I've always felt bad calling you that."

"It seems clever to me," said the golem.

Will shrugged. "I'm not one to remind a friend of his shortcomings by insulting him. Just because you have a little dick doesn't mean people should mock you."

"Joke's on you, Will. Janice gave my little soldier his own nickname, 'Ponderous Pete.'"

He chuckled. "Did you think the logic through there? She might be trying to tell you something. If you're 'Tiny' because you're big, then—I'm sure you see where I'm going." A long laugh came from the golem, and Will grinned. It had been a long time since they'd spent time together, and he'd almost forgotten one of his favorite things about his big friend—Tiny was never too big to laugh at a joke, even when it was aimed at him.

The phase spider didn't seem to catch the humor, however. It had been chittering at them and nervously edging back and forth, looking for an opening to escape. There wasn't one, or so Will had thought, until it suddenly bounded upward, flipping in the air to catch hold of the cave ceiling. As big as the creature was, he couldn't see how it kept from falling down, but the monster skittered agilely forward and leapt again, landing at the cave entrance—behind them.

It wasn't quite far enough, though. Tiny already had his greatsword out, and he spun and stepped toward the beast, bringing the blade into a wide and deadly arc. Will had been about to use a force spell to block the spider's exit, but the massive demon-steel sword made him fear the spider's defensive magic might not be enough, so instead he threw up a point-defense shield to prevent the sword from connecting. "Don't kill it!" he shouted.

That was all the time the arachnid needed. It continued its run, and a second later, it was beyond the area filled with ghostly flames. Will used another force-spell, even though the distance now made it an expensive choice. The phase spider shifted to the material plane and then dodged around the small force-shield. It was less than thirty feet from where Sammy and Rob stood.

Tiny hadn't expected the shift and was already running after it, forcing Will to chase him in order to bring them both back to the material plane—costing them precious seconds. Meanwhile, the spider was bearing down on Will's cousin—well, and Rob too, but Will wasn't worried about the vampire. He cared about his old schoolmate, but vampires were like jigsaw puzzles; you could always stick them back together.

Sammy put a force-dome around herself and Rob, but as usual, it was only good for a few scant seconds. She dropped it when the spider was halfway through and cast another. And another.

Tiny had stopped, realizing the futility of his charge, and Will caught up to him, bringing them back. They were standing some twenty feet from Sammy and Rob, and as her latest force-dome came down, she panicked, and Will knew very well what would happen next. He saw it in her eyes a split second before it happened, and he tried to warn her with a shout. "Don't burn—!" Knowing it was too late, he created a sonic shield around himself and the golem.

Short of dragonfire, Sammy's flames were the hottest thing in the world. In fact, they were what he had used as a stand in for dragonfire when he had been training to face Lognion. Yet even as good as his shield was at diverting the roaring torrent of flame, he still needed to add a cooling spell to keep the radiant heat from flash-cooking him inside his defensive shell. Without the wisdom of past experience, he would certainly have died.

Tiny's golem body would have been fine, but Will's instincts weren't always completely logical. As Will's vision cleared, he searched for the spider's burnt husk, and failed to find it. The bright light from the flames had left an afterglow in his eyes that prevented him from spotting the ghostly shape quickly enough. The spider had retreated into the ethereal, and now it shifted back, its fangs just inches from Sammy's nose. It had phased while already in motion and was biting at her right shoulder.

Again, Will's combat reflexes were fast, but not always smart. He used a force-lance, hoping to spoil the attack. It struck the spider's abdomen and did essentially nothing. He was hoping Sammy would put up a shield of her own, but in that ill-omened instant, she froze.

Only Rob made the right move, rocketing into Sammy and shouldering her aside with such speed that Will heard bones snapping from the force of the impact. The venom-rich fangs sank into Rob's chest and then its mandibles closed in from the sides, crunching through ribs as it reared back to shake the vampire like a dog with a new toy.

Tiny reached them a moment later. He'd dropped the sword and now loomed over spider and vampire. If Will narrowed his eyes to slits and used a lot of imagination to pretend that Tiny's golem body was the size of a man, then the spider would be roughly the size of a large dog in comparison—a large dog with eight legs. In that situation, Rob would be the size of a four-year-old child.

Tiny's golem body took hold of two of the spider's front legs as he tried to pull the spider back and away, but Rob was still locked in its jaws. Rather than try and shift his grip and risk losing the creature, Tiny twisted his demon-steel hands and ripped the two legs completely off the arachnid's body.

With a chittering scream, the phase spider shifted back into the ethereal, taking Rob with it. Will followed—alone. He couldn't afford to take Tiny with him and leave Sammy unguarded.

Although it only had six legs now, the phase spider could still run, but its speed was hampered by the vampire it was holding. No, not holding—Will could see now that it had been trying to drop Rob, but his friend had clamped his strong hands on either side of the mandibles, holding them closed on his ruined chest. He was denying the spider the use of its fangs and slowing it down by forcing it to carry his weight.

Will would have smiled if the sight hadn't been so gruesome. He used the grave-digging spell to create a hole beneath one of the spider's legs and a point-defense shield to briefly block another, causing the spider to stumble. That gave him the time he needed to catch up.

"Not to worry! I've got this," Rob gurgled cheerfully as he spotted Will. "Just this bit, though, not the rest. I saved all that for you." His words came out in wheezing gasps punctuated by high-pitched noises as the spider's mandibles occasionally bit down, crushing his ribs inward.

The monster turned, facing Will and threatening him with two of its remaining legs, but he was undeterred. With two legs down, the fight was much simpler. Stepping in, he unleashed a wind-wall spell at half power. It blew the liquid grey turyn away from one side of the spider's body while simultaneously tearing away some of Rob's considerably more delicate skin. He blocked one leg with his metal shield, another with a point-defense spell, then brought his buzzing axe down hard against one of the legs the spider was walking on. It passed through the exoskeleton as though it were made of butter rather than hard chitin.

The grey turyn flowed back, and he repeated the pattern. Soon another leg was gone, amputated midway along its length. Rob was unrecognizable. Will was getting low on turyn, as the wind-walls took quite a bit, even at half power, but he pressed on. "You've got this," cheered Rob. His scalp was hanging in front of what remained of his face, obscuring an even worse sight.

The spider shifted back, and Will followed it. Another wind-wall and another leg was taken. The spider shifted back to the ethereal before Tiny and Sammy could fully react. Will followed again. It collapsed when he took the next leg, having only two left.

As tired as he was, the spider must have been tired too, for the defensive turyn didn't reappear, allowing him to cut off the remaining two legs without needing to expose Rob's battered corpse to any more tearing winds.

His eyes were gone, but as the spider shuddered to the ground, Rob could sense a change in the battle. "Did we win, Master?"

Panting, Will shot back, "Don't call me that."

"Sorry. Habit. The lich would grind my bones if I didn't address him that way." His voice was already sounding steadier as his lungs healed, even though he was still firmly in the grip of the spider's mandibles.

"Doesn't that hurt?" asked Will.

"The bone-break spell hurts worse than anything you can imagine," said Rob.

"I can imagine a lot," said Will, "but at this moment I'm referring to the spider chewing on your mangled body."

"Oh, that. Not as much as you might think. Grim Talek's training—if you can call it that—made things like this much easier to bear. Speaking of which, my strength is fading. Is it safe to let go yet?"

"One second." Straightening up, Will circled the spider, trimming what remained of its legs back so that none were longer than a few inches. As he went, he used two broadly purposed medical spells. One was made to stop blood loss, and the other would encourage the rapid growth of scar tissue.

"What are you doing?" asked Rob. One of his eyes had returned, increasing his curiosity.

"I'm using medical spells to minimize blood loss, or in this case, to minimize hemolymph loss," he replied.

The vampire sniffed. "I don't see anything but that sticky blue crap oozing out of it, and that's not blood. Trust me, I'd know. I'm so hungry I could eat you right now—but I wouldn't, of course. No need to worry."

"The blue stuff is spider blood," explained Will. "Hemolymph is the technical term. Unlike ours, it's based on copper instead of iron, hence the blue color."

"Then it should be green," argued the vampire.

"Did you even pass alchemy?" retorted Will. "Copper can be red, black, green, or blue depending on the oxidation state." He frowned. The blood-staunching spell seemed to work, but the spell for growing scar tissue was a bust. *Time for plan B.* He took out a flat knife and used a metalsmithing spell to heat it up until it glowed. "Sorry, spider. If I'd known I was going to have to do this, I would have skipped the other spell, but I was trying to be humane."

"You can't be humane to a spider," said Rob. "You'd have to be—arachnidane? Is that a word? Ow!" The phase spider bit down on him when Will began cauterizing the stumps. "What are you doing?"

"Leggy has lost a lot of hemolymph and I'm worried he might die, so I need to give him a regeneration potion. So I'm caut—"

"Are you insane? You're going to heal this thing? Leggy is a stupid name, by the way. Trust me, this thing is all teeth."

Will sighed and kept at it. "Cauterizing the stumps should keep the legs from regenerating. Also, spiders don't have teeth."

"His name is Toofus. Toofus the Doofus," pronounced Rob. "There, it only took me a half a second to come up with a better name than 'Leggy.'

You're welcome. Ow!" Rob's arms gave out, and the spider's mandibles released him partway before biting down again. This time, they went far enough to sever the vampire's spine. Rob screamed briefly but quieted down almost immediately after. "See, I think he likes the name."

"Sorry," said Will, hurrying. "I'd like to drain the turyn from him, but then the regeneration potion might not work." He wanted to smack himself then as another realization hit him. Rob's latest pain had been completely unnecessary. Without its defensive grey turyn, Will could probably attach a source-link spell and paralyze the creature. Will tried and nearly failed. The spider's source felt foreign and slippery, but after a few seconds, Will made the link. *So maybe I was smart not to try that during the fight.*

With the source-link in place, he first paralyzed the beast, then relaxed its jaws so Rob could pull himself away. After he'd done that, he summoned a hypodermic syringe filled with a regeneration potion, an idea he'd gotten from Dr. Lorentz. To his chagrin, the spider's legs immediately began growing back. His impromptu cautery had been insufficient to stop them from regenerating.

Rob now sat some fifteen feet away, pale and gaunt. Most of his wounds had closed, though his face was still recovering. His skin slid back and forth like a snake, trying to find the right position to settle. To Will's eyes, the vampire looked dangerously emaciated, and he should know. He'd kept one locked up for several years, draining its blood for use in Dragon's Heart potions. His friend was well past the point that Will would have expected most vampires to devolve into animalistic hunger, yet he was still making bad jokes. *He really meant it when he said he'd gained control of it,* Will realized.

"You're gonna have to lop them off again," remarked Rob.

"I can't keep doing that. Leggy is low on stamina already. The shock might kill him." Will readied himself to cast a shield, then summoned a clay jar filled with pig's blood. The shield had been in case Rob lunged at him, but his friend simply went motionless. He threw the jar, and Rob's hands shot out to catch it with frightening speed.

"Thanks," said Rob, his lips curling in disgust as he sniffed the cold animal blood. He turned it up immediately, loudly slurping as he spilled the sanguine liquid in his haste. Will looked away.

He focused on drawing turyn while he waited on Rob to finish and regain his composure. Leggy seemed to have fallen unconscious while the regeneration potion did its work, but Will maintained the link to keep him paralyzed. While all that was happening, he considered the next steps. When his power had recovered sufficiently, he moved over and put a hand on Rob's shoulder.

"Aww. I love you too, buddy," said Rob immediately.

Will rolled his eyes. "I'm going to send you back to Sammy and Tiny. Let them know it worked and that I'm safe. I'll be back shortly. Since Leggy regrew his legs, I don't want to wait any longer before locking him up." He started to cast the spell, then paused and stepped back. "Actually, let me clean you up first." Selene's Solution restored Rob to a state of pristine hygiene, though it could do nothing for the great tears and rents in his clothing.

Rob looked at him with big doe eyes. "You're so thoughtful."

Will summoned a blood-cleanse potion and drank it. "I'm being careful. A lot of your insides were scattered around. Here." He withdrew two more blood-cleanse potions from his limnthal and handed one to his friend. "Give this to Sammy, just to be safe. She was just a few feet away when you got eviscerated."

The vampire's expression turned sour. "Who's the other one for?"

He patted the spider. "It's for Leggy. I don't know if arachnids can catch vampirism, but he gnawed on you for quite a while. Better safe than sorry."

"I think you love Toofus more than me," said Rob, then shuddered. "I don't even want to think about what a vampire spider would be like."

Will touched him and used a spell to send the vampire back to the material plane. Then he turned back to the arachnid. Originally, he'd planned to pack the legless monster into his limnthal. His captive vampire had survived there for some time, but with the return of the phase spider's legs, he didn't feel good about the idea. He had no way to restrain the creature, and if it somehow recovered before he summoned it back...

Instead, he would maintain the source-link to keep it paralyzed while he took it directly to its new home. Putting his hand on the monster's cephalothorax, he teleported them away.

CHAPTER 39

It was midday, and Will's mother nearly went into shock when she saw what he had brought with him. "Sorry, Mom! Didn't mean to scare you."

The beacon in his secret lair wasn't strong enough for him to teleport to it from more than a few miles, so he'd had to orient on Erisa for his first teleport. He gave his mother a hopefully reassuring smile, then teleported a second time, arriving in his sanctum sanctorum. He used a force-travel-disk spell rather than an elemental one to avoid damaging the floor and loaded Leggy onto it. Then he took his prize down the hall and into the relatively new prison he had built.

It was a ten-foot by ten-foot cube, carved into the bedrock. While most of his secret lair had paneling or faux masonry to conceal the fact that it was underground, this empty cube still showed the rough-hewn surfaces of the rock it had been cut from. It had solid stone on all sides but the entrance, and within it had a crosshatched network of black bars that covered the sides.

The metalwork was rough and crude, but he'd been in a hurry and working alone. Will had had to simultaneously keep the turyn drained from the metal while using other spells to heat and weld it. If the original bar stock hadn't already been formed in the shape of thick square bars, he would never have finished it in time.

The cell door was crude too. It was simply a square-framed section of bars that had chains wrapped around it at two of the corners to serve as rough hinges. On the other side, two more chains served to keep it firmly in place—or as hinges, if he chose to undo the chains on the other side. All of it had come from the salvage Evie had taken him to in her home plane, and Will counted himself fortunate that demons seemed to like chains. He never would have been able to make them on his own.

Demon-steel was incredibly difficult to work with.

Once he had one side of the door undone, he brought the travel disk carrying Leggy inside and deposited the spider there. He checked it over once more, searching for wounds, and found none. The regeneration potion had done a thorough job. Through the source-link, he could tell it was recovering, though it would likely remain unconscious for some time.

Stepping back out, he laboriously hauled the door into place and replaced the chains, looping them several times before locking them with complementary demon-steel locks. The demon-lords had really enjoyed locking things up.

Will admired his handiwork. The fact that his lair had been underground was fortuitous. The ethereal plane mirrored the material plane in all ways except those that had changed recently. His spider would be unable to planeshift since the entire area they were in was underground. In the ethereal all of it was solid bedrock. Unless it could chew through demon-steel bars, it wasn't getting loose.

It was time to get back to the others. Will slipped his awareness slightly out of alignment with his body, but before he could shift his focus to Sammy, he heard a voice in his mind. *Why?*

Startled, he looked at the spider. *Was that you?*

In the astral plane, minds could communicate directly and language was irrelevant. Now that he was paying attention, he felt the source of the next reply. It came directly from the phase spider. *Why have you done this?*

Will blinked. *You're sentient—and astrally sensitive?* It had never occurred to him that the spider might be intelligent.

Yes. Why do this? Your cruelty is monstrous.

Taken aback, Will struggled to formulate a response. *You tried to eat me.*

I did not dismember you and set fire to your stumps. The regrowth of my limbs was scant relief when I realized you likely intend to cut and burn them again. Such torture is unimaginable.

Will frowned, then repeated, *You tried to eat me.*

So? You are food. Do you not eat as well?

Will turned in place, scratching his head. "I can't believe I'm in moral discussion with a spider—and losing." In truth, he'd already felt a little bad about the lengths they'd gone to in order to capture it, and now that he knew it was a thinking being, he felt worse.

I have to go, but I'll be back later with food if you like. What would you like to eat?

You, answered the spider, predictably.

He rolled his eyes and teleported back to Sammy and the others. "Guess what!" he said loudly.

None of them were interested in guessing. "Why did you go after the spider by yourself?" demanded Tiny.

"Because I couldn't leave Sammy alone. You saw what happened."

"One mistake and it might've taken your head off," growled Tiny. "If you thought it was too dangerous to leave your cousin alone, you shouldn't have gone after it. You're a father, remember?"

Rob raised his hand. "I appreciate you coming after me."

"You were never in any danger," said the golem.

The vampire's face took on a wounded expression. "I feel pain. Being chewed like that hurts, though not quite as much as your words."

Will walked around the golem so he could see Sammy better. She was lying next to a tree with a cloak rolled up to pillow her head, though she was still conscious. Her eyes were half-lidded. "Are you all right, Sammy?"

"She took a regeneration potion already," said Tiny. "The vampire broke her collarbone and ribs when he knocked her out of the way."

"There was no time to be gentle," protested the vampire in question.

"I wasn't blaming you," rasped the golem's voice. "Your choice was the right one. Unlike his."

Will was already kneeling beside her, but he turned and glared at Tiny. "Why don't you take that demon-steel greatsword and shove it up your metal ass? Maybe you'll knock the stick loose that's been up there for the past thirteen years." Without waiting for a response, he turned back to his cousin.

"I'm fine," she told him. "Been through worse."

"Why did you stop casting force spells? All you had to do was keep refreshing them until we got to you. Did you panic?"

Sammy's eyes slid to one side, toward the ground. "I only had three prepared."

He sat back on his heels, surprised. "You can't reflex cast any force spells? What about the point-defense shield? I told you to keep practicing it."

"I do. It just hasn't gotten there yet," she replied, visibly embarrassed.

"It's been over a decade. How much are you practicing?" he demanded.

Anger crept into her response. "We've been at peace all that time, and I've been busy. Most of us don't spend every waking second worrying that someone's going to break down the door and murder everyone in sight. I'm not like you."

"What does that mean?" asked Will.

"All you think about is the past, about killing or being killed. That's why you can barely sleep at night. *I'm* thinking about the future, and it's *good*, Will. I've built a business empire to rival the oligarchs themselves. That takes a lot of thought and effort."

Wounded, he struck back. "Using the money from my potions."

"They aren't worth that much anymore, Will! They stopped being relevant to my income years and years ago. You live in the past so much you don't even know how far prices have dropped. I've been paying you the old rates out of my own pocket, to help you pay for your hospital and the school." Angry tears were welling up in her eyes.

"Ouch," whispered Rob.

Will was stunned. "I never asked for charity, or pity. You should have told me. There's plenty of other ways for me to make money. I just didn't know."

"Because all you think about is death. Yours, mine, Oliver's—you live in a constant state of fear," said Sammy.

"And look what happened today! You nearly died, for lack of a single spell. If I hadn't—" he paused, then amended his words. "If Rob hadn't shoved you aside, you'd be dead."

"Just to put in a word," said Rob, looking at Sammy, "my presence was a product of your morbidly obsessed cousin's paranoia, so his mental illness *does* have some occasional upsides."

"It was his mental illness that put Sammy in harm's way to begin with, not to mention risking his own life," said Tiny dourly.

Rob stared up at the golem and held a finger to his lips. "I don't think you're helping," he hissed.

"None of this is helping," said Will. "Let me get everyone home. I have work to do, and I don't have time for arguing." He looked down at his cousin. "I'll pay you back the difference for the potions. How much did you really get?" Then he remembered his discussion with Tiny a few weeks back. "Twenty-five? No, that's probably the end price, so twenty maybe?" He started doing the math in his head. If she'd paid him five times what she sold them for then he owed her…

"I don't want your money, Will," said Sammy. "I was glad to support what you're doing."

"By giving me…" he double checked his math mentally, then finished, "eight-thousand gold more than you received? Are you nuts?"

Rob stumbled, almost falling despite his vampire reflexes, and the demon-steel golem's head swiveled to stare intently at the arguing cousins. Will had once been privy to the accounts that now belonged to Duke Shaw and in those days, the yearly budget for the Arenata estates had been around thirty-thousand gold. Eight thousand in the hands of a solitary person was an unthinkable sum.

Sammy was angry enough to shake off her sleepiness and sit up. "It was a pittance to me! Especially for what it gave you, and even more for what you've done for the people in Trendham."

Will stared back at her. "A pittance?"

She nodded. "And eight thousand is just for the last batch. Think about what I've sold for you over the last four years. The prices were dropping steadily the entire time."

His brain seized up temporarily. "Why?"

Sammy's complexion had turned a splotchy pink and her eyes were red and swollen. "We're family. My money is yours, but you would never just accept it. You're too proud, Will! Everything I have, I owe in part to you. You saved me when the Darrowans killed our family. Your mother kept and raised me. You brought me to the capital and taught me magic, and when we left, it was your potions that paid for everything. Is it too much for me to want to repay some of that? Do you have any idea how disgustingly wealthy I've become?"

"I'm a little curious," admitted Rob, but everyone ignored him.

"Accept no debts," muttered Will.

Sammy looked ready to spit. "You don't have any, idiot! *I* paid you for those potions and it was worth it. There's no debt between us."

"I'll rep—"

"If you try, I'll melt that gold and pour it over your head." Sammy's hair had somehow escaped her braids and was standing out in random places. Combined with the wild look in her eyes, it made her look simultaneously frightening and comical.

Will could tell she meant what she said, and his stubborn pride faded, replaced a second later by an involuntary chuckle. He suppressed it, but then his cousin caught his humor and started to laugh even as she wiped away angry tears. Soon they were both laughing.

Tiny and Rob watched, silent spectators, but after a couple of minutes had passed, the golem spoke up. "I hate to interrupt your laughing fit, but I need to get back before someone notices."

Rob's expression was flat and his voice serious as he added, "I'm free all day, and I'm still curious about how rich Sammy is."

As usual, no one bothered to answer him. Will took them each home. For Rob and Tiny, he teleported to Darla, who had hidden in the carriage house where the demon-steel golem was stored. For Sammy, he teleported to Evie, who had patiently waited at Roc's Roost for them. The cat happily returned to her usual doings once they arrived, and Will said his goodbye to Sammy. "Stay safe, and *please* practice the point-defense shield."

By unspoken agreement, neither of them mentioned the money. Sammy nodded, then embraced him. "I will. Give Olly and your mother a hug for me."

CHAPTER 40

Once again, Will teleported, orienting on his mother. She was sitting down with a cup of tea this time. *Chamomile, probably,* he thought with a smile. Erisa always went for chamomile to soothe her nerves, though if he'd upset her enough, she might have used valerian as well. Valerian was a soporific, so she generally avoided it except at bedtime, but the sight of a giant spider was a bad shock for anyone.

He arrived in the doorway that led to the main room. That put him in plain view of where she sat at the dining room table but left enough room that he was less likely to startle her. Erisa's eyes widened momentarily, but the teacup remained steady in her hands as she took in his appearance.

"Sorry for earlier, Mom. I didn't mean to bring the spider into the house, but I had to improvise."

Erisa was waving at him, pointing toward his bedroom. She was whisper-mouthing her words, "Go change!"

He frowned, quietly mouthing his reply as he started in the direction she indicated. "Why?"

"We have a vis—" she began mouthing back.

"Hello! Oh my!" Cora stood in the kitchen doorway, holding a teacup of her own. Her eyes were watching Will with clear interest. Before he could say anything, she remarked, "Why am I not surprised?"

Will had no idea what to say. He'd dismissed his axe before teleporting, but he was still armored well beyond any reasonable explanation that could conceivably include a kitchen worker. The shield was still strapped to his arm, battered and torn, its bronze inlaid runes now spoiled from the phase spider's attacks. If Cora was any kind of merchant worth her salt, she would know that the once-enchanted shield alone was worth as much as the house they stood in—or at least it had been worth that much. The mail hauberk, coif, steel cap, and linen gambeson weren't worth quite as much, but they were still enough to buy at least two draft horses. *Please don't let her know what demon-steel is,* Will prayed silently. Its value was practically incalculable, and there would be no explaining such a thing.

"Ahh...!" Will said eloquently. He closed his mouth, then gracefully opened it again to add, "Ahh ha! You!" He pointed in Cora's direction. "I was hoping you'd show up."

She lifted one brow in amusement. "But not today, obviously. Should I come back some other time?"

"No!" said Will loudly, raising his voice more than he had intended. Some of his secrets were definitely spoiled, but he wasn't about to let Cora leave again without getting the chance to talk. Her appearances were rarer than hen's teeth.

The trader laughed. "I didn't mean tomorrow. Maybe just a few minutes? I could step out while you change and wash up. I'll even pretend I didn't see anything, and we can start today's reunion over again."

Erisa was standing. "Actually, I need to go into town and pick up a few things, then I need to check on Layla Simmons. Her due date is coming up soon, so she'll be glad to see me."

"You don't have to do that, Erisa," started Cora, but Will's mother held up a hand.

"No, honestly. I really need to go out." Erisa headed for the door, but as she passed Will, she gave him a smile and a quiet word, "I won't be back until dusk. I'll catch Oliver when he gets out of school so he can carry the shopping for me."

Will knew exactly what his mother was implying. "Mom! That's not—you don't—"

"You two have a nice long chat," said his mother, and then she was out of the room.

"Sorry about that," said Will.

"Your mother is a delight, Kelvin. No need to apologize." Cora's eyes were still moving up and down, doubtless studying his gear and assessing its relative worth. Then she frowned. "What's the blue stuff?"

"Hemolymph," he admitted, feeling awkward.

"I have no idea what that is," she replied honestly. At some point she'd crossed the distance between them. Her eyes looked closely at his mail. "Half-riveted, half-welded rings, that's quality mail." Her hand drifted to the skirt, fingers trailing through the long tear there. "Something significant had to happen to do that," she observed.

"It's been like that for a long time," lied Will.

"Is that why the torn edges are so shiny?" Cora's lips quirked into a half-smile. "I knew there was something about you, kitchen boy. I could smell it." She inhaled then. "And it wasn't the smell of armor, but I had a feeling."

Her closeness made him aware of her in an entirely new way. "I thought you were going to pretend you didn't see anything."

She looked up at him with unblinking eyes. "I never left, and you're still wearing armor covered in—what is that, monster blood?"

"Would you believe me if I said no?" *Why the hell am I so turned on?* he mentally chided himself. *Is it because of the adrenaline? They say near-death experiences make people horny.* He looked into Cora's eyes, and he knew it was more than that. He'd felt this way before. Recent combat or not, he'd been drawn to her from the first time they'd met.

"I might, if you let me help you take it off." There was a challenge in her gaze.

Will couldn't take his eyes off her, noticing every movement, including the surreptitious way she had just licked her lips. "Perhaps you should let me do that, and bathe. This stuff smells pretty bad."

"It would," she agreed, "but that's new linen, isn't it? Aside from the smell of rust, it hasn't had time to start smelling of old sweat."

It was his first time wearing the gambeson, but her observation surprised him. "You're more familiar with armor than I expected."

"I told you my ex-husband was a dangerous man." She inhaled again. "I always hated the smell, but right now, it's a bit nostalgic. I am glad it's not an old gambeson, though."

Her head was tilted slightly back as she spoke, and Will's hand moved before he could think, following the nape of her neck to brace her as he lowered his lips to hers. Fire flashed through him, bringing new life to his flesh and erasing his fatigue. He took a step back, meaning to break away, but she clung to him, continuing the kiss.

Will reached back and opened the door, then kicked it shut again as they backed through it. The heavy belt that kept his hauberk cinched tightly around his waist fell to the floor. *When did she manage that?*

He leaned forward, thinking to begin the awkward shaking dance that would allow him to shimmy out of the hauberk, but Cora stopped him, her hands moving to his neck. "Coif first," she told him with an amused smile. Her fingers unlaced it and lifted the heavy mail from his head, followed by the padded hood, exposing his sweaty, matted hair.

With that done, he could lean forward and start trying to get the hauberk off. Normally, he did it alone, but Cora's expert hands caught the ends of his sleeves and helped him slide his arms out, then she grabbed at the mail where it was bunching around his shoulders. With her skillful aid, the mail came off with ease. "You've done this a few times," said Will.

"I told you. I like the dangerous ones, and you, Kelvin Wiltshire, are definitely a dangerous man." She pushed him back then. "You do need a bath, though."

"Would you like to know another secret?"

Cora's eyes brightened. "Is it magic?"

He frowned. "You already knew?"

"I wasn't sure, but I saw the shield just now, and when I was here last time Durin showed me the ward runes hidden around the edges of your room," she answered.

"Your dwarf has good eyes," Will noted. Reaching out with his right hand, he grazed her neck with his fingers, then let it trail down to her bosom. He watched the quartz stone set in the gold band, but it remained clear.

He thought he'd covered it well, but Cora noticed something in his face or demeanor. "What was that?" she asked. "Were you testing me?"

Rather than deny it, Will nodded.

"And?"

"You passed," he said quietly, a faint sadness showing in his eyes.

She smiled then kissed him again. Will held onto her, prolonging the kiss until he could wipe away the tear that had formed in the corner of one of his eyes. The fire inside him continued to grow. "What was the secret?" she reminded.

"You already guessed it."

"I guessed magic, but I don't really know what that means in your case."

"I'm a wizard," he clarified, then with a dramatic wave of his hand, he cast Selene's Solution, cleaning his body, hair, and the linen gambeson that he still wore. "A bath is nice, but this is quicker."

As the magic passed over him, Cora's eyes grew hungrier. She was unlacing the sides of her dress with fingers that were now clumsy from her haste. "Damn it. Why did I wear the dress?"

He hadn't really noticed until then, but Cora's hair was carefully done. It had grown to a medium length since he had last seen her, and it was gathered up and tied behind each ear with blue ribbons. The dress she wore was a sky blue and embroidered with yellow thread, creating geometric designs at the neck, cuffs, waist, and hem. It was the kind of attire that wealthy women wore casually, and commoners wore on holidays.

In the past, she'd always worn trousers and simple tunics, though she'd had them tailored to fit her shape, but Will wouldn't have cared even if she had shown up wearing naught but a burlap sack. "Were you trying to impress me?"

"That's it," she agreed. "Did it work?"

He was out of the gambeson and shucking his trousers while she was still struggling to loosen the laces enough to get the dress up past her waist and shoulders. Will finished first and began tugging on her sleeves, working in a manner not unlike what she'd done for him with the mail. When the dress came free, she straightened up, standing now in nothing but a thin linen shift. Will was bare.

He pulled her in, feeling her curves through the soft fabric as he answered, "No. It didn't work. I don't give a damn about what's on the outside." Reaching down, he lifted the hem, pulling the shift up and exposing her skin. "It's what's on the inside that counts." A low growl rose in his throat as he looked upon her.

Taking his hand, she backed toward the bed. "I have an idea, regarding things being inside or out."

"That's not what I meant, exactly," he replied, "but it's an excellent idea."

***

The two of them were dressed and well put together by the time Erisa and Oliver returned hours later at dusk. Will cooked a quick meal for everyone and then suggested a nighttime walk to Cora. She readily agreed. Will did his best to ignore his mother's smirk.

"We won't wait up for you," Erisa told him.

Oliver frowned. "You're not coming back soon?"

Feeling awkward, Will answered, "We might have a drink and stay out late." *Or all night.* He wondered if Cora had anyone waiting with her wagon or if it was empty.

She gave him a hint with her reply, "Very late, probably."

The night air was cool as they began their walk, and Cora's first question got right to the heart of the matter. "Do you really want a drink?"

"No." His eyes were bold as he stared back at her.

"Me either."

"Is your wagon—?"

Cora grinned. "It's empty." She took his hand in hers. "This way."

"What happened to Durin?"

"He went back to Delgath. Said Terabinia smelled too much of elves now. He didn't like all the bluet people are using now."

That caught Will's ear. "Did he say why?"

She shook her head. "I asked, but he didn't have a better reason than the fact that it's elves selling it. Tradition is very important to the People of Stone."

"And hating elves is a tradition?"

Cora nodded. "It's such an old one I'm not sure they even know why anymore, although Durin claims it's because his people were once slaves to them, ours too."

"How long ago?"

She shrugged. "I'm not a historian. I don't think Durin knew much more anyway. Whenever it was, it was so long ago that no one remembers it."

"Before the dragon then," muttered Will.

"Before what?" she asked.

"Before recorded history," said Will. "The elves lived here, but after the dragon came, they left."

"Are you talking about the dragon they say burned Spela?"

He nodded.

"Nobody really believes that, do they?" she asked him.

Will gave her an odd look. "You don't?"

"None of the people I've met who claimed to have seen one were the sort I'd believe."

"Didn't the queen put out a proclamation? She made it public. The old king was a dragon in disguise, until the Black Duke slew him and put her on the throne."

Cora laughed. "I read the notices, and it's obvious that you didn't."

"What does that mean?"

"The queen's proclamation said that her husband killed the dragon, though apparently the Black Duke helped somehow. It's been a long time since I read it, but I never took any of it seriously."

"She's the queen, though."

Cora gave him an odd look. "Do you believe everything the oligarchs say? There were almost no witnesses that saw the dragon, not in Terabinia anyway, and almost all the ones who supposedly saw it in Shimera were conveniently burned to death."

"Then what do you think happened?"

She shrugged. "I have no idea. Everyone saw her husband go mad before he killed her father. The fact that they created some fanciful story about him actually being a dragon that they killed in secret months later was probably just a justification for it. For a while I thought it might have been simply an attempt to paint the prince consort as a hero before she had him conveniently eliminated."

"You think she killed her husband?"

"Not now!" laughed Cora. "His reappearance ruined that theory."

Will replied, "I feel like you ought to know more about it than that."

She gave him an odd look. "Why?"

"You're working for the crown, aren't you?"

"I sell spices."

"And information," he said, amending her answer. "But I get the feeling you're more loyal to Terabinia than you'd like people to know."

"A spy, you mean?" she asked, eyes wide. Will said nothing, just returned her gaze in silence. Gradually, her mock-surprise faded, replaced by a faint smile. "I have no idea what you're talking about," she answered dryly.

"Mm hmm." Will saw a large shape around the bend in the road. "Is that your wagon?"

"Yes."

"What happened to John and Mary?"

"The couple working for me?" she asked. He nodded and she continued, smiling, "I paid them to find lodging tonight."

Will raised his brows. "You were pretty confident then. What if I hadn't been interested?"

"You were interested," she replied. There was no doubt in her voice.

"I might have been away. You'd have wasted your money."

Her features took on a hungry look. "It was worth the risk. I got my money's worth."

Will grinned. "I don't think I've gotten mine."

"What?"

"Yet." Pulling on her hand, he caught her as she fell, then put one arm beneath her knees and lifted her up. She let out a 'whoop' and kicked for a second as she left the ground.

"What are you doing?"

"You walk too slow," he answered, taking large strides toward her wagon.

Cora buried her face against his neck, then nipped him gently. "You're so impatient."

"You were gone a long time," he answered, looking down. "I've missed you."

Her tone was serious as she replied, "I've missed you too."

CHAPTER 41

The night was warm and sweet. The two lovers remained together until dawn, talking about everything and nothing at the same time, though neither of them asked any of the obvious questions. Cora showed no curiosity regarding the revelation of his magic, though she did ask one question about the blue blood that had been on him.

"Should I worry about the blood I saw when you came home?"

"In what sense?" he responded cautiously.

"In the sense that you might encounter a violent end before I return again."

"No. That's the first time I've needed armor in a very long time, and I don't expect to need it again for even longer."

She nestled deeper into his shoulder, resting her head on his chest. "That's good."

"You're not curious about what happened?" he asked quietly.

She looked up at him, peering over his chin. "If I asked, would you tell me the truth?"

"No. But I'm willing to invent an entertaining story if need be."

She smiled in the darkness, running her right hand over his chest again, as though reassuring herself of his presence. "You haven't said anything about my side job. It doesn't worry you?"

"No, should I be worried?"

Her fingers tightened against his skin, and Cora pressed her face hard against his side, as though she wanted to crawl inside him. "Never," she whispered with emphatic intensity.

"You're not tempted to make any mentions of a strange man and his family living in Lystal?"

"I've never spoken of you to another soul. Why should I? You're my solitary joy, my private treasure."

Will ran his fingers through her hair, lifting it to his nose and inhaling her scent. "You haven't guessed my identity, have you?"

She rolled over on top of him, pressing as much of her skin against as his as possible. "I don't allow myself to think on it. I don't want anything to spoil our brief moments."

"This is a dream," he agreed, "fragile and easily broken."

"Let's pretend it can last forever," she told him. "Sadness can wait for the dawn."

***

She left in the morning, and Will sank into a quiet depression for the next several days, though he tried to stay busy to keep his mind off of it. His mother noticed despite his best efforts. "What's wrong with you?"

"I'm the world's biggest hypocrite," he muttered, too softly for her to understand.

"What?"

"I miss her."

"Then fetch her back and make some grandchildren to liven this place up," replied Erisa.

"It's not that easy."

His mother studied his face. "She doesn't want children?"

Will was looking in his mother's direction, but his eyes stared through her. "She loves children, but she can't have any."

"You can adopt. Oliver's been a blessing."

"She can't live with us, Mom."

Erisa's faced twisted in confusion. "Why not?"

"We both have responsibilities."

"That's stupid, and I know for a fact there's nothing preventing you from settling down with a wife. If she's not free, find someone who is. There's a world full of women out there."

"I'm in love with her, Mom."

"You barely know her. She's been here what, three times?"

"I need to get to work," he said, trying to deflect the conversation.

"At what? Lettler's had that new cook working in your place for weeks now. How long does it take you to do—what are you doing with that spider? Dissecting it?"

"His name is Leggy, and no, I'm not dissecting him. We've come to an arrangement."

Erisa stood up from the table. "It can *talk*?"

Will nodded. "I wouldn't say we're friends, but if things go well again today, I'll be taking him home in another day or two."

His mother looked toward the ceiling. "I pray to the Mother, it's somewhere as far from here as possible. Across the ocean isn't even far enough."

He smirked. "Leggy is from Darrow, but there's probably a few of his kin to be found in most of the mountains around Hercynia."

"And that killed my desire to ever venture into the mountains again," she said.

Will finished his morning tea and teleported to his private workshop. He wasted no time checking on his eight-legged associate, although it was a little annoying that he had to slip partway into the astral every time they wanted to talk. *How are you today?*

I would be better if you let me out of this cage. I have cooperated with your demands and given you my promise.

Will felt bad about that, but he didn't relent. *I'm sorry, but I have to be safe. I believe you, but not enough to risk losing you before I learn as much as I can.*

Surely you know lies cannot exist when we talk this way?

Will had never really thought about it consciously, but he intuitively knew it to be true. Speaking through the astral was essentially direct communication between souls. Any attempted falsehood would be immediately apparent. *I hadn't thought about it,* he admitted. *In any case, if you teach me well, this will be over soon. Do you need more food?*

The sheep you brought will last me several more days.

Will glanced at the silk-wrapped body hanging up in the corner of Leggy's cell. Knowing that the animal inside was still alive made him want to shiver, but he gave no visible sign of his discomfort. He teleported through the bars so that he could stand next to the arachnid.

Then he slipped partway from his body again. *I'm ready,* he told the spider, then returned fully to himself so he could watch Leggy's work more carefully. Standing so close to the dangerous creature was nerve wracking, especially with no armor, but he had little to fear. They'd spent several hours working side by side already, and the beast had shown no sign that it might try to betray his trust.

He'd also been clear in their early negotiations that he had other abilities at his disposal. The armor and spells he'd used in their previous encounter had been deliberately chosen to avoid killing the phase spider. Will hadn't been so rude as to make a specific threat, but he was ready with a wind-wall if necessary. Combining that spell with a quick use of his sonic shield would almost certainly render the phase spider into large mess of grey chitin and blue vital fluids.

Without touching the astral, he couldn't hear Leggy's response, but the spider held up one leg to indicate where it would start. Its defensive turyn appeared there a second later, before slowly creeping along the limb to meet up with more of the silvery liquid that was appearing from different places. Will watched with his turyn sensitivity as high as possible, trying to observe the flow of turyn inside the spider as well as what happened on the surface.

Will had successfully replicated the strange turyn he'd first seen used in one of the vampire Alexander's spells many years ago, but doing what the phase spider did was an entirely different matter. After nearly being killed by one of Leggy's kin years ago, he had tried repeatedly to use the special turyn as a flexible body armor many times, but had no success.

He'd actually had a dream for something similar since his early days as a student at Wurthaven after he'd learned Arrogan's demon-armor spell. That spell covered the user in a layer of positive turyn that was antithetical to the negative energies the demons survived on, protecting the caster from turyn poison and acting as an offensive form of armor in combat against demons. Will rarely used the spell now, since his ability to convert turyn from one frequency to another had grown to such an extent that even traveling to Hell itself was fairly safe for him, but it had given him the idea to create other types of magical armor, and the first that had come to mind was creating a force spell that would cover the user in a force effect that protected the user from every angle yet still allowed them to move freely.

He'd soon learned that such a thing was impossible. Force spells had certain advantages, but they always created forms and shapes that were rigid and immutable. The closest thing to what he had envisioned would be a small force-sphere that surrounded and moved with the user, and such a thing wouldn't allow the caster to interact with the environment. Nothing could pass through the force effect, whether it be weapons or spells.

Meeting (and nearly dying to) a phase spider had opened his eyes to entirely new possibilities. The special turyn they secreted and covered their bodies with was nearly identical to a force effect, but it had different properties in several regards. It was impermeable to most things, but unlike traditional force effects, it was flexible and permeable to gases. While that allowed the spider to obtain oxygen normally, it also meant the phase spider's defense was vulnerable to violent gusts of wind sweeping it away.

It was also corrosive to normal force effects, making it an impressive tool when facing wizards or sorcerers who relied on force spells for their defense. Will still vividly remembered the day he had killed Lognion's human puppet. The man had used his vast supply of energy from his elementals to feed a force-dome that allowed him to mock Will for a considerable length of time. Will had only gotten through by using brute force and the nearly limitless rivers of power that flowed through the sky above them.

Such tools weren't always available, even to him, and they never would be for someone like Oliver. His son needed something more practical and accessible.

Leggy finished his demonstration, and Will slipped partway into the astral again. *You're circulating it!* Will announced.

Yes.

It never occurred to me before, but you aren't just secreting the energy and discarding it, you're actively reabsorbing it at the same time, Will added.

Your sight is keen. Perhaps now you understand why you cannot hope to recreate what we do naturally.

There I disagree, replied Will. *Show me again. I've seen nothing to dissuade me so far.*

Very well.

They ran through the demonstration again, and again. Eventually, Will requested that the spider use different parts of its body, the abdomen, the cephalothorax, different legs, and finally its entire body at once. Each time, he observed and tried to understand the currents that flowed beneath the arachnid's hard chitin exterior. By the end of the day, he was certain.

I can do it, he told the spider. *I just need time to practice.* He demonstrated by briefly creating the silvery turyn around his right arm from hand to elbow. It was rough and unrefined, giving his arm a bulbous appearance as he circulated the turyn from elbow to fingertips. A large part of his difficulty lay in the fact that he couldn't reabsorb and recirculate the power the way the spider could. Instead, he had to rely on creating an external flow. In this case, he was sending the turyn down the outside, from elbow to fingers, then rolling it under and bringing it back on the inside, though still outside his body. The complex motion made it difficult to control, as well as giving the silvery turyn a bloated, bulbous appearance.

Afterward, Leggy had a few things to say. *Your version is crude, not to mention unstable.*

Unstable. How so? asked Will.

Repeat what you did, but do not be alarmed when I touch you. It will not be an attack.

Will did. He wished he could talk to the spider while he worked. It was annoying to have to stop each time and shift his perspective slightly, but he wasn't able to do detailed work on something new while keeping his spirit slightly disjoined from his body. Once more, he created his awkward copy of Leggy's defensive barrier, mentally steeling himself so he wouldn't jump when the spider lifted a leg to gently touch his arm.

His silvery turyn replica collapsed and fell apart. More conversation followed. *Why did it do that?* he asked. *I'm sure I did exactly what you do, even if it looked rough.*

The circulating flows must remain apart. For us, we move the other half within our exoskeleton, but you are doing both halves outside your skin. Any external force that jostles it will bring them together and disrupt your defense.

Will wanted to swear, but he was still happy for the knowledge. Some of his ideas wouldn't work without extensive changes, but the most important one still had possibilities. He had a lot of experimentation ahead of him to confirm his thoughts. *Is there anything else you can teach me?*

You have the essence of it, though I do not think there's any way you can make use of it. You were not born in the correct body.

That brought another unrelated question to his mind. *Do you think my kind are ugly?*

On the contrary, you look delicious, replied Leggy. *But if it will ease your mind, I have been thinking about our interactions. I will not feed on your kind again, barring starvation.*

Will nodded. *I've rethought my views on your kind as well. Now that I know how intelligent you are, I regret some of my actions. Is it the same for you?*

No. It is simply apparent that your kind are too dangerous to make an enemy of. I will warn my future hatchlings to avoid eating humans.

Will would take what he could get. *I appreciate that. I'll take you home now. It's been a pleasure working with you.*

The feeling is not mutual.

I can't say that I blame you, replied Will.

CHAPTER 42

Oliver's sixteenth birthday came and went, without a word from his father about his desire to become a wardsman. Oliver brought it up, but his dad always had something else occupying his time and thoughts, or so he claimed.

"Ask me in a few weeks," was all Will would say on the subject, leaving Oliver increasingly frustrated.

He was resolved to take the first opportunity he could find, though he wasn't sure what he would do regarding his age. While sixteen was a customary starting age for many jobs and apprenticeships, he still needed parental approval until he was eighteen. Even if he had a way around the problem of his age, he would need to go to Bondgrad. The illustrious House of Ink was located there.

Although each of the oligarchs maintained their own semi-private militaries and groups of wardsmen, the tattooed warriors were all trained and given their ink there at the House of Ink. To enter, one had to be chosen and sponsored by one of the oligarchs, and after completing the training, receiving their tattoos, and passing the trials, the new wardsman would be released to fulfill his contract with the one who had sponsored him.

The House of Ink charged a hefty fee for their training, and if a candidate was unlucky enough to fail, they could be held liable for the debt incurred to their sponsor. Usually that meant ten years of indentured servitude to their sponsor, a fate only slightly better than outright slavery.

Oliver wasn't worried about failure, though. He knew he was good enough. Gaining a sponsorship was the only real obstacle he could see. For that, he would need to travel to the capital and present himself at the House of Ink on the first day of any given month. That was when they allowed interested parties to test themselves against the trainers to prove their worth, or at least their potential. Only the best were accepted. Failing that meant the person interested in a martial career would have to lower their expectations, perhaps seeking service as an ordinary man-at-arms, or finding work as a merchant-marine.

Given the fact that the oligarchs tended to maintain only a tiny fraction of their troops as wardsmen, most who hoped to gain such a prestigious occupation were doomed to disappointment.

Oliver mulled these things over as he walked to school. Going to school felt silly as well. He was already sixteen, and Gabet's Academy had no formal graduation to be concerned with. Students went until they found employment or their families took them out. In spite of his troubles during the early years, Oliver had already mastered the essentials that were coveted by most who went there: reading, writing, and numeracy. He could count and do sums, as well as other essential operations. He'd even learned the basics of bookkeeping, which was a prized skillset among the students who came from families that owned businesses.

Technically, he could apply for an apprenticeship with an independent accountant, of which there were a few, though most merchants handled their own accounting, or he could seek a job in any number of places that valued literacy and penmanship. *Become an accountant, or maybe a scribe—Dad would love that,* he thought bitterly.

He was still several blocks from the school, but seeing it in the distance only depressed him. His best friend, Doug Rushton, had already stopped attending. Doug's father worked at a factorage owned by the Lentam family. The Lentams owned the majority of everything in and around Lystal, since the Lentam oligarch was heavily invested in mining, fishing, and transport. Doug's dad had gotten him in as a bookkeeper, and that had been the end of Doug's schooling.

To Oliver's surprise, he saw a familiar figure waving to him in the distance. He'd recognize the lean beanpole frame of his friend anywhere. Doug was still small, relative to the average, but he'd gained enough height that he wasn't considered short, though at five-foot-seven his head only came up to Oliver's shoulder.

"Alver! Hey!" called the other teen.

Oliver jogged to reach him sooner, smiling as he got close. "Hey, Doug. How've you been?"

"Bored, but there's some excitement in Lystal today." The smaller boy waggled his brows.

Oliver leaned back, feeling skeptical. "Really? Nothing happens here."

Doug nodded. "Yeah, I guess that's true. So I suppose you aren't interested in seeing Blathe's wardsmen."

"Blathe?" Lloyd Blathe was an oligarch, or one of the 'Five,' as some people called them. Most of his interests lay in timber and logging, so the Blathe family had operations in various places around Trendham, but their business was handled mainly in Kemp and Dulence. While the Five didn't have official territories, Lystal was generally regarded as primarily a part of Lentam's sphere of influence. "Why would Blathe's wardsmen be here?"

"Recruitment. They're looking for candidates to sponsor." Doug gave him a meaningful look.

Oliver frowned in disbelief. "They've never done that before. You have to go to Bondgrad to—"

Doug was already shaking his head as he interrupted, "The Ruling Council voted last week. Strommen sent out notices. The wardsmen brought copies. They've posted them around the main square."

Brent Strommen wasn't one of the Five, but he was the Prime Minister elected by the council to oversee Trendham's government. Technically, that meant he held the most power, but only as long as he retained the approval of the Five. In disputes between them, he was the final arbiter, at least until a new minister was elected by the council. "Notices of what?" asked Oliver.

"Increased recruitment. The Five have been authorized to double the size of their forces in the coming years. They'll be hiring and training more armsmen of all sorts, but today they're looking for wardsmen candidates," said Doug.

"But why Blathe?"

Doug shrugged. "I don't know. Maybe it just happens to be his men that are here. Or maybe they're going to share. I just thought you'd want to know."

Oliver stared at the ground. "I can't go. I'm supposed to go to school."

"Still? You've already passed your birthday."

He shrugged, then looked at his feet. "Dad won't let me. He said he might, but he hasn't given his approval, yet. I'm not sure he ever will."

"So, what? You're just going to sit around on your ass until you turn eighteen?"

"What choice do I have?"

Doug's answer was immediate. "Skip school."

"I'm not old enough to join on my own."

"You can still watch them testing potential candidates. I'm sure everyone who isn't nailed down will be gathered to watch." Doug paused, then asked, "Do you have any money? You know there will be betting too."

Oliver shook his head. "No. Don't you have a job now?"

"I'm an apprentice, which means I get paid almost nothing to take shit from everyone and sleep in a closet."

"Your dad kicked you out?"

"No. But if he did, I'd have to sleep in the closet. Seriously. They have a closet for apprentices who don't have a bed to sleep in."

"But you don't actually sleep in it."

Doug sighed. "No, of course not. I'm still at home."

"Then why say that?"

"It's poetic license. Stop being so picky. Do you want to come see the fighting or not?"

"I do, but…"

Doug grabbed his arm and turned him to face a different street, one that led toward the center of Lystal. "But nothing. What happens if you miss one day?"

"The headmaster will probably report it to my dad, then I'll be grounded."

"And? Anything else? What's he going to ground you from? Being bored? Grounded lasts a few days, but this is your only chance to see the wardsmen in Lystal."

Oliver's feet were already moving as Doug pulled him along. "Why did the council vote to increase the military allotments?"

"They didn't say in the notice, but it's probably because they're worried about Terabinia invading or something like that."

He'd already given up any pretense of resisting and walked freely beside his friend now. "Why? We've been at peace with them since forever. I'd have thought it would be Faresh."

"Faresh isn't the one taking our ships."

"And Terabinia is?"

"They deny it, of course, but who else could it be? Faresh doesn't have much of a navy, and it's gotten beyond anything you'd expect from pirates."

"What do we expect from pirates?"

"I dunno. I'm not a sailor. But everyone says it's too much. I heard Terabinia is even considering closing the border. They keep claiming they're the victims, but no one believes it."

"Huh." Oliver's attention switched to the crowd in front of them. The number of people in the street had grown denser as they walked, and now they had to work hard to make any progress. Glancing to the sides he saw some people had climbed onto roofs and balconies to get a better view of what was occurring in the main square.

A wooden stage was there, used for different purposes throughout the year—announcements were often made there, as well as plays and skits during the harvest festival. More rarely, public punishments were meted out there, but today it was being used as a small arena. Posts had been driven into the hard ground around it, and ropes strung between them, creating a makeshift fence around the raised platform. Within it, two men fought, while two others stood casually by, watching with mild interest.

Three of them were shirtless, despite the chilly fall air, and the reason was quite obvious. They'd removed their tunics and set aside their cloaks so the crowd could see the tattoos that covered their torsos. Symbols covered their chests and backs, while lines flowed outward, following the lines of their arms. More symbols marked the joints, elbows, wrists, and even their fingers, and though the men's lower halves were still covered, it was obvious the lines went down their legs as well.

Wardsmen, thought Oliver with a rush of excitement.

The two watching were wardsmen, and they looked to be in their thirties, while only one of the two fighting had tattoos. The other was a boy Oliver had met a few times, but didn't know well, the son of a farmer that lived near Lystal. Leif was his name, though Oliver couldn't recall the teen's last name. He was backing up nervously, blood already running from his nose.

The man responsible for his bloody nose looked to be younger than the other wardsmen, perhaps in his late twenties. He had dirty blond hair that had been cut short, and a lean, rangy build. Were it not for the tattoos, Oliver would have been tempted to bet on Leif. The farmer's son had a heavy build and muscles that came from real labor. He was young enough to be quick and flexible, but his broad shoulders hinted that his punches would be nothing to laugh at.

But the skinny wardsman was laughing, showing bad teeth and what seemed to Oliver to be a cruel personality. "Had enough, boy?"

"Not yet," said Leif, wiping at his nose again, trying to stop the blood that was dripping down across his lips and chin. "You said two minutes. I can last."

"Stop backing up then," said the wardsman, malice in his eyes.

"Don't hurt him too bad, Gavin. We haven't found five yet," called one of the wardsmen that watched from the side.

"Not my fault this town is full of nothing but hicks and sheepfuckers," responded Gavin, taking his eyes off Leif for a moment.

Leif tried to take advantage of the distraction, suddenly reversing his direction and moving forward. He aimed for the body, but the wardsman had been waiting for him to try it. Barely taking his eyes off the man he was talking to, Gavin took a deceptively quick step back, causing the young man to overextend, then the wardsman bounced from his backfoot, springing forward and delivering a brutal punch directly against Leif's temple.

The sound was shocking, reminiscent of two pieces of hard lumber being knocked together. Leif instantly went limp, and Oliver hoped the other boy wasn't dead. The location of the hit was a dangerous one. *A fist shouldn't sound like that, even against his skull,* observed Oliver silently. *Do the tattoos make his body harder?*

"Fuck!" swore the wardsman who'd been talking to Gavin. Moving quickly into the improvised fight square, he knelt beside Leif. After a moment, he sighed. "Still alive." The look he directed toward Gavin was one of irritation and long-suffering. "No thanks to you." He waved to a couple of onlookers. "Take him over there and see if you can revive him. If he lives, we'll take him."

A half-hearted cheer rose from those who'd been rooting for Leif's success. It was obvious that many in the crowd had mixed feelings about the near-lethal nature of the previous bouts.

Gavin spit on the platform. "You're soft, Len. We don't need candidates like him."

The older wardsman shook his head. "He had enough guts to get up here after seeing how you fight. He'll do fine." Len studied the crowd, then added, "This would be easier if you'd ease up. We won't get many willing to step up if you keep trying to kill 'em."

Gavin gave the senior wardsman a look of disgust, raising his voice to make sure everyone in the square could hear him. "That's the point of being a wardsman. Fight hard, die young. Anyone not willing to risk dying to join shouldn't be one of us to begin with. You're getting old and soft, Len." He looked over the crowd. "Five have tried so far, and two we'll take! Anyone else willing to chance getting his skull cracked? Surely one of you sheepfuckers has the balls to try!"

The third wardsman, who'd been silent until then, moved up. "Take a break, Gavin. I'll take the rest. I can't blame them for not wanting to step up here with a mad dog."

"Damn it, Sean! Don't steal my fun."

Sean nodded toward the fence, then repeated his words more slowly, "Go, take a break." From the tone, it was clear he was the wardsman in charge, and while Gavin didn't hide his anger, he obeyed. The leader said to the crowd, "Who else? You'll face me, and I'll do my best not to kill anyone, whether you pass or not." He offered a smile that was meant to appease the crowd's sour mood. His eyes roved over the square and then fell on Oliver, who stood a head above the people around him. "You look like a sturdy lad. Care to try your luck against old Sean?"

Oliver was full of mixed emotions. Hesitation because he knew he wouldn't get permission to join, some doubt because of what had happened to Leif, and an equal measure of anger for the same reason. He started to shake his head no, but Doug spoke up first, "He'll do it!" His friend shoved him toward the platform.

"What are you doing?" hissed Oliver.

"You've got this. I know it," said his friend.

"Your friend doesn't look very confident," said Gavin from the side, a sneer on his face.

And just like that, Oliver forgot his reasons for hesitating. He began pushing his way forward, determined to teach the rangy wardsman a lesson in civilized behavior. Sean smiled as he approached. "I like that look better. Want to test yourself?"

Oliver met his eyes. "I do, but I'd rather fight him." He pointed at where Gavin lounged to one side.

"Fuck yeah!" crooned Gavin.

The lean wardsman was halfway to the center of the platform when Sean's hand came up against his chest, pushing him back. "You've done enough for one day. I'd rather not have to wait a week for the new candidates to heal before they can start training. Go sit down."

Disappointed, Gavin started to turn back, but Oliver spoke up. "He's a good boy, isn't he?"

The wardsman turned and leapt, his fist lashing out to catch Oliver with a sucker punch, or rather, he tried. Oliver took a quick step sideways, putting the leader between them. Gavin couldn't correct the angle of his attack without hitting his senior, and instead was forced to pull back, having missed in front of the crowd. Oliver laughed.

Sean was less amused. "Mother damn you, Gavin! You're asking for it. I'll have you—"

"Fuck it, Sean. Let me fight the bastard, he's asking for it," snapped Gavin.

"I'm willing," said Oliver loudly. "But I'd rather use practice swords than fists."

"You think you know how to use a blade, sheepfucker?" sneered Gavin.

"Enough!" barked the senior wardsman. "I'm not letting you beat an entrant to death. You'll stick to fists." He turned to Oliver. "Is that good enough for you, Mister I-have-a-death-wish?"

"His body is hard as iron," said Oliver evenly. "Without weapons, that's a bigger advantage than with."

Sean lifted one brow. "You noticed that, eh?" He gave Gavin a dark look. "Think you can fight without using ink?"

Gavin growled. "I won't need it."

"Fine, no tattoos, and we'll see how long this young ox can stay on his feet," pronounced Sean.

"If I knock him down, can we use practice swords?" asked Oliver.

Sean rolled his eyes. "Sure, lad. Sure, just try not to bite off more than you can chew. If you've got the quickness to go with those muscles, you might make a good candidate. I'd rather that than have to explain another one of Gavin's 'accidents.'" The older man stepped back.

Before the leader had gotten more than halfway to the side of the platform, Gavin came at him. He moved slower than he had before, but he was still suspiciously quick. Oliver didn't know if the man was using his tattoos or not, but he wasn't worried. He'd been expecting the move. Taking a tiny step to one side, Oliver turned and moved his head just enough that the punch merely grazed his chin. It looked at first as though he might have taken the blow, but as Gavin's momentum continued on, it was obvious he hadn't.

Oliver's left hand caught Gavin's right arm just above the elbow, and he helped the man along, preventing him from regaining his balance and keeping him in line for a rising palm strike from his own right hand. It landed just under the wardsman's chin, rocking his head back and lifting his heels from the ground.

Oliver's hand stung, as if he'd struck a wall instead of a man, and he was sure the wardsman had used his defensive magic. The blow should have been enough to take the fight out of anyone, but he could tell the wardsman was merely surprised. Gavin tried to step back as he came back down, but Oliver's right leg had already been positioned behind his left, and instead he fell on his ass.

Oliver smiled down at him. "Think you know how to use a sword?"

Gavin bounced up from the ground as though he was made of springs, but Sean was already there with a hand on his shoulder. "That's enough, Gav. He knocked you on your ass. Losing your temper won't make you look better."

Len spoke up from where he'd been watching. "The kid's quick for his size."

Sean nodded. "You pass. Move over there." He pointed to the area where a man with a black eye sat beside the still-unconscious Leif.

"You said we could use practice swords if I knocked him down," said Oliver stubbornly.

Sean's eyes widened. "Are you stupid, lad?"

"That's what you said," agreed Gavin with a malicious smile. "It's not my fault the sheepfucker has a death wish."

"How old are you, kid?" asked the wardsmen's leader. "I can't let a minor—"

His blood was up, and his reply came instantly, "Eighteen." Gavin's eyes lit with delight, and a few minutes later, Oliver found himself standing opposite the lean wardsman, a heavy practice sword made of ash in his hand. This time, Len and Sean made sure they were properly separated and made certain they were both ready before the match started.

Gavin appeared to be a few inches under six feet tall. He was probably a little above average, but the other wardsmen were bigger, making him appear small. Oliver was several inches past six feet, and it had been a while since his dad had measured him. He might be pushing six and a half feet by now. He thought he had a rough estimate of the wardsman's speed, and he had the advantage of reach, so unless the tattooed warrior was a master swordsman, he figured his odds were good.

They came together, feinting, striking, and parrying with a speed that few in the audience could follow, but the two of them were just feeling one another out. Gavin grinned at him. "You should have sat down with the other sheepfuckers, boy. I'm going to hurt you."

"You can try."

The wardsman sneered. "I'll stick this piece of wood right up your ass, just the way you like it."

They moved together again, their wooden blades clacking loudly as they strove to land blows, but several seconds in, Oliver's foot came down on something rough, and he stumbled. Gavin's blade whipped out, hitting his right thigh with all the force the wardsman could manage. The opening had been unexpected, so he wasn't able to hit as hard as he would have liked, but the pain that shot through Oliver's face gratified him nonetheless.

Oliver was limping after he jumped back to avoid a follow-up. He nodded at his opponent. "Good shot. Point to you."

Gavin laughed. "There's no points here, boy. You'll be flat on your back and begging me to stop before I'm done with you." He made a rude gesture, sliding his wooden blade in and out through a circle of his fingers.

Oliver's smiled through his pain. "Is that what you want me to do? All you had to do is ask."

Laughter rippled through the crowd, and the wardsman's face reddened. Lunging forward, he launched a frenzy of blows. Oliver let himself be forced back, limping as he went, but he'd been ready with a plan already. The insult had merely been the bait. He'd trained for years with his father, and using an injury to his advantage was nothing new. The other man had no idea how much or how little his leg really hindered him. So he exaggerated the limp.

At the same time, his focused defense was making Gavin even angrier. The wardsman needed to land another blow to show his superiority, and to stop the laughter from the crowd. Oliver smiled at him as he retreated, playing up his amusement for the sake of the audience. When his leg folded and he started to fall, the wardsman didn't hesitate.

Gavin brought his weapon around in a sweeping blow that was meant to land against Oliver's head or neck, and given the force he was using, Oliver had little doubt that the wood would cave in his skull, but his fall didn't continue. Instead, his supposedly weak leg firmed up, pushing him forward and inside the arc of Gavin's swing. The other man reacted with blinding speed, but Oliver's had cost him his balance. As he rapidly stumbled back, Oliver's wooden weapon whipped around to hit the same place that Oliver had been wounded, Gavin's right thigh.

Knowing that the wardsman cared nothing for points or skill, Oliver held nothing back. He expected the blow to land with a thud, but the wardsman's body was like stone. A loud crack echoed across the square, and Oliver's practice sword exploded, sending shooting pains up his hand and wrist. All he had left was a jagged stump of wood in his hand.

It was obvious, to Oliver at least, that his opponent had cheated. He'd expected his blow would leave the man unable to walk, or possibly even broken his leg, but instead Gavin's stone-like resilience had destroyed Oliver's weapon.

Oliver could tell it had hurt, though; he saw the pain in the wardsman's face, but it was replaced an instant later by pure fury as Gavin went berserk. Roaring, the wardsman attacked, swinging his wooden blade with all the speed and force he could muster.

The crowd was yelling so loudly now that it filled the air, yet over it all, Oliver could hear the wardsmen's leader shouting for them to stop. "It's over! His weapon's gone! By the Mother, stop, damn you!"

He would have liked to obey, but his opponent was hell-bent on murder, so Oliver did the only thing he could. He fought. His own adrenaline was pumping harder than ever before, and his body moved faster than ever before. It was that or die, and his heart demanded life.

Oliver backed for three steps, acting as though he would be driven into a circling retreat. That's what anyone else would have done. Nothing else made sense. A normal person retreated in the face of superior speed and strength, and the wardsman was the very picture of fury in motion. But years of practice overrode his instinct to run. Three steps. That was all he gave.

On the third, he reversed course and stepped back in. Without a weapon to guard, he took a hard blow against his shoulder, but that was a cost he'd chosen to pay. The wardsman would beat him to death if he allowed things to continue as a sword fight. Punches weren't good either, since he was liable to break his hands against the man's granite-like skin. But Oliver was bigger and possibly stronger. No matter how hard the man was, he had to be able to bend his joints to fight. Oliver's longer arms and legs would make it even easier to wrestle the man down and tie him into a knot.

But first, he had to get Gavin to the ground.

As the other man's sword pounded into the meat of his shoulder, Oliver bent his knees, then drove forward with the stump that remained of his practice sword, aiming for Gavin's solar plexus. Normally he would have used a punch, but again, the wardsman's hard skin would probably break his hand, so he thrust with the wooden handle, putting his offhand behind the hilt for extra force. If he could drive the wind from his opponent's lungs, he could wrestle him to the ground. Then, hopefully, the wardsman's superior would stop the fight.

The jagged end of the practice sword punched through the wardsman like a hot knife through butter. He felt it enter the other man's body, tearing through skin and fascia, liver and arteries, until it struck the hard bone of the wardsman's spine, where it finally stopped. Oliver's right hand was halfway embedded in Gavin's belly, still gripping the wood as blood slowly dripped down his wrist.

Oliver's mouth fell open in horror, and as he looked up, the wardsman's face held a similar expression. Gavin's eyes never left his as the man's legs buckled and he collapsed to the ground. Unable to draw wind, the wardsman silently mouthed two words, 'fuck you,' before going completely still. His dead gaze kept Oliver paralyzed as a hush fell over the square. A few seconds later, someone screamed. "He's dead! Olly killed him dead!"

"He shoved a broken sword through his belly!" someone else yelled, and after that, everything else was drowned by the noise of everyone in the crowd shouting all at once.

Oliver had let go of the sword handle and now stared down at his blood-covered hand. His fingers were trembling. "I don't understand," he muttered. "It shouldn't have gone in."

A shadow fell over him, and Sean stared at Gavin's corpse. Len was there too, standing on the other side of the kneeling teen. The wardsmen's leader shook his head. "Fuck me if this isn't all I need today."

"It wasn't supposed to go in," repeated Oliver, looking up at them, hoping for some reassurance.

Sean's eyes were hard as he stared back. "Anytime you shove a weapon at somebody's gut, you'd best be expecting it to go in."

Len spit on the ground. "Dumbfuck Gavin, killed by a dumbfuck kid. Ain't that just fucking poetic."

"Live fast, die young, that's the motto," said Sean with a sigh. His gaze fixed on Oliver again. "How old are you kid? Are you really eighteen?"

Numb, Oliver answered, "Sixteen."

"Hah, just a few years younger than Gav there. He turned twenty just a few months back," said Len.

Twenty? Oliver had thought the man looked nearly thirty. If so, how old did that make the other two? They looked to be mid-thirties—did that make them twenty-five, or were they even younger?

"Damn shame," said Sean. "Even dead, Gavin's fucking up our recruiting efforts. You'd have made an excellent wardsman, kid."

"Wait, what's going to happen to me?" asked Oliver.

Len patted him on the shoulder. "Sixteen means you'll face the law as an adult."

"But I'm not eighteen," protested Oliver.

"Doesn't matter, kid. Not when the charge is murder. You'll hang for this," said Len. His hand tightened slightly. "Don't think about running. I ain't got nothing against you, boy. Gavin was an asshole, but I'll put three feet of steel through you if you try to run."

"Murder? I wasn't trying to kill him!" pleaded Oliver. "You saw what happened. I was just trying to wrestle him down so he wouldn't beat me to death. I didn't even have a weapon!"

Sean shook his head. "The big hole in Gav's belly says otherwise."

The town watch arrived a minute later, and together with the wardsmen, they escorted Oliver to the city jail. Doug stood watching helplessly, unable to stop them.

Chapter 43

Will sat across from his son, staring at him through iron bars. He rubbed his face with his hands for the second or third time but said nothing.

"I'm sorry, Dad. I didn't think this would happen," said Oliver quietly.

His father's first words weren't what he expected. "How do you feel?"

Oliver's lip began to tremble. "Bad. I wasn't trying to do that. I didn't mean to kill him. You believe me, right?"

"I believe you, but that's not the point," said Will. "I always hoped I could keep you from this day, but it looks like I failed."

"You can tell them, though, right? You know a way to convince the magistrate, don't you?"

"I'm a cook, Olly. My word isn't going to do much. What were you thinking?"

"I was thinking it wouldn't go through him like that," said Oliver desperately. "He was using some kind of magic that made his skin hard. It should have stopped me."

"Iron-body transformation," said his father. "At least that's what the spell is called. They might have a different name for it." He sighed. "What should have stopped you, was *you*. Are you telling me you didn't have any other options?"

"No! He was trying to kill me!"

"What about before that?"

"Before?" Oliver looked confused.

His father's eyes were dead as he looked back at him. "They said you had already passed their test. But you insisted on fighting that man with wooden swords, didn't you? Why?"

Oliver looked away. "He was an asshole. Did you hear about what he did to Leif? He nearly killed him right before that."

"So, you decided to teach him a lesson. How is that working out for you?" asked Will.

Oliver blinked. "Dad, I'm sorry! I didn't mean for that to happen! I feel like I want to throw up. Please! You don't know what it's like. The blood...!" Tears ran down his cheeks.

His father's expression darkened, and his voice came out in a low growl. "I know *exactly* what it's like, you fool! I've told you about some of the things I went through. I still remember the first man I beat to death, slowly, in the snow, just so I could take his clothes to keep from freezing to death. And now you, you will remember that moment for the rest of your life, however long that is. Right now, it doesn't look like you'll have much time for regret."

"Dad! Please, that's not what I wanted."

"I taught you to fight to keep you safe. Now I've got one more man's blood on my guilty conscience. If I could, I'd take your place, son, but I can't. You're a man now, at least in the eyes of the law. Doesn't matter what I think." His father stood up, then stared down at him. "You should have accepted your win when they said you passed. Better still, you never should have gone to the square and fought to begin with. You know what you can do—you shouldn't have had anything to prove. Even worse, if the magistrate knew what I've seen you do with just a practice sword, you wouldn't even have a case. I've *seen* how hard you can hit. It's lethal."

Oliver stared at the ground, but he looked up when he heard the rustle of cloth. His father was removing his shirt, then he turned around.

"Look at my back. Do you see the scars?"

Oliver had seen them before, but he'd never said anything. His father had always been careful to keep his shirt on. He'd assumed it was from embarrassment when he was little, and after learning some of the details about his father's past, he'd thought it might have been punishment for a crime. He'd never dared to ask about the long stripes that decorated Will's back. He nodded.

"Do you see them?" hissed Will.

"Yes," said Olly softly.

"Let them be a lesson. I kept these scars so I wouldn't forget. I took the lash so someone else wouldn't." He pulled the shirt back on and turned back around. "I *could* have fought. I *could* have taught them a lesson instead of taking the whip, but I didn't. Do you know why?"

Oliver shook his head.

His father's answer emerged from his throat like a curse. "Because a *whipping* wouldn't kill me, but if I'd fought, a lot more people would have died. The soldiers trying to arrest me hadn't done anything wrong, but I would have killed a lot of them. The woman who I was trying to protect probably would have died as well, or at the very least her family would have been punished for my resistance. The *point*, if you're listening, is that fighting is never a decision to take lightly. You don't do it unless the cost of not fighting is greater than your life, or the life of whoever you're trying to protect. You *don't* fight to prove a point, or teach people lessons!

"You chose that fight, and now a man is dead. Do you think he learned? Will he be nicer now?" Will stared at him through the bars. After a minute of silence, he sat down and put his hands in his face again. "I'm sorry, Olly. I know it's hard hearing this, and I know what your intentions were, but this is the real world. Actions have consequences."

"Are they really going to hang me?" asked Oliver finally.

Will sighed. "Probably. The whole damned town saw you make a fool out of that wardsman before you decided to drive a wooden stake through him like you thought he was a vampire or something."

"Does that really work on vampires?"

"No," said his father immediately.

Oliver seized on one last secret hope. "Dad, you won't—you won't let them hang me, right? If they decide to, you can…" He wiggled his fingers suggestively, trying to mimic a spell being cast.

"How powerful do you think I am, Olly?"

Oliver stared at the ground. "I don't know. I didn't think wizards could do much before, but you've scared me a few times. You can put people to sleep, or paralyze them. I know that. What if—"

"What if I put the guards to sleep? Then unlocked your cell? We'd have to walk out of here then. There's more guards outside. How many do you think I can handle?"

"Well, if we're together, I can help," said Oliver. He made a fist. "I bet I can take on a few."

"So, after I break you out, we'll fight our way through? They'll have weapons. How likely do you think it is that someone else will get killed? Pretty damn likely. Is your life worth some man not going home to his own family? What happens to his children, his wife? Think they'll understand? And then, when we get home, what do we tell your grandmother? Should we just pack a bag and run? She probably wouldn't be in trouble, but how is she going to live if we're on the run, wanted men?"

Oliver's face crumpled. "I wasn't thinking."

"No. You haven't been thinking at all today. Listen up, son. Even if a miracle happened and they decided to let you go free this minute—this isn't over. That man you killed? He probably has relatives, and they'll never forget your name. Trust me, I know. I was nearly assassinated, *twice,* once by a widow mourning her husband, and another time by the parents of a dead boy. People carry grudges for a long time when someone they care about is killed."

"Even the wardsmen who were with him didn't like him," said Oliver.

"So?" Will glared through the bars. "Everyone has a mother. I've known some evil bastards in my time, and even the worst of them had *someone* who wanted to even the score when they died. Stop making excuses or trying to rationalize your way out of this."

Frustrated, Oliver threw his arms wide. "What do you want me to do?"

"Learn," said his father. "Don't try to justify what you did. Take responsibility. You can argue when you face the magistrate, but don't make excuses to yourself. You've killed a man. That means something. Learn that, so that if you're lucky enough to get through to the other side of this, you don't make the same mistake again. You said you feel bad. You should. Focus on that feeling so you never forget."

"I won't, Dad. I can still feel it, when the wood went through him. But I don't know how to get past it."

Will's expression softened, and he reached through the bars to take his son's hand. He held it for a moment, squeezing gently. "You don't get past it. You learn to live with it. I never wanted this for you, and seeing it breaks my heart."

Oliver looked up and saw something that broke his heart. Tears were running down his father's cheeks. "Dad, I'm sorry."

"I love you, Olly. No matter what happens, I'll always love you. Don't forget that." Will pulled his hand back and turned toward the door.

Oliver watched him go, unable to respond, despair gripping his heart. It felt like the end of the world when the door closed. "I love you too, Dad," he said softly.

***

Erisa was waiting when Will came through the door. "Well? Did you get him out? Surely, it's just a mistake. Olly wouldn't hurt a fly. I know he didn't do it on purpose."

Will's look was dark when he met her eye. "He didn't start out trying to kill someone, but he did it anyway."

"What? No! Why? There had to be a reason!" she protested.

He nodded. "He was too stubborn to take a beating. He wanted to win so bad he wouldn't let himself lose. I'm sure the fellow was an asshole, of that I have no doubt, but it was Olly's bad judgment that got the jackass killed."

"William, you're scaring me. What's going to happen?"

He sighed. "They'll want him to hang."

His mother stiffened. "You're not going to let that happen. Tell me what you're thinking?"

"About where we're going to live after this! We won't be able to stay in Trendham. That leaves what? Faresh? Barsta? How do you feel about the desert? Or what about barbarians? We can't go back to Terabinia. Do you fancy Shimera? Things are a mess there since I killed off the main demons they worshipped." He walked over to a cabinet and pulled out a bottle. "For tonight, I'm going to have a cup of wine and mull over our options."

His mother nodded. "I just needed to hear you say it. I don't care if we have to move, but I'm not losing my only grandson. When will you—?"

"I'm not doing anything until they give a verdict, and that's probably a few days away, maybe a week."

"You're going to leave him in there for a week?" she asked, visibly upset.

"He killed a man! At the very least he should reflect on what he's done!"

His mother glared at him. "And you haven't done as much yourself?"

Will sighed. He didn't have the energy left to be angry. "The first one is the worst. He needs time to understand, to let it sink in. If I just go in there and burn the place down, he won't learn a thing."

"What if they don't sentence him to hang?" she asked after a minute.

"I don't think that's likely."

She shook her head. "He's young, and Douglas told me that some of the people watching thought he was just defending himself. The magistrate will hear their opinions. What if he chooses a lesser sentence?"

"Like prison?"

She nodded.

Will shrugged. "Even better. I'll have more time to decide when and how I'll get him out. It might do him good to have a month or two to rethink his choices, anyway."

"William!"

He refused to engage after that, and once the wine had taken the edge off his anxiety, he started making plans. He wasn't pleased about any of it, though. He couldn't move his workshop—it was far too big—but he wouldn't be able to teleport to it if they moved half-way around the world. Making a beacon that would allow that wasn't feasible without a lot more time and resources. *I've spent so much time carving it out and building everything,* he thought sourly.

And then there were his other projects: the school, the hospital. How would he continue those? Could he? Sammy could probably help, but he didn't want to ask. And what about Sammy? She wouldn't move. She'd already made a new life in Trendham.

Another thought kept cropping up, despite his efforts to push it aside. It shouldn't matter, but it did. *How will Cora find me if we move again?*

CHAPTER 44

Five days passed, and during that time Oliver saw more people than he expected, though most of them were drunks being locked up until they were sober. His grandmother visited on four occasions, but she invariably cried, and that made him feel even worse. She did tell him things would get better, but she made no mention of how, and he got the feeling it was simply something she said because she couldn't accept the alternative.

There was no breakfast and no supper. The jail served one meal near lunchtime, and it was nothing to brag about. Usually, it wasn't more than thin broth, half a loaf of hard bread, and a wedge of cheese. Meat wasn't served at all.

He was told not to expect to go before the magistrate until Tuesday, but Sunday evening, two guards came to his cell, accompanied by a wardsman that he recognized, Sean. Clearly, they weren't taking any chances after seeing him fight in the town square.

"Hold your wrists out toward me," said one of the guards. Oliver did as he was told, and shackles were put on him. Then they opened the door. "Out."

"Where are we going?" he asked as he stepped out. The sun was already setting, so he couldn't imagine what was happening so late in the day.

"Shut it," said the older guard.

He didn't push his luck, and a few minutes later, he found himself standing at the front desk, where he'd initially had to give his name and surrender some of his belongings. The man sitting behind it pulled out a pair of boots and set them in front of him, followed by his belt, pouch, and a small knife. "These yours?"

He nodded. "Looks like it."

The man pushed a piece of paper toward him. "Sign here."

He signed, feeling awkward with the shackles on his wrists, and then Sean instructed him to put his footwear back on. "Are we going somewhere?" asked Oliver.

One of the guards glanced warily at the wardsman, then answered, "You're a lucky bastard. Magistrate sent word your charges have been dismissed."

Oliver blinked. "What? Dismissed? So, I'm free?"

Sean gave him a nasty smile. "Free as far as they're concerned. You belong to Lloyd Blathe now."

"Huh? But I haven't been tried."

Everyone laughed. "No charges, no trial," said the wardsman. "You have a problem with that?"

Oliver held up his wrists. "I'm still in shackles."

Sean looked at the guards. "I've got it from here. You've done your part." Once they were gone, he held up a key. "You belong to Mister Blathe now."

Oliver frowned. "What does that mean? Am I a candidate?"

"You're whatever he decides you are. At the moment, you're property."

"Are you saying I'm indentured? I haven't signed anything." Slavery was illegal in Trendham, but being indentured was nearly the same thing.

The wardsman chuckled again. "Don't try my patience, boy. You're only sixteen, remember?"

Oliver's mind was racing. If he was being taken as an indentured servant, someone would have had to sign the contract. Only one person had the legal authority to do that. "My dad?"

Sean nodded. "You're not as stupid as you look. Dear Daddy signed you over to Mister Blathe, so you're not his problem anymore."

Shocked, Oliver stared at the wardsman for several seconds. "He wouldn't do that."

The other man pulled out a leather bundle and unwrapped it. Within was a heavy sheet of parchment covered in official-looking language. At the bottom of the page were three signatures. One belonged to the magistrate, one was that of Blathe's legal representative, and the third was signed 'Kelvin Wiltshire.' Oliver recognized his father's handwriting.

The wardsman grinned at him. "Until we get to Bondgrad, your ass belongs to me." He motioned for Oliver to stand, then led him outside, where a black carriage waited on them. "Get in."

Glancing around, the streets were nearly empty, and Oliver saw no one he knew. *They can't just take me away at night, can they? I haven't said goodbye to anyone.* His mouth opened, and he could only ask, "Why?"

"If your choice was between seeing your kid hanged or sold, which would you choose?" said Sean. He didn't wait for an answer, though. "You've got about two seconds to get in that carriage before I see how much you like getting a shot to the kidneys."

There was nothing wrong with his brain. Oliver climbed the short steps and got in the carriage. Sean sat opposite him and promptly fell asleep, so he held his questions. The carriage rolled on through the night, and somewhere in the middle of it, Sean woke up again. Finally, Oliver asked, "Why am I still in shackles?"

"So, you don't try to escape."

"I wanted to be a wardsman to begin with. Why would I escape?"

His captor laughed. "You think you're going to the House of Ink to be trained?" Suddenly uncertain, Oliver nodded. The wardsman laughed louder. "You're going to Mister Blathe's copper mine, near Dulence."

"But—"

"Shut up," snapped the wardsman. "You cost Mister Blathe a valuable asset when you killed Gavin. Dumbfuck though he was, it still costs a pretty penny to train and ink one of us. Executing you serves no one, but my employer is a smart man. He'll have you work the mine until you've repaid him what he lost, plus the money he spent bribing the magistrate to get you turned loose."

Oliver gaped at the man. "How long will that take?"

"Ten years? I doubt you'll live long enough to find out." Then the wardsman kicked him in the chest. Oliver saw it coming, and he might have tried to dodge, or at least lessen the blow, but that would only enrage the wardsman. Sean's boot caught him square in the sternum, painfully driving the wind from his chest. "That's for talking again after I told you to shut up. You can ask questions when you meet the mine boss. He loves to talk to promising young men like yourself."

***

The foreman at Blathe's copper mine was named Tulley, but he did not, in fact, enjoy talking. The only communication Oliver saw the man engage in involved yelling, and it was purely one way. Any response, any question, anything but immediate obedience was answered with pain, swift and certain.

He was quartered in one of five stone bunkhouses built near the entrance to the mine. The mine itself was in a sunken rocky depression that served as a very effective wall around the perimeter. A stone-paved road led up and out, but there were guards and two wardsmen standing watch at the gate at all times.

Planning an escape would have required free time, though, and Oliver had precious little of that. Each man had an iron shackle welded around his right ankle with a ring attached. At night, a chain was passed through the ring, connecting each worker to five others in a row. The ends were locked to rings in the floor at either end of each row of beds. Oliver only had enough slack to climb into bed.

Bathroom breaks were at dawn, and if anyone couldn't hold it until then, they were punished. Oliver's first week was miserable due to that, but his body quickly adapted to the schedule. During the day, he was chained to the man who slept in the bunk on his right. His partner was named Clarence, but he wasn't given to talking.

Throughout the daylight hours, they used shovels to load the gravel-like ore that other men chopped out into iron mine carts. When the cart was filled, they pushed it up and out to be unloaded. Then they went back down and repeated it all over again. It was simple labor, and Oliver would have thought nothing of it, but after the first day, his hands were a mass of painful blisters.

The foreman had expected that though, and he was given linen strips to wrap his hands in until they healed. That was the only mercy he received, and the healing was slow, because he was still expected to work.

At first, he held out hope. *Dad will find me. He'll get me out.* It seemed obvious to him that his father had gone along with selling him to save his life, but there was no way he'd leave his son to rot in chains. By the end of the second week, his calluses had come in, and his hope had started to die.

Despair was a sad trade for it.

The only bright spot in all of it was the food. Apparently, Lloyd Blathe believed in feeding his servants well. Or as Clarence put it, "Starving men do shitty work. Cheaper to feed us than replace us." They were served two meals a day, a modest breakfast and a large supper that always included meat, bread, and copious amounts of vegetables. The cooking was nowhere near as good as he was used to, but Oliver ate everything he was given, and if anyone had leftovers, he would eat those as well. Surprisingly, it wasn't uncommon for those sitting with him to offer him extras.

He was the biggest man in the mining camp, and while no one went out of their way to befriend him, neither did they give him any trouble. That was quite contrary to what he'd expected, but Clarence had explained it well, "Mister Blathe doesn't suffer damage to his property. If someone can't work, he doesn't make money. If you're the reason someone else can't work, you're gone. Anyone that fights doesn't last long."

"Gone?"

His partner had run a finger along his throat to illustrate the point. Oliver hadn't asked him for any clarification beyond that.

After the first month passed, Oliver had given up hope completely. He followed the routine and he tried not to think, for thinking only led to regret and pain. Some nights, he would open his eyes and see something staring in through the bunkhouse window above his bed. It had frightened him at first, until he recognized it as an owl. After that, he looked forward to seeing its large, golden eyes looking in. It was the most interesting thing that was likely to happen to him on any given day.

It wasn't until the start of the fifth week that things changed. It was midafternoon when the foreman came down and unchained him from Clarence. "Come with me."

He knew better than to ask why. Oliver followed, glancing back once as a silent goodbye to his partner, who would have to continue working alone. When they emerged into the sun, he stood blinking, then saw three men waiting for them. Two were wardsmen, as evidenced by the tattoos that were visible on their hands and necks. The third was probably the most finely dressed man that Oliver had ever seen. The gentleman wore a fine white linen shirt that was topped by an embroidered coat. His trousers were perfectly tailored, and he wore shiny black riding boots that came almost to his knees. A riding crop was in his hands. "Is this him?" asked the gentleman, pointing at Oliver with the riding crop.

The wardsman who answered was Sean, and he was the only one of the three that Oliver recognized. "Yes, sir, Mister Blathe."

The man rubbed his chin. "He's big, but too big. He'll be slow."

"Trust me, sir, he isn't."

"You really think he's a granling?"

Sean nodded. "Yes, sir. I'd swear to it."

"Show me."

The senior wardsman met Oliver's gaze and motioned for the others to clear a space. "Try to knock me down, kid."

Oliver rolled his shoulders to stretch them out. "I'm not in the best shape right now."

"A fight never comes when you're ready for it. If you want out of here, show them how fast you are," said the older wardsman.

Oliver took one step, then ducked and backed away just as rapidly, narrowly avoiding the foot his opponent had aimed at his head. That was new to him. He'd learned basic front kicks, mainly to the body or knees of an enemy, but the high-arching sweeping side kick was entirely unknown to him. He'd avoided being laid flat by just a hair, and his eyes widened at the realization. *How is it possible to kick like that?*

He didn't know, and now wasn't the time to attempt it. He moved in again, ready this time. Oliver's elbows were tucked in and his forearms ready to guard his head. Against most foes he would keep them lower, to guard his body better. Headshots were dangerous, so most avoided them, but he knew the wardsman could reinforce his body, making the attack less risky. He kept his own hands open to increase his options.

"Come on, boy! Don't pussyfoot around!" said Sean, prodding him to attack.

Oliver took a step, starting a jab, but the other man had chosen the exact same instant to come forward as well, aiming a fist at Oliver's jaw—and his belly. He'd already started moving to slap the headshot aside with one hand when he realized Sean's left was also heading for his midsection. It was a sneaky attack, and the wardsman moved with a speed unlike anything he'd seen before, even from his prior fight with Gavin.

Oliver bent slightly, while simultaneously rotating to the right, pivoting above his forward leg, causing the body blow to miss. If he'd understood what the wardsman would try, he could have capitalized on the moment, but as fast as Oliver's reactions were, he wasn't balanced well enough to take good advantage, though he did manage to shove the wardsman's shoulder as they passed. A half-second later, he'd centered his weight and was racing to attack the wardsman as he turned back to face him.

He had the initiative now, so he used it, pressing his own attacks. Oliver gave it his all, moving so quickly it made his bones ache. He kept his hands open, though, using palm strikes even when he aimed at the body, but despite his superior speed, he couldn't quite land a hit. The older man was as cunning as a fox and slipperier than an eel. He slipped each blow and dodged when he couldn't, as though he knew where Oliver would aim before he even moved.

Ankle hooks failed as well, but Oliver kept up the pressure, his arms snapping forward with lightning speed as he forced the other man to continue backing up. The moment he let up, the wardsman would start counterattacking, and from what he'd seen already, Oliver wasn't sure he had enough experience to avoid them.

He's breathing hard, thought Oliver. *If he slows at all, I have him.*

Then it happened. The wardsman reacted too slowly, and Oliver's latest body punch went through. Oliver was still using a palm strike, but he put everything he had into it. As he'd expected, his blow landed against what felt like granite. Pain shot up his arm, and a loud crack rang out. Then the world went black.

Oliver woke, but his eyes were still closed. He was in bed, chained up as always. *That dream was so real.* Then he realized that the world was orange, as though the sun was on his face, but that didn't make sense if he was sleeping in the bunkhouse.

"—never seen the Viper pushed so hard. He was practically being chased around the yard," said a voice nearby.

"Don't let him hear you say that or you'll be the one being chased," said another man's voice.

"You weren't there, Glenn! The kid was moving like he was using ink, faster really," said the first voice.

"Didn't keep him from being knocked the fuck out, though, did it?"

"He cracked Viper's ribs!"

"No fucking way. He wasn't using his ink then," argued Glenn.

"He was," protested the first man. "The kid hit him with an open palm. Sounded like someone breaking a tree branch when it landed. Viper's fist landed a second later and dropped the kid, but he couldn't breathe after that. Blathe had him loaded into the carriage before leaving the kid with us."

"Hmm. Well, I guess that explains why his arm is swollen."

Gradually, Oliver realized he was moving, or rather, he was being moved. The surface he was lying on was bumping and shifting under him. Opening his eyes, he squinted at the sun, then turned his head to one side. He appeared to be in the bed of a wagon.

"He's awake," said the voice belonging to Glenn. Oliver saw now that the wardsman appeared to be a forty-something without much hair and the beginnings of a large belly. Tattoos were visible on his neck, peeking out from beneath the collar of his tunic. The other man was in the driver's seat, and seemed to be younger, though he also had tattoos.

Oliver tried to sit up, but the world was swimming around him, and a wave of nausea washed over him. His left arm was throbbing from the elbow down. "Where are we?" he asked.

"On our way to Bondgrad!" said the driver cheerfully.

Glenn's reply was more muted. "We're taking you to the House of Ink."

"Why?"

"Probably because Mister Blathe decided you're worth more to him with tats than busting rocks in a mine," said the driver helpfully.

"Shut up, Sid," barked Glenn, who was apparently the senior wardsman. "Last thing I need you doing is speaking for our employer."

"It's true," responded Sid.

"Says you, but if it gets back to Blathe and he doesn't agree with your assumptions, it'll be both our asses," growled Glenn.

Sid sighed. "You're such a buzzkill, Glenn. Fine." He leaned back to look at Oliver, then asked, "Are you really a granling?"

Oliver replied honestly, "I don't know what that is."

"A kinasheet genius," clarified the driver.

"A what?" asked Oliver.

Glenn coughed. "The word is kinesthete, Sid. Do I need to spell it for you?"

"I was sounding it out so the kid would understand," lied the driver.

"No you weren't, cuz that's not how it's said," argued Glenn. Then he turned to Oliver. "A kinesthete, sometimes called a kinetic genius, or if you're into the old lore, a granling, is someone with a natural gift for movement, or combat."

"It means you're fast," offered Sid.

"Shut up, Sid," ordered Glenn. "I was talking." He refocused on Oliver. "Fast, graceful, strong—basically a natural athlete."

"Oh," said Oliver. "I've always been quick, if that's what you're saying."

"It's more than just quick. It's the kind of speed only a wardsman or a monster could hope to possess. At the House of Ink, there are masters who are that fast, but they train for years and years to achieve it," explained Glenn.

"Master wardsmen?" asked Oliver.

"Trainers. Wardsmen like us don't live that long, usually."

"Fight hard, die young!" snapped Sid, lifting his fist in the air with a grin.

Oliver frowned. "The trainers at the House of Ink aren't wardsmen?"

"Some are, like Daikor Sean, the man you fought earlier, but the *master* trainers are un-inked. Usually retired military who didn't want to go back to civilian life and had a talent for fighting."

Oliver frowned. "You're saying ordinary people train wardsmen? Can they beat them in a fight?"

Glenn sighed. "You're getting the wrong idea. Generally, no, they couldn't win a fight against one of us, but if you give a master his chosen weapon and fight on his terms, it's possible. Think of a sword master, like Master Thun. He's almost fifty, but he's trained with blades his entire career and he moves like he's got ink on him. He doesn't have the rest of our advantages, but if you put a sword in his hands and fight without armor, he's good enough he might gut one of us. When you get to the House of Ink, remember to show respect to anyone they introduce you to as a 'master.'"

"So what's a, die core, or whatever you called Sean?"

"Daikor," corrected Glenn. "It's one of the ranks we use. Wardsmen don't slot into the military hierarchy. We have our own ranks. Most, like Sid and me, are Enrads. We completed our training and got inked, but that's all. The really good ones get promoted to Gavel, and if you live long enough you might be lucky enough to reach Daikor like the Viper."

"He means Sean, the one you fought," supplied Sid. "He's been around a long time. Practically a living legend, since he's as quick as a viper."

"Shut up, Sid," snapped Glenn reflexively.

"How old is he?" asked Oliver.

"Ancient," replied Sid, ignoring his partner's command. "He's pushing thirty-nine."

"Thirty-seven," said Glenn. "Also, shut up, Sid. I'm tired of correcting your mistakes."

"You must've woke up on the wrong end of a whore today, ya grumpy ass," replied Sid.

"Wrong end of what?" asked Oliver.

"A whore," repeated Sid. "It means he woke up with his dick in her stink hole instead of—"

"Damn it, Sid! Shut the fuck up. I'm tired of listening to your stupid shit," swore Glenn.

Sid pulled at the reins, causing the mule pulling the wagon to slow. "Holy Mother! Did you see that owl? Look!" He pointed toward a tree on the right side of the road. "It's fucking huge."

Oliver was still supine, and consequently unable to see over the side of the wagon, but Glenn turned his head. "I don't see anything."

"It flew the second I looked at it," said Sid. "Biggest damn owl I ever saw."

"Probably just a vulture, knowing how stupid your pox-ridden brain is," replied Glenn. "Get moving. We're not paid to sight-see."

Oliver made another attempt at sitting up, and this time he succeeded, although his stomach still turned over and he fought to keep from vomiting. Then he noticed that the iron shackle had been removed from his ankle. He pointed to it. "Does this mean I'm free?"

Glenn started laughing, and a second later Sid joined in. "Ain't none of us free, boy. But with some luck you'll be a wardsman."

"Fight hard, die young," repeated Sid. "Freedom is overrated. We ain't gotta worry about gettin' old. Wardsmen live fast and die young, but while we're here we eat the best and fuck as much as we want."

That wasn't exactly how Oliver had envisioned life as a wardsman, but it didn't sound terrible. He glanced at Glenn to see what the wiser of the two thought of his companion's words. For once, the man didn't tell Sid to shut up. Instead, he grinned. "It ain't all bad. Sid's right there. Live long enough to get your ink and you'll be up to your nose in pussy and pie."

"Or stinkholes if you're like Glenn here," added Sid.

"Shut up, Sid."

CHAPTER 45

The House of Ink wasn't so much a house as a complex of buildings that occupied an entire city block within the city of Bondgrad. There were entrances on all four sides, but only the main one was open to the public. The others were locked and used only by those who worked there. The largest building faced all four streets, forming a walled stone box that enclosed the entire block. Oliver heard someone else describe it as an 'enclave,' and the name did fit, for the House of Ink was like a small, self-contained city within the city. Inside the outer building were numerous smaller buildings, gardens, training areas, and storehouses.

The candidates were housed in small cells located within the outer building, with each man having a private cubicle that was barely large enough to hold a single bed and a tiny writing desk. That section was called a dormitory, but the size and spartan nature of the 'cells' reminded Oliver more of a prison. Ironically, he'd had more room living in the bunkhouse at the copper mine.

The instructors, administrators, cooks, servants, and other employees lived in other sections, and some of them doubtless had better quarters. Oliver had thought Sid and Glenn might live there as well, but they'd left soon after bringing him in. Wardsmen were the product of the House of Ink, not its residents, although a few apparently returned to teach if they'd lived long enough and hadn't had the decency to die of premature aging yet.

"Our days start at the first light of dawn. Dress and wash your face before then. You'll hear the bells ringing when it's time to come down for breakfast. The dining hall is close to the eastern yard. Just follow the others, they'll all be heading that way when the bell rings," his tour guide told him.

The man started to leave, but Oliver caught his sleeve. "Are you a candidate too?"

"Heavens no. I'm just a secretary. Good luck."

"I didn't catch your name," said Oliver, stopping him again.

The man frowned. "Franklin, but I doubt we'll meet again. It was just chance that I was on door duty today. I normally don't leave the offices much." He turned away and was gone.

Oliver went into his cell and sat down on the bed. He occupied himself for a few minutes by examining the contents of his room. The desk held little more than writing implements and a few sheets of paper. He thought that was somewhat unusual for a place where they were training warriors. But if there were to be any lessons regarding penmanship or numeracy, he was confident he was better prepared than most.

A small chest at the foot of the bed contained not just one, but four identical sets of clothing. It seemed like an excessive amount. Each set included loose trousers and a short-sleeved tunic. There was also a single heavy overtunic for cold days and multiple pairs of socks. Although the clothes were made to be baggy, when he tried on a set, he found them to fit close to his body. *I must be bigger than the average.*

A knock came at his door, and he opened it. An extremely fit and muscular youth stood in the hall, and Oliver guessed they were close to the same age. While Oliver was a head taller, the other teen wasn't lightly built, being close to six feet tall and probably around two hundred pounds of what was mainly muscle. Unsure what to say, Oliver merely waited.

The two of them stared at one another for an uncomfortable period of time that stretched from a few awkward seconds to more than a minute. The stranger didn't seem to blink, so Oliver matched his intensity, and the two young men continued to stare. After what seemed like five minutes, his visitor turned and walked away, having never said a word.

Mystified, Oliver closed his door. "That was weird."

Another knock came and he opened it again. The same youth stood in the entrance, grinning this time. "I'm Alex."

"Oliver," he replied.

"Alver?" said the other boy, mispronouncing his name the way the Trendish always did. "That's a strange name."

"I was born in Terabinia," explained Oliver.

"You sound normal."

"I grew up in Lystal."

Alex nodded. "Makes sense. Trema here." He pointed a thumb at his own chest.

"Do you like the sea?" asked Oliver. It was the first question that occurred to him, since Trema was a port town, and he hadn't really seen the ocean except once when he was little.

"Nah. The trees are short there and the salt makes everything metal rust and the water makes everything else rot. Inland is better."

Oliver nodded. "I've never heard anyone put it that way, but I can see your point."

"Most people feel the opposite," said Alex with a shrug, "but they're probably dumb."

"Are you a candidate too?"

"Yep. I started a week before you. Headmaster Ving said I should show you around."

"That seems smart," said Oliver. "Now?"

"If you want. There's not much to do until morning." He looked Oliver up and down. "Your clothes are too small."

"I noticed," agreed Oliver.

"Bring them with you. I'll show you where to exchange them. There aren't many here your size, but I'm willing to bet they've got enough on hand so that you don't immediately rip them."

Oliver rolled his shoulders, then swung his arms. "I don't think they'll rip."

A hand blurred toward his face, and Oliver ducked sideways, then took a step back, bringing up his hands in a defensive posture. He waited to see if Alex would attack again, but the other boy didn't move, instead remarking, "You're quick."

He relaxed. "It seems like it."

"We spar in those clothes daily. They'll definitely rip. Come on." Alex turned and started off down the hall.

Oliver didn't quite know what to make of his new acquaintance. The other boy seemed friendly in an odd way, but he liked his way of communicating. Doug had always been full of words, too many words. Alex didn't belabor the obvious and seemed to just say everything directly in a way that made sense.

After helping him exchange his clothing, Alex led him outside and took him on a tour of the buildings, pointing out the dining hall, practice areas, and the large yard where they would assemble after breakfast. Every day they lined up there for general assembly, and any announcements or general speeches would be given to them then. Ordinarily, they simply answered role call and went to see their assigned trainers, so it wouldn't take more than fifteen minutes.

Along the way, Alex introduced him to ten or so others, but Oliver wasn't sure he would remember their names the next day, and he quickly realized that the reason the other boy didn't introduce more people they passed was simply because he was new as well. Just learning the layout and location of all the important stuff was enough for his brain that day, anyway.

Eventually, Alex led him back to the dormitory and wished him goodnight, but before he left, he aimed a swift punch at Oliver's midsection. Alex was quick, but not like the wardsmen, so Oliver dodged easily. With a wave, a smile, and no explanation, the other boy went back to his own room.

The next morning, Oliver was impressed by the food. It still was a far cry from his father's cooking, but it was miles better than the food at the mine, and apparently the House of Ink also believed in feeding their candidates plenty of food. Judging by the muscles on even the skinniest of candidates, Oliver could understand why. Young men ate a lot, and these ate even more than most.

At assembly, everyone responded with 'present' when their name was called, and as expected, the man holding the roll sheet mispronounced his name. "Alver Wiltshire!" After he'd responded, the man glanced up. "See me after I dismiss everyone. I have your assignments."

He did as he was told, staring off into the distance while he waited. Idly, he studied the trees around the yard and noticed a large owl once again, sitting in the shadowy limbs of a large oak tree. He stared at it until the instructor called him again, handing him a short list of four names with a time beside each.

"Are you familiar with our bells?"

"They seem to ring a lot," Oliver observed with honesty.

"First bell is breakfast, second is general assembly. The third bell is at nine, that's when your first assignment is." He pointed at the first name on the sheet, which had the numeral nine written beside it.

"Trainer Long," recited Oliver.

"Fourth bell is at eleven." The man pointed at the second name. "Fifth is noon—you'll go back to the dining hall. Sixth bell is one o'clock." He pointed at the third name. "Then seventh is three, and that's your last assignment. The eighth bell is for supper. You won't want to miss that, as I'm sure you'll be very hungry by then."

"Thank you, sir," said Oliver with a nod. "I forgot your name."

"Singer. Instructor Singer."

"Oh." Singer was listed at eleven. "I'll see you at fourth bell then," said Oliver.

"Try to wash the sweat and dirt off before you come. My class will be the only quiet one you'll have." With that, Instructor Singer walked away.

Oliver felt satisfied with how things had gone so far, until he realized he had no idea where Trainer Long's class was, and everyone else seemed to have vanished while he talked to Instructor Singer. He raced along, asking everyone he passed and just managed to get there before the third bell rang.

As it turned out, his first 'class' was a sparring session. Long taught unarmed combat, which meant some wrestling, some boxing, and a lot more unorthodox maneuvers that wouldn't be allowed in any civilized sport. The young men were paired off with others roughly the same size and given basic instruction in wrestling before they were turned loose on one another. There were sixteen of them in the group, so the numbers worked out, but the closest one to Oliver's size was several inches short of him, and probably twenty pounds lighter. With his size and unusual strength, it wasn't much of a contest for Oliver.

The class with Instructor Singer turned out to be in basic penmanship and arithmetic. Many of the candidates couldn't read when they first arrived, and their math skills often didn't go beyond simple counting. After briefly examining Oliver's abilities, Singer told him he wouldn't be coming back the next day. "You know as much as we require. I'll have a replacement for you tomorrow morning."

At sixth bell, he reported to Trainer Brimley, who taught military formations, tactics, marching, and a good bit of history as well. "Some think this class should be held in a room with pen and paper, since a lot of it is strategy and tactics, but I prefer a hands-on approach. You'll get the history and other bits as we go, but the most important things for you to learn are the drills. Modern war relies on coordination and organization. To that end, you won't be much good on a battlefield if you don't understand how to march, what the formations are, and how they're used. Therefore, I intend to drill you as I would new recruits. Spears and shields are over there."

Their weapons were full size, but padded, and while Oliver thought he'd be bored at first, he soon learned that what his father had taught him didn't mean much without practical experience. Drilling and marching in unison was more difficult than he expected, and it was something he'd never been able to practice.

Seventh bell took him to his final class, with Trainer Martin. It turned out to be another combat class, this time focused on using staves. Again, they were paired up, and once again, Oliver was way ahead. The quarterstaff was the first weapon his father had ever practiced with him, and was probably the one his dad was best with. Even without his speed he would have been well ahead of the others.

Of more interest to him, after the class finished, he observed several of the other students launching surprise punches at one another. The attacks seemed to happen at random, during conversations, greetings, goodbyes—it didn't matter. If a blow landed, there was no retribution, though the one who failed to dodge usually groaned.

Oliver asked his sparring partner, a fellow named Gryn, as he was leaving. "Why do people keep trying to hit each other at random?"

Gryn immediately took a swing and missed, then he lived up to his name and grinned. "They should have told you when you came here." He reached into a small pouch at his waist and pulled out a small wooden token that was painted red. "If you tag someone, they have to give you one of their chits. Collect fifty and you can turn them in for a gold crown. You should have gotten five to start with when you arrived."

That was news to him. "No one told me. Who do I go to for the first five?"

"The bursar's office, next to the quartermaster."

"Thanks." Oliver knew where the quartermaster was, since Alex had taken him there to exchange his training clothes. Unfortunately, the bursar turned out to be much less helpful.

"Sorry, not falling for it," said the portly man. "Bring me fifty and I'll pay you, but I can't count the number of times someone says their chits were lost or stolen."

"That's not it," complained Oliver. "I never received any."

The man shrugged. "Not my problem."

He narrowed his eyes. "If I tag you, do I get one?" He jerked slightly as though he meant to swing at the man.

"No! Is that a threat?" The administrator seemed disturbed by the thought.

"No one explained the system to me either. It just seemed like a possibility," said Oliver with a malicious half-smile.

"Instructors and other staff are off-limits," said the bursar stiffly.

Oliver gave the man a look of extreme disappointment, which was entirely sincere, then left. On the way back to his cell, he came across Alex and gave the other teen a punch to the shoulder that sent him stumbling into the nearest wall.

Alex gave him a sour look, then fished out a red chit and handed it over. "They told you, eh?"

Oliver nodded, then asked, "You were supposed to explain it to me, weren't you?"

His new friend gave him a sly smile. "They never actually *told* me to tell you."

"How many do you have?"

"Three," said Alex with some embarrassment. "I got up to seven, but then a few of the others started tagging me every day. Once you know there's someone that you're better than, they can become a steady source of chits, so it turns into a hierarchy of sorts. The only way to avoid losing them all is to improve, or learn to avoid the ones who are good enough to tag you regularly."

"How many times can you score on the same person?"

"Once a day."

Oliver nodded. "I'd let you have this one back, but you didn't tell me until just now, so I'm keeping it."

Alex frowned. "I never asked you to give it back."

"I figured you might get sour, since you won't win any from me," said Oliver with a confident smile. He had a new goal in life.

CHAPTER 46

The next day he was assigned to the Small Blades class to replace Penmanship and Arithmetic, but again he found the material ridiculously simple compared to what he had already practiced. Even on the rare occasion that there was something new to learn, his superior reflexes made up for his inexperience.

Throughout the day, he approached every student he passed, and by eighth bell he'd amassed forty-seven chits. Every time he patted the fat little pouch at his waist, he smiled with satisfaction. The second day he did even better, collecting another forty-nine.

By the third day, other candidates began avoiding him, and on several occasions, he found himself in a footrace to catch fleeing targets. Fortunately, he was also an excellent runner. His size was a bit of a disadvantage, however, and some of the tall, lean candidates were more trouble than they were worth to chase down. Instead, Oliver took to ambushing those who were prone to running.

At the end of the week, he turned in two hundred chits and collected four gold crowns. It was more money than he'd ever seen before, and it made him wonder how much his debt to Mister Blathe was. Could he buy his way free, and if so, did he want to? He was getting what he'd always wanted, but the idea of owing the man money bothered him. *"Accept no debts,"* that was the motto his father had always drilled into him.

On the first day of the second week, he was switched to a different set of class assignments, Advanced Unarmed Combat, Long Blades, Improvised Weapons, and Archery. Archery was the only one that challenged him at all, though he did have some experience there. At the end of the second week, he was again moved into different classes, and now he was being matched against students who were on the final stretch before receiving their tattoos.

It was still too easy.

At the end of the first month, he was called to the office of Instructor Singer, who he then discovered was also the man in charge of organizing the training schedule for candidates in the pre-ink section. The older man leaned forward at his desk, lacing his fingers together. "What am I going to do with you, Alver?"

"Sir?"

"You don't fit in our training regimen very well. Who taught you before this?"

He hadn't thought about how to answer that before, but remembering his father's obsessive efforts to remain anonymous, he suddenly felt reluctant to answer, so he lied. "My granddad."

"Your granddad?"

He nodded.

"Was he a retired sergeant or a military instructor?"

Unwilling to push his luck, he went for ignorance. "He never told me. Said he didn't like to talk about his time in the army. He died a few years ago."

"I see," said Instructor Singer slowly. He stared at Oliver for several seconds, then sighed. "Well, in any case, I've no choice but to move you to Supervised Instruction."

He frowned. "It's all been supervised, hasn't it?"

"Yes. It's just what we call the final leg of the journey before you get your ink. You'll need to spend time with a personal trainer who can assess your individual strengths and weaknesses, then shore up the areas you might be lacking. I'm assigning you to Trainer Martin."

"Thank you, sir. How long will he be teaching me?"

"Until he decides you're ready for ink. Most of the time, once a candidate is put in Supervised Instruction, it's anywhere from a couple of months to a year, so congratulations. You've made your way through the early part of the program faster than anyone since the Viper."

He recognized the name. "Do you mean Daikor Sean?"

Singer lifted one brow. "You've met him?"

"Yes, sir. He picked me up from the mine."

The instructor nodded. "That makes sense. He was a granling like yourself."

"So he went through the early classes as quickly as I have?"

Singer smiled. "Don't tell anyone I said this, but no. However, you should bear in mind that he came to the House of Ink from the streets of Bondgrad. The only previous learning or instruction he had had came from the poor and homeless. Even so, it was remarkable to see how fast he mastered every form of physical training. If he hadn't been illiterate, he would have gotten through almost as quickly as you have."

He nodded. "I had no idea."

"If you repeat that to anyone, I'll call you a liar," said Singer with a serious expression, though he broke into a faint smirk a moment later. "He's a little sensitive about his past, so if you meet him again, I wouldn't mention it to him."

"Am I likely to meet him again?"

"Lloyd Blathe is your sponsor, so I would think so. Once you finish, you'll be entering Mister Blathe's employment. Sean will probably be your direct superior, but all that depends on Mister Blathe. I shouldn't offer assumptions."

***

Trainer Martin was a lean whipcord of a man without much fat on his frame. He was just under six feet tall and probably weighed no more than a hundred and sixty pounds, but he walked with a confident, graceful air about him. Given the fact that he had no tattoos, Oliver was surprised to discover the trainer was extremely quick. The man looked to be in his forties, yet he moved with a speed that Oliver could only match by pushing himself close to the limit, the point at which his bones and tendons would begin to thrum with pain.

After their first unarmed sparring session, he asked, "You don't have tattoos. Are you a granling?"

Martin rubbed his mustache, a habit the man had whenever he stood still for too long. "Because I'm so quick?"

Oliver nodded.

The trainer smiled briefly. "No. In my case, it's merely the product of a lifetime of effort."

"Oh."

"Did you think because you're special, no one could match you?"

Actually, yes, but Oliver shook his head no. "No, sir."

"Many people have talents, Mister Wiltshire. Some can add ridiculously large numbers in their heads with ease, some can remember anything they've ever read, and some, like yourself, have a natural talent that enables them to learn to move with perfect efficiency. The rest of us have to work for it, but that does not make us less. With focus and extreme discipline, many of the candidates here could emulate your speed someday."

After fighting wardsmen and candidates alike, Oliver had begun to question some of his previous assumptions. "Then why do they give them tattoos, if it makes them live shorter lives? Why not just train them to be like you?"

"I read your file when they told me you would be my student," said the trainer. "You fought the Viper, correct?"

"Yes, sir."

"And you struck him hard enough to crack his ribs."

"I'm not sure."

"You did," said Martin with absolute certainty. "If you had used your fist, what would have happened?"

"I knew not to."

"It was a body shot; most would use their fist."

Oliver sighed. "The wardsmen make themselves really hard. I'm guessing it's from their tattoos."

"Exactly. If he hadn't, you would have ruptured his liver as well, probably killing him. It's called an iron-body transformation, and it is one of the most used abilities that wardsmen possess."

"So they get the tattoos just for that?" asked Oliver.

The trainer chuckled. "Not at all. The main reason is that it takes ten years or longer for someone to master their body as I have, and I still don't quite match your gifts. For example, if you're truly a granling, you likely have the ability to increase your endurance and strength as well. I can make myself somewhat stronger, but I doubt it would be close to what you can. The point, though, is that no one has the time or money to spend keeping a stable of martial artists who do nothing but train for decades at a time. Not to mention the fact that the results are variable. Some men train for years and still never reach the peak of human capability. There's a lot of variability in human potential. You were lucky enough to be born with what seems to be an extreme amount of potential and talent."

"So the tattoos are just a shortcut, is that what you mean?"

Martin nodded. "Yes, mostly, but they grant other useful abilities. Not only do wardsmen have extreme speed, strength and endurance, but they can climb like spiders, and see in the dark. The iron-body transformation is probably one of the most useful combat abilities they gain, however, and it isn't just defensive."

Oliver stared back in confusion. "It isn't?"

"If you had had it when you fought the Viper, you could have used your fist instead of your palm, and against someone without it, you could have used your fingers as though they were spears."

He shuddered as he remembered the feeling of a wooden practice sword sliding into Gavin's body, followed partway in by his hand.

Martin nodded. "Now you see. Not only that, the iron-body transformation is enough to prevent most cuts, and though an arrow will sometimes penetrate your skin, it won't go in deeply."

"Do you wish you had the tattoos?"

"No. I have a family. That wouldn't have been possible for me otherwise."

"The tattoos make them sterile?"

The trainer laughed. "No, in fact they leave a lot of bastards behind, but most wardsmen don't live long enough to raise children."

"Could I be a trainer, like you?" asked Oliver.

Martin shook his head sadly. "Your sponsor wouldn't agree to that. Far fewer trainers are needed than wardsmen, and as a granling, you are too valuable to waste. You'll last longer than the usual wardsman."

His father had told him that, but mainly because he had finished the first compression. As far as Oliver knew, no one here knew anything about that, or wizards in general. "Why?"

"Granlings always do. Since your abilities are natural, it doesn't age you the same way tattoo magic does. So only the iron-body, climbing, and night-vision magics will accelerate your age. That's why the Viper is so much older than the other wardsmen you've met."

Oliver remembered something Glenn had told him. "He's thirty-seven, right?"

"Late thirties, I think, but I don't know his exact age," said the trainer. "Most wardsmen are lucky to get past their twenties." He stood up. "Enough talk. Time to get back to work."

Days passed and turned into weeks as Trainer Martin took him through a variety of weapons and combat styles, and for the first time, Oliver felt as though he was actually learning something. There was still a feeling of hesitancy, though, and after a month was done, Martin took him aside for another chat.

"This is as much as I can do."

Oliver had enjoyed their time, and he knew he had much more to learn, so he protested, "No, I've learned so much, but there's—"

The trainer lifted a hand and Oliver fell silent. "I know, but it isn't safe for me to teach you more."

"Why not?"

"I need the iron-body tattoo to safely train you at the speed and intensity you need, and you need it in order to safely be trained. In other words, I'm recommending you receive your tattoos. After that, you'll be given a new trainer, a wardsman, who can continue your education with less risk of serious injury or death."

Excited as he was to hear the news, Oliver disagreed with the reason. "I wouldn't hurt you, sir."

"Not on purpose, candidate." Standing up, Martin held out his hand. "You'll do well. It's been a pleasure, Mister Wiltshire."

And with that friendly dismissal, Oliver was left to his own devices. He wandered back to his cell, unsure what to do. He still had most of the day left to him. On the way, he saw Alex.

"Hey!" said the other youth.

Oliver gave him a dull look and a wave.

"What's wrong?"

"Nothing. I was just told I'm getting ink," he answered.

"Wow! That's great! Must be the fastest anyone's ever managed it," said Alex enthusiastically. Then he grinned. "I know a lot of people will be glad to see you go."

"Why?"

His friend held up a red chit. "Now maybe some of us can collect more than a few of these without you taking them away."

"I'm not leaving, just getting tattooed."

"Yeah, but after that you won't be part of the game. Maybe they have something similar among the newly inked trainees? You should ask, or maybe they'll tell you afterward. I guess that's what the teachers are for, anyway, right?"

"You're rambling," said Oliver.

Alex seemed uncomfortable, and he shifted from one foot to the other, as though his bladder was overfull. "I'll miss you," he blurted out, then gave Oliver a rough hug. "Don't tell anyone."

"Umm, sure," he answered, unsure why anyone would be embarrassed by a hug. Then again, since he'd come to the House of Ink, he'd never seen any contact between the candidates that didn't involve attempting hit the other person. Maybe it wasn't customary.

CHAPTER 47

The next morning, after breakfast, Oliver waited in his room. No one had told him what to do, and he no longer had a schedule. A knock came at the door, and when he opened it, he found a face there that he vaguely recognized. "Franklin?" It was the young man who had first escorted him to his room the day he arrived.

"You remembered," said the young man.

"You said I wouldn't see you again," said Oliver.

"I guess I was wrong. Are you ready?" After he nodded, Franklin continued, "Follow me."

He did, and Franklin led him across the entire breadth of the House of Ink, through the yards and gardens, until they reached the opposite side. On the way, he spotted the owl again, watching him from a tree, but he said nothing. They entered the stone building through a set of double doors and then went down a set of stairs into a lower level. They entered a long hallway and followed it, passing doors on either side, but they passed no one else. The area seemed empty of people.

An iron-bound oak door waited at the end of the hall. "Here we are," announced his guide. Then he unfolded a small sheet of paper and consulted it, before saying, "Inside your flesh will be forged anew and your skin will bear witness to your new life. When you leave, you will be a wardsman. Fight hard."

"Die young," responded Oliver automatically. It was a phrase he'd heard often during his time at the House of Ink, and although he hoped to live much longer, he couldn't help but admire the passion that filled their motto.

The door opened, and he stepped inside. Four men stood there, naked but for loincloths, their bodies covered with the tattoos Oliver had seen dozens of times before. They pointed to a place in their midst, and once Oliver was there, they began removing his clothes. "Bathed and washed, you will be reborn in ink," they chanted.

Naked, he was taken to a steaming tub and bathed. Through it all he did nothing, as the men pushed him under, then scrubbed him from head to toe, including places he would rather no one else touched. His heart sped up at those points, but he managed to avoid embarrassing himself.

Once he was dry, he was taken to another chamber and told to lie on a stone bier. Then the wardsmen moved to stand at the four corners of the room. Seconds later, an old man entered, followed by two assistants carrying a variety of equipment and tools that Oliver had never seen before.

"Hail Hengist, master of ink and blood," announced the wardsmen.

The old man nodded, then looked down on Oliver. "You will be with me the rest of the day and into the night. As I work, you will feel pain, some of it mild, and some intense, depending on the region. You will remain silent and observe through it all. Do you understand?"

"Yes, Master Hengist."

"Very well, then we shall begin." The ink master nodded to his assistants. "Strap him down."

Oliver hadn't expected that, but he held still as they brought out heavy leather straps and wrapped them around his wrists and ankles, securing them to iron rings located at the base of the stone bier. One of them lit some incense while the other laid out a series of bowls and basins. Pigments and oils were mixed, and Hengist sharpened a metal tool while Oliver watched.

The old man seemed set to begin when a new figure appeared in the room. The wardsmen reacted in surprise, but then sank to the floor like puppets with broken strings.

Oliver stared at the stranger, a young man in his late twenties with dark hair and a heavy but well-disciplined moustache. The ink master was the first to speak, "How did you get in here? Who are you?"

"My name is Doctor Lorentz, and we are here to assist you with the procedure."

"What have you done to the guards?" demanded Hengist.

"Nothing," said a slightly deeper voice, one that Oliver recognized. *Dad?* But his father was nowhere to be seen. "They're merely sleeping."

Doctor Lorentz nodded, and as Oliver followed the direction of his eyes he realized someone else was standing beside him, though he couldn't quite make his eyes focus on the other man. Lorentz spoke next. "He will need to be asleep for this." Then he lifted his hand in Oliver's direction. Something strange passed through Oliver, but nothing happened. "It's not working," said Lorentz with a note of consternation.

"He's completed the first compression, like yourself. It will take a stronger will," said the deeper voice. "I'll take care of it."

"I don't care who you think you are, you can't be here!" complained Hengist, but his voice cut off immediately after.

Oliver desperately tried to focus on the face of the other man, but his eyes didn't want to cooperate. He felt something connect inside, and then the world started to go dark. As his consciousness faded, Oliver heard the other man's voice coming to him, as if through a tunnel. "Pay attention, Hengist. Mister Blathe wants this one done differently. Today you will assist Doctor Lorentz and myself."

"Blathe doesn't dictate what goes—" Again the ink master's voice cut off without warning.

"You may speak when I allow it. Your compliance with my instruction is mandatory. I'll compel you, if necessary," said the deeper voice.

Lorentz spoke next, his voice fading into the distance. "We'll need to open him up first."

***

Oliver had to pee, badly. Opening his eyes, he saw that he was lying in bed, back in his cell. Or had he even left? *Was it a dream?* He started to move and felt a strange sensation across his body. He looked down and examined himself. His chest was covered with arcane symbols, and lines traced up and down his arms and legs, with more runes at every joint along the way. He recognized the tattoos, and a feeling of excitement welled up inside him.

"I'm a wardsman now," he said softly. *But what was that dream? Was it real?* Hengist had said he would be awake throughout the procedure, but the only thing he remembered was the arrival of two strangers. Had they put him to sleep?

Standing up, Oliver looked himself over more thoroughly. Even his groin had been tattooed. *Glad I missed that.* He touched himself carefully, expecting pain, but there was none. "It should hurt," he muttered. "The skin should be red and sore around the tattoos."

It wasn't, though. Although everything was sharp and precise, it looked as if it had been done weeks ago. On his writing desk, he spotted a jar and a note. Inside the jar was a pungent-smelling salve. He read the note:

> *Apply this ointment each morning and before bed. Apply extra if you bathe and your tattoos should heal within a week. Do not attempt to use your new abilities until instructed.*
>
> *~Hengist*

"They're already healed," muttered Oliver. "Shouldn't you know that?" *What happened to me?*

A knock came at the door, and he opened it. One of the first wardsmen he had met stood there, Daikor Sean. Oliver dipped his head in respect. "Daikor."

The other man smiled. "You've learned respect since we last met." He stepped inside, and it was then that Oliver realized he was still naked. He started to look for some trousers, but his superior ordered him to stop. "Let me look at you."

Sean studied him closely, peering closely at his skin. "So, it's true. You're already healed."

"Do you know what happened to me? Some people barged in when it started. I don't remember anything after that."

The wardsman studied him silently for several seconds. "Mister Blathe told me that he arranged for you to receive a different set of tattoos, but I'll confess, yours look the same as mine. As for what happened when you saw the ink master, you know more than I do. He did tell me that your skin would be finished healing before I arrived, though."

He remembered hearing his father's voice, but he didn't want to give that information away, so Oliver held his tongue. Instead, he dipped his head again. "Daikor, if you would excuse me. I'm not sure how long I slept, but I need to take care of certain necessities."

The senior wardsman nodded, and Oliver ducked out of the room and jogged down the hall. He returned a few seconds later and grabbed his trousers, then left again. It was several minutes before he came back.

"Feel better?"

He nodded, then asked, "How long have I been asleep?" His urine had been dark, and from the sun he could tell it was almost noon. He'd gone to be inked early in the morning.

Sean shrugged. "I'm not sure. But I was told you were to be given your ink day before yesterday."

Oliver's eyes widened. If that was true, then he'd slept for close to thirty-six hours.

"Hungry?" asked the other man.

He nodded. "Yes, sir."

"I won't bother you long then. Fifth bell will be ringing soon. Don't do anything today. I want you to rest. Definitely don't use your tattoos. I want you to wait for that until we begin training. That will be the day after tomorrow. Understand?"

"Yes, sir."

"Rest well and eat plenty today. Tomorrow evening, Sid and Glenn will come pick you up. Do you drink?"

Oliver blinked. He'd had wine or ale with dinner on many occasions, but he'd never drunk enough to feel much of anything. If he'd stayed at home, he probably would have, since the taverns in Lystal would serve him after he turned sixteen, and Doug would definitely have insisted. "I'm not sure," he answered. "But I'm willing to try."

Sean smiled. "Once a wardsman's tattoos heal, it's a tradition for his brothers to take him out and celebrate. I have duties to attend to, but Sid and Glenn will be more fun. Just be careful what you let them talk you into."

"Sir?"

The viper chuckled. "Need me to spell it out for you?"

"I don't want to get in trouble."

"Drink as much as you want. You've been locked away here for months, so you'll probably want to drain your balls too, and that's fine. Boys, girls, whatever you please, they'll lead you to it. Don't chew chaka, or any other drugs for that matter, and don't get into fights, and for Mother's sake, don't kill anyone. Is that clear?"

He hadn't intended to try chaka, but the Viper's other remarks led him to some new thoughts. "Boys?"

Sean sighed. "That was figurative. Anyone younger than sixteen is off-limits. Stick to the brothels and you'll be fine. It's their job to make sure their employees meet standards and get health checks. Don't be tempted to pick up any of the women standing on the street; that's how you get the pox. The ink on your dick won't save you from that."

The wardsman paused, watching him. When Oliver didn't respond, he asked, "Any other questions? I'm not going to explain how your dick works."

He shook his head. "No, sir."

Sean nodded, then backed out of the room. "Fight hard."

"Die young," replied Oliver, and then he was alone. Despite himself, all he could think about was what he might discover at a brothel. He wasn't even sure what he wanted to discover. He'd never really thought about the subject of girls, and the idea of similar games with his own sex was entirely new to him.

He spent the rest of the day thinking about it.

CHAPTER 48

"Hellooo!" yelled a familiar voice.

Oliver grinned as he opened his door for Sid. "I wonder why you're here," he said with a deadpan expression.

"The fuck you do! Let's go! Glenn's so excited he's liable to bust a nut, get drunk, *and* shit himself before we get back downstairs."

Oliver frowned, then smiled a second later. "Really? He doesn't seem like the excitable sort."

The wardsman paused as if thinking, then replied, "That's because you've only seen him when he's sober. Trust me. Sober he's a pain in the ass, but with a few drinks in him, he's just an asshole."

"Where is he?" asked Oliver.

"Waiting on the street. He prefers to be in the open."

"Why is that?" They were already heading for the stairs.

"I think he worked at a dairy when he was younger. Probably saved 'em money by curdling the milk with his face. Nowadays he has to settle for frightening women and children with his smile," explained Sid.

"Is that why you came in?" Sid gave him a puzzled look, so Oliver added, "Because you were tired of scaring women and children with your looks?"

"Nice try, kid. Keep working on it," replied Sid with a wink. "Try again when we meet some girls, and I'll do you a favor and pretend to laugh. Maybe they'll think you're funny."

As they stepped onto the street, Glenn nodded and offered a grunt at their appearance. Then he turned and started walking. Oliver looked askance at Sid, and the other man smiled. "He hasn't had a drink yet."

"Where are we going?"

Sid opened his arms wide. "This is your night, me boy! Nothing but the best, so our first stop will be Breville's Cock!"

He'd never heard the name before, so Oliver simply nodded and smiled. "Sounds good." After a ten-minute walk, though, he noticed something odd. "Why is there a rail on either side of the road?"

"Cuz we're on a bridge," answered Glenn, offering his first words of the evening.

"Breville Causeway!" announced Sid, then he pointed. "That tall building ahead is Breville's Cock. We'll wet our throats there." Glenn nodded, seeming satisfied, then Sid added, "He likes getting his throat wet from a c—"

"Shut up, Sid," ordered Glenn.

A few minutes later, they were standing in front of a wide street facing bar that led into and beneath the massive building. Everything seemed familiar, and at last it clicked into place in Oliver's mind. "This is Roc's Roost!"

Sid took a bow. "According to legend, that may well be its name, though the truth is lost to history."

Glenn motioned toward the bar. "I see a couple of seats. Let's grab them. It's usually tight in here."

"What about the downstairs bar? It's got views of the river," said Oliver.

The two wardsmen both stopped and gave him strange looks. Sid put a hand on his shoulder. "Alver, me boy, how would an innocent lad like yourself know about the iniquities of the river bar?"

"Iniquities? It's really nice," countered Oliver.

"Have you been here before?" asked Glenn doubtfully.

Realizing he might have said too much, Oliver tried to think quickly. "My dad's a cook, but he worked here when I was little, before we moved to Lystal."

"Ahh," said Sid, breathing out in a long sigh. "That makes sense. I thought you might be a rich kid's son for a second there."

Oliver gave him a wry look. "I wouldn't have been sold to work at the mines if I was, now, would I?" Inwardly, he was trying to calculate the odds that he would run into his aunt. He loved his Aunt Ess, or Maddie as she'd told him to call her at Roc's Roost, but he didn't know if she knew about the events of the past months. Even if she did, he wasn't sure if he wanted her to know that he was out for his first night of drinking and debauchery.

His aunt was always fun, but he could only imagine her disappointment if she knew he was headed to a brothel. He was worried enough about her seeing him drinking. His thoughts were interrupted when someone's hand touched his shoulder. Turning, he saw what might have been the most beautiful woman he'd ever encountered. She was small, petite to the point of almost being tiny, with light brown hair that shimmered gold in the last glow of the sun. Her dress seemed to cling to her indecently, and her smile was almost feral, showing off her canines.

For some reason, Oliver almost expected her eyes to have vertical pupils, like a cat, but although the irises were a golden green, they appeared perfectly human. "Excuse me, young man, have you been here before?" she asked.

Sid's eyes were close to falling out of his head. "No, but I'll come more often if it means I'll see you here."

The stranger gave him a quick glance. "You look like you've come too many times already." Then she winked and returned her gaze to Oliver. "Wait here. I have a table downstairs."

After she moved away, Glenn elbowed him. "How much money do you have?"

He frowned. "Two crowns and three silver pennies, but Sean said you were paying."

"I was, but you have no idea how much they charge down there." He looked at Sid. "Maybe we should duck out before she comes back."

"And miss the fun? Did you see that woman? I'd pay gold just to smell her hair, or better yet to sniff—"

Glenn punched his partner. "Exactly my point. We're about to be milked."

"She can milk me all night long," leered Sid.

"Of our money, you moron," groaned Glenn.

"Listen, I know you like 'em hairy, but let me have this, Glenn. Please! I want to die happy," begged Sid. "I'm sure there's some pretty men down there for you too. Maybe the enchantress has a brother! Did you think of that?"

"She wasn't even talking to you," growled Glenn. "She was too busy looking at Prince Muscles here." He elbowed Oliver.

"If you gentlemen will follow me, your table is this way," said a smooth, feminine voice.

Oliver turned. Dark hair, dark eyes, and pale skin greeted him. The woman who was waiting on them looked familiar. Glenn gave her a suspicious look. "And you would be?"

"Cecilia. I manage the river bar." With a smile she gestured, then led the way, hips swaying hypnotically as she walked.

"That's two," whispered Sid. "This place is a gold mine."

"No, we're the mine," hissed Glenn. "That's why people call 'em gold diggers."

Oliver simply followed while they argued. In the worst case, he still had nine gold crowns he'd left in his room. If they spent too much, he felt sure they would let him go collect the rest of his money from the House of Ink.

The river bar wasn't as crowded as the street-level bar, and a steady breeze blew in from the long balcony that overlooked the water below. Plants decorated the railing, hung in baskets, and occupied planters in every corner, giving the place an arboreal atmosphere. The customers were better dressed and the noise level was lower, in part because of the lighter density of people, and partly because of the music. A small stage on the wall opposite the balcony had a solitary minstrel playing a stringed instrument as he sang.

Oliver found his eyes drawn to the man, who seemed to shimmer in the indirect lighting. He stopped as they reached a corner table and focused on the player. The music fascinated him, and the musician's long fingers fairly danced across the strings as he played. "Enjoying the music, or the beauty?" asked a voice beside him. Oliver turned and saw the strange woman who had first approached him standing nearby.

"B-both?" he stuttered. Glancing over, he saw that Sid and Glenn were preoccupied as Cecilia seated them. "Who are you?"

She smiled, and he wondered at her age, for she seemed both young and old. Judging by appearances, she could be anywhere from sixteen to twenty, but something in her eyes told a different story. "Since you don't recognize me, I probably shouldn't say, but you should think of me as family, or perhaps as your fairy aunt." Her eyes sparkled with hidden mirth. "I told Maddie you were here."

His eyes widened in alarm. "No! Why? How do you know about—"

She lifted a slender finger to his lips. "Shhh. She'll be here soon. Just play along. Tonight is *your* night." She spun him around to face the table, so he sat down, but when he turned back the strange woman was gone.

Sid glared at him. "Lucky bastard." Then he grinned. "Next time she comes back, ask her to sit with you. I'll tell her the other chair is occupied."

"It's just the three of us," noted Oliver.

Sid pointed at his lap. "She might take a seat the way your luck is running." He nudged Glenn.

"What?" said the other man.

"Stop staring at the bard and pay attention. This is Alver's night," said Sid.

The other wardsman sighed. "Can't help it. Have you looked at him?"

Oliver nodded. "He stands out. His hair is shining."

"I like his hands," offered Glenn, holding up his own rough fist. "Long, graceful fingers."

Sid was listening to the two of them, then remarked, "Damn, Alver, I didn't realize you were on Glenn's side of the fence."

Oliver blinked, then answered honestly, "I'm not really sure."

Sid laughed. "It's easy. When you look at people, which ones make you want to wade into a bedroom battle?"

"Umm…"

"How about the lady that you were just talking to?" asked Sid.

Glenn broke in, "Someone like her doesn't count. She even had me thinking about crossing the aisle."

Sid nodded. "I can't argue. She could probably make a dead man rise. How about you, Alver?"

She had in fact caused a reaction, which only made him more confused, but Oliver didn't want to talk about it. He was saved by the arrival of his Aunt Ess, which caused Sid to completely forget his train of thought.

"Oliver! You should have told me you were coming here!" she said, motioning for him to stand. "Look at you! Daryl's boy is all grown now!"

It took him a second, but then he remembered his father's alias was Daryl here. It was all getting to be too much for him to keep track of. He nodded and smiled, remaining mute as she hugged him. She whispered in his ear, "Your father will be glad when I tell him I saw you, and your grandmother especially. She's been a mess since you left." Pushing him away, she appraised him once more with her eyes, then turned her gaze on the others. "Your food and drinks are on the house tonight."

Sid almost shouted, and Glenn's face showed visible relief. Then Cecilia reappeared, moving to stand beside Oliver's aunt. "Would you gentlemen like some drinks, or perhaps something to eat?"

Glenn seemed surprised. "You serve food?"

Cecilia smiled. "Only down here. The street bar is drinks only, but here, we cater to all your needs."

Oliver's aunt spoke up. "They should definitely start with food. It's Oliver's night. He just got his ink."

Cecilia nodded. Her eyes had already been studying Oliver. "I'll be sure he has a good time."

Oliver's aunt froze for a second. "He's *Daryl's* son, Cici. Keep that in mind."

The manager seemed puzzled. "Daryl?" After a moment her face lit up. "Oh, *that* Daryl?" Her expression changed as she got back to business, describing what food they had on offer.

After the two women had left and the ale had arrived, Glenn leaned over to Oliver. "Who was the redhead that's paying for our drinks?"

"Her name is Madeleine. She's the one my dad used to cook for," he answered.

Sid raised one brow. "She looks your age, Alver. Seems hard to believe."

Oliver shook his head. "No. She's probably in her thirties."

"Damn well preserved then," muttered Glenn, then he paused. "Wait, did you say her name was Madeleine?" When he nodded, Glenn asked, "And she's staff here or…?"

"She owns Roc's Roost," said Oliver.

Glenn spit out his ale. "That's Maddie Brightblaze?"

He shrugged. "I don't actually know what her last name is."

"Fucking Brightblaze?" exclaimed Sid. "Glenn, are you sure?"

"This is her place," said the other wardsman. "He said her name is Maddie, I just wasn't thinking." His eyes went wide as he stared at Oliver. "She hugged you!"

Sid scooted closer to Oliver, waving his hands as if to draw the air from the young man to his nose. Then he leaned in and sniffed Oliver's shirt. "I can smell it—gold and spice."

Oliver was giving Sid a confused look, then tried to put a few inches between them. "What are you doing?"

"Trying to get some of Brightblaze's luck. It must be all over you after that *warm* embrace she gave you," answered Sid.

Seeing he was still confused, Glenn explained, "She's the richest woman in Bondgrad, probably in all of Trendham. She could sleep on a bed of solid gold if she wanted."

Oliver gaped at them. "Is that a joke? I'm missing it."

Glenn chuckled. "How much do you think Roc's Roost is worth? It's the largest public house and hostel in Bondgrad, and it's located right on Breville's Causeway, right in the fucking middle of the capital. She owns it, and from what I hear, she owns a lot more as well."

"What kind of cook is your dad?" asked Sid. "If she liked him enough to pay for our drinks, he must've been something special."

The food arrived, followed by more ale, and then wine. The combination of music and alcohol relaxed Oliver, and once his companions quit bubbling over the fact that he knew Maddie Brightblaze, he began to really enjoy himself. An hour passed, but midway through the second, Sid tapped his shoulder. "We should go before we get too drunk."

"Leave here? It's free," Oliver responded in disbelief.

Glenn snorted. "That's the problem. He hasn't spent any money. His coin is burning a hole in his crotch."

Unsure what he meant, Oliver's face was blank until Sid grinned and began gyrating his hips. "I'm on fire. Let's quench these blades."

A minute later, they were making their way up the stairs and toward the street, but Oliver didn't manage a clean escape. Somehow, his aunt spotted him again. "Hey, Olly!" He stopped and saw her coming his way. Though the place was packed with people, all eyes were on her, and the crowd parted to give way for Maddie Brightblaze. She leaned in and spoke softly. "Are you heading out for the usual merriment wardsmen enjoy after getting their ink?"

His cheeks burned and Oliver froze in place.

"Relax, I'm not going to say anything to your dad. He's a prude, anyway." She took his hand and put something in it. "Show this at the door and they'll take care of you."

Oliver glanced down. He held card that had been dyed a vivid crimson. It had a large gold 'M' emblazoned on it. "Are there men at the door?" The street bar had numerous arches open to the street. There was no door to speak of. Usually, people paid the waitress or at the bar, at least as far as he understood things.

His aunt laughed. "Your friends will understand." Reaching up, she touched his hair fondly. "I can't believe how you've grown. I should have been there to see more of your childhood." Her face turned serious. "Keep the card and make sure you don't lose it. Show it to anyone in the city and they'll know you're one of mine. Doesn't matter what or why, if the watch gives you trouble, show them the card. If you shop the markets, show the card." She winked and turned away.

Sid stared at the red card, then hissed. "Put that away. Don't show it until we need it."

He frowned. "It's just paper."

"It's worth a hell of a lot more than gold, and there's some who'd cut your throat to get it, if they thought they could get away with it," explained Sid.

Glenn coughed. "Only if they thought Brightblaze wouldn't find out. Nobody crosses her."

They moved out into the street and walked westward, and for a moment Oliver simply enjoyed the cool breeze playing against his flushed cheeks, then he asked, "You keep talking about her like she's a scary person. She's just running a business."

Glenn put a hand against his chest, stopping him in his tracks. "Listen. I don't know what your real relationship with Brightblaze is, but you need to be aware of a few things, since you seem dangerously ignorant." He lifted his thumb and pointed back toward Roc's Roost. "That woman is *not* to be trifled with. She's dangerous, and she's a wizard in case you weren't aware. A few years back, one of the crime bosses tried to make her pay rent to him. He took his men and hired a wardsman just to be safe."

"Chet Burgen," said Sid, spitting on the cobblestones. "I don't miss that piece of shit."

Glenn nodded. "Yeah, he was scum, but he was one of us." He glanced back at Oliver. "Chet was one of Mister Blathe's wardsmen, same as you and me, but he was greedy. Dag hired him to cut Brightblaze up if she didn't cooperate."

"Who is Dag?" asked Oliver.

"That was the crime boss's name," answered Glenn. "Anyway, they went up to the top of Roc's Roost, and she met 'em alone. When Dag started making threats, she didn't take kindly to it. When Dag came down later, he was stark naked and didn't have a single hair left on his body. His men were naked too, and Chet was never seen again."

"What hap—?"

Before he could ask the question, Sid blurted out, "She burned him to ash!"

"Shut up, Sid. I'm tellin' it," snapped Glenn. "They *say* she burned Chet to dust in less than a second. One minute he was there, the next he was gone."

"Just gone!" agreed Sid, nodding enthusiastically.

"Damn it, Sid. I ain't gonna tell you again," growled the senior wardsman.

"Sorry."

Glenn took a breath. "As I was saying, they told everyone she burned him up in a flash. Some don't believe it, but they believed something bad happened. Dag's hair grew back, but it was pure white after that, and he never said a cross word about Maddie Brightblaze again. Blathe eventually had to fire him years later when it turned out Dag had apparently been feeding information to Brightblaze on the sly.

"She was already doing well before that, but afterward, there was no stopping her. Even the oligarchs steer clear of anything Brightblaze has an interest in, and that includes our employer, but it's better if you don't mention her at all in his presence. In fact, be damn sure he never sees that card, or you'll be out like yesterday's trash," finished Glenn.

"If you don't want it, I'll take it," said Sid, grinning. His partner gave him a hard look, and he reconsidered. "Actually, now that I think about it, I couldn't use it. If Brightblaze found out I had it, I'd be toast, and if Mister Blathe found out, I'd be in deep shit."

"Maybe I should get rid of it?" said Oliver hesitantly.

"She gave it to *you*," said Glenn. "I say use it. If anyone takes offense, they'll have to take it up with her. If Mister Blathe finds out, you can just tell him the truth. Worst case, he'll fire you, but he wouldn't do worse cuz it might piss her off."

Oliver nodded and they resumed walking. After a minute, he asked, "Can a wizard really do that, burn someone up in an instant?"

Glenn shook his head. "Not that I've ever heard. When you train with Daikor Sean, he'll talk about what they can do, but the gist of it is you treat 'em like shitty crossbowmen. Most of them are about as ill-prepared for a fight as a banker on holiday. Usually, they have spells that can hit you at range, like a bowman, but they're slow and most of them can't aim for shit, especially when things get hairy. Personally, I think she drugged 'em and took a razor to Chet's throat and then used it to take the hair off Dag. He was just too embarrassed to admit it."

Remembering how his father had fought after revealing the fact that he was a wizard, Oliver thought the story about Aunt Ess might be true, although he had trouble reconciling the notion with his memories of her. She'd always been kind and silly. When he was little, she had danced around the yard with him and played along with his endless games. He'd seen her more as a big kid than as an adult.

"There it is," said Sid with anticipation, "the Velvet Glove. The finest brothel in all of Bondgrad, probably in all the world. Within, they boast of whores so beautiful that kings would beg to sleep with them." He winked at Oliver. "Don't worry, though. They cater to all sorts. Show 'em that card, who knows what they'll do? Maybe you can sample them all!"

CHAPTER 49

From the outside, the Velvet Glove looked like a very successful public house. It had wide double doors, and there appeared to be a large bar serving drinks inside. The differences were subtle at first. The interior was much quieter than a tavern, and the number of women was markedly greater. Taverns usually held mostly men, except upscale places like the river bar they'd just been in, where rich men took their wives and mistresses for entertainment.

The lounge around the bar had cushioned chairs and low couches where people could lie back and relax while they socialized in small groups. As he studied the room, Oliver soon realized that each group revolved around one or two people, who were probably the customers. In most cases, that meant a man sitting with one or two ladies, but in a few others, it was a man sitting with other men, usually younger, better-looking men.

Everyone seemed cheerful, and laughter was constantly in the air, as the patrons and employees joked and talked with one another.

In short, it was nothing like what he'd expected. Rather than a bar or a whore-house, it seemed more like Oliver's ideal, a place where friends and lovers could relax, drink, and laugh. He never would have guessed the real service being offered, until he noticed one of the women leading a client upstairs.

An older woman greeted them from the bar. "Come inside, don't be shy!"

Sid needed no further encouragement, and they followed him to the bar. When they got there, he grinned and nodded at Oliver. "Show her."

Feeling awkward but trying to act sly, Oliver pulled the card out and held it up with two fingers. The madam's eyes showed recognition. "May I see that?" When he hesitated, she reassured him, "Only a fool would try to steal it from you. I just want to make sure it's real." After she'd turned it over to look at both sides, she handed it back, giving Oliver an appraising glance. "So young to be so favored. I'm Annabelle Withy. My house is yours tonight."

"Does that mean we get a discount?" asked Sid hopefully.

Chapter 49

421

The madam looked over at him. "Are you with him? If so, there's no charge. Brightblaze will cover the cost."

Curious, Oliver asked, "Have you met her?"

"Who?" she asked.

"Maddie."

The woman lifted both brows. "Not personally, but everyone that does business in Bondgrad deals with Maddie Brightblaze. No one cheats her, not twice anyway. Would you like some wine?"

"Got any elven wine?" asked Glenn.

"Of course. I keep all the best vintages here. No one leaves disappointed." After she had brought out a bottle and filled their glasses, she gestured toward the rest of the room. "Find a place to rest and make yourselves comfortable. The loveliest companions in all of Trendham will visit you shortly. Talk, drink, or invite them upstairs, the night is full of endless possibilities here at the Velvet Glove. Do you have any preferences?"

"Blonde, brunette, redhead, I'm very open-minded," answered Sid.

Glenn elbowed his partner. "She meant men or women." With a wink, he added, "I like 'em well-fed and bearded."

The madam laughed. "Actually, I meant both. Whatever you like, we try to please." Her eyes turned to Oliver. "And you?"

Caught by her gaze, Oliver blushed. "I—uh—I'm not sure. I've never, ah—"

Annabelle's expression brightened with enthusiasm. "This *is* a special occasion for you, isn't it? Don't worry, sweetheart. We'll get you sorted out. Take as many upstairs with you as you please, and if you decide you need someone with some experience, don't hesitate to let me know."

They found a comfortable corner and sat down, enjoying their wine. As promised, a few minutes later, young women and a few men began wandering over, and they behaved so naturally that it felt much less awkward than Oliver would have expected. Newcomers would stop and introduce themselves, sit down, and if encouraged, they would begin to get close.

Still nervous, Oliver didn't meet anyone's eyes, but instead watched what Sid and Glenn did. Glenn remained polite but brusque with the first man who stopped by, but when the second appeared, he smiled, and soon the two were sitting close beside one another, chatting like old friends. *Friends who feel comfortable enough to put their hands in each other's laps,* thought Oliver.

Meanwhile, Sid was already sitting with two young women, but Oliver noticed the wardsman kept glancing up at Annabelle, who still stood behind the bar. Leaning over, he whispered, "Isn't she past her prime for you?"

The wardsman grinned, answering in a normal voice, "Alver, me boy, you've yet to learn. Experience is worth more than perky breasts. A woman like that could probably drain your balls in five minutes flat and have you begging for more."

The woman sitting between Sid and Oliver, a lady named Lacie, nodded along. "Are you talking about Mistress Withy?" When they nodded, Lacie smiled. "She trained everyone here. No one knows their way around a fat cock like she does. That mouth of hers can do things you wouldn't believe."

"She doesn't see customers anymore, does she?" asked Oliver.

"Only when she wants to," admitted Lacie. "If you're shy, I can ask her for you."

"Ahh—," Oliver didn't know what to say. He was nervous, but something about the madame felt reassuring. If he had to choose, it might be easier to relax with someone older. Then he felt someone sit down beside him.

"Hello. I'm Nicole." He looked over and saw a lovely young woman with dark skin that proclaimed her Fareshite heritage. She gave him what seemed to be a genuine smile. "Oh, you're quite the handsome one, aren't you? I love your shoulders." Her hand touched his neck and traced his jaw.

Anxious, Oliver tried to be decisive. "Would you like to go upstairs?"

***

It was over in minutes, and although Nicole had wanted to stay, reassuring him that at his age he would soon recover his vigor, Oliver finally convinced her he was done. She left, and he lay naked on the bed, reviewing his feelings. Alex's face had popped into his mind several times during the experience.

Everything had worked, but he'd felt embarrassed and uncomfortable. It had almost been a relief when it was over. Now he didn't know what to do with himself. If he went back out, Glenn and Sid would wonder why he was already finished. He didn't want to cut their evening short. Closing his eyes, he let himself drift for a while. Without intending to, he fell asleep.

Sometime later, he heard the door click and saw Annabelle shutting the door. She had changed into a robe that left little to the imagination as she walked over and sat down at the edge of the bed. "Are you all right?" she asked, her voice warm.

His reflex was to lie, but something about the older woman made him feel safe. "I don't know."

She nodded. "Nicole said you seemed tense. That's often the case the first time."

"I don't think that was it."

Annabelle moved over, putting her arm around his shoulders and running her fingers lightly through his hair. Her robe parted as she moved, exposing more of her chest. "Tell me then. Just relax, and I'll listen."

"I didn't feel a connection."

She nodded again. "That makes sense. You came up here so suddenly. That's why we have the bar, so people can get comfortable."

"I think I have to be friends with someone," he said, agreeing.

"Nicole should have gone slower. That's not your fault. Do you feel comfortable with me?" she asked.

Meeting her eyes, he nodded. "Yes. I'm not sure why, but you feel familiar."

"Good. Does it feel comfortable when I do this?" Her hand trailed lightly down his stomach, then brushed his inner thigh, sending a faint thrill through him.

Breathing a little faster, he answered, "Yes." He could see her eyes watching his manhood like a predator eyeing a meal.

Her hand moved again, grazing him. "I think you're coming to life. Would you like me to keep going? It's entirely up to you."

"Only if you want to," he told her.

"Are you worried this is just business?"

He nodded.

"Don't be. Sometimes it is business, but I like to think of myself as a healer. These days, I choose when I want to help someone. Does that help?"

"Yes." Her hand gripped him then, making him gasp.

Smiling, Annabelle whispered in his ear, "Tell me your name so we can be friends."

"Oliver."

"That's a lovely name," she replied, then suddenly her hand stopped. "Wait. What?"

"It's a Terabinian name," he told her. "Most people call me Alver since they can't seem to say it properly."

"I know that," she snapped in irritation. "I'm Terabinian originally. How old are you?"

"Sixteen."

Something like panic showed in her features. "Who are your parents? Do you know them?" Annabelle closed her robe and cinched it tightly around her waist.

"My dad's name is Kelvin," he said uncertainly. "I never met my mother, though. She died when I was little."

"Oh, thank the Mother!" she swore.

Oliver frowned. "But her name was Annabelle too, which now that I think about it, makes this seem a little weird." He tried to laugh.

Annabelle had her hand on her forehead, her eyes staring at him from beneath it. "Fuck me backwards. This can't be happening. What was her last name? Tell me it wasn't Withy."

His brow furrowed. "I'm not really sure. Dad told me, but I've forgotten. You can't be her anyway. She's dead."

"Was she from Barrowden?"

Oliver nodded.

Annabelle bounced up from the bed as though something had bitten her. "That son of a bitch!" Her eyes were boring a hole in his chest. "You're my son."

Oliver slid sideways across the bed like a snake, covering himself with the sheets as he fell off on the other side. "No, wait, no!" He pointed a shaking finger at her. "You cannot be her, and I can prove it."

She gave him a dubious look, cocking her hip and resting one fist atop it. "How?"

"I told you my father's name was Kelvin, but that's not his real name! So, you're definitely mistaken."

"No, his real name is William Cartwright. Do you have any idea how small Barrowden was back then? I was the only Annabelle, and I'm damn sure he was the only William there, but he isn't your father, anyway."

His panic vanished, replaced by a strange rushing sound, as though a great wind was passing through his ears. "What did you say?"

"I said I am most certainly your mother, you poor bastard."

"No, the other part."

"I never *fucked* William Cartwright, is that what you want to hear? I tried, but the self-righteous prick wouldn't lower himself to sleep with a prostitute." She seemed to be growing angrier by the second. "Your actual father was a Darrowan soldier, a big, hulking brute of a man who I sincerely hope is roasting in hell."

Oliver blinked. "No, my dad is William Cartwright, so you have to be wrong."

"I was taken when the Darrowans invaded. Didn't he tell you about that?"

He shook his head, then repeated, "My dad is William Cartwright. My mom died when they invaded."

"No," she replied sadly. "She was taken and raped. Then I was used as a prostitute for months. The only reason I can even guess at who your real father is, is because of how damned big you are."

"You're lying."

"Oliver, have you looked in a mirror? You realize you don't look like him, don't you? Will is tall, but not *that* tall, and certainly not that wide. You're built like an ox. Look at my eyes. They look like yours." She took a step, as if she meant to close the distance.

He scrambled to his feet, backing up. "No, they don't."

For some paradoxical reason, that made her laugh. "Listen, I know this is fucked up, but it's true. The woman who raised you is named Erisa, right?"

Cold fear washed over him, and he continued to shake his head. When she started to move around the bed, he jerked and took another step. "Don't come near me!"

"It's me, Olly," she said softly. "I know you don't deserve this messed-up situation, but it's true. I carried you. I birthed you. I fed you from these breasts." She lifted one of her now-covered mammaries to emphasize the point.

"Don't!" Bile rose in his throat. He'd been admiring her breasts only minutes ago. "You are *not* my mother. She's dead."

Hurt registered in Annabelle's face. "You'd rather have a dead mother than find out she's a whore, right?"

"Yes!" he shouted. "You were just touching my—ugh! I can't say it! I think I'm going to vomit."

"Get over yourself," she snapped. "It's not the end of the world. Just forget about it."

"How? Can you?"

"Of course. After you've seen a hundred, they all look the same. It's not much different than seeing an arm or a leg."

He gaped at her. "That's fucked up! *You* are fucked up!"

A malicious look came into her eyes. "Really? Want to know something else even more fucked up? Your so-called father paid for this place."

"What?"

She was nodding as he stared at her in horror. "That's right. He paid me a hundred gold crowns and set me up in this fine establishment, just so I would steer clear of you. I wanted to see you, but he wouldn't have it! Told me he'd kill me if I said a word."

"No, he wouldn't do that."

"He damn well did!" she swore. "I'll admit, I was a mess after you were born. I was half-crazy and I couldn't think straight. Erisa took care of you when I left, but I came back! I came back, and you were gone without a trace. The house was burned to the ground. What was I supposed to do? Then, years later, when I saw your father here in Bondgrad, what did he do? I begged him to tell me about you, to let me see you, and he all but spit in my face."

"You really met him here?"

Seeing the doubt in his eyes, she lifted her chin. "I did, and he paid me to keep quiet."

"But he works as a cook. He doesn't have that kind of money. He doesn't live here either. How would that happen?"

Annabelle grinned evilly. "They're all the same. How do you think any man meets a whore? How many times did your so-called dad make trips to Bondgrad? I can give you one guess as to why he would travel here, where no one he knows could find out. I'm sure he was feeling pent up and frustrated as hell from pretending to be your father all the time, but here he could let it all out and no one would know how the oh-so-righteous William Cartwright likes to get his kicks. It was his luck and my fortune that he ran into me, otherwise I'd still be sucking sailors' dicks down by the docks." She saw the shock in his eyes and went on, "Which is exactly what he was looking for that day, until he realized it was me standing on the corner!"

The walls seemed to move as her words landed on his ears, and it seemed ironic to him that the room could breathe but he could not. Oliver took a step back, and then another, until he felt the wooden shutters of the bedroom's solitary window behind him. Unthinking and unfeeling, he reached back and pulled them open.

Remorse filled his mother's eyes. "I shouldn't have said that. I'm just angry. You hurt my feelings, Oliver."

He turned and jumped, realizing too late that the Velvet Glove had glass windows behind the shutters. His body crashed through, and long shards of glass fell with him as he dropped from the second story to the alleyway. Some of it sliced into him, but he hardly noticed the pain. A large owl took flight from the roof across the street, but he paid it no heed.

Annabelle shouted to him from the window, "I'm sorry, Oliver. Come back! I didn't mean to say those things! It was the truth, but I shouldn't have said it like that."

Oliver ignored her, ignored the pain in his feet, and started running. His clothes, his money, even the red card, all of them were still in the room, but he no longer cared. He simply had to get away. He ran blindly for a while, leaving bloody footprints behind as he tried to outrun his mother's words. When he finally came to a stop, he found himself standing in front of the main entrance to the House of Ink, though he wasn't aware of having headed there.

The man who opened the door was Franklin, and though he seemed slightly shocked at Oliver's naked and bloody appearance, he only said one thing. "I know it's your night to celebrate, but please tell me you didn't kill anyone."

Oliver shook his head. "Jumped out a window."

"Are you drunk?"

"I wish I was."

"Whose blood is that?"

He blinked. "Mine. Why?"

"Do you need to see the healer? You might need stitches," said the other man.

"I think I'm all right. I'll wash up and come back if I need help." Emotionally, Oliver was numb, but he no longer felt any physical pain. Glancing down, he saw that he wasn't leaving bloody footprints either.

Franklin waved him on. "Fine."

Unconcerned with his nudity, Oliver marched up the stairs and down the halls. It was late anyway, and almost no one was out and about. He went to the dormitory and when he came to a stop, it wasn't his door that he stood in front of. He knocked, and Alex opened it.

The other teen's eyes widened for a second, then focused on Oliver's face, reading his expression. "You're hurt." He stepped back from the door, letting him inside, then he closed the door. "I see blood. Are you wounded?"

Oliver shrugged. "I'm not sure."

"Sit down on the bed. I'll be right back." Alex disappeared, but returned a few minutes later with a washcloth, a basin, and a pitcher of cool water. Without asking, he began wiping away the blood on Oliver's skin. "I'm not finding any cuts."

For some reason, Alex's unquestioning kindness brought back the pain. He could feel his eyes welling with tears. Glancing up at Alex with lost eyes, Oliver mumbled, "There should be some. I jumped out a window."

"That's dramatic," replied Alex, before sitting down. "Want to tell me why?"

"No."

His friend nodded. "Fair enough." He put his arm around Oliver's shoulder. "Does this help?"

He nodded.

"Can I do anything else?" Alex's eyes were still and serious.

Looking over, Oliver felt something. "Tell me you're not my mother."

With a smile, Alex replied, "I am *not* your mother."

Leaning over slowly, Oliver kissed him. In the rush that followed, he forgot the miserable events of the day, for a short while at least.

CHAPTER 50

The next morning, Oliver woke in a sweat. The tiny bed in Alex's room was too small, forcing them to remain close together, not that he minded. His friend opened one eye and grinned blearily at him. "Sleep well?"

"Not at all," he replied. "Thanks to you."

"It's not my fault. You were too good at it."

Without thinking, he answered, "Like mother, like son."

"I can see why you never tell jokes. Blech!"

Sitting up, Oliver looked for his clothes, then remembered where he'd left them. He could buy new clothes. He was never going back there. "It wasn't really a joke."

Seeing his clothing dilemma, Alex pointed at his footlocker. "I'd loan you some of my clothes, but they won't fit you." Then he frowned. "What do you mean?"

"I found out my mom is a prostitute."

"What? Say that again! What?"

Oliver began to talk, slowly at first, and it all began to come out. He couldn't stop, didn't want to stop. Alex was his only real friend, the only person who could listen. So he told him everything, from beginning to end. The only thing he reserved was his father's name and the fact that he was living in exile, but he told the rest, including the fact that the man he'd thought was his father was also a wizard. He omitted everything about his Aunt Ess, though.

It felt good to finally get it off of his chest, to share some of his secrets, and when he finished, Alex hugged him. "How in the hell did you stay sane? That's the miracle in all this."

"Am I sane?"

"You found my door. I think that's a sign of sanity."

Oliver frowned. "Really?"

"You knew I would listen. You knew I would care, and that means you want to survive. That's a good thing."

He motioned to his friend, then back to himself. "Is this a good thing?"

Alex nodded. "I think so."

***

Will didn't see the message from Sammy on his enchanted tablet until the next morning:

> *That bitch Annabelle hurt him! Didn't realize she was here, but I've a fix for that.*
>
>   ~S

He frowned, pushing down a surge of anxiety. Slipping out of his body, he checked on Oliver first and was surprised to find him in bed with a stranger. *I didn't expect that,* he thought, but most importantly, it looked as though his son was unharmed. The two young men seemed intent on their conversation.

Refocusing, Will sought out his cousin and found her pacing back and forth in the garden space atop Roc's Roost. Standing beside her was a humanoid wolf-like creature of monstrous proportions that looked as though it had been pulled straight from a lumberjack's worst nightmare. The beast stood over seven feet tall and was covered in thick, black fur, and although it was bipedal, the head was distinctly wolfish, with a long snout and teeth that dripped saliva onto the ground. Thickly muscled arms ended in humanoid hands tipped in long, deadly claws.

Being in the astral realm, he felt the connection immediately, and knew the monster was Tailtiu, though he would never have recognized her in the flesh. Her voice emerged in a deep, husky snarl. "My way is best. I have not killed in ages, but for her I will feel no remorse."

Whatever had happened, Tailtiu was clearly furious, but apparently, Sammy still had a clear head if she was keeping a tight leash on the ex-fae. Will felt confident in her maturity, until she spoke. "Fuck that! The cunt needs to burn!"

"It will be over too quickly. I can draw it out, so she truly suffers," argued Tailtiu.

There were flames in Sammy's eyes as she replied, "Do you have any idea how painful being burned to death is? I wouldn't start with her, anyway. First, I'll empty the place and turn the Velvet Glove into an inferno. There won't even be a stone remaining when I'm done—nothing but ash! I'll have her watch, and *then,* only then, will I start on her."

"I have been burned, badly," agreed Tailtiu. "But the pain recedes after the skin is gone. The body goes into shock. The pain I will inflict is far better."

"Better than me burning her tits off, one at a time? How?" demanded Sammy.

The wolf smiled, revealing vicious teeth, but what she did next made Will doubt his sanity. Tailtiu thrust her hips forward, displaying a monstrosity unlike anything he'd ever seen. Between her legs was something like an eel, if eels were covered in bony barbs. It writhed, then straightened momentarily and hissed. "Those who live by the cock, die by the cock."

What in the fuck? thought Will, horrified. Averting his gaze, he looked to Sammy, again hoping for sanity, but she was studying Tailtiu's phallic appendage with malefic fascination, rubbing her chin with one hand. "I won't lie. I feel nauseous just looking at it, so I think you may be on to something. Is there some way we can add flames to it?"

"I'm not good with elemental magic," said Tailtiu. "Besides, though it would look nice, flames would accelerate the end too much."

Sammy nodded. "I defer to your wisdom. Clearly, you are the master here. I'm still going to burn her tits off, though."

"After I—"

Sammy nodded again. "Yes, of course. I'll wait until you think the time is right."

Unable to wait any longer, Will teleported. "I'm going to need an explanation."

Tailtiu reacted first, giving him an enthusiastically terrifying smile and turning to give him a good view of her groin. "William! Behold my war-cock!"

Seeing it in person was even worse. Will reacted defensively, trapping Tailtiu within a force-cage. Then he took a step back to ensure he was well out of range, since it was obvious her phallus could fit between the bars. Disgusted, he looked back and forth between the two women. Of the two, Sammy was easier to look at. "What is that thing?" he demanded.

Sammy raised one brow. "You know Tailtiu is a proficient shape-shifter."

"A female one," he pointed out, trying to keep his eyes away from the writhing terror.

"It's terrifying isn't it!" said his fae aunt happily. "Look upon the instrument of justice!"

His cousin's eyes narrowed. "You think penises are special somehow? If she can grow wings why should a dick be any more difficult?"

Will threw his hands up. "I don't really care about that. I'm more concerned with the fact that it has teeth! Why?"

Tailtiu chuckled. "For the same reason you do, so it can chew."

His stomach turned over. "Please put that thing away. It's making me ill."

"But you haven't seen the details yet. You're too far away. Get rid of this cage so I can show you my masterpiece." Tailtiu's enthusiasm knew no bounds.

"I'm going to burn it off if you don't—is it looking at me? By the Mother! That's just wrong!" he exclaimed.

"I thought the eyes were a nice touch," said Sammy. "Go ahead and change back for now, but keep the details fresh in your mind, so you can recreate it when we get there."

Downcast, Taitiu obliged, while Will focused on his cousin. "What in the world is going on? I checked on Olly, but he seems fine."

Sammy tapped her chest. "In here, Will. She ripped out his heart and stomped on it!" Her hair developed flowing streamers of flame as she spoke. "I didn't even know she was in Bondgrad, and she was right under my nose! I practically sent him to her!"

"We're talking about his mother, correct?" he asked.

"I said 'Annabelle' in my message—who else would I mean?" she snapped. "He met her at the Velvet Glove last night. Are you starting to get the picture? Do you know what almost happened?"

"Velvet Glove, what's that?"

"A brothel," explained Tailtiu. "He was happily fornicating until *she* showed up."

Will turned on his aunt. "I asked you to keep an eye on him! What were you doing?"

"Watching! Why are you shouting at me?" exclaimed the ex-fae.

On the verge of apoplexy, Will shouted again, "Because my son was in a whore house! You were supposed to protect him!"

Tailtiu was confused, but she shouted back anyway, "From sex? What else should I worry about? Is breathing allowed? You make no sense!" She pointed at Sammy. "She's human, and she sent him there, so why are you upset?"

Will took a deep breath, then held up one hand. "Let's table this for a while." He turned to his cousin. "You sent him to a brothel?"

Without an ounce of shame, Sammy answered, "No." Will continued to stare, and finally, she added, "He was going out on the town."

"You gave him your card," offered Tailtiu.

Sammy's eyes darted toward Tailtiu, and irritation flashed across her features. "My card is good anywhere in the city." She met Will's gaze with confidence. "He was celebrating his tattoos. He shouldn't have to waste his money in taverns."

Tailtiu nodded in agreement. "Wardsmen always wet their blades in the brothels after receiving their ink. It isn't her fault."

Will glanced at his aunt. "And how do you know that? You spent almost ten years in the ocean before I asked you to come back."

His aunt answered honestly, "Samantha told me."

"What's more important is what happened while he was there," said Sammy firmly, ignoring the accusation in Will's glaring eyes. "She told him you're not his father."

His anger vanished, replaced by a cold lump in his stomach. "You're sure she told him?"

Tailtiu nodded. "I heard them through the window. They were about to mate when he told her his name."

Will's jaw fell open, and he rounded on his aunt. "He was about to—with his mother—and you didn't think he needed protecting?"

"I didn't recognize her," said Tailtiu. A few seconds later, she added, "Do humans not do this?"

He closed his eyes. "Tell me what happened and exactly what was said."

"We've been trying, but you keep interrupting," complained Sammy, but she flinched when she saw the reaction on his face. Gesturing to Tailtiu, she said, "Tell him what you told me."

Tailtiu's memory was excellent, and it was a short tale. By the end of it, Will was sitting on one of the stone benches, his head in his hands. Sammy stood close by, and though it looked as though she wanted to put a hand on his shoulder, she drew back instead of risking contact. "Now you see why she needs to die. No mother should say things like that to her child. It's unthinkable."

Numb, Will answered, "She's his mother."

"Exactly," said Sammy with conviction.

Despair on his face, Will looked up at his cousin. "She's his mother. How do you think that will go over with Olly? Think, Sam!"

Her voice was cold. "He won't know."

"If the Velvet Glove gets burned to the ground, he'll know," said Will. "He's not stupid. And spare me your other plans. No matter what you do, *you'll* know. That's why I couldn't do it."

"So, you did meet her? I thought she was lying about that," said his cousin.

Will nodded despondently. "It was true. I gave her the money too, but I didn't know what she would do with it. Not that it matters. I thought she'd waste it and end up dead in an alley."

Tailtiu interrupted, "If you were starved for sex, why not call for me?"

"Huh?" Will couldn't find a way to make her remark line up with the conversation.

"She said you were coming to Bondgrad to hire prostitutes," explained his aunt.

Will sighed. "That part was a lie, obviously."

"Oh."

"That woman still needs to be punished," growled Sammy, flames reappeared in her hair.

He glanced at her, clenching his will. The flames went out. "No."

"Let go of my magic," hissed Sammy. "I'll do as I see fit, and if you think—"

"Touch her and I'll tell Mom," he replied.

Her aunt was the closest thing to mother she had, and Sammy's skin paled. "You wouldn't dare."

"Try me."

Sammy seemed to deflate, and Will relaxed his hold on the turyn around them. She sat down next to him, and they remained silent for some time, brooding over dark thoughts. Will had already freed Tailtiu, who was now in her usual human form. She sat down on the other side of him, and the three stared at the grass together.

Eventually, Tailtiu broke the silence. "Just to be clear, we are *not* killing her, correct?"

"Correct," said Will.

His aunt sighed, and the silence dragged on while the sun rose higher in the sky. Then she asked, "What did you think of my war-cock?"

"Very creative," said Sammy quietly. "I doubt I'll sleep well for weeks now."

Will nodded, then continued her thought, "I've seen things impossible to comprehend, and there are at least a dozen secrets in my head that could end the world tomorrow. I dream of horrors and have nightmares regularly, and that—that was an entirely new level of awfulness. It would almost be worth not stopping the two of you, if it would let me erase the scar of that wretched vision from my soul."

Tailtiu rocked on the bench, smiling faintly and swinging her feet with satisfaction. "Thank you." She stood and walked to the railing, then transformed into a large owl and flew away.

"Where do you think she's going?" asked Will.

"Back to watch Oliver, I imagine," answered Sammy. She leaned sideways and bumped him with her shoulder. "You can be quite poetic when you want to be. It makes no sense that you're still single."

"I met someone."

She eyed him with surprise. "Really? Are you talking about Vonnie?"

He shook his head. "No. I like her, but I—I can't get past this one."

Sensing the frustration in his voice, Sammy frowned. "Something's wrong with her, isn't it?"

"Probably several things," he admitted.

His cousin rolled her eyes. "Why can't you just pick someone normal? Does she at least have two arms and two legs?"

Will snorted. "She's got those."

"Just two of each?"

He nodded.

"What's the problem then?"

"She can't stay with me. She travels. I'll only see her every year or two—if I'm lucky."

"That's not too bad," she replied. "So long as she's not a princess and doesn't have a dragon for a father."

He laughed. "A dragon's no problem. I've killed one once already."

"I'm sorry I didn't tell you about the prices changing. Someone started undercutting me in the rare potion market a few years ago."

Will nodded. "You were right. It would have hurt my pride."

"I should have told you anyway."

"Yeah, but I've no right to judge, as demonstrated by the recent debacle my lies have wrought."

Sammy watched him, her green eyes thoughtful. "I'm filthy rich. Richer than you were when you were a duke. I might be the wealthiest single person in Trendham, and if I'm not, it won't be long before I am. I want to share it with you. Will you let me? Or will your pride get in the way?"

He patted her knee. "It makes more sense for you to take over the finances for the school and the hospital. I'm constantly working in the dark, and anonymity scares people. You've got the skill and the people to manage it better anyway. I should focus my time on other projects."

"What about Erisa, and Oliver?"

Will frowned. "Mom is happy in Lystal. I don't think she wants more, but you can ask her. Oliver needs to find his own way. He's young and talented."

"Don't you want to help him?"

"Of course I do, but it's just like me and the price of potions. He's got his own pride, and if he doesn't, then he needs to develop it. He'll never be happy if he's constantly sheltered."

"You haven't talked to him in months."

"I doubt he wants to see me right now."

Sammy's cheeks colored as her temper began to rise. "Don't you dare start sulking and ignore him like you did me. He's still young, and he will always need his father."

Will looked at her, then nodded. "I won't, but I'm going to give him a little time."

"Not too long."

He smiled at his cousin, thinking again how beautiful she was. Not physically—that was obvious to anyone—but her spirit remained kind and compassionate, despite all the things they'd been through over the years. *There's a lot to admire in her heart,* he told himself. "You should have been a mother, Sam."

"What?"

He nodded again. "You heard me. It's a shame. You would be great at it."

Normally she would argue at that point, but his cousin went quiet instead. After a minute, she responded, "I thought about it for a while."

"After we came to Trendham?"

She shook her head. "Before and after—after we went back for the trolls."

"Emory?"

Sammy looked at him, embarrassment written on her face. She'd argued with him about Emory for some time before they'd left Terabinia. Now she was admitting the lie. "Go ahead and say it."

"Say what?"

"I told you so."

He put his arm around her shoulder and squeezed. "You're both going to live for centuries. There's plenty of time."

She gave him an irritated look. "Men like him don't wait around. He's probably already got a wife and children."

"You don't know? Tabitha could likely tell you."

"I'm not going to ask," she said firmly.

"So why didn't you nail him down when you had the chance?"

"I wanted more, plus you and Oliver needed me, and Aunt Erisa." Will stared at her from the side of his eye but didn't comment. After a moment, she exclaimed, "He deserved better!"

"Than you? Sam, I'm starting to think you're delusional."

She sighed in exasperation. "He's a nobleman. I was nothing."

"You're one of the few third-order wizards in the entire world."

She rolled her eyes. "There will be more. I know I talk big, but I don't always believe what I say about myself. Emory had—has—a gentle heart. I'm all over the place, like wildfire. He needs someone smart, someone stable. Someone who can make him happy. I wanted adventure, he wanted a family."

"But you've changed your mind."

"The glamor of the city gets stale after a while. I can have anything, but it seems worthless now." She gave him a shy look. "Can I confess something?"

"Sure."

"Part of why I was so obsessed with money and success was that I wanted to prove something."

Will frowned. "To whom?"

"Emory, myself, I don't know! It just seemed like if I became successful enough, maybe I could finally believe I was worthy."

Hugging her tightly, Will rested his chin on her head. "Oh, Sam, that's the stupidest thing I've ever heard you say."

"I know, believe me." After a minute, she stepped away, glancing at the sky. "It's almost noon. Are you hungry?"

When he agreed, she had lunch brought up to them and they had a quiet meal before he returned to Lystal.

***

Late that night, long after even the hardiest carousers had gone to bed, Annabelle Withy sat in her room, combing out her hair and staring at the mirror on her dressing table. The past few years had been good, but now her heart felt dull and empty. Meeting Oliver had shaken her to the core. *And as always, my temper and my mouth ruined any chance I had of knowing him,* she thought.

She glared angrily at her reflection. "You're a complete bitch, but half the fault is on Will's head. If the self-righteous ass had told him the truth, none of this would have happened." Her thoughts ran in circles. *Better yet, he should have come back for me. They left Terabinia purposefully, to keep me from finding them.*

"I know where he is now, though," she said to the mirror. "Once he's calmed down, I'll talk to him." She imagined her son coming to live with her. A wardsman would be good to have around, far better than any normal guard. She had considerable respect already, but with a wardsman for a son, none would dare look down their noses at her.

A knock came at the door, and she frowned. It was late, and none of her employees would dare disturb her without a good reason. Standing, she crossed the room in several quick strides and opened the door. In the hall, she saw a man, possibly the most beautiful man she'd ever seen, but it was late, and she was tired. "Tomorrow, love. It's far too late." She started to close the door, but he put his hand on it.

She shoved, but his size and strength were undeniable. Irritated, she glared at the stranger. "One yell from me, and the men downstairs w—" Her words cut off with a squeak as the newcomer's hand shot out, taking her by the throat and squeezing tightly. Moving forward, he carried her back into the room, kicking the door shut behind him.

She kicked, but her struggles had no effect, and after a few seconds, Annabelle relaxed. When the stranger pushed her back onto the bed, she glared back at him with eyes full of spite, then threw her robe open. Wheezing, she managed to speak. "You think I'm afraid of you? I've been here before, and nothing you can do will hurt me."

As she'd expected, the stranger quickly removed his clothing, but then something strange happened. His skin crawled, sprouting black hair as his body expanded, and a feral growl escaped his throat. Annabelle stared, fixed by the horror of the transformation, from man to some terrible man-wolf hybrid. The creature smiled, showing long fangs. "You hurt someone yesterday, Annabelle." The voice emerged with a deep rasp to it that sent shivers down her spine. "You hurt someone precious to me."

The fear stole her breath, her reason, and any hope of escape, not that she had any. Hyperventilating, Annabelle's arms and legs flailed as she tried to move away, but she couldn't find enough coordination to move more than an inch. Something dark and glistening rose from between the monster's legs. When her eyes finally focused on it, she began to scream, but her tortured throat made the sound weak and impotent.

It brushed her thigh, and something sharp cut into her skin. Wide-eyed and frothing, she kicked, but the beast caught first one ankle, then the other. "Today is a warning. Leave this city, leave Trendham, and never let me find you. If you speak to my child again, I will devour you from the inside out, beginning with your womb." The horrifying phallus raised its head then, hissing at her with a mouth full of needle-like teeth.

Mercifully, she lost consciousness.

When she woke later, she thought it must have been a nightmare, but her throat was sore. Looking in the mirror, she saw a bruise forming there. Checking her leg, she saw a small cut on her thigh. Trembling, she looked around the room, trying to think, then she saw the door, where a message waited, scrawled by sharp claws.

From the womb out.

She screamed again, and this time her voice was loud enough that it woke everyone in the Velvet Glove.

CHAPTER 51

Oliver began training with the Viper the next week. Daikor Sean moved back to the House of Ink, taking quarters in the section reserved for employees and instructors. He never gave Oliver a schedule, but from the time he finished breakfast until the evening meal, he was given few respites. Some days, if he failed to meet his trainer's expectations, he wasn't even allowed to break for lunch.

Oliver loved it. Before then, the closest the House of Ink had come to his childhood dreams had been the time he spent with Trainer Martin, but with Daikor Sean, he could finally train in earnest. His first lesson had been in learning the proper state of mind to trigger his iron-body transformation, and things had only gotten better from there.

By the fifth day, he decided he had never been happier. Fighting, food, and Alex filled most of his time, allowing him to block out the memory of what had happened just the week before. It was Friday morning before breakfast when a commotion in the hall caught his ears, along with everyone else's.

"Get out of my way or I'll burn the hair off your balls," came a woman's voice.

Alex opened his eyes, still half-asleep. "What's that?"

Oliver had already gotten to his feet. "I think it's my aunt."

His friend rubbed at his face. "I don't think they let women in here."

"Are you sure?"

Alex shrugged. "I've never seen one here."

The sounds were coming closer, and Oliver was certain he recognized Aunt Ess's voice. He pulled on his trousers and started searching for his tunic. "Oliver! Where are you?" More voices followed, then he heard her again. "Well, he's not there. Which one of you knows where he is?" A few seconds later, he heard, "No, I don't give a damn what time it is."

Footsteps outside the door heralded a knock seconds later. "Olly, are you in there?" Before he could react, the latch moved and the door opened. His aunt stepped in with a smile. "There you are." Her eyes fell on Alex a second later. "Oh! I'm sorry. We haven't been introduced."

She held out her hand, and Alex accepted it gracefully, as though it were the most natural thing in the world for him.

"Alexander Engelman, at your service."

"Madeleine Brightblaze, but if you're a friend of Oliver's, you can call me Maddie," she returned. She studied Alex's features for a few seconds. "Do you play any instruments, Alexander?"

"No, but I'm told I have a pleasant voice," said Alex with a smile.

Oliver was surprised. "You can sing?"

Alex nodded.

Sammy grinned. "If you're good, with those eyes and that jawline, you could make a fortune. Learn an instrument and I wouldn't have any doubt."

"Thank you, Miss Brightblaze, but I'm set on becoming a wardsman,"—his eyes darted to Oliver—"like my friend."

"Who's your sponsor?" she asked.

"Mister Pummen."

Oliver watched, having unexpectedly become a spectator. He'd learned several things in a span of seconds, and he suddenly wondered why he hadn't known them before. His aunt continued, "That's a shame. Oliver's with Blathe. You'll be going different places once you finish here."

Alex nodded, then glanced away with an air of self-consciousness. Oliver finally spoke. "Have you been thinking about that? It didn't even occur to me."

"That's still months away," said Alex. "No use worrying now."

"Oliver, I need to talk to you," announced his aunt, then she looked back to his friend. "Is this your room, or his?"

"Mine," said Alex.

She nodded, turning to Oliver. "Let's talk in yours for a few minutes. Is that the one over there? They pointed me that way, but when you weren't there…"

"Yes."

She led him across the hall and down several doors, then opened his door and pulled him inside. From the hallway, Oliver heard someone let out a wolf-whistle. His aunt heard it too. "Excuse me a moment, Olly." Opening the door, she stepped back out. "You! Yes, you! Oliver is my nephew, you degenerate. Do you know who I am? You're about to find out. If you even think about starting any rumors, or even tease him, I'll come back and burn every hair off your ugly ass."

Oliver was frozen in shock. Whoever his aunt was berating said something he couldn't hear, and then he caught the distinct sound of flames. *My life is over. She burned one of the candidates to death.* A very unmanly shriek echoed down the hall.

His heart restarted a moment later when she resumed, "Say that again and it won't be your trousers next time." She stared down the hallway for several seconds, then came back in and closed the door. "Now, where were we? Olly? Are you all right?"

He shook his head. "No. I don't think so."

His aunt's features softened. Moving closer, she put her arms around him. He remained stiff, but didn't resist the embrace. His Aunt Ess looked at him, her face barely coming up to his chest. "When did you get so tall?" she asked.

He shrugged.

"Do you know why I'm here?"

"No," he answered woodenly.

"I heard about what happened at the Velvet Glove." The world began to swim in front of his eyes, and a rushing sound filled Oliver's ears. He didn't know how to respond, so he stayed silent. "That woman said some things, and I'm here to make sure you know the truth."

He pulled away, ignoring the hurt expression on her face. "The same kind of truth you and everyone else has been giving me since I was a kid?"

"No. But it will be the real truth. The truth your father has been too afraid to share."

"Apparently, he's not my father."

Her hand came up in anger, but then she dropped it and turned her face away. She dabbed her eyes with one sleeve, then looked back. "Is that really the truth? Is that what your heart says?"

Oliver's jaw moved uncertainly, but then he firmed it up again. "She knew his name. She knew Nana's real name. She knew the truth."

"She told you her version of it. A version full of jealousy and spite. Will you listen to mine?"

"There's only one truth. He either is, or he isn't," said Oliver angrily.

"No, there's more to it than that."

"Everyone wants to color things in their favor, but facts are facts. Why should I believe anything you say now?" he demanded.

"Because my truth is colored with love, and love is what started all this. Love is what made your dad lie, so it needs to be considered if you're going to judge his choices. Can I tell you the truth I witnessed?"

Oliver was so upset he couldn't reply. Angry tears threatened to spill over onto his cheeks. His aunt continued, "He didn't have to be your father. He *chose* to be. Most of what that woman said was true, but she twisted it. What happened to her was terrible, and Will didn't even know she was alive until he found her imprisoned in the Darrowan camp. He brought her out and made every single one of them pay for it. The man who sired you was probably among them, and I wish I could be sorry for his death, but they killed most of my family too. I hate what they did, and I can't help but hate the men who did it.

"Annabelle lived with Erisa until she gave birth to you, and Will wasn't there. He only saw you once or twice before we moved to Trendham, and Erisa was already comfortable raising you as her own child. Annabelle had already run off, and none of us knew where to find her."

His voice was thick when he tried to respond. "She said you left to make sure she couldn't find me."

"She'd already been gone over a year," said his aunt. "And we left because we didn't have much choice. Despite what you might think, your dad had a lot on his plate at the time. No one really knows all the things he did, not even me, but he helped a lot of people. When we got to Lystal and you asked him if he was your father, there was only one answer his heart could give."

"I asked him?"

She nodded, tears streaming from her eyes. "Yes. You did. And *that* was the moment he became your dad. Not because he knocked up some girl he didn't know, not because he owed anyone anything, but because he loved you and he knew you needed a father—a real one. That's why he's your dad, and that's why we're family. Do you understand?"

They were both crying, but Oliver managed one more question before his voice broke completely. "Then why did he sell me?"

She was crying into this chest now. "Because he's stupid and he didn't tell me what was going on." She pounded on him with her fists for a moment, and Oliver was struck by how small his aunt seemed. She'd always seemed larger than life, but now she looked like a child beside him. Finally, she looked up, her face swollen and puffy. "Your father's going to have to answer that question, but think about a few things before you say anything dumb to him. Where are you right now?" She didn't wait for an answer. "Is this what you wanted? It certainly looks a lot like it."

"I was in a mining camp for over a month."

"And? Do you think you did nothing wrong?" He had nothing to say to that. His aunt had a few things to add, though. "He had someone watching you every minute of every day, but he's such an idiot, he wouldn't have done anything unless someone tried to do you serious harm. Your grandmother is still furious with him, and I only found out recently." She shook her head, then wiped her face again. "Sometimes I think I'll never understand his way of thinking."

Something had opened inside him, like a weight had finally fallen away. "I think I understand."

His aunt seemed confused. "Huh?"

"It makes sense to me."

"How?"

"It wouldn't have meant much if he'd given it all to me—or used your money. He gave me the chance to earn it for myself." Oliver gave her a timid smile.

She returned it with a lopsided smile of her own. "You're both cracked in the head."

***

His training continued, and a few days later, his father appeared without noise or fanfare. Unlike his aunt's visit, it seemed as though no one noticed the strange man in the House of Ink. One moment he was alone, and the next his dad was there, standing across from him in his room. Oliver wasn't sure if he'd teleported or walked in, but he was there.

They talked for a while, but only shared a few tears. The worst of that was already past. Mostly, it was just a relief to see one another. His father repeated some of what his aunt had said, but he stumbled over the worst parts and failed to mention anything that might excuse him for what had happened. "It's all right, Dad. Aunt Ess told me about what happened to my mother. So did Annabelle, but I know it wasn't your fault."

"I burned that camp, Oliver. There were thousands there."

"I know."

"I made sure most of them couldn't escape. Do you—do you understand what I'm saying? He was—that man, whoever he was—he was probably there."

"I only have one father," said Oliver. "The one who chose me."

They talked more after that, primarily about Oliver's training and his close friend Alex, who was hopefully going to receive his own tattoos in just a few months. "You're very close to Alex, aren't you?" asked his father.

Oliver nodded.

"As long as you're happy."

Oliver's eyes widened. "Dad—"

"Yeah, yeah, don't blow smoke up my ass. I don't care if it's serious or not. Only time will tell, but if he's going to be part of your family— *our* family—I'll want to meet him eventually."

Oliver stood still. "Fair enough."

"About your tattoos…"

"Hmm?"

"They aren't like the ones most wardsmen have. I made some changes."

Oliver gaped at his father. "*You!* That was you there! I thought I dreamed that."

Will nodded. "I couldn't leave your future in the hands of some halfwit apprentice with little to no knowledge of magic and some superstitious tattoo tradition that hasn't changed in centuries."

"Daikor Sean has been teaching me the visualizations to activate strength, speed, and endurance, but none of them work," exclaimed Oliver.

"You don't need them. Waste of space. How about the night vision?"

His trainer had said the same thing, but he still felt sour about it. "My night vision works."

"Underwater breathing, climbing?"

Oliver nodded. "I just take a deep breath and I'm fine for a long, long time. He's going to show me how to use the climbing tattoos tomorrow."

"Good. I added a few other things, but you should probably keep them a secret. They're more of an advantage if no one knows." Will rubbed his hands together. "Have you cut yourself yet?"

"When I jumped out of the window," said Oliver with some embarrassment. "I bled some, but I never found the cut."

His father smiled from ear to ear. "Excellent."

"Can I regenerate? Like those potions?"

Will shook his head. "Hell no, don't ever think that. It'll get you killed. Full regeneration is costly and leaves you vulnerable. It would take all your turyn and leave you weak and sleepy at best. What Doctor Lorentz and I did was add a number of specific healing techniques. Ordinarily, they'd be impossible to put in a ward or an enchantment, but the tattoos map out your body in a way that fits perfectly with the technique."

"So what can I do?"

"Your cuts will seal themselves relatively quickly, and even more importantly, your muscles and tendons will repair themselves when damaged. Same thing with your bones."

Oliver tilted his head to one side. "That sounds just like regeneration."

"Trust me, it isn't," said his father. "Bruises are still going to suck, and your organs won't heal. If someone sticks a piece of steel through your belly, there's a very high chance it will kill you." Will held up a hand suddenly. "Not from infection, though! I managed to replicate the effects produced by blood-cleanse potions, so you won't have to worry about your wounds turning sour. Let me tell you, I had to work hard to convince Tiny to let me see the Terabinian research. The muscle and bone stuff was meant for their Iron Knights, but they couldn't get it to work with the armor. It's perfect for tattoos, though."

"So, skin, muscles, bones, and no gangrene, is that it?"

"Poison too," said Will with a grin. "No need to worry about poison."

"And all of this just happens when needed?"

"Yep."

"You didn't give me anything I can *use*? No active abilities?" Oliver was trying hard to hide his disappointment.

Will gave him a dark stare. "Do you know how many men I've seen die from bleeding out? Or survive that, only to lose an arm or leg because we didn't have enough medicine to keep their wounds from going bad? You don't even have any idea what it's like to break a bone, do you?"

"Well, not exactly but—"

"On the battlefield," interrupted Will, "with a hundred enemies still trying to stick a spear in your side! I once had a vampire stick a sword straight through my damned spine!"

"I can heal from a severed spine?"

Will frowned. "Well, no—but that's not the point! You've gotten me all flustered. Ungrateful whelp! I have half a mind not to tell you about the other things I added."

Oliver's ears perked up. "Other things?"

His dad grinned at him. "Have I ever showed you my camouflage spell?"

"Camouflage?"

"You can blend in with your surroundings."

"Do I have to get naked?"

"No, why?"

"My tattoos are on my skin," said Oliver as if it was the simplest thing in the world.

"That would be the stupidest thing in the world then," snapped Will. "How would you wear armor? I wouldn't have included it if it wouldn't work on your clothing too."

"We don't wear armor most of the time," Oliver informed him. "We use the iron-body tattoos."

Will rolled his eyes. "That's all well and good, but I've used that spell plenty of times. If you're planning to be some sort of fancy bar bouncer or guard ladies when they go to the privy, that's fine, but if there's ever a real fight, you're going to want something better than that."

Oliver felt attacked. He'd already learned to use it in numerous ways, offensively and defensively. The main thing was skill and preparedness. He started to say so, but his dad was already waving his hands. "Save it. Hold out your arm and imagine liquid silver flowing over your skin."

"What?"

"Like quicksilver. Have you seen quicksilver before?"

"No."

Will nodded. "Good, because that shit is poisonous as hell. That's why I never let you see my alchemical workshop when you were growing up. It wouldn't hurt you now, though. Damn it, I'm getting off topic again."

"What else is new?"

Will eyed him for a moment. "You're not too old for me to put you over my knee."

"I'd like to see you try. I'm half a head taller than you," said Oliver with a gleam in his eye.

"You're going to be awfully embarrassed when you have to explain to Alex how your daddy had to give you a spanking at the ripe old age of sixteen," returned Will. The two of them glared at one another intensely for several seconds, until Will broke and a smile stole across his face. They both laughed for a minute before he finally continued.

"Imagine water, but instead of blue, it looks like metal. Think about it flowing down from your elbow to your fingers," said Will.

Oliver tried several times before he felt something happen, then he saw it. "Oh wow! Wow. What does it do?"

"It's complicated. So you're going to have to put up with listening to me for a while, but if—"

"Can I do it all over myself?"

"Yes, but—"

"I'd suffocate, though, right? So I need to use the underwater breathing tattoo and hold my breath first."

"No. Will you shut up and listen?"

"I'm just excited," admitted Oliver.

Will ran a hand over his face. "May the Mother give me patience. It's gas permeable, otherwise the spiders wouldn't be able to diffuse air through their spiracles. That's also the main weakness, since air spells can disperse it temporarily."

"Spiders?"

They talked for half an hour, and Will answered endless questions before Oliver was satisfied, but eventually the bell rang, and they were out of time. Will promised to come back in a week and explain further, but Oliver had one burning question that wouldn't wait. "How long have you been working on all this?"

Will paused, then answered, "Since the day I promised you could be a wardsman if you would try the compression training."

"You didn't even want me to be one. You were hell-bent on making me a wizard instead."

"I hoped so, but I didn't know what would happen, so I had to think ahead."

"That was almost a year ago."

His father nodded. "A wizard prepares. Plus, it soon became clear when you couldn't handle turyn sight."

"But you must have spent a lot of time and resources on all this. You said the healing stuff was based on secrets from Terabinia, didn't you?"

Will nodded again, and creases appeared in the corner of his eyes. "A wizard prepares, but a father makes sure. I couldn't let anything happen to my boy."

They hugged again, and for the first time, Oliver was late to his morning meeting with Daikor Sean.

CHAPTER 52

A year went by, and the world kept turning. Oliver spent half of it training with Daikor Sean and entered service with Lloyd Blathe. In the meantime, Alex received his own tattoos and had begun his own intensive training. Fortunately for Oliver, Blathe spent a considerable amount of his time in the capital, so he was able to visit Alex frequently.

For Will, things settled into a new routine, and he returned to working a regular schedule at the Laughing Goat, though he only worked two days a week now. He considered those days his 'weekend' since he still enjoyed cooking as his primary hobby. His real work was done during the other five days. He expanded his lair, using construction and excavation spells collected from the library at Wurthaven, and when he couldn't find a spell appropriate to the task at hand, he designed his own. His skills in spell design and spell theory had grown so much that in many cases he could create novel spell solutions in less time than it took to record them. He was continually filling new journals, and on several occasions, he created spells, used them, and forgot them before remembering to write them down.

He did his best to make sure that didn't happen, but it didn't bother him too much. Recreating a spell he'd made once before wasn't an arduous task.

In part, his speed and success were due to the fact that new spells weren't nearly as dangerous for him as they had once been. Back when he'd studied Spell Theory under Professor Dulaney, he'd been continually cautioned on the dangers of untested spell designs, with good cause. A spell construct that produced an unforeseen resonance could explode, or if it was given too much or too little turyn, it might become unstable, and the consequences could range from silly to lethal.

A third-order wizard had much less to fear, though. Will's magic resistance made it unlikely he would be hurt by anything an unbalanced spell produced, and his growing confidence made mistakes less common as time went on. His worst fears were for his environment, or more specifically, for his books and alchemical tools. Glassware was expensive and difficult to replace, and books were obviously very flammable.

Consequently, he designed several very reliable wards to protect his books and journals from both flame and explosions. The luxpress made it easy for him to design an enchanting template that he stamped into the inside of every cover, and the ward was so well balanced that it would last nearly forever, unless the item protected was actually exposed to a fire or an explosion. There was a visible mark at the bottom of the spine which told Will if any of his volumes needed to have their turyn replenished, so he didn't have to worry over rechecking them or setting a schedule for book maintenance. He always knew at a glance.

The glassware was more problematic. While he could easily design protections for glass, the magic involved could potentially interfere with the potions he brewed. He thought the problem to be a tractable one, but his skill and intuitive grasp of alchemy were nowhere near as great as his ability with spell design. It would probably require great mastery of both to create protective wards that wouldn't affect the alchemical process. *Maybe in a few decades,* he told himself. He still had a lot more he wanted to do in the areas he was currently interested in.

Besides, the last time he'd had a spell construct explode, he'd been able to contain it with his will alone, just as if he was suppressing the magic of another practitioner. The arcane was his home, and a shark needn't fear the waters it swam in.

The elves had established an embassy in Terabinia, and it was their influence that he suspected when it came to the drop in potion prices, but he couldn't prove it. While they were very open in most of the products they traded, namely bluet, the supplier flooding the market with alchemical products was well hidden. He made one or two half-hearted attempts to trace them back to their source but gave up soon after. Numerous go-betweens and shifting sale locations made it a difficult task, and he wasn't that concerned about it, anyway.

The only thing that made him think he should eventually invest the time was the fact that it could potentially be a way to locate Grim Talek. The lich had remained hidden since Will's departure from Terabinia, and it was very possible the potion sales were coming from him.

Cora visited in the spring, spending two days this time. Will canceled everything for her, and wasted not a single minute. His neighbors probably noticed the two of them during their walks, as he was well known as a bachelor, so the sight of him walking hand-in-hand with a woman was news. He didn't care, though, and neither did Cora. They simply waved and smiled at anyone they passed on the street. *No one here knows either of us, anyway.* Will was confident in his long-standing alias, and Cora... *Her secrets are her own,* he decided. He already knew he didn't want to know them. The truth would destroy their brief happiness.

The second evening, while they were curled up together in a nest of blankets in her wagon, the conversation turned to the wider world. "Things have gotten tense lately," she said unexpectedly.

"There's been a lot of unrest over lost ships," agreed Will.

"It's more than that," she told him. "I'm hearing rumors that the Five are considering severing their trade agreements with Terabinia."

"They love money too much for that. Terabinia is their largest market."

"Don't be too sure. Some say they might even close the border."

He hadn't been paying much attention to politics, and until then, he hadn't regretted the choice. It was one of the best things about not being the prince consort in Terabinia. "Is it that bad?"

Cora nodded. "If the border closes, I won't be able to trade in Trendham." The unspoken meaning in her eyes went deeper. If the border closed, she wouldn't be able to visit *him.*

"I like the sound of that even less."

"You like it here, don't you?" she asked, a certain wistfulness in her eyes.

That look pained him, for he knew she wanted the same, but he answered honestly, even though it might sting. "I miss Terabinia, but I've never been more at peace. My son is grown, Mom is happy, and I have all the time in the world to put into my own projects. It's bliss, being unknown."

She laid her head back against his chest. "I'm happy for you. I wish it could be the same for me."

Will felt a tightness in his chest. He wanted to tell her it could be, but he knew better, and broaching the subject could easily destroy the illusions they both were choosing to believe in. "It will get better in time," he told her instead. "As long as we can see each other like this, the world isn't so bad, is it?"

"It's been growing steadily worse over the past few years," she answered, her voice full of melancholy. When she looked back up at him, her eyes were liquid. "I've never asked anything of you, have I? I haven't pried into your life, or your secrets."

A lump formed in his throat. "You haven't, and I love you for that. I know it can't have been easy for you."

"I don't know if you have any influence with the Five—"

"I don't," he said, interrupting her.

Cora nodded. "Very well, you don't then. But if you did, or if there was anything you could do or say to improve relations between Trendham and Terabinia…"

"I don't talk to the Five," he insisted. "They don't know me, and more importantly they don't know where I live, and that's how I'd like it to stay."

Her mouth opened briefly, then closed again. "I'm sorry."

"Don't be. You're doing the best you can."

"You haven't asked about my other job—"

"And I won't."

She nodded. "But I'm doing everything I can to prevent a war, you know that, right?"

He squeezed her shoulders. "I know."

"It's all I can do to protect you," she said quietly, "to protect this life you've created here."

"You worry too much about a lowly cook. Lystal is far from harm's way no matter what happens," he said, trying to sound reassuring, but the expression on her face was still full of uncertainty. Sitting up, he met her eyes and spoke with sincerity. "I'll protect what I have here; that's not your job. You're already working hard, and I trust you always will. No matter what the future holds, I'd never lay the blame at your feet."

After a moment, she nodded, and the two of them relaxed into the cushions again. "What do you think about Terabinia these days?" she asked.

He cocked his head and lifted one brow. "You mean since I left it?" She nodded, and he thought about his answer for a few seconds, then answered, "Queen Selene has surprised everyone, but not me. I never had any doubt she would rule with justice, kindness, and mercy. While a lot of the noblemen doubted her governance, I knew she had more skill than anyone else to handle the job. I fully expected her to dance circles around their childish plots and ploys, and she's made fools of her enemies at every turn.

"Best of all, she's kept sight of the real goal, taking care of her people, and because of that Terabinia is more prosperous than ever before. It would take me a while to list all her accomplishments, and I've no doubt the list will only continue to grow longer as the years pass by."

Cora was smiling when he looked back at her face. "I asked about Terabinia, and all you talk about is their queen. You sound as if you might be infatuated with her."

"Far more than that," he admitted. "I'm completely smitten, just like everyone else who hails from there. You must spend too much time traveling and eavesdropping in foreign lands. Go home and spend some time in Cerria or Myrsta's taverns. You'll hear the people talking. They love their queen more than life itself."

A tear rolled down her cheek, and she nodded. "Perhaps I'll do that." Lifting herself up on one elbow, she brought her lips to his for a short but sweet kiss, then she told him, "I love you, Kelvin Wiltshire, and whoever else you may be."

"I love you too, Wilhelmina Dewitt, and whoever you may be," he answered with a smile.

Her eyes narrowed. "Whoever I may be, I told you I don't like that name! What are you supposed to call me again?"

"Oh, right! I forgot. Carol, is it? Or was it Coral? I keep forgetting. Maybe I should just call you Wilma—that's the usual nickname for Wilhelmina, isn't it? It sounds nice too."

Growling, she wrestled her way on top of him. "I think you'd better think hard, or I'll have to jog your memory."

His eyes were bright as he replied, "If I say your name *and* think myself hard, will you jog something else for me? Cora…"

CHAPTER 53

Spring came the next year, and James Wellings greeted it with a sense of anticipation, as he did every spring. It had been a long day, but he looked forward to returning home, though he didn't rush. The walk from Wurthaven to their house was a pleasant one, especially so now that the trees were beginning to bud new leaves. In another week, the walk would be even lovelier as bright green began to overtake the skeletal branches.

People passed him going in either direction, since most of them had a greater sense of urgency in reaching their destination, but James liked to stroll. He whistled a tune as he went, thinking of what might await him at home. Edward was fourteen now and showing the awkward signs of incipient manhood. Elaina and Christopher were twelve and eleven, respectively, making James wish he could stop their time, for they were at the perfect age in his mind. The littlest, Talia, was nine, and she wasn't so little anymore. Skinny as a reed, the girl was an incorrigible tomboy and was just as bad as her brothers when it came to getting mud on her clothes, or bringing frogs into the house. Her older sister, Elaina, was constantly scolding her.

Best of all, Tabitha would be waiting for him—or not. She was frequently busy when he arrived, but the smile that would slide across her lips when she spotted him at the door always lifted his spirits. James considered himself fortunate in every way that mattered, and the fact that he also enjoyed his work was almost too good to be true. The students inspired him, much as his own children did, and thanks to the recognition he'd received for some of his recent papers, he would be taking on a new role in the coming semester as a lecturer in the Engineering and Artifice Department.

The future was so bright nothing could spoil his mood, not even the man who roughly bumped into him without looking. "Begging your pardon!" James sputtered, or would have, but his lungs weren't cooperating for some reason. His body stumbled as the stranger's arm pumped back and forth like a piston, driving a fist repeatedly into his chest.

No, not a fist, he realized as his eye caught a glint of metal reflecting in the afternoon sun, *a knife.* Drops of scarlet flew by in slow motion as James fell. Strangely, he felt little pain, but he wanted to cough as liquid filled his lungs. They still wouldn't work, though, making it difficult for him to even do that.

The real pain came as he hit the cobblestones, but James wasn't paying attention to that. His focus was on his assailant. The man had already turned away, slipping his knife back into his coat as though nothing had happened. "Death to the queen! Justice for Trendham," said the stranger as he began walking quickly away.

I'm dying, thought James, but it was too sudden for him to be angry. Instead, he thought of his family. What would they think when he didn't come home? Worse, who else might show up at his door? If he had been targeted, he knew why, and Tabitha and the children would be even better targets. His eyes focused on his murderer, and he reflex cast a spell. The range was a bit long, costing him a considerable amount of turyn, but the force-lance tore a fist-sized hole through the killer's back.

"Tabitha," he tried to whisper. He had to warn them. His body was growing cold, and the white shirt he wore was soaked with crimson. A woman screamed from across the road, probably at the sight of him. James lifted himself up on his arms, but immediately regretted it as he grew faint and his arms trembled. Sinking back down, he looked at his right hand. It was trembling and covered in blood, but all he cared about was the signet ring on his index finger. It wasn't the original, the one he'd inherited from his father. That ring sat in a box at home. This was a replacement; one he'd designed himself. Concentrating, he used his thumb to twist it around, then pressed hard against the top of the Wellings family crest.

Had it worked? He couldn't tell. *I should have seen a flash of turyn,* he realized, but he hadn't. His trembling fingers weren't responding properly. *Or maybe it's my eyes. Everything is so dark.* Darkness closed in around him, but only for a moment.

A woman was looking down on him with the kindest eyes he had ever seen. "Don't be distressed, child. You've earned some rest."

"You're the Mother," he said, glad to find his voice finally working. "I wasn't sure you were real." Then he felt a sense of panic. "I have to warn them."

"You did. Rest easy."

He nodded. "I'll miss them."

"You'll see them soon, James."

"Then it didn't work?"

"Time is meaningless. Five minutes or fifty years, it will seem the same," she told him.

Chapter 53

***

Darla was making her own way home, arms full as she carried two large sacks with her, one of flour, one of beans. She wasn't much of a cook, but she didn't have to be, Galen, the man who ran the orphanage was a decent hand in the kitchen. He was even older than her, and one of his legs didn't work well, but his thick arms still had plenty of strength in them, more than enough to care for the children that lived there.

When she had first met the man, she'd been suspicious. In her experience most who professed to care for the poor and dispossessed were liars, or worse, predators who used those weaker than them to improve their reputation while they took what they wanted from their charges: money, food, or sex.

Laina had been the first to break through her cynicism, introducing her to those who truly believed in the lofty goals of the Mothers of Terabinia. Of course, it had also helped that Laina had been beautiful and charismatic, but Darla had been younger then.

After Laina's death and Will's exile, she'd been a little lost, but Darla had tried to continue Laina's dream by doing what she could for the charity. That was how she'd met Galen, a hopeless man who seemed intent on spending his days caring for the children that others had cast aside. Over time, she'd begun to trust him, and rather than just bringing food donations from the Mothers to his door, she'd wound up moving into the orphanage with him.

Darla suspected that Galen might harbor a romantic interest, but he'd never made any overtures. Despite his coarse exterior, he was uncommonly good at reading people, and he probably sensed her disinterest in that regard.

She loved him though, in all the ways that mattered, and if he'd expressed desire, she'd long ago decided she would humor him. Not out of pity, but simply because he reminded her of Laina. Love was love, and she regarded it as a shame that he'd been born in a body that failed to arouse her other interests. Thankfully, he had never broached the subject.

Galen was only ten years older than her, but Darla suspected he thought of her more as he did one of his children. That sort of thinking was typical of him, and she was certainly just as broken as any of the other wayward souls he'd collected around him over the years. Either way, she didn't mind.

She had a family.

Her route home shouldn't have taken her through the wealthy neighborhood that Tabitha's home resided in, but she always took the longer walk in order to get a look at the streets around the house. It wasn't much of an effort, and Darla sometimes felt guilty for not doing more. If anything happened to Laina's remaining family, would she be willing to forgive Darla's lack of dedication?

It was a foolish question. *She would have wanted me to be happy, and she would have loved what I'm doing with my remaining years,* Darla told herself.

Her legs were tired, and her back was sore. Taking a longer route home was one thing, but doing it with forty pounds of dried goods in your arms was a chore. Darla had already passed forty, and her past life had left her with aches in many of her joints. Ignoring the discomfort, she pressed on.

A group of men were loitering on the street corner near Tabitha's house, and Darla took note of them as she passed. Clothing, smells, the way they spoke, there was something off, but she couldn't put her finger on what bothered her. Midway down the block ahead, she saw another three men talking, though they were standing on the opposite side from the Wellings' residence.

There were more people than she expected to see there at that time of day, but they weren't doing anything suspicious. Groaning, Darla put down the sack she carried and leaned her back against the decorative iron fence that surrounded the front yard. It was barely more than four feet high, and served little purpose to Darla's thinking. The only enemies the fence would stop would be a riotous mob of grannies. Rubbing her back, she looked around briefly and then discreetly brought out the metal tablet Will had given her, then wrote:

Men outside T's house.

The message was short because it had to be, and she only sent it to two people: Will and Tabitha. If she spent too much time, she would seem suspicious. Tucking the tablet away again, she lifted her load and stood. She had a decision to make.

There was still no reason to think anything nefarious was about to happen, but the hair on the back of her neck was standing up. Glancing behind her, she assessed the men on the corner, then the three ahead of her. None of them were paying much attention to her.

Go home and you won't have a problem, she told herself, but instead she crossed the road, heading toward the group of three. *I don't have to confront them, but a closer look might tell me the truth.*

And if the truth was that the men weren't casual bystanders? Then she'd have another decision to make. Taking on seven men would be a stupid thing to do, even for her. She had quit wearing the Arkeshi mail vest under her clothes many years ago. Carrying that extra weight when she was young was probably half the reason her knees and back were so often painful. The only weapon on her was a six-inch knife she kept under her blouse.

It won't come to that, she decided, ignoring her instincts.

"Would one of you boys mind taking a minute to give me a hand?" she asked as she came up to them.

"Lady, you don't look like there's anything wrong with you," said the youngest-appearing man.

"I hurt my back a few days ago," she said, stumbling slightly.

When it looked as if she might drop her sack, the older one, who stood closest to her, put a hand out and caught the sack. "Careful."

The young one glared at him. "Vince, don't waste your time helping this cunt. She's a turdian anyway."

Vince glared back. "Terabinian or not, she's old enough to be your mother. Show a little respect."

Darla studied them as they spoke, then she leaned over, putting a hand out to steady herself. She missed his arm and accidentally put her hand on his side, though he was covered with a broad cloak. Through it, she could feel a sword hanging at his side. She'd already made up her mind that they weren't soldiers, watchmen, or anyone else who should be carrying such a thing, and the remark about Terabinians clinched the conclusion.

Instigators, spies, or assassins. Those were the options her mind offered. So long as it wasn't the house across the road, she wouldn't interfere. Seven was too many, even in her prime, and she was practically unarmed. "I'm sorry for bothering you, then," she said to the one who had helped her. "I'll get out of your way."

As she started to take the sack back, the city bells rang, announcing to all who could hear that it was five o' clock. The young one rose up on his toes, excited. "That's the signal. It's time."

A multitude of things flashed through Darla's mind. But first and foremost among them was the fact that whatever terrible deed they had planned would happen then and there, which meant that Tabitha's family were almost certainly the ones being targeted. Regret was next, but her hands were already moving. Thought was the enemy of pure and efficient action, and some lessons would never leave her.

Stumbling again, she covered the motion of her hand pulling the blade from beneath her shirt. Sadly, the nice one had to be her first target. If he'd been in simple clothing, it would have been much easier, but she'd felt hard leather beneath his cloak. Leather she could pierce, but it would be slower, less accurate, and would almost certainly cost her too many of those first precious seconds of surprise. Worse, it could be brigandine or something she couldn't stab through.

That meant she had to aim for places she knew would be unarmored, and there was a separate set of risks down that path, mainly revolving around the risk of missing.

As Vince looked down to steady her, Darla's hand snapped up, with her left hand under the elbow to give it extra force as she drove the dagger under his chin and into his skull. He started to fall as she withdrew and turned. With luck, the others would freeze, giving her more time.

The middle one did, but the rude young one was already reaching out to snatch her away from his friend. His eyes probably hadn't registered the attack yet; he was simply an asshole. His movement complicated things, though. Darla took his hand in hers, passing the blade to her other hand as she did. Holding his wrist steady, she drew the blade in a rapid circle around it, severing veins, tendons, and arteries.

As the young one started to scream, she stabbed the quiet one. She didn't know if he wore any protection, so she went for the leg. Very few soldiers wore armor on their thighs. Even on a battlefield most didn't, relying on mail that hung almost to their knees, if they had it. Only officers would have full leg armor, and this man certainly wasn't anyone important.

It helped that he was taller than her, not to mention slow. Her blade went in a few inches above the knee, and Darla stepped in and around him, ripping the blade through the muscle behind his leg. He'd be crippled for sure, but her true goal was the popliteal artery. Severing that would kill him soon afterward unless he received immediate aid.

The kid was screaming bloody murder now, which suited her just fine. If Tabitha hadn't read her message yet, the noise would serve just as well.

The man she'd just crippled started to fall, but he knew he was in a fight now. Twisting, he tried to catch her under his right arm. Stabbing upward, she hit his forearm, but the blade snagged between the bones. She didn't waste time trying to pull it free.

She only had two options. If she followed him down, she could speed up his demise, but she would be entangled for far too long. Stab wounds didn't kill quickly unless you hit the heart or brain, and she no longer had a blade. Dying men often possessed incredible strength, and she might be badly hurt before she could exit the struggle.

With a feeling of regret that she didn't have time to claim his weapons, she ducked and turned, pulling the man's cloak around him. Darla's eyes widened as she saw the loaded crossbow he'd been concealing within it. Her fear came not from him, as the dying cripple would be hard-pressed to aim with a wounded arm and a bad leg.

It was the others that worried her. If *one* of them had such a weapon, it was likely that some of the others did as well.

Darla dropped into a roll, but her body wasn't as supple as it had once been. She executed the move, but something popped, and she felt pain shoot through her back and side. Adrenaline overrode the pain, and she continued forward into a sprint for the corner of the building they were in front of. She needed cover before someone could aim in her direction. The first four men were shouting, though she didn't spare them a glance.

She rounded the corner only to come face-to-face with another five she hadn't seen yet, and in the back of her mind, she registered the knowledge that she was unlikely to live much longer. A novice might have reversed course, but that way only led to certain death. Instead, she dove down, hurling herself into the legs of the man leading the charge from the alley.

In the course of her career, she'd survived a number of unlikely events and seen others die to freak moments of chance. She hoped the man who fell over her would catch the quarrel that must surely be headed her way by now, but luck was on his side, and the bolt whizzed over his head. *I saved his life,* she realized, savoring the irony.

"Gods be damned! Watch out, she's fast!" someone yelled, as Darla leapt upward. She was hoping to put her head into the second one's chin, but her luck seemed to have run out. The young fighter jerked his head to the side and pushed her away to get some space.

That suited her just fine. A grapple would have been the end. The man's belt knife was in one of her hands now. Borrowing the momentum from his shove, she let it carry her backward. The one she had tripped was just beginning to rise, until her foot came down on his hand. She felt bone crack under her heel, and during the seconds that the pain blinded him, she pulled a second knife from his belt.

At last, she felt moderately armed. If she'd had her mail vest and a short sword, she would have been even happier, but some things were not to be. The four men on their feet had fanned out, surrounding her. Two had their swords out and a third held a mace in his hand. The fourth was still lamenting the loss of his knife, when he should have already drawn another weapon.

Darla chose him.

As she dashed toward him, he jerked back, so she turned to meet whichever one had seized the moment to strike at her from behind. With luck, it would be only one of them. Fights were chaotic and proper coordination was rare.

Usually.

Both swordsmen were swinging, one high and one low. She managed to divert the high blow away from her chest, but the second blade cut deeply into her thigh. Blood poured down her leg and a smile found her lips.

"And so, I die," she said, showing her teeth. "Dance with me." She pushed off with her good leg and brought her arms around in a swirling motion. The blade dance was hardly practical in a real fight, but she knew her life was fading fast, and with only one leg she wouldn't be able to maneuver.

Her slashes caught the man who had slain her by surprise, and he swung wildly to try and ward her off. One knife skidded along his weapon, pushing it aside, while her other hand slashed through his shirt. It didn't find flesh, but Darla was quick. Her guard hand was coming back, and she cut a horizontal slice through his nose.

Arm, wrist, shoulder she delivered painful cuts too quickly to be stopped. Her killer panicked, and she ended her ceremonial display with a real strike, driving one blade directly into his eye. Lightning ran up her spine as the dead man's friend drove his sword through her back, but she twisted, ignoring the searing pain.

Unable to withdraw, the man released the handle, stepping back at the sight of her dreadful smile. Darla tried to follow, but her leg folded, and she hissed in frustration. She only wanted one more. Knowing she'd never reach him, or anyone else, she threw the knife in her hand, then followed with the other. It was a foolish move, but she didn't have any others left. *Please, grant me one more.*

The first knife struck at a bad angle and bounced away. The man had flinched as it came at his face, but the second blade was just behind. It cut through his cheek, exposing the bone of his jaw.

The mace crashed into Darla's shoulder, driving her the rest of the way down, but her eyes were on the man with the cut cheek. "If you live to see tomorrow, you are blessed, for you have seen the Arkeshi fight and lived." The mace came down again, crushing the side of her head. More blows followed, but she wasn't there to receive them.

"Little sister, you lived well," said a deep male voice.

"My lord," said Darla, grateful for her good fortune. "I had feared I wouldn't find a place at your side. My life has been nothing but peace for years."

The man standing over her wore black and red leathers and his chin sported a dark, close-cut beard. Darla knew him instantly, for he was Marduke, the lord of death and shadows. Despite her soft life, she had died as an Arkeshi, with blood on her blades.

"The peace was the best part, wasn't it?" he asked, reaching down to lift her up. "Did you think I care nothing for life and love?"

She blinked in confusion. "That is not what we are taught."

"Perhaps in the next life you will find better lessons, but you have nothing to be ashamed of in this one," he told her.

"I will be reborn?"

He nodded. "When you are ready, but for now there's no rush. Come and dream; keep me company for a while. Do you like to dance?"

The only dance she knew was the dance of blades, but she nodded anyway. In her heart, she had often dreamed of dancing the way normal folk did, with bright songs and merry smiles. Glad tears ran down her cheeks as she followed him into the light.

CHAPTER 54

Tabitha was reading in the parlor, but the text in front of her eyes made them want to close. James had asked her to proof his latest paper, and while she always tried to be enthusiastic about his passion, the details bored her to death. Her children were milling about the house, restless and waiting for the inevitable circus that generally followed their father's arrival after work.

She smiled thinking about him, and for not the first time, she wondered how such a ridiculously silly man could write such a boring technical analysis on the topic of ward balancing. It was as if two separate men lived inside her husband's head.

The city bell rang, and she knew it would only be a few more minutes, but as she tried to return her attention to the page in front of her, she heard shouting in the street. Reflexively, she rubbed at the ring she wore on her right hand, a beautiful replacement James had given her for her wedding ring. In the years since regaining contact with her brother, they'd been careful, but she didn't really expect real trouble.

Rising from her seat, she crossed over to the window, but she stood to one side before moving the curtain. Men were fighting in the street, but it wasn't obvious why. A smaller figure started running, and she wondered if someone had stolen something. Before she spotted the weapons, the glass turned a deep shade of purple, and a loud chime rang out inside the house. Looking down, she stared at her ring. She hadn't activated it, but the diamond had turned blood red.

That meant James had used his, even though he wasn't home yet. Already alarmed, Tabitha's heart raced at that thought. Wherever he was, her husband knew they were in danger, which might mean *he* was in danger.

Moving toward the hall, Tabitha was already yelling, "Edward! Elaina! Talia! Christopher!" Lyle, the cook, was the first face she saw, though.

"What's happening?" he asked.

"We're going into the basement. Find Neicy and the children. Quickly!" Moving to the base of the stairs, she continued yelling, "Christopher! Elaina—" Her oldest daughter's head appeared before she could finish. "Mom? What's wrong?"

"Where's Talia?"

"In our room," answered the girl.   •

"Get her and get to the basement. Open the door if you're the first one there. Hurry! Christopher!"

"Yes, Momma?" he answered, standing directly behind her.

She was already so flustered she nearly struck him, but Tabitha caught herself. "Where's Edward?"

The eleven-year-old shrugged. "I dunno."

"Find him and get—no, forget that. Go down to the basement and get in our special room. I'll find him," she ordered. It had only been a minute since she'd looked out the window, but a new chime sounded and continued at a steady beat. Someone had crossed the fence.

Tabitha and her husband had had long discussions about how their precautions should work. They lived in the largest city in Terabinia, and it wasn't uncommon for children to climb or jump over the fence. Even adults occasionally snuck into the back garden, usually to grab fruit from the trees. For those reasons, the wards outside were purely defensive. The glass changing color was an indication that reinforcement wards had activated, making the windows difficult to break.

Something hard slammed into one of the front windows, and she jumped. At that moment she was wishing they'd included something offensive, even if it put strangers and pets at risk. Elaina and Talia passed her as they came down the stairs.

"He might be in the garden," said the oldest girl. "Should I look?"

Tabitha shook her head. "Get down there, now." Mentally, she tallied them all. Three were on the stairs, Lyle and Neicy with them. Edward was the only one missing, and if he was outside, he would need to use the outside cellar door. The front door and the garden door would no longer open for anyone, even Tabitha.

That was another of their hard choices, meant to prevent either of them from being forced—or used—to breach the house's defenses. The cellar door was the compromise. It was also locked automatically, but it could be opened at the touch of anyone in the family, providing them with an alternative escape route. She and James had gone over it countless times with their children, making sure they understood, but in that moment, she didn't feel confident.

The cellar was separated from the basement, with its own secure room, but she hadn't heard the signal that anyone had entered it. Tabitha ran up the stairs, hoping he was asleep in his room. If Edward wasn't there, her only way into the garden now would be to jump from one of the second-floor windows. She heard a roar from somewhere outside, the sound of a large beast of some sort, and a second later, the house shook as something slammed into it.

Ignoring it all, she reached the boys' room and went inside. It was empty, so she ran to the window and looked out onto the garden. Her eyes moved desperately, until she finally saw him and her heart stopped. Edward was on the stone path leading toward the cellar, but he was lying face-down and something dark was pooling beside him.

Again, she heard the roar of some mysterious beast, but it was apparently on the other side of the house, probably near the front door. Meanwhile, the garden was full of strangers carrying weapons. Four of them stood around Edward, with axes and swords in hand.

Tabitha never heard the glass break as she passed through it, nor did she consider the height from which she leapt. None of it mattered to her. Stretching out her arms, she used the talent she had kept hidden for so long, grateful she had found a use for it. Feathers sprouted from them as massive wings grew, turning her fall into a glide that allowed her to land near her son, but they didn't remain wings.

Even as her feet were almost to the ground, they changed, along with the rest of her body. An axe thudded into her side, but Tabitha was already beyond such pain, and the weapon was small in comparison to her growing bulk. She lashed out with a thickly muscled arm that was rapidly being covered with heavy scales, and the axe wielder fell. The blow had broken something in him, and he screamed as he went down.

Quarrels slammed into her, but they only made her angrier. Men were shouting and running, surrounding her, but that didn't last long. With the sweep of one long arm, her talons caught two, disemboweling them and giving her room. The others backed up, and three men farther back were hastily reloading crossbows. Tabitha stretched out one hand, and the fingers elongated with incredible speed, crossing the distance and impaling the crossbowmen.

An explosion sounded from somewhere, and some of the men clapped their hands to their heads in pain. The pressure wave had popped their eardrums, and a moment later, Tabitha realized her own world had gone completely silent.

She didn't care.

In less than a minute, she finished slaughtering the invaders, and her only regret was that she couldn't hear their screams. Looking around warily, she shrank, her body expelling crossbow bolts and the axe that had been left hanging from her back. To her surprise, a spear fell to the ground as well. She hadn't even noticed it. Blood was everywhere, some of it hers, as a wave of exhaustion swept over her.

Tabitha's flesh mastery was an interesting talent, as it not only allowed her to shift into a plethora of forms, but it also made self-healing a trivial task, but it still suffered from certain drawbacks. The healing robbed her of energy, though it wasn't as bad as what a regeneration potion would have done to her. Her natural talent was more efficient than artificial alchemy, but it still would have been better if she had armored herself *before* being stabbed and hacked so badly.

Better still, I could have used the spells I've been practicing like a fool for the past five years, she chided herself. She'd lost her mind when she saw her son on the ground. Ranged elemental magics and simple shields would have accomplished the same slaughter and cost her much less blood.

"Edward, can you hear me? Eddie? Please." She was leaning over her son, afraid of what she would find. Already, she could see the bolt sticking out of his back, just over his kidney.

Her ears finished healing, and she heard a painful groan. That was when her heart began to beat again, and color returned to the world. Summoning a potion from her limnthal, she tried to lift her son into her arms.

That earned her a shriek of pain as the bolt shifted in his back. For a moment, she didn't know what to do, but she could hear more fighting and snarling coming from the front of the house. She could either pick Edward up and run for the cellar door or try to administer the potion first. She had no idea how bad the wound really was—she had no medical training—but there was no doubt in her mind that it was serious. He might die from the rough treatment if she simply grabbed him and ran.

At the same time, hurting him pained her heart, but she saw no other choice. Unstopping the potion, she dribbled a few drops around the wound, then turned his head and got the rest into his mouth. Closing her eyes, she ripped the barbed weapon out of his back. Under any other circumstances, it was a terrible idea and in her usual form she wouldn't have had the strength.

Edward's scream tore at her heart, and he vomited up most of the regeneration potion. She summoned another and forced it down his mouth, heedless of his choking. She had no idea whether the few drops she'd put on his back were enough, or if the small amount he'd swallowed would do the trick.

She knew nothing, and without certainty, fear kept its grip on her heart, until finally she saw the wound begin to close. Tabitha released Edward's mouth, and he vomited again. Heedless of his pain, she lifted him again and ran for the cellar. Only after they were inside and the door had shut behind them did the tightness in her chest start to unclench. She created a light and found the inner door, a heavy, iron-bound oak door set in stone.

She dragged her son inside and closed it behind them, watching the wards activate, sealing them inside. They were safe, and a light above the door told her the other room in the basement had been shut and sealed as well. It would take time and serious magic to get into either of their safe rooms, time no enemy would have unless the capital itself had fallen.

Tabitha had one real concern left: James. She summoned her enchanted tablet and looked to see if he had written a message, but the only thing she saw was a warning from Darla. She hurriedly wrote out a new message, sending it to everyone who had a matching tablet.

> *Our home is under attack. Children and others are safe in basement room, Edward and I are in the cellar. There were at least twenty in the garden, most of them dead now. Not sure what happened in front. There was an explosion.*

She held her breath after sending it, then sent another message. This one for her husband alone.

> *James, where are you? Are you safe?*

It had only been minutes since the attack began, but her eyes began to well with tears. Whatever was happening, he probably couldn't stop to read or send messages. She'd been too busy herself, until just then. Unable to help herself, she sent him a new message.

> *I love you. Please be well.*

Alone in the dim light, Tabitha watched her son sleep and tried to stay calm. There was nothing else she could do.

***

Blake Word had just left the queen's side and was returning to take a rest in his own room. He was old now, but he still served with pride. Selene had tried to send him away with a title and a small grant of land, but he always refused.

"I've watched over you since you were a girl, and I've no intention of stopping now that you have a crown." That was his regular response, and he meant it, but the truth was that he had no family left and nowhere else to be. Selene was the closest thing he had to a daughter, and whether she knew it or not, she needed him.

Maybe if Will had stayed, he thought, but that was wishful thinking, and the look he'd seen in her eyes the day her husband had left cemented Blake's decision in stone. Everyone else saw only a monarch when they looked at her, cold, distant, and powerful. None of them saw the woman who worked endlessly to provide for her people. None of them knew the loneliness she endured, or the tears she cried when no one was there to see.

Even Blake rarely saw them, but regardless, he knew when she cried. The signs were always there for someone that truly knew her.

The ground jumped beneath his feet. It was followed a split second later by a dull boom. Blake recognized it as an explosion immediately, and his hand went to his side automatically, but there was no sword there. Weapons weren't allowed near the queen, and he was no longer an armsman. There were already plenty of men bearing arms.

Looking over the balcony, Blake saw a number of guards looking at one another uncertainly. None of them were sure what had happened. "To arms! There's an attack!" he yelled at them. Glancing back toward the queen's chambers, he saw two of the Driven step out of the walls where they normally hid. One lifted a hand and stone grew over the doorway, while the other created a force-barrier to protect the two of them and the entrance as well.

Confident that Selene would be safe, Blake ran to the stairs and started down. He had to slow then, for going down was harder on his knees than going up. They ached and groaned at the abuse as he hurried.

On the main floor was a vast, open room that served as a ballroom on formal occasions, but currently it had soldiers and servants running to and fro. Alarm bells were ringing from the towers outside, and news hadn't yet reached the palace as to what had occurred. Blake fast-walked across the open space until he reached the main hall that led to the enormous double doors that served as the palace's main entrance. In the hall, a number of weapons decorated the walls, heirlooms of fallen heroes. Most of them were old but the servants kept them in good condition.

Ignoring the breach in tradition, Blake snatched a rapier from its display and headed for the doors. He needed to get outside so he could see what was happening at the bailey, or whether the problem came from one of the towers.

The doors exploded inward, and the blast wave that followed picked him up and tossed him on his ass. Pain shot up his spine, and the world went quiet, but Blake scrambled back to his feet as quickly as he could.

Smoke and dust filled the now-ruined entrance, and from the cloud, armed men piled into the hall.

Unable to hear himself, Blake shouted an alarm, "Invaders in the hall!" He regretted not having chosen a different weapon, though it would have been difficult for him to wield anything heavier. He'd become thin and frail over the years, but adrenaline lent strength and speed to his arms.

The first ones through were fools, as they usually were. The better fighters would be behind them. The enemy didn't appear to be soldiers, however, though they did wear mail shirts. There was nothing military about their bearing or their movements. From what he could see, they might as well be farmers given some armor and a weapon.

Knowing his blade wouldn't pierce mail, he aimed for the legs and knees, using the higher attacks only to force his opponents to back away. People instinctively feared a blade near the face. He'd crippled three, as he backed down the hall, and he hoped that the guardsmen behind him would reach him soon, but he didn't dare look away.

Spearmen were entering now, and Blake cursed, then called out to the palace defenders again, "Invaders in the hall! Defend the queen!" His old legs couldn't move fast enough as he backed up, and the spears were thrusting toward him.

Unable to hear, his only warning that help had arrived was the look in the eyes of his attackers. The spears heading toward him shifted to meet a new foe, and then someone huge passed by. Blake recognized the man immediately, for it was the Black Duke.

Sadly, the duke wasn't in the armor that had earned him his name. Today he was merely human, though the man was still enormous. John Shaw, known to his friends as Tiny, raced into the face of the enemy, a six-foot-long greatsword in his hands. Black veins crawled up his neck and across his cheek and the backs of his hands, the visible signs of the Dragon's Heart potion he'd taken.

The strength and speed of a vampire, combined with the size and weight of Tiny's sizeable frame, made him almost as frightening as he would have been in the demon-steel armor. His blade swept several spears aside, and he side-stepped the point of the one he missed, then his back cut ripped through the line in front of him. Hands and arms fell away, spewing blood, and while the blade didn't cut through mail, when it did strike an enemy chest, its force sent them tumbling to the ground.

Spears broke and men screamed, playing out a silent battle in front of Blake's eyes. Moving forward now, he did his best to keep the invaders from circling behind the duke, and blasts of fire informed him that the Driven had finally arrived. The queen's elite sorcerer-guards quickly turned the tide.

Blake lifted his blade and cheered, jubilant at their victory. He'd never expected to fight again at his age. He knew he'd accounted well for himself, and if any of the servants ever looked at him with pity again, the others would soon educate them, whispering tales of how the queen's worn-out manservant had fought and helped hold the entry hall.

Younger men could handle the rest, for he was out of breath. Tiny glanced at him, concern on his face, but Blake waved him off. "I'm fine," he said, still deaf.

The big man ignored him, shaking his head, and as Blake's legs gave out, the giant warrior caught the older man, helping to ease him to the ground. There was blood everywhere, and Blake could see that Tiny was talking to him, but he couldn't understand.

"I'm fine, just out of breath. Don't put me down here; there's blood all over the floor—" he complained, but stopped as a pain gripped his chest. Blake grimaced. "Never mind me, this happens now and then. Just got too excited." Then the world went dark.

When Blake opened his eyes again, there was a new face in front of him, a stranger in red and black, who despite his fierce appearance seemed to radiate a sense of peace. He'd never seen him before, but he still felt familiar somehow, then Blake groaned. "Ah, fuck. Am I going to Hell now?" Marduke's appearance could only mean one thing.

The dreamer smiled at him. "There isn't one, just so you know, but given what I've seen in your heart, I'm sure you'll find this pleasant."

"Sounds like some wishy-washy bullshit if you ask me," said Blake with a snort. "What killed me? Was it a spear?"

The man smiled. "No. You were too good for that. Your heart gave out."

Blake grinned. "Too right. I'd have been embarrassed as hell if I had let some amateur gut me." He paused. "Is she—is Selene safe? That's all I want to know."

The dreamer nodded. "She's safe. They'll be putting that rapier you used back on the wall with an extra placard beneath it, and there will be songs sung for you in the years to come."

"I don't give two shits about any of that, as long as she's safe," said Blake, and rising to his feet, he followed Marduke into the light.

***

The Queen of Terabinia strode down the hall close behind the Driven, ignoring the advice of those who wanted to protect her. She had nothing to fear, though they didn't know that, and the closest she came to the appearance of danger was a crossbow bolt which she stopped with a shield. She was angry, but orders needed to be given.

"Don't kill any that you find alive," she called out. "I need answers." Ahead of her, she saw Tiny, kneeling beside a smaller figure. She started to order him to his feet, until she recognized the man he held.

Inside, a long, cold scream echoed in her heart, but her face showed almost nothing. Her tears would wait for closed doors and spells to soundproof the walls. Before she could say anything, a runner found her and hastily gave her his report from the men at the front bailey. Another reached her immediately after, and minutes passed while she took in the information being brought to her from various messengers.

She listened calmly and gave quick orders, sending them back with her instructions, and through it all, her friend and mentor, Blake Word, the father of her heart, grew colder on the ground. Somewhere in the recesses of her mind, the scream never stopped.

When she had learned enough, that the city was safe, that the palace invaders were dead and the walls secure, she told the next messenger to wait and put her hand on Tiny's shoulder. "John."

Tiny looked up, and his face was a terrible thing to see. His eyes were red from the potion, and black veins still marked his skin, but the quiet sorrow he projected was somehow worse than those things. "He's dead, Your Majesty."

Her lip almost quivered as she answered, "I know. I'll have him taken and treated with honor, but first you need to go home. Take a squad with you, and some of the Driven as well."

The duke was already on his feet. "What's happened?"

"There are reports of smaller attacks all over the city, mostly at the homes of our nobles."

Tiny was up and running before she'd finished.

***

Tiny didn't wait for a squad, or the queen's elite guard. He ran for the gate, and the instant he set eyes on a horse, he aimed for that instead. A soldier sat atop it, and although he realized who was ordering him down, he was too surprised to move quickly enough. Tiny reached over and dragged the man off, then mounted. He kicked the suddenly overburdened equine into a trot and then a canter. He wanted to gallop, but there were too many people in the palace yard. He couldn't get up to full speed until they reached the street, and even then he had to shout to warn people to get out of his way.

Chapter 54

Ten minutes later, he was home, and his fears came true. The guards who should have been standing at the street entrance were dead, and the iron gate open wide. The front door of the house had been shattered, as if by a ram, and two more guards were dead there. He strode through the house, stepping over the bodies of servants and calling for his family.

"Jan! William! Emmet! Where are you?" His despair deepened as his ears got no response. The house was empty of anyone but the dead. He headed for the back door. The garden was just beginning to put out flowers now, and with the warmer weather, he knew his wife liked to spend more time outdoors.

The back door was still in one piece, but the top corner was missing, and black char covered the ragged edges. "Jan! William! Emmet! Is anyone there?" His voice sounded desperate to his own ears as he shoved the door out of the way.

His eyes beheld a scene of horror. Dead men lay everywhere. Broken bodies missing heads, arms, and legs were scattered all about, draped over benches and topiaries alike. Blood had spattered the pavers, and the familiar smell of death hovered in the air.

Visually, it was shocking, but audibly there was near silence, except for the soft sounds of someone crying. Jogging forward, he found them behind the garden shed.

The seven-year-old Emmet stood silent beside his mother, his face blank with shock. Janice was sitting, her head and torso bent over their oldest, William, whose head was in her lap. Her shoulders were shaking, and Tiny knew it was her weeping that he'd heard.

Tiny felt empty, as though every bit of feeling and emotion had been drained out of him as he walked up beside her, numb. He already knew the truth. If their son was living, she would have spoken. If he was wounded, she would have already healed him or given him a potion. Looking down, he could see blood soaking into the grass. Janice had covered William's chest with her shawl, but the crimson had already soaked through, and at one edge he could see intestines. His child had been gutted like an animal.

"He's dead, John," she told him through clenched teeth, her voice shaking in time with her shoulders. "They killed him, and I didn't even know until it was too late."

Slowly easing to his knees, he knelt beside her.

"I told him he could plant the roses for me," she said. "I didn't know. I should have made him stay in."

Unable to respond, Tiny began to weep alongside her.

"I came this way as soon as I heard them, but I wasn't fast enough. I wasn't here for him."

"There was no way you could predict this," he finally managed to say.

A long, wracking sob finally escaped her chest. "I'm his mother! I was supposed to protect him!"

"We'll find the ones responsible," he told her.

Drawing deeply, Janice's next words emerged with venomous fury. "I *know* who's responsible. I heard their words before I killed them. 'Justice for Trendham' is what they were saying. It's the Trendish that did this, and they were coming for us, and the queen."

Tiny's jaw tightened. "They'll regret this. I'll engrave the lesson in their bones."

Finally, she looked at him, with red-rimmed eyes to match his own. "This means war, John. They have to pay for this." Her hands were pulling on the edges of his coat, as though she didn't know whether she wanted to embrace him or pound on his chest.

He pulled her in tightly, and she screamed into his chest while his own shoulders began shaking. After a minute, Emmet touched his arm and he pulled their youngest in close between them as they cried together.

CHAPTER 55

Will teleported as soon as he noticed the messages, but he arrived on the front lawn of Tabitha's house fifteen minutes after everything had already ended. He'd had to teleport to Evie, since Tabitha had locked herself and the children into rooms hidden behind heavy wards.

Bodies were to be found in every direction, but the biggest concentration seemed to be near the front door of the house. At least fifty men had been ripped to pieces there, and several showed signs of being partially eaten.

Evie showed no signs of remorse as she cleaned herself, though the white fur around her mouth was dyed pink now.

The front door and part of one wall had been blown inward by a massive explosion, and given the lack of a certain smell, Will presumed it was from an enchanted spellbomb. He slipped partially out of his body so he could commune with the Cath Bawlg.

What happened?

I took a nap, she responded. *The explosion woke me up, but I think there was some fighting before that.*

Are you sure?

Evie nodded, pointing her nose in the direction of the street. *I didn't kill those.*

He'd already received new messages from Tabitha, so he wasn't worried about his nieces and nephews, and he'd told her to stay put until he was certain things were safe outside, so Will crossed the street to look at the evidence. The scene confused him until he found Darla's body in the middle of it. Her head had been crushed and repeatedly battered, and it wasn't until he checked under her clothing that he was finally sure it was her. The Arkeshi tattoo was unmistakable.

"I shouldn't have asked her to keep an eye out for them," he muttered quietly. He wasn't sure if she'd been watching or if she'd just wandered into it, but if she hadn't been near, she would still be alive.

Evie stood beside him, having taken human form. Despite having perfected her human transformation, the blood stains that covered her seemed more gruesome now. "A warrior's death is her own. You cannot claim it."

Will eyed the cat-turned-woman. "Have you been reading books? You sound wiser every time we talk."

She shrugged. "I cannot nap for more than two-thirds of the day. I get restless."

He would have laughed, but Darla's death had darkened his mood. Next, he circled the house, finding the slaughter in the garden. His sister had done an impressive job, though if she hadn't told him she'd been there, he would have thought it was another of Evie's battles. None of the men looked to have been slain by spells. *I'll have to ask her about it once everything else is settled.*

Stepping through the shattered front entrance, he searched the interior of the house using both spells to locate hidden and camouflaged creatures and his unique visual abilities. Then he checked again, before finally messaging Tabitha that it was safe to emerge.

The color of the glass changed as the defensive wards shut down and his sister entered through the back door, carrying Edward in front of her. Her body was thicker and heavier than it should have been, and after a second Will realized she had transformed it in some way. Shape shifting was a talent he'd never been successful with, and there were very few spells that dealt with it. Almost all shifting was done with wild magic, which was how his aunt did it. Evie's transformations were similar, though her extradimensional nature made it difficult for him to sense the magic she used. He resolved to ask her about it, but the question could wait for another day.

Tabitha gently deposited her oldest on the couch in the parlor and then went down into the basement to let her other children and the servants know it was safe to come out. Minutes later, they were all together in the front parlor, and everyone was talking at once. The younger children were especially loud, and no one could really blame them. Nothing so terrible (or so exciting) had ever happened during the span of their relatively short lives. Even the sight of their ruined front door did little to dampen their enthusiasm.

Their mother remained quiet through it all, and it wasn't until little Talia spoke up that the others realized something might be wrong. "Where is Daddy?" she asked.

"He hasn't gotten home from work yet, sweetie," said Tabitha, but though she did her best to maintain a calm front, they sensed that something was wrong. Christopher and Talia both grew quiet.

Elaina did her best to be positive. "I'm sure he'll be home soon. He probably just had extra work to finish."

Will wasn't so sure, and Rob hadn't responded to his most recent message yet, so he didn't know if the attack on the Wellings' home was unique or part of a larger event. With a growing sense of dread, he reluctantly announced, "I'll see if I can find him," but before he could slip into the astral, Christopher began yelling.

"There's a man in the yard! He's carrying Daddy!" The eleven-year-old had been staring through the ruined front entrance, so everyone rushed over to join him, but Tabitha reached him before anyone else.

She hissed when she saw the vampire nearing the house. Rob's clothes were covered in blood, and by the look of James' limp body and blood-soaked shirt, most of it had come from him. A growl rose in her throat. "What have you done to him?" Her already thick body began growing, and scales began appearing on her skin. Sharp spines emerged from her back, and claws emerged from her hands. "How dare you!" she shrieked in a voice that was already deep and raspy.

Will's eyes widened in alarm, and though he instinctively clenched his will, it did nothing to stop his sister's shapeshifting. No matter how strong he was, the magic within her was beyond his control. Glancing at Rob, he could see by the look on his face that he hadn't been the one to hurt James. He had the look of a reluctant messenger.

But Tabitha wasn't thinking clearly, and she'd been suspicious of Rob from the start. Will realized he might need to restrain her, but his options were limited. He couldn't keep her from shifting, and most magic wouldn't get past her resistance. Although he was technically stronger, their relative strengths were too close for him to attempt a source-link.

That left him with physical barriers or potentially lethal attacks to choose from, and he wasn't about to risk Tabitha's life—not even if Rob had been mortal—so he put a force-cage around her as he ran forward. "He didn't do it!" he yelled.

Tabitha threw herself against the bars of force, clawing at them to try and get through. Will felt his turyn beginning to drop as she strained against them. He continued to move closer, making it easier to maintain the spell, but if she kept fighting, he knew he'd have to consider something different. "Put him down and back away, Rob. I need to calm her down first," he called over his shoulder.

Rob was already doing that anyway, laying James out on the torn-up grass as he responded, "He's not dead." His voice was loud enough for everyone to hear, and silence reigned for a moment afterward.

Tabitha went still, and Will rushed over to examine his brother-in-law.

"Is it true?" she said, her body slowly shrinking.

Will nodded and dismissed the force-cage. "He's breathing. I think he's just asleep. I don't see any wounds." He glanced up at Rob. "Regeneration?"

The vampire nodded, holding out an empty vial, one of several Will had given him, but there were tears in his eyes. "It's my fault. I was there and I didn't even realize until it was over. He was almost gone before I got to him."

"No, you did fine," said Will. Tabitha was already beside them, and her children swarmed around her and their father seconds later.

Once she was certain her husband was alive, Tabitha began looking for answers. "How? What happened?"

Rob had already backed away and crossed the fence, so he was off their property. From the sidewalk, he answered, "I've been following him each day."

"Why?" demanded Tabitha. She glanced at Will. "Did you tell it to do that?"

Will shook his head. He'd done nothing but give Rob make-work assignments to listen to people in taverns, along with warnings to stay well away from the Wellings' house. He'd only given his friend the regeneration potions on the off-chance they might come in handy. He had a surplus now that he was no longer selling them.

"I didn't know what else to do," said Rob, holding up his hands in a gesture of peace. "I'm out of the yard now, by the way. Sorry for crossing the fence, but I didn't want to put him down out here." He continued to back away.

"Stop," ordered Tabitha. "I want to hear what happened."

Rob stopped, his eyes moving to Will for advice. Will nodded, and after a moment he spoke again. "Will told me to stay away from your home, so I have. Just so you're clear. I haven't been spying. He hasn't given me much to do, other than wander around and listen to people, so I wanted to do something more. Since I couldn't come *here,* I thought maybe I could help by looking out for your husband, so I started following him in the mornings and evenings, on his way to and from Wurthaven.

"A stranger bumped into him during his walk home, and I didn't even realize what had happened until he fell down and blood started going everywhere. He killed his attacker, but he'd lost so much blood he nearly died. I thought I'd be able to protect him, if someone decided to hurt your family, but I was wrong. I'm sorry." Rob stood waiting after he finished, clearly unsure what to do with himself.

Will could see a multitude of strong emotions in Tabitha's expression, as though she was fighting with something inside herself. Finally, she looked at her brother and asked, "He's safe?" Will nodded, and she asked, "How safe?"

"He won't hurt anyone," said Will. "He hasn't for many years now."

Steeling herself, Tabitha crossed the yard and went to the street gate, which was still shut and locked. All their attackers had gone over the fence rather than bother with it. Opening it, she approached Rob carefully, then stopped a few feet away. "I think I've misjudged you," she said evenly. "Is it safe to come closer? Your instincts won't—?"

He nodded. "I'm already covered in blood. If I was going to lose control, it would have been when I found your husband. I'm very sorry for what happened to him, and I'm sorry if I scared you, but—"

Tabitha shook her head and stepped closer. "Please, you've done nothing wrong. I'm the one that owes you a debt of gratitude." Reaching out, she took Rob's hands in her own, then lowered herself to her knees and bowed her head. "I've done nothing but cursed you since learning of your existence, and I was ready to kill you myself just now, though you've done me no wrong. Instead, you brought back the most precious thing I have. I can only hope you'll forgive me."

For his part, Rob seemed shocked and appalled as she knelt in front of him, and he looked at Will as though worried he might be in danger of being set afire. He pulled lightly on Tabitha's hands—to draw her back to her feet—but she didn't cooperate until she had finished her words.

Then she stood and asked, "Will you please come in?"

"I couldn't—"

Tabitha's gaze was insistent. "Please. My home is in shambles, and I would feel safer knowing you are there with us."

There was much to be done, but once everyone had settled down, Will took them all to Lystal, including the servants. He asked that they not ask about the location and that they stay inside. Of course, the house was too small for so many, so he immediately followed by taking them to his hidden sanctum, which was much larger. He had already added a section to serve as living quarters for future wizards, but it was unfurnished, so he went back to the Wellings' house and collected the children's beds and a few other necessities.

Lyle and Neicy went back the next day, to stay with their own families, but James, Tabitha, and their children spent the rest of the week. It was a full day before James and Edward were awake and fully recovered, but once they were, Will's brother-in-law had endless questions about the secret workshop and its many halls and rooms. He was especially excited to learn that he and Tabitha were the first 'council members' to finally see it.

Rob was simply happy to be included. He'd lived in relative solitude for nearly two decades, so being accepted among people, much less a family with children, felt strange and novel for him.

The last night before Will took them back to begin reconstructing their home, he had a quiet conversation with his sister.

"I've been meaning to talk to you about what you said to Rob," he told her. "It was a kind gesture, but it felt like too much."

Tabitha shook her head. "No. It wasn't. Do you remember when Mother found out you were our brother?"

Those memories were all too vivid. Agnes Nerrow had soundly rejected him, as though his blood made him a traitor. She'd refused to believe his good intentions, and everything he'd done in the past for them was suddenly recast in the light of negative assumption. Her relationship with him had gone from motherly to hostile, and there'd been no convincing her he should be treated any other way. Tabitha's own relationship with her mother had become strained because of it. "I do," he answered.

"I won't be like that," she said firmly. "I make mistakes, but if I find out I'm wrong, at least I can admit it. He still terrifies me, by the way. It's all I can do to keep myself from showing it, but it's getting easier. As each day passes, I can see how earnest he is, so I hope in time I'll be able to adjust."

"You didn't need to kneel, though," offered Will.

"I hated him, William, just because he existed. Not because of who he was, but for *what* he was, and what I assumed about him. You told me otherwise, but I wouldn't listen or even consider the evidence. What if he hadn't kept an eye out for James? Knowing how we felt, he shouldn't have bothered. My antipathy could have cost my husband his life. I very much owed Rob an apology, and he deserved to have everyone see it. I'm not too proud to kneel and ask for forgiveness."

He put an arm around her shoulders. "You might be the best one of the three of us."

She is, agreed Laina. It was the first time she'd spoken in ages.

Tabitha glanced at him. "You mean, you, me, and Laina?" When he nodded, she asked, "Is she still—with you?"

"I hear her voice now and then. It's been over a year, but she just agreed with me about you," he told her.

Tabitha let her gaze wander. "I wish I could hear her. I'd give anything to see her again."

CHAPTER 56

As the news of the events percolated through Terabinia, a number of things happened. The border with Trendham was closed, and the call for levies went out. The army mobilized and began to prepare.

Trendham and Terabinia had been accustomed to peace for as long as anyone could remember, and many people had relatives living in the neighboring country, but now anyone with a Trendish accent was treated with suspicion and contempt. All Trendish civilians, traders, sailors, and temporary visitors, were summarily ushered out, and in some cases hotter heads prevailed, leading to violence.

As Terabinia's army marshalled itself at the border, Trendham's Prime Minister, Brent Strommen, had no choice but to respond in kind, and the Council of Five quickly agreed. War was brewing in the air, and most seemed to welcome the news. There had been growing discontent in Trendham over lost ships for years, and now Terabinia's claim that they had been attacked seemed like a false pretext to excuse imperialist expansion.

A week after the attacks, Will went back and paid a visit to Janice and Tiny. He teleported to Tabitha first, then walked, and although his first impulse was to sneak in, it seemed in bad taste given recent events. And so he found himself in front of a locked gate beside the street, waiting for an answer after explaining himself to the guards.

They'd given him strange looks after he'd announced himself to them as 'William Cartwright.' It was the first time he'd openly used the name in sixteen years, and he was dressed in simple clothes. One of them had laughed in his face, but Will had simply waited until the laughter died down. Then he'd insisted again, "Tell them I'm here. I'll wait."

A long staring match had ensued, and if it had been any other time, he would have expedited matters by forcibly persuading the guards. He'd already heard about the death of Janice and Tiny's oldest, however, and the last thing he wanted was to make matters worse by assaulting their guards. So he endured jokes and insults and continued to politely insist, until finally one of them relented, warning him, "If His Grace finds out you're out here making mock of him after what's happened, things will go hard for you."

Will nodded. "I'll wait."

With a sigh, one of the guards left to relay his message. "It's your funeral."

A full twenty minutes after his arrival, they opened the gate and escorted him in, and both of the guards were looking quizzically at each other, unsure what had happened. The men at the door opened up, and he went inside while the gate guards returned to their posts. He didn't even bother to offer them an 'I-told-you-so' as he entered.

Janice met him at the foot of the stairs. She looked tired, and there were dark circles under her eyes, which complemented the black dress she wore. Her eyes were intense as she stared at him, and he wasn't sure if it was anger or sadness that motivated the stare until she threw her arms around him.

"Where have you been?" she demanded. Her voice sounded as though she was already on the verge of tears.

"That's something a lot of people would like to know."

Stepping back slightly, she squeezed his upper arms with her hands, as though confirming his solidity. "It was rhetorical, but just so you're aware, we already know you're in Trendham."

Tiny, he thought immediately. "Does Selene know?"

She hugged him again, then moved away. "Of course. She's the one who told me."

His mind was already racing as he wondered who knew what, but he knew better than to ask reckless questions. Those might give away even more information. Instead, he waited, an expectant look on his face.

Janice sighed, then explained, "I was furious with him when I found out you visited him here. I was even more upset with you for not taking time to let me see you." She gave him a cross look. "My stubborn husband never would have said anything if you hadn't asked to see those research notes."

Will relaxed slightly. "Notes?"

She rolled her eyes. "Don't play dumb. You should have known he wouldn't betray his oath. John got permission before asking me to copy them."

Thinking through her words, he decided it was likely that Tiny hadn't told them his precise location. It sounded as though he'd pretended Will had found him first. *He must have told them Trendham to satisfy their questions, but he wouldn't say more than that,* reasoned Will. If so, it meant there was much less chance that the location of his home in Lystal had leaked out, but it led him to other questions. He kept his thoughts to himself, though.

Reaching out, he patted Janice's shoulder, observing the ring he wore carefully. "I should have known he'd do that," he replied. "I wish I had come a long time ago. It shouldn't have taken something like this before..." He stopped, unsure how to finish. "I've missed you both. I know it's a hollow offering, but if there's anything I can do..."

She had looked away, dabbing at her eyes. "Will, thank you, but let's not talk about it now. I'm barely keeping my head above water and I just—I can't—I'd rather hear about you."

He nodded and she took his hand, leading him upstairs. "Is something wrong with the parlor?"

"My study is more private. The less we're heard, the better," she told him.

"Where's Tiny?"

She waited until they were inside her office and had closed the door. Will saw wards come to life, and force-screens and anti-eavesdropping magics became active within the walls. For his own peace of mind, he'd already been erasing the sound of their voices beyond the space between them, but he didn't feel the need to mention it.

"He's at the palace. Things have been pure chaos since the day of the attacks," she answered at last.

Will nodded. "I've heard some rumors, so I've been—"

"Do you know something?" she asked quickly. "I was hoping you came with good news."

"I meant rumors about the city, about what happened here. Was there a pattern to who they targeted?"

Disappointment showed in Janice's face. "Not that we could tell. They targeted noble houses and the palace. You heard about Tabitha?" He nodded. "Her home was the least important of those attacked, yet they spent more men and resources there than anywhere else, other than here and the palace itself."

"You think it was because of me?"

"I was hoping you could tell me. You're the one living somewhere in Trendham. Of all the attacks, her house was the most unlikely one, unless they wanted to get to you. All the other homes belonged to powerful people."

"They might've known about her relationship with Selene..."

Janice seemed dismissive. "I'm sure you know Tabitha hasn't set foot in court since the day you left. Most think she fell out of the royal graces when it was put out that you had died. The only other rumors I know of are those claiming she's an enemy of the crown now. There's no reason to think the Five would see any merit in targeting her, other than because of you."

"The Five? You don't think the oligarchs have a hand in this, do you?"

Her face tightened with suppressed anger. "How could they not? Their cries of 'death to the queen' and 'justice for Trendham' were heard by hundreds of witnesses."

"That's no proof—"

Janice interrupted him, "Most of them died, but we took some prisoner. They were all Trendish, and to a man, they were fanatics convinced that Terabinia has been capturing and torturing Trendish sailors. Some of them even claimed we've been raiding villages on the border. All of it was lies. *You* tell me why they would believe such things?"

"I've heard rumors like that floating around, but it wouldn't convince hundreds of people to sneak into Terabinia and throw their lives away," he argued.

"Unless they were motivated," agreed Janice. "They had someone urging them on. Someone paid for the mail shirts they wore. Someone gave them weapons and made the plan; someone pointed them straight at us."

Will ran a hand through his hair. "I highly doubt it was the Five."

"Then who was it, William? You tell me! I would love to hear it. I'd love to know who sent those men to gut my son!" Janice's voice rose to a near shout, and veins were standing out at her temples. "I'd really hoped you would know something, but if not, that's fine too. We'll find out on our own, and every single one of them will be hanged for it."

He was shaking his head. "We'll find them, but it's going to take time. You have to be patient if—"

"No! You be patient!" she snapped. Janice was standing up behind her desk now. "It's my son who was murdered, not yours. If you want to do something, go back home and find the ones responsible. Bring me their heads and hearts—I want them on this desk!"

Stunned, he had no response.

"That's what I thought," she said after a moment, sitting down again. "If it was the Five, they'll pay, and if it wasn't, we'll find out who it is after we turn Trendham upside down and shake it until all the rot and corruption falls out." She stared at him for a moment, studying his expression. "You look like you want to say something."

"I do, but I don't have an answer. All I know is that war isn't the solution."

After a hasty intake of breath, Janice stopped herself, putting both of her hands face-down on the desk in front of her. Will could see the frustration written in her features, mixed with a deep exhaustion that comes from wrestling with heavy emotions for days on end. "I know this isn't your fault, William, but I'm—I'm tired. Thank you for thinking of us. I wish you could have met our William."

It was an obvious dismissal. Will reached out to put his hand atop one of hers. "Listen, Janice, I—"

She pulled away, rising from her seat. "I'm sorry, William. I'm not fit for company right now. I think you should go." She left unspoken the obvious finish to her sentence. She wanted him to leave before she lost her temper again. "Please."

He went, and he even exited via the door like a normal visitor would. No sense in creating strange rumors or leaving the guards to wonder if he was still hiding somewhere inside. Will waited until he was a block away and out of sight before teleporting home to think.

He had worried about seeing her again after so long, but Janice's greeting had been warm. Now he understood why. She'd seen a possible ally in her quest for vengeance. Whatever else he might be, the Stormking was an attractive piece to have on one's side in a coming war. Once she'd realized he had no interest in punishing the people of Trendham, she'd had no more patience for small talk or sentimental reunions.

Janice was a frightful thing now, a mother with a wounded heart. There was little room in her heart for anything but retribution against those who had slain her son, or those who she thought were responsible.

Will went to Bondgrad next, first checking on Oliver before going to find his cousin Samantha at Roc's Roost. He'd already visited her a few days before, to give her the news regarding Tabitha's family.

Once again, he climbed stairs, following her up to her rooftop suite where they could speak in private. She had no good news for him.

"Nothing," she said, summing it up in a single word. "I haven't found even a hint of anyone who might have organized something like what happened."

"We should start by figuring out who stands to gain from this war," he told her.

Sammy nodded. "Fine. That sounds great. Tell me who that is, because I'm coming up blank."

He felt the same, but he had to ask anyway, "You can't think of anything that might benefit even one of them?"

She shook her head. "No. War is bad for business unless you're an arms trader. None of the Five make significant money selling arms or armor, and even if they did, it would be damn stupid to try and increase business by bringing war to their own doorstep."

"Then it would have to be a third nation, such as the Fareshites or the Shimerans." He didn't bother mentioning Barsta. The tribes that ruled it were small and numerous without any central controlling power.

Similarly, the dwarves in Delgath had little interest in the outside world, although they did do a brisk trade in weapons and armor. "You mention arms traders. What about the dwarves?"

Sammy shrugged. "All right, how? As far as I know, they don't have much in the way of magic, aside from their skills in smithing and enchanting. Have you seen any dwarves wandering around Trendham convincing people to sneak into Terabinia and kill people?"

"Actually, I have seen one."

"Really?" she seemed surprised. "I've dealt with lots of merchants and traders and never seen a single dwarf. They're famously xenophobic, and even more so now that the elves are back."

Thinking about it, Will did find it suspicious how he'd met Durin, especially considering the company the dwarf had kept, but he still couldn't find a reasonable explanation for how the dwarves would have created something on the scale of what had happened in Cerria. The number of Trendish men who had snuck into the city for the attack had numbered in the hundreds.

Even more mysterious was the fact that neither of them could find any sign of who the men had been. Janice had been confident that they truly were Trendish, but if several hundred men had snuck away to Terabinia, no one seemed to know who they were. There weren't any outcries about numerous men abandoning their homes and families.

None of it made sense. Will wished he had a list of the names of the men that had been captured, but they were dead now. The few that hadn't managed suicide had been hanged three days after Selene's investigators had finished extracting whatever they could. If they had even a small list of names, he'd have to ask Janice for it—either that or go directly to Selene.

Returning to the conversation at hand, Will replied, "I met him shortly after the Redweep Fever started. He helped save my life."

Sammy waggled her brows. "I thought it was your girlfriend that did that."

"He was with her," said Will. "Apparently she sometimes goes as far as Delgath and even to Barsta on her route."

His cousin frowned. "Trading spices? Is that what you told me before?"

He nodded.

"The spice trade revolves around Faresh and Darrow. There's some things sourced from Terabinia too, but no one goes to Barsta or Delgath for spices."

Will shrugged. "Then they're probably good places to find customers, right?"

Sammy shook her head. "No. Not at all. The dwarves apparently don't care much for anything grown above ground, other than meat and barley for their beer. The Barstans might want them, but they're difficult to trade with and have no money to speak of. What did you say her name was again?"

"Cora Dewitt," replied Will. "She said she knows you. That's how I met her. She found me when I was offering money for information about how you were doing, back when we weren't talking."

"I don't know anyone by that name," said Sammy. "I'm sure I'd remember a trader who was friends with a dwarf, or at least have heard of her. That's not common."

"Her actual first name is Wilhelmina, or Wilma, but she doesn't go by it."

Sammy looked concerned. "She's sounding more suspicious by the minute. Are you sure you should be talking to her?"

Telling his cousin that Cora was actually a Terabinian spy or informant wouldn't help allay her fears, so he didn't bother. He certainly couldn't tell her the deeper truth that lay hidden behind that. That was a conversation for another day. Will smiled reassuringly. "I trust her. I can't really explain why, but I do."

"Are you sure? Because the last woman you got romantically involved with was raised by a psychopathic dragon and sacrificed children to turn herself into a lich. You don't exactly have a good track record."

Will gave her a sour look. "Says the woman who fell in love and ran away."

"You can't argue that Emory isn't a good person, though," she countered. "Did you know his talent developed?" Before he could say anything, she went on, "It's plants. He always wanted something impressive that would make him unstoppable on the battlefield, but he's best with flowers. He spends several months a year traveling around Terabinia, helping farmers get the most from their crops."

He could hear the pride her voice as she spoke. "How did you find that out? Did you finally ask Tabitha if he's married?"

"No!" exclaimed Sammy. "I just asked how he was doing, and she told me about his talent."

"But she didn't mention whether he had a family?"

"No, and I didn't ask."

Will nodded. "You're far too mature for that, I'm sure." He wondered why Tabitha hadn't told her more. Sammy and his sister had been best friends at one time. It wasn't possible that she hadn't realized why his cousin was curious. Did that mean Tabitha knew he was married and wanted to spare her feelings—or was she hoping to tempt Sammy into revealing the truth of her heart? He wanted to shake his head; women were too complicated for him to figure out when it came to certain things.

"Smart ass. Why don't we get back to the important questions? You don't think your lover and her dwarf are suspicious?"

"She's more than just a lover," he protested. "And no, I don't think she has anything to do with it. If anything, she's probably just as confused as we are."

"You should catch the dwarf alone and interrogate him," she suggested in a playful tone. "Maybe he could tell you why she likes small men."

He knew she was teasing, so he didn't bother entertaining the joke. "I'm sure if you asked Durin, he'd say it was the elves. Cora said that's why he went back home. Too many elves around. His people have a longstanding distrust regarding elves."

Sammy grinned. "Probably jealous of how beautiful they are."

"Have you seen them?"

She nodded. "There's been quite a few in Bondgrad. They've set up an embassy here, same as in Cerria."

"What if—?"

She shook her head. "Will, they're beautiful, and they smell—if you only knew. Every time I see one, I get the most wicked thoughts."

"Like you want to go to Terabinia and kill people?"

"No, stupid. Like I'd like to get rid of my clothes and find someplace dark to experiment."

"Huh." He remembered Selene telling him something similar, when she'd been forced to live with the elves while Aislinn was hiding her from Lognion.

"If I could convince one to work at Roc's Roost as a performer, I'd have unbelievable crowds. An elven bard would be the ultimate draw."

"You've already got the place filled to capacity most of the time," he told her.

"True. I'm more worried about what would happen if a competitor managed to hire one. They could steal a lot of my business."

"And then you'd be poor," joked Will.

She gave him a look that said he was being ridiculous, then reached down and made a mildly disturbing grabbing gesture with her hand. "Maddie's Cock is just a small part of my business these days, but it's still the jewel in my empire."

"Maddie's Cock?" Will shook his head as he laughed. "Are you renaming it?"

She winked at him. "No, but I'm sure someday they will. Eventually, historians will look back and realize my legend has become much bigger than Breville's."

"I hope Emory is happy to see it with you someday," said Will with a smirk.

They both laughed, then talked some more, but neither came up with anything solid, aside from continuing to look for answers. Will had little hope they'd find any. There wasn't much time.

"You realize Emory is going to be there, don't you?" he asked. "When all this comes to a head."

Sammy's expression darkened. "Yeah."

"I'd rather you not be there."

"I'm pretty sure I didn't ask for your opinion."

Will met her eyes and didn't look away. "Do you really think you can turn your flames against Terabinian soldiers?"

"Maybe it won't come to that," she answered, looking to one side.

"That's wishful thinking. There's liable to be thousands of soldiers on either side, and everyone seems to be screaming for blood right now, here and in Terabinia. If you show up, you'll be forced to take a side."

She chewed her lip. "This is my home now. These people didn't ask for this."

"So what will you do?"

"If someone's crossing the border to attack Trendish cities, I'll stop them."

"You'll be fighting against our homeland then. You'll be fighting Emory too."

Sammy closed her eyes. "So be it." When she opened them again, she asked him the same question. "What are you going to do, then?"

"I'm not sure, but I'll probably be happier if you aren't there to witness it. Same thing for Oliver."

"We really can't stop this, can we?" she asked.

She'd finally said it, putting the ugly truth out there in front of them both. Will shook his head sadly. "That's the terrible thing about the sort of power we have, Sam. People think we can do anything, but when it comes down to it, all it does is allow us to kill a hell of a lot more people than anyone else."

"We could turn the tide, though."

"You remember the trolls," he reminded her. "This time, the tide you're talking about is built of human flesh and bone. 'Turning the tide' sounds poetic, but if you're standing there on that field, you'll see it's just senseless carnage. No one wins. You'll have to lay waste to thousands to rout them, and then you'll be hated by every wife and mother in Terabinia for generations to come—not to mention our friends."

"So you think I should stand by and do nothing? Wait to hear news of Trendham's crushing defeat? What happens when their army reaches Bondgrad?"

"More slaughter," he said with a sigh. He'd been a conqueror before, and he knew how hard it was to prevent the types of things that happened when soldiers fresh from death and blood found themselves loose in a city of those they'd defeated. "But at least you won't have your name on anyone's tongue, cursing you and crying for vengeance."

"I'll know," she told him. "That's all that matters."

"You say that because you've never been the one that everyone hates."

"Neither have you."

In his case, that was only half true. Will had made plenty of enemies among the citizens of Darrow, and more among the nobles in Terabinia. He'd also managed to alienate a good number of friends, and he doubted there were any demons singing his praises. Or fae, for that matter. But in essence, she was correct. He was still regarded as a hero by many in the Terabinian army, and probably by some of the citizens—maybe. There were plenty who blamed him for Ethelgren's destruction in the capital during the vampire plague. He stared at her for a while.

She doubled down. "Not *everyone* hates you. Just a lot of people."

"Most," he corrected. He'd forgotten the Shimerans; he was universally reviled by them. They blamed him for the dragon's incineration of Spela.

Sammy gave him what was probably meant to be a brave smile, but he could see the anxiety in her eyes as she replied, "Maybe you need some company. We can share the burden of being the most hated people together."

"You're a mess, Sam." He stood and made it obvious he was heading home. "Stay home. I won't be coming to pick you up."

"That's exactly the kind of shit that ruined things for you with Tiny. Don't piss me off, too."

"I'm used to it. Don't be there. You'll just regret it." Then he teleported home. The best thing about teleportation was that he could always get in the last word.

CHAPTER 57

Things grew steadily worse over the next week, and it was clear to everyone on both sides that war was an inevitability, and the main question lay in where it would begin. The land border was an unlikely option, for despite its length, it was dominated by mountains and the few passes that crossed it were small and impractical for an invading force. Watch posts were set along all of them, and any attempt to bring a large force through one would result in a logistical nightmare as the defender could bottleneck the invader easily. That geographical feature was one of the longstanding reasons a war between the two nations had long been discounted as too impractical.

The queen's army had taken advantage of the border in a few key ways, however. Since the Trendish were fighting a defensive war, they couldn't afford to ignore any point of entry. Terabinia had a much larger standing army, and with the fresh levies, she could afford to position a few companies at each pass in order to tie down a portion of the Trendish army. A few companies forced into guard duty meant little for the Terabinians, but it was a more meaningful reduction in force for the Trendish.

The oligarchs knew this, but it wasn't something they could do much about.

The main threat would come from the sea. The North Sea was an unlikely possibility, since it was still partly frozen, and both nations kept the majority of their ships in the Central Sea. Again, the advantage here lay with the Terabinians, who had a much more capable navy. The Trendish had no hope of preventing entry into their waters. The queen therefore had a multitude of options for where to begin landing her troops.

The most aggressive path would be landing near Baricia, and after pacifying the port city, the Terabinians could use the river to move barges filled with supplies upriver to supply their army while it marched toward Trema. After that, they could make for Dulence and go downriver from there to Bondgrad itself. On the face of it, one might think that entailed three battles before reaching the capital, but Baricia was the only city along the way with any significant defense.

Trema and Dulence would be a bonus for the invaders, as they would likely be able to resupply themselves along the way.

Landing near Karda was probably less attractive. That port wasn't quite as heavily defended as Baricia, but the Terabinians would face a long overland trek to reach Bondgrad after taking it. With only small villages and farmland along the way, their supply line would be more vulnerable to ambush along the way, and an army with no food was no army at all. Military might and the strength of Terabinia's magical auxiliaries would mean little if the army starved. The Trendish had been fighting similar battles with the Fareshites to their south for centuries, and they had plenty of experience fighting that type of war.

The military experts thought Baricia was the most likely target, with a broad landing along the coast between Karda and Baricia. With that in mind, they marshalled their forces near Trema and sent a portion south to Baricia. The majority, including Oliver and Lloyd Blathe's forces, went overland to the coast. They would follow the coast and respond to any reported landings. The hope was that they could destroy as many of the Terabinians as possible before they could land in significant numbers. The coastline was far too long to defend in its entirety, and the enemy had too many ships to prevent their arrival, but if they could make it costly enough, they hoped they would weaken the queen's army enough to enable them to hold Baricia.

Naturally, as often happened in war, none of this played out as expected, and the plans of both Queen Selene and the Five had to be tossed in the fire. An unusually strong and highly unlikely series of spring storms struck as the Terabinian navy entered the straits that led to the southern coast of Trendham. The Terabinian sailors did their best to navigate the rough waters, but when the wind grew too strong and twenty-foot waves were crashing onto the decks, they were forced to make land in the forested region north of Karda.

Once ashore, they were committed. The majority of their ships had survived, but most needed repairs, and once the men and equipment had been unloaded, the idea of reloading and setting sail again from the wilderness coastline was a logistical nightmare. Most of the now-emptied ships were sent home.

As a landing site, it was probably the last place the Royal Marshall would have wanted to begin a war. Not only would they need to trek along rough coast and through virgin forest, but Karda lay on the other side of the River Larbon. Approaching from the northern side meant they would face a contested river crossing.

Four divisions had landed, and despite the lost ships, the queen's army still numbered over twenty-thousand strong. In comparison, the oligarchs were thought to have only one division's worth of professional soldiers, with a similar number of poorly trained and hastily marshalled militiamen. The Trendish had some weak wizards and only a few sorcerers, so it was expected that they would be at a serious disadvantage in any battle unless the Terabinians were heavily outnumbered.

John Shaw, the Black Duke and Royal Marshal of the Queen's Army, chose to send one regiment of roughly eighteen-hundred men back toward the mountains. There was a small pass near them, and caught between the Terabinians on each side, the defenders there would quickly fall. Securing the pass behind them would ensure a stable if somewhat anemic supply line from their homeland.

With the rest of the army, the marshall began marching for Karda, and as scouting reports began coming in, the oligarchs soon discovered that the queen's banners had been seen with the marching army. Selene herself had come with the Royal Marshal, not content to wait at home during the war.

The news was greeted with both joy and despair. Joy by those who thought her death or capture might enable a quick end to the war, and despair by those with access to better military intelligence. Most of the common soldiers thought of the Terabinian monarch as little more than a figurehead, not realizing her personal power.

The Five knew better, and it had long been suspected that Selene had likely inherited her deceased father's immense collection of elementals. It became steadily more probable that after an expensive and costly battle, they would almost certainly lose Karda. Depending on what they had left after that, they would have only a small chance of winning the war that followed that first defeat.

Being businessmen, the Five would have been inclined to surrender, despite the patriotic songs of freedom that they encouraged among the people to increase morale. Aaron Pummen suggested it, but the others voted him down immediately. They knew the Terabinians were coming for vengeance, and even if the war ended in a quick surrender, their enemy would demand a price to be paid in blood. The oligarchs would be the obvious choice to pay that price, as well as their families. Even if the queen did allow trials, they would be nothing more than pretense. Someone had to be punished.

It was evening in Karda, and Oliver was standing by the woefully inadequate city wall, staring out at the campfires that dotted the dark expanse on the other side of the river. He wore a knee-length chain byrnie and a steel cap, and he had an enchanted steel buckler tied at his hip in such a way that he could quickly retrieve it. A spear that was a foot shorter than him sat couched in his left hand, while a double-edged short sword was on his left hip, both were enchanted for strength and improved cutting power. His father had insisted on replacing or personally enchanting practically every part of his armor and weapons.

Alex stood beside him, similarly geared, though most of his items weren't enchanted. The smaller man did have an enchanted shield, also given to him as a gift by Oliver's father. Will had apologized for not having time to do more.

Alex punched Oliver's shoulder. "Think it will be tomorrow?"

Oliver turned to him, worry in his eyes. "I don't know."

"What's wrong? Fight hard, die young. This is what we trained for."

Oliver shrugged. "I'm not sure I like our motto anymore."

"You're the best of us. Don't tell me you're getting cold feet," said Alex, trying to sound cheerful.

"Being the best, that was a good goal before, but now I'm afraid of what I might lose." He met Alex's eyes, and they both knew what he meant.

"Don't be so serious. Tomorrow could bring anything."

"Look at the fires," said Oliver. "They go on forever. We can't win against that."

"They say the Stormking is probably on our side. Those storms couldn't have been coincidence. If he shows up, who knows what might happen?" suggested his friend.

Oliver finally gave him a faint smile. "My friend Doug, from home, he's probably listening to all the news hoping to hear about the Stormking. He's probably thinking the same thing."

"He's probably here," said Alex. "What did he do?"

"He's a bookkeeper," answered Oliver. "I'm sure he would prefer to read about this than see it firsthand."

"He's the same age as you?" When Oliver nodded, he continued, "He's probably here then. Almost everyone our age was forced into the militia. Unless he's rich, he's here."

That was a bleak thought. Oliver didn't like his own chances, but everyone knew the bulk of the casualties usually fell on the militia. They had the poorest gear, the least training, and were always given the worst positions. It was better to lose the amateurs and preserve the professional soldiers. "I hope not," was all he could say, though.

"Well, like I was saying, if the Stormking shows up, we might have a chance."

"He's Terabinian," said Oliver. "Even if he's against the war, he's not likely to oppose his own country."

"Supposedly the queen banished him," said Alex. "Maybe he's got an axe to grind."

"He was married to her," said Oliver, shaking his head. "Even if he didn't agree with her, I can't see him fighting his own people."

Alex's eyes lit up. "Hey! Did your dad ever meet him? You said he was in Cerria when they had the vampire plague, and he was an officer in the army too, right? Being a wizard, if he was any kind of important, he probably met the Stormking in person."

Oliver chuckled. "If he did, I bet they weren't friends. He's got a bad fear of storms, so hearing you say that, I'm beginning to wonder if that may be why."

"They were on the same side, though."

"Yeah, but from all the stories, it sounds like the Stormking is completely ruthless. Doug told me he attacked his own men on several occasions if they failed to obey him instantly, and supposedly he publicly humiliated some of the noblemen, like my dad. If one of them was my dad, or a friend of his, that might be exactly why we moved here." The more Oliver thought about it, the more it made sense to him, and he was surprised he hadn't thought of it before.

"You said your dad was a good fighter, though, right?"

He nodded. "Yeah. He's probably good enough to be one of the trainers at the House of Ink. Toss in some spells, and he's really deadly."

"Then I'd think the Stormking would have liked him."

"Do you like all the other wardsmen?" asked Oliver with a smile. He already knew the answer. The requirements for entry into the House of Ink meant that most of the candidates were proud, aggressive, and more than willing to fight one another for dominance. In other words, almost all of them thought at least half their comrades were assholes, and none of them agreed on which half was which. Once he saw Alex had processed his message, he added more. "Plus, my dad's almost a pacifist. I thought he was afraid to fight when I was little, but it turned out he was just *very* against violence. That's also why he made sure he was never there when they tried to force him into the militia."

Alex nodded reluctantly. "Yeah. I wouldn't want to say anything bad about your dad, since I'm really grateful for this shield he gave me, but as young as he is, he should be here with us."

Oliver felt his temper begin to rise, but he held it down. "Listen. He's been through some shit. I understand why he doesn't like war in general, and this war in particular. If he shows up, it'll be on his own terms, but I won't fault him if he doesn't. He's got principles, and he does his damnedest to live up to them, which is more than I can say for ninety-nine percent of the men here right now."

"Hey!" said Alex, a conciliatory tone in his voice. "I didn't mean it like that. You know I'd never think anything bad about your dad. I just wish he was here."

Oliver relaxed. "Me too. Honestly, he'd make me feel better than some insane Stormking. I wouldn't trust him, but I know my dad. He's solid. If he was here, he'd probably be in the tents with the oligarchs, telling them a better way up to set up the order for battle."

They continued talking for some time, until their watch was done. Alex returned to the area set aside for Pummen's elite, and Oliver went back to Blathe's. Neither slept well.

CHAPTER 58

The Terabinians hadn't had time to build siege weapons, but Karda didn't have enough fortification to really require them, and the Terabinians' magical superiority made magical assault spells entirely feasible.

Before they even attempted to cross the river, massive balls of fire rose from the enemy positions and arced through the sky. Oliver had been ordered to remain beside his employer, so he saw the man's surprise as they watched the fiery assault begin. "So, they really are out for blood," whispered Lloyd Blathe. His face paled as their doom approached.

At the midpoint of their arc, the meteoric balls vanished, winking out as though they'd been nothing but an illusion. Oliver glanced at his employer. "What happened t—?"

He never finished his question, as a sound struck them with a force and fury so great, he thought someone had broken the world in two. Everyone in Karda fell to their knees, but the effect on the Terabinians was even worse. The small amount of cavalry they had reared, the horses tossing their riders, while the foot soldiers collapsed, many of them rendered senseless. Those that were still conscious clapped hands to their heads and screamed in pain as blood ran from their ears. Thousands of the Terabinian soldiers, those closest to the river, had had their eardrums ruptured.

The sky, which had been hazy and grey before, turned dark as the wind picked up and lightning started to flash between the clouds. A murmur rose among the Trendish, as people began to talk. There was little doubt that the Stormking had come. Some gained hope, and others trembled, uncertain whom he would support.

From nowhere, a man appeared, striding over the water of the River Larbon, and if anyone doubted his identity, the lightning that cloaked his form made it plain who he was. The Stormking walked until he reached the midpoint, then stopped, and a voice crossed the waters, finding the ears of anyone who could still hear.

"Soldiers of Terabinia, go home. This war profits no one. You will find only death here. The men you would kill today are not responsible for the crimes against your country. March back to the mountains and I will not hinder you. Remain here and you will not see another day. The choice is yours."

Oliver was astounded by the clarity of the Stormking's words across such a distance. Whatever magic he used, the Stormking's voice sounded as though he was speaking from only a few feet away, without the need for shouting. Stranger yet, he recognized the voice, or thought he did. "Dad?" he muttered. Surely, he was mistaken.

Stretching up and leaning out, Oliver ignored the risk of arrows and did his best to get a good look at the man standing on the river as if it were solid ground. The Stormking was facing away from him, but after a minute, he looked back over his shoulder and even at over a hundred yards, Oliver's sharp eyes could make out his features well enough to tell. "Fuck me, I'm an idiot. That *is* Dad." A thousand things began crossing through his mind, and he felt like the biggest fool to have ever lived. The things his cousins had said, the way his father had hesitated before telling him he was a wizard, even as he had repeated his name for Oliver to mull over. His father had spelled it out for him, and he'd still been too stupid to see the obvious truth.

A whisper emerged from his lips. "He's not afraid of storms. When he's afraid, he creates them."

Lloyd Blathe moved closer. "What did you say? Do you know him?"

Oliver looked over in surprise, but shook his head. "No."

His employer sighed. "I've met him three times, always unexpectedly, and this is the first time I've seen him in the light." Blathe stared directly at Oliver. "The last time, he made mention of you, but I couldn't figure out why."

"Sir? What did he say?"

"Nothing I care to repeat, but if you know him, or have any clue why he might be interested in you, I would appreciate it if you told me."

And at long last, Oliver understood his father's constant, obsessive need for secrecy and anonymity. He already knew what his father would say about the oligarch's question. If Blathe knew he was Will's son, he would become a bargaining chip at best, or a target at worst. That was why his father had thrown himself on Blathe's mercy and sold him, rather than resort to threats or extortion to keep Oliver out of the hangman's noose. Not because he had to, but because it would put a target on his son's back if anyone knew the Stormking favored Oliver for some reason.

Oliver shrugged. "I've no idea. Maybe he knows I'm a granling?"

Blathe sighed. "You're special, but rare as they are, I wouldn't think that would be enough to catch his eye."

Their conversation ended as a loud shout echoed across the river.

* * *

Will rose early that morning and walked through the Terabinian camp, watching and listening. The army camp was nostalgic for him. The routine was still much the same as it had been when he'd served as a private contract, and the sounds and smells were all too familiar. He wandered without fear of being stopped or questioned, and even went near the officers' tents.

He wasn't listening to gain any real intelligence, he merely wanted to make sure they intended to attack that day. Once he was sure of that, he made his way back to the river shore and waited. When the time seemed imminent, he camouflaged himself and used a water-walking spell for his entrance. Appearing suddenly would enhance his theatrics, but he didn't want to waste turyn unnecessarily. The camouflage and water-walking spells were far more economical than a teleport, and would achieve the same result.

He had alternatives, but the magical assault was ideal, so he smiled when the fireballs appeared and began arcing out over the river. His will blanketed everything, and the elemental spells became his. He might have used the power to directly fuel his rebuttal, but instead he leveraged the turyn to create a link with the storm above, then drew on its power to create the sonic boom. He kept it focused toward the Terabinians, but gave the Trendish a taste as well. In the negotiations that hopefully would follow, he wanted them to fully appreciate their position.

Will delivered his message and waited to see how they would respond. He wasn't surprised when he saw the black bulk of Tiny's golem striding along the shore, bellowing orders and trying to restore order. The metal monster stopped and pointed at him.

"William! How could you do this?" yelled the Royal Marshal.

Will sent his reply softly to Tiny's ear, or at least to where he thought the golem perceived sounds. "Take them back, John. I won't allow this war."

"Do you think we wouldn't consider this possibility? Stand aside or I won't be responsible for what happens to you!" yelled Tiny.

"My family was attacked as well," responded Will. "But this is not justice."

"My son is dead!" The Black Duke stared silently at him for a timeless moment, then lifted his right arm and pointed directly at Will. When he dropped it, the arrows began to fly.

It wasn't just arrows, however. That would have been simple foolishness. Some of the arrows were enchanted and some weren't. Several heavy ballistae were fired as well, and while their aim was focused on him, there were so many missiles, it was more of a volley, ensuring he couldn't depend on a short-range teleport to avoid it, and a point-defense shield would similarly be useless. They were wise not to use elemental attacks, for obvious reasons, since he would simply use their magic for his own spells.

Ideally, they would have used force-effect spells, but the distance was too great, and that would have spoiled the trap. Force-spells affected both the material and the ethereal plane, so transitioning to the ethereal wasn't viable if attacked by a force-lance. The Terabinians wanted him to try and use the ethereal plane to escape, for a second, nearly identical volley was happening there.

His friends knew him well, but none of them really understood just how easy it was for Will to see both planes at the same time. He didn't need a spell for it, and he'd routinely scanned the ethereal as he'd walked around the camp. He'd watched their second force move into position in the ethereal plane just before dawn.

A wind-wall spell, force-dome, or some other barrier spell would have been an obvious choice, but he expected that they had accounted for those things as well. His best option was to not be there, but he was worried that Selene might have figured out a way to trap him during a teleport. He couldn't know what he didn't know, and his wife was devilishly smart.

In his hand, he held a small ivory cube, the same one he'd once used to trap Grim Talek. It was designed to allow him to deploy a complex ward without laying out strips of cloth or spending time drawing runes, and it produced a cube-shaped effect. Much like a force-dome, Erica's Barrier could serve as either a prison or a last-ditch defense. Pressing his turyn into the cube, the ward expanded around him, and Will ceased to exist.

Erica was the only name he knew for the tenth wizard who had written in the book of secrets he'd inherited from Arrogan. She'd peered into the void and gone insane. The ward was based on one of her attempts to protect herself from the results of her insanity, but it also introduced anyone who used it to the same madness. A large part of the reason for Will's nightmares over the years came from the fact that he'd caught a glimpse of something the first time he'd used it.

He reasoned that he'd already been infected with the same mental illness, so he probably didn't have much to lose from doing so again—he hoped.

As the cube expanded, it severed the space it contained from reality. Will and the air around him literally ceased to exist, for they were outside and beyond existence itself. From the banks of the river, he seemed to vanish, but from within his ward, he was given a view into the endless nothing that surrounded reality itself.

There was nothing there, no light, nor even the blackness one might consider as the absence of light. It was simply null, and over the years since his first experience of it, he'd had lots of time to ponder it. The universe he lived in was a product of the dreamer, the goddess Temarah, or perhaps Marduke, depending on who was asked. Will had met them both, and Marduke had explained it a bit. Every sentient being, every soul, was part of the same singular entity, and the dream was the world they created together.

Cutting himself loose from reality in such a way, his awareness of the void would then stir and create things from the formless emptiness. To forestall that, Will did the best he could and closed his eyes and ears. Nothing could touch him inside Erica's Barrier, not even the void. Only his mind was at risk, or so he hoped.

Eyes shut, he waited, with no way to receive knowledge of the world he had exited. His link to the storm had been severed, but he was burning inside from the power he had saved for that moment. Minutes passed, and he grew impatient as the pain from that stored turyn began to grow. Hopefully the Terabinians would have exhausted their attacks before he returned.

Removing his power from the cube, he let the ward collapse, and light flooded in. Will surrounded himself briefly with a force-dome as his eyes readjusted. Ropes stretched across the width of the Larbon and men held onto them as they pulled themselves across. On the Trendish side, he could see massive, barbed steel anchors that held them in place on the opposite shore.

He wasn't sure whether they'd used spells or some sort of ballista to launch the spear-like anchors, but that no longer mattered. Arrows and spells alike flew over the river to try and keep the defenders from focusing properly on the men in the water. Men were dying behind the walls and in the water as bowmen on both sides aimed and found their targets.

Will released the force-dome, substituting it with a hemisphere that gave him a clear view of the sky, then sent the rest of his energy toward the clouds. It returned seconds later, bringing with it the strange awareness of so much more than he could describe. Connected to the firmament, the storm itself became an extension of his body, and it contained a vast ocean of power that would have burned him to a cinder if he had tried to possess it within his human form.

Glowing with vivid actinic light, the Stormking called, and the wrath of the heavens answered. The bright flash that followed blinded everyone staring in the direction of the river, but those who looked a second later saw the water itself glowing as the lightning faded away. The ropes spanning the water were on fire, and the men floating dead in the water gave off the stench of burned flesh. Hundreds had died in an instant.

"I have warned you once," said Will, casting his voice into the distance.

Horns blared, and the queen's banner advanced, accompanied by a white flag. They stopped well away, still more than a hundred yards from the shore, but Will could see and hear them clearly. Selene wanted to parley.

He waited, watching while the Black Duke walked back to talk to the queen. The massive golem returned minutes later. "The queen would like to parley," he shouted.

"A temporary truce then," said Will. "Meet us in one hour, on the spot where you now stand. A guarantee of safety must be given until all parties have returned to their current positions, after this meeting."

"If Her Majesty agrees, I will return." The demon-steel golem marched away and returned a short while later, and the agreement was made. "In one hour, on this spot," said Tiny.

Will nodded, then teleported to his cousin, Sammy.

CHAPTER 59

The Five had been delighted when Madeleine Brightblaze announced she would give them her unwavering support. Everyone knew she was a wizard, and it was also understood that she possessed uncommon magical strength, but none of them had the slightest inkling of what she was truly capable of. Her wealth was so great that there was never any consideration of the idea that she should serve alongside the wizards conscripted from the mage's guild. Consequently, she had been allowed to remain amongst the officers and the oligarchs, offering advice regarding the Terabinian magical capabilities. No one really knew what to do with her, so thus far she had remained content to act as an advisor.

She had several purposes of her own. Will had convinced her to remain passive, guarding the oligarchs and military leadership, and more importantly protecting Oliver. Her location also made it easy for Will to reach the Trendish command if he needed, not that they were aware of that.

When he arrived after teleporting from the river, he was greeted by gasps and raised brows. None of them knew the secrets behind how he teleported, so the fact that he was closely connected to someone in the room was unknown to them. Will gave his cousin a professional but indifferent nod after he arrived. "Madeleine, I am glad to see you are well."

"Maddie, you know the Stormking?" asked Brienna Marlow, the only woman among the Five. "Why didn't you make us aware of this?"

Sammy shrugged and started to reply, but Will spoke first. "I met her once decades ago, during the war with Darrow." Waving his hand dismissively, he continued, "I am here for one reason. I've arranged a parley with the queen. One of you should attend to represent the interests of Trendham."

Jak Coires was incensed. "You can't agree to things like this without first con—" His words died in the air.

"It wasn't a question," said Will. "Choose among yourselves or I will choose for you."

Douglas Lentam watched Jak's angry but silent face with alarm. "Maddie, stop him!" he ordered.

They'd discussed the potential for such a thing previously, so Sammy wasn't surprised when a blue-tinted force-dome surrounded her. The color had been added purely to make it plain to see for the non-magical oligarchs. She affected a look of outrage, but made no real attempt to escape.

"Argue with me and your successors will be taking your places much sooner than expected. Choose a representative and meet me here in slightly less than an hour. Your chosen representative may bring two guards or assistants, but no more," announced Will. Then he teleported again, this time to where Evie waited, hidden a short distance up the river. Once there, he camouflaged himself.

What will happen now? she asked.

It was rare for her to initiate conversation on her own, but it was a day for rare occurrences. "I'll talk to Selene, face-to-face."

She brought this horde here. She may not listen.

"First, I'd like to say that the Terabinian military is not a *horde*. Second, I don't believe she wants this. In fact, I'm sure she doesn't."

You haven't seen her in many years. You don't know her heart.

He shook his head. "You're wrong. Tiny, Janice, and most of the other leadership may have let their emotions run away with them, but Selene calculates everything. She acts according to what she thinks will bring the most good for the largest number of her citizens. Always."

Yet she was emotional enough to cast aside her humanity to save your life, said the cat.

"I've spent the majority of two decades thinking about that," he admitted. "My wife is a little insane, there's no doubt, and when I left, she pleaded with me, claiming her decision was for me. I believed her then, but I couldn't stomach the thought. Whether she realized it or not, I think the real reason she stooped to murdering children was more because of her principle of striving for the greatest good for the greatest number."

That still doesn't make sense.

"It did to her, and she's proved it out since then," he replied. "She knew what she would do as queen. It might have been a selfish act, for herself, or for me, but deep down, she also knew she would be a better ruler than anyone that's ever sat on the throne before. She's always polite and well mannered, but trust me, deep down, she knows exactly how much smarter she is than almost everyone else."

You called her your wife. Was that a slip of the tongue?

He stared at the grey cat ruefully. Evie's skill when it came to understanding people was constantly improving. "Maybe."

If you seek to reconnect with your old mate, what will the new one do?

Will laughed. "You're worrying about some things you shouldn't. Let's focus on the war."

But the war is with your old mate.

Will shook his head. "No. It's not. The war is with the people convinced they need justice, and with the calculation in her head. She's here because she's convinced that this will lead to the greatest good. Given a better alternative, she'll accept it in a heartbeat."

Your people are too confusing.

He nodded. "I agree with you there."

***

When the time was right, Will teleported to the set place, bringing with him Lloyd Blathe and the two he had chosen to accompany him. He wasn't happy about the oligarch's choices, though. Oliver stood on one side of the man and Sammy stood on the other.

They were on a flat sandy stretch beside the river and immediately before them stood the black metal golem and Emory Tallowen. The queen had remained farther back, waiting until the exact moment, but she could see the place where they stood. Once the time had been reached, she teleported to stand between her two vassals.

Will made the introductions, though he could already see the surprise on Selene and Emory's faces at the sight of Sammy standing there with him. The golem couldn't show expressions, but Will supposed that Tiny had also recognized Oliver, though it had been a few years. He gave Sammy's name as Madeleine Brightblaze, though he wondered if Emory or Selene would care enough to maintain her secret. Either way, it wasn't material to the discussion.

If this goes bad, there's no good outcome, thought Will. *The only person standing here that I don't care about is Lloyd Blathe.*

"Your Majesty," said Lloyd without bowing. "I would have preferred you visit under friendlier circumstances."

Selene inclined her chin slightly. "Then you should have sent us a friendlier invitation."

"Whoever perpetrated the attacks against your nobles, we had nothing to do with it," answered Lloyd. "I cannot stress that enough."

"We sent you the names of those we managed to capture, yet you've failed to provide any evidence it wasn't you that aimed them at our people," she returned. "And if it be that you are innocent of this, then you must accept your responsibility for your incompetence in the governance of Trendham."

"We haven't had enough time," protested Lloyd. "I've only found information on two of the names, and both of them are men who were lost at sea more than a year ago. I cannot work miracles."

Emory glanced at Selene and waited for her nod before he spoke. "You claim they were sailors while pointing the finger at Terabinia and claiming piracy. We've endured the slander of false blame against our navy for years. This excuse is pitiful."

"Call it what you will, it's the truth, and it's all I've got. All this killing won't serve justice or help you find your culprit," said Lloyd.

"Because he stands before us already," grated the Black Duke. "My son is dead, and you have the indecency to stand before me claiming to know nothing of his killers."

Selene lifted one hand, then spoke. "Whether you are guilty or not, it is clear that you cannot be allowed—"

Will stepped in front of the oligarch. "Before you say something you'll regret, I think you should add my presence to your scales before you weigh the balance and make a decision."

She had avoided looking at him since arriving, but now Selene's eyes fixed on his. She seemed cold and distant. "*You* should not be here at all."

"You had to know I wouldn't ignore this," Will replied. "Can we speak privately? Just the two of us?"

Between Emory and Tiny, he got two immediate cries of "No!" and "Absolutely not!" Lloyd also showed surprise, though he limited himself to a simple "What?" Oliver and Sammy both looked unhappy, but neither spoke.

"Very well," answered Selene. She silenced their objections with a harsh look, then faced Will again. "How would you like to do this? A simple force-dome?"

She left unspoken the fact that if either of them created the force-dome, that person would be unable to use other force-spells until they dismissed it. She was immortal, but Will wasn't, and if he cast the spell, she could then easily dispatch him with nothing more than a force-lance.

"I'll cast the force spell," said Sammy.

"Perhaps I should," countered Emory. They stared at one another, realizing that they'd each volunteered to avoid putting the other at risk.

Will sighed. "So much distrust here. Her Majesty and I are old friends. There won't be any betrayals." He glanced at Selene. "I'll put up the protections if you don't mind, and I'll include a sound-shield and something to hide us from view. Is that all right?"

Selene's brows went up, then she nodded.

Heedless of the fact that he was leaving himself open to attack, Will sealed the two of them within a force-dome, then erected a sound-shield and a special screen that reflected light, making it appear as if they stood within a mirror. Selene's features immediately became more animated.

"Why are you here? Why? You know better," she told him.

"Because I had to be."

"Leave the politics to me! Isn't that why you left?" she exclaimed.

He held up his hands. "I've thought about that a lot, and there's some truth there, but let's think through what's happening today first."

She stared at him with angry eyes, but finally nodded. "You think you have a different solution, one I'll accept?"

"I'm not sure, but I'm certain that forcing me to annihilate an army isn't going to improve things for Terabinia," he replied.

She looked as though she wanted to pick him up and shake him. "William, you know me. Do you think I would be pressing forward if I didn't have an answer for that? I'm trying to protect you. I've *been* trying to protect you, but if you stay here, you won't walk away."

He ignored the threat. "You know this war will only bring suffering and hardship to the people of Trendham."

Selene nodded. "For a time, but when that's past, I will remake it. I didn't want this, but the attacks in Cerria have forced my hand."

"You're the queen. Turn them around and go back."

"They'll dethrone me if I do," she returned. "You have no idea how angry they are."

"They can't hurt you."

"It doesn't matter. I can't rule if Terabinia falls into civil war. Currently, my only choice is to prosecute this war on the faith that I can eventually do more good here than the harm this war will cause. Otherwise, I'll lose my throne and everything I've worked for will fall to ruin."

"As much as I believe you'd be a good ruler, I can't let you do that."

"Stupid tregbor! Why won't you ever listen?"

Will blinked. "What was that word?"

"Does it matter? You're desperate for death, and nothing I can say will dissuade you. Don't make me do this to you. Not you. Please."

"Yes, it matters," he insisted. "What was it that you said?"

"Tregbor. It's an elven word for mage."

Selene had spent almost a year living among the elves, but she'd never used any of their language in front of him before. "Did you learn that recently?"

"No, but I've been learning more since the elves opened diplomatic relations. Why are we talking about this?"

"Because I think I've figured out our problem. It's the elves."

She stared at him as if he'd lost his mind. "I don't remember you being this dense. You're just grasping at straws. The elves have no cause and no means. I have to act based on facts and reason, not rash emotions."

Will narrowed his eyes. "You think I'm jealous of that elf prince from way back when?"

"I never said that. Show me your proof if you're so certain it was them."

He studied her for a moment, feeling uncertain and—torn. "Before that, we need to settle something between us." He held out his right hand toward her.

Her eyes glanced at it, lingering on his ring, then returned to his face. "That won't prove anything." But she stretched out her hand anyway.

Clasping her hand, he felt a thrill at her touch. Meeting her gaze again, he said, "I love you."

Selene flinched. "You abandoned me. Do you think saying that will—"

"Not by itself," he admitted. "But there's more to say."

Her eyes smoldered with anger and the beginnings of tears. "Do you know how long I waited for you, expecting my death at your hands? For the longest time, that's what I wished for, and I deserved it. When you rejected me, I had to face the truth, and you were right, but you never came back to finish it. I wanted to die, just to see you one more time."

She sighed. "Eventually I gave up and got on with making the best of it. I can't change what I did, no matter how much I wish I could. You should have killed me then, because now I'll be forced to kill you instead."

Will's face showed his sadness. "For a while I thought I should, but I never had the heart. I knew I couldn't do it and I figured I'd end up where we are today, with you being forced to kill me instead."

She blinked, and a tear rolled down her cheek. "You idiot, I've been trying to protect you for all these years. I could never have killed you. You've never understood m—"

"It took a while, but I learned eventually," he interrupted. "It's not too late. I still love you, Cora." Selene's eyes went wide, and he pulled on her hand, drawing her closer. Will leaned in, until their noses were almost touching. "Did you hear me?"

"I'm not sure." Selene's features were a mixture of sorrow, confusion, and longing. She didn't believe her ears.

"I said I love you, Cora Dewitt."

A second tear fell, then a third as she asked, "You knew?"

"Not at first. That's partly why I wouldn't let you have your way the first time we met, but I felt something from you then." Raising one hand to her cheek, he kissed her lips lightly. "I don't think I can live without you anymore. It's been too lonely, and only seeing you every few years is torture."

"How?" was all she could say at first. Then she lifted his hand. "This shouldn't have told you anything. The stone didn't even change color."

"James and I figured out a way, and I designed this one to only show the color I wanted so you wouldn't be suspicious. I knew you had no source from the first time I touched you with it."

"But you said nothing. You were never a good actor, Will."

He smiled and kissed her again, lingering only a second. "I've improved. Plus, for a short time I was a little worried you might be Grim Talek."

She frowned. "I don't think he's ever taken a woman's body, not that anyone has seen him in years."

Will shrugged. "As old as he is, I wouldn't put it past him. I doubt he cares about such things. Just be glad you're a good kisser. Cora's lips were very convincing."

She kissed him then, her hands holding tightly to his, but after a few seconds, she pushed him away. "This doesn't solve anything. You have to leave, otherwise I'll regret what I do today for the rest of my wretched existence."

"I heard that word, tregbor, once before. That's why I was so insistent," he told her.

"Does it matter?"

"A troll called me that—one of the trolls Sammy and I exterminated in Terabinia."

Selene was thinking hard, but she still wasn't satisfied. "That's not enough."

"I checked with the trolls in Muskeglun. None of them knew the term. Clegg asked among all the tribes he knew. Those trolls learned it from the ones who sent them to Terabinia."

"But why?" she asked. "What motivation would they have for that? How would they benefit from a troll apocalypse? If Hercynia was populated by nothing but trolls, they would have no one to trade with, and that still doesn't link them to the Trendish terrorists."

"The dragon is gone, Selene. That's why they're back. They resumed trade because it was safe again, but it's more than that. This was their world before Lognion came. Isn't that what Durin told you? The dwarves were their slaves, and very likely, so were we. I think they want it back." She looked uncomfortable when he mentioned Durin's name, so he asked, "What was he doing with you? Was he an ambassador, a diplomat, something else?"

"A prince," she said quietly. "Cora escorted him partway on his trip to meet with me. Things did not go well."

"Because he tried to warn you," suggested Will.

"He wasn't rational. His people have an ingrained hatred for the elves. I lost my temper finally and sent him away."

Will frowned. "That's not the Selene I know. You've always used people's prejudices against them, brokered deals with enemies, or put them against one another to further your own goals. You're too much of a politician to just send a valuable asset away because he irritated you."

"I was under a lot of stress at the time, but..." She looked hesitant. "It doesn't matter now. It's too late, Will."

"It's not," he insisted. "And it makes more sense the longer we talk. They want our world for their own, and the trolls were a simple way to accomplish it, until I screwed up that plan, but they're masters of the long game. They're setting nation against nation to weaken us. Lloyd said some of those Terabinians were lost sailors. Who else could have been taking those ships? We know the elves have a sizeable merchant fleet. They could just as easily have a full navy, and they clearly have considerable magical resources. The bluet alone is proof of that."

"You're saying they've been taking people...?"

"And twisting their minds. I don't know much about mind magic, or it could even be illusions, but it makes sense to me that the elves do. How else could so many be convinced to commit to a suicidal assault? I wonder if the bluet has anything to do with it?" He glanced up. "Tiny told you what I found, didn't he?"

"About what?"

"Bluet."

"Nothing. Why?"

"It's connected to the astral somehow, but I can't figure out what it means. It's like it has a soul. If you isolate it from the astral, it decomposes entirely. I showed Tiny. He said he would share the information with you and Janice. I was hoping one of you might have some insight."

"It's far too late now, Will."

"Too late for the truth? I know you can see the pattern here, and if Tiny didn't say anything it makes me suspect he was influenced somehow as well."

"Too late for you, for us. You never should have come here, and your son—how could you bring him as well?"

The look in her face communicated far more than simple regret. "You've already set the trap, haven't you?" It was more statement than question. "I saw the first, and I saw the men you had ready for this one. Can't you just call them off?"

Forlorn, she answered, "No. It's not mine, and they're already here."

"Who?" After a moment, he came to a realization. "The elves?"

"It made sense somehow, and I was certain you wouldn't do this. This parley, it gave them a perfect time and place."

He couldn't believe his ears. "You've betrayed the truce?"

Selene shook her head sadly. "No, but the moment it's over. It's over, for you, for them."

Will was thinking furiously. "But you're here as well, and Tiny…" He stopped, realizing the two he'd named were still perfectly safe. Selene wouldn't die—only her body could be harmed—and Tiny wasn't really there at all, not in the flesh. "What about Emory?"

"Emory is a fool. He never listens to reason. His best hope is that he won't be targeted," she answered.

He sighed. "This is another indication that your judgment has been altered. This isn't like you."

"It's exactly like me, Will. You know that," she argued.

"No. You would make sure that *you* were in control. Not some new ally. You're not this trusting. You've never let anyone else take command, certainly not when it came to something so personal."

Selene looked defeated, and it wasn't something he'd expected to see. "Perhaps you overestimated me. I question myself more every day." Her lips firmed up. "I promise you, though. I'll remember this. Every moment. Once it's over, I'll find the truth and make those responsible pay for it."

"The elves, you'll make them pay for it," he corrected.

She blinked, then replied hesitantly, "Yes."

"Did you forget what we just talked about?"

"No, but lately I've been more forgetful, it seems."

Frustration rose in his chest. "It's the bluet, or the presence of the elves themselves. You have to stay away from both, or you won't be able to do anything. They're affecting the way you think."

Selene stared at him. "How should I do that? They're in our camp. Bluet is used everywhere. We don't know how they could do any of this, and I'm still not sure I believe you, and even if I did, you're already dead. The moment we leave here, it's over."

Will stepped in, wrapping his arms around her. "I love you. No matter what happens." He pulled away slightly, focusing on her face. "You trust me. Don't you?"

"Yes?"

"You love me. I know you do. Cora told me so," he said with a smile.

Finally, she nodded.

"Tell me how it's going to happen. Together, we'll find a way through it."

She did, and after she was done, Will had to admit that the plan was thorough. She and the elves had considered just about every contingency in his arsenal, and this time even cutting himself off from reality wouldn't be much of a help. They'd be waiting for his return. *Plus, I can't put Olly or Sammy at risk of the same illness that torments my dreams.*

Will wasn't ready to give up, though. He was too stubborn for that, and his family was on the line. The elves had planned well enough for him, but there were cards on the table that they still hadn't seen. "Selene, how much do you like being queen?"

"I hate it, but there is no one else. My duty is to my people."

He liked her arrogance. *No one else who can do the job as well as she could.* That had been her meaning. "Don't you wish you could escape?"

"Like you?" she said ruefully. "Cora was the closest I could come to happiness. The throne is the price I pay to atone for what I have become."

"You aren't governing now. The elves are."

He saw a spark of anger in her features, but it passed quickly. "And how would you remedy that?"

"By doing what I should have done long ago, my love. I'm going to kill you." Leaning forward, he kissed her one last time.

CHAPTER 60

As the force-dome and Will's other privacy measures disappeared, everyone's eyes focused on the two of them. His eyes swept the area, looking at both the material plane and the ethereal. The number of men in the ethereal had increased dramatically, though most of them were over fifty yards away, and a line of them at a hundred yards completely encircled the place for the parley. *Those would be the mages,* thought Will. Selene had been right; he, Oliver, and Sammy were almost certainly fucked.

He'd made sure he had a healthy amount of turyn before coming, but he wasn't connected to the sky, and it was unlikely he'd have the chance to do so. The elves would attempt to starve him of power in much the same way he'd once used Erica's Barrier to starve Grim Talek. He'd have to make the most of every bit of turyn available to him.

It was the worst possible situation for any wizard. Limited access to turyn and an abundance of physical threats. Once things started happening, they would be swarmed by the elite fighters hiding in the ethereal.

In contrast, the Terabinian half of the parley was in much better shape. Selene had a vast array of elementals to draw from, and Tiny was completely invulnerable to practically anything that could be thrown against him. Anything that *could* bring to bear the type of force necessary to damage the demon-steel golem would potentially trigger an explosion that would destroy both the golem and everything else for half a mile around. Will had options that might do such a thing, but Oliver and Sammy wouldn't survive, and he wasn't prepared to kill most of the Terabinian and Trendish forces either.

Teleportation wouldn't be possible. The mage perimeter would establish a force-sphere around the entire area that would serve multiple purposes. It would prevent escape, protect the ritualists from attack, and limit the turyn available to him while their warriors sought to cut them down.

If that wasn't bad enough, Tiny would be a nightmare, and Emory could potentially limit the ways in which Will could use force spells himself. If he tied himself up with one, Emory could take the opportunity to remove his head with a force-lance.

Add in the fact that Sammy and Oliver had no idea what to expect, and that the queen had to be dealt with first, and it made his prospects for seeing another day look pretty dim.

As all eyes turned to him and Selene, Will smiled. "We had a very productive discussion, I think." He glanced at Sammy. "Did you have a chance to talk to Emory? If not, you should probably take the opportunity to catch up. I'm sure he would like the attention." To Oliver, he added, "We'll probably need the spider's blessing to get through the rest of the day."

He gave them a second to process his words. Emory frowned, and the golem watched him intently, but Will remained relaxed. Looking up at Tiny, he had one more thing to say. "You'll realize in time that this was a misunderstanding." Lifting his left arm, he gestured, drawing their attention to his movement, but it was his right hand that they should have watched. His old falchion appeared in it, and with a firm but precise swing he brought it across in front of him, sweeping Selene's head from her shoulders.

The move was so unexpected that everyone froze in surprise and horror for a timeless moment as her head toppled and fell. The golem started to move, and Emory screamed reaching for his magic.

Will had a firm grip on the turyn around them, preventing any use of normal spells and magic, and in the distance, he felt the force screens go up and blend together as the elven mages in the ethereal invoked their barrier ritual. Force spells worked both ways, and it didn't matter which plane they were on, for they affected both. The shield sealing them in had a certain solidity to it, as though they had tapped into a ley line to supply it with power.

Emory struggled for a moment before thinking to attempt a force-lance, but a force-dome appeared around him a second before, courtesy of Sammy. Will dropped the falchion, since it would be useless against the golem. Tiny was already bringing his greatsword to bear in a sweeping blow, but before Will could do anything, a figure made of what looked like molten silver slammed into the metal monster, knocking it back. Oliver had leapt across ten feet in a single leap, his body covered in the phase spider's special shield, and his shoulder struck the golem's upper body at just the right moment to overbalance it.

Free for a moment, Will summoned a handful of vials and dropped them on Selene's body. A single force-lance shattered one, and the corpse went up in a blazing funeral pyre. Decapitation wouldn't force her out, but incinerating the body should do the trick, and alchemical fire didn't have to contend with her magic resistance.

Emory's prison was filled with green vines that covered the interior, swelling and putting pressure against the enclosure. Whether he could break free would depend on who tired first, him or Sammy, but the complicating factor was the multitude of armored figures sprinting across the open ground toward them.

Lloyd Blathe watched the proceedings in shock and horror, knowing he was most surely about to die.

Will took full advantage of the fact that he was the only one currently able to use elemental spells. They weren't far from the river, and the ground was damp, which made liquefying the earth under the golem's feet a simple task. It was a spell not too dissimilar to the gravedigging spell he had used for so many years, but rather than excavating the ground, it flooded it with any water available and agitated it into a slurry.

Oliver had just dodged another swing of the greatsword, and he leapt away as the earth dissolved into mud, while the metal monster sank in until most of its body was swimming in mud. With luck, it would take Tiny a considerable amount of time to work his way free of the morass.

"Guard your aunt!" ordered Will as he summoned his staff. Five feet of oak appeared in his hand, and once he activated it, three feet of steel blade appeared from one end. A dangerous hum filled the air as he brought it around to threaten the elven soldiers that were almost upon him. He backed toward Sammy, and Oliver circled around to the other side of her.

Lloyd Blathe had fallen to his knees and seemed to be wishing he could crawl into the earth itself. If he'd been wiser, he might have moved to stay near Sammy, but Will wasn't going to waste time on the man. He was already using his point-defense shield at a rapid-fire pace, stopping bolts and arrows from reaching them.

As they converged together, Will gave the orders that he hoped would save their lives. "I can guard the three of us briefly, but we're going to need Oliver to get us through the shield that's keeping us trapped. It's too strong for me to break without using something that would kill us all in the process."

Oliver was already leaping forward and back again. Blood was running the length of his spear, and three of the elven warriors were already on the ground. The enemy wore an unusual type of armor that seemed to mix sections of lamellar plates in some places with mail in others. Plates covered the chest, shoulders, thighs and shins, while mail joined those sections and covered rest of their limbs. Their bodies were somewhat leaner than the average man, and in comparison to Oliver, they looked like thirteen- or fourteen-year-old boys attacking a grown man.

The metal of their armor was unusually pale, almost seeming white, and it shone with an unusual luster. Whatever it was made of, it was light, for they didn't seem to be hampered by any noticeable weight. Oliver hadn't bothered trying to penetrate the plates, but while the mail seemed unusually resilient, a strong, quick thrust could drive the head of his enchanted spear through to find flesh.

If they had fought like normal men, Oliver could have slain them in droves, but they were unusually quick and well acquainted to working in groups. He was far faster and stronger, but now that the noose was closing, he found it harder to go on the offense. Any movement away from his aunt left her vulnerable to attack.

"I can't hold him much longer," shouted Sammy, referring to Emory. "Should I make space with some flame?"

"Save your strength. On the count of two, both of you touch my back, and Sammy, you release your shield. I'll move all three of us. We'll be in the clear for a second or two. Focus on getting us through the enemy's barrier then, Oliver. I'll keep them off us. Sammy, that's when you might think about causing a little mayhem, but after we get through might be best." He waited a second, then began, "One, two…" The force-dome containing Emory vanished, and he felt two hands on his shoulders. Will teleported, taking them across the field to the edge of the screen keeping them contained.

The elven warriors had converged around the center, so they were temporarily forced to reorganize and run toward the side they had teleported to. The fifty-yard gap would afford them a few seconds of peace. "Make us a hole, Olly!" shouted Will, moving in the opposite direction, toward the onrushing elves. "Stay between us, Sam, and make sure you don't get too close to me." Will began launching a steady stream of light-darts in groups of five at Emory, who initially tried to stop them with a point-defense shield. Since the missiles arrived in groups of five, he caught one in the leg and another in one arm as his shield couldn't protect his body all at once. Emory switched to a force-hemisphere to guard his entire body before the second batch arrived. Still unable to use other magic, he glared at Will in frustration.

Meanwhile, Will's buzzing staff swept around him in arcs, its blade cutting through elven armor with only slightly more difficulty than it had with flesh and bone.

"I can't do much, Will!" shouted Sammy. "You're keeping me suppressed as well as Emory!" She was firing off force-lances to stop or kill elves that tried to move around and flank her cousin, but small, focused attacks wouldn't be enough for long.

At the same time, Oliver's silvery form was pushing against the elven force-screen. Despite the seemingly vast amount of energy that fueled the barrier, the liquid turyn encasing his body ate into it like acid, and a hole began to open in front of him. The elf on the other side stared at him in horror but couldn't take his focus away from the ritual they were using to sustain the barrier.

"I'm almost through," shouted Oliver, gritting his teeth. "But I don't think the hole is going to stay. It's healing around me as I pass."

"Keep going. If you get through, kill some of the mages and it should fall apart," yelled Will. Close to being overwhelmed, he relaxed his hold on the turyn and stopped launching light-darts at Emory. "Now, Sammy!"

Emory and Sammy both reacted at the same time. Emory dropped his defense and leaned toward them. Vines grew and raced across the ground toward them, while at the same time Sammy unleashed an inferno. It was an unfortunate match for Emory, whose vegetative attacks shriveled and turned to ash in an instant. At the same time Sammy's rolling wave of flame passed over and around Will without touching him. Her control was so perfect that even the heat seemed to avoid him, but for the elves, it was a different story. The metal of their armor was left intact, but heat flash-cooked them within it, killing everyone within twenty yards of them.

Oliver got through the barrier, and it healed itself behind him. He'd lost his spear a few minutes prior, but with sword and buckler, he charged at the nearest elf maintaining the ritual. His victim stopped his efforts with the barrier and tried to flee, but Oliver cut him down from behind and headed for the next, who was only twenty feet away. The barrier began to flicker as it became unstable.

And then he met the Iron Knights of Terabinia for the first time. They had been running up from the Terabinian line to reinforce the elven mages, and though they weren't organized, two stood in his way to his next target. Oliver dropped his spider-shield and focused on speed. Hopefully, his mail and the iron-body transformation would be enough if he miscalculated.

The Iron Knights were armored from head to toe in the first full plate he'd ever seen, offering him almost no weak points to aim for. The joints were a possibility, and places like the neck. One-on-one, he would have tried, but with two, he'd only be opening himself up to attack, so he didn't try. He darted forward, blocking one sword with his buckler and then dodging to the side. His opponents were quick, but Oliver's muscles and bones were aching from the speed he was pouring into every movement. After dodging to the side, he turned and spun, lowering his body and sweeping his shin into the back of one knight's leg. The Iron Knight fell, and Oliver rose from the spin and continued on, thrusting his sword into the next mage's terrified face.

The Iron Knights were well defended, but they couldn't match his speed and agility. As the second mage fell, the barrier began to collapse. Oliver turned to run back to his father and aunt, while the remaining mages reeled. The destabilized ritual sent vast currents of turyn rolling back into them, and they collapsed under the strain.

And then the Stormking was free.

The failed ritual was the perfect fodder for Will. He felt Sammy and Emory both contesting for a share of the now-free turyn, but he took the lion's share, doing his best to starve Emory without keeping Sammy from replenishing her stores.

Thunder cracked in the sky above them, and thousands of Terabinian soldiers cried out in fear. Adrenaline and power surging through him, Will began to laugh, and then the world went white as waves of lightning crashed down on everyone within a hundred yards, sparing only Sammy and Oliver.

The elven warriors died instantly, as did the Iron Knights and unconscious mages. Emory protected himself with a force-dome, but it only stopped the first wave. The second and third crashed through, and he collapsed to the ground. The only one still functional was the Black Duke, who was nearly out of the mud pit now.

"Men of Terabinia, your queen is dead, your champion defeated, and your allies lie in ruin. Flee now or I will give you no mercy." Stretching out his hand, Will used a force-push with the power of the heavens behind it, launching Tiny's demon-steel golem into the middle of the River Larbon, where it sank into the depths.

Sammy moved to stand on his left, her body cloaked in living flame while Oliver stood on his right, once again covered in the ominous silvery energy of the spider-shield. It was little wonder that the armies of Terabinia turned and began to rout. Those at the front ran through the rear ranks, and the fear in them infected the rest. The continuing booms of thunder above spurred them on.

Moving forward, Will and his companions returned to the still-burning remains of the queen. "Burn the rest, Sam," he told her. "Make sure there's nothing but ash, and then I'll scatter it to the wind. I want nothing left for them to find."

Her flames were far more effective than the alchemist's fire had been. She finished in less than a minute, but then her eyes fell on Emory, and a gasp escaped Sammy's lips. "Oh, no. No, no, no, no!" Half-running, she knelt beside the man she had once loved.

His body was limp as she lifted his head. Burns tracked across his skin in strange lines left by the lightning. She checked the two places he had been struck by light-darts, but the wounds were shallow. His magic resistance had protected him from the worst. "You have to be all right, Em," she whispered. "You had a shield up and the lightning was magical. You have to be alive."

Will knelt beside her, while Oliver stood guard over them. Putting two fingers against Emory's throat, he felt for a pulse that wasn't there. Ignoring the fear in his heart, he summoned a regeneration potion and poured it into his old friend's mouth. Then he put his hands on Emory's chest and sent a quick pulse of electricity into him.

It was a long shot, but if he could revive him, even for a moment, he hoped the potion would do the rest.

"He's breathing!" shouted Sammy, practically into his ear. Tears were running down her cheeks.

"I'm not sure how bad his injuries are, but the potion should fix most of it, I hope," said Will. *Maybe.*

"What do we do now?" asked Oliver, watching the Terabinians as they abandoned the field. Behind them, cheers echoed across the river from the defenders inside Karda.

Will glanced at his son, feeling exceptionally proud. Lightning still flowed over Will's face and body, but he was barely aware of it. "Sammy will need to make sure Emory is stable, and someone will have to take charge of getting him home. Tiny can handle the job, but he's going to be hopping mad when he finally gets out of the river. I just hope he'll listen to me." As he spoke, he noticed Lloyd Blathe's body on the ground a short distance away. "Also, it looks like your employer didn't survive. Once I finish talking to Tiny, you'll have to take his body back."

A few minutes later, ripples appeared in the water some distance from the bank. Gradually, a massive black helm rose out of the water as Tiny's golem marched back onto the shore. Will stood waiting for him. Neither said anything for several seconds.

"Emory is hurt," said Will at last. "I gave him a potion, but he's not going to be conscious for half a day at least, maybe longer."

"Do you have any idea what you've done, William?" asked the golem. "We were friends. Emory was a friend. Selene was your wife!"

"You have two choices," said Will. "Last time we had a moment like this, you wouldn't take the time to hear me, so I'm hoping you'll give me a moment to explain. Listen if you still have any respect for our friendship. If not, you can take Emory and try to reorganize your army. I'm sure they need you right now."

The golem stared at him for several tense seconds. "You have five minutes, then I'm leaving."

Will talked, and after five minutes, Tiny was still listening. After fifteen, he collected Emory's unconscious form and began walking in the direction of the retreating Terabinian army. Will looked at Sammy and Oliver. "It's time for me to disappear again. Do you want me to take you home with me, Sam?"

She shook her head, glancing at Oliver. "No. Olly still has to return Lloyd, and I want to make sure he's treated as a hero rather than blamed for a death that wasn't his fault. The Four, plus whoever Blathe's successor is, will probably want some reassurances and help sorting out what to do from here. Maddie Brightblaze can make a difference."

Will wanted to hug them, but thousands of eyes watched from across the river, so he merely nodded. "Send me a message if they give you any trouble. Good luck." With that, he teleported back to Evie, and then took her with him back to his home in Lystal.

After a long bath, he ate dinner with his mother, and that evening he slept the sleep of the dead. If he had any nightmares, he was too tired to notice.

EPILOGUE

In complete darkness, Selene opened her eyes. She was in the ritual chamber, deep below the streets of Cerria. Directly above her was the old Arenata residence, which had once belonged to her and Will. These days, it was known as the Shaw residence, since Janice and Tiny now owned it.

She was cramped, which was to be expected. The chamber was never meant to hold a creature her size. She'd spent years restoring her body and making it whole, though she'd never known if the day would come that she would need it. Today was that day.

It was tempting to simply tear and dig her way to the surface, but that would destroy the house above. Despite her frustration, she couldn't do that to Janice. Instead, she drew on the power of half a dozen elementals and used it to empower a gate spell. The spell was complex, and it had taken even Selene years to master it.

Few had the power necessary to create such a thing with just a spell; the turyn demand was too great. Aislinn and Lognion were the only ones she'd observed doing so in the past. Of course, the secrets of both gates and teleportation spells had only come to light a few decades ago, when Will had bargained with his grandmother to receive the journals of the Wayfarer's Society that she had recovered.

In general, it was expected that most casters would require a ritual with multiple assistants to open such a gate, but Selene possessed thousands of elementals. She had no lack of turyn to draw upon, and her immortal existence meant she had little to fear from overextending herself.

The gate opened on the streets of Cerria not far away, just outside the stone building that the elves had purchased for their embassy, and screams echoed from people on the street when they saw her massive reptilian head emerge from the tear in space. In her current body, the buildings looked like dollhouses. The gate closed behind her, and she lifted her head to the sky, filled her lungs, and roared.

It felt good, so she tried her voice next, enjoying the deep rumble it emerged in. "I smell elves. You were brave to return to this world. Did you truly think me gone?"

With massive claws, she tore their embassy apart and smashed the pieces into dust. She caught those who managed to escape before the building fell and mashed them into red paste. Once she was done, she turned and carefully made her way down the street, navigating her way until she found the eastern gate. As she went, her body damaged numerous homes and store fronts, but there was no help for it. She hadn't learned to fly yet, and she wasn't about to attempt it with an entire city watching.

Pushing through the gates, she regretted the damage to both them and the walls, but there was no avoiding it. Once outside, she headed for the mountains. Hopefully there she would have the privacy to learn how to control her wings.

***

Back in Lystal, life hadn't changed, although the news that the war had ended abruptly and without any real losses was a surprise and a joy to the citizens. It would be weeks before all the young men who had been taken into the militia returned, but the news was greeted with a lot of joy by the families of those who had left.

The Laughing Goat had suffered a slump in business with so many called off to war, and it wouldn't recover until most of the young men had returned, so Will took an extended vacation. Almost a month to the day after the fateful events in Karda, he spotted a familiar wagon rolling up the road toward his house. The sight of it lifted his spirits.

He waited on the porch until it pulled up in front of the house. A lone figure sat in the driver's seat, and she waved when she spotted him. Cora had returned.

Will walked over and waited, offering a hand to help her down. "I've missed you."

She smiled back. "It's been a long month."

"Think you'll stay a while this time?"

Cora glanced at him with her head angled to one side, shading her eyes from the sun with one hand. "I was thinking about it. Promise you won't cut my head off?"

He blanched. "Please tell me it didn't hurt."

A look of horror came over her face. "The most painful thing in my life. It was excruciating, and the pain from the fi—" she paused when she saw the expression on his features, then relented with a laugh. "I told you I wouldn't feel a thing. Why are you doubting me?"

"You weren't the one that had to do the cutting and burning," he replied sourly.

She waved her hand dismissively, "That body was long dead. I had practically no sensation left in it." Lifting one hand, she rubbed her neck. "If you decide to kill me again, however, let me know in advance. This body is still very much alive."

"I'm still curious about that. Who was Wilh—"

She stopped him with a finger against his lips. "Don't. She stirs sometimes, when she hears her name. Call me Cora, or Selene if no one is around."

Will frowned. "She's still in there?"

She nodded. "I'm a guest, so even if I don't go back to Terabinia for a while, I can't stay too long. I promised to return her by the end of the month."

It was already the last day. "This month or—?"

"Next month, obviously," she reassured him with a smile. "Although I will need to factor in travel time, so we have two weeks at best."

Will shook his head. "Screw that. I can't believe you wasted two weeks driving that wagon. I'll take you back myself."

"You sound a little greedy. I'm not sure I'm prepared for that kind of commitment," she told him, a twinkle in her eye.

He laughed. "Are you saying you won't marry me again?"

She shook her head. "Half of my weddings that involved you ended in disaster. I'd be a fool to risk a third. As far as I'm concerned, we're still married, unless you're still clinging to the 'death do we part' argument."

Will kissed her, and when he finally came up for air, he sighed. "Much better."

"I can't believe you kissed me in that dead body. Yuck. If you were willing to do that, it makes me wonder what other things you've touched with those lips."

He laughed, then winced. "It wasn't too bad, although your lips were cold. To be honest, I was so wrapped up in my emotions I hardly noticed the difference."

Her expression was incredulous. "I knew you had no taste in women." She glanced toward the house and spotted Erisa watching them from the window. "Are we going to tell your mother the truth or—?"

"It would be easier if we didn't," he replied.

"So you're just going to let her think you're a huge man-whore?"

Will frowned. "Why would she think that?"

She patted her chest. "My host needs the money, but she's not going to agree to me taking much more of her time." Seeing the alarm in his face she quickly explained, "There are others. I just can't expect one woman to give up her life."

"Oh." Will was still working through the ramifications of what she'd revealed. He was happy to know that Selene wasn't killing women to steal their bodies, or enslaving women to maintain a living body, but the whole situation was still odd. "So you'll be in different...?" His words trailed off as he realized what she was getting at.

Selene nodded. "That's right, playboy. Your mother's going to have questions if you keep bringing different women home for weeks at a time."

"I'll think about it," he told her. "All the switching does sound inconvenient, though. You don't have anything more permanent?"

"The body you cut and burned is the same one you met me in after killing Lognion."

"And it's been dead all this time?" he said, gaping.

"Necromancy has a lot of nice tricks. The preservation spells are fantastic, otherwise you'd have had a lot more to say about kissing me than that my lips were cold. You'd probably have needed a clothespin for your nose."

"I always assumed you would just replace them." Will stopped when he saw the pain in her eyes.

"I might have, but for the things you said the day you left. It hurt, but you were right. After that, I was determined to avoid killing anyone, so I did my best to preserve what I had. Honestly, once I had the preservation spells perfected, it was easier than replacing it."

"And yet you came here, as Cora," he pointed out.

"Dead flesh can't feel much. I felt a little crazy the first time I came here. I was sure you'd find me out somehow, but I couldn't help myself. Experiencing life again after so long, it was like a drug. You have *no* idea how frustrated I was when you rejected me on my first visit."

Will was rubbing his chin. "So you don't have a backup now? You can't just keep paying people, can you? And how do you get them to agree?"

Selene smiled. "I do have one—rather large—spare body. We'll need to figure out a place to store that one. As for the women, there's only been three so far, and I've just had servants hire them after a little research. The others were simply told they'd be working at Rimberlin House for however long. I would meet with them, and from that point they remember nothing. When the contracted time is over, I turn them loose and pay them. They go home with some missing time and a fat bag of coin."

"I've got a nice place to put Lognion," said Will. "I can't wait to—" He paused, seeing the disgust on her face. "What?"

"Don't call it that. I'd rather not remember him at all. It's just a body."

Will nodded. "Anyway, I've got an expansive lair. I'll add a room to hold the dracolich. I'm more concerned about how you're going to keep finding volunteers."

She stared at the ground. "It won't be easy if I give up the throne. People ask a lot more questions if you aren't royalty."

He gave her a suspicious look. "I haven't been to Cerria since that day, but it sounds like you're saying people don't know you're dead."

"Janice is sitting in my place. We told them you slew an imposter disguised as me." She smiled, then added, "I'm obviously too smart to risk my life in a parley with the enemy. I'm not dumb, William."

"And I suppose I am?" he said ruefully.

"I consider it part of your charm."

"I figured out who you were pretty quickly," he countered.

"You didn't know at first."

"I suspected. That's why I made the ring."

"That was clever," she admitted. "But half the credit goes to your brother-in-law. No one's ever figured out a way to type someone's source like that before."

"Speaking of clever, how did you find me? Did you have Tiny followed?" he asked.

Selene shook her head. "No. I underestimated him. I had people watching him in Cerria, but that was all. I found Sammy instead. When I came to Lystal, I really was looking to find whoever was paying for information on her. I counted myself lucky when it was actually you."

"How long were you looking?"

She raised her brows. "Before that? Years. But only when I could get away. I never told Janice what I was up to. I was too embarrassed."

That made him feel sad, and a little guilty. "I'm sorry. I should have trusted you, or given you a chance."

"You were right," she said immediately. "I'm still haunted by what I did. I felt terrible all over again after I did find you. I didn't deserve a second chance, and tricking you—it was wrong, but it was all I had."

Will shook his head. "I'm seeing it the other way around. I'm not sure why you didn't move on after I left, even if it was simply for political reasons."

"To remarry would mean an even bigger deception, and I would have had to start killing to maintain it. Forcible possession kills the host after a few months—that's what Grim Talek told me, before he left. Any man sleeping with a corpse would notice, so I'd have to replace my body and reshape the flesh every few months. Do you think I could do that?"

Will looked away. "For a while I thought you might be capable of anything."

She sighed. "Maybe I am. I'm sure you know I'm not normal, not even close—but the only thing that has ever kept me anchored—is you. I couldn't tell anyone what I had become. Janice and Tiny knew, and I could see the looks they gave me when they thought I wound't notice. They were repulsed. Even Janice doesn't trust me, not completely. I was trapped and alone. That's why I couldn't help but look for you, even though that meant I was even crazier."

Something else occurred to him. "Your host, she doesn't have, is she, is there someone waiting—?"

"A husband?" Selene smirked. "No. She had almost no family. Most of the story I told you about Cora is true, it's part of why I chose her. I empathized with her past." After a pause, she added, "You should tell me what you prefer before I find a new volunteer."

"What do you mean?"

She put her hands on her chest suggestively. "More here? Less? How about the hair?"

"I'm happy with you as you are."

Selene let out a sigh of exasperation. "That's what you said before I did this to myself. Are you saying you didn't prefer one over the other?"

He couldn't see any safe answers. "I like the person behind the eyes."

"What about red hair? I was thinking of looking for a svelte redhead next time."

Will lifted his brows. "That could be—interesting."

"Sick. I knew you had a thing for your cousin," she accused.

"What? You suggested it, not me!"

"It was a test, you pervert. I think I'll have to choose a blond now."

Will held up his hands. "That's fine too."

"Laina had blond hair. You really are a deviant."

He rolled his eyes. "Well, I am infatuated with my dead wife, so I can't say I'm exactly normal."

"If you ever want to do more than kiss me while I'm in a dead body, that's the end of our sexual relations. I'll tell you that right now," she responded.

"Does it count if it's a dead dragon body?" he asked.

Selene froze, her face showing disgust. "That's really disturbing."

Will refused to relent. "You started this sick game, and you can't handle it? Too bad. Besides, I've already been inside your father once before."

She visibly paled. "Stop. I'm going to vomit."

"A necromancer with a weak stomach?"

"I've only been in this body for a week. I'm extra sensitive for a while after switching to a live body."

Will gave her a suggestive look. "How sensitive, exactly?"

She laughed. "Your mother is waiting to say hello, so it's going to be a while before you get a chance to find out. Let's go inside."

Will took her hand, and together they walked toward the front porch. "Oliver is going to lose it when I introduce you as his stepmother one of these days."

Selene stopped. "Do you think he'll be upset by me?"

He gave her an evil grin. "No, but I think it would be best if I introduce you while you're a dragon."

"That's just mean, Will," she said, shaking her head.

"Opportunities like that only come along once. It would be a shame to waste it."

"How is he doing?" she asked.

"Much better. Sammy bought his contract from Blathe's successor, so he's working for Madeleine Brightblaze now. So is his friend—Alex."

"Who is Alex?"

"It's going to take a while for us to catch up, but before I tell you about your stepson, we need to go in. Mom looks like she's about to die of curiosity."

Smiling, they entered the house together, and the rest of the day proved to be one of the best Will could remember in quite some time.

***

That night, Will woke from a dead sleep, his heart racing as he gasped for air. He was being haunted by the woman he'd seen before, and this time her body had been an ever-shifting horror of tentacles and scaled appendages.

But unlike most nights, there was a hand on his brow. "It was just a dream," Selene told him. "Breathe easy. I'm here."

Normally, his paranoia would have kicked in, but instead his heart rate slowed and he began to feel calm. Embarrassed, he looked at her in the dark. "This is why I sleep alone."

"I'm not leaving," she told him. There had been some discussion earlier on the topic.

"I'm dangerous. Sometimes I can't tell whether I'm awake or not."

"You've already decapitated me once. How bad can it get?"

He sighed. "*You* might be fine, but Wil—Cora might not."

Selene showed no remorse. "Hosting me is a risky job. I trust you, and I'm not leaving."

Will pursed his lips but decided not to press the argument. Selene changed subjects. "If you're awake, let's talk a little."

He sat up. "I meant to ask you about the elves. How did they react?"

"After I crushed their embassy and made a few flights over the countryside, I'm hoping they'll decide they made a mistake coming back, but I don't know yet," she answered. "I may need to take more direct measures."

"I've been thinking of traveling to their world," said Will.

"I don't think that would be wise."

"It was less wise of them to piss me off," he responded.

Selene sighed. "No one knows how to get there. No one has ever found a congruence point, probably because it's somewhere at sea."

"You went there once." He pointed out.

"Aislinn made the gate, and I knew nothing about that type of magic back then. I couldn't make one to get back unless I went again. Not that I would help you do something so obviously reckless."

"That's fine. I can get there on my own."

She studied him in the dark. "I know better than to try and stop you, but if you do this, at least take someone with you. Your son seemed extremely capable."

"I wouldn't risk him." Will already knew Selene couldn't come. She would need to bring her phylactery to travel between worlds, putting her at extreme risk, assuming she was even willing to be that far from Terabinia and the responsibilities of the throne. "If I try my way, I can't take anyone anyway," he told her.

"How would you do it?"

He smiled. "Walk onto one of their ships and wait for them to return. They aren't the only ones who can be sneaky."

"That's an incredible risk. I don't see the point."

Will wasn't comfortable with his idea either. One of the secrets he'd inherited was a spell that could cause an entire plane to unravel. "I'm tired of other races and beings thinking our world is free for the taking," he told her. "The fae, the dragon, the demons, how many times do we have to persuade others to leave us alone? I might know a way to stop the elves from bothering us for good."

"That sounds very—final. I don't like the sound of it."

"You might not be the only crazy partner in this relationship," he replied. "I'm not saying I *will* do anything, but I think I need to assess them. Depending on the threat they represent, there are a number of options I might choose."

"You talk like a king rather than a lone wizard living in the backwaters of Trendham. You already ran from being prince consort; why are you trying to take on a responsibility like this?" she asked.

"As a queen, you're an excellent role model," said Will, "but I'm the First Wizard. I may not be involved in politics, but when it comes to humanity, and our world as a whole, it's my job to make the call."

"You're still intent on this wizard's council thing? Who do you have on it?"

"Tabitha, James, Sammy, myself. I was hoping to talk to Emory, but I'm not sure how he feels after what happened. I think all the new first-order wizards should be made a part of it, no matter what country they are from."

"They're all my subjects, currently," said Selene. "What about me?"

"You're not technically human anymore. I'm pretty sure that disqualifies you."

"Aren't you the one making the rules?"

"I'll have to think about it."

"Maybe I can change your mind," she said softly.

Will rolled over. "I'm tired."

She shoved his shoulder. "Really? You just had a nap."

"I'm a frail mortal."

"I'm not," she whispered in a husky voice.

Will glanced at her over his shoulder and got caught in a kiss. "You'll be the death of me."

Selene growled softly. "Almost certainly."

Keep an eye out for the next book in the series:

Daughter of the Dragon

Books by Michael G. Manning:

Mageborn
The Blacksmith's Son
The Line of Illeniel
The Archmage Unbound
The God-Stone War
The Final Redemption

Embers of Illeniel (a prequel series)
The Mountains Rise
The Silent Tempest
Betrayer's Bane

Champions of the Dawning Dragons
Thornbear
Centyr Dominance
Demonhome

The Riven Gates:
Mordecai
The Severed Realm
Transcendence and Rebellion

Standalone Novels:
Thomas

Art of the Adept
The Choice of Magic
Secrets and Spellcraft
Scholar of Magic
Disciple of War
The Wizard's Crown

ABOUT THE AUTHOR

Michael Manning was born in Cleveland, Texas and spent his formative years there, reading fantasy and science fiction, concocting home grown experiments in his backyard, and generally avoiding schoolwork.

Eventually he went to college, starting at Sam Houston State University, where his love of beer blossomed and his obsession with playing role-playing games led him to what he calls 'his best year ever' and what most of his family calls 'the lost year'.

Several years and a few crappy jobs later, he decided to pursue college again and was somehow accepted into the University of Houston Honors program (we won't get into the particulars of that miracle). This led to a degree in pharmacy and it followed from there that he wound up with a license to practice said profession.

Unfortunately, Michael was not a very good pharmacist. Being relatively lawless and free spirited were not particularly good traits to possess in a career focused on perfection, patient safety, and the letter-of-the-law. Nevertheless, he persisted and after a stint as a hospital pharmacy manager wound up as a pharmacist working in correctional managed care for the State of Texas.

He gave drugs to prisoners.

After a year or two at UTMB he became bored and taught himself entirely too much about networking, programming, and database design and administration. At first his supervisors warned him (repeatedly) to do his assigned tasks and stop designing programs to help his coworkers do theirs, but eventually they gave up and just let him do whatever he liked since it seemed to be generally working out well for them.

Ten or eleven years later and he got bored with that too. So he wrote a book. We won't talk about where he was when he wrote 'The Blacksmith's Son', but let's just assume he was probably supposed to be doing something else at the time.

Some people liked the book and told other people. Now they won't leave him alone.

After another year or two, he decided to just give up and stop pretending to be a pharmacist/programmer, much to the chagrin of his mother (who had only ever wanted him to grow up to be a doctor and had finally become content with the fact that he had settled on pharmacy instead).

Michael's wife supported his decision, even as she stubbornly refused to believe he would make any money at it. It turned out later that she was just telling him this because she knew that nothing made Michael more contrary than his never ending desire to prove her wrong. Once he was able to prove said fact she promptly admitted her tricky ruse and he has since given up on trying to win.

Today he lives at home with his stubborn wife, teenage twins, a giant moose-poodle, two yorkies, a green-cheeked conure, a massive prehistoric tortoise, and a head full of imaginary people. There are also some fish, but he refuses to talk about them.

Printed in the USA
CPSIA information can be obtained
at www.ICGtesting.com
LVHW061137270824
789408LV00005B/220/J

9 781943 48147